PRETTY WOMAN

From the topmost ducat-gold curl to the tip of her toes, Countess Elizabeth Bartholdy was the most beautiful and youth-filled damsel any man could ever dream of. She simply had to smile and lower her long sooty eyelashes to have most men agree to do anything she asked of them.

The guard on Prince Vlad of Basarab's elegant prison was made of sterner stuff than most. But he was still a man. And too slow to react, when she put her hand where no lady would have done.

That instant of hesitation killed him, as the razor-sharp talon-like steel tips to her claws slipped through the cloth far more easily than the proverbial hot knife through butter. A few inhuman things could survive those venom-tipped nails. No human could.

She sheathed the claws again, as he fell with barely a whimper. She paused for an instant to enjoy the look on his face.

There was a cost to turning your own body into the perfect assassin's killing tool, but Elizabeth had paid that price long ago. More than a century before.

She opened the door to the chambers of the captive duke of Valahia with a smile on her lips. Mindaug had given her a time and place at which he would still have to be alive and, for best effect, virginal. At the time and a place when the shadow ate the moon. After that, he could be abused and die.

Much Fall of Blood

Mercedes Lackey
Eric Flint
Dave Freer

MUCH FALL OF BLOOD

Copyright © 2010 by Mercedes Lackey, Eric Flint & Dave Freer

A Baen Books Original

Baen Publishing Enterprises
P.O. Box 1403
Riverdale, NY 10471
www.baen.com

ISBN: 978-1-4391-3416-0

Cover art by Larry Dixon

First paperback printing, February 2011

Library of Congress Control Number: 2010005098

Distributed by Simon & Schuster
1230 Avenue of the Americas
New York, NY 10020

Pages by Joy Freeman (www.pagesbyjoy.com)
Printed in the United States of America

To the Tasmanian devil

The Great Powers Of Europe

Muscovy

Mongol Khanates

Territories Controlled by the Knights of the Holy Trinity

The Grand Duchy of
Poland
and
Lithuania

Norseland

Baltic Sea

Vilna

Kiev

Black Sea

Warsaw

Hungary

Budapest

The Balkans

North Sea

Berlin Vienna

Prague

Holy Roman
Empire

Adriatic Sea

London

Mainz

Milan

Rome

Aquitaine

Paris

Genoa

Orleans

League of
Armagh

Mediterranean Sea

Atlantic Ocean

Map of the Balkans

PROLOGUE
June, 1540 A.D.

A PLAIN ON THE SOUTH BANK
OF THE LOWER DANUBE

The ochre dust hung in the air, heavy with the smell of sweating horses. It muffled the yarring yells and the thunder of hooves, a little. But only a little. Kildai's willow-root club sent the head flying, bouncing away from the pack of riders shouldering their horses forward. It hooked, by the hair, in a small bush. Kildai's pony was smaller than the average Mongol horse, but very quick on her feet. Good on her turns, and she could accelerate. He broke from the crush and leaned out of the saddle to club the head onward toward the post.

Just before he was knocked out of the saddle, he saw Gatu Orkhan talking to a man in a hooded cloak on the high dais. It was odd how some moments were caught like a fly in the amber of memory—perfectly preserved when all else faded and decayed. A strand of lank blond hair hung out of that hood. The native Vlachs—some of them at least—had the occasional blond head. As did the Rus. But what would either be doing here, at the great kurultai, on the high dais? The Mongol traditions of their forefathers might be dying away in everyday life, here in the lands that remained to the Golden Horde, but not on this occasion. That was not a place for a slave. Not now.

The sight distracted Kildai even in middle of the great game.

Being knocked senseless was the smallest price you could pay for that. But he would swear that something had actually knocked him out of the saddle. Something that felt like a great hand.

CATICHE, SLOVENIA

Count Mindaug had achieved the remarkable. Not only had he escaped Jagiellon and found other—admittedly dangerous—protection, but he had spirited his library away, too.

His hostess did read. But she was not fond of research. She drew her power from elsewhere. From a bargain which she still dreamed—foolishly, vainly— that she could avoid paying the price for, eventually. Jagiellon had merely become one with, and been largely consumed by, that which he had sought to entrap and use for power. The powers and knowledge their masters had accumulated in planes beyond human ken and understanding was enormous . . . and devouring.

No one could talk Count Mindaug into such folly. The written word was less powerful, but drew from far wider sources. He had laid his plans skillfully. Eventually, he would risk another throw in the game of thrones and powers. Besides, it suited his own vanity to believe he could deceive both creatures of outer darkness and fallen angels. He knew that was probably just vanity, but it appealed to him, nonetheless.

He studied the passage in the small book again. The book was not bound in dark leather taken from some creature of the night, nor written on a fragile parchment of human skin. But it ought perhaps to have been, because the matters explained therein were compellingly evil. Mindaug had long since learned that content, not form, mattered. He was glad that this fact had bypassed so many of his peers.

He got up from his seat in the book-filled small apartment the countess had set aside for him. That was a calculated insult on her part, and one that had failed to put him in his place. The books there contained a far wider realm than she herself controlled. The details of this magic . . . well, he doubted she would read them. But she had a fascination with blood, for obvious reasons. She would not care what came of her experiments, of the lusts generated or the offspring created. But he, Mindaug, would control them. The keys to that control were right here in this book.

Unlike his former master, the Black Brain who had taken possession of the grand duke of Lithuania, Elizabeth did not care for the less than immediate and proximal things. Power over the rulers of Hungary was sufficient, as long as her comfort and vanity were ministered to. Mindaug did not threaten her directly with his machinations, but when she finally paid her price, or if Chernobog finally took on one foe too great or too many, Mindaug would be ready. He would return to his lands on the edge of Kievan Rus. The throne of the Grand Duchy was a short step from there.

Alternatively, if certain variables came to pass, he might instead become the power behind the throne of Hungary. That would be less satisfactory than seizing power directly in Lithuania, of course, but it might do well enough. Unlike most of those he maneuvered against, Count Mindaug had no interest in power for its own sake. His was ultimately a cautious nature. He needed power—preferably great power—simply because he could ill afford to let anyone else have it. Such had been the great lesson his life had taught him.

But first he needed to persuade the countess that she needed the blood of the Dragon. As was his way, honed by long practice in the Grand Duke's court, he would do it by telling her that she needed something else. It never ceased to amaze him how those who had vast, immense power seemed very often to be so stupid. He supposed it had something to do with having untrammeled power, and having it for so long.

JERUSALEM, IN THE LANDS OF ILKHAN MONGOL

Jerusalem the golden lay behind him, outside, with its noise, and heat, and smells. It seemed as far away, right now, as fabled Cathay. Eneko Lopez knelt in a small chapel, a simple, humble place, as befitted the faith of the humble, because in the face of God, all men, even the greatest, are as dust motes.

He saw how the dust motes danced in the sunlight of the Levant, as the light shone through the high slit window. Dust motes... Yet the Father cared for and numbered even the least of those motes, he knew. Eneko knew too that pride had always been his weakness. Here, at last, on the hill of skulls, where the greatest had humbled himself, given himself as a willing sacrifice, Eneko knew that he had been weak, and that despite this, he was still beloved. It was no great moment of epiphany, but rather the blossoming of a slow-developing plant. Perhaps he was lightheaded with hunger from his vigil, but the path, so obscure, now seemed clear.

Alexandria.

Alexandria, the seductress of the east, luscious, perfumed and corrupt. And home to the greatest library on earth, a repository of more thaumaturgical knowledge—good and evil—than anywhere else. Yes, he had been instructed to go there. But Eneko Lopez was not a man who took any instruction without weighing it against his conscience. After all, why would God have given a conscience to man, if not to be used? But now it seemed clear: those who had used ecclesiastical magics to defend the Church had formed their centers in the areas where Petrines or Paulines held most sway. They had left largely unguarded and unused the city of Saint Hypatia. It must not remain so. Knowledge, not politics, would be their sternest bulwark against evil, as Chrysostom had said.

Politics. He sighed and stood up, shaking his head. It had ruled the Church as much as it did secular society, though less so under the current Grand Metropolitan than previously. To be fair, the wisdom of the current Holy Roman Emperor in this matter could not be denied. Eneko had been sent here to pray for the Holy Roman Emperor's soul. He had done so. Eneko had also prayed that the soul might remain within its fleshy envelope as long as possible, for the sake of the people of Europe and of the Church. Eneko had played his role in keeping the second in line to that throne alive, and, while he'd had doubts of the boy at first, he'd come to realize that the spirit of Prince Manfred of Brittany might be large enough for the task. If it had been only a question of physical size Eneko would have had no such doubts. Eneko had less knowledge of Prince Conrad, the direct heir. But the Hohenstauffen line had proved that the imperial eagles often bred true. He would just have to pass on his stewardship now, for as much as the young prince might dream of the fleshpots of Egypt, Eneko was sure that their paths would diverge here.

Despite the relief that he felt now that he saw his path clearly, he was also a bit saddened. He would not have thought it possible that he would miss Manfred of Brittany, a few years before.

In another part of the great holy city, in a shady courtyard scented with orange blossom, Eberhard of Brunswick, representative of the States General, emissary of the emperor Charles Fredrik, thought of his time among the Celts. The advantage of dealing with the Celts had been that they used chairs. When one dealt with the Ilkhan, one lounged on cushions or sat cross-legged on them. Yes, Jerusalem was considerably warmer, and much less damp than Ireland, but he missed having a backrest, especially as it would seem the Mongol officials were just as long-winded as the Celts. Admittedly the wine he was being served was better than the beer in Duhblinn.

The platitudes were...platitudes. But the undercurrents were disturbing. The Ilkhan Hotai the Ineffable, to judge by his emissaries, wanted something. And when the master of all the lands between here and Hind wanted something, he usually didn't need to pussyfoot around about asking for it, even if politics here were conducted in a more subtle fashion than among the Celts or the Norse. Despite his wizened body, he was a man of immense influence. The Ilkhan's slightest word could mean death and destruction to thousands. This had to mean that Hotai thought that the Holy Roman Empire wasn't going to like the request much.

"As you know," said Bashar Ahmbien, "we are not a great maritime people."

What he said was true enough. It was the mastery of the horse that made the Mongols the dominant force of the east. Light, fast cavalry, great bowmen and superb tactics.

But of course Eberhard politely demurred. "You are a developing maritime force, rather."

"Perhaps—but the vessels of more powerful forces are reluctant to allow us to develop further."

This was dangerous talk. The Mediterranean needed yet another sea-power about as badly as the Holy Roman Empire needed Jagiellon as the Grand Duke of Lithuania.

"Ah," said Eberhard.

Ahmbien cocked his head, obviously weighing that noncommittal "Ah" for any possible information. It didn't tell him very much. "Yes. We have found this irksome in the Black Sea."

That was somewhat better, Eberhard felt, although far from anything to relax about. But Ahmbien plainly understood this, too. "It is not, you understand, our desire to control the seas. We've found ships very poor places to maneuver our horses. But we would like to talk and trade with our kin."

"The Golden Horde," said Eberhard, cutting to the chase. This was both dangerous and yet potentially advantageous. The Golden Horde had become isolated on the lowlands to the east of the Carpathian Mountains after the death of Batu Khan. To the south, the Bulgars, Thracians, other mountains tribes and Emperor Alexius in Constantinople cut them off from their fellow Mongols in Egypt and the Levant under the Ilkhan. Hungary and Slavic tribes and Vlachs vassals of the Grand Duchy of Lithuania blocked their movement to the north and west.

The Holy Roman Empire truly did not mind if they blunted their swords on Grand Duke Jagiellon's minions to the north. Even if they won, well, that would—at least in the short term—be no bad thing. The Mongols had proved to be excellent rulers, once the initial wave of conquest had passed with its atrocities and barbarities, often less greedy in taxation than former rulers, and happy to allow freedom of religion and trade. Even their justice was frequently an improvement.

Local satraps were varied, of course, and some were oppressive and greedy. But the shadow of the Great Ilkhan rested on them. They did not dare go too far. Eberhard knew that a Mongol war with King Emeric of Hungary would be a desirable thing, although it would be better if that merely resulted in the death of King Emeric, and not the destruction of the buffer-zone that was his kingdom. But, weak reed and traitor though Alexius was, giving aid to cause the downfall of Byzantine Emperor Alexius was not desirable. Besides . . . the Black Sea . . . the Venetians were good allies, and they relied on the trade out of the Black Sea to some extent.

"You are too astute for us, noble lord," said Ahmbien, a hint of a smile peering out from behind his moustache, a moustache that would have done the hind end of a wild Irish moorland pony proud. "The Golden Horde. The descendants of Batu Khan. It would appear that some months ago the issue of succession became paramount. We believe this is of interest to you. The leadership is divided among the clans. Since the death of Batu Khan the Horde have increased their numbers and look for fresh lands. Part of the Horde favors expansion to the south."

Eberhard tried not to tense, like a terrier at the mention of rats. And failed.

His host inclined his head at him, just slightly. "And the faction we feel has a just claim would break out through the lowlands to the north and east. Our support would carry weight among the clans."

Eberhard exhaled. Of course, there was no way of telling if Ahmbien spoke the truth or not. But at least the Ilkhan were presenting the information that there were two factions, which they had no need to do. "Of course," he said.

"We understand each other, then. An agreement of mutual convenience as it were," said Ahmbien, tugging his moustache.

"Indeed. But I fail to see what this has to do with us. Or with maritime prowess?"

"We have always been able to send messengers across the Black Sea. Not easily, but by indirect routes—Trebizond, by sea northwards to Kerch, across the Krym and then on into the lands of the Horde. We receive news the same way. Our last five messengers have failed to return. So have the ships they sailed on. We believe a great fleet is being assembled in the Dniepr gulf. We have word of at least three hundred round ships, and many galleys."

There could only be one destination for such a fleet. Byzantium.

And whatever else the Holy Roman Empire might disagree with the Ilkhan about, this they had in common. The Ilkhan did not want the allies of Prince Jagiellon to take Constantinople. Neither did any other Mediterranean or even European power. "How long has this been underway?" asked Eberhard.

"Perhaps three years," said Ahmbien.

The reasons behind Jagiellon's adventures against Venice suddenly became much clearer. The Mediterranean without Venice's galleys would present a large soft underbelly. Smaller powers—the Genoese and others—could be picked off piecemeal. Jagiellon had been moving pawns on a board so vast that others had not been able to see them all. When he had failed in Venice, he had just gone on building ships. But by now ... they should have sailed.

"The tribesmen of the Golden Horde raided deep into the north. They captured and burned a fleet of barges. Barges full of flaxen sailcloth and rope," said Ahmbien, as if reading his mind.

"Ah!" said Eberhard. "The fleet would have sailed after the failure of the attack on Corfu, but couldn't?"

Ahmbien nodded. "By next spring they will sail, unless the ships are destroyed."

"Can they be?" asked Eberhard.

Ahmbien shrugged. "The raid cost Prince Jagiellon's allies dearly. But it cost the Horde still more. Batu Khan was killed. Thus the Horde did not take and keep but returned to their grazing-lands to hold a convocation of the tribes, to choose a new leader, as is our tradition. Ghutir, the son of Batu, was named as the new khan. But he died. Magic and poison were both blamed. Now, the succession is clouded. There is Gatu, the son of Batu's younger sister, the grandchild of the Orkhan Berke. And there is a cousin, one Kildai, who is the great-grandson of Batu Khan's older sister, and is descended from Ulaghchi Khan on his mother's side. It is complex."

"Always seems to be," said Eberhard dryly. "And one of these would go south, and the other north. It would seem that being flanked by the same enemy would be unwise for anyone, let alone a master of tactics like the Mongol."

"You speak soothly," said Ahmbien with equal dryness. "Except ... Gatu, we believe, has no intention of being flanked ... by enemies."

It took a moment for this to sink in. "I think I need to go and prepare certain messages, Your Excellency," said Eberhard. He struggled to stand up, his knees complaining about the long time spent sitting on the cushions.

The Bashar Ahmbien waved him down. "Sit, my guest. I have more to tell you, and a proposal to make. I wish to introduce you to the tarkhan Borshar." He clapped his hands. A servant appeared, bowed. "Summon the tarkhan Borshar of Dishmaq," said the old man.

Borshar, when he arrived a few minutes later, was a tall shaven-headed man with the customary Mongol forelock. He showed not a trace of expression on his broad face. He bowed perfunctorily. Eberhard had met many functionaries in his long and varied life as an official of the States General. He was good at reading men. Borshar just came across as inscrutable. Eberhard did not like that.

Ahmbien coughed delicately. "The Ilkhan would take it kindly if you could prevail on your Venetian allies for us. Relations," he smiled wryly, "are better between yourselves and them than between us and them. We need the good tarkhan taken to the lands of the Golden Horde. We believe that his presence can influence matters in a mutually beneficial fashion."

Eberhard raised his eyebrows. "One man?"

Ahmbien shrugged. "And his escort, naturally. We have found one man in the right place can make a large difference. Of course it would help if that one man carries the word of the legitimacy of a marriage and the support of the Ilkhan."

"Legitimacy?"

"The marriage of the elder sister of Batu Khan. It happened in times of war, and without the formality it should perhaps have been accorded. The claim of Gatu to the Khanate rests partially on the shoulders of that uncertainty, and partly on the youth of Kildai."

It sounded good. That was enough to make Eberhard suspicious.

"Letters of safe conduct, according those who accompany the tarkhan the status of escorts to an envoy, will of course be provided, under the seal of the Ilkhan."

Eberhard did not raise his eyebrows in surprise. But he wanted to. That was a signal privilege. The Mongols were legendary for the degree of safe-conduct accorded to such emissaries and their escorts.

❀   ❀   ❀

It was as luxurious a boudoir as Manfred had been able to contrive. She had taught him a great deal, reflected Francesca, and not just about sex or politics. Whether the knowledge of fabrics and cushions was really essential to a man who might one day yet rule the Holy Roman Empire, and definitely would rule the rough Celtic halls of Brittany, could be debated. But Francesca de Chevreuse had no doubts about it being of value. Both politics and sex were enhanced by such things. How many pointless wars were born, accidentally, out of a poor night's sleep or an uncomfortable seat? While dukes, kings and emperors might claim to rule by divine right, that did not appear to protect them from occasional peevishness. She'd gotten to meet several of the great men, first as a courtesan and later as Manfred's leman.

She bit her lip. Being Manfred's leman had been a comfortable life and an interesting one. She had a great deal of power and influence, even with the emperor himself. It would take very little effort and feminine wile to maintain the status quo. But in a way, this life was a gamble. And she was an intelligent gambler. It was time to get out of this particular game, while she was still winning. The emperor might have looked indulgently on his nephew's mistress, even used her as his agent, while she was a transient feature of Manfred's life. But she knew, too well, that the throne would not tolerate her installing herself as the power behind the prince.

Manfred was changing. Command on Corfu had altered him. He didn't realize it yet, but he was ready to move on.

She'd seen it before as a courtesan. She recognized the signs now.

Therefore it was time for her to move on, too. Quickly and neatly, retaining the contacts and friendships that she'd established. Alexandria called to her. It was supposed to be a warm, cultured and seductive city. Well, that sounded just like her sort of place. She gave a wicked little chuckle. Besides, the city would need something to counter Eneko Lopez and his companions' piety.

Manfred came in quietly. For a big man he could move remarkably silently when he chose to. "I thought you might be asleep," he said.

The solicitousness too was unlike him. Manfred was not inconsiderate, or even particularly self-centered, for a prince of the blood. Erik had seen to that. Manfred could be very considerate—when it occurred to him that his normal way of life might be less than pleasant for someone else. That much she had tried to teach him, along with politics and a less brute force approach to everything.

"A glass of wine?" he asked pleasantly, running a big hand down her spine.

Francesca swallowed. She'd dismissed many lovers before. Some of them had been powerful, big, violent men. She'd taken appropriate steps to deal with that sort of problem, and moved on. Anyway, she had no such fears from Manfred. Why then, was she afraid? It suddenly came to her. Yes, he was powerful and influential. But she was afraid of hurting him. That was not something that had ever bothered her before. She'd spent a long time with Manfred, though, longer than with any other lover. Long enough to know that he too had his soft spots, and where they were.

"I thought you were still in church," she said.

"The bishop got tired of me. He threw me out."

Manfred smiled. "The Church loves me . . . and loves me to leave when I sing."

He walked across the room and poured out two goblets of wine. "The truth is that I had a feeling I should come up and bid you farewell."

She gaped at him.

"I didn't want you to go without at least saying goodbye."

Her eyes narrowed. "Eneko?"

He handed her the goblet. "He's as mum as an oyster, my dear. You know that."

"Then how . . . ?" She was never at a loss of words. Suddenly, she found them scarce.

"You said so, a while back. And I've been seeing the signs. I was taught by a selection of women, Francesca. As well as you."

"You've learned a bit too well," she said wryly. "What do you intend to do about it?"

"Help with the organization. I've learned over the years that you usually do exactly what you plan to do. And I value you too much, both as a friend and a lover, to stand in your way."

"It is not fair to play emotional games, Manfred." Her voice was slightly gruff in spite of the superb self-control she prided herself on.

"Nothing is fair, Francesca. But I'm not good at games. I'd rather hope that I could see you in Alexandria one day, than be stupid enough to try to keep you."

"You've grown a lot, Prince."

"I hope not. Getting armor altered is more complicated than you may realize. Now, do I lock the door to keep Erik out for a last few minutes or not?"

"Oh, I think I can spare you more than a few

minutes, and make it last a little longer than that too," said Francesca, lowering her lashes.

Erik Hakkonsen, bodyguard and mentor to Prince Manfred of Brittany, forced the attacker's blade point into the wood of the door behind him. In the process he might just have broken the man's fingers. Erik hit him with the pommel of his knife to silence him. The last thing that he wanted was to attract extra attention. Narrow alleys were not his choice of fighting ground. Kari was still fighting with the other two. Erik grabbed both of Kari's opponents by their loose garments and slammed their heads together. Hard.

Kari looked reproachfully at Erik as he dropped the two limp bandits. "What did you do that for? It was shaping into a nice little fight."

Erik shook his head at the young Vinlander. Kari's family were sept and kin, at least by Erik's understanding of the duty he owed to Svanhild. Erik therefore owed a duty of care to the boy. He'd not expected that to mean taking care of a tearaway, who, while less inclined to go drinking or whoring than Manfred had been, liked fighting. Kari fitted Jerusalem like a bull-seal fitted a lady's glove.

"If you want to fight there are plenty of knights. And there is me," said Erik.

Kari grinned disarmingly, showing a missing tooth. "The knights fight like knights. And as for you... I like to win sometimes. I thought you were busy watching over the *Godar*'s nephew?"

"He's in church. On his knees. Where you will be shortly. Those men did not want to fight. They wanted to kill and rob you."

Kari shrugged. "Who else could I find? I don't like picking on drunks. You said that that was unsporting."

"One of these days you will also remember that I said picking fights with back-alley murderers would get you killed, you young fool." Erik took him by the ear and led him toward more salubrious parts of the city. With Manfred, Erik had thought that he was hard done by having had to locate all the taverns and brothels in any town. Kari took things to whole new level. He could be looking for a fight anywhere.

BUDA, THE KINGDOM OF HUNGARY

From the topmost ducat-gold curl to the tip of her toes, Countess Elizabeth Bartholdy was the most beautiful and youth-filled damsel any man could ever dream of. She simply had to smile and lower her long sooty eyelashes to have most men agree to do anything she asked of them.

The guard on Prince Vlad of Basarab's elegant prison was made of sterner stuff than most. That was not surprising, of course. You would want such guards for the grandson of the Dragon. But he was still a man. And too slow to react, when she put her hand where no lady would have done.

That instant of hesitation killed him, as the razor-sharp talon-like steel tips to her claws slipped through the cloth far more easily than the proverbial hot knife through butter. There were a few inhuman things that could survive the venom that tipped those nails. No human could.

She sheathed the claws again, as he fell with barely a whimper. There was a slight clatter from his sword. She paused for an instant to enjoy the look on his face. She loved that look of startlement and betrayal. It suited men so well.

Her fingertips were once again without blemish, her nails beautifully manicured. There was a cost to turning your own body into the perfect assassin's killing tool, but Elizabeth had paid that price long ago. Long, long, long ago. More than a century before.

She opened the door to the chambers of the captive duke of Valahia with a smile on her lips. There was something about killing that awoke certain hungers in her. But magic required that she should not use the boy within to satisfy those lusts. He had other value to her. Mindaug had given her a time and place at which he would still have to be alive and, for best effect, virginal. At the time and a place when the shadow ate the moon. And her control of herself was superb. After that, he could be abused and die.

The prince in the tower had not spent long hours mooning out of the windows or singing to passers-by. Heredity had shaped him into a silent man—that and a lack of company, perhaps. Besides, neither were practical options. There were no windows he could see out of.

King Emeric had seen to it that his hostage lacked for nothing—except his liberty, and the freedom to use his mother tongue. The prince had had instruction in several others, Frankish, Greek, Aramaic. He had had tutors for these subjects, of course, Hungarian ones. But other than those and the silent guards, he saw few people, and certainly none of his own age or speaking his own tongue. He had kept the language alive somehow in his memory, reciting the stories and songs of his childhood—silently, under his breath every evening. He had been forbidden to speak or sing them aloud.

He'd done so at first to escape the crushing fear and loneliness of being a small boy taken far from everything he loved and knew, and imprisoned here. And then terrified out of his wits—after being beaten and shown slow death—an act of brutality that as an older, more logical man, he understood had been to ensure that the king of Hungary had a suitably cowed vassal. Instead, his spirit had been shaped by the experience into a secretive but fiercely resistant one. A spirit that sometimes indulged in cruel and wild fantasies of revenge, but more often just longed to be free.

As for sanity...was he mad? Sometimes he wondered.

As prisons went, his apartments had every luxury— except windows. There was a narrow arrow slit high up on the wall above the stair. From a certain angle, he could see the sky through it. Not direct sunlight, but daylight, and sometimes cold breezes wafted in from the outside world, strange in their scents, unfamiliar in their chill.

By the age of twenty he had, to some extent, forgotten the world outside the walls. Not forgotten a desire for it, no, never! But forgotten the details of it. Books, for all that he loved them, were not the same. And Father Tedesco, his most frequent companion, was more inclined to talk of the glories of Heaven, than the glories of the world outside.

Vlad heard someone outside the doors, and wondered if the old priest had come to visit him again.

There was a faint clatter and the door swung gently
open.

It wasn't the elderly priest.

It was a vision.

An angel.

Naturally she had come to save him from this hell.
So why was he so afraid?

THE SOUTHERN CARPATHIAN
MOUNTAINS

The hills echoed with the howling of the wolves. The
slim, dark-complexioned man with the silver earrings did
not appear to find that a worrisome thing. He slipped
along the ghost of a trail as silently and as surefootedly
as a wolf himself. The full moon shone down casting
spiky shadows on the pine-needle covered forest floor.
The wyvern was just a slightly more spiky piece of
darkness. Spiky darkness with red eyes that glowed
like coals. Wyverns could shift their opalescent colors
to match their surroundings. Here she did not have to.

"So, old one. The blood moon time is coming. The
signs say she will capture him," said the lithe man,
looking warily at her.

The wyvern nodded. "She will watch over him
carefully. And she has killed many of our kind." It
spoke his tongue. That was part of the magic gift of
the creature. A small but vital part.

"Blood calls. We must answer. We have a compact to
honor. Blood to spill." His teeth flashed briefly at that.

"You are too fond of blood, Angelo."

He shrugged. "It is in my nature. My kind needs to see it flow. Life is just the song of the hunter and the hunted."

"There is more to it than that," said the wyvern.

"Not for us. Prey or predator, all part of the one or the other, and part of the same."

The wyvern was a hunter herself, and understood the wolfish Angelo and his kin better than most. "But which one is the boy? Hunter or the hunted?"

Angelo laughed humorlessly. "We will just have to see, won't we? And she considers all of us prey. Him more so than us."

The old wyvern sighed. "True." She bowed her head. "Strike cleanly."

Angelo drew his blade. It was an old, old knife, handed down from generation to generation. The flakes of razor-edged chert were still sharp. The magic would not allow metals to be used for this deed, the start to the renewing of the compact. It came from a time of stone, tooth and claw. "When have I ever done otherwise, old friend?" he said grimly. "It is the least I can do."

Afterwards he gathered the blood, and cradled his burden, cut from the creature's belly. The wyvern was one of the old ones, a creature woven of magics, not designed by nature. There was no other way to get her egg out. The wyvern had to die so that the new ones could be born. And the young wyverns were needed, if the old oath was to be renewed.

Blood must flow. It was all in the blood.

The wolves howled as he walked the trail back towards the tents. Angelo howled in reply. By morning they must all be gone. They were not welcome here any more. The local residents did not approve of the gypsies. Angelo found that funny. They were not the recent incomers, traveling people from the south, barely in these lands for a few centuries. They had roved this land for always and always. But the "gypsies" were a good cover. The old ones had adopted some of their ways, just as real gypsies had taken on some of the ways of the pack.

Well, it should be a year before they came back to this part of their land, in the normal course of events. Of course this year might be different. Angelo stalked out of the woods and slipped past a neat farmstead as silently as he'd come. Somehow, the dogs chained there still barked. It was, he supposed, inevitable that they would know he was near. Dogs did. It was an old kinship, even if they were estranged now.

Instinctively, Angelo surveyed the property. The hen-coop beckoned, but he had more important things to do than harvest it. The camp must be broken, and that took time; time they could not spare. They must be miles away before dawn. The evil old woman had her creatures, too. They would bring her word that the old wyvern was dead. She'd been investigating the subject of the Dragon's blood, and word got around.

The settled ones deemed this their property and the gypsies to be trespassers and something of a nuisance. Amusingly enough, that was just how Angelo and his clan regarded the settlers. A nuisance that was cluttering up part of their ancient hunting range. The settlers were too numerous to eliminate, but the tribe made up for it as well as possible by preying on them, as wise predators do, not too much or too often. That way prey went on being prey, and available.

❦   ❦   ❦

Gatu Orkhan stared narrow-eyed at General Nogay. "I will need more gold. Much more."

"I have been told that this can be provided," said Nogay. "But gold, Orkhan, is not all we need."

Nogay knew his master to be a weak reed. A good fighter, true. A general who had used his forces well, carefully pitting them against foes he could beat. But while he might have blood of khans in his veins, he lacked that which made men love him.

Lithuanian gold from across the northern border, gold landed in secret on the beaches to the east, had helped. But thanks to the legacy of Ulaghchi Khan, the clans—especially the traditionalists such as the powerful Hawk clan—frowned on ostentation, away from feasts and weddings.

"Yes. We will need more magics," said Gatu, misunderstanding him.

Nogay contained his sigh. He was no magic worker. No shaman who could move through other realms. He had simply used some simple spells provided by his northern paymaster, Grand Duke Jagiellon. The spells required certain rigid conditions—clear sight of the victim, and items of the victim's essence—hair, nail clippings, skin. He'd killed for his master before, with these tools. And he'd been very careful to make sure that he had some hair from Gatu, and he disposed of his own hair and nail-clippings in the fire.

PART I
July, 1540 A.D.

Chapter 1

Sitting back in his chair in his office in the Castel *a terra* of the Citadel of Corfu, Benito Valdosta raised his eyebrows. "And you want me to come out to your estate for some hunting but not to tell anyone. Giuliano, how stupid do you think I am?"

Giuliano Lozza had begun to acquire a little layer of comfortable plumpness again that had made the recruits in Venetian Corfiote irregulars call him *Loukoúmia*. Marriage to Thalia, and with a babe on the way, had eased some of the bitter lines that the murder of his wife and child had brought to the face of the former guerilla-captain. Giuliano had turned down the offer of the job of captain-general of the island without a second thought. He was more interested in his olives, his grapes and the possibility of a pack of plump children to spoil. It would be easy for a fool to forget that the *Loukoúmia* was a master swordsman and strategist.

Benito was only a fool some of the time, and this wasn't one of them. Giuliano smiled. "Spiro told me I might as well be direct with you. It's a dangerous business, Benito. One I wish I was not involved in."

"Then why are you involved, Giuliano? Just what is going on?"

"Listening ears, Benito," said Giuliano quietly. "Trust me. For old time's sake."

Benito sighed. "I've got responsibilities, Giuliano."

"She—they'll do without you for a day, Benito," said the swordsman-turned-olive-grower, understandingly.

Benito looked at the crib in the corner of his office. Times changed. He now had an office, not to mention the crib. "But will I do without them?" he asked wryly. "Very well. Tomorrow."

Giuliano shook his head. "Tonight. It must be tonight. The wind is right," he said, cryptically, "for the kind of game we're after."

The wind was setting westerly. Good for Albania, if not wild boar. The hairs on Benito's neck prickled. "I'll be there."

"So will our old friends, Taki and Spiro."

That confirmed his suspicions. Every second local male was called Spiro, and every fourth, Taki. The conversation would mean nothing to a listener who was not aware that their mutual friends Taki and Spiro were the skipper and the mate of a small fishing boat. They were principally fishermen, anyway, although it could be argued that they were actually principally drinkers of mediocre to bad wine, and incidentally extremely good seamen and fisherman. Like all skippers around these parts, Taki fished for some targets that were best fished for on moonless nights, landing goods when and where duties were not collected on cargoes. Benito would have trusted them with his life. He'd had to before.

Whatever was going on, it had forced a man who

would rather grow olives to mess with politics. A man who would rather farm than adorn the most powerful military and second most powerful political office of the island. It had to be worth looking into. Corfu was a Venetian possession, but it was also a small island close to Byzantine Greece and the wild mountainous tribal lands of the Balkans. As much as the tribal clans up in Albania and the hinterland accepted any one leader, it was Iskander Beg, the Lord of the Mountains. Iskander Beg had held off both the Byzantines and Hungary—no small feat.

Some of the tribes had occasionally raided Corfu in the past. Corfu was a soft place compared to their iron hills. The Venetians, and the local magic, had made that an expensive exercise—but the cost had been counted by both sides. As the temporary deputy governor, Benito wanted to avoid any more attacks. Corfu needed a time at peace to recover and grow. An enemy might see this as a good opportunity to attack.

Benito had put out feelers to Iskander Beg, with those who did a little legitimate trade with southern Illyria. He had not expected a reply from this source. He smiled ruefully to himself. He should have. He'd learned a great deal about politics in the two months he'd waited for Venice to send out a new governor, much of which he hadn't wanted to know. The underlying principle seemed to be that nothing in politics was ever straight or direct.

He sighed and looked at the clock. He had yet another meeting with the surviving Libri di Oro, the aristocratic landlord parasites that Venice had created from the Corfiote nobility. Created, and then made rotten and idle. They would pour platitudes on him, when what most of the ticks wanted was for him to drop dead, and the opportunity to get their old lives back, with as much extra land-loot as they could steal added to their wealth. Benito would be polite in return, although he wanted to break them. Going off in the dark with Lozza would be a relief. He hoped that it would be to do something stupid and dangerous. At least he would be more in control then.

The water was black, nearly as dark as the mood on the boat. Even the wisecracking Spiro was less than himself.

"You realize," said Giuliano, "that if this goes wrong, Maria will kill all of us tomorrow." He was being perfectly literal. She would, and Giuliano understood Maria's "wifely" role with Aidoneus better than most Venetians. His wife believed firmly in the Goddess, and had told him where things stood.

Spiro looked at the dark mass that was Illyria, straight ahead. "If it doesn't go right, there won't be a tomorrow."

Taki, sitting at the tiller-bar snorted. "The Lord of the Mountains keeps his word. Relax. And give me some more wine."

"You've had enough," said Thalia. She'd refused to remain behind.

"I'm still upright. So how can that be true?" asked Taki cheerfully.

"If we sail back, then I have every intention of not being upright," said Spiro. "So we need to save a half a cask."

"Never put off drinking until afterwards, just in case there is no afterwards," said Taki. But he didn't insist on more wine. Instead he guided the fishing boat toward a pair of lanterns set up in a dark cove, lining them up very carefully.

A little later Benito Valdosta sat at a rough oak table in a small shepherd's hut, facing the beak-nosed lord of southern Illyria. The humble setting did not seem to bother the man. Lesser men might need regal trappings so that one did not confuse the king with a hill-shepherd. Iskander Beg claimed descent from Alexander the Great of Macedon, and he didn't need fine clothes or a rich hall to tell you who he was. All Iskander needed was enough light for a man to see his eyes.

They burned. And looking at them, Benito knew that he had found a kindred spirit, albeit one reared in even harsher soil than he had sprung from. This was not a man who would be cowed by threats or worried by the odds against him. On the other hand, he looked very shrewd indeed. This was a good thing, Benito decided, because what Benito had in mind was more like commerce than devilry.

"Once," Benito said, "there was a road from here to the Adriatic."

"The Via Egnatia. From Phillipi or Christopolis to Appolonia or to Dyrrachium. Durazzo, as the Venetians call it. Days past. A route for conquerors," said the Lord of the Mountains, dismissively. Yet . . . was that a hint of a smile under his moustache? And, whatever else he was, ignorant of history he was not. Iskander also spoke good Frankish for a hill-chieftain in a remote, mountainous piece of nowhere.

"The Romans built it to conquer Illyria. Did they succeed?" asked Benito airily.

Iskander gave a snort of laughter. "Oh, for a little

while. You can never really conquer the land of the eagles. People try."

"The Byzantines are that foolish," said Benito idly.

Teeth gleamed through the moustache. "Not often. The emperor tells them to be. The field commanders do not, in reality, try very hard any more. We've discouraged them."

Benito grinned back. "Then why worry? I gather we share a love for Emeric of Hungary."

The Lord of the Mountains nodded. "He does seem to have had a sharp lesson from you in Kérkira. And another for crossing my land without my permission."

Benito clicked his tongue. "A pity he succeeded."

Iskander Beg shook his head. "Not really a pity. He's a fool. And it is better to have the fool we know for an enemy, than to have him succeeded by a man of competence. Emeric's mouth and vanity are worth a good thousand soldiers to us." Iskander's eyes narrowed a little. "On the other hand, I have been told that your death would be worth a great deal of gold, besides several thousand warriors."

Benito smiled urbanely at the Lord of the Mountains, showing no sign of the tension he felt. "You don't have to flatter me."

The Lord of Mountains beamed. "I like you, boy. And I have just upped the value that was put on you."

"You gave your word," said Giuliano.

"And my word is good," said Iskander Beg. "Even if we stand to eliminate two dangerous enemies at one stroke."

"We do not have to be enemies," said Benito.

"You are not Illyrian. You are not of my tribe. Therefore you are my enemy."

Benito was beginning to get a feel for the way the man thought now. This was more than just a declaration of Illyria's superiority and isolation. It was a subtly worded invitation. "And how does one join your tribe?"

The Lord of the Mountains tugged his moustache. "Three ways. By birth. By marriage. And by challenge."

"It's a little late in the day for the first two. So what is the challenge? The usual thing, eh?" Benito's smile was all teeth, and did not reach his eyes. "To drink a bottle of slivovitz, kill a bear and make love to the most beautiful woman in the village. And later the challenger staggers into the village terribly scratched and says: 'Now where is this woman I have to kill?'"

The Lord of the Mountains laughed. "You'd do better to take your chances with the bear than trying your charms on our women. No, it is a simple challenge." He pointed out of the door into the darkness. "A test of stealth to start with. I will put my men on the hill. I will go to the summit. You must join me, without being caught."

Benito's heart fell. Even after the time he'd spent with the Corfiote irregulars, Erik Hakkonsen had rated him almost as silent a woodsman as a blind horse with bells on its harness. But what did he have to lose, beside face? "Surely. Send your men out."

"They'll try to cut you rather than kill you. I'd do the same if I were you. No point in being part of the tribe with a *gyak* on your head."

Benito looked at the men he would have to avoid. Looked at their knives. Wished it could have been the bear that he had to cuddle. The twenty or so of them slipping away into the forest had longer claws. Erik should be doing this, not him. This was not the

thick Mediterranean scrub of Corfu or the lowlands
of Illyria, but an actual forest in the steep limestone
gully that led down to the river. Or bare, open rock
and thin heath that wouldn't hide a field-mouse.

"I will go up there," said the Lord of the Mountains, standing up lithely and setting off without a
backward glance.

"Benito, you are crazy," said Thalia. "The Kyria
Maria will kill me if I let you go."

Benito shrugged. "You have to understand the man,
Thalia. He is testing us. Testing Corfu. To fail will
be bad. To not even try will say that we are soft." As
quietly as he could he slipped away into the woods.

It wasn't quietly enough. He never even saw the
man, just saw the flash of steel.

They might be able to move like ghosts, but no one
had taught them how to use the blade. Being fair, it
could have been that the man had wanted to cut, not
kill. The Illyrian hadn't expected to have his blade
pushed into a tree, and to have himself thrown hard
over Benito's hip. Iskander Beg's man had the breath
knocked out of him—but the weak cry and the crashing
were enough. Others were coming. So Benito stepped
around the vast boled tree and swung up into it.

He hadn't been as unobserved as he'd hoped. There
were five of them coming out of the shadows. They
sounded cheerful enough as they helped his victim to
his feet.

And then they started climbing after him. Benito
moved higher, farther out among the spreading branches.
Dawn was not that far off and visibility up here was
better. They were good woodsmen, but terrible climb-
ers. For this business, a childhood spent scrambling

over the roofs of Venice was far better training than woods and mountains.

Benito waited until the closest man was within a nervous two yards of him. The branch cracked and Benito dropped to a lower branch, with a laugh. The backspring had the pursuer grasping branches frantically. Benito moved out on the lower branch.

Another three men. He waited as they climbed the tree too. And Benito jumped.

As roof jumps went it was a small one—not more than four yards and to a lower branch. It was a branch in another tree, however. Moving fast now, Benito went down that tree, leaving the swearing Illyrians behind him. Someone fell, by the sounds of it.

That had cleared at least eight of them out of his path. Benito abandoned stealth and ran, uphill, cursing tree-roots. He had about three hundred yards to cover.

Fortunately, he saw and heard the pursuit—and climbed the next tree. He repeated the trick—not waiting for the fellow to get high before dropping into another tree. And down. And then a few yards on. Up again, unseen.

He watched as one of the Illyrians passed below. It was tempting to drop on the fellow and teach him to also look up occasionally, but he was here to get up the slope, not to have fun. And Benito had to admit that he *was* having fun. He had missed this.

Better not to let fun distract him too much. The trouble was that treed gullies inevitably got narrower and steeper at the top.

He found a nice weighty dead branch, and, climbing up to where he could at least see the crescent moon, he flung it down slope. That done, he dropped out of the tree and began moving laterally, out of the forested gully. There was no cover out there.

No cover for the solitary guarding Illyrian either. The fellow was staring at the forest, sitting on a rock cleaning his fingernails with his knife. Benito had less than seventy yards to the top. There were times for subtlety and times for speed—and a good solid branch he found lying on the ground.

Benito tossed a loose rock downhill and to his left, and started running as soon as he heard it clattering. The momentary distraction gave him twenty yards before the Illyrian saw him and ran at him, yelling. There were other shouts from behind him. Benito didn't look back. He just used the branch like a lance, and the moment's shock of impact to sidestep. And then to keep running for the last twenty yards.

Where a rude shock awaited him.

He might even have been caught right there, if it had not shocked his pursuer just as much. There was no one there.

Benito simply turned and ran the other way. He swore quite a lot, too. There was a perfectly good path down the slope to the hut that took him a few minutes, instead of the half hour he'd spend in blundering through the woods.

The Lord of the Mountains was sitting on the bench outside the hut, with one of his own men, and the other Corfiotes. Benito had had the hill to help him get over his bad temper at being so neatly gulled.

Iskander hadn't actually said he would *be* at the top of the hill. He'd just said that he'd go there. Well, if the Illyrian thought he could teach a Venetian how to make deals with weasel words...

"Giuliano," he said conversationally, panting just a little, "disarm that bodyguard."

The bodyguard was undoubtedly one of the finest fighters in all Illyria. Giuliano Lozza was still easily his master, especially since the bodyguard plainly wasn't expecting such a command.

While the distraction occurred, Benito stepped up to Iskander and touched his shoulder. "Reached you," he said. "But I think I will leave you alive, because you are more trouble to Byzantium and to King Emeric than I'd realized you would be."

Iskander Beg smiled. "The blood feud you'd cause by killing your own kinsman and chieftain would hardly be worth it."

He stood up, planted his hands on his hips, and watched the panting band straggling up to the hut. "Well? Do you still think the Venetians are soft? And that we should raid now while Kérkira is war-weary and weak?"

The remark provoked a fair storm of laughter. Knives were sheathed. Benito found himself surrounded by the group that had tried to catch him, grinning and backslapping. Iskander joined them. "Come. Now we will talk. And drink slivovitz, kinsman."

Sitting and drinking the clear plum liquor at dawn was not something that Benito wanted to do every day, but today it seemed fitting. "I rule at least in part by guile," explained Iskander, sitting a little apart and talking to him. "The tribes are fiercely independent. But they will follow a clever leader who has won their respect. This story will go around. It will grow in the telling. People will say how cunning the Lord of Mountains was ... and that this Venetian was a match for him. Like a fox, but with honor. That is important here. There were some that said it would be the right time now to attack Kérkira. In spite of the magic."

"It's not something I would attack. That magic destroyed Emeric," said Benito, keen to reinforce the idea, as little as he approved of the Goddess and her cult.

Iskander Beg shrugged. "The Illyrians drove the Pelasgian mother-worshippers from this land to Kérkira. They have long memories in these mountains. They remember the land moving and the sea coming and killing their ancestors. They remember that magic, and saw that it was still active. Now my people have two reasons to keep away—magic and a leader they can respect. So: Tell me now what you plan for the Via Egnatia. It would not be good for the trade of Kérkira for it to operate again."

"I think it can be made good for Corfu," said Benito, "for Venice, and also Illyria. Ships, especially round ships carry more cargo. But...if I am right, the Byzantines will seek to bar us from the Bosphorus. From the Black Sea trade. Trade is like the muscles of your hand. If you don't keep using it the hand grows weak. It loses its cunning. It's what happened to Via Egnatia. Once a little part of every caravan that passed along it stayed here in Illyria. Most of the bulk went on to be sold, but enough remained here—paid by travelers, to be a goodly amount of wealth. Still, it was a small part of every rich load. Some chieftains saw profit in robbing travelers, taking the entire load rather than just a little. So fewer travelers risked the road. So it became less friendly—and now no one uses the old trail. I want to open it up again. If we can reach some agreement with the Bulgars or the Golden Horde, Venice could still move cargoes of silk and spices from the east through Trebizond, even if Constantinople is closed to Venetian shipping. Raiding is fun, but the real profit lies in trading."

"Spoken like a Venetian," said Iskander.

"Yes. It has the advantage of being true, too," said Benito dryly. "Look. We have this night put the final veto on to any Illyrian ideas of war with Venice. You did not want it anyway. Why not use the situation to our mutual advantage as well?"

Iskander Beg was silent for a while and then answered. "Because the chieftains of the Illyrian tribes from here to the edges of Macedonia obey me out of choice. Fractiously. I really have little power over them. And raiding is a way of life here. But I will think about it."

Benito rubbed his chin thoughtfully. It was something that had bothered him once...to be his father or his grandfather's offspring, and not to be himself. But since then—now on this hillside, again—he'd proved himself. And a weapon was a weapon. You used it when you needed it, before worrying about where it came from. "You may have heard of my grandfather, Duke Enrico Dell'este of Ferrara."

"The Old Fox," said Iskander. "I have done my best to study his tactics. Just because I live in the mountains of Illyria does not mean that I am ignorant, Benito Valdosta."

Benito was sure by now that wherever this man had lived—and he'd bet it wasn't just in the mountains of Illyria—that he was anything but ignorant. "We talked about the Swiss mercenaries once. He said the greatest warriors came from places where nature shaped and honed the men from birth, and frequent combat had tempered them. Harsh places. He also said that the people of such places win battles, but lose long wars."

Iskander raised his eyebrows. "While I accept the first part of his statement—my people have to be as hard as the rock of our mountains or they would die, and they spend what spare time they have in feuding—I do not intend to lose my wars. All our wars here are long. So why does the Old Fox say that we will lose?"

Benito knew then that he had been right to bring his grandfather into it. Enrico Dell'este would be taken seriously on this subject, by such a man. Benito Valdosta would not be. Not yet.

"Two things. Firstly, numbers. The warrior of the harsh lands can kill five times as many soft lowlander soldiers—but there are fifty men from the fat fertile lowlands to one from the harsh mountains. And the other factor is money. It is hard enough to scrape a living off these bare hills, let alone buy good weapons or keep a large standing army. The second sons of the mountains, and cold northlands too, go off raiding or as mercenaries because there is not enough food or land."

Iskander grunted irritably. "I accept that the Old Fox is right on this. But I have a people and a land to hold, and, yes, to reclaim that which was taken from us. We shape our fighting around harvests and fieldwork. Short sharp raids are our way."

"And you need the grain and cattle and sheep of

the lowlands to keep your people alive in winter. But you cannot press your advantage, because the food needs to get home. So, you win each battle . . . and lose the fertile valley lands, because you cannot hold them. Or if the tribe moves to soft lands, they too become soft and lose their battles."

Iskander raised his chin, and stared down at Benito, eyes narrow. "So, Benito. The Old Fox's grandson does not lead me down this path only to tell me that I cannot win. How do we avoid this trap?"

Benito smiled. "I told you. You sit astride a trade route. In the long term, trade will bring your people far more than the loot from one raid, or even from one trade caravan. You can keep the second and even third sons home, as warriors. There will be fighting on the borders."

"More when there is a rich prize like a trade route to be seized, or competition to be blocked," said Iskander.

Benito drank some of the plum liquor. "Nothing is for nothing," he said with a grin.

Iskander nodded. "You speak very persuasively. What does Venice gain from this?"

"A route around Alexius. More traffic. And someone who will lose much trade if they go to war with us," said Benito.

"Clever," said Iskander.

"It's this stuff we are drinking. Enough of it and anything sounds clever." Benito swayed to his feet. "I just hope Taki really does sail better when he's drunk or we may end up in Vinland instead of Corfu."

Chapter 2

"Magic is not some cheap fairground trick, for the entertainment of fools, easily done and cheap in the price it asks," said Eneko Lopez, calmly but firmly. "And you know we do not act for earthly thrones or powers."

"This isn't exactly an earthly power," said Manfred wryly.

"It still means mixing in the affairs of governments, princes and kings, to say nothing of emperors."

"And what are the alternatives, Eneko?" asked Manfred. "That we should all sit on our hands waiting for the lightning to fall? You know as well as I do that Jagiellon has motives which reach far beyond mere geographical conquest. At least you should know that, seeing as you have told me so."

Lopez lowered his heavy brow and peered at Manfred from under it. "Don't play your semantic games with me, Manfred of Brittany," said the cleric grimly. "God gave us responsibility, so that we might use it. Not so that we could rationalize doing just what we wanted to do."

"Well," said Manfred, "at the end of the day it is your decision." He turned and walked out.

Erik followed, looking rather bemused. "I thought that you were going to make sure that he sent a message to the emperor?" he said, once they were outside.

"I have," said Manfred grinning, showing his large square teeth. "You cannot force someone like Eneko Lopez to do something by telling them that they must."

Erik raised an eyebrow, "So you tell him that he must not? That's Kari-level logic."

Manfred shook his head. "I set it out with impeccable logic and then leave it to him to sort it out with his own conscience. I am pretty sure that in the next few minutes he will be consulting with those brothers of his, and will be in magical communication with Rome. Word will spread very rapidly from Rome. We have a good network that picks up information from there. I can pretty well guarantee that word will be carried both to Mainz and to Venice within the next two weeks if not sooner."

"Where did you learn to be so devious?" said Erik, shaking his head. "The right knightly behavior is to have threatened to knock his head off and then to have a good half an hour argument and shouting match about it."

"Would that have achieved anything?" asked Manfred, grinning. "I mean, it sounds like a lot of fun and very traditional, but Eneko is really not someone you can force to do anything. What we really wanted was for him to contact Mainz magically. He's not going to do that, no matter how we try, but this way we might get him to at least tell Rome."

"If it catches on, we could have the development of a new age of reason," said Erik dryly. "But I don't think the Knights of the Holy Trinity are quite ready for this."

"It's the weight of all of that armor," said Manfred. "It weighs down on their heads—"

"And stops the brain from working," finished Erik. "It's an interesting theory, Manfred, but I know as many hidebound warriors on the plains of Vinland as I do among the Knights of the Holy Trinity, and they don't wear armor."

"A good thing, too. Next thing I know you'll want me out of my armor. And I'm built to carry it. I must admit I really feel more comfortable in it. But I thought I'd beat you to your favorite argument about steel affecting our brains."

"I detect the fell hand of Francesca," said Erik with a wry smile. "I wonder how long the effects of her training will go on affecting you?"

"She is not someone that I am going to forget in a hurry," said Manfred, quite somberly.

"True," agreed Erik. Privately, he thought that his task was going to be considerably harder now. But there was also no doubt that Manfred was considerably wiser than he had been when he had first encountered Francesca, both about intrigue and in dealing with people. Much to his surprise, Erik regretted that she was going to be going to Alexandria and would not be continuing to journey with them. He had come to accept that she was an ally, and in her strange way, a kind of friend. But all he had said was that they had better tell the knights of Manfred's escort that they would be leaving Jerusalem quite soon.

Manfred nodded. "Eberhard is just waiting for some letters that will accredit the Mongol tarkhan as a diplomatic emissary of the Ilkhan. The Mongols are very stringent about the way that diplomatic missions are treated. I gather that the protection afforded to him would even extend to us if we were caught up in some fracas in their territories."

"Mighty generous of them," said Erik sardonically.

"It harks back a long way," said Manfred sententiously. "Apparently some minor emperor sent back the head of a tarkhan to Genghis Khan. Genghis declared war and hunted the emperor down, finally killing him on some remote island in the Black Sea. Believe it or not, I actually read about it. If they knew about the reading back in my father's court I would be a laughing stock. It's all the fault of you and Francesca. You have rotted my brain and kept me from the strong drink that would have preserved it. I need some wine to set this right."

"Any excuse," said Erik, "but I must admit that I am fairly dry, and the water in this town would give a camel the flux."

"Excellent," said Manfred. "Let us go and find Falkenberg. That way we can combine drinking with telling him that Eberhard is going to have us escort a party of Mongol diplomats."

"I am sure that will delight him," said Erik, grinning wryly.

"Well, I suspect the drinking part will."

In the cell that he had been assigned in the Hypatian monastery, Eneko Lopez might well have guessed that he was being manipulated. He was an astute man and had much experience of the ways of the world. However, Manfred's predictions were quite correct, too. Eneko had very little option but to warn the Grand Metropolitan in Rome that the earthly arm of the spiritual evil to the east was going to threaten the entire Mediterranean.

Soon he and his brothers were busy setting up the candles for the wards. In reality, this was neither the most demanding nor the most difficult of magics. However, he did believe that magic should not be used lightly under any circumstances. Kings and princes seemed to have trouble understanding that every little thing they wanted done was not of the greatest urgency.

The monks chanted in unison, raising the wards. Eneko wondered whether this development should change the way that he saw his future duty. Perhaps Rome would see it that way. On the other hand, Alexandria was as much a city of the Mediterranean as was Venice or Rome. Unless he misread the intentions of the demonic force that had possessed Prince Jagiellon, it only sought geographical dominion in order to gain control over other things which were not of this world. What it sought could as easily lie hidden in the myriad scrolls and ancient books of magical lore in the great library at Alexandria. Eneko did understand that power left its mark on the very stones of places. It was almost as if the magic leached out into the surroundings, polluting them and changing them. Sometimes for the better, or, depending on the nature of the magic, the worse.

He shook himself away from these thoughts. It was his turn to perform the rituals. He could ill afford to be distracted. Even thus protected by angelic wards the practice of magic reaching across great distances was still a very dangerous pastime, in which the practitioner was at great risk of interception and harm by hostile magic workers.

Chapter 3

"We must hurry," said the blond woman. She seemed not much older than Vlad himself, and was extraordinarily beautiful.

The door to his gilded cage swung invitingly open. The prince hesitated. "Who are you?" he asked.

She curtseyed. "This is no time for formal presentations, Your Highness. I am countess Elizabeth Bartholdy of Caedonia in Valahia, as well as of estates in other lesser places such as Catiche. I have come to save your life. I will explain once we are away from here."

It sounded tempting. But King Emeric had himself explained that Vlad was more in a protective custody than just being a mere hostage. "The guard?" he asked, looking at the fallen man, sprawled at the doorway.

"He is drugged. I am afraid I had to put something in his wine."

He looked very dead to Vlad. Death always had an odd fascination for him. He curbed the desire to bend down and feel if the man was cold. Dead animals were.

"Your Highness," said the beautiful young countess,

with just a hint of asperity. "Your father is dead. You have no further value as a hostage. The only reason that you are still alive is because King Emeric is away on a military adventure. I know that messages have been dispatched to him, asking for orders about your future. And even if the king decides to keep you alive, your principality will no longer be yours. In the Duchy of Transylvania, the Danesti prepare to put a pretender on the throne. Your loyal boyars need you."

Father Tedesco had said that Vlad's fascination with death was unnatural, a recurrence of the evil that had haunted his grandfather. Sometimes Vlad thought that was true. That he was the Dragon, reborn.

She touched his hand, her hands soft and cool. He had not been touched by a woman who was close to his own age for many years now. It sent an odd frisson through him, not wholly pleasant, yet compelling.

"We must go now. The carriage is waiting," she said.

He followed her out of the doorway and into the passage. She locked the door, and dropped the key onto the sprawled guard. It was all strange and dreamlike. He'd imagined walking down that passage. He found imagination had deserted him. Left him numbed, and a little afraid.

"Where are we going?" he asked nervously. He'd dreamed of fleeing his captivity often. But it had been a vague, nebulous dream, based on the geographical knowledge and observations of a ten-year-old boy. He wasn't even sure where home was, now.

"First, we flee Buda," she said. "We will go north to my castle in the little Carpathians. We can find shelter in several of the nunneries I have founded, on the way."

Nunneries. Well, she must be a good woman then, thought Vlad, trying to quiet his unease. The unease was not helped by the fact that she had taken his arm and was walking so close that her hip brushed against him.

She led him to a small door, which opened at her touch. Vlad had lived in near isolation since he was a young boy, but he was sure that such a portal should be locked and guarded in any castle. This one appeared to be guarded by a solitary shoe, lying on its side next to the doorframe.

It was very bright outside. Vlad blinked and screwed up his eyes. The sun on his skin was hot. It had been years since he'd last felt that sensation.

"I don't like the sun much myself," said the countess, pulling a soft lace veil over her face and urging him forward with a gentle tug. "So bad for the complexion. But we shall have to do something about your pallor. Only a prisoner or a bled-out corpse is that white-skinned, and it will not do to have you too obvious. We have several days of travel ahead of us. The roads, alas, are not something Emeric gives a great deal of attention to. I have one of the new enclosed carriages from Kocs. It will help to hide you from the sunlight."

Vlad's mind was still tumbling along with his emotions. Part of him wished to scream and dance. Another part suggested that it was all very big and open and bright, and he should turn and run back to the tower in Buda castle that had been his world for so many years. But bright and hot or not, the sun felt wonderful.

Nervously, he walked down the narrow path, away from the castle. Away from the wide Danube and the row of pikes and the flesh-tattered bones of the impaled victims that Emeric ornamented his view with. That was something Vlad's grandfather had also been infamous for. Vlad wanted to turn and stare, but she led him onward, walking calmly, until they came to the first houses, set along a narrow street. Already Vlad was aware that his boots hurt. He exercised regularly and vigorously, but only with the armsmaster in the confines of his prison. He had not walked so far since he had been a child. There were horses waiting, held by a terrified-looking groom. Horses too had grown smaller, thought Vlad bemusedly, although he knew that this simply could not be the case.

Fortunately, he had not entirely forgotten how to ride. Looking at the strange world he found himself in, Vlad was desperately glad he was not attempting this alone. He had absolutely no idea where he was going, except that it was downhill and away from the castle.

It just felt wrong. He should be going east, or at least following the river. The Danube would lead him to Valahia, to his father's duchy. His now, he supposed. But surely his rescuer knew where she was going? He would just have to put his faith in her.

They rode on, keeping in the shadow of the houses.

The wind carried a shred of strange lilting music to him from the open door of a tavern. His head said he must stay close to the countess. But his heart wanted to dismount and find that musician. He had not heard anyone play that tune since he had been a child, carefree and happy with his mother in Poienari castle. He could not remember where he had heard it there, but he could remember the tune clearly, and he also remembered that it was important, somehow. Terribly important.

His companion must have heard it, too. She turned and looked, and although the veil hid her features, he could sense her anger. "We need to ride faster," she said.

This already felt fast enough to someone who had not ridden since he was ten. But Vlad gritted his teeth and urged his mount into a trot behind her.

The music echoed in his head. It was still there when a footman helped him to dismount in a very ordinary courtyard, where four horses were already poled up to a large-wheeled carriage. At first he thought that it must be a huge vehicle. But then he realized that the man holding the door and bowing to them had an out of proportion head and was very small. He was child-sized, although bearded.

The countess gave Vlad no time to marvel at the fellow, but had him join her in the carriage. Her strange little dwarfish servitor lifted the steps, closed the door, and then made the carriage sway as he climbed up onto the box. The curtains—a rich, dark red velvet, were drawn closed. The coach clattered and swayed out of the yard. The interior felt as claustrophobic as his prison had. Vlad reached to open a curtain, to see the wonderful world out there. She put a restraining hand on his arm. She had a very strong grip for such a slight thing, Vlad noticed.

"I would like to see. It has been so long since I last could see any other places."

"Later, Prince. For now it is not safe. Now you can simply enjoy being alone in the darkness of my carriage with a beautiful woman." She gave him a sideways look, smiling. "I am sure you would like to kiss me, now that we are private and together."

The idea seemed both delicious and dangerous. Except . . . he was not all sure how to do this. She was very soft and scented against him. "We must not go too far," she said throatily. "Yet."

"It is as you said, Angelo," said the saturnine man. "She has him in her clutches. She takes him north, to her lair. But he heard the call. I saw him turn when you played it."

Angelo nodded. "It is in his blood, and that blood will answer. Now, somehow, we have to get him loose from her. We have only three days. Tonight she will stop at her nunnery. She needs her blood."

"We need blood too, Angelo," said Grigori with a toothy grin. "At least meat. A cow or a sheep."

Angelo shook his head. "A chicken will not be missed too much and will have to do for us. She doesn't want dinner. She needs pain and blood to sustain her youth. Now, brothers. We need to run. If we have a chance, we must take him."

Grigori grinned again. "I'll hamstring him, you tear his throat out. Mind you he doesn't look like he'll give us much of a chase. He looks to be a pale, weak thing."

Angelo looked grim. "*She* will chase *us*. And it will be no quick death if she catches us."

They followed the coach, discretely, at a safe distance. It was hard, deep in the farmed lands, away from the forest. But at least it was twilight, and anyone who saw them might assume that they were just great dogs, running.

Chapter 4

"I was not in any real danger, Maria. They take honor seriously over there. And now we have a peace agreement, and maybe more."

"With them," Maria hissed, glowering at him. "Illyrians! How could you!"

"Given a choice between another war right now, and reaching an agreement that could keep the Corfiotes sleeping peacefully in their beds, I thought that it was not a bad idea," said Benito calmly.

"The Illyrians drove the great Mother's people to take shelter here. Made us call on the Lord of the Dead to put the sea between us and them! Kérkira's women can never forgive them. There can be no peace between us."

"Maria, you have an Illyrian rug on your floor. You bought that happily enough, thinking that you had got a bargain. This is a business arrangement too, and Petro Dorma will be well pleased, I think. Besides, you were born and bred in Venice, not here. The people of Venice's canals are 'us,' not the women here."

Benito tried to keep his own voice completely cool.

He had no love nor trust for Corfu's ancient religion. He tolerated it. Barely.

"They are my people now," she said stiffly.

Benito was too tired for an argument. He shrugged. "Then maybe you should actually ask them what they think, instead of getting on your high horse and talking for them. Thalia seemed to think that it was a good idea."

"Oh." That seemed to take the wind out of her sails a bit. "You've been drinking."

Benito nodded. "Slivovitz. For breakfast."

Maria sniffed. "Don't they have food?"

"Ewe's cheese and bread that's rich in stones," said Benito, feeling a tooth. "Trust me. I needed slivovitz to be able to eat it. Seriously, Maria. Illyria is a hard, poor country. I'd rather they weren't using us as a larder to raid. Let them trouble Emeric and the Byzantines instead. Besides, you'd like the Lord of the Mountains. I must see that you never meet, or you might run off with him."

Her eyes filled with sudden tears. "You know that's not true, Benito. I love you. It's just..."

"It's just that I didn't tell you before I went," he said skating away from the other man in her life, the Lord of the Dead. Aidoneus was always somewhere in the back of Benito's mind, as was the fact that he would have to lose her for four months, come winter. It made their relationship just that bit more tricky, along with the fact that the Church would not marry them, as a result. That drove her further into the arms of the Mother-Goddess worship and paradoxically toward Aidoneus. Life was never simple.

"Partly," she said. "And partly..."

"I know. And now is there any chance of real food? Without rocks or slivovitz? And how is our baby?"

"Grumpy and sleepless without her father. And fast asleep now, having kept me awake half the night. I suppose I could find you a bite to eat. There is some cold frittata."

Benito grinned and hugged her. After a moment she responded. "Our time together is so precious, 'Nito. And I miss you like fire when you're away."

"Better away for one night than fighting a war again," said Benito. "But yes. I missed you, too. I need you, remember."

She nodded, and buried her face in his shoulder. Together, a little later, they walked to Alessia's crib. Benito felt his face soften as he looked down on her. "Did she give you a hard time last night?"

"She's your daughter," said Maria. "So, yes. And I was worried about you. Boars can be dangerous."

"They're not a patch on an Illyrian with a sense of humor, or sailing with Taki after Spiro's finished the wine. Come, let her sleep a bit longer, and let me get some real food. And then maybe..."

Maria smiled wryly. "And then she'll wake up."

"She's trying to prevent any competition for your affection."

Later—when, as predicted, Alessia was awake—Benito went back to his office. Inevitably, there were a slew of minor matters that people thought would be better if he dealt with in person. Perhaps some of them would, at least for the people concerned. He also had to go and talk to Belmondo. The governor was in semi-retirement, but still wielded some influence back in Venice.

Benito was keen on having Belmondo's wife—and the old man himself, purely as an ancillary—shipped off to somewhere like Vinland. So far, Renate De Belmondo seemed to have understood that in choosing to accept Benito's Maria as a willing bride for the Lord of the Dead, and, what was almost worse, having put Alessia at risk, she had made for herself an implacable enemy. An enemy who would take her slightest misstep as a reason for dire consequences.

Renate may possibly have had reasons, and made innocent misjudgments in an effort to do her best. Benito could see that now. But he was never going to tell her that. He'd learned to believe in checks and balances to power, no matter how good that power was. It was faintly amusing to know that Renate and the nonhumans of the island considered him to be a check on their power. They were a little afraid of him. Bringing Maria back from the kingdom of the dead had engendered some respect from them, it seemed. That was good. Nonhumans had advantages over most mortals. Reminding them that they shouldn't abuse their powers was no bad thing, Benito felt.

Chapter 5

The sun beat down like a hammer from the cloudless sky of Outremer as they rode toward Ascalon. Well, Manfred had to admit that the hammer part could also be from the amount of wine he had drunk last night. The glare off the polished armor added insult to the throb in his head. After the departure of Eneko Lopez and his companions—one of whom was a very odd companion indeed, Francesca de Chevreuse—and a small escort of the Ilkhan's warriors, things had gotten a little rowdy. Manfred, in between wishing for a drink, had time now to think about that escort. It would seem as if the Ilkhan's local representative, the Bashar Ahmbien, was sparing no effort to please the delegation from the Holy Roman Emperor. They even had a writ of safe conduct as the escort of an emissary, with the seal of the Ilkhan himself.

Ahmbien also had spared no effort in seeing they got on the road out of Jerusalem quickly. He had even intervened to deal with some awkwardness resulting from Erik having assaulted three of the local constabulary while they had been trying to arrest young Kari.

"It was a misunderstanding," Erik said. Looking genuinely embarrassed he admitted: "I took them for back-alley knifemen."

Manfred enormously enjoyed his gentle reproach to Erik. He hadn't had many opportunities. "Tch. As if those assigned to patrol the bad parts of town ever indulged in that kind of thing! Anyway, luckily you didn't kill them. The Ilkhan takes a dim view of that. Their cracked heads will mend."

"I am sorry. I will pay weregild."

"I already have." Manfred did his best to shake his head in a good imitation of disappointment. "I do hope word of this never reaches Iceland. Think what your poor mother would say!"

Erik peered at him suspiciously. "You have no idea, Manfred. Mama is . . ."

Manfred's composure failed then, and he collapsed into helpless laughter.

Erik did a very fine bit of glowering before starting to laugh himself. "I should have left them to arrest Kari. The best place for that boy is in jail, or out on the open prairie. I can't imagine what possessed the Thordarson clan to bring him along."

"Maybe they thought there would be enough space for him to be a horse-borne hooligan. From what I've heard, the Vinlanders are used to more space and less people."

Erik nodded. "It is what calls to me about the place. There are mountains and valleys and plains . . . and then more. It is so vast and fertile."

"And warmer than Iceland and far from your mama, after she hears that you assaulted three officers of the law."

Erik pulled a wry face. "There is truth in that. She is very strict in her interpretation of right and wrong. She would never have accepted Francesca."

"You had enough trouble at first."

"I was wrong," Erik said simply. "I will miss her, you know."

"Not as much as I will," said Manfred, with a wicked grin.

Erik blushed. He was still, even after Svanhild, very prudish about some things. Manfred smiled. He'd had a pleasant few minutes giving Erik a hard time. It was a good thing that they hadn't killed the Bashar's officers, though.

Erik rode beside him now in silence. That suited the way Manfred's head felt, but headache or not, certain things were niggling at his mind.

"Just who is this Borshar Tarkhan?" he asked, pointing an elbow at the Mongol group who rode ahead of them. "I got the official story from Eberhard, but frankly it just doesn't wash."

Erik looked at the column ahead. "Eberhard says he claims to be a diplomat, but thinks that he might just be something else. I do not know the language yet, but look at the posture of his escorts. They fear him. He is a non-Mongol, yet he outranks them."

"A spy? Something else? And we are escorting him? People might take it as our stamp of approval if he causes trouble, Erik." Something else got through to Manfred's mind. "What do you mean 'know the language yet'?"

"I have decided that my penance will be to learn this language. It would have stopped me being an embarrassment to you yesterday, with Bashar Ahmbien's officers."

"Erik, get over it. I wasn't embarrassed. Amused as hell, yes. Jerusalem has been less than funny. I know you well enough by now to know perfectly well that you just made a mistake, an understandable one."

"Nonetheless, if Eberhard is right, I want to understand what they're saying. We have a new horseboy."

Manfred blinked. "What?"

"A brat Kari found for us. He speaks fair Frankish, and fluent Mongol. I will be taking lessons."

"As long he also actually knows which end of a horse produces manure and which end bites, and keeps the tack in good order, we can use him. Although getting Kari to choose a horseboy may turn out to be a mistake."

"I hope so," said Erik. "I hope he'll be more trouble than he's worth. I have made Kari responsible for the boy. He says he has no parents. That may give Kari something to do besides get into trouble himself."

Manfred shook his head. "The problem with clever ideas is that they have a habit of not working out quite the way one plans."

David, the son of Isaac, was the horseboy in question. He, too, was finding out that the trouble with clever ideas was that they didn't always work out quite as one planned. It had seemed such a good scheme. True, the Mongol overlords had very short tempers with horse thieves. With thieves of any sort—the Yasa code was harsh. Thieves died, even if they were young thieves.

But that was for those who stole horses from them. They were fairly disinterested in horse theft from visiting crusaders—as they referred to the people of the Holy Roman Empire. They had a grudge there. They were none too keen on their vassals being great horsemen either, and taxes discouraged horse ownership amongst the non-Mongol commons. There was still a market for stolen horses, though, and these foreigners had some very fine animals. And, it would seem, no idea that they might need close guarding. He could lead off a string of them from the stables to a buyer from Samaria and be back in Jerusalem—why did this foreigner think anyone would ever want to leave Jerusalem?—by morning. Even if they did come looking for him, he would just be one boy among many in the backstreets of Jerusalem.

Then he'd discovered the first problem with being hired by someone who didn't speak Frankish too well. There appeared to have been a misunderstanding. He'd thought that he was being hired to work in a stable in Jerusalem. He'd been unable to bolt when he discovered they were saddling up for the ride out of the city. Well, he disliked being out of the city, but he could steal horses out here just as easily, and use one to get himself back home.

Then he'd found that the column was being escorted by the Bashar Ahmbien's guard. He could take a chance on foreigners, but no one messed with the Ilkhan's men. There would be no help for it but to leave on foot as soon as he got the chance. His older brothers would laugh at him. Likely his father would beat him—as if he hadn't recommended him to this man who barely spoke Frankish, let alone Mongol.

David scowled. It was after midday. He should be peacefully asleep. And he'd never ridden this far before. He was going to have to cross a lot of countryside before he got back to civilization again. He'd have to see what in the way of light goods he could steal to make the exercise worthwhile.

"I feel we should be walking," said Eneko. "Or at least walk from Bethlehem."

"I will go by ship," said Francesca calmly. "In case you had any delusions about me being pregnant and on a donkey."

There was startled silence. "That's quite close to blasphemy."

"I just said it was out of the question. You were the one playing at being Joseph. Besides, piety is a state of the mind, not of the feet."

There was a snort of unwilling laughter. "You do have quite a knack of putting men in their place, Francesca de Chevreuse."

"They get so lost otherwise," she said placidly.

Chapter 6

"His *suns* soul roams the lands of Erleg Khan, my daughter," said the shaman, calmly. "I must call it back to join his other souls here under the bowl of heaven."

Wherever Kildai's soul was, it was nowhere pleasant. Bortai's younger brother muttered, but his eyes did not open. If you opened them, the pupils remained wide, even if you took him out into the brightness of mother-sun.

The shaman of the White Horde smiled comfortingly. "The windhorse of this boy is strong. His souls are strong, too. It will return. It may take time. Erleg Khan's world below is wide, far wider than this."

Bortai sighed and looked at the doorway. "Parki Shaman, you know as well as I do that the one thing that we do not have is time. Gatu calls for the election of a new khan now."

The shaman shrugged. "It may take greater skills than mine. My master Kaltegg, who was your father's shaman, had more—"

Two warriors bundled in through the door. The blade of the leader's sword embedded itself into Parki's neck. The target was in itself more shocking than the deed. Once, no one would have dared to raise a hand to the shaman of the White Horde. Now, with the old ways dying, someone had killed him. But Bortai had no time for horror.

She had time for a knife instead. The killer had no opportunity to free his blade before she cut his throat. Her father had believed that it was time the people returned to the path set by Chinggis Khan. To the traditions of the Mongol. That meant that she knew how to use a knife, a lot better than some low half-Vlachs scum.

Her father's insistence on a return to the secret history and the Yasa had gotten him killed. Her, it had kept alive.

Alive for the moment, at least. She was still armed only with a knife, and dressed in a deel, facing a foe with a sword and wearing a leather and steel mailcoat. He swung, the blade passing through the flames. She could not restrain her gasp of horror. Even those who had given up the old faith for Islam or Nestorian Christianity would not do something like that. A Mongol knew that it would mean their death.

Belatedly, that occurred to her attacker also. He looked at the fire, and that instant of distraction was enough for her. He died, as she'd intended, quietly. She cut the felt at the back of the tent, and, picking up her unconscious brother, slipped out into the darkness.

Already the kurultai encampment was noisy with the sound of drunkenness. Kildai was only fourteen, but he was a solidly built boy. She knew that she could not carry him far or fast—but that now was the time to follow the ancient maxim of Chinggis Khan to the letter. She must flee, and survive. There would be time to gather others to their standard if they lived. But Gatu had obviously decided that they would be better quietly dead.

Kildai was a problem in his unconscious state, though. He would have to travel in a cart, and that would be difficult. There were of course many carts in the section of the kurultai that was devoted to her Hawk clan. But, by the action taken, getting back there was unlikely. Even if they did, if they broke camp now it would be noticed and would lead to a confrontation that they could not afford at this point. Gatu's men would be waiting, patiently, for the last of the White Horde, the clan of the Hawk, to flee the boundary markers of the kurultai. The guard duty for the camp worked according to a strict rota, and the clan on guard tonight were no friends to the Hawk clan. She could not go back. They would be waiting, she was sure.

Instead, she made her way across the camp, keeping in the darkness between the gers, until she came to the Fox people. They were Blue Horde, but their grazing was poor, and they had a constant raiding warfare with the Bulgars. She put Kildai down in the deep shadow, stripped off most of her jewelry, and left it next to him in her sable muff. It would not do to appear too wealthy. She took a deep breath and walked forward between the fires they had set for visitors and traders. The small group drinking kumiss were silenced by her arrival.

She put her hand on heart and bowed. "Respect to the hearth and the Fox clan."

They still drank kumiss and set up guest fires, so they probably still held to tradition. Tradition would require a greeting and an offer of sustenance before any form of business could be discussed. The delay irked her, but it could be used to her advantage.

The Fox clan elders would assume she was avoiding being stolen by her intended groom. That was a game they would revel in. Being hard to capture was still honorable. Chinggis Khan had declared an end to wife-stealing, and while he lived that had been strictly observed. But he was centuries dead and, like drinking, wife-stealing was a much beloved Mongol custom.

Eventually, the niceties having been observed, they got down to negotiation. Bortai was terrified that her brother might wake, alone and in the dark and as confused as people were, after a blow to the head. But she kept a steely calm. "I need three fine horses, such horses as the great Fox clan ride."

The clan elder shook his head sorrowfully. "Alas. Horses... We could offer you a pony. For twenty dirhan in silver."

She shook her head equally sorrowfully. "A prince's ransom. I am a poor woman. What of a gelding and mare?"

The bargaining went on. She dropped some comments about the leader of the Jaghun her father wanted her to marry. She was afraid that even the small piece of jewelry she offered might be too much, or a piece they might recognize. But at length she got what she wanted—which was anything but three horses—and they got a good price on a covered cart that had seen better days, with an ox. The cart would be in bad repair, and it was most likely the ox was

young and still balky and undertrained, or close to
its deathbed. But they expected her to be caught in
fairly short order, so there was no point in parting
with the best. There was a fair chance that the ox
would either be left on the plain or become part of
her new husband's property.

Now she had to deal with the delicate matter of
getting Kildai into the cart, unseen. She really had
no idea how to manage that. But fortune favored her.
No sooner had the beast—young and balky, as she'd
predicted—been poled up, than a loud fight broke
out. Her Fox clan helpers hurried off to watch. They
were fairly drunk by now and entertainment at night
in the kurultai was scanty. She went back to find
Kildai and found that he had moved. Rolled over, or
been rolled over.

Her heart was in her mouth as she felt for her
fur muff that she'd left the rest of her jewelry in. It
wasn't there!

Anger blossomed like fire in her. What had they
come to, the great Golden Horde? She assumed that
someone had thought the boy drunk, maybe a thief
himself, and had robbed him. She cursed furiously.
Kicked something. It was the muff...but there was
no jewelry in it.

Feeling around she found a solitary bangle that the
thief must have dropped. Maybe there was more, but
time conspired against her. She slipped the bracelet
onto her wrist, carried Kildai to the cart, loaded him
into it, and led it off. There would still be sentries
to pass. But discipline was fairly lax. She'd planned
to bribe a night-watch sentry. Now...she might have
to kill one.

She made her way to the edge of the vast encampment. Once outside those limits, the rules of conduct for the kurultai would no longer apply. She could see a sentry on horseback, silhouetted against the night sky. There might be foot patrols, as well. It had not occurred to her to find out before the kurultai. Like the problem of how to deal with a mounted guard, that had not been something she had ever given any thought to.

The sentry was mounted, and had a lance, a bow, a sword. She had a knife and a bullock-cart.

And he was not going away.

She led the cart forward. Sometimes boldness was the only approach.

The guard rode over. "Where are you going, woman?"

She bowed. "Greetings."

"I asked you a question." He leaned over and grabbed her by the hair.

She grabbed his wrist and jumped, and then hung. "Hellcat!" he swore, struggling to keep his balance. But he was a Mongol horseman, not easily dislodged from the saddle. She kicked off two footed from the pony he was riding. It whinnied in protest, and he lost his grip on her hair—well, mostly; some stayed in his hand—as she fell free. She rolled under the cart.

Then the fool committed the cardinal sin of any cavalryman in combat. He dismounted. And fortune, or the tengeri, favored her. He dived under the cart too, to try and catch her, startling the ill-trained young bullock. She rolled out of under the far side of the cart while the heavy wheel rode over his arm. He screamed, but she already had her foot in the stirrup, and swung up onto the pony. She had the advantage now, as he staggered to his feet, clutching his arm.

Mongols train their horses to be weapons, too. And the guard had much that she and her brother would need to survive. She rode him down. Then she used his own lance, which had been strapped to the saddle, to make sure that he was dead. Only when she was certain did she dismount, tie a rope to him and drag him to the cart. That took nearly all of her strength to get him onto it, to lie next to her stentorianly breathing little brother.

She tied the pony to the tail of the cart, and then led the bullock off into the darkness, following the heavily worn and rutted track to the southwest, away from the lands of the White Horde and the Hawk clan. In short, away from the direction of safety—but that was also where Gatu's men would search first. By mingling her tracks with those of the other clans who had come from the southwest she would make it harder for them to track her.

A bullock cart could not move very fast or very far. And they only had one pony. A family needed at least ten, and a hundred sheep, just to survive. They would have to eat plants. The thought was enough to make her blench, despite all she had been through that night. The shame and disgust would simply have to be borne.

It was a long night. When she stopped to rest and water the bullock and the pony at a copse next to a small stream, she had time to check on her brother, and to examine the dead man.

He carried the typical gear of an ordinary horseman. Knife, sword, a small hatchet and a leather surcoat, varnished and sewed with iron bosses. His captargac had some boiled horsemeat, a small bag of millet, a small clay pignate and grut—four or five days food for them before she would have to resort to roots, berries and leaves, and whatever game she could kill.

She left the body in the copse, covered with leaf litter. She would have given him a better burial, but time pressed. A bullock-cart does not move very fast and distance was her only friend, tonight. In the morning—or sooner—the body of the shaman Parki would be discovered. Then there would be a hue and cry. Gatu's men too would be out looking for both her and Kildai.

Thinking about it now, she was sure it had been Gatu's intention to present the murdered bodies of both her and Kildai and a couple of dead scapegoat killers, to the clan. With no leadership, the Hawks and their adherents would have fallen in behind Gatu. Now...his plans too were awry. The death of shaman Parki added to that. Many had fallen from the old religion, but shamans were still revered and respected.

It was possible that the great kurultai might break up, with no decision on the khanship reached, and with clan fighting clan. She could only hope the Hawk clan survived. The clan was in a very poor position— without leadership, the sub-clans might desert to join others. There were some cousins with a claim to the clan-head but, thought Bortai, none who would do more than to enable the Hawk clan to survive, at best.

In the pale light of dawn, Bortai found a small fold in the landscape and hid the cart in among the scrub oak. She tethered the ox and pony where they could graze and reach the stream. Then, too exhausted to do more, she lay down next to her younger brother. His face was pale, but he was still breathing. She put an arm around him, and she slept.

She woke briefly as a party of horsemen rode past on the lip of the hill. She could hear their voices carried on the breeze. They were angry voices, but the words were indistinct. She held the hatchet, and waited. One whicker from the pony and they were lost.

But the riders rode on, and lady sun shone down from father blue sky.

Chapter 7

David was saddle sore, tired and a long way from Jerusalem. Too far for him to run in one night. And that dark-haired son of Baal that had hired him still wanted work from him!

"You want me to do what?"

Kari cuffed him. "Every night. It gets done, see. If I have to chase you to it again, I'll beat you. Do you know *anything* about the care of horses? You ride like a bag of corn. You barely know which end bites and which end makes manure."

David decided right then that running off, with or without something for his trouble, could barely wait until everyone was asleep. Only they didn't seem tired.

It was a cold and gray dawn when Kari shook him awake. "Get up, lazy boy. There is work to do." Kari seemed cheerful to be up before the sun. David was not. He must have fallen asleep, and he was so stiff he could hardly move.

Kari looked at him trying to stand up and began to laugh. "You're not really a horseboy, are you?"

David stared poisonously at him. "No, lord."

"Then why did that big fool of a stable master tell me you were?"

David did not point out that his father was no stable master, although right now he would agree that he had been a fool to have done this to his youngest son. "Can I go? I will even give you the money back." He never thought he'd say that. But it would be worth it.

Kari laughed. "No."

"What...?" David gaped.

"Ha!" Kari shook his head. "And make me have to tell Erik that I messed up? Are you crazier than me? No, you are going to become a great horseboy. Now get moving. The more you move, the less stiff you will be."

The only direction David wanted to move in was straight down back into sleep. But with Kari standing there he could hardly do anything except to stagger towards his chores.

A few minutes later the Frank, Erik, came in to the stable, still in a quilted jacket and carrying a thin-bladed sword. "No training this morning, Kari?" he asked, setting aside the blade and taking off the jacket.

Kari poured oats into a nosebag. "No. New horseboy to train instead."

Erik laughed. "I hope he makes your life a bloody misery."

"Then he'll be a short-lived horseboy."

Other Frankish knights began arriving. They had all plainly been hard at some form of exercise, and were sweating freely despite the cool of the morning. David soon realized that he was there merely to care for the spare remounts. The knights had each come to see to their own horses. What kind of Frankish lords were these?

Later he asked Kari. He got a cuff around the ear for his question—but also some answers. "Firstly, I am not a Frank. I am from Vinland. And secondly, these are the Knights of the Holy Trinity. The Knights are a militant order, brat. They may be Frankish lords, but right now they are monks in armor. They also believe a knight must have a close bond with his horse. It is his first and greatest weapon in battle."

David had heard of the Knights. Who had not? It just hadn't occurred to him that these men with the three crosses on their surcoats were part of that order. They fought up in wild northern parts, which in his limited knowledge of the world, must be at least three days' ride from Jerusalem.

Vinland...he wasn't too sure where that was. A wild land somewhere to the west, full of monsters and barbarians. He took a long look at Kari. Well, that fitted.

"Why are they here?" he asked. "Are the ogres and trolls of the north coming to attack our master the Ilkhan?"

Kari shrugged. "I am just Erik's blood-retainer, now. Or so he has told me. It is some affair of state, brat. Of no interest to you or me."

David had heard of affairs of state. Just quite what they were he was less sure. But he suspected high-paid whores. He found the idea very interesting indeed. The Mongol escort's slaves and servants began trickling in to the stable area to see to the horses. One had a steaming piece of new bread. David was suddenly aware of a pressing need for food. He'd fallen asleep before anyone had eaten the night before. "Do we get to eat?"

Kari looked at him critically. "When you've finished with the horses, yes."

"Chartering vessels for this lot is going to be less easy than it was in Venice," said Manfred thoughtfully. "I don't have Francesca to smile at Petro Dorma, and the Venetians are going to look askance at fifty armed Mongols and their horses."

Eberhard shook his head. "Only nine will be going on with us. This is something of an honor guard. But yes," he said, his old eyes twinkling, "even I miss Francesca. Although it is her wit and her knowledge of statecraft that I miss."

Manfred grinned. "Old man, I saw you look at her statecraft, if that is what she kept on her chest. And I'll bet we miss her more than she misses us. She'll be breast deep in intrigue already, mark my words."

"Breast deep..."

"She never got neck deep. Always liked to be able to see above the common herd of players. I'd like her here to watch this emissary." Manfred began to chuckle. "Mind you, just think what she will drag Eneko Lopez and his friends into."

"The priest and the courtesan. An unusual pairing," said Eberhard, smiling.

"That depends on the priest," said Erik. "But those two are well matched, I would say. She'll add some worldly wisdom to his saintliness and he will add some his piety to her...uh...breasts."

Eberhard nodded. "It's as well that those two are numbered among the Empire's friends."

Manfred rubbed his jaw. "I wouldn't put it that way, exactly. Eneko Lopez is a friend of God. As long as the Empire is on God's side—at least in his eyes—he will stand by us through thick and thin. But only God will save us if we become like Aquitaine. I've heard him on the subject. As for Francesca...she is a wonderful woman. A very, very clever woman. I wonder if I ever saw what really motivated her. It wasn't just money. She could have become very rich, at least in the short term, by betraying the Empire. She knew who would pay—I know, because she pointed enough of them out to my uncle. She sees, or at least saw, that her interests aligned to the Empire—when it might have been of short-term benefit to see profit elsewhere. Now..." He shrugged. "I know she will be in contact with my uncle's agent in Alexandria."

"You're very dispassionate about it," said Eberhard, impressed despite himself. His brief had been to teach Manfred something of diplomacy and statecraft on this journey to the Holy Land. At first he'd thought it hopeless...

Manfred shrugged again. "She said princes need to be."

Erik said nothing, but he knew Manfred well enough to know that his charge was still a little hurt by Francesca's departure. Manfred was deeper than he let people guess. And his armor was more complex, too. Perhaps Francesca and Manfred had not been soul mates, as he and Svan had been, and God knew how it still burned him even now to think of her, but Manfred had stuck almost faithfully to Francesca for longer than Erik would have thought possible. In a way he was comforted that Manfred was a little wounded. Dispassionate might be what princes had to be, but it was not what a man must be. And a prince needed to be a man, first, or he might become a monster like Jagiellon. Maybe errors in love were a small price to pay to avoid that.

But all he said was, "Time to ride before it gets too hot again."

"To think I longed for warmth in Ireland," said Eberhard, looking out at the cloudless sky.

"Too much of anything is a bad idea." Manfred speared another piece of meat from the wooden platter on the table.

"Tell your stomach that also applies to breakfast," said Erik. "The sooner we go, the sooner we'll get there."

The sea was near to mirror flat when they came in sight of Ascalon, gleaming as if some knight's poor squire had just polished it, with reddish tints from the setting sun. Erik saw how the new horseboy—who had possibly the worst seat of any rider Erik had ever seen, bar Benito—gaped at it, his mouth wide open. For once, the scrawny foxy-eyed boy didn't look like a thief looking for a target. He just looked stunned and very young.

"What is it?" asked the horseboy.

"The Mediterranean. They call it a sea," said Kari, sneering, "but it's hardly worth it."

"But . . . what is it?"

"Salty water. The tear of the giantess Ran."

"Can't be." The boy swallowed. "It's even bigger than Jerusalem."

"And has more fish, too. Some big enough to eat a man whole."

The foxy expression returned to the boy's eyes. "I'm not some stupid Frank."

Kari grinned. "You just thought you were a horseboy. Really, we're keeping you for bait."

"Kari," said Erik.

"Well, he's not much good as a horseboy," said Kari with a shrug.

"And too scrawny for good bait," said Erik. "Now, someone who hasn't come to drill for the last few days is more likely to have a bit of fat on him for the sharks."

David decided that they were all crazy. He ignored them. But he wanted to get to that "sea." It called to him. He wanted to touch it. Tears...ha. There was not that much salt in the whole world. But to see it and touch it! The stories he would tell his older brothers.

The world was a bigger place than he'd realized. Bigger even than Jerusalem, although he would never admit that in public. Ascalon itself was barely worth calling a town, though, he thought, with a lofty sniff. They rode on into the gathering dusk, towards the port. The air smelled very strange. He recognized the garbage and horse-dung scent of Jerusalem. But it was overlaid with fish, tar, and a smell that he'd never come across before.

It smelled salty.

"The bad news is that going on to the Black Sea, let alone chartering a vessel to take Borshar there is simply not feasible," said Eberhard. "The Mongols are not welcome in Byzantium—with good reason, to be fair—and word is out that the Venetian traders on the Golden Horn are virtually under siege again. Alexius is not going to allow Venetian vessels to pass through the Bosphorus to the Black Sea. He may let the eastern trade convoy that has gone to Trebizond back out because to try to trap them again would mean war, but it's going to take a fleet bombarding his palace to get the Byzantines to let Venetian vessels sail up the Bosphorus."

"Get hold of the fleet in Trebizond and get them to transport these Mongol gentlemen to the lands of the Golden Horde first," said Erik. "The Mongols have this very admirable system of pony-messengers."

"It won't work." Eberhard shook his head. "I suggested that. It appears the eastern convoy did not make a long stop in Trebizond. Normally they stay for months. But this time...well, Venice may know something we don't. The vessels unloaded, took on what cargo was ready, and put to sea. Ahmbien had them watched, and used that system of riders to keep him informed."

"Then," said Manfred, standing up, "I think we need to sail for Venice. I suspect Alexius's capital is about to feel the weight of Venetian bombards. The question is what do we do with this Borshar Tarkhan?"

"I suppose we need to ask him."

They found the Ilkhan delegation on the balcony. Borshar Tarkhan rose and bowed. "Greetings. I gather your endeavors have not met with much success," he said in perfect Frankish.

He was expecting that, thought Erik. Their spies must make Francesca envious. "Yes. We plan to go to Venice itself—"

The tarkhan interrupted. "I am ordered to accompany you if that is the case."

Erik wondered why Eberhard looked as if he had just swallowed something really nasty. As they walked back to their quarters in the inn, Erik decided he'd better get on with learning some Mongol. It made him uncomfortable not to know what these people were saying among themselves. And he was, first and foremost, Manfred's bodyguard. Anything that made him uncomfortable was a warning sign.

Chapter 8

Vlad's head was in a turmoil. He was, by nature, a very precise person. Enough people had told him so, from King Emeric himself to the servants who had marveled at the geometric positioning he liked of the few accoutrements in his room. He could not understand why everyone would not wish their world so ordered. He liked to know precisely how things worked. In the small world of his tower in Buda castle, that had been easy enough. Some things, like his careful dissection, had upset and revolted Father Tedesco. But birds were free. They flew to the tower, to the high window, and away at their own choosing. He had merely wished to understand how it was possible. He had gained some understanding of just how they beat their wings and how the feathers flared from their wings. And of how thin and frail their bones were, even compared to mouse bones.

He had done penance for that.

He wondered now if he should do penance for this. He would have liked to have Father Tedesco to advise him. To try to make sense for him of all the unfamiliar emotions. The woman lay against him, her body softly curved and warm and scented. She had drawn his hand onto her thigh and now her fingers trailed across the skin on the back of his hand, barely touching him. How she could maintain such control as the carriage jolted and swayed on its leather springs was something a small part of his mind was fascinated by. The rest of his mind was overwhelmed by the sensations she was creating as she traced strange patterns with her perfectly manicured fingers.

After a little while he decided that he really didn't like it. It made an odd heat within him, not entirely a pleasant sensation. He felt as if he might take her into his arms or tear the fine fabric and lace away from her breast. It was beyond his rational control. That too he did not enjoy. So he pulled his hand away.

She laughed throatily. "Do you not like me, Prince?"

He blushed and stammered some reply. Was he being terribly rude? Was this how men and women conducted themselves outside of his tower? He had been escorted to King Emeric's throne room several times. There had been women and men there, but he did not recall noticing anything like this. Nor in his reading. Nor in his distant memories of growing up.

For the first time in many years, Elizabeth was both surprised and intrigued. Her senses were enhanced in such a way that she saw and felt things denied to ordinary mortals, just as their so-called salvation was denied to her. Pah. What had she ever cared for that? There was a virginal innocence to this boy that was almost intoxicating to her. It could only come from rearing him in such isolation from the world.

There was a darkness in him, too. Not at all like her carefully cultivated darkness, with its rewards and price, but wild savage darkness, more like some volcano of power and passion held in rigid check. And he had great strength. Power, for which he had paid no price. Power enough to pull away from her spell of binding and subjugation as if it had been a mere spiderweb. She had used sigils of dark magic that should have made him her slave.

She knew that his blood had value in magical terms, but she had merely seen him as bait. Bait for an ancient, rare and magical creature, useful to her plans. Now she realized his blood might be even more valuable than she'd believed. Possibly even worth keeping within his veins for a while. Who would have thought that mixing blood could have that effect? She might have to experiment with it herself. Of course, if it only affected offspring it would be of little use to her.

She would set Mindaug to investigate the matter. He needed work. She would watch Mindaug more carefully than Chernobog had been able to. Elizabeth had less interest in geographical power than Chernobog, but there were aspects to this strangely powerful pawn in that area, too. So much—besides pain and betrayal— had become ennui as the years passed. This would provide a fascinating distraction. She would have him in the end. She would enmesh him and strip him of his innocence and then his power, and enjoy a brief period of lust and darkness with him before all was done. But in the meanwhile, let the prey think he had sprung the trap. That he had got away.

"What shall we talk about, Prince Vlad?"

He was silent for a while. "My homeland," he said.

"And please, I need to open these curtains. The swaying makes me feel sick."

Both requests surprised her a little. She disliked bright sunlight, and the countryside. So dull, only good for hiding things in. And her knowledge and interest in Carpathia's countryside was sketchy at best. "It is mountainous. There are a great many trees."

"Pine trees. I have run and hunted there often," Vlad said longingly.

He had been taken from home when he was ten, she knew. He must have been somewhat differently raised than the boys of the royal house in Buda. "You remember that?"

He shook his head. "I dream it. I dream it often."

And that, to one such as her, was more worrying than his resistance to her entrapment.

They panted and lolled in the shade of the small copse on the hillock, three rangy, gray-eyed men, in ragged, patched clothes that spoke of travel.

"Why could she not have chosen a cooler day for it?" said Grigori, wiping his face with a multicolored kerchief. "Or gone by night. Running at night is safer and more pleasant."

Angelo shook his head. "Not from her. Remember who she is. And this is not our home range. It is hers."

"I am just glad that the roads do not run too straight. At least it's cooling off. Do you think that she will go on through the night, or stop at her nunnery?"

"Stop, I think. The horses are tired and there is nowhere else here she can get a change. Not that I know of, anyway. I have scouted this country, but I know it less well than I like." Angelo handed a wineskin to his companions. "Drink. I see dust. It will be the carriage."

"Is he definitely still in it?"

Grigori wiped his mouth and handed the wineskin on. "Hard to tell through the curtains. The carriage has been out of our sight a number of times. Would she fear pursuit enough to set us a false scent?"

Angelo peered toward the dust. "She is old enough and devious enough. But she is also arrogant in her power. All we can do is follow until we can get close enough to get the scent of him. And getting too close may be foolish, too. I have watched her kill."

The enclosed carriage clattered closer along the road. But now the drapes had been drawn aside. They could see him clearly despite the distance, his skin pale and his hair as dark as that of his grandfather, the Dragon, with the same heavy moustache. His face was lean and long. His expression, troubled.

They watched as the carriage and the outriders passed some quarter of mile away. Their keen eyes noted details. Details others might not have spotted, but they were hunters. The offside horse was beginning to go lame. The countess would have to slow down soon.

Angelo got to his feet. "That'll make the chase easier. She'll be there at nightfall now, not before."

"It's an ill time to get there. We could strike before?"

"If the chance arises." Angelo sniffed. "The weather is on the change. That may help us tomorrow. Come, brothers. The chase calls."

A shepherd boy walking back to his flock with a hat full of blackberries saw a carriage and outriders pass.

He waved. No one waved back, but that was hardly surprising. Then he dropped his hat and stood staring.

Those looked like great gray wolves loping across that field. Surely there were no wolves here? He felt suddenly very frightened and alone, and aware that his flock was farther away from him than it should be. He stood indecisively for a long moment. And then, without stopping to pick up his hat, let alone the wild berries, he ran in the opposite direction from the wolves or the carriage. The carriage had outriders, doubtless with bows or guns. Let them deal with the wolves.

In the carriage, Vlad's companion had fallen silent. He did not mind. There was the vista. The air outside. It helped with the queasiness from the swaying. There was just so much space. He saw a boy in one of the fields waving his hand. It took him a few moments to work out that the young fellow was greeting him. He waved back, smiling for the first time on this momentous, terrifying, exciting, confusing day. But for some reason the lad was running away as fast as his legs could carry him.

"What was that, Prince Vlad?" asked the countess, turning her wonderful smile on him.

"A boy. He waved and then ran away. Am I that frightening?"

She shook her head. "Peasants. They are afraid of everything. Anyway, we are near the nunnery of Saint Anna. We can rest there for the night."

"They will allow men within their walls?"

"I founded it. I still provide a generous stipend for it. We take in poor girls and orphans from Arrabona. Even some waifs from Buda and Pest."

"That is Godly work."

She crossed her hands in her lap and looked demurely down at them. "They have no one to turn to."

How could he have doubted her? He knew so little of this outside world. Father Tedesco had told him of the poverty and the needs of the poor. He had known little about it when he'd first come to Buda. But the subject had been one of the old priest's more frequent topics.

The area must be rife with bandits, thought Vlad, surveying the grim, gray-walled compound, with its church and cloister. The abbess who greeted them was scarcely more cheerful looking. And she was large. As big as most men, with hands like slabs of pork.

She bowed very respectfully to the countess. "All is prepared, your ladyship."

Countess Bartholdy smiled regally. "Good, Anna. We will have worship and rest. See that my men and the horses are suitably looked after. You have prepared a chamber for my guest?"

The abbess nodded. She turned to one of the women standing in her wake. "Illona, lead the gentleman to his chamber. See that he has warm water to wash with."

Illona looked as if she had missed all the meals the abbess had found. She beckoned, and Vlad followed her, in through a heavy studded door and up a long passage to a flight of stairs leading to an upstairs chamber. They passed a kneeling girl painstakingly sweeping the stone flags. The girl must have had a dreadful life. There was a beaten air about her. A look of fear. She cowered away from them in the passage. Vlad realized that, despite the terrors Emeric had inflicted on him, perhaps his captivity had not been so evil.

The room was large and luxuriously appointed, with an enclosed bed hung with fine red cloth. "Most comfortable looking," said Vlad.

Illona nodded. "Her ladyship keeps it for her companions. Warm water will be brought to you, shortly."

Looking over her shoulder—he was far taller than she was, far taller than most men, let alone women—Vlad was surprised to see the girl staring fearfully at him. A novice, he assumed.

She looked so afraid. He wanted to comfort her. "That girl..." he said, gesturing.

Illona smiled for the first time. You could not often say that a smile disfigured a face, but in this case it was true. "That one is for her ladyship's service. I will send you another."

"I just wanted say to her that God will care for her. She is safe in the arms of the Church now."

The woman Illona seemed surprised. But she turned away without saying anything.

Later that evening, Vlad dined with the abbess and the countess. They ate venison and he enjoyed it very much. The wine too was as red as blood and strong. Wine never seemed to make him drunk, as he had seen in others and read about. It—or the long day—made him sleepy, however, and he was glad to make his excuses and retire to his chamber, where he soon fell into a sound sleep.

He was wakened by a scream.

Definitely it was a woman, screaming.

He thought he had better go and see. But the door refused to open. And the window too was barred.

The moon shone down and he looked out. He had

quite a prospect from here. He could see the chapel. He could swear that was another scream coming from there. He watched for a while. And then he saw a light—candles—in the darkened chapel. They came out in the moonlight—some thirteen people, carrying something between them in a blanket. One of the carriers, simply by her size, had to be the abbess. Another, oddly, walked like a man. A third was plainly the dwarf.

They all wore hooded cloaks—except the last figure who walked behind them. Even in the moonlight, Elizabeth Bartholdy was beautiful. Her blond hair looked white in the moonlight, and her face serene. Somehow, she looked even younger than she had before. He wondered if he should call out and ask what had happened. But it seemed as if she was in control of the situation, so he just stood there, silent, watching as they walked into the cloister. As they passed below him, he thought that it looked rather like someone was lying on the blanket, but their candles did not provide enough light for him to see clearly.

After they had gone, he stood there for a long time looking out across the open landscape beyond the monastery walls. Yes, there were bars. But at least he could see. And the air smelled cleaner here.

In the distance something howled, a strange wild sound.

He almost felt as if he should howl back. He even found that he had taken a deep breath to do so, before shaking himself, and thinking how foolish he was being.

Then, because everything was still, he went back to bed. On the way he kicked a metal shackle set into the wood. It bruised him, and perhaps because of the pain or because it had been such a strange and experience-filled day, sleep took a long while coming.

And when it did, he found himself in the old familiar dream of running through the scent-rich forest. Of the hunt.

But somehow, this time, he was the prey.

They left early the next day, breaking their fast just before dawn. Most of Countess Elizabeth's retinue looked as tired as Vlad felt, even if they were probably not as stiff. Vlad's muscles hurt as he struggled up into the carriage.

The countess herself, on the other hand, looked positively sparkling this morning, her skin radiant and full of a youthful glow. She smiled at him. "It does not look as if you had a good night. Unfamiliar beds do that to me, too."

"What was happening last night?" asked Vlad curiously.

"Why, nothing. Should something have?" She lowered her lashes and looked at him from under them, with a little smile on her lips.

"I woke up when someone screamed. I tried to get out but I was locked into my chamber. From the window I saw a party come out of the chapel. Why was I locked in? What were you doing?"

She laughed musically. "Why were you locked in? You silly boy! You are a man and this is a nunnery. If they had their way they'd have chained you to the bed, too."

"Oh, is that what the shackles are for?" he asked, pleased to have had the mystery clarified.

She looked at him enquiringly with just an element of calculation in her gaze. "Shackles?"

"Yes. There are four set into the wood of the bed. I barked my shin on one, so I noticed."

"Goodness. I wonder what those are for. Perhaps for chaining a dog or something. I was merely joking, Vlad. I did not want to trouble you with that sad business last night. The poor girl was possessed of an evil spirit. We had to scourge her and pray with her to exorcise it."

"Oh. I will include her in my prayers, then," said Vlad. "Is she free of it now? Will she be all right?"

"She will recover. Pain is a necessary part of the process," said the countess. "Do you really have to have the curtains open, Prince? Of course I am a weak woman and not as robust as you. The breeze is so injurious to a lady's complexion. It's almost as bad as the sun."

"Once they cross the Danube we must strike," said Angelo. "If we let her get him to her fortress we will never get him away from her. Even another night could be too late."

"They will take a ferry. We could sink it, and snatch him from the flotsam." Grigori grinned, showing very white teeth.

Angelo shook his head. "She has a bargain with the Vila."

"Then we need to plan to get across by boat," said Radu. "Besides, Grigori, you get tired after swimming half a league."

Chapter 9

The crowd of voivodes and hetmen in his throne room were doing their best to look brave and great. To the iron eyes that looked out at them from Jagiellon's mask, they were neither. They were, however, the right sort of tools for his tasks. Greed and fear made great levers to drive them about his purposes. He kept them in balance between fear of their fellows and fear of him. And when he called, they came, like the cowed dogs they were.

Of course, there were a few who had attempted to avoid the summons with various excuses, and had sent representatives. They would be punished appropriately. They entertained something Chernobog disapproved of, and did his best to eradicate: the folly of hope.

Still, there was one emissary whose master could not be punished. Or, at least, could not be punished... yet. The fact that the emissary was here, and being seen in public, was an endorsement of sorts, as the remains of the Golden Horde were not yet vassals. But soon they, and the Bulgar Slavs, would fall in line. Constantinople and Alexius posed no challenge.

Chernobog's geopolitical machinations followed a very different logic from that of his merely mortal foes.

There was power in the geography, both on a physical and a spiritual plane. Other powers and their minions, such as that accursed Elizabeth Bartholdy, did not fully grasp that. They would. But by then it would be too late.

"Nogay Tarkhan." Jagiellon greeted the emissary with what for him was considerable affability. The man still stood too straight. He bowed. He had not abased himself. "And what news from Gatu Khan?"

"He still remains Gatu Orkhan. The kurultai broke apart before his election could be finalized."

Jagiellon stood up slowly. He was a huge man and he towered over the tarkhan. He turned to the assembled lords of all of the vassal tribes and states to the east and south. "You are all dismissed," he said. "The tarkhan and I have things to discuss privately."

Nogay stood stock still, perhaps alarmed by the hasty departure of the others. Some of them were known to him. Many of the southern clans which owed fealty to Jagiellon were blood relations of the clans within the remnant of the Golden Horde that lived on the western shore of the Black Sea. The Crimean Tatars were close kin. They were intermarried too with Bessarabians under Jagiellon's sway.

When they were alone, Jagiellon resumed his seat. He had stood solely for the purpose of intimidating the tarkhan with his immense size. That done—satisfactorily, he gauged—he had no desire to remain on his feet. The Black Brain found the grand duke useful, and the man had become so heavy in middle age that standing for any length of time risked damaging his lower limbs.

As he lowered himself into the throne, a slight scuttling noise drew his attention to the side. A rat had emerged from a hole in a corner of the throne room and was staring at him, its whiskers twitching with caution.

Caution only, not fear. Rats had little to fear in the Grand Duke of Lithuania's palace. As a matter of policy, Jagiellon made only minimal attempts to suppress the rodents. He kept just enough feral felines to prevent the rats from overrunning the palace altogether. He—or rather, the demon who controlled him—found that a multitude of rats had the effect of frightening his subjects, in a subtle kind of way. Perhaps they feared their overlord might feed them to the rats in the cellars.

As, indeed, he had done on a number of occasions.

Once the grand duke's eyes moved away, Mindaug sent the rat scurrying along the wall. As soon as Jagiellon began to speak, he would have the rat move close enough to overhear the conversation.

Mindaug leaned back in his chair, his eyes closed, visualizing the scene in far-off Vilna through the rat's eyes. There was some peril here, of course. Mindaug would be subjected to considerable pain in the event Jagiellon took notice of the rat again and decided to kill it.

That was a minor danger, however. First, because it was unlikely that the grand duke would succeed in such a project. As a young man, Jagiellon had been a truly formidable physical specimen. His reflexes had been astonishing for someone his size. But age and sedentary habits—not to mention his gross culinary indulgences—had added so much fat to his frame that, though still immensely strong, he was no longer as quick as he'd been years earlier.

The grand duke was still surprisingly quick, for such a huge man. But not likely to be quick enough to catch a rodent. Even if he did, the pain inflicted upon Mindaug would be intense but brief. And there would be no lasting damage. The method Mindaug was using to control the rat had some problems. The effort of controlling the noxious little creature was considerable; the effort of trying to filter meaningful words through its tiny brain harder still. After two hours, Mindaug would be mentally exhausted. But the great advantage was that Mindaug could sever his connection with the rat—or have it severed by another—without suffering any permanent injury.

No, the real danger lay with the Black Brain, not the monster's human shell. There was always the possibility that Chernobog's suspicion would be aroused, should he notice that a rat in his palace was behaving oddly. The demon himself was not given to using small animals as spies. Those methods were too humble and subtle to appeal to his basic nature. However, he would know that such was possible, for someone with sufficient knowledge and skill.

There weren't many in the world who had that knowledge and skill. But Chernobog was likely to know that his former servant Count Mindaug was one of them—and he had a grudge against Mindaug. Which was reasonable enough, of course, given that Mindaug had betrayed him.

Should the Black Brain come alert, there was the real possibility that his demonic power—which, unlike his human sheath's body, was not subject to fat and unexercised muscles—could move fast enough to catch Mindaug before he could extricate himself from the rodent. Should that happen . . .

Well. The result would be most unfortunate. The best Mindaug could hope for was that Chernobog would be satisfied with locking the count into his rodent form with no hope of escape. In which case, Mindaug's lifespan would become that of a rat—two years; three, at best—and, still worse, it would be a life emptied of all interest. Even if Mindaug could maintain his intelligence in those circumstances, which he thought unlikely beyond a few weeks, what good would it do him?

Count Mindaug's great interest and passion was knowledge, and knowledge required the ability to read. It was hard enough to make sense of spoken words through a rat's little brain. Mindaug had never been able to get one of the wretched rodents to learn how to read. That was their greatest limitation as spies.

Cats were worse. Dogs, hopeless. Some day Mindaug planned to experiment with owls. In addition to their superb eyesight, he thought their talons might be suitable for turning pages.

He had the rat right behind the monster, now. He commanded the little creature to scuttle underneath the throne and then hold perfectly still. Partly, to avoid any risk of detection; mostly, so Mindaug could concentrate on the coming task. Filtering sense through a rat's brain really was quite difficult.

Later, after the grand duke had finished with his agent in the Golden Horde, Jagiellon called for the

voivode from Odessa and the admiral from the secret
vast shipyards he had built close to the mouth of the
Dniepr where his fleet was being assembled.

The voivode had no doubts about the fragility of
his position, but he had news that he believed would
please his master. "We have begun pressing sailors,
Grand Duke. They are river men mostly, but at least
they have been on board a vessel before. We have
thirty round ships and some seven great galleys, and
nearly forty galleys now outfitted. The galleys are
doing patrols already with the other vessels and the
crews are learning their trade."

"I will send fresh levees. Ten more galleys must be
in the water before winter," ordered Jagiellon.

The voivode bowed. "It will be done, Prince."

"The men to be transported on the round ships
will begin to arrive in the last weeks of March. See
that their the camps are prepared."

"Could I ask the numbers, Prince?"

"Some thirty thousand. That will be adequate for
the purpose. The first four thousand will arrive with
the barge fleet from Kievan Rus with the cordage
and sailcloth. Now go. I am going to select from the
candidates who have been sent down from the north."

The voivode of Odessa looked both curious and
afraid. As well he might, Jagiellon thought. The man
was too efficient for his own good. Unfortunately, he
was also too efficient to kill right now.

This was a problem for Jagiellon, and one which
he had become faced with all too frequently. Ruthless ambition and greed had provided some of his
best vassals, but such a vassal always wanted to be
overlord. It was necessary to watch them, intimidate

them, and occasionally reduce their ranks. This voivode was very close to that brink.

The grand duke was not overly concerned with the matter, however. In long years, only Count Mindaug had succeeded in escaping the Black Brain's culling. And someday he expected to catch Mindaug and be finally done with him.

Mindaug kept the rat hidden under the throne until well after nightfall, then let an hour pass after the grand duke left the chamber before he had the rat emerge.

That done, he sent the rodent in search of one of the palace's handful of cats. That took no more than five minutes.

The feline was presumably surprised to find a rat doing all but leaping into its maw, but its brain was not big enough to retain the memory for long. The chance that the Black Brain would detect anything amiss was essentially nonexistent. Even the chance that Chernobog would have detected the lingering traces of Mindaug's presence in the rat had been minuscule.

Minuscule—but not nonexistent. Mindaug valued methodical caution above all other virtues.

The pain was intense, true. Cats were efficient killers, but not merciful ones. But the moment passed, soon enough, and Mindaug was able to concentrate on what he had learned.

He was not surprised by the scope of Chernobog's ambitions. Still, he had not realized how extensively the Black Brain had succeeded in penetrating the Golden Horde. Mongol society was not easily subverted by outsiders, even ones with the grand duke's powers.

That much was simply a matter of abstract interest, at the moment. But Mindaug could no longer ignore the possibility that his present refuge might become threatened. Countess Elizabeth was extraordinarily shrewd, but she had two intellectual blind spots.

The first—inevitable in such a foul creature—was that she had delusions concerning her ability to postpone forever having to pay the price for her bargain.

The second was that she consistently underestimated the sometime effectiveness of purely human political and military action. Mindaug thought that blind spot was also due to the creature's foul nature. No matter what methods were used, successful action in the political and military spheres required a great deal of effort. Among Elizabeth's multitude of vices, laziness took its rightful place also.

So. It was time for Mindaug to consider his alternatives.

Chapter 10

Benito Valdosta read the message from Petro Dorma very carefully, for the third time. The orders contained therein came as something of a relief, in part. They would get him away from a myriad of petty problems, and might stop him from murdering some Libri d'Oro idiot.

On the other hand, the idea of leaving his wife and daughter while he led a naval campaign was considerably less than attractive. However, unless he misread the time line, it could just work out. The Byzantine emperor would be expecting both trouble and relief in spring. If Benito had his way, he'd have trouble long before. In autumn, if possible. There was always the risk of storms. On the other hand it would be a very unwelcome surprise for His Imperial Idiocy.

It could be a worse surprise for the fleet in the Dniepr. The most serious flaw in this plan could be the arrival of the Golden Horde. Benito wished that he had more knowledge of what was happening in the lands of the Golden Horde, to the west of the Black Sea. He began to toy with the idea of spying or at least surveillance, possibly from the lands of Iskander Beg. He wondered just how Petro Dorma had come by all his information in the first place, and if Benito would be able to access those channels. The old established order in Venice tended to regard him as a loose cannon. "I can't imagine why," he thought to himself, with a chuckle, getting up to go and collect a map of Constantinople from a cupboard. He could imagine Admiral Dourso's delight at the news that Benito Valdosta was coming back to the Arsenal.

However, that was a trivial problem compared to the one he was going to face when he broke this news to Maria. That would require a lot more than mere military tactical skill. It might just involve the ability to dodge flying china. Living with Maria could be a lot of things, but it certainly was never dull. He considered the best possible ways of approaching the subject. Regretfully, he decided that sneaking off without telling her probably would not be worth the pain. In the end, the truth might just serve him best, even though he doubted that it would serve him very well.

Still, the problem would have to be faced, and soon. Petro wanted him back in Venice within three weeks.

Maria watched her daughter indulging in the traditional pastime of chewing her toes. She had begun to worry about winter. That was a thought that was never too far from her mind. She would have to leave Alessia and Benito and go down into a vast and unearthly realm to spend her four months with Aidoneus, the Lord of the Dead.

She really, really did not wish to go, but that was the bargain that she had made. No matter that she had risen to be a scoulo wife, and now the wife in all but name of the acting governor of one of Venice's most valuable colonies: she was a canaler born. There was a code of honor that went with that. Canalers had very little, except for that code. They made their bargains, and they lived and died by them.

She sighed. Honoring her bargain also meant that she was going to have to leave her daughter with Benito for four months. She knew he was surprisingly capable. But that did not make it any easier.

Benito came in, without his usual smile, but with a piece of paper in his hand. "Read this," he said, handing it to her.

Maria had learned to read late in life. It still took more concentration than she felt happy about, but Kat's letters from Venice had made her a little more practiced. Still, she had to read this message twice. She closed her eyes, and put her hand to her head. "I thought that we had won some peace."

"The only kind of peace that Grand Duke Jagiellon will ever recognize is total surrender to his will," said Benito. "And that is not a peace I would have my daughter live under. I saw what he did to Caesare. He must be stopped." There was a certain implacability to that statement, a grimness that belonged to a man far older. At times like this, Benito frightened her a little. And yet this was what made him the man that he was. A man who had literally gone to hell for her and brought her back.

"Yes, but why must it be you that stops him?" she asked plaintively.

Benito grimaced. "Because Petro Dorma thinks so. Of course I'll have Admiral Dourso as well."

"You are not to kill him," said Maria sternly. "And anyway, if there is danger Corfu needs you."

"If Jagiellon succeeds in taking control of the Bosphorus it won't just be Corfu that is in danger," said Benito. "His armies will ravage everything from Alexandria to the gates of the Mediterranean. This is a fight we must take to him. We must destroy his fleet. We really need to deny him access to the Black Sea if the Byzantine empire is going to be a weak reed."

"Oh? And why don't you just conquer all of the known world while you're about it?" Maria had never entirely come to terms with the sheer size of the world. Part of that was because she had spent her formative years in the narrow canals of Venice. In a way, her world had been defined by the confines of the Lagoon. Travelling first to Istria and then to Corfu had changed her perceptions a little, but there still seemed far too much world to get her head around.

One thing that she was sure of: the Black Sea was both far off and large. Yet she also knew that Benito was almost impossible to stop once he got going.

He chuckled. "I think that the whole world might take more than two or three months. I might just have to settle for Constantinople."

She was taking this far too easily. Benito knew that he ought to just be grateful and not to pursue the matter. But he loved her very much, too much just to take the easy way out.

"Explain why you are not throwing dishes at my head," he said gently, taking her into his arms.

She was silent for quite some time, leaning into him. Eventually, she said slowly: "I suppose it's because I wished that you and Alessia would go to Venice while I was . . . away. Kat and your brother Marco are there. They will be good to our daughter. Also, Petro Dorma is the Doge. He is responsible for the well-being of all of Venice. I do not think he is a man who would lightly ask this of you. He must have real reason to fear. And the canals are still full of my relations. But," she said fiercely, "this is my Corfu now. Mine. You will see that it stays safe." That was a strict instruction.

He nodded. "Too many people have bled and died to keep it free and safe for us to neglect it now."

"And you will be careful?" she said, her eyes narrow.

"I never promise what I can't deliver," he said with a wry grin. "I promise I'll take reasonable care. Well, as much as possible."

"Huh!" she snorted. But she did not pull away from him. Instead she snuggled closer. "Alessia has fallen asleep. And I don't think you have to go back to that office just yet."

Benito knew just how much work there was waiting for him. But, all things considered, it was probably less important than staying here right now. So he picked her up, the muscles he had built up while working in the Arsenal paying a handsome dividend, and carried her through to their bed. Briefly, he thought about where he would get good maps of the Golden Horn, but then he focused on more important and immediate matters.

Chapter 11

They got out of the carriage in order to be ferried across the Danube. Vlad enjoyed that brief respite. The open air was full of strange scents carried on the morning breeze. Although he would never have dreamed of saying so to his angelic seeming rescuer, he found the scent that she used cloying. She had insisted on keeping the curtains in the carriage closed this morning.

The far side of the river was the site of a small town. Vlad hoped for some breakfast, and, by the hopeful looks they had cast at the inn, so did the outriders. But Elizabeth showed no signs of hunger or a desire to stop. As soon as the horses were poled up, she had the coachman drive them onward at a spanking pace.

"I have never been that fond of large amounts of running water," she said. "It makes me feel a little queasy."

"I quite understand," said Vlad, sympathetically. "You are such a delicately built lady that I wonder how you can travel so fast. I remember that my mother always insisted that we spend a day resting after she had been traveling for a day. We sometimes used to travel to Corona. That was considered a two-day journey, but Mama always made it take four. It used to drive my father nearly mad."

She looked at him rather strangely. "I would not have thought that you could remember so much from so long ago."

"I remember it very well, although it sometimes seems as if it is somebody else's life I am remembering. I was lonely and afraid when I was first sent to Buda. All I could do was tell myself stories of what it was like before. I did not speak very good Hungarian and the people would not speak to me in my own language. Not even Father Tedesco, and he was very good to me. I remember the woods and the mountains. I long to see the mountains again."

"And so you shall," said Elizabeth. "My castle—one of my residences, the one which we are going to—is set on the edge of the mountains, although I must admit it lacks some of the delights of civilization. I am fond of the liveliness of the capital myself. But there are certain advantages to a residence in a rural fastness. For one, it will be a good place to hide you."

"Do you think that King Emeric will be looking for me?" asked Vlad warily. Emeric had terrified him when he had been a small boy. He had learned to control and hide that fear. But he had seen just what Emeric did to his enemies or to those who dared to disobey him. They died slowly on the pikes set outside the castle.

That was something that Father Tedesco said that Vlad's grandfather, the Dragon, had been infamous for also. Perhaps for that reason, Vlad had found it strangely fascinating. But it was not something that he wished to experience, personally.

"Undoubtedly," said Elizabeth. "Do not worry, Prince

Vlad, we will keep you hidden. As long as you stay with me, you will be quite safe."

"Does that mean that I will have to stay hidden indoors? I had hoped to at least be able to go out hunting again."

Elizabeth laughed at him; a musical tinkle of sound. "You poor boy! We will not have to confine you that much. Of course there will be certain magical protections set in place. And anyway there is not much game close to the castle. My late husband hunted to excess, I am afraid. He always claimed that it was to get rid of the wolves, but I suspect that he just liked killing things."

"Oh," said Vlad. "My father liked wolves."

She sniffed. "Nasty creatures. And very hard on the sheep."

Vlad had to admit that was probably true.

The carriage rolled on in relative silence, unless you counted the creaks and rattles as the carriage swayed on its leather springs along the badly surfaced road. The horses were clearly tiring, as they were now moving considerably slower.

Suddenly the coach lurched, and the horses broke into a gallop.

The coach swayed even more wildly and the coachman was plainly fighting for control. Vlad found himself flung about and clung desperately to the leather strap. Elizabeth, however, seemed perfectly in control. She leaned forward and tapped on the small window. Somewhat jerkily, it was opened. "What is happening out there?" she asked sharply.

"Don't know, milady. Horses panicked," said the struggling coachman.

After a while, he managed to bring the lathered horses under control. He opened the little window again. "Sorry, milady, the offside wheeler is going lame. And all of the horses are tired. We'll need to rest them and see if we can find another team. There is a small inn in the hamlet about a mile ahead. Can I stop there?"

"If you must," said the countess, looking mildly irritated.

"Perhaps we could get something to eat there?" asked Vlad.

"I doubt if they will rise to much above pörkölt, which will mostly be cabbage. But nonetheless what you say is true. I have been very remiss in looking after you. We shall have to see what this little place offers. But do not expect too much."

Vlad did not know what to expect at all. However, whatever happened, he would be out of the stuffy swaying carriage for a while. Her scent was making him want to sneeze. He also felt as if he hadn't seen a meal for days. He was not too sure just what "pörkölt" would prove to be, but he would like to try it anyway.

The dwarf, who had also been on the box of the carriage with the driver, clambered down and lowered the stair. He handed the countess down into the crudely cobbled courtyard. She looked around. There was a dung heap. Scrawny chickens ran about. A pig peered at them from one of the empty stables.

"I think that I will get back into the carriage," she said disdainfully.

Vlad emerged and stood blinking slightly in the bright sunlight. "I need to stretch my legs," he said. It was also fascinating and different.

She nodded. "Ficzko, accompany the prince." She climbed back into the carriage, and lay back on the velvet upholstered seats. She took a pomander from her reticule and sat swinging it under her nose.

The dwarf bowed to Vlad. It was a rather exaggerated bow, that did not go well with his sardonic grin, or his raised eyebrow.

"Come and survey your kingdom, O great lord," he said. There was a faint mocking tone to his voice. Vlad took a strong dislike to him, although it seemed beneath him to detest a man who barely came up to his elbow. Vlad felt that he should rather be sorry for Ficzko, with his large head and small body. But the dwarf's attitude did not make it easy. Neither did the faint sneer he wore.

Vlad walked out into the village street. One street was all that there really was to the entire village. Still, it was a joy to stretch his legs and walk, knowing that he could walk as far as he wished. The countess's dwarf had to run to keep up with him.

And then he heard it again. A strange, lilting, wild music, played softly. It was coming from a narrow gap, a pathway between two of the roughly thatched village houses. Had this been a city, it might one day have achieved the status of being an alley.

Ficzko darted forward to stop him walking towards it. "Your Highness, you must not go down there! It is those filthy gypsies and their evil music."

Vlad found that he remembered the gypsies from his youth. They had always seemed so colorful. He wondered if these were the same gypsies that the dwarf was referring to. The music was suddenly enormously compelling. He had to go to it!

There was a yell and the thunder of hooves from behind him.

The carriage horses and several others came running past, chased by some enormous doglike creatures, gray and terrible. Vlad turned to see what was happening, not knowing quite what to do. The dwarf turned also, startlement writ on his ugly face. As they did so, a dark-haired man in bright ragged clothes stepped out from around the corner.

He raised a pipe to his lips and began to play.

The dwarf rushed at him with an incoherent cry of rage. The piper merely stuck out a foot, and sidestepped. The dwarf landed headlong in the mud. The piper bowed slightly to Vlad, without stopping his playing. Then he turned and put his boot on the middle of the dwarf's back, pushing him back down into the mud. Face down in the mud the large-headed little man scrabbled for his dagger.

The dwarf succeeded in drawing it, but the piper casually kicked it out of his hand, sending it several feet off into a puddle. Then the piper stopped playing and gestured to Vlad, signaling him to come closer.

Vlad was painfully aware that he did not have as much as a knife, let alone a sword. He stepped forward to help Ficzko. "Let him up."

The piper shook his head. "It is you I have come to help, Drac. This one is an enemy. He would stop us if he could." He spoke, not in Hungarian, but in a language that Vlad knew, but was rusty with disuse. A language that Vlad had not heard spoken in more than ten years.

Vlad stopped, eyes wide. *Drac?* He remembered the term. Some people had called his father that. The peasants and the tradesmen in the small villages.

"No time to explain now. We need to get away."

"Who are you?" asked Vlad warily. This made no sense. He should run back to the countess now. Yet... the music called to him. Told him he was right to trust this odd man. It felt right, in a way that his flight had not.

"A friend." The piper grinned. "You might say we share some of the same blood." He laughed. It was a strangely infectious laugh. "And now we must flee."

Vlad wavered, torn between the appeal of the man and his native language, and caution. His instincts said to trust the man, in a way they had not with his angelic-looking rescuer, even if logic said otherwise. The piping had unleashed something strange in him. Something deep and powerful.

"Is there danger?" he asked. "And what about the countess? Should we not try to rescue her too?"

For an answer the piper raised the pipe to his lips again and played a brief trill. "It is you they want, Drac. They will chase you. She is safe."

His Vlachs must be more rusty than he had realized. The man must be referring to the enormous creatures that had driven off the horses.

Well, if he could act as a decoy and draw the pursuit away from his rescuer, that was plainly his duty. It was only the dwarf, and the way that the stranger had treated him, that gave him pause. He still had his boot planted on the dwarf's back, holding him down in the mud.

He stepped uneasily forward. Ficzko kicked out viciously—at Vlad. "I'll kill you!" he yelled, and he was definitely yelling at Vlad rather than at the man who might be a gypsy. Vlad was confused. The dwarf must be a traitor!

"Clearly one of your enemies, Drac. We will leave our little foe here," said the stranger, putting the pipe into one of his many pockets. He leaned down, took the dwarf by the scruff of his doublet and deposited him into an empty horse trough. He flung him quite hard. Ficzko lay there and groaned.

The gypsy took Vlad by the elbow, and led him around the corner. Two horses were tethered there.

"You don't think that we should rather go back and rescue the countess?" asked Vlad.

The gypsy shook his head. "Trust me, Drac." He looked very earnest. "I swear by the blood of the old one, if you do not flee with me now, you will be kept a prisoner and die, probably very slowly. And your people need you. Your land needs you. But we must ride now. We will never have this chance again. You will be much more closely guarded, if we fail."

Out of his distant past, Vlad plucked a memory of his mother protesting to his father about the gypsies camping at the foot of the cliff below Poienari. And his father saying that they might be thieves and rogues but the sons of the Dragon could trust them, even when they could trust no one else.

Vlad mounted. If it was he who was being pursued, then let them follow him. The countess had risked much to free him. Two things were important: that he repay her for that, and that he should stay free.

They rode hard cross-country along a break of trees which screened them from the village. The gypsy rode with casual skill, Vlad with grim determination. As a boy, he had been in the saddle very often. Even if the horses had shrunk he had not forgotten the skills entirely.

Presently, the gypsy slowed his horse to a trot. They came to a small copse left on the edge of a field. Two other men in similar bright ragged clothes were waiting, holding two horses that looked rather familiar.

They mounted up. "What took you so long?" asked one, grinning. "We thought the two of you had decided to stop for lunch."

That reminded Vlad of the hunger that he had complained of on stopping at the hamlet. Alas, he had never even tried the "pörkölt," or anything else.

It appeared that his new escort had no intention of letting him eat, either. They rode on, pushing the horses hard. The route they were following kept along the bottom of a shallow depression and next to a marshy stream. It also kept them away from the skyline. Vlad realized that they must surely be locals to know this area so well. It would be very difficult for anyone to follow them by sight.

But he had little spare concentration for possible pursuit. Lack of practice at riding, and not having eaten since very early that morning were having an effect.

"He's going to tumble out of that saddle soon, Angelo," said one of the other riders.

The dark, gray-eyed gypsy looked at him. "True. We need some shelter, Grigori. Somewhere we cannot be seen too easily."

The man he had referred to as Grigori pointed. "There is a haystack and an old barn just over the lip. Maybe half a mile. Or there was last time I was here."

"And how many seasons ago was that?" asked the third gypsy sardonically.

"About five, I think. But stone barns tend to stay

to the same places, although they keep moving the haystacks."

"It's getting across the lip that worries me," said Angelo. "Grigori, let me hold your horse. Go back and see how far back they are."

The lithe, curly-haired gypsy slipped off his horse. The more Vlad had looked at that horse the more he was sure that it was one that had been ridden by one of the outriders. The man loped off with a long-legged easy stride. He looked, to Vlad's blurred vision, almost like some great predatory animal gliding away.

But Angelo did not let the rest of them stop. He pressed on, leaving Grigori to catch up.

Vlad decided, when Grigori caught up with them a few minutes later, that the man must run like the wind. "Can't see them," he panted. "I'd say that they were a good two or three miles back."

He vaulted into the saddle with an ease that Vlad could only envy. "Let's go and find that barn," he said. "There was a good place for rabbits close to it."

Somehow, Vlad managed to stay in the saddle until they reached the shabby stone barn. But as they arrived, he felt himself starting to fall.

He could not remember how he came to be lying against the edge of the haystack, with his collar loosened. But there was the delicious smell of cooking meat.

"A stupid idea to light a fire if you ask me," said the gypsy whose name Vlad had not yet discovered. "As well to tell the foe where we are."

"They are not very good at eating raw meat," said Angelo. "And smoke is a clear scent marker to you, Radu, but not to them. Ah. I see the Drac is awake. Do you need your rabbit very well cooked, lord?"

"I would eat anything right now, cooked in any way, or even not cooked at all." Vlad took the wineskin that Grigori held out to him.

Grigori laughed and punched his companion in the ribs. "We could have given it to him raw, after all. Maybe even with the fur on."

Angelo, in the meantime, was cutting slices off the rabbit which they had been grilling over the open flames of a small camp-fire. He speared them on the end of the knife, and handed it to Vlad. "Eat, Drac," he said encouragingly.

Vlad swallowed some of the wine from the wineskin they held out to him. It was far from the finest vintages. In fact, it was something he would have turned his nose up at a few days ago. Now it tasted powerful and magnificent.

The rabbit flesh was extremely rare, barely more than charred on the outside. Grains of coarse salt clung to it. Vlad did not think he had ever tasted anything finer. He washed it down with some more of the red wine from the wineskin. "My thanks," he said, already feeling better even after the first few morsels.

"Cut him some more," said Grigori. "I have seen a wolf eat slower."

"But not you," said Radu, taking out his knife and cutting some more of the meat to hand to Vlad.

"Eat up and be quick," said Angelo. "We have a way to go before we reach a secure place. Once we are in the mountains we can take things a little slower, but here we are too easy to find. And trust me, Drac, you do not want them to find you."

Very shortly, far too soon and after far too little food, Vlad found himself being thrown up into the saddle again. They had to do that, because he found that his muscles had already begun to stiffen. He still had had no chance to establish just who they were and where they were taking him.

They pressed on, going back down into the shallow valley and riding on into the gathering darkness. The horses were tired now, only able to walk. Vlad was beginning to wonder if they had successfully drawn the pursuit after them and away from Elizabeth. He was beginning to wonder about the nature of the huge creatures he had seen driving off the horses. He was beginning to wonder also about his good-natured gypsy companions, and just where they had suddenly come from and how they had come by the horses.

Most of all, he was wondering just when he would be allowed to get off his horse. By the time they finally stopped, though, he was too exhausted to wonder much at all. All he wanted to do was to rest and to eat. And sleep. Yes, sleep, and he did not care if he had to sleep on the ground—just as long as it was somewhere off a horse.

However, they must have made some allowances for his royal blood. The gypsies found him a haystack to sleep in, which they plainly considered the height of luxury. And that night, so did he.

In the pale predawn, the gypsies rousted him out of the haystack, and they set off again. Somewhere they had acquired fresh horses. The saddles were still the same, but the horses were not. The gypsies were skilled in choosing cross-country trails that avoided dwellings. The countryside was changing around them. Ahead were ridges spiked with pine trees.

Vlad could not remember very clearly just what his home had looked like. He hoped that Poienari Castle would loom suddenly from one of these ridges, but they seemed too small to be the mountains that he remembered. Perhaps that was like the way horses had shrunk in the time that he had been locked away. The mountains of his memory had definitely seemed both bigger and bleaker than these. Still, the sight of the ridges lifted his spirits, even though it did nothing at all for his aching thighs and sore posterior.

They rode up into a valley and off towards a scattering of rocks. Hidden among these was a narrow cave entrance. "We should be safe enough up here," said Angelo, reining in. "Radu, you take the horses on and let them go a few miles from here. Most likely they will find their own way home."

Vlad was unsure about what was happening to his life, but apparently he had fallen among horse thieves. He deeply and intrinsically disapproved of dishonesty. After he had begun to speak, it occurred to him that this was perhaps not the wisest time to berate the gypsies, but he did not think first.

"Did you steal those horses?" he demanded.

The gypsies looked at him and then began to laugh. "He is the Drac, all over again!" said Angelo.

"Answer my question," he said sternly, feeling faintly foolish, but still determined.

"Well, Drac, it's more like this," said Angelo. "If you needed a horse from one of your tenants, you would use it. By our way of thinking, all of this was our range, and we're entitled to some of the produce, let alone to borrow a horse or two. We had a hard time explaining this to your grandfather, or so the stories say. He made a few grim examples of some of the boyars and German merchants. That made him very popular."

"Made him popular?" Were they being sarcastic? he wondered.

"Yes, with the peasants," grinned Grigori. "And after one or two really good examples, the level of honesty in Valahia improved dramatically. He is a hero still today among them."

That was a very different story from the ones that he had heard from his Hungarian captors. "I thought he was hated and feared."

"By some people, yes," said Angelo. "He was a little mad."

The gypsy made it sound as if that was a positive attribute. Perhaps it was, for ruling a small mountain kingdom. "See those horses get back to their owners," Vlad said sternly. Then it would not really be theft. More of a loan.

They grinned. "They have some extra horses now anyway, better quality than this crow-bait."

Vlad wondered where those horses had come from but decided that he would let it be. "What do we do now?" he asked.

"Rest, eat, and stay away from those who will be hunting for us. Work our way along the mountains until we can get back to the heartland, to the real mountains. To your homeland, Drac."

Chapter 12

In terms of raw power, both of intellect and in the actual ability to affect events, it would be hard to have eclipsed the people gathered in a quiet and rather nondescript salon in the Doge's Palace in Venice. Both the Doge, Petro Dorma, and Duke Enrico Dell'este were more than capable of a display of pomp and finery, if they thought it would serve their purposes. But unlike many rulers, they understood that these were just tools, not ends in themselves.

Besides, they had no need to try and impress the other people present. The Venetian Council of Ten knew them all far too well. Marco Valdosta, and that which walked with him in spirit, were unlikely to even notice finery and rich throne rooms. They both saw far deeper than that. Count Von Stemitz had seen more Gothic splendor in Mainz. And Patriarch Michael, speaking for the church in Rome, had his eyes set on far more spiritual glory. Only Admiral Doria, the Duke of Genoa, unfamiliar with the group, was in the least surprised by the lack of ostentation in the quiet private salon.

"Eneko Lopez is not a man to send such news without being very certain of it," said Patriarch Michael, in reply to the admiral's question.

"I have heard of him," admitted the admiral. "He has a reputation for being a somewhat inflexible man. You will pardon my saying so, but the church has for so many years refused to send such communications. Why should it be different now? How can you be sure that this message is a real one? We have always enjoyed much better relations with the Byzantine Empire than Venice has. Our trade with the Black Sea is more extensive than Venice's. We would surely have been aware of any such fleet."

The patriarch nodded. "It would be very difficult, if not impossible, to be absolutely certain that no form of magical interference has taken place. Nonetheless, the clerics in Rome are very skilled, and have the greatest ecclesiastical protections that we have been able to devise, Admiral. They are as sure as they possibly can be that the communication came from Eneko Lopez in Jerusalem. He sent word of a threat to many nations and to the Church itself. That would be why he has decided to do this."

"It is just that... Yes, our ships are restricted in their access to certain ports. But we would surely have known from our agents if something of this size was happening. We trade with the Golden Horde, too. The Black Sea is something we know well."

As Petra Dorma was all too well aware, the Black Sea was the region in which Genoa had most of its influence, other than the trade in their local Ligurian region and their colonies on Corsica. The admiral was unlikely to forget that Venice was its largest commercial rival in the Mediterranean. Both sides had used war and a plethora of dirty tricks to try to gain the upper hand.

However, the new duke had gained his place after the old duke had supported (largely tacitly, it was true) the blockading of the Venetian fleets. That had seriously angered the Holy Roman Emperor. Charles Fredrik had not yet taken substantial steps against Aragon and the Aquitaine. But when he had had an opportunity to intervene in the election of a new duke in Genoa, he had let it be known that he favored the captain-general of the fleet—and besides having the military might of the Holy Roman Empire to use as influence, much of the trade to and from the north flowed through the port.

Venice was the predominant power in the Mediterranean, but the Genovese would dearly like to change that situation. Petro could only hope that the admiral saw a greater advantage in cooperation rather than playing a spoiler's role, which the Aquitaine was particularly infamous for. That was why they had not been asked to send a representative to this meeting. For the Aquitaine, their own immediate interests always came first. Of course, the Aquitaine would couch it in seductive terms; that, and the seduction itself were what they were best known for.

"We would be prepared," said Petro, "to conclude certain treaty arrangements concerning the use of the Golden Horn, and also access to ports on the Black Sea. We would not be offering such concessions lightly, Your Grace."

The Genovese duke looked somewhat taken aback. Such directness was unusual among Italian principalities.

But he was an admiral first and a duke second, and plain speaking had value to a seaman. "It could certainly seem that you are in earnest," he said. "Look, it is not that I doubt your sincerity, Doge. Or the fact that I doubt a message could have been sent from Jerusalem. But much of our trade depends on cordial relations with the Byzantine emperor. We have a somewhat different strategy to that of Venice. We have never occupied any of his territory. Should we now descend on Constantinople, as part of an attacking fleet, that relationship could not be reestablished."

Personally, Petro Dorma doubted that Emperor Alexis was going to manage to keep the throne under his incompetent backside for too much longer, even if Venice and her allies left him alone. Whoever took over might not remember those who had supported Alexis with any fondness. But before he could think of a tactful way of pointing this out, the Old Fox came to his rescue.

"There is no need for an attack on Constantinople," said Enrico Dell'este pacifically. "All we need is safe passage for the fleet. Should your friend the emperor grant us that small boon there will be no form of conflict. The fleet could even sail under your flag at that point."

To put it mildly, that was a very flattering offer, and not one that Admiral Dourso of the Venetian fleet was going to take kindly to. Admiral Doria—now the Duke of Genoa—was plainly quite taken with the idea. It would elevate his status a great deal.

"But what possible reason could we have to do such a thing?" he asked thoughtfully.

"Piracy!" said Duke Enrico. "It's always a problem, is it not?"

Patriarch Michael raised his eyes to heaven. "Deceit serves no one, my son."

"There cannot be five years between us, Father," said the duke with a smile. "And if it proves false, both Venice and I will be punished."

"And if there is no fleet in Dniepr bay? What becomes of our bargain then?" asked Admiral Doria.

"We will honor them," said Petro. He knew that Venice was unlikely to prove forgiving if this was indeed a false alarm. Doges had been unseated before, especially as a result of costly and unsuccessful military adventures. But he would honor his bargains. He could only hope that whoever came after him had the common sense to abide by it also.

He had great faith in Eneko Lopez, however, and did not think that this would turn into a false alarm. Besides, there were several other reports from Venice's agents, both in the Black Sea, and more particularly in Constantinople. This just added a final bit of weight to those reports.

Suddenly Admiral Doria began to chuckle. "I foresee that you will have great problems with my old enemy, Admiral Dourso."

Petro coughed. "We have taken some small steps in that direction. A fast galleass has been dispatched. I have recalled a young and very able commander from Corfu."

Enrico Dell'este turned to him sharply. "Benito! What do you wish to do, Petro? Put hot coals down Admiral Dourso's breeches? Benito nearly drove him mad in the Arsenal."

"Well, yes, but he has habit of getting his own way," said Petro Dorma. "Benito fights to win. He will not let things like petty rivalries stand in his way. And the sailors who sailed with him before, will, it appears, follow him to hell and back. If he says that the fleet will sail under the Genoese flag, then not many men will disagree."

Admiral Doria raised his eyebrows. "This is young Benito Valdosta?"

Duke Enrico nodded. "My grandson." There was more than a trace of pride in his voice. "He is something of a hooligan. But a good leader of men."

"And my brother," added Marco, a little defensively.

"I have heard of his . . . ah, adventures." Admiral Doria sounded a bit dubious.

"He is a great deal more respectable these days," said Petro Dorma, smiling. "Although not everyone believes that. It's quite a reputation to try to live up to. So we like to keep him out of the way on a nice quiet island until we need him."

Chapter 13

Elizabeth Bartholdy was in a towering rage. Whip in hand she stood astride the dwarf's recumbent body. "You fool! How could you let him escape?"

Ficzko whimpered.

"Answer me!" she shrieked. But he was beyond answering anyone. The only footman that remained cowered back against the wall. The others had all set off on foot after the horses. The remaining footman looked as if he would very much like to join them.

As abruptly as Elizabeth had lost her temper, she recovered it. She turned to the footman. "Put him in the carriage."

Gingerly he picked the small man up.

"On the floor, not on the seat," she said. "Then go and procure me a private chamber in that inn. I will need nine candles." She did not explain what she would need the candles for. But then, as he had been in her service for some years, he could probably guess.

In truth, she was more furious with herself than she was with her little henchman. She had heard them playing their vile music in Buda. They masked themselves well by pretending to be gypsies, but she knew them for what they were. She should have realized that it was some kind of spell. A summoning of some sort.

Why had he been so proof against her magics? He had seemed the simplest of men, yet somehow he had resisted her. That was extremely unusual. She had not wished to use the full force of her powers on him. But next time... Next time, she would bind him. Both with physical chains and with the spells of binding, of lust, and of her other strengths, pain and blood. Now she must perform workings in order to track him.

The footman returned. "The chamber has been prepared for you, my lady. I could only get you tallow dips. This is a poor place. It is all they had."

She tossed the whip back inside the carriage. She was aware of watching eyes peeping around the coarse drapes. They would have watched her beat the dwarf. They would suspect what she was going to do in that chamber, and they would perhaps balk at her demand for a suitable sacrifice. She cared little for their knowledge of her activities. Such small and poor folk could do nothing to her. Yes, her activities here would feed rumor, but that already existed. She had the power and the influence to override any consequences it might cause—and the rumors also sent her recruits.

She reached into the carriage. A little blood would do for a minor working. She would just have to summon a suitable sacrifice. She drew her hand across Ficzko's back, which came back sufficiently red. She muttered a minor cantrip. That would keep him loyal, despite the beating. The dwarf was useful to her. He was one of her oldest cohorts, entrapped by desperate feelings of inadequacy both about his size and his sexual prowess. He had been a willing and, indeed, an eager participant in her activities. He enjoyed the power. Perhaps that came from being so small.

In her other hand, she took the cushion that Vlad had been leaning on. An item of clothing would have been better, but she had to make do with what was available. Then she went inside to the low-beamed room and drew the drapes. She had no need of light to set up the circle of tallow dips, and to prepare to call the inn's cat. She stationed the footman at the door. She could open a window for the victim.

Later, while she washed her hands in the basin she had had the footmen fetch—the little brute had scratched her—she pondered the information that she had gathered. The direction scarcely surprised her. The distance did. And so did the fleeting image of a vast gray wolf. It occurred to her then, that they too had betrayed themselves. She had hoped—indeed all of Count Mindaug's researches had led her to believe— that Vlad would be the perfect bait for the ancient creature that she wished to entrap. If anything, the changers had proved that. Now all she had to do was to catch him and hold him. It was a game of cat— she looked at the body of the sacrificial animal—and mouse. She would enjoy that. And she might even enjoy playing with the little mouse for a while.

They were games that she had had more practice at than anyone else. She had had more time to perfect them. Her hands crooked briefly into claws. Yes, she would enjoy playing with them and she would make the game last; tease them with pain and with hope, even though they had no chance of escape. As for the lupines and their powers, she must get Count Mindaug to research the problem. He had managed to bring the greater part of his extensive library with him. Elizabeth had always disliked books, preferring to follow her researches with assistance from the bargain that she had made, but she would acknowledge that there was value hidden in those dusty tomes. She just preferred someone else to extract it.

Unlike Count Mindaug, she could think of nothing more dull than that vast repository in Alexandria although it did sound as if she would enjoy the rest of that city. One day she might even go and visit the fabled jewel of the Nile delta. Later, when she had finished this current business.

Chapter 14

Maria was standing outside on the battlements of the Castel *a terra*—it was one of little Alessia's favorite walks—when she saw Manfred and Erik come up the hill from the newly anchored galleys. They were not hard to recognize. White-blond heads such as Erik's were rare, and so were people of Manfred's bulk. She smiled and took the now sleepy child back to their apartments in the vast castle complex.

She had been very sad to leave the house that she had shared with Umberto. But practicalities had dictated. The house was part of the living given to whoever was in charge of the little Arsenal. Spare houses were few in the citadel. It would have been unfair to deprive the new master sent out by Venice. Yet there were ample accommodations in both the Castel *a terra* and the Castel *a mar*. The governor traditionally lived in the Castel *a mar*, but that had a tunnel that led into the caves in which the island's age-old Goddess temple was hidden. Benito, she was sure, had engineered matters so that all the possible apartments in the Castel *a mar* were either more inconvenient for his work and ill-suited to Alessia's comfort, or were occupied by people whom she would have felt guilty to have him evict.

There were some rooms available, it was true. Rooms that were on the small side, and up several flights of stairs. These rooms in the Castel *a terra*, on the other hand, were so much more comfortable and had a fine view and a pleasant breeze. Benito could be very subtle when he chose. Of course, it would need a little more than mere inconvenience to take her away from the Goddess. But the living arrangements did stop her from spending quite as much time with Renate De Belmondo as she would have otherwise.

Not that the priestess was not available to her, or that she could not visit her. But it was a little more difficult, and there was always a wary look in Renate's eyes when they met. Renate had been accustomed to huge power. It had been kindly and gently wielded, but the priestess had been accustomed to having the final word, and being deeply respected for this. Maria had to smile. Benito was not too good at respect for anyone.

Maria could accept that Renate De Belmondo had made innocent misjudgments. But, older and wiser now, she could also see that Lady De Belmondo had been grooming Maria for the role that she now found herself in. Something that Benito said rang very true: Aidoneus should choose his own brides, and court them just as other men did. Too often, intrinsically unwilling brides—girls schooled into complaisance, or desperate and miserable—had taken up the half almond. That had not been good for Corfu, and it had not been good for the Goddess or her priestesses either.

Of course, Maria thought wryly, it hadn't been for

the benefit of those ill-suited brides that Benito had
wanted Aidoneus to go and choose his own girls to
woo. Still, the situation had had a curious side effect:
the priestess had let it be known that Maria was her
chosen successor, as well as the living bride. Women
came to talk to Maria now. In many cases she simply
sent them on, but there were some things that she felt
better qualified to help and arbitrate with. Renate De
Belmondo was *Casa Vecchi Longi*. As well-meaning as
she might be, she had never known poverty or want.
Most of the Goddess's worshipers on the island were
peasant women. They had never known anything but
poverty. Maria understood the choices they had to
make better than Lady De Belmondo. She'd had to
make them herself, as often as not.

As time passed, she found that word had plainly
got around: more women came to consult her. And
it became more and more difficult to actually manage to do her own housework. Someone would just
do it for her. That was not something that she'd ever
thought she'd miss. On the plus side it did mean that
entertaining became very easy. She'd felt guilty about
it, and the small gifts, too. But she understood all
too well that to refuse would hurt their pride. And
when pride is almost all you have, it is very precious.

She was very sure that Benito would bring Prince
Manfred and Erik Hakkonsen to visit their apartment. Once it would have terrified her to have such
elevated people in her home. Now, she looked forward
to it, with some pleasure. Besides, when you came
down to it, they were remarkably human. Perhaps
not ordinary—well, definitely not ordinary—but still
people, despite their rank.

Benito was trying to deal with the mountain of things that had to be sorted out before he left, when someone knocked tentatively on the door to his office. Benito ground his teeth in fury. He had given very strict instructions that he was not to be disturbed. He refused to even look up from his desk.

"Who the hell is it this time? Tell them to go away, Spiro!" he shouted to his secretary. He recognized that timid knock.

Instead, somebody opened his door. "And there I thought you would be pleased to see us again," said Erik.

The carefully sorted papers and documents went flying. Benito nearly knocked his desk over and landed on his face in the process of vaulting it. Erik grinned from the bear hug, "You're really not suited to desk work, Benito. You nearly broke your neck there. A fine way to treat it after all the care we took looking after you during the siege."

Benito attempted—and failed—to throw Erik over his hip, grinning so widely that his ears were in danger.

"You've gotten fat and sloppy since I've been away," said Erik, also beaming. "We need to practice again."

"Excellent," said Manfred from where he was blocking the doorway to Benito's secretary's office. "Then he can beat you up for a while. I need a break."

"What would you prefer?" asked Erik, cracking his knuckles. "Fingers? An arm?"

Benito had stepped back and stood looking at the Icelander, while still holding on to his upper arms. There were lines on that handsome clean-cut face that had not been there before. But at least Erik was able to smile again, even if there was a sadness in his eyes that Benito suspected would never quite go away. Erik was back his to dry jesting, too.

He also plainly understood the way that Benito was looking at him. "I won't say that time heals, Benito. But you get used to it."

Not knowing quite what to say, Benito just nodded. There was some things that went beyond saying anyway. Suddenly, only having to part from Maria for four months of each year seemed a very small price to pay for getting her back. He knew that Erik would have settled for that, or made any other bargain, to see his Svanhild again.

"Let's go and get ourselves a drink," said Manfred gruffly. "Even some of that vile *kakotrigi*."

Benito laughed. "It's not that bad. Actually, I am getting to like it."

Manfred looked into the office. "Want some help getting this lot into the fire? Best thing you can do with papers, honestly."

Behind Manfred, Benito's secretary flapped his hands as if he were a large panicking goose, trying to take off. Erik beckoned to the man. "Pick this lot up. Sort it out. Make sure that he has any relevant bits that he has to actually read clearly marked. And if you get any wrong you can explain to me just why your life is of any further value."

Manfred chuckled. "When you finished sorting them out I think my uncle could use your help in Mainz. No wonder Icelanders are known to be such prudent traders. It's the way they keep records. Now let us go and find some wine." he said to Benito. "We've got quite a lot to tell you. And you might as well enjoy your *kakotrigi* now because I have a feeling that you are going to be joining the Venetian fleet shortly."

Benito gaped at him. "How in Heaven's name did you know that?"

Manfred nodded to Erik. "See? It seems that Eneko Lopez got a message through after all."

Erik scowled at Benito. "You had to say that, didn't you? Now he'll think he's an expert at manipulating the likes of Eneko Lopez."

Benito snorted with laughter. "There are some people that it just doesn't pay to try to fool. And he is one of them."

"Now you're making his head even bigger. Let us go and find this wine. I dare say you have some in your quarters. It's more likely to be private than a dockside tavern."

"Besides, I'll get to make eyes at that pretty wife of his," said Manfred with a grin. "I like to live dangerously."

"And she is the dangerous one," said Erik.

"I knew that," said Manfred. He punched Benito on the shoulder, in what he probably thought was a gentle manner. "You didn't think I was afraid of the hero of Corfu?"

"It's my wine, and my wife," said Benito, rubbing his shoulder, and leading them off. Privately, he found it heartwarming that they thought of Maria as his wife. That was more than the Church was prepared to do.

Chapter 15

"How did you know that they were coming?" asked Benito, looking at the wine goblets and the platter of pickled squid, olives and wedges of frittata.

"Who cares?" Manfred cheerfully ambled forward and bowed to his hostess, gesturing at the food and bottles. "You should be grateful, you dog. It matters not if she consulted the entrails of a seagull, or received a divine visitation. She has provided wine and food. And, as usual, I'm starving."

Erik came forward also and bowed and kissed her hand. Maria blushed slightly. In the canals, a friend would have given her a hug and kissed her on both cheeks. She decided that it was time he learned some canal manners. She stepped forward and hugged him. He hesitated a moment and then hugged her back. "Gently," she gasped. "I'm not a bear that you have to squeeze to death."

It was his turn to blush. Manfred pushed him aside. "I should have gotten Francesca to give you lessons. This is how you do it." He enclosed Maria in an embrace only fractionally less bearlike, but also with a kiss on each cheek. "Better?" he said cheerfully. "Mind you, he's a braver man than I am, is Erik. I was more wary about hugging young Benito's wife. At his age men are very possessive."

"Well," said Benito, "I would be jealous except that Erik told me that you were starting to become senile and not really responsible for your actions anymore."

Maria laughed. "Don't worry, Benito. If they become too familiar, I will make them hold Alessia. I have found that she controls most men better than I ever will."

"And how is the young charmer?" asked Manfred, looking at the rocking crib.

"She likes to be moving when she goes to sleep," explained Benito.

"Like her father, she has restless bones," said Maria. "She sleeps best if she is very tired and we are traveling."

"Of course it could just be that she likes the rocking motion," said Benito, "but that does not allow it to be all my fault." He grinned and assumed a posture of deep dignity. "We fathers have our responsibilities."

"We have a few of those, too," said Manfred. "Currently, in the shape of a group of Mongols from the Ilkhan that we are supposed to do something useful with. We're hoping to put them on a ship heading for the Black Sea. We thought you'd be the best person to deliver them."

Benito blinked. "What?"

They explained.

"So," said Manfred, "we are relying on you to get these Mongols to the lands of the Golden Horde. Hopefully, that will stop Erik muttering incomprehensibilities at our rather useless horseboy."

"What?" said Benito again.

"I was trying to learn some of the Mongol tongue," explained Erik. "The horseboy is supposed to be teaching me. In exchange, he avoids doing any work. He's better at that than at teaching, I'm afraid."

Benito rubbed his forehead thoughtfully. "I think I may be able to deliver your Mongol emissary, and possibly without mobilizing a fleet and subduing Constantinople."

"Don't tell me," said Manfred, grinning. "You have a new plan which avoids ships entirely. You're going to disguise us as Magyars and persuade Emeric of Hungary to send us there with a personal escort."

"That's not a bad idea," said Benito, "but not quite the one I had in mind."

"No doubt something worse. Why do we always fall in with these lunatics, Erik?" Manfred helped himself to more wine. "I mean, he's better than that mad bastard up in Telemark. The Turk would have attached all of us by leashes to the feet of well-trained eagles and flown us across. Screaming, because that's what we did mostly when involved with his clever 'solutions.' I suppose we should be grateful. With Benito, at least we just end up as nervous wrecks, shaking a lot."

Benito had heard about their misadventures with a certain Jarl Cair in Telemark. They sounded a little too magical to him, and far too involved in matters he understood less well than warfare or thievery. Cair was a problem he'd rather not face, by the bits that Erik had left unsaid. Fortunately, he wasn't likely to be his problem. Telemark was a long way from Corfu or Venice. "While it does involve crossing the land of the white eagles, I hadn't yet decided to attach you to any of them. I cannot say that it isn't tempting though, as an idea."

"And where are you going to find enough eagles to carry something that size, especially in armor?" asked Erik, jabbing a thumb at Manfred.

"He means Illyria," said Maria. "The land of the white eagles."

"I see he hasn't gotten any less crazy since we met him," said Erik. "It would probably be easier to disguise us as Magyar. From what I've heard, it would take a fairly large land army to fight its way across the Balkans. And the terrain is hell. Straight up-and-down, apparently. Rough on anything except the locals. Bad for a big slow-moving field army."

Benito smiled. "There used to be a road, a Roman road across. As it happens I have been in...ah, negotiations with Iskander Beg. The Lord of the Mountains, as they call him."

"What he means is that he went and did more crazy things, and got himself accepted into one of their tribes," said Maria tartly. "I was very angry with him, and he's been trying to persuade me ever since that there are great advantages to us being close friends with our ancient enemy."

"Well, there are some advantages, if they have stopped trying to kill you," said Erik.

Benito laughed. "I wouldn't go that far. Illyrian ideas of hospitality are enough to kill most people. But I do think it would be possible to have them take your party of Mongols off your hands and escort them across the mountains. That would solve one of the tactical issues that's really been bothering me. Forcing our way through the Bosphorus is going to be tricky enough. If we find that the Byzantines have been reinforced while we're in the Black Sea, things could become very awkward indeed—especially if we've suffered losses."

"Planning your campaign already?" asked Erik.

"He's collecting maps," said Maria. "Some of them smell."

"And none of them are too accurate," said Benito grumpily. "Or at least no two of them seem to agree with each other exactly. I'm hoping that they'll have better quality maps and more information in Venice. There has to have been more to this than one message from the Ilkhan."

Manfred nodded. "I think you'll find that is true. Petro Dorma and the Council of Ten maintain a pretty effective and widespread network of spies and assassins. So does the Holy Roman Empire. You know it often only takes one keystone piece of information to make it all fit together. From what you say, they've been conferring. It may even be that this confirms information that hasn't come back. Jagiellon uses some means which are denied to the rest of us to maintaining his security. And working in his territories is a high-risk profession."

"Petro is not exactly a rash individual," said Erik. "I think you can guarantee that he knows more than just the information we sent from the Ilkhan."

"I hope so," said Benito. "What we have now is not much to plan a campaign upon."

"Why don't you come down and discuss them with Falkenberg and Von Gherens? You wouldn't find much better advice," said Manfred. "Just so long as you bring the wine with you. They're too expensive for me to provide for at the dockside tavern. For men of God, the Knights drink far too much."

"I've noticed that you only complain now that you're paying," said Erik. "And they drink far less than you do. We also need to discuss the possibility of sending Mongols across the Balkan mountains with the tarkhan himself. He's not the easiest of men to read or get along with."

Manfred grunted an agreement. "The Mongols keep to themselves. A couple of the warriors speak a little Frankish. So does the tarkhan. But he doesn't talk to anyone."

"I suppose keeping to himself is part of what an envoy has to do," said Erik.

"Huh," said Manfred. "Old Eberhard can and will talk to anyone, usually at such length that they will pay him to go away. And my uncle says that he is one of the most effective diplomatic envoys in the Empire."

"Still, talkative or not, we could use the Mongols not coming south." Benito paused. "Actually, what we really want is information from the Black Sea. Or better still . . . An alliance with the Golden Horde and we would have successfully isolated Alexis and flanked Emeric, and threatened Jagiellon. By a stroke of diplomacy we would have won more than the Knights of the Holy Trinity have in the last fifty years."

"Remind me not to get you to explain that to Falkenberg!" said Manfred, laughing. "Still, the idea is not without some temptation. I wonder if we can send old Eberhard with the Ilkhan's Mongols to the Golden Horde?"

"He is not that bad," said Erik. "A bit prosy, that's all. But he has served you very well on occasions. Bought us a lot of time."

"He's good at that," granted Manfred. "I'm still in

favor of sending him to treat with the Golden Horde, though. It's as good an opportunity as the Empire has had to make contact with them. As usual, Benito makes a good point."

"It wouldn't work," said Erik. "They are very hierarchy conscious. Well, in a way. They believe any Mongol is the social equivalent of a noble among other people. They would only treat prince to prince. That's always made finding ambassadors very hard. Eberhard was telling me about it. Actually, he was telling both of us about it, but you were asleep."

"The Empire has at least half a dozen impoverished principalities in it," said Manfred. "A fair number of princes should be willing to take on lucrative and nonenergetic employment."

"Eberhard commented on that also," said Erik dryly. "It's true enough that there is no shortage of princes. However, can you think of any one of them that you would trust to buy a horse for you without them coming home with a three-legged donkey? That is, assuming that they didn't drink away the money before they even got to the horse fair. Most of them are not impoverished for no reason."

Manfred grinned. "Prince Heinrich of Swabia. The perfect choice. He could be guaranteed to come home from the horse fair with a fine pair of dead ducks and a price on his head. As a diplomatic envoy, he would make a very fine hat stand."

"Curiously, the very example that Eberhard mentioned," said Erik.

"I do see the point," admitted Manfred. "Still, in terms of value to the Empire, and the fact that the Mongols have a very strict code of honor about the treatment of diplomats, you'd think my uncle could have found someone."

Erik shrugged. "The problem is also one of finding the right opportunity to talk actual business. According to Eberhard, they're experts at talking for a very long time and not saying anything."

"If *he* thinks that they're good at that, then heaven help any ordinary prince," said Manfred. "So will you see what you can do about our Mongols for us?"

Benito nodded. "It might be best if I went in person," he said nonchalantly.

"Not all the way to the Black Sea!" Maria said sternly. "Petro Dorma himself has sent orders for you to go to Venice."

Benito pulled a wry face. "True enough. On the other hand, we could get such a lot out of somebody from our side going along to have a good look. It's mostly going to be sea battles, this campaign. Except of course for Constantinople. I've a mind to use stealth there, if at all possible."

"It shouldn't be," said Erik.

Manfred took a deep pull at his wine glass. "We're talking about Emperor Alexis here," he said. "Anybody else would take preemptive measures. Among other things, Alexis believes that he's a military genius. He's also still deeply in debt, and likely to stay there. It might be easier just to buy our passage to and fro."

Benito shook his head. "Not if we are in a bidding war with Jagiellon. Then Alexis could afford to trade the two of us off against each other. By reputation, Alexis does not stay bought."

"So Eberhard said," said Erik. "You really have to give up sleeping when he talks, Manfred."

"I think I was half awake for that part," said Manfred. "So tell me, Benito, are there any delightful young ladies with acrobatic skills you'd like to introduce me to here?"

"There had better not be," said Maria.

Benito laughed. "I've gotten respectable these days." He paused briefly. "From this I gather that Francesca went through with her plans to go to Alexandria?"

"Unfortunately," said Erik. "I thought that I had persuaded him out of that sort of behavior. It appears that I hadn't, and that it was just Francesca's influence."

"I wouldn't have called it influence, myself," Manfred said. "More like affluence."

Everyone laughed, Erik while blushing. Benito found that quite funny. After all, Svanhild had been even more "affluent" than Francesca. "I am sure," he said, "that all the ladies of our beautiful isle, some of whom may easily be both acrobatic and even possibly well endowed, will be delighted to make your acquaintance, now that Francesca's gone."

"Quite a few of them were interested even when she was around," said Maria, with a secretive little smile. "They are going to be a bit more aggressive about it this time, I think."

Erik groaned. "I hope we can get these Mongols heading off across Illyria as soon as possible. Then I can get him back on the ship and out to sea where the worst I have to worry about is predatory mermaids."

Benito drained his glass and stood up. "Drink up," he said. "Let's go down to the ship and meet your Mongol envoy. As acting governor, it falls within the realms of my duty to offer him and the Knights of the Holy Trinity the hospitality of the Citadel."

"Excellent." Manfred rubbed his hands. "That means they'll be accommodated and drinking at your expense."

Erik laughed. "You know, I don't think the *Godar* Hohenstauffen realized just what a great thing he was doing for Manfred's education when he insisted to the abbot of the order that Manfred should be suitably accompanied—and then gave Manfred a fixed budget."

"And gave me a minder," said Manfred sourly, "to make sure that I didn't settle accounts in the traditional knightly fashion."

They went down to where the knights were disembarking their mounts off the vessels, and giving the animals some much-needed exercise. Benito was cheered by the enthusiastic greeting he got from the knights. He was also soon being overwhelmed with advice on how to capture a vast wealthy city.

"The biggest weakness of the Byzantine Empire is that it is heavily dependent on mercenaries. Buying the Emperor Alexis is an expensive waste of time," said Von Gherens. "Buy his army out from under him."

That was an idea that had not even occurred to Benito. Of course, some of the emperor's troops would be torn from levies from within the eastern Roman empire. Very possibly, he would have a mercenary but intensely loyal personal guard. Petro would know all of these details, but it was an avenue that was still worth following up.

The discussion centered on the weaknesses and strengths of Constantinople and the Bosphorus and Dardanelles. Siegecraft was something the Knights were expert in, and, as they had taken to Benito during the siege of Corfu, they were all too willing to teach him as much about it as they could. A number of them had been to Constantinople and had looked on it with very professional eyes.

Eventually, Benito was able to make his escape and be introduced to the tarkhan Borshar. The man was reclining on some satin cushions under a makeshift awning on the deck, while one of his servitors fanned him. Several of the Mongols lounged about. The air was full of the scent of some form of burning herbage. Perhaps the tarkhan found the odor pleasant. To Benito, it smelled like a weedy field being burnt off.

Borshar rose slowly to his feet, when one of his honor guard announced their presence. He wore his hair in the Mongol fashion, shaved except for a long forelock, but that was where the similarity with the Mongol guard ended. Borshar had a bony and slightly hooked nose, a long face, and heavy eyebrows like two straight bars that sloped slightly downward towards his large ears. His eyes were deep set, brown, and, it appeared to Benito, a little out of focus.

The tarkhan bowed, a mere inclination of the head. "Prince Manfred, how can I assist you?"

"The boot hopefully is on the other foot, Tarkhan," said Manfred. "Let me introduce you to his Excellency, Milor' Benito Valdosta. He is the acting governor and military commander of this charming island. He has, we hope, a way in which you may fulfill your mission."

Benito bowed politely. He could see how the man had gotten under Manfred's skin. Still, perhaps it was just a foreign culture. The way things were done among the Mongols. "I am honored to meet you," he said, in his best attempt at the tongue-mangle that Erik had taught him on their way down to the ship. This did get a reaction. It drew an incredulous smile from the Mongol warrior who had announced them, and it made the envoy's mouth drop open for an instant. He closed it, but looked considerably more alert now. "I am afraid," said Benito, holding up a hand to stem a flood of incomprehensibilities, "that is all of your language that I speak."

"Your greeting," said the tarkhan, "is surprising. So . . . Why did you tell me that my mother was a tortoise?" His eyes narrowed.

The Mongol guard seemed to find the situation utterly hilarious. He had dropped his spear and was clutching his knees, doubled up with laughter. It did not seem that the tarkhan found it quite as funny. On the other hand, neither did Erik or, right then, Benito. Several of the other Mongols had stood up, and the joke was repeated when the Mongol guard had enough spare breath. It was apparent by the reaction of the others, that however affronted the envoy himself might be, his entourage thought it a capital joke.

"I do apologize," said Benito. "I was told that it meant that I was honored to meet you." Inwardly he wondered furiously how the hell he could get out of this situation. Had he started a major diplomatic incident? Was the man going to try to kill him? Manfred was laughing as hard as the Mongols by now, and would be scant use in any defense. Erik looked ready to kill someone—which also was not what they needed right now. "It would seem that I was gravely misinformed."

"And your informant is going to wish that he was never born," grated Erik.

The tarkhan tugged his moustache. It was short, black and bristly, unlike his companions' luxuriant affairs. Then he smiled. It did not extend to his eyes, but at least he smiled. "Perhaps we should confine ourselves to speaking in Frankish."

"I think so," said Benito with relief. "Anyway, other than that...um...useful phrase, I don't know any Mongol. It's not a phrase that I think I will have the opportunity to use again. What I had come to say is that we have concluded an agreement with our neighbors across on the mainland. I believe we can arrange for you to travel across Illyria, to the lands of the Golden Horde. Would that be an acceptable solution for you? You could arrive within weeks. If you wait for a sea passage, it could be many months."

The envoy stood impassively, not even blinking, for a few long moments. Benito decided that it would be very dangerous to gamble with this man. It was almost impossible to tell what he was thinking. Then the tarkhan said, "I will have to consider this. You will allow me time to think. You are proposing a somewhat different route and method than the one which I was instructed to follow."

"Certainly," said Benito. "I will need to establish that you can be granted safe passage. That will take me a few days. We will meet again formally and officially soon, hopefully without any more such interesting incidents. In the meanwhile, can we possibly sit and have a glass of wine together? I'm sure that we have much to discuss of mutual interest to the Ilkhan Mongol and the people of Venice." Benito gave the tarkhan the benefit of his most winning smile. "It is sometimes easier to discuss these things informally over a few glasses than to deal with them in the full light of protocol."

"I have not been given the authority to reach

agreements with the Republic of Venice," said the tarkhan disinterestedly. "And I do not drink alcohol. I will let you know what decision I reach as to the possibilities of traveling across land to the Khanate of the Golden Horde." He waved as dismissively as any emperor, and they were left with little choice but to bow and leave.

Chapter 16

"In the 58th year since the Khagan Temujin, the Princess Khutulun wrestled with Khan Ulaghchi. As was the custom, one hundred horses were bet upon the outcome," sang Bortai, softly, as she gathered berries. "But the great khan bet a thousand horses."

She faltered briefly. A thousand horses! She traced her lineage directly to Khan Ulaghchi, the greatest and most powerful of the khans of the Golden Horde, whose dominion had extended across all the Cuman Khanates, the Volga Bulgars, the Bashkir lands—from the Carpathians in the west to the Alatau Mountains in the east, and across the limitless steppe between. He had drawn tribute from the Kievan Rus princes and been visited by delegations from across the world. He had had a thousand horses to gamble. But he too had barely survived fleeing his uncle Berke, with no one but his warrior bride beside him.

Ulaghchi had survived. Had then conquered. But had he ever had only one horse? There was no doubt that that period of hardship had shaped Ulaghchi and his loyal Khutulun. That was what had made him

determined to keep the Mongol people true to their
traditions, no matter what other tribes they assimilated.
Ulaghchi's rule had lasted for over half a century, and
his influence was still felt now, hundreds of years later.
He had set out the rules of conduct that still gov-
erned the noble houses, enforcing Chinggis's rules on
drunkenness, drawing back to the shamanistic roots of
their faith. Taoism, Buddhism, Christianity and Islam
were tolerated, but they were for non-Mongols. The
Mongols were above these things, true only to the
everlasting blue sky, guided by the spirits.

Ulaghchi's was a great dream to follow. But with
only one horse, and an unconscious brother, the clan
scattered and possibly destroyed, it also seemed a
very far-off dream. As much of a dream as getting
Kildai to Kaltegg Shaman, whom Parki Shaman had
recommended before he was killed.

Out of the corner of her eye she spotted a movement
in the shrubbery on the far side of the little stream.
She tensed, staying absolutely still herself. Then, after
waiting far too many heartbeats, she slowly turned her
head, making no sudden movements. There was a roe-
deer doe there, barely thirty paces away. A big step
from any other game she'd seen so far. There had been
a rabbit that she'd bagged yesterday. She had chopped
it finely, cooked it into a broth with some millet and
salt and herbs. But that deer would be enough food
for days... If she could get a clear shot at it. What an
idiot she was. A few moments ago she'd been singing,
quietly, it was true, but still behaving as if she were safe
in clan-lands and not on the run from their enemies.

She strung the bow and selected an arrow, being
careful not to make any sudden movements. She took

careful aim. She was not as good a shot as her little brother was, or even as her older brother had been. And missing was not an option. That was enough food to see that they could stay hidden all day for a while, and only move at night.

She gave thanks both to the spirits of the wood and the deer. And then swore, as the deer crashed forward. She shot anyway, and fought her way forward through the blackberries, knowing that she was tearing her deel, but too angry to care. Now she might lose an arrow as well. And then she stopped dead.

For there, not forty paces away was someone else, doing exactly the same thing. He had caught sight of her and froze, just like a deer that hopes you have not seen it. Just as she was doing.

His clothes were more ragged than hers—and that thing could hardly be called a bow. And he was tow-headed, and plainly terrified.

What was a slave doing here, with a weapon? That was something a slave would be killed for, even now. Realistically, everyone knew that slaves did a little poaching, trapping small game, using a shepherd's bow or spears that were little more than sharpened sticks. But this slave—with that bow, and having slain a deer...

He had to be a runaway. No wonder he was so scared. Bortai had instinctively put another arrow to her bowstring, after launching the first. He was going to break and run any moment now. She could see the way his eyes darted, looking for cover, looking for the best way out.

"Stand," she said.

He didn't. He fell to his knees instead, his eyes

wide and wild. A week ago she would hardly have noticed. But now...she could hardly help but be aware of some fellow feeling, if not sympathy. The Vlachs was young and gaunt to the edge of starvation. It was a pity he'd cost her a clean shot at the doe, but perhaps he could be of some use. There was, to be honest, much that a slave would know that she as a Mongol princess did not. Things which would be useful in helping both her and Kildai to survive.

"Spare me, noble lady," he said tremulously. "I was just so hungry."

"So was I," she said crossly, "and now you have cost us both our dinner. I suppose the beast is a good league off by now."

He shook his head and pointed with a shaking hand. "No, lady. You dropped it."

Well, that put a very different complexion on the matter. She felt almost inclined to let him run, as a reward. But she could ill afford him being caught and telling someone about her.

The best thing would be just to kill him, but she couldn't quite bring herself to do it. "Well, then, you'd better come and carry it back to the cart."

He blinked. Then a lifetime of obedience took over. "Thank you, lady." He set down his crudely made bow down and began walking into the thicket. For a moment, Bortai wondered if he would bolt. She would have as soon as she had cover. But then, she had not been a slave all her life. The Vlachs seemed to accept that he was back in servitude. Oddly, his face, so terrified a few minutes before, had eased into an expression of relief.

That made sense, in a way. Slaves did not make

decisions. Slaves simply did what they were told. They
were fed, and housed, perhaps no better than a dog,
but that was the owner's problem and prerogative.
The runaway might have lost his freedom, but he
had also been freed from responsibility that he had
no idea how to deal with.

And she might as well be killed for stealing a
slave as far stealing a horse. She'd taken the horse
in fair combat, but she doubted if the orkhan would
accept that.

The doe had managed to stagger on a little way
before it fell, but had not gone too far. Looking at
it, honesty forced Bortai to admit that it was the
slave's heavy crude arrow that had pierced its eye
and killed the beast. Her arrow was merely lodged
in the hind flank.

"Where did you learn to shoot like that?" she asked
suspiciously.

He looked at her with frightened eyes. "I think I
was just lucky, lady." He hesitated. "I did shoot...when
I was a little boy. Before..." His voice trickled off.

That did explain it, partially. Those born into slavery
were more docile than those taken on raids. Raiding
deep into the mountains did yield some new slaves.
It was not something her clan had had much part in.
Ancient law forbade the holding of Mongol slaves, or
even those of part Mongol blood. With their territory
being in the north, the Hawk clan had mostly clashed
with other clans farther north, those now under the
sway of minor khans who owed allegiance to the
Grand Duke of Lithuania.

Other clans might hold the law in scant regard.
But the Hawk clan was rigid about such things. That

made them respected, certainly. But Bortai suspected they were also regarded as thinking themselves a little too good for everyone else.

The slave could be lying about the luck. Slaves did lie. Honor did not have to be their path. Either way, they would need to pick up that bow of his. She might need him to use it again, no matter whether he was supposed to or not.

It was a good-sized mature doe. "Take the hind-quarters," she said, "we'll clean it back at the cart." The carcass would draw flies, but she wanted to be close to Kildai, just in case he woke.

They carried the doe back to where she had hidden the cart, pausing to collect his makeshift bow. She had to shake her head at the thing. It was just a yew bough with a string, made, by the looks of it, from flax. What could he be able to do with a real composite bow?

They hung the carcass in a tree to flense it. Then, abruptly, the slave sat down. He tried to stand up again, but failed.

"When last did you eat?" asked Bortai, looking at him, sitting and swaying.

"Not for some days, lady," said the man, trying to rise again.

"Sit," she said firmly. "I have one unconscious man on my hands. I do not need a second." She dug in the captargac. Mixed up some of the grut and ground millet with some water in the bark bowl she had contrived. "Here," she said. "Eat that."

He took it, confusion and gratitude vying for space on his face. He had plainly had the kind of master who would never have given food to his slaves with his own hands. There were some like that. "Thank you, lady," he said. "I thought you would beat me."

"For falling down from hunger? No wonder you ran away."

He looked at her with very frightened eyes. So he might, since the penalty for running away was death. But that was likely to be her own reward if Gatu or Nogay and his men caught up with them. Of course they would probably amuse themselves with her first. Try, at least. She would have to see how many of them she could kill. It was more honorable to die in combat.

"You will not send me back? Please, lady." His voice was shaking.

"With whom?" She pointed at the cart. "With my brother?" She knew in a way that she was being foolish, telling him that she was alone. But he was so afraid, and so weak. She took out her knife, and began to cut open the doe's belly. He staggered to his feet, and began to help to haul the intestines out. "If I am caught..." he said quietly.

She interrupted. "They will kill you. Do you think they would treat me any differently?"

"Oh." He was silent as this sank in. He hauled the liver out. "Can I set this aside, lady?"

She nodded.

"It does not keep very well," he explained. "We can dry some of the meat, but we must eat the organ-meats soon."

It appeared that the runaway slave had thrown his lot in with her. In a way, a small way, that was comforting. "I know that much. What is your name?"

He looked startled anew. "Ion, lady."

She had never introduced herself to a slave before.

They all just knew who she was. Presumably they found out from other slaves.

But she saw no reason to go into detail. What he did not know, he could not betray. "I am Bortai." It was a common enough name.

He bowed awkwardly, plainly as unfamiliar with this situation as she was. "I know. Princess Bortai of Hawk clan."

So much for keeping her identity a secret. "And how do you know so much?"

He looked warily at her again, as if afraid that she would hit him. "It was my task," he said. "I was supposed to follow you. To tell my master where you went."

She looked at him. He was just such an ordinary looking slave. Of course they weren't supposed to bring slaves to the kurultai. But many people did. Would she have noticed anyone following her? Anyone as unobtrusive as this? Now that she thought about it, she could see where slaves would make excellent spies, if they were capable and bold enough. That was a lesson to be remembered.

"Who was your master?"

His terror returned full force. "You will not send me back? I will be a good slave to you." His eyes were as wild as when she had first encountered him.

"Don't be more foolish than you have to be," she said tersely. "I just want to know by whom and when you were ordered to follow me."

"Lord Nogay. He showed you to me at the start of the kurultai, high lady."

Nogay was one of Okagu's followers. "And where did you lose track of me?"

"At the ger of Parki Shaman. I saw Lord Nogay's men go inside. I heard... But when I dared look you had gone. There were only the dead. I was very much afraid. I ran to Lord Nogay. It took me too long to find him. I did not know he was with the soldiers watching the Hawk clan's gers. He was very angry. He took most of the men from the watch and went looking for you. When he and his Jaghun came back from looking for you, the fight with Hawk clan had already broken out, and they had fled."

That meant that at least some of her clan had escaped.

"Lord Nogay began to beat me. I knew that he would not stop until I died. But he did stop, when someone brought him news that a sentry had been found dead. He let go of me, and I ran."

No wonder he had looked at her with such terror.

"I did not know where to run, but the camp was in uproar. There was much fighting. Many clans fleeing. Much chaos in the dark. Some fires had broken out. I ran. I hid. The next night, I ran again."

"Where did you think you were going?"

"To the mountains. I came from there."

He should have been going west, then, not south. Bortai suspected that the direction that he had been traveling in was merely away. Her own decision had been slightly more logical, at least in the short term. She'd gone the opposite direction from that which any logical person would have thought: toward the lands of the Hawk clan. That was direction in which the greatest search would have been instituted.

The direction she'd taken instead would hopefully throw off the pursuit, at least for a short time. It was also the shortest distance to the security of the Bulgar hills.

Dubious security, to be sure. She had a good chance of being enslaved, just like Ion, or merely raped and killed by the Bulgars. Relations varied. In some places, border clans had peaceful arrangements. In others, more commonly, raiding continued both ways.

She might be lucky, she might not. But at least there would be no systematic search for her and Kildai in Bulgar tribal lands.

Between her and Ion they lifted Kildai up a little, and gently spooned small quantities of broth into his mouth. The quantities had to be very small, or he simply coughed and spluttered. Bortai was not too sure how much of it was actually getting into him., but he did seem to be swallowing something.

Looking at him, Bortai felt very alone and very afraid. A warrior princess like Khutulun should be ready to deal with usurping orkhans. But the clans of Golden Horde always insisted on a male khan, except as a temporary regent for an underage heir. Ulaghchi the Great had left a legacy of deep reverence for Mongol tradition. That could work both for and against them. Many of the clans would support Kildai because of that tradition. Though young, he was still of age. But they would not support her, while he was unconscious.

She refused to let her mind even think about her little brother being dead.

That night they moved on again. Of course, any decent herdsman could have tracked them. But the land hereabouts was riven with tracks, mostly recent. It was, Bortai admitted to herself, very much easier to break camp and to yolk the ox with help. And now she could ride and scout while Ion drove the cart. That was a great deal better and safer than driving the cart blindly.

They still traveled only a league or so that night, but she was able to find a good patch of woodland to hide in. In this area the wooded steppe was more wood than steppe. That was good for hiding, and bad for traveling fast.

This was a better sited hiding place, and there were two of them. That still should not have meant that she could sleep so deeply. But two nights of fear and stress and traveling, compounded by wary and uneasy sleep during the day, had taken their toll.

She had not even realized that she had fallen asleep. She had just meant to lie down for a few minutes in the shade under the cart. She was awakened by the sound of voices. Unfamiliar voices, and harsh ones.

Her first thought was that the runaway slave must have betrayed her.

Chapter 17

"The complexities of the situation," said Eberhard of Brunswick, "are such that I wish you had brought me into it earlier. Yes, Benito Valdosta, I accept the point that you're making about the vulnerability of a fleet in the Black Sea without control of the Dardanelles and Bosphorus. In my youth, I too served with the Knights of the Holy Trinity, in the Swedish campaigns. I have some grasp of military matters, even if I admit that I lack the depth of perception that you seem to have. But it is of enormous diplomatic importance to use the leverage that we now have with the Ilkhan, especially when it comes to the opportunity to visit and treat with the Golden Horde. Prince Manfred is in the unusual—and, I might say, unprecedented—position of being accredited as part of a Mongol diplomatic mission." He sighed. "I had hoped to prevail on his Imperial Majesty to let the prince and the Mongol party be part of the fleet. It's not a negotiating position we are likely to be in again. The Mongols have some strong ideas about the necessary status of envoys."

Manfred sat down with complete unconcern about the

effect that his bulk might have on the spindly furniture in Eberhard's cabin. He put his hands together, steeling fingers. "Of course," he said, "there is one simple possibility. I am empowered to act in my uncle's name. I carry his seal. Instead of trying to hold on to the Mongol envoy and his party so that we can accompany them on what will be the sort of naval engagement that delights Benito, we could simply accompany them across the Balkans. That way, we could very possibly achieve Benito's end and what you say would be my uncle's purpose."

"That is an entirely ridiculous suggestion, my Lord Prince!" exclaimed Eberhard, for once shocked out of his normal diplomatic speech. "Uh, with all due respect. The risks to your person..."

"Are considerably less than the risks I faced in Venice, Telemark and later in Corfu," said Manfred bluntly. "Not only do the Mongols have rather demanding requirements as to the status of envoys from non-Mongols, they are also famous for the courtesy and sanctity they require others to accord to their envoys. I am in the enviable position where the Ilkhan would be obliged to go to war against the Golden Horde if anyone touched a hair on my little head."

"It is only so little," said Erik, "because it contains so little of the stuff required to think inside it. There is the small matter of the Balkans. We are down to fewer than two hundred knights. One hundred and seventy-four, to be precise. That is insufficient even by their own delusions of prowess to cross those mountains."

Benito coughed. "If you think you are safe in Mongol hands...well, I think the one thing no one will argue about is that Iskander Beg is also a man of his word. True, the word—short phrase, rather—is usually 'I will kill you if you cross my lands.' If he decided that you would not cross the mountains of his kingdom, you would not. But it isn't. He has agreed to let at least one convoy take the old Roman Road. If that works out, there will be more. The Illyrian was honest enough to say that there might still be trouble from bandits or a chieftain who decided to do his own independent raid. But even fifty of the knights would be more than a match for that."

Erik frowned and said thoughtfully, "And we are as much honor bound to see that the Ilkhan envoy gets to the lands of Golden Horde, as they are to treat us as diplomatic envoys. We promised to get them there. There are only ten of them. Not enough for the crossing without us."

"They did rather trick us into it, didn't they?" said Manfred, grinning at Eberhard.

"I concede that it is possible that the compliment that they paid us by giving us such status could have been for an ulterior motive," said Eberhard. "But we stood to benefit so much from the status in any dealings that we had with the Golden Horde—"

"I see this as a way of turning it to our benefit, now," said Manfred.

"I still think the idea is fraught with danger," said Eberhard. "Erik, tell him it would be folly."

Erik stood there sucking his cheek. Eventually he shook his head. "No, *Ritter*." He looked at Benito. "You forget that I have been involved in several of this young madman's crazy solutions. He has a way of seeing solutions, solutions that will work, where other people would charge in blindly and lose. I see a great deal of danger in a sea assault on Constantinople. I see even more danger in getting Manfred back from the Black Sea, if Constantinople is reinforced. I also see no benefit to the Empire in this envoy arriving after the election of a new khan. It seems to me that that is very likely to happen."

"Besides," said Manfred quietly, "this has the potential to seriously damage two of our greatest foes. I think there is little else that I could do which would help the Empire as much. I have decided."

Once Manfred had actually taken that kind of decision, Benito knew that there was little point in anyone arguing. And no one did. Discussion then moved to practicalities—how to feed and provision the expedition, and how to pay for it. After listening for a while, Benito cleared his throat. "If you will all excuse me," he said, "I had better go and see about contacting Iskander Beg. Of course, it is entirely possible that the man whose mother is a tortoise may decide that it's a bad idea."

Erik scowled. "I'd forgotten about that horseboy."

Benito grinned. "I may tell you, as the acting governor of the island, that the murder of horseboys is not permitted. It was a damn fine trick. It's just a pity that he had to catch me with it instead of you."

"Death would be far too fast," said Erik. "In fact, I think that I will go and look for him right now. As Benito has just pointed out, our planning is premature."

He stood up, blond, lean and very deadly looking. Benito wondered if he would ever have tried playing such a practical joke on the man. Possibly—when he'd been thirteen and convinced that he would live forever. He had to feel some sympathy for the horseboy.

❀   ❀   ❀

The horseboy was not there.

David was already making his way through the streets of Corfu town. He had had no intention of being anywhere close to the blond foreigner when he found out that he had been taught some choice Mongol insults and not the useful phrases he'd thought he was learning. As luck would have it, David had been lazing and listening in to talk of the tarkhan and his Mongol guards when it had happened. If he had not realized just how serious the trouble was that would result, it would have been one of the finest bits of revenge of his life. And now . . .

Now he was back in familiar territory, even if this was a town still scarred by the battle they had apparently had here over the last winter. He only wished that it was a larger town. But a town was still better than all the miles of emptiness—both of water and on land—that he had come to discover the world outside Jerusalem held. That was a lot of emptiness, and he wanted none of it. He would have to somehow get on a boat and go back home. Jerusalem must be missing him.

As he walked through the streets, his sharp eyes taking in the details of the shops and stalls, he wondered what the local penalties for theft were. From what he had heard, there was nowhere in the world that was as strict as the Ilkhan. Well, it was said that the Golden Horde were even more traditionalist. If there was anywhere in the world that David did not want to end up, it was in their backyard. Thieving was a dangerous enough way of living in Jerusalem, where he and his family had many contacts and knew the local scene very well. Pilgrims and foreigners could be preyed on, provided one was careful.

What he really needed was a local informant. He picked on a likely looking ragged boy, greeting him. And was rewarded by a high speed stream of incomprehensible gibberish.

Maybe life was going to be a lot more complicated than he'd thought. He felt a bitter sense of resentment and betrayal. Why hadn't anyone told him foreigners didn't all speak Frankish?

It was only after the foreign urchin had run off that he realized that his pouch was missing. He swore and ran after the boy, but the boy knew where he was going and David did not. Soon, he was forced to give up the pursuit.

Well, he had wanted to know just what sort of penalties for theft they had here. At a guess, he had just been shown—the hard way. If he ever found the little brat again somebody else would be learning the hard way. Grumpily, he set off to acquire some lunch. To a sharp Jerusalem boy that could hardly be much of a challenge.

Benito was back at his desk in the Castel *a terra* when Erik came to see him several hours later. "It's too soon for me to have word back from Illyria," he said. "And thanks to you I now can't find two essential pieces of paper, and my secretary is a gibbering wreck. Besides that, I haven't heard a word from your Mongol friend."

"It's not that," said the Icelander. "I've got Kari out scouring the streets. But if that horseboy has run off into the countryside it might take us weeks to find him."

"Ah!" Benito leaned back in his chair, and managed not to smile. "I did warn you about killing him, Erik."

"Neither Kari nor I have laid a finger on him," protested Erik. "And it's not because we didn't want to. But apparently he ran off before we'd even finished talking to the Mongol. Several of the Knots saw him go. None of them had the brains to stop him."

If Erik was calling the Knights of the Holy Trinity by the derisive term "Knots" he was genuinely furious—and by his expression, worried also.

Benito had long since given up deliberately baiting the likes of Erik Hakkonsen. Danger seemed to seek Benito out, without him going looking for it. "Relax, Erik."

"I'll need some help, Benito. A word with some of your Schiopettieri, and possibly the loan of some of your troops."

"I said, relax. I already sent a messenger down to your vessel. You must have missed him by a few moments. I have your runaway horseboy. He will need to be a little faster and sharper, if he's going to cope with being a thief in the big city. He can't even cope with swiping bread and squid on Corfu. I'm tempted to give him a few lessons myself. In the meantime, I'm just doing for him what you and Petro Dorma did for me. He's enjoying a little bit of a frightener in my cells. I have a few of the lads yelling at him in Greek."

Erik shook his head as if to clear it. "Yelling in Greek? Why?"

"I figure that I owe him something for nearly causing an international diplomatic incident. And if you think I'm being too harsh, the boy can count himself lucky to still have his fingers and face intact. Stealing anything from Mamma Kasagolis is just plain stupid. If a patrol hadn't been passing by at the time he'd have been beaten half to death. As it was, he did acquire a few lumps before they figured out that he really wasn't able to understand Greek. They brought him here, because as the podesta I deal with foreigners. I figured out that he was your horseboy, but I pretended not to understand a word he said. So what do you want to do with him? You can collect him now, if you like."

Erik began to laugh. He laughed until he had to sit down. When eventually he got his breath back, he shook his head. "The Mongols virtually stamped out crime when they conquered Outremer a couple of hundred years back. This brat is undoubtedly what passes for a thief in Jerusalem. He might even be quite good at it by the standards of a city without much crime. I think he's experiencing some culture shock. Can you have your men lead him out and show him the gallows?"

Benito raised his eyebrows. "Don't you think that's a bit much?"

"No, I don't. It's going to be a while before he gets back to Jerusalem. There are a good few places where he could get himself into just that much trouble, or get us into it. I don't have the skills to teach him to be a thief who can survive, and you don't have the time. So I will have to frighten him into a bit of honesty, at least for a while."

Benito smothered a smile. "And this has nothing to do with him teaching you that a respectful greeting is 'your mother is a tortoise.' You know, it could have been much worse. He could have had you—or in this case me—proposing some form of interesting sexual liaison."

"Then I would not just have had you show him the gallows. He could have tried on the noose for size," said Erik grimly. "I think you can let him spend the night ornamenting your cells. Kari and I will come and fetch him early in the morning."

"I'll temper justice with mercy," said Benito, nodding. "I'll have someone explain to him that the gallows will be where he's heading, unless someone from the ship is prepared to come and take him away. That'll give him some reason to be grateful when you do turn up. It's more than he would have gotten in most port cities."

Erik snorted. "He'd be lucky not to have ended up dead in an alley in quite a lot of them. At the very least someone would have knocked him on the head, and slit his pouch."

"I gather," said Benito with a laugh, "by his plaintive complaints and protestations, all of which I pretended not to understand, that someone *did* relieve him of his pouch. He is taken aback by the dishonesty of us foreigners and how we victimize visitors."

"Isn't it strange," said Erik, with a smile, "how the biter seldom likes to be bitten?"

"It does give you a different perspective on it," admitted Benito. "Not that it works as a perfect cure for everyone. People are inclined to see things from their own point of view, regardless."

"It worked on you," said Erik. "But then, you always were almost too smart for your own good, Benito." He smiled as he said it.

Benito shrugged. "Anyway, you'd better take this, if you're going to take that horseboy with you." He held out a slim book.

"What is it?" asked Erik, a little suspiciously.

Benito did his best to look aggrieved, in a saintly sort of way. "Why does everyone always think the worst of me? It is a book of Mongol-Frankish translations from old Belmondo's library. Some common words and phrases. And the same in their script."

"I'll show it to the boy and tell him he has to be a bit more careful now," said Erik, taking the book.

Benito sighed. "Erik, the time you've spent with the Knights of the Holy Trinity is affecting your thinking. Don't even *think* of showing him the book. You let him go on teaching you. But you check the words yourself, with the book he doesn't know you have. And then you make him say them to one of the Mongols, if they don't quite match the book."

Erik raised his eyebrows. "You're starting to make the Old Fox look positively straightforward."

"It's so obvious," said Benito, shaking his head.

Chapter 18

After King Emeric of Hungary's reverses in the attack on Corfu, and the devastating losses of their retreat across the Balkans, he had had little appetite for campaigning. But if he was to repair his armies and keep his tax base intact, he had to take action against the upheavals that followed.

He used a restive province to cow the others and demonstrate the penalties for rebellion. He brought overwhelming force to bear and left behind in village squares some pointed reminders of what could happen to those who displeased him. Sharp reminders, with people impaled on them. He'd also found that to be an effective way of getting the message across. True, a lot of the peasantry had fled, and it would be some time before the province started to yield dividends again. But a king could not be expected to hunt down every peasant.

So, he was in a buoyant mood, joking with his commanders as he rode back toward the royal castle at Buda, at the head of a column of his invincible Magyar heavy cavalry.

The messenger who arrived was relieved to find him so cheerful. King Emeric had a habit of executing messengers who brought him news that he did not wish to hear. And even the stupidest messenger would know that the king was not going to enjoy this piece of news.

By the shift in expression on the king's face, from laughter to a narrow-eyed stare, Emeric had read the messenger's expression too. "Well? Spit it out. What is wrong, you fool?"

"Your Majesty, I am sorry to be the bearer of bad news . . ."

"Your face told me that already," snapped Emeric. "Now what is it?"

"Your Majesty, it would appear that Prince Vlad of Valahia has escaped from his quarters."

Emeric pursed his lips, and sat still a while in the saddle, in thought. Then he said, "I imagine you would not have brought me this news if he had been recaptured. How did he escape?"

"It would appear that he had outside help, Your Majesty. The guards were all murdered. None of them appear to have even tried to defend themselves. Three were stabbed, and another four appear to have been poisoned. Some of them died in what appears to have been extreme pain. We must conclude that some form of treachery or magical means were used."

"Spare me your conclusions," said Emeric. "Tell me instead what measures have been taken to recapture him. I think it is time that I dealt with the Vlachs for once and for all. Having a suitable hostage has kept them from being too restive, but with Vlad's father now dead, I had wondered what steps to take next.

It would appear that the matter has been taken out of my hands."

"Your Majesty, we have sealed all the roads going east. Patrols are scouring the countryside between the roads. We have taken in several suspects known to have Vlachs sympathies. They are being put to the question."

"Well, at least they were measures not entirely devoid of sense. Although inadequate. You need to send a message to my aunt, the Duchess Bartholdy. Also, I will need reinforcements sent to our garrisons at Irongate, Poienari, Beszterce, and Caedonia. They are to seize the dowager princess and her daughter and have them conveyed to my court. Once news of this leaks out, we will have unrest in the Duchy of Valahia. Have my secretary write the orders for you, and bring them to me for my signature and seal. You may carry them back to the castle immediately. Baron Arbalar will take the appropriate measures from there."

The messenger bowed. "Yes, Your Majesty."

He was too relieved at keeping his head to even dream of protesting that he had just ridden for ten hours, and that he and his horse were in no state to ride directly back to the castle. He could always get a new horse somewhere. He had used up four remounts so far. And being too sore to stand tomorrow was better than sitting on a sharpened stake now.

However, by the time that Emeric's secretary had finished scribing the letters and the tired messenger took them to the king for signature and his seal, Emeric had changed his mind. "I think instead," he said tearing up the neatly penned letter, "that I had better go and speak to Elizabeth myself. You will proceed back to

Buda, and pass on my orders there. I will take part of my column to go north to visit the countess."

The messenger was relieved, again, that the king would be going north and not him. One did not work in Emeric's court for as long as he had without becoming very wary about the stunningly beautiful Duchess Bartholdy. There were certain unpleasant rumors about her seemingly eternal youthfulness. Emeric's court was always awash with rumors, but the ones concerning Elizabeth were unusually persistent.

That might just be a pipe blown by jealousy, of course. She was truly beautiful. But the messenger had no desire to find out if they were true or not.

Emeric had plenty of time on the three-day ride to Elizabeth's castle in the northern Carpathians to think about the situation that Vlad's escape created for him in Valahia. There were complexities involved, and considerable potential both for exploitation and disaster. The area to the west of the Carpathian mountains was fertile and valuable. There were a number of settlers there from other parts of his territory. They at least would be loyal. And it was country that was suited to his kind of military operation. But the area inside the arms of the mountains themselves was almost entirely loyal to the house of Valahia, with the exception of the Székely seats. It was also not a good area in which to try military conclusions with an army like his, so dependent on heavy cavalry.

Perhaps it was time that he threw his weight behind the Danesti—a rival and related clan. One never knew if they would prove any better, unfortunately. However, no matter how good a refuge the Besarab had in the mountains, they needed the flatter lands to sustain themselves. The mountains were dirt poor. All very well for producing a few sheeps' milk cheeses, but not much good for outfitting a troop of cavalry.

It would appear that someone had half crippled her pet dwarf, Emeric noticed, when he was shown in to the duchess's presence by a limping Ficzko. That would not improve her humor. He was a horrible little man, but he had been in her service—in more ways than one, Emeric suspected—for many years.

In private, Elizabeth showed the King of Hungary none of the respect that she would accord him at court in Buda. "Well, Emeric?" she said impatiently. "I am rather busy at the moment. What is the problem, this time?"

"And why should there be a problem, Aunt?" he said, in an attempt at hauteur which failed completely. He knew that she was not actually an aunt, but more like a great aunt. Or even great-great-aunt. He also knew that she had manipulated and controlled his father and very possibly his grandfather, too. He knew full well that she had arranged his father's death, so that he could ascend the throne. Like a spider she had controlled the web of power that was Hungarian politics for the better part of the last century. She still looked as if she was barely twenty. Of course most people believed that it was her mother, and grandmother, who had been so influential in their time.

Emeric maintained the fiction that he was independent of her power. And, in fact, he had done his best to try to become that. At least in Buda, they would question her orders now. But that was a small step, and one he was well aware of the danger of taking.

"Because you only ever come to see me when you *are* in trouble, Emeric," she said coolly.

That was probably true. But then, she only came to Buda to interfere in the running of his kingdom. He almost always did her bidding in the end. That didn't mean he had to like it.

"This time, it is more your advice that I want. I do not think we are in trouble yet. Vlad of Valahia has escaped from his quarters in the castle. I was going to have to release him anyway. With his father's demise, the Vlachs are calling for his return to take the throne. I was going to insist that we had his mother as a hostage instead, and marry him off to a suitable lady of my court. A Hungarian or possibly a Slovene. Now the matter is rather out of my hands. There is that clan of cousins, the Danesti..."

Elizabeth smiled warmly at him. That was enough to sound some alarm bells, as well as allowing him to relax slightly. He could still ill afford to openly antagonize her, so it was good to see the smile, but it was a little worrying that he might find himself as a cog in her machinations. Emeric was well aware that Elizabeth was involved in some very black magic indeed. As black as it got, in fact. And in his heart of hearts, he knew that he was not a great and powerful practitioner of those arts.

"This time you were wise to come and speak to me before you did anything rash," she said. "There is a great deal more to the house of Valahia than just a petty principality. There is power there. Power that we should harness for the Kingdom of Hungary. And Prince Vlad must be very innocent, the way you've kept him sequestered. More innocent and ignorant than a convent-reared babe."

He knew her well enough to understand that she was not talking of dynasties, or the right to command vast armies, or rule by hereditary right over great swathes of Europe. She was talking about power in a less earthly sense.

That could still, of course, give him both the armies and the rule, which was what he wanted. But Elizabeth had always been rather uninterested in those, even though he was sure that she intended to keep the magical power mostly to herself.

"I have ordered some of my troops to seize his mother and sister and have them sent under escort to Buda. I will have the girl married off as soon as I get her there. I'll find a suitable nobleman. Perhaps one of the Slavs or Croats."

The countess shook her head. "It is very unlikely that your troops will find them there. If they—whoever 'they' are, which still needs to be determined—are well enough organized to seize Prince Vlad from Buda, they will have taken steps to get his mother and sister out of harm's way as well. You should have taken some measures with the girl earlier."

"She's barely thirteen."

"A fine age," said Elizabeth. "I'm sure that you would have found more than one noble ready and willing to do their duty for the kingdom. There are enough greedy little lordlings that would marry a cesspit if you told them to, and not a few of them would prefer it if the girl was young."

"I've just been busy. I did not expect the Prince of Valahia to die just yet. I certainly didn't expect his son to escape his captivity."

"We need to look at steps that can be taken to

capture Vlad. I must tell you that I need him alive, Emeric. If necessary you can kill him later, and put the Danesti on the throne. I think them a shaky reed for your purposes, though."

"The instruction will be given." She did not explain why she insisted that Vlad be taken alive, and Emeric did not enquire. The answer was likely to be one he didn't want to hear—assuming she answered at all.

"You are very unlikely to catch him by ordinary means," said Elizabeth. "If he has help, and that help has arcane skills, ordinary patrols and check-points are not going to catch him. He will certainly be disguised, and will probably be well informed as to their whereabouts."

She sat back in her chair. "I think that you're going to have to leave this in my hands for now. By all means invest more troops in Valahia. Prepare for unrest. Make a few suitable examples of some of the peasantry. The local boyars have little cause to love the house of Valahia. The commoners however, are another matter. Let them feel the weight of your authority. I will need some of your troops. Mostly cavalry, I think. I believe I can locate him by magical means. Restraining him, and whatever partisans he has been able to gather, will take quite a few men. I will need to operate in secret. I'll want some of your light cavalry as well, and an officer with no scruples and the ability to follow orders. But he needs to have some brains too."

Emeric felt as if he was being given the orders. But as always, with Elizabeth, he felt powerless to resist her plans. He wondered, not for the first time, if she had put some kind of compulsion on him. But surely she would never have dared to do that. He was, after all, the king.

After Emeric had left, Elizabeth sat, thinking. She had been unsure, when he arrived, if he had found some trace of her abduction of Vlad. A competent magic worker could have divined what had been done. Of course, she had left a few traps, demonic traps, that probably would deal with all but the most competent of magic workers.

There were few of those left in Hungary. The Church was docile in Emeric's domain, and Elizabeth had hunted the pagans far more relentlessly than any Christian fanatic ever had. She had made very sure that Emeric had little access to anything but dilettantes in the field of magic, especially the darker arts. She'd had to kill a few who had attempted to seek his protection.

But he might have found someone in his rather futile militaristic efforts that she had not yet found out about and neutralized. He had done so before. There was a streak of deviousness in the boy. That was about all that was left of the old bloodline. She ought to breed from him soon. The original line had been a strong one. She'd seduced her own brother to make sure that they bred true. It still gave her a tiny frisson to think of his utter horror when he had discovered what he'd done, and just how she'd manipulated him and forced him, and that limp wife of his too, into deceiving the court and the world.

She smiled. He'd been driven to take his own life, in the end. She'd seen to it that he died unshriven, with the full burden on his soul.

The role of great-great-aunt suited her better than that of great-grandmother. She wondered if she should do it again. It would be easy enough: the compulsion had been set in place during rituals that Emeric did not even remember, back when he had been about four years old. He'd been charmingly innocent and terrified.

But perhaps it was just as well to thin the blood. She'd had to kill the others far earlier in life. They'd become suspicious and rebellious at a younger age than Emeric, shaking off some of the enchantment. Emeric was so vain that he considered his person sacred.

Anyway, it would appear that everything had worked out for the best. Emeric had given her the troops she desired to herd the bait with. When she was ready, she would catch both the prey and the bait. Both had their uses. She stood up in a fluid movement, almost catlike, refreshed by her deliberations. She must go and speak to Count Mindaug. It was he, and his endless literary researches, that had brought her the knowledge of what she needed for bait. Mindaug didn't know that she had been trying to catch one for the last fifty years. Like pagans, the nonhumans were creatures to be used and then destroyed. Except the Vila, who were too useful to be destroyed.

She had even met the original Dragon of Valahia briefly. Such an opportunity that she had missed, perhaps. But there had been something about him—despite his reputation, which had interested her—that had made her uneasy. Besides, he had undoubtedly been more than a little mad.

Belatedly, her thoughts turned to the younger sister that Emeric had mentioned. Just the right age. Very probably a virgin. That would be particularly valuable blood for refreshing her youth. Royal blood, and with a nonhuman taint. Best drunk straight from the still-warm victim.

Emeric wanted to waste such a resource on marriage to one of his vassals. Her need was greater. She would have to have the girl snatched, if Emeric succeeded in capturing her.

"They were relatively common creatures once," said Mindaug. "Many were created."

He wore, Elizabeth was amused to discover, eyeglasses here in his book-piled chambers. Perfect vision—indeed, better than perfect—had been part of what she'd demanded for her side of the bargain. She recalled that she had once been prone to terrible headaches, back when she too had read, seeking a way—any way—to avoid the creeping ravishes of time on her beautiful skin.

"So you have said. And the pure essences extracted from that blood will have value to me and my works. But I become more and more interested in the effects of the blood in admixture with humans. Vlad may be bait, but he is powerful too in his own right."

Mindaug looked down at the book in his hands as a way to avoid looking directly at her. "Yes," he said. "It said so in the book I showed to you. Creatures of mixed blood are dangerous, as they exist outside the constraints of either humans or the others, with some of the powers of both. So are the creatures which cross the lines between the nonhuman realms. But they are not easy to create."

"I have some experience at forcing matings of nonhumans of air and water, and some success with the offspring," said Elizabeth.

Count Mindaug reflected that it was odd that he, like so many of the other nobility of Europe, was related to this woman. As a class they were, he reflected, more inbred than was wise. Perhaps that was where her madness came from. There could be no doubt that there was madness there, underlying her vanity and the strange desperation that had led her down this course. She enjoyed killing and pain. Count Mindaug did not. They were necessary tools and he was adept at using them. But, like his point-filed teeth, they were about survival, not choice.

So was helping her with her preparations here in this bleak, stone walled and cold "nunnery" that she had as an adjunct to her castle. At the same time, he was preparing certain spells in case he would need to make a rapid physical departure. He had, as yet no second country or a protector to flee to. He'd been quietly searching for both. Hungary looked to be the best possibility, as little as Mindaug wanted to be in the proximity of that realm's vicious and sadistic king. But if things went awry—if Elizabeth Bartholdy decided that he was a threat, for instance—he could disappear rapidly. True, it would only take him as far as his crowded library in her castle in Catiche. But he could use more ordinary and physical ways to flee from there. It would take her or anyone a while, even with demonic aid, to find him.

Mindaug continued to study the plainly bound book. It struck him that demondim might take a multitude of forms, including appearing to be paper.

Chapter 19

Bortai heard his voice then, sounding just a little arrogant—something she wouldn't have thought the slave capable of. "What do you want here?" he asked. "My master is away, and the young master is asleep. Go before you wake him." He spoke as if he had been a family retainer for fifty years, confident in his value to the clan.

Bortai was surprised to hear the strange voices modulate. "We just want to know what you are doing on our lands," said one.

"When the kurultai broke up, we were separated from our clan," said the slave. "We are returning to them. We merely travel through. That is permitted."

"We are looking for a woman..." That was a different voice.

"There are no women here," said the slave in a tone of some shock and disgust. He did it well, as if they had suggested that the cart was some kind of cheap brothel in one of the small settlements. "Even my master's wife is three years dead."

"We must look," said the first of the strange voices. "Stand aside, slave."

Bortai rolled quietly to the far side of the cart and drew her knife. Up to that moment, there had been some chance that the interrogators might back off. But they would see Kildai. They would find some of her things in the cart. The runaway slave could hardly stop them.

"No," Ion said. The slave's voice shook, but he did the unthinkable. She could see them now, two ordinary warriors from one of the poor clans from the south that had allied itself to Gatu. One had dismounted and had stopped just short of the slave, an incredulous look on his face. His hand rested on his sword hilt. But he faced just a solitary slave. He was hardly expecting trouble, even if Bortai could see that the slave had a stout stick in his hand.

While one man remained mounted they were in grave danger. But he was relaxed, slouched in the saddle. She measured the distance with her eye. She could throw a knife fairly well, but doing so would leave her unarmed. Still, she saw no alternative.

And then, once again, the slave's precipitous and unexpected actions affected her aim. He hit out at the warrior with his cudgel, dividing her attention for a moment. She was too late to stop the throw, although she did pull back from the intended force of it. As a result, she did what no good Mongol would ever do. She hit the flank of his horse instead of him. At least the weakened throw meant that the knife did not sink itself to the haft as she had intended.

But as far as the horse was concerned, a giant and vicious horsefly had just bitten it. It screamed, reared, turned and tried to bite the spot. Not surprisingly, the horseman lost his seat.

Ion almost lost his head. His blow with the cudgel, while unexpected, was hardly the most effective blow ever struck. The warrior barely staggered, and an instant later had drawn his sword and struck back. But sheer fury made him clumsy with his stroke, so that the slave was able to block it with his cudgel. The cudgel lost the top hand-length, and, almost dropping it, Ion stumbled back. He would have died seconds later if Bortai had not kicked the warrior's legs out from under him.

The warrior still had his sword, but not for long. As he rose, Ion stepped forward and managed another wild swing with the truncated cudgel. That hit the warrior on the forearm just short of his elbow. The sword flew out of his hand and embedded itself in the wood of the cart. Bortai was on to him before he could draw a knife.

Wrestling was one of the noble arts, one in which she might not exceed the skills of the legendary princess Khutulun, but was easily a match for some poor ordinary warrior. However, there was still the other man, who had gotten to his feet, drawn his sword and was running towards them.

Ion turned tail and ran. Bortai knew now that she had little choice. She had to kill the first man very quickly. They had staggered to their feet. She did not wish to throw him and lose grip. Instead she swung him between herself and the second man and he took the sword thrust intended for her. His companion's own fury made him clumsy also.

A moment later, Ion made sure that the other warrior had no opportunity to strike again. Ion's crudely made arrow skewered the man just as effectively as it had the doe.

The warrior screamed, staggered and fell as she

pushed his blood-gushing companion away from her. Ion advanced slowly, another one of his homemade arrows on the string.

Bortai did what every good Mongol woman would do in such circumstances. She picked up a knife and cut their throats, neatly.

Ion dropped his bow, and stood there, holding on to the edge of the cart. His face was white and his teeth chattered. He looked to her as if he would fall over at any moment.

But they were more urgent things to be done. One of the Mongol horses stood, as Mongol horses had been trained to stand when their riders alit. The other...

She would need to see how far it had run. "We will need to saddle up. No, I will just take this horse. But you had better yoke the ox." She was already in the saddle, and looking to see if she could see any sign of the other horse.

"Lady Bortai, we must flee," he said, his eyes wild with fear again.

"If we can't catch the horse, we'll have to. Whatever happens, we are going to have to take steps not to be tracked. Or not to be tracked too easily. Within the next day they'll start looking for these two. If I can find the horse, we'll have to bury the bodies."

She put her heels to the pony's sides. Fortunately, she did not have far to go before she found the other horse. Her first thought was for the injury that she had caused. It was a nasty wound, but probably not serious. She led the horse back, looking for her knife, which had obviously fallen out. But she found no sign of it. That in itself was irritating. There had been a good stone on the pommel.

When she got back, the cart had been hitched up but there was no sign of Ion. He might have run off, but she would give him the benefit of the doubt for now. Last time that she had assumed that he'd run off he had used that bow of his to good effect. It wasn't lying in the cart or on the ground. So it was a safe assumption that he'd at least taken that with him.

Bortai hitched the horses and began to unsaddle them. Sure enough, Ion appeared warily from behind a tree and began to help. He was still obviously very afraid.

"You did well back there," she said.

He shuddered. "I did not actually know what to do," he admitted.

"Hit much harder," said Bortai gruffly, some level of combat aftershock beginning to take hold. It was better just to keep doing things.

A slave was not supposed to take up arms. But if he had not done so, she would probably have been dead and Kildai would have been killed not long afterward. It would seem to her that Nogay had wasted a very loyal servitor—but then perhaps that was why he had been entrusted with following her.

"We need to do something with these bodies," she said. "And maybe move just a little bit."

The slave looked at the bodies and shuddered again. "We could take them to the edge of the stream where there is a steep bank. We could cave it in on top of them."

She made a face. That was too close to the water. Disrespectful of it. But they had to do something, or the carrion birds would show others just where these two had met their demise. "Not in the water," she said.

He shook his head. "Well clear. There was a little hollow that I was hoping to hide in myself, Lady Bortai."

So, once they had looted the bodies of anything useful, between them they dragged the corpses to the undercut bank. Sooner or later, unless they had rain, someone would probably track the missing two warriors. They would find the spot where the killing had happened. It was very possible that they would find the bodies too. Hopefully the cart would be a few days away before that happened.

A little later, they moved the cart and the horses. As they were unhitching it again, Kildai gave a weak moan. His eyes opened wide, and then closed again. Bortai dropped the yoke and ran to him. But it did not appear that he was going to do any further waking up just yet. She hoped, desperately, that he would stir soon. They had three horses now. Once he could ride they could abandon this cart.

She was not going to abandon the slave. If he was caught he would be killed. The man had risked a great deal to save her and Kildai, and behaved with rare courage too. Such loyalty had to be respected.

She wondered if he could ride. In the meanwhile, she must see to that poor horse. It would need to be stitched and poulticed. Fortunately, she knew how to do both. She felt scant sympathy for the clansmen that had hunted for her. They would have killed her and Kildai, and taken their severed heads as proof. But horses were different. A horse did not choose the use it was put to.

At dusk they must travel on again. They would seek to mingle their trail with that of other bullock carts. But never again would she allow exhaustion to override her caution. They could take turns to sleep. Ion might not be as keen eared as a sentry, but she would teach him to watch the horses. A horse was more keen eared than any human, especially for the sounds of other horses. If whoever was not on watch slept a little distance away with a bow, they could wreak havoc on any enemy. They could certainly deal with foes in ones and twos.

There was nothing like victory, no matter how unlikely, and how much by the favor of the spirits, to dispel fear and despair. With Kildai stirring, she almost dared to let herself hope that they could survive.

Chapter 20

"So, Benito, you want to send a column of Knights of the Holy Trinity down the Via Egnatia," said Iskander, as the two of them sat on a log looking out toward Corfu. "Do you want to start several wars?"

Benito thought carefully before replying. "I suspect that knowing they could be flanked might also restrict certain ambitions. If I were Alexis, I would make haste to open the sea route, before the principal source of my income dried up. But then I am not Alexis."

"I would have reason to know fear, if you were," said Iskander. "But there is also Emeric of Hungary, to say nothing of the Grand Duke of Lithuania."

Benito shrugged. "Seen from your point of view, King Emeric is at war with you and will remain at war with you for as long as he lives. The fact that you may be allying with some of his enemies is hardly going to change that. If anything, it may make him a little more wary. As for Jagiellon, the Mongols are at the moment a buffer between you and him. I have explained why we are escorting these envoys from the Ilkhan to the Golden Horde. If we fail, you will have

Jagiellon's proxies on your doorstep. If we succeed, you will have a buffer zone."

"That is a better argument than all the rest," admitted Iskander. "But there is no need surely for the Knights to accompany them. I tell you truthfully, some of my people will be very uneasy about that party, so large and heavily armed."

"By all means, match them with an equal number. The truth is, and I am being frank here, we dare not have anything go wrong in getting those envoys to the lands of the Golden Horde. We are honor bound to see that they get there. If we fail in any way, we will have acquired a powerful enemy. And to be honest again, some of the tribesmen in these hills are, by your own admission, barely under your control. They might try their luck with a small party of Mongols, no matter who they were escorted by. They're not going to—not one little tribe by itself—try it against the Knights. I think the Knights' reputation has penetrated even here." He smiled at Iskander's slightly troubled face. "If at a later date some tribesmen raid a caravan the matter can be dealt with without destroying any chance of other traders using the Via Egnatia. But this first journey must succeed."

Iskander stood up, and took a deep breath. "I risk my own standing among the tribes. Have I your word, as a kinsman, that the Knights of the Holy Trinity do not come as a reconnoitering force? That they will, unless attacked, refrain from conflict?"

Benito did not smile, even though he wanted to. This was serious. "I have never been as happy to give my word. You don't know them as I do, Iskander Beg. They are monks in armor. They will serve where their abbots tell them to serve. And they will obey orders, even to the death. They are a bit boneheaded, to be honest, but one gets used to them." He said the last with a disarming grin.

Iskander laughed. "Well, there are a fair number among my own tribe that would fit the boneheaded part, but they're not much good at taking orders. We tend to go our own way up here. Where there are two of us, there are three different opinions. I will provide an escort and scouts."

"And I will see that they pay, and pay handsomely, for food and lodging where it is available. We will have to discuss this, Lord of the Mountains. If possible they do not want have to take a baggage train with them. It will not be easy to get it over the mountains in a hurry."

Iskander smiled. "As it happens I have a number of very fine Hungarian tents that I could have set up along the way. Their previous owners had to abandon them."

"So sad for them. I think that we could decide on a mutually agreeable fee for this. There really isn't much of a market for second-hand tents."

Iskander laughed. "Maybe not on Corfu. But they are promising material for fine cloth up here in the mountains. Delicate blouses for the ladies, and things like that."

"Probably linen for the Lord of the Mountains' bed too."

Iskander shook his head. "The canvas is a little too soft for that. It might make me soft too. To avoid it I will have them put up for a traveling band of Knights. No one will want to use them after that."

"Well, seeing as we would be doing you a public service, you wouldn't want us to pay for the use of them then, would you?"

"You chaffer like a Venetian, Benito. Not a member of my tribe," said Iskander shaking his head, with his brow wrinkled in sorrow, and his mouth held prim. "Just think of the poor women who will lose fine blouses."

"Well, it's the duty of the king to help to guide them away from vanity and vainglory. But, before we get to serious dickering, I need to make sure this journey is going to happen."

The Lord of the Mountains raised his eyebrows. "Surely," he said, "they can see your impeccable logic?"

"It's hard to tell quite what the envoy is thinking. We did not exactly get off on the right foot."

Benito told Iskander just how the horseboy had misled Erik, and just what had followed. Iskander's teeth gleamed white through his moustache. "This boy will go far, if he lives long enough."

Benito laughed. "Right now all he wants to do is get off my God-forsaken island, and get back to his nice safe Jerusalem, where he is apparently counted one of the biggest rogues. Or thinks he is. Anyway, just as soon as I hear from our Mongol envoy, I will send you word."

Iskander Beg nodded. "I will arrange it all. It is possible that I may decide to accompany this caravan myself. I will of course expect you, kinsman, not to tell them who I am. You're quite right. Much rests on this first caravan succeeding. But I would not have word of my presence get out. You are not the only one whom enemies would like to see dead."

"A good idea, I think. There have not been many

caravans of such value. At least, not ones where several great powers would pay so much just for the heads of the people on it."

"I know," said Iskander. "I think you should put it about that the Knights are outfitting to go overland to Rome. That might be best. You have my word, and you have my honor: they will get through my territories alive, while I remain alive to see that they do. You may tell the Knights and the envoy that. Even outside of Illyria, my honor is known."

Benito took his hand firmly. "I am proud to be adopted into your clan for that reason. It is a reputation that goes back many centuries."

Iskander smiled wryly. "Centuries... One day I will tell you the entire story, Benito Valdosta. It is much more complicated than you realize. But let us just say that there are few enough men of honor. We should stand together, because, clan or no clan, we are brothers of a kind."

"I know," said Benito simply. He felt an affinity with the man, and with his tiny beleaguered quarrelsome people, who still—against the odds—defied great powers both to the north and the south. It was clear that the liking cut both ways. He felt almost as if he was dealing with the elder brother Marco might have been, if they'd shared the same father. It might not be logical, but Benito knew that he could trust Iskander. He also knew why Iskander was Lord of the Mountains. Men would follow him, even these fractious hill-tribesmen.

The Mongol envoy's eyes looked sharp and slightly hooded. But at least he was smiling, which was an improvement on anger. "Of course, I will require certain guarantees. It was with such contingencies in mind that I asked that Prince Manfred and his Knights be accorded the status that was given to them by Bashar Ahmbien. But I believe that as long as he accompanies us the Ilkhan would not take it as an affront. I would be able to complete my mission. Thus all our parties would be satisfied."

Eberhard looked doubtful. "It is still fraught with some risks, Borshar Tarkhan. The person of Prince Manfred, for all that he thinks this is a good idea, is not one the Holy Roman Emperor is likely to put in harm's way again."

Borshar looked mulish. "It is a point of honor, *Ritter*. Either we are accorded the appropriate escort, to which you agreed, or we do not go."

"Let us have no further discussion on this matter," said Manfred firmly. "I have decided, and I am authorized to speak for the Emperor. In this case I will speak for him about myself. The risks you speak of are small. Iskander Beg is known to be a man of his word. So are the Mongols, especially on matters of diplomatic protocol, and the safety and treatment of envoys. That, I believe, covers us. We will accompany you."

Borshar bowed respectfully. "You conduct yourself with honor, Prince."

"I hope so," said Manfred. "It is the hallmark by which my mentor," he gave an ironic smile at Erik, "says great men and great nations are known. He sets a high standard for us."

"I shall see that meetings are arranged between yourself and the new khan of the Golden Horde," said the tarkhan. "As you are a man of rank and honor. If we can talk now of practicalities, we speak of a journey, overland, of some sixty leagues, I believe."

"More," said Falkenberg. "It's mountain country. But part of the route follows an old Roman road, and Benito has arranged provisioning and accommodation. We should, even estimating conservatively, have you there in twenty days. We are preparing for the journey with some extra packhorses. It has been set about that we will make a landing at Bari and that we will proceed overland to Rome and then on to Venice."

"That is slow travel by Mongol standards."

Von Gherens eyed him frostily, but said nothing.

Chapter 21

For Vlad, the days had passed in something of a blur. In fact, it was the countryside that had passed in something of a blur, and mostly they had passed through it in the dark. When they had stopped, especially in the first few days, he had simply been too exhausted to do more than eat and sleep. He had not cared quite what they had eaten, or that they had slept in haystacks, or caves, or a ruined barn. There were always fresh horses, and a change of horses. He was aware that this was not how noblemen usually lived, but at first he had not protested. At least the gypsies seemed to know where they were going, and just how to avoid the patrols. But after a week he was becoming fitter, and, he noticed that the party had visibly relaxed.

"We come to the edge of our range here," said Angelo. "We are still far from our heartland, but people around here gave some allegiance to your father. We will have a rest day tomorrow."

"Is it Sunday?" he asked.

The gypsies looked at each other. "I don't really know," said Grigori. "You tend to lose track of the

198

days after a while. Town people keep track very well. We will have to find one and ask."

"I need to go to church," said Vlad, guilt washing over him.

The three gypsies looked at each other again. "It's not a place that sees us very often," admitted Angelo.

"You have less reason to fear for your souls than I do," said Vlad.

They did not seem inclined to argue with him about that.

"We will take a room at the inn," said Angelo.

The thought of sleeping in a bed was almost intoxicating. Vlad felt that he'd been something of a burden on their journey, that they could have traveled faster without him. He hoped that soon he would be back in some measure of control of his own destiny. He just wished that he knew what that destiny was, besides merely staying alive. The countess had said something about his father being dead, and his boyars needing him. He seemed to remember that his father had been furious and bitter with the boyars, and had said that they hated him just as much as he hated them. But Father Tedesco had said that time healed all wounds. Perhaps they had forgiven and forgotten.

After a week of hard riding and sleeping rough, all without any sign of fresh clothes or ablutions, beyond a splash in a stream and getting thoroughly wet crossing various rivers, a bath was going to be very welcome. They had not crossed a single river at a bridge, or by using a ferryman. The gypsies certainly knew how to find any ford. Some of the crossings, however, had involved a fair amount of swimming. That wasn't quite as pleasurable as washing in warm water, especially as they kept to the high ground, scantily populated, and heavily forested. The water in those wilderness rivers was bitterly cold. The gypsies hadn't seemed to care, so Vlad had not let them know just how cold he was finding it. Now, the prospect of warm water, a soft bed, clean linen, and possibly some clean clothes...

The innkeeper took one look at them, and picked up a big clumsy cudgel studded with bits of iron. "Get out of here!" he hissed, swinging the cudgel menacingly.

"We have silver to pay for food and lodging," said Angelo.

The innkeeper's expression did not soften. "Stolen, I'll warrant." He eyed them narrowly, still swinging his club. "Get out of my sight, you gypsy filth. If you come back, I'll break all of your skulls, you thieving vermin."

Vlad wished that he had that basic accouterment of a gentleman, a sword. He had been taught to fence. Indeed, he'd maintained a rigorous regimen of arms training for years, as much for the value of the exercise as the skills themselves. Of course, as a prisoner—say better, a hostage—he had been required to return the weapons to the armsmaster after each lesson and go unarmed again. Vlad knew full well that if he had a sword he could have killed this idiot in two seconds. A mace, in three.

"My good man," he said to the innkeeper, very coldly. "You forget that you are speaking to your prince. I have traveled long and far and we have offered you money. I have scant patience with those who abuse my subjects."

For a moment, it looked as if his hauteur had succeeded. The innkeeper's jaw and the cudgel both fell.

Unfortunately, the innkeeper did not lose his grip on the cudgel, and recovered his jaw. He bobbed a sardonic bow. "Your Royal Highness! I didn't realize it was you."

The innkeeper turned slightly to address the two inmates of the tap-room—an old man, white bearded and rheumy-eyed, and a solid looking prosperous farmer, "Next he'll be telling me how lucky I am to have King Emeric, my sovereign and overlord, favor my humble establishment. Get out, you gypsy scum. You and all your filthy friends. Get out of my sight before I spatter your brains."

Something snapped inside Vlad. Vlad had been a hostage, but a nobleman, and treated as such. Even the gypsies treated him with respect. He could not remember quite how it happened afterward, but heartbeats later he had the innkeeper by the throat and held up at arms' length. He had no idea where the strength came from. The man was both large and fat—but just then holding him seemed entirely effortless. In fact, he was only using his right hand to do so, having using his left to strip the innkeeper of his cudgel.

"You will treat me and my companions with courtesy and respect, you cur." He flung the innkeeper away from himself, to land sprawled and dazed against the far wall. Vlad stood there, his arms folded, and waited.

The man sat up slowly, fearfully. He felt his throat. His eyes were wide and round. The other inhabitants of the tap room had gotten to their feet, shocked by the sudden violence. "Why didn't you help me?" croaked the innkeeper.

The large farmer looked at Vlad warily—but the little old man limped forward and knelt.

"The Dragon has returned," he said reverently. "My

prince. I served with the pikemen at Khusk, when we broke the Hungarian charge. I was wounded there. You gave me twenty forint and ten acres of land. God has answered our prayers." There were tears on the old lined face. "Forgive me, Sire. My eyes are old, and I did not quite believe them. God has been good to me. I have lived to see your return."

He turned slightly to see the burly young man standing gaping. "Janoz!" he said sternly. "Boy, come and give your homage to our sovereign lord!"

Vlad had been told by several people that he had grown into the spitting image of his grandfather. That had been a man no one was indifferent toward, but either hated or loved. Mostly hated by the boyars and loved by the commoners, from what Vlad could tell. Of course, there were exceptions either way. Countess Elizabeth, for example.

Hated or loved, the Dragon had always been feared. His justice, even to those who thought it just, was invariably savage.

Plainly, this old man thought Vlad and his grandfather were one and the same. He'd just referred to one of the prince of Valahia's greatest victories, when he had given the Hungarians a very bloody nose at Khusk. That victory had won a decade of peace for the lands this side of the Carpathians. It had also won the ruler of Valahia a reputation among Hungarians as a merciless and cruel madman—even by the standards of a nation ruled by Emeric.

Valahia's Transcarpathian lands were too small and poor to stand indefinitely against the might of Hungary, though. The Dragon had held them off, but his successor has been made of weaker stuff. Vlad's father had been—by his own admission and by the bitter complaints that Vlad could still remember—little more than a figurehead, a proxy for rule from Buda.

Vlad reached out a hand to the old man and raised him up, as the large Janoz came forward uncertainly. The old man kissed his hand, smiling tremulously up at Vlad, though his tears still flowed. "If only my Rosa was alive to see this," he said.

Vlad was left without anything easy to say. He had never, that he could recall, had to deal with adulation before. And he certainly would not have expected it because an old man took him for his ferocious grandfather. Perhaps that was simply the reverence of an old trooper. His grandfather had treated his common soldiery well, by all accounts Vlad had heard. Apparently, the loyalty endured.

Vlad knew very little about ruling, but this struck him as something worth remembering.

"Lord..." said the young man, coming forward. His tone was respectful, if not reverential. He might not accept his father's conclusions, but he did accept that Vlad was no gypsy vagabond, despite appearances. "He is old. He wanders in his mind sometimes."

"His mind is a lot sharper than this stupid innkeeper's!" said Angelo, laughing.

"He has mistaken me for my grandfather," said Vlad. "I am sorry."

It took a few seconds for the implication of this statement to sink into the younger man's head. Then he too knelt, his eyes wide. "My Lord Prince...they seek you. They must not find you here."

"Who is looking for him?" asked Grigori.

"Soldiers," said the local farmer. "Some Magyar.

Along with a troop of Croats. They were here the day before yesterday. Asking if we had seen you."

"They are closer behind than we realized," said Radu grimly.

Angelo nodded. "I am surprised they dared to ask here. Rumor will spread."

"They do our work for us," said Grigori. "Telling people the prince is free. They will rouse the country."

"We must get him away from here," said Janoz. "Keep him hidden and safe from the Hungarians. Prince Vlad, my father served your grandfather. I would be your man. We need you, my prince. Drive these foreigners out, and make our land safe again."

"You need to raise an army, Drac," said Angelo with a twisted smile. "I think you just found your first recruit."

The young man nodded earnestly up at him. "And I have four brothers, Sire. I am the youngest. And there are the Teleki brothers. And the Bolyai. And I would think among the boyar Klasparuj's peasantry..."

Vlad raised him up. "I accept your service. But right now I am tired, thirsty and I want to know if today is Sunday."

Janoz looked puzzled. "No, Sire. That was yesterday." He turned to the innkeeper. "Get up! Bring food and good ale. And the prince wants warm water."

"Have you run mad?" croaked the innkeeper, still massaging his throat. "He is no prince. Prince Vlad is locked up in Buda. This is a gypsy."

"I was able to make my escape," Vlad said tersely, restraining himself. There was a kind of madness pressing at him that wanted to take this fool and crush his throat. Vlad was quite sure right now that if he gave in, he would do it quite easily. Crush the throat and probably the spine in the process.

He'd always been strong—so, at least, he'd been told by his armsmasters. But now, he felt as if he possessed the strength of an ogre.

He took a deep breath. "I have been hunted hard and far. But now I am ready to begin to turn the game against them. And I want warm water, a razor, soap and a towel. We may not be able to stay here in safety, but I will wash and shave. And we will have something to eat. And all of this will happen very quickly or I shall wring the life out of you. I have suffered you in patience long enough."

Whether the innkeeper believed him, or whether he saw the way Vlad's long fingers twitched and remembered their iron feel on his throat, it had the desired effect. "Yes, lord." The man scrambled to his feet and left for his kitchen at a staggering run, belly and dewlaps quivering.

Angelo pointed to Janoz. "Follow him. Make sure that he does not season the food with henbane. I've no love for all this washing, but food and beer are going to be very welcome."

Vlad nodded. "And you, old sir, are going to sit down and tell me how things are going in the principality. I have been locked up in a tower in Buda. I need to know what is happening here. I need to know what my people need."

Vlad was vaguely surprised at himself. But he found that he really did wish to know these things. "I will not forget that you were the first to welcome me home, and that your son was the first to offer himself to my service."

Vlad found that he could scarcely have picked on a more eager informant. In a cracked old voice, the veteran told him of increasing taxes and—worse still, from his viewpoint—of Emeric's campaign of creeping Hungarianization of Valahia. He was encouraging settlers into the country with generous offers of land or permissions, to displace the local people, especially the tradesmen. The foreigners were naturally more loyal to Emeric than to the Prince of Valahia. They were given privileges and licenses—for instance, smithy permissions, which were refused to metalsmiths that had been working here for centuries.

There was an outraged shout from the kitchen. Vlad and the gypsies went through to find Janoz struggling with the innkeeper, and the back door open. "He waited till my back was turned and then tried to sneak off," panted Janoz. "He tried to tell me earlier that we must call the magistrate."

Vlad found that the strange fury was rising in him again, like some inner dark tide. Perhaps it showed in his eyes because the innkeeper made a desperate attempt to break free—and succeeded. Unfortunately for him, not into the stable-yard outside, but toward the pantry.

The innkeeper snatched up a long knife from the butcher's block, and that was where Vlad's memory of the incident stopped. When Vlad next came to himself he was holding the man, now limp and upside down, with his face pressed hard into a bucket of slops.

He blinked. How had he come to be doing this? He hauled the innkeeper out of the bucket and stood him upright. The fat innkeeper toppled over, very slowly. Looking down, Vlad noticed that his own hands were bloody. So was Janoz, who was sitting on the floor, his face white, blood leeching onto his shirt.

Vlad stood irresolute for a moment, not knowing quite how he had come to be where he was, and not knowing quite what to do next. Fortunately, it would appear that the gypsies did have some idea. Grigori knelt next to the injured Janoz and tore the shirt aside, exposing the wound in his chest. It gaped and bled, blood coming in bubbling thick spurts. His father hobbled up, horror and despair on his face.

"He took the blade intended for the prince," said Angelo.

Vlad too knelt next to the wounded man. "Get us a physician. Run, man." He looked at the face of the young man. "And a priest!" he yelled after him.

They carried him through to the taproom and laid him on a settle. His father held one hand, and Vlad the other.

The village had no physician. The midwife was doing her best, as the priest gave the man the last rites. Someone had gone to call Janoz's kin.

"He is trying to say something." The priest leaned in. So did Vlad. The dying man turned his head to the latter. "My Prince," he said weakly. "Mira..."

And that was all he would ever say in this world.

"Who did he call for?" asked Vlad a little later, as they drew the linen over his face.

"You, Sire. And his wife."

Vlad was silent. Then he said, heavily: "He had a wife?"

"A wife and a young son, Sire," said the old man.

"I must see them. I swear this," said Vlad, his voice

cracking. "If I come to rule, that son will have lands so wide that he will not see the borders from his home. Your son was my first man. I will never forget that."

"You killed the scum with your own hands, Sire. Drowned him in his own kitchen's filth. Justice is served, at least."

"I should have killed him earlier," said Vlad bitterly. "If I had, a fine man would not have died."

The old man nodded. "I just wish I could have died in his place. I am old. But he died well and with honor, my Prince," he said shakily.

Vlad put a gentle hand on the old stooped shoulder. "He died with great honor, and acted with courage where many a knight would have failed. I will see him remembered for it, and honored. I swear to this. And now will you have someone take me to his widow. I must speak with her."

"He is becoming more of a prince by the moment," said Radu in a slightly grumpy tone. "He has not yet understood that we are not his subjects."

Angelo shrugged. "It is the place, and the blood, and of course the old magic. It runs stronger in some than others. It runs dangerously strong in this one. And the light and darkness are closely balanced in him. When he is killing, the dark could dominate."

He took a deep breath. "We need to renew the compact. The old one did not die in vain."

"She did work some of her magic on him," said Grigori. "I can smell it about him."

Angelo shrugged again. "He has to be strong enough to throw that off, or he will be too weak for the blood pact. We can but bide our time."

Grigori nodded. "Still. He accepts responsibility well. And he is stronger than his father."

"We just need to hope that he is more stable than his grandfather. Breeding these bloodlines is not easy," said Radu.

"True," said Angelo. "But what other choices do we have? We need them. We need the compact. There are more human settlers every year. And we need space to run."

"I need space to run now. I need to hunt, properly," said Grigori, who was if anything, far more wolf than human.

In the little church Vlad kept vigil by the corpse. He prayed for his man's soul. He prayed for his own soul, too. Something dark was rising in him. Something he was not sure he could control.

And part of him wanted to let it free.

Chapter 22

Duke Enrico Dell'este stood and pored over the layer of maps that almost entirely covered the vast expanse of table that he had commandeered. So far the only final strategic decision that he had been able to reach was that he needed a bigger table.

"As I said to Lodovico, it's all very well," he grumbled to Petro Dorma when the Doge came down to inquire how his planning was going, "to talk of strategies and of how we will deal with various obstacles. But you cannot plan in a void of information. We have so little knowledge of what is actually happening in Byzantium, let alone the Black Sea. We don't know for sure quite what Genoa will bring to the conflict. We don't know if the other states appealed to will contribute any forces at all."

"I have here a digest of some of the latest reports to come in from our various agents," said Petro. "Some ships just got in, bearing word."

"I would appreciate it still more if they would bring that jackanapes of a grandson of mine back here. What have they to say?"

"The most interesting one comes from Puglia, of all places. It would seem that Emperor Alexis is trying very hard to recruit some mercenary commanders. Fortunately for us, his reputation precedes him. His promises are worthless. And he has very little hard cash to offer."

"I can think of a few that it might be worth our while to pay to have go to his 'rescue,'" said the Old Fox. "Most of the condottieri are not worth half the money they are paid. And what else, Doge Dorma? You have asked me to help with your strategy. I cannot do this without information. In northern Italy I have a fine network of spies and agents. I know who is buying supplies to outfit campaigns. I know who is moving where. But I really cannot afford to do the same for Byzantium and places farther afield. My pouch is not as deep as that of Venice."

"And I wish that the Council of Ten would agree to let me spend quite as lavishly there, as you do here," said Petro. "But for what it is worth, now that we know what we are looking for, we have confirmation from Odessa. Some of Jagiellon's troops are building up in a camp outside the city. And although the agent I have there has not been able to leave the city, he has some rumors of a fleet. Several shipwrights have disappeared from the city, taken in the early morning by soldiers of the voivode. On the other hand we have no news from the Golden Horde, except via the same agent. They were due to hold their kurultai—that's essentially a vast electoral meeting to choose a new khan—in a week's time. The kurultai typically go on for a while, but even so, they must have a new khan soon. Other than that, Alexis prepares himself for conflict, but is trying to do so in secret. We have a great deal of detail about that, and about the defenses prepared for Constantinople."

"I truly hate trying to plan a campaign with such extended lines of supply and communication. By and large the fleets are going to have to operate completely independently. The Black Sea fleet is still sitting in Trebizond. We could have used their strength. I am not even sure just when they will be able to sail. I cannot get a straight answer from Admiral Dourso."

Petro laughed. "Benito will get answers out of him, or if not from him then from the masters at the Arsenal, as I found last time. Benito was good at it."

"I am glad to hear that I am good at something, anyway," said Benito Valdosta, from the doorway.

"Benito!" bellowed Enrico Dell'este. "You hell-born boy! What has taken you so long, eh?"

The gruff comment was completely at variance with his beam of pleasure. He had spent most of his life carefully distancing himself from his two grandsons, for their own safety. It was likely that Marco Valdosta would succeed him. The boy would do well, would be much beloved by the populace—the root of Dell'este power. But there was no doubt that the younger brother—as much a devil as the older one was a saint—filled a larger place in Enrico's heart. True, given half an opportunity, Enrico would kill the man who had fathered the boy, for what he had done to his errant daughter. But that was not Benito's fault. Enrico had moved far past any feelings of that kind. The boy had proved himself every inch a Dell'este!

He wore the colors of the house of Dell'este on the tassels of his sword-scabbard, Enrico noted with pride. He hugged him, fiercely. "I ask again, what has kept you so long? Petro, let us have some good wine!"

"Lodovico kept me. And some good wine. Quite a lot of good wine. If I have any more I will be awash, and I will want to see the town, instead of concentrating on these maps. Lodovico sent me here, eventually. I have yet to find my brother. Lodovico has gone in search of his daughter and son-in-law for me."

"As far as I know," said Petro, "he is treating patients at the St. Raphaella chapel."

"I should have guessed," said Benito. He pointed at the table. "I have been collecting maps myself. But you have a few more than I do."

"Still not enough, and not enough information either," said Dell'este grumpily.

"Well, I have some more. And I have taken some steps." Benito bowed to the Doge. "Which I hope you'll approve of. Time being of the essence, I did these on my own cognizance."

"Why am I suddenly afraid?" asked Petro Dorma with a small smile. "What have you done?"

"You know the letter that I sent you about Iskander Beg? About reaching an agreement to reopen the Via Egnatia to trade."

Enrico raised his eyebrows. "You did not tell me about that, Petro."

"It is a commercial possibility," said the Doge. "The problem lies with the Bulgars, if we wish to use that route to access the Black Sea. Otherwise, it is probably cheaper and easier to move cargoes by sea rather than overland to Constantinople."

"You should occasionally see things in other terms besides commerce," said Enrico dryly. "If it is possible to cross the Lord of the Mountains' lands with a decently large land army..."

"It will not work," interrupted Benito. "Iskander Beg is not going to allow foreign soldiers to use his land as an access route. For starters, it would probably break his hold on the mountain tribes. For a second, he has to live with two nations that are hostile to us on his borders. We do not intend to try to hold Constantinople. At least, I hope not. Iskander Beg would be left with a furious neighbor. He can hold the Byzantines, or Hungary. But if they both attacked him, which they would if they saw him in close military alliance with us, the Illyrians would at best be severely punished."

"True enough," admitted the Old Fox. "But we could at least use the Illyrians to gather some decent intelligence."

"Well," said Benito, "I hope that I have done that and a little more. There are commercial possibilities too. I gather you had a message delivered from Jerusalem by magical means."

"Yes," said Petro. "The more conventional paper confirmation arrived by fast galleass a few days ago. It filled in some of the detail that was missing from the magical communication. Our friend, Prince Manfred of Brittany, has been a busy man."

"Not as busy as he's going to be," said Benito. "I have sent him and the remaining Knights of the Holy Trinity across the Balkans, to escort a party of Mongols and the Ilkhan envoy to the Golden Horde. Apparently, he is in rather a unique position to negotiate with them, and the Ilkhan Mongols can hopefully shift the election of a new khan for the Golden Horde in our favor."

Petro pulled a wry face. "It's too late for that, I'm afraid. They've had their electoral meeting."

"I knew it was too good an idea to work," said Benito irritably. "Well, at least Manfred is in a good position to negotiate with whoever they have elected khan. He may still save us some fighting. And at least he is safe as a diplomatic envoy among them."

"Like the fleet sitting at Trebizond, I wish we could get hold of him to tell him what was happening," said Petro.

"Ah. The fleet has already left Trebizond," said Benito. "Apparently the Mongols tried to negotiate a passage with the Venetian vessels. But they had already sailed. I heard that from Eberhard."

"That's very early. Something must have been worrying them. They can hardly have full holds yet," said Petro.

"Those two factors considerably alter our strategies," said Enrico. "I presume you've arranged for information to flow back with your devious Illyrian friend. Can he be trusted, by the way? Never mind, that's a stupid question. You would hardly have sent Manfred of Brittany off with the Illyrians otherwise."

"Yes to both questions. Iskander Beg is both a devious and dangerous man. He's also an extremely honorable one, in my judgment. The greatest danger that we could suffer is that someone could kill him. He makes a wonderful thorn in the side of Emeric of Hungary." Benito smiled. "He admits, by the way, that he left Emeric alive after the Corfu campaign, because he would sooner have an enemy he knows is an incompetent idiot, than have to deal with the successor who might be more able."

The Old Fox raised his eyebrows. "A sensible man, if not one of nature's optimists."

Benito shrugged. "There is little enough about his land to encourage optimism. It's hard and poor, most of it. And the tribesmen thrive on raids and feuds that go on for generations. But he is a thinker, and a clever and learned man, despite where he lives, and his rustic people. He has studied your campaigns, by the way, Grandfather. I think if he had more resources, and possibly more people, Byzantium and Hungary would have to watch that they were not consumed by him. I would rather have him as a friend than an enemy. Venice might be wise to let him profit a little from the overland trade, even if it costs us some short-term profit. But, if Manfred can reach some accommodation with the Golden Horde, that would open up a route to the lower Danube." He smiled at Petro's expression. "Yes, I thought that would appeal."

"Petro, you look like a fox dreaming of unguarded hen roosts," said the man who was called the Old Fox himself.

"He's probably," said Benito speculatively, "dreaming of the possibility that Alexis will successfully bottle up the sea route to the Black Sea ports. That would exclude the Genoese, and any other traders, and give Venice a large advantage, if not a virtual monopoly. Even for a year or two, that could make an almost obscene amount of money."

Petro eyed him suspiciously. "If you should ever consider entering the services of another state, Benito, I will have a hard time persuading the Council of Ten that you are not a practitioner of black magic and an enemy of the Venetian Republic, and a suitable target for our assassins. And that," he said to Enrico, "is by way of a joke, my friend. So you can take that expression off your face. Venice loves him far too much. He's just too astute for his own good."

"I took business-cunning lessons from the best," said Benito, grinning at the former head of the trading house of Dorma. "So how is my old enemy Admiral Dourso slowing things down this time? I must get across to the Arsenal later. I have some friends to chase along."

"I'll walk with you," said Enrico Dell'este. "We can take a canal-boat. It will be better if you surprise them, the way you surprised me."

A little later they were out of the Doge's palace, and away from the easy listening of spies. Benito turned to his grandfather. "Your man Antimo Bartelozzi, grandfather. Would there be any possibility of sending him to Constantinople? On a certain commission for me... well, for Venice. I'll have to talk to Petro about money."

His grandfather looked at him strangely. And shook his head. "You can't send a man to a place where he already is, Benito."

"I should have guessed."

The Old Fox clapped his favorite grandson on the shoulder. "And I should have guessed you'd ask. Petro knows, but not whom."

The sun was setting. Benito paused for a moment, to gaze upon the sight. Some trace of melancholy must have come to his face, for Enrico asked: "Thinking of your friends?"

Benito hadn't been, actually. He'd been thinking that mid-summer would soon enough pass, and that

before too many more months went by Maria would
vanish into the underworld. There, she'd spend the
winter as the wife of Aidoneus.

As always, the thought was...hard to handle. But
Benito didn't want to get into *that* discussion with his
grandfather. So, he nodded his head.

"Yes. I have no idea when I'll see Prince Manfred
and Erik again."

If I ever do, came the additional thought. But he
left that unspoken. There was enough of melancholy,
for the moment.

The Old Fox clapped him on the shoulder again.
"Some wine, I say!"

Benito smiled. "Splendid idea."

PART II
August, 1540 A.D.

Chapter 23

The trail was wreathed in mist that was cold and damp; it clung and eddied about the riders, swirling around them. For Dana of Valahia it was just the final chapter of this entire terrifying misadventure. Why had Mother decided that they had to leave at midnight? She was exhausted, and so was her horse. If they'd left quietly just after complin or even a little before lauds they'd have got just as far from Poienari Castle by now. As it was, it was a miracle they hadn't been caught.

Actually, they had been caught, while leaving through the wicket gate. Fortunately, by one of their own guards, not those horrible disrespectful Hungarian boors that King Emeric had sent just after Papa died. The guard commander had kept his silence. If only he'd come with them instead!

Dana could only curse her brother Vlad and his escape. Before that, Mother had talked resignedly of an arranged marriage, which Dana didn't look forward to. But wasn't that better than running away and living like vagabonds, hoping the Danesti cousins would hide them? Mother thought it better than letting them take her daughter as a hostage, too. Dana wasn't so sure anymore.

They'd gotten lost, in the dark down in the valley, out of the moonlight. Dana would have sworn there was only one trail and the one fork. But the solitary scared manservant was no better at finding the trail than she was. They should have taken the fork. It would have taken them up the steep switchbacks to St. Tifita's chapel, and then back down onto this trail twenty miles farther on.

Instead, just when they could not afford the time, they had taken the long trail. She had told her mother that they had passed it. Told her at least three times. Bertha had not been listening. She was too sunk in panic, too afraid. And now, the dawn was just starting to come on. Any moment, the sun might break through the mist.

They had not yet come to the point below St. Tifita's where the shortcut would have come out. They came around the corner, and found the trail blocked. Now, just when they could least afford to lose even more time! The trail was full of multicolored carts, donkeys, ponies, geese, even a few goats. And lots of raggle-taggle gypsies, their bright eyed dirty children herding livestock, the adults tending the carts.

"Get them out of our way," said her mother, her voice slightly shrill. "Quickly."

The manservant pressed forward, yelling at the gypsies and flapping ineffectually at their livestock, their jeering children, and the stolid horses drawing the carts. Nervously, Mama began pushing her way after him. Dana followed, trying to keep her horse as close to her mother's as possible. They hadn't gotten very far into the crowd when a tall old man with wavy white hair and a crooked beak of a nose leapt down from the seat of his cart and grabbed the two bridles.

"Unhand our horses, gypsy!" Mother was making a determined effort to sound autocratic and in complete control. It was rather spoiled by the squeak at the end of the last word.

"Just trying to help, lady," he said in a deep gravelly voice, his eyes under those heavy brows bright and sharp. He didn't look like he had ever helped anyone in his life. Or been polite to them either. But he did doff his hat.

"Let go of our horses. We are in a hurry, varlet," said the dowager duchess.

He shook his head. "The boys saw the Hungarians climbing the trail to St. Tifita's, lady. They're ahead of you. And coming up behind you on fresh horses. But we can hide you."

"Are you mad?" Her voice squeaked again. Then she slumped in the saddle. "Oh God. There must be another trail . . ."

"For goats, maybe." The gypsy raised an eyebrow at their mounts. "Not for spoiled horse-flesh."

"But you're gypsies . . ."

"We don't mind lowering ourselves a little," said the gypsy. "For the House of Valahia, that is. We have an arrangement with your family, you might say. It's why we are here, lady. Word came from the north that the Drac has returned to his own. We come to honor a bargain."

Dana had worn old clothes at her mother's instance. Mother too was dressed in an old riding habit that she would not normally be seen dead in. They both wore hooded cloaks. How did this man know who they were?

"Bargain...?" said Bertha.

"With the old Drac." The silver-haired gypsy grinned. "He gave us the right to camp on the field below the cliffs of Poienari Castle." That seemed to be a joke.

"Mother..." said Dana.

"Be quiet. I must think. Dear God." Bertha turned to the gypsy again. "Drac. In the north. Do you mean... my son?" There was hope and fear in her voice.

"Yes. He comes to fulfill the old bargain, maybe. The Hungarians kept your man from it."

There was a shrill whistle from the ridge. "That's Radu. The Hungarian troopers are arriving. He can hear them from the ridge."

"Mother, my horse is going lame. Let them hide us," said Dana.

The gypsy nodded. "Good girl." As if she wasn't the daughter of the dowager princess of Valahia and the sister of the prince, but one of the ragamuffin children crowding around them!

He reached up a hand. "Here. Let me help you down, and then you get into my cart with my Silvia. No time to change your appearance now. Hide under the sheepskins."

The gypsy helped her down from the saddle, and someone else helped her mother down. They were hustled to the bright-painted cart hung with a clatter of pots and kettles, and pushed inside by a little woman who looked every inch a fairy-tale witch.

"You keep still," she hissed. "Climb under the skins in case they look inside."

Looking back, Dana saw that the saddles and tack had already been stripped off their horses, and some brat was smearing her beautiful gray with mud. The old woman pushed her forward. "But our saddlebags..." protested mother. Gypsies were thieves. Everyone knew that. And they had as much silver as they'd been able to gather and mother's jewelry case in those saddlebags.

The old woman cackled. "Stay alive first. Then you worry about your saddlebags and your pretties."

There was a pile of old sheepskins and blankets in the cart. They ducked under the hanging bric-a-brack of a traveling pot-mender, and bunches of drying herbs and tools, to reach them. The old woman lifted the skins up, and the two of them slipped underneath.

The skins were probably full of lice, thought Dana. But at least she and her mother were lying down. Dana felt her mother cling to her. What had happened to the footman, she wondered? Somehow she doubted if the gypsies' hospitality extended to him.

Then they heard the sound of hooves. Hard-ridden horses. "Stand aside, you scum!" yelled someone in Hungarian. Did he think that the gypsies would understand? By the yells and the braying and the gabbling of the geese, the soldiers were making them understand.

"You!" shouted a voice authoritatively.

"Yes, lord?" It was the gravelly voice of the man who had hidden them. It would appear that he at least spoke Hungarian.

"Have you seen anyone come past this morning?"

"No, lord. Not since last night."

"When?" demanded the Hungarian.

"It was dark. We heard them come past, riding hard."

"Hell's teeth! What other trails are there around here?"

"I do not know, lord. Many, maybe. We only come here once a year. To the field below the castle."

"Is that where you're headed now?"

"Yes, lord. We stay for three days and then we go on."

"Not a day too soon, I'll bet. We're looking for two women. A woman with gray hair, a little stout, and a girl you can't make a mistake about. White face, and dead straight black hair. She'd be about on the edge of womanhood. If you see them, send word up to the castle."

"They beat us if we go there, lord," the gypsy said dubiously.

"Tell them you have a message for Lieutenant Hasrafa. Now get yourself out of our road!"

They waited in the dark for a few minutes. "You can come out now," said the crone. "They're gone."

"We must get onto our horses and go," said Bertha. "They'll catch Hermann. He will tell them..."

The old woman snorted with laughter. "He's lost his horse. The boys have led him up into the gorge. The horse won't tell them much. And by the time he gets back to the castle we'll see he doesn't either." She peered at Dana. "You look all in, little one. When last did you eat? You can tell old Tante Silvia. I have four granddaughters your age."

"Where are we going?" asked her mother fearfully.

"Poienari Castle. We have the right to camp in the field at the base of the cliff."

"But we just fled from there..."

The old woman smiled wickedly. "If you are going to steal a chicken, the best place to hide it is inside the owner's hencoop while he looks everywhere else."

Chapter 24

"This," said Falkenberg, "is not the kind of country you want to have to cross with siege cannon."

Erik looked at the mountainside and the trail that had wound its way up. It was beautiful country, in a stark kind of way. "It's certainly not the kind of place you'd want to try to cross if there were hostiles ready to ambush you."

Falkenberg nodded. "Even with a lot of light cavalry scouting for you. There are too many good spots to drop arrows or rocks onto the trail."

"It's a good thing that we have the locals scouting for us." Manfred pointed to two of the Illyrian escorts on the upper arm of the hairpin bend. "Although it does raise the question of why they should feel the need to."

Erik shrugged. "It's a bit like the feuding tribes and clans in the mountains in Vinland. Most of them have some kind of grudge with their neighbors, usually so long ago that they've forgotten quite what it was about. They'll come together to fight a common enemy, or to raid a profitable target, but the rest of the time they fight each other. Just to keep in practice."

"I'd rather that they fought with each other than with us. They've got no armor to speak of, but this is good country for archery and ambushes." Falkenberg surveyed the slope with a professional eye. "Still, I will grant that whoever this Iskander Beg friend of Benito's is, he can organize. We are making better time than I'd expected."

David rode close behind the three knights, listening. He was scared half out of his wits. He had thought that he was adapting to the strangeness. But that had been in the closed confines of the ship, where he'd still been his normal confident self. He'd recaptured that confidence quickly enough once he got over the initial shocks, and had done some learning: basic things like how to muck out well, and how not to try anything clever on Kari.

That hadn't stopped him taking enormous delight in setting up the tall blond *Ritter* with the Mongol lessons. On thinking about it, though, that had probably been quite stupid. Kari, who in David's opinion would pick a fight for fun with a dragon, treated Erik with serious deference. But David had really thought that in among the rubes in the tiny town on that god-forsaken island, that he would be cock-of the-whoop. Then that old woman had caught him. He'd been pathetically grateful at being rescued by what passed as the local police! If word of that ever got back to Jerusalem he'd probably have to stay away for ever.

And then there was the very young man that they called—so respectfully—Milor' Valdosta. He'd been laughing at Jerusalem's finest, David was sure. Well, he was sure of it now. At the time he'd been terrified.

He'd been, David had to admit, nauseatingly grateful to see Kari and Erik. Even if they were going to beat him. Which they hadn't, oddly enough.

And then, just when he thought he could reassert his self-confidence with yet another neatly placed language trap, Erik had set him up. Thank God that he had made him use the phrase on Lord Tulkun. The Mongol was too plump and too good-humored to take it the wrong way. Besides he understood far more Frankish than he ever let on. But Erik now seemed onto his tricks.

And Erik and Tulkun were clumsily talking. David had resolved to be a lot more careful in the future. He was going to listen and learn a little before he tried anything.

He was so busy listening and learning that he nearly got himself killed when things next went wrong.

"Scatter!" yelled Erik.

David blinked. What was "scatter"? Some kind of wild animal? Then, as the column of knights divided and spread, putting their heels into their huge mounts with the calm skill of professional soldiers, who know when to obey orders, he realized that what Erik meant. *Scatter because someone is shooting at us, and there are a lot of arrows in the air . . .*

The knights were armored. He wasn't.

Both the Mongol party and their Illyrian escort had drawn bows. The difference was that the Mongols were already riding hell for leather and the Illyrians were trying to still their horses. Several bangs and puffs of smoke testified to wheel-lock pistols being used.

David's horse did not like the noise. It was not a warhorse and had not been training for battle. Ironically, that probably saved his life. The horse reared, and David fell off.

A black-fletched arrow cut into his shoulder as he sat up, just as Kari galloped past and snatched him off the ground. "You damn fool! Didn't you hear Erik? Pamolai's claws! How badly are you hit?"

Almost fainting with pain, David tugged at the arrow. "Leave it. It'll have to be pushed through," Kari said, pulling his horse up behind a huge boulder. Somehow he managed to dismount, still holding David in one arm. "Erik said that he wanted you to be a lesson to me," said Kari grimly. "The first bit of decent action we've seen, and I'm babysitting. Now let's see that arrow."

He tore aside the cloth of David's cotte and shirt. "You're a lucky brat. It'll have to wait a few minutes but you'll be fine. Those Mongols are the finest horse archers I've ever seen. Better even than the skraelings on Vinland's plains. I think there are some very surprised and very dead Illyrians."

The knights had divided neatly, according to their training. Manfred's bodyguard kept in tight formation around him. The rest of the heavy horses thundered up the pass. Their attackers had hidden in some rocks where they had thought that they could escape up the next hairpin zigzag. What they hadn't anticipated was just how fast the knights' horses could gallop once they got moving. They also hadn't anticipated just how agile the ponies of the Mongols could be. The Mongols had not stuck to the trail—and they were capable of shooting very accurately from the back of a cantering horse.

The panicked ambushers tried to flee. But the

knights were less than a hundred yards off by then. That was not enough time to get their own mounts up to full speed. The rushing wall of lance points caught up with them and swept them off their horses.

There was little for the Illyrian escort to do, except dismount and cut throats, which they seemed to do with great relish. In the meanwhile, the Mongols were scouring the mountainside. The entire ambush had resulted in one dead packhorse and one injured horseboy—and fifteen dead bandits.

"We were supposed to panic, and flee, and then they'd loot the pack-train," said the Illyrian captain, kicking one of the bodies. "It's a favorite trick around here. What gave you warning, Lord?" He asked Erik curiously.

"I heard the arrows coming," said Erik. "One of them had a loose fletching. It makes a characteristic noise."

The Illyrian looked at him with wary respect.

Erik too had learned something in the ambush. He had heard just how well the Mongol could shoot from a moving horse, and now he had seen proof of it. That, and the agility of the men and their ponies had probably made a good few of the Knights of the Holy Trinity reassess them. Admittedly, this was a hand-picked and elite group, both of Mongols and of Knights.

He turned to Kari. "You'd better start teaching that hell-born brat some basic military discipline and skills. I'll not have his death on my hands and conscience, just because he sits around going 'huh?' when he's told to move. I'm surprised he didn't try to argue about it."

"The very thought that had gone through my mind," said Kari, swatting David relatively gently on the uninjured shoulder. "Mind you, we could just use him for target practice. That way he would at least die for a purpose."

Erik favored both of them with twisted half smile. "On second thoughts, let Von Gherens and Falkenberg train him. They have not enough work to do. They normally instruct novices."

Iskander Beg, masquerading as the captain of the party's Illyrian escort, watched and listened. He had been somewhat embarrassed by the ambush that his men had missed. Fortunately, it had failed spectacularly, and he'd learned a little more about the two parties he was escorting. Enough to realize that there was a large difference in quality between these Knights of the Holy Trinity and King Emeric's heavy Magyar cavalry. The spiky armor might look archaic, but there was nothing archaic about their drill. He had noticed that, even though they were on the march, they still practiced every morning. The fact that they, and not a pack of servants, tended the horses was interesting. Benito had said they were a monastic order, but still...

He was glad that they were mostly engaged in combat in the far north.

The Mongols were less of a surprise. In the uncertain border region near the Danube, where you could as easily encounter Bulgars, Hungarian patrols, and the occasional Golden Horde Mongol, the Illyrians had had first-hand experience of Mongol horsemanship and archery. It would appear that, despite differences in dress and appearance, these Ilkhan were much the same as their cousins in the Golden Horde. Iskander did not think that he would like them for southern neighbors. Better that the Byzantine Empire remained as a buffer between him and them. He had a feeling that they would be intolerant about raids and far better at dealing with steep hill country than the Byzantines.

Still, best to be shot of the lot of them. This had been, in terms of gold, a profitable exercise. Benito had been quite right about that. But there was also something to be said for keeping them out of the heartland of his people. Although that that could just be prejudice. And a little embarrassment.

Chapter 25

Vlad had arrived in the village as a vagabond. Now, it would seem that he was their prince. But he was deeply troubled over what he had done. He was even more troubled that he could not remember doing it. And the death of the freeman—the first man to ever volunteer to serve him—cut him to the quick. Yes, the fellow was barely a step up from the peasantry, not that different from the servants who had been assigned to him in Buda—but being there at his death, Vlad had realized that he was human, too.

The priest had been little help with this inner conflict. He was a simple country cleric, as much afraid of Vlad as was possible without physically turning tail and running. The villagers and the small farmers and handful of peasants seemed to hold their prince in a kind of reverent awe. Not respect. Not even terror, as he had partly expected.

He'd thought at first that it was merely the reaction from an old soldier, who had reason to know gratitude. But it seemed to be a general reaction. The local point of view obviously differed greatly from that of the Hungarians.

The other thing that Vlad had found deeply troubling was the fact that, except in name, he still was a vagabond. And it appeared that in the world outside his tower, money was a real need. Not, it would seem, for himself, or at least not now. He had been given the finest raiment the village people had to offer— spare breeches and a cotte from the priest, who wore a cassock most of the time. They were black, as befitted the priest's profession. He was given a special shirt saved for weddings by a small landowner. With those gifts, Vlad had come to understand poverty a little better. Someone labored over cleaning his old clothes while another had darned his shirt, marveling over the fineness of the cloth.

Food, too, was their gift, as was drink. He'd been unprepared for the fiery plum liquor. He was even more unprepared for the women who seemed to be making certain overtures. He was uncertain how to take them.

But there were other things. They had come to him, that very afternoon. Two of them, young, tousle-haired and scared. "We wish," said the slightly shorter of the two, "to join your army, Drac. We can fight."

Vlad had been startled. Yes, Janoz had volunteered to be his man, but it hadn't strictly occurred to Vlad that that meant soldier, or that the Prince of Valahia's presence in the Carpathians meant certain war.

"I . . ."

"You will need them," said Angelo. "You will need a lot more than just them," said the old soldier. He seemed to be escaping from the grief of losing his son by casting himself into the role of Vlad's advisor. Vlad absorbed it all like a sponge. Perhaps he was coming at rule from a different and wrong perspective. It was not something Emeric had had him tutored in. He would take whatever advice was available, and gratefully.

"You will need a lot more men, and good weapons, Sire. The best you can hope for around here are a few boar spears or an old halberd or two."

"I had not thought about all of this," said Vlad humbly. Yes, the man had just been a peasant levy, but he still knew more of war than his prince did.

"Well, Sire..." The old man rubbed his temples. "In my day, this was good country to recruit from. There were lots of bowmen needed, and most of the boys around here can pull a bow fairly well, although light bows and fowling pieces are what they have mostly used. But these days, seems to me, you need arquebuses. They can be had, there are some fine weapons being made, especially by those damned Poles, but they'll cost you a fair amount of gold. You will need cavalry and some cannon, too. You'll not find any of our people who would make fit cavalry, Sire. The only trained men are in the service of the boyars."

"My sons will come to join you, Sire," said the old man proudly. "Only, I was hoping we could get some of the harvest in. There is Janoz's widow. We'll need to provide for her, too, and it will be hard."

Vlad knew that it was in fact his duty to provide for her, now. Father Tedesco had instilled that in him. Perhaps the old priest had been looking to his own future, but Vlad had already seen, first hand, the value of loyalty. The problem was that at the moment he had not as much as one silver piece to his name. Money rested in two groups in Valahia: the tradesmen and the nobility, not the peasants, villagers or a handful of small freeholders. Somehow he must win the support of at least one of the groups of the powerful and wealthy.

A liveried serving man knocked respectfully at the door of the inn which had, by force of circumstances, become his headquarters. The old soldier scowled at the newcomer. "And now, Benedickt? I thought you had become too good for us village people?"

"I have a message," said the servant loftily, "from my master for Prince Vlad. He would offer the duke hospitality. Where do I find him, you old fool?"

The insolence galvanized him. "You speak to him," said Vlad coldly. "And I suggest if you wish to keep your head on your shoulders, you rapidly learn some respect for your betters."

The lackey did a double take. Quickly he assessed the posture, tone and attitude of the man he was facing—and bowed hastily. "I beg your pardon, Sire. I just came in out of the brightness. I thought it was only the old...ah, gentleman."

Vlad had noticed one thing about himself. Although he had been out in the weather, and even some sunlight, his skin was not browned like the gypsies or the locals. His skin was very pale and his hair and moustache were jet black. If this fellow could see the old soldier in the somewhat dim lighting in the inn, he could certainly see Vlad.

Still, he reminded himself sharply, the boyars could provide him with cavalry. And as the major landowners, they had money. He knew that much.

"Very well," he said. "I will come."

The man bowed again. "The master will have a horse sent for you."

"That would be appreciated," said Vlad, thinking that the boyar Klasparuj was very well informed.

Later that afternoon, two footmen returned with a spirited black stallion, tacked up with a beautiful saddle of the finest leather. It was such a horse that Vlad had always imagined he would ride. The joy of mounting it set aside any doubts that he might have had about the wisdom of visiting the boyar. So, accompanied by a footman on a bay gelding—itself a horse that was a long step up from most of those he had ridden in the last week—he set off for the home of the local overlord.

There was certainly nothing lacking in the welcome he got at the fortified manor house. Klasparuj himself came out to greet him, bowing deeply, and kissing his hand. "It is indeed as the rumor from the peasants had it, my Prince. You honor my humble home."

The boyar's home looked to be a remarkably fine and richly appointed to Vlad. Not up to the standards of the royal palace in Buda, of course, but the man was plainly a very well-to-do nobleman.

"Thank you," said Vlad. "I was not sure what support I enjoyed among my nobles. I am going to need your assistance and your loyalty."

"Of course," said the boyar, bowing again. "Come in! Come in! My cook has a wonderful way with blue trout. I think it good enough even for the capital. I have been there, you know."

He was not quite babbling, but plainly more than

a little nervous. Vlad reminded himself that the boyar, like most such, was a provincial. A wealthy one, obviously, but he had probably never entertained anyone of Vlad's rank before.

"Buda is so magnificent. Beautiful. The reflection of the castle in the river! Not to mention"—this came almost with a giggle—"His Majesty's taste in pole-ornaments." Then he seem to recall himself. "But I am a terrible host. Let me give you some wine! Arpad!"

He gestured to a hovering servant, who was waiting with a tray holding large goblets. Next to him was a man holding an ornately enchased silver beaker. That was the same man—Benedickt, if Vlad recalled correctly—who had come to deliver the message. He poured red wine into the goblets.

The boyar took his wine and immediately raised it in a toast to his visitor. "Your health, my liege. May you reign long and prosperously!"

They drank. It was strong, heavy red wine.

"Ah!" said his host. "Bull's blood, Benedickt, see that the prince's glass is filled!"

"I am not reigning yet," said Vlad, feeling a little uncomfortable in his borrowed peasant's Sunday black wool and simple linen shirt, while his host was wearing embroidered puce velvet. "But I do hope to enlist your aid—"

"Of course. Of course. You have only to ask, my liege. Come, though, and meet my family."

They walked through into a large salle. A sulky looking plump boy in his late teens stood there, dressed in the height of last year's court fashion in Buda. Sitting next to him on a settee was an older woman—clearly his mother, from the resemblance—wearing a

rust-colored high-waisted velvet overgown, with a fine
saffron linen shift puffing out from slits in the sleeves
and showing at the neckline. It was an opulent gar-
ment, although she filled it too generously, especially
the low, almost transparent shift studded with seed
pearls. So it seemed to Vlad, at any rate—but then,
he had been allowed little contact with women by
Emeric. Perhaps he was mistaken.

"Anselm, Clara," said the boyar. "Come and make
your bow to the prince. My Lord, may I present
my wife and son, ardent supporters of your cause.
Benedickt. See that we have wine."

More goblets were produced, more wine drunk, as
they waited to be called to dine. Vlad could only hope
that they would be quick about it. He was very hungry,
and everyone, including the factotum Benedickt, was
keen to see that his glass was full.

His hostess had begged him to come and sit next
to her on the settee. Vlad wished now that he had
remained standing. She seemed to find reason to touch
him every few words, to run her fingers delicately
along his arm, and to urge him to drink more wine.
The woman puzzled him. It had been many years
since he had been a guest in the home of another
person. He really could not remember this sort of
behavior. But he'd been a mere boy, interested in
boyish things, and heartily bored by social events. His
brief encounters with the Hungarian court and the
women thereof had not suggested that this was the
way they behaved. But perhaps things were different
here in the provinces?

He still found it embarrassing. Possibly awkward,
as well. The boyar seemed eager to commit his men

and money to Vlad's cause. He really did not want the man taking offense about his guest's conduct with his wife.

"I wish you would tell us about what they are wearing at the court," asked the young man, surveying his own raiment. Vlad had never given his clothing a second thought. It was set out for him and he was dressed by his valet. Vlad had found the dresses of women more interesting to look at. He was, naturally, aware of the prevailing mode. But his own dress was not something that he had ever been much interested by.

"Don't bother the prince," said his mother, taking the opportunity to pat Vlad's hand again. "The prince needs more wine, Benedickt."

He didn't. Fortunately, a butler came and called them to eat just at that point.

"I'm afraid," said his hostess almost as soon as they'd taken their seats, "that we have very little to set before you tonight. Some good fish. The blue trout is our pride, but other than that, we only have some venison, some broiled boar, sweetbreads, and a brace of roasted duck."

Vlad did not point out that for the last while he'd been lucky to dine on rather ill-cooked rabbit, and a few scrawny chickens that his conscience pricked him about. The gypsies might possibly have bought them, but he rather doubted it. Instead he just said: "That sounds delightful."

"Can we give you another glass of wine?" she asked, leaning over and brushing her breast against his shoulder. Somewhere in the conversation it had come out that the lady Clara was considered a great beauty. Plainly she had not compared herself to the radiant

Lady Elizabeth. His image of beauty, he feared, would be forever colored by Countess Bartholdy's flawless perfection.

It was a very long meal. Vlad had been awake a long time and ridden many leagues, and the turmoil of the happenings at the inn had not permitted him to rest. The combination of food and lots of wine was making him worried that he would quietly slide under the table, snoring. He could remember some of his father's guests doing that. Now he understood why.

On the other hand, if he remembered right, most of those had become quite rowdy before doing that. Wine did not seem to have that kind of effect on him at all, however. He was just very tired.

Apparently, his hosts must be aware of the effects of so much wine. They were watching him closely, possibly in fear that he would start becoming rowdy.

He must make the extra effort. He needed them. "I think that I need some air," he said, his voice reflecting that inner tiredness.

He pushed his chair back. He noticed that his solicitous host had done the same, as had his son, and Benedickt the majordomo had come to draw his chair out for him. Slightly embarrassed by all this attention, he was paying less of a mind to his feet than he should have been. He hooked one on the chair leg and stumbled.

"Seize him, Benedickt!" shouted his host, surging forward. Moments later, a surprised Vlad was bowled over by his host, his host's son, the majordomo, two other footmen, and even his host's wife. She, admittedly, did little more than try to kick him on the shin.

"By God, he has even more of a capacity than his accursed grandfather was supposed to have!" grunted his host.

"His other appetites are less," said the lady of the house disdainfully.

The boyar snorted. "I was never so embarrassed as by your behavior. You conducted yourself like a harlot."

"You told me to do so, Klasparuj," she said angrily.

"Yes, well, I thought he would be less likely to notice us plying him with drink if he was distracted by a little flirtation. I did not mean you had to engage in that kind of coquetry! Now, go and get us some rope. We need to bind him fast. It will be some hours before the Croats can be here."

"Send one of the footmen," she said sulkily, turning her head away. "I have done enough for you. I cannot see what the fuss is about, anyway. I mean, look at him! Dressed like that!"

Black fury began to rise in Vlad. It had all been a deceit! His memories of the boyars had been correct. He was beginning to feel that he should never trust in anything but his first instinct.

"Emil. Go and fetch us some rope," said the boyar. "I have wasted a great deal of good wine capturing him. It's all superstition. We could just have tied him up when he got here. I hope King Emeric is going to be generous."

The footman got up, and the black tide within Vlad surged also. They were not holding him particularly tightly. He had been so surprised he'd not done any struggling, and they obviously thought him almost comatose with drink. Calling on the furious strength that was welling up inside him, he flung them aside.

Or at least, he succeeded in kicking the majordomo away, and cracking together the heads of the plump son, who was holding one arm, with the footmen who held the other.

That left only the boyar himself. He clung fast to Vlad's back, even as Vlad struggled to his feet.

The boyar kicked at his legs, making Vlad stagger back toward the vast hearth. Vlad tripped over one of the fire-dogs and fell backwards, into the burning logs.

His fall was cushioned by the man on his back—who screamed and let go.

Vlad stood up, in time to see the plump son swing a chair at him. Vlad sidestepped—and fell over the boyar, who was crawling out of the huge fireplace, screaming in pain. The man's clothes were on fire. The chair smashed on the edge of the fireplace—and part of it flew into the fire, knocking a log out.

The boyar rolled desperately. He crashed into the wall and the long drapes. Flames licked up from his burning clothes onto the drapery.

The majordomo had fumbled a clumsy wheel-lock pistol out from wherever he had hidden it. With shaking hands, he pointed it, as Vlad advanced from the fireplace. Vlad was far too angry to be afraid.

The pistol boomed. Vlad kept coming forward. If it had hit him, he didn't feel it. But the woman screamed and clutched her throat and sank to her knees, before pitching forward.

The majordomo stared at the tableau in horror.

"It is not a good enough bullet to kill the prince of Valahia. Mere lead won't do it," said Vlad, still walking toward the table, ignoring the screaming and terror. He picked up a branch of candles, and flung it like a javelin at the second footman, who was trying to pull a halberd free from a display of arms. It missed, but as he ducked the footman swung the halberd wildly and knocked over another branch of candles. The candles in the branch Vlad flung had all been extinguished by the speed of his throw. But these remained alight, and the tallow burned in a shallow puddle on the large kist. It must have dripped inside, and whatever was inside was very flammable too. It went up in a tower of flames.

Somehow the heat got through to Vlad. He shook himself, took stock of his circumstances, and realized that he was in a burning building. The son was trying to get past him, and Vlad let him flee. The boy was running the wrong way, up the passage.

The footman and majordomo had fled. Vlad could not leave the boyar and his wife to die. The boyar was farther away. He would gather him up, and grab the woman and run.

The boyar must have been half crazed with the burning, because he took one look at Vlad and somehow staggered into a run . . . back towards the burning drapes. Vlad allowed himself just a moment of indecision and then turned. If the man could still run, he could save himself. He scooped the woman up in his arms. She was voluptuous and heavy, but Vlad had no difficulty carrying her. He kicked aside the still swinging door and stormed out into the hallway. The front door was open, and the roof on fire.

No one likes or trusts the gypsies. But these men had brought the prince here and he had plainly exerted his hold over them too. So when the gypsies told the

villagers to gather their weapons and come to the
fortified manor of the boyar Klasparuj, they came.
Boyar Klasparuj was a hated landlord. Grasping and
cruel, he and his men were feared.

Their prince was already loved and respected.
"He killed Gregor the innkeeper with his own hands
for what he did to Janoz. Drowned him in his own
kitchen filth. And you know, he went himself to the
house of the widow Mira..."

If the prince wanted them, armed, his word was law.

They were waiting in the darkness when the fire
began erupting through the roof. Angelo turned to
Grigori. "He has called the wildfire."

The second gypsy nodded. "It's never a good thing
to wake in a building."

The door burst open and some liveried footmen came
running out, yowling like scalded cats. Angelo stopped
one. Hard. "Where is the prince?" he demanded.

"Dear God. I shot him!" quavered the man.

"What?!" demanded a villager. "Benedickt..."

"But he didn't die," said the man, his voice shrill.
"He just didn't die! I shot him dead. And he just
kept walking towards me. He said lead would not kill
him. It had to be royal metal. We gave him so much
wine it would have felled an ox, but he wasn't even
drunk. He's a demon—"

"Not a demon," said Radu. "Drac. He is the Dragon,
reborn."

As he said this a figure came staggering down the
stairs, his hair and clothing aflame, a kist in his hands.

And then, as part of the roof fell, sending a plume
of flame into the sky and illuminating everything
with sharp red light, Vlad came out of the doorway,

a woman in his arms. The flames curled up hungrily behind him, highlighting the prince in his austere black, his face very white. Red blood ran from the voluptuous woman's throat, and down onto her breast.

The villagers surged forward. Vlad put her down. "She is dead. They tried to betray me, Angelo." He looked at the flames and said tiredly. "The fire will spread. You'd better see to the horses in the stables. We'll need good horses. They had sent for King Emeric's men."

Villagers ran to do his bidding.

"What of this one?" Radu pointed to the fallen figure that had staggered out, aflame, just before Vlad appeared.

"The son. Let us see if anything can be done for him."

But he was no longer breathing. His hands had burned onto the kist he'd carried.

"He abandoned his parents to fetch that," said Vlad.

"The manor strongbox must have been important to him," said Angelo dryly. "Well. We'd better get to those horses and leave."

Vlad shook his head. "No. I have money." He kicked the strongbox. "I have horses and I have men. I see that the men have weapons with them."

"We thought you might need freeing."

"I might have," acknowledged Vlad. "But I dealt with that. I have had enough of just running. I have a funeral to attend tomorrow. Let us deal with these Croats tonight. It will make them less eager to follow me."

Angelo looked at the burning building. At the peasants with pitchforks, boar spears and bows. "They'll kill this lot, Prince."

Vlad shook his head. "We will not give them the opportunity. These people know the land here. The Croats do not. And they expect a prisoner. One man. They will not know what to expect."

Grigori rubbed his chin, thoughtfully. "I think that after tonight, they will expect the worst."

Radu snorted. "The tale will grow somewhat in the telling."

"Oh yes," said Angelo. "A dark and fearsome tale. A legend."

Chapter 26

Standing at the burned out shell of the manor house. Elizabeth tapped the riding crop against the cheek of the soldier. "Now tell us again, remembering *all* the details."

The trooper looked warily at the perfect complexion and classically beautiful face. She smiled, perfect rosebud lips curved. "I'm waiting."

"Lady, there really is no more. We got the message from the boyar Klasparuj. We rode back, guided by the messenger. We had no suspicion that it would be a trap. The locals are sullen and uncooperative, but no one would have dared to raise a hand to His Majesty's troops. They all do what we want. At most they just won't help us. But this one led us into an ambush, damn him."

"Of course he did not live through this," said Elizabeth.

The soldier nodded. "Captain Kouric ran him through, right there."

"I wonder if stupidity is infectious?" said the countess. "How are we supposed to question a dead body?

You kill them *after* you have the answers. Now we are going to have to find someone else to give us that information."

Captain Kouric looked wary himself. He had come to realize that the countess could be even more vicious than King Emeric, but that she was also much more astute. Of course—although Kouric would never have said this aloud, even to his closest friends—being more astute than Emeric was not hard.

She noticed. She noticed far too much for comfort. "And now, Captain? What else have you done that I'm going to dislike?"

He cleared his throat nervously. "His Majesty's orders. Any village that shows resistance, we are to execute as many of them as we can find."

"And you've sent some of your men to do this?"

He nodded, sweat beading his forehead.

"Send the rest of your men after them," she said coldly. "Now. If they've killed anyone, you'll be hanging alongside them in the village square. I need to know what happened here. If that means executing dull-witted soldiers of your force, I really don't mind."

He left at a run, yelling for his men and horse.

Elizabeth stood there tapping her quirt on her palm. The tiny slivers of glass embedded in it had no effect on her skin. There were ways, of course, of getting the information, even from the dead. If need be, she could get the burned timbers and blackened stones to tell her. But what she needed was a little more complex. Entrapment always took bait, and she would bet that Vlad had made loyalists for himself. She was not too sure quite where he had got himself a military force.

The Croats were Emeric's second best troops. They could not have been defeated by mere peasant levies. Vlad must have successfully recruited some of the boyars. That in itself was odd. Emeric, on her instruction, had treated them well. The trans-Carpathian lesser nobility were a fair way towards being more loyal to him than to their actual overlord.

But there was always some petty noble looking out for the main chance. Apparently, this boyar Klasparuj must have been one of them. The surviving Croats said that they had not burned the place. It was possible that they weren't lying. On the other hand, they had a reputation for arson—to the point where Emeric had had to forbid it during the last campaign. Arson was a shortsighted practice, unless one used it to burn people along with the structures that could be useful later.

She walk over to ashes. Someone had died here. She could feel it. Died terrified.

"I got there in time, you ladyship," panted the captain. "They were still rounding people up into the village square. Nobody has been hurt. At least not too badly."

"I trust you did not mention my name. Remember, I am not here. I am strictly incognito in this affair."

"Uh." The captain looked as if in avoiding the mud puddle he had stepped into a cesspool. "I did say that your ladyship had ordered them freed." She tapped her quirt on her hand again. "But I didn't use your ladyship's actual name."

"I have told you that it is necessary for me to keep an apparent distance from the search for Prince Vlad. Now, thanks to your foolishness, I will have to remove myself from this area. I will need you to bring me those of the boyars who have provided you with the best support. I will need to interview them."

"Yes, your ladyship. What can we do about the attack on our men?"

"Why, be very happy that you failed to execute the villagers. The last prince was a fairly timid man. But this prince's grandfather would have impaled your troops and set them on the border as a warning. This one seems more like that. Learn to play a longer game, Captain. In good time you will get your opportunity."

She paused for a moment, reminding herself not to fall into the same error. "I've rethought my strategy here. I did indeed order you not to kill the villagers. That made you very angry, that I should suddenly have arrived and told you to take this action. See that you tell quite a number of people that."

"And the boyars, lady?"

"Have them come and see me," she said, turning away. "I need to interview them, to find ones that are suitable."

She did not say what she wanted them suitable for, and the captain wisely did not ask.

Captain Kouric rode his showy roan down the village street. He noted four of his men's horses outside the smithy. Now, horses do throw a shoe every now and again, but the captain had an excellent memory—for horses, anyway. Two of those horses had only been reshod yesterday, and those were four that should have been out on patrol. He stopped his horse and tied it next to the others and went inside. Two of his soldiers, who would normally not have deigned to lift a finger if a civilian could be made to do it, were working the bellows while the smith drew a crucible from the furnace with long tongs. The other two were readying a series of bullet molds.

"And just what is going on in here?" he asked sharply, almost causing the smith to drop and crack his crucible full of molten silver metal.

"Nothing, Captain," said one of the troopers hastily.

"Just making some more bullets, sir," added another, as if Kouric could not see that.

He raised his eyes to heaven. "And since when did you need a smith to do that? And why do you need to do it right now?"

"Uh. We thought it might be useful, sir, to have some spares."

"Always a good thought," said Kouric, his eyes half lidded. "But why did you bring the work to the smithy this morning, when you're supposed to be on patrol?" His voice, silky and pleasant, might have fooled those who knew him less well than his own troops.

"Uh. We only heard about this late last night, sir. And we can't get our fire hot enough..."

Kouric had seen them melting lead often enough to know this to be a lie. He merely raised his eyebrows at them.

"Well, sir, it's not lead. It's ... it's silver, sir. It is that or gold, and most of us haven't got much gold.

"'Tisn't my fault," said the smith. "They told me to melt all their silver pennies. I just does what I'm told, sir."

"Silver bullets? You are melting your own money into silver bullets?" demanded the captain incredulously. "Have you all gone mad?"

The soldiers had the grace to look embarrassed. "It's the only way to stop him, sir. A common metal won't do nothing to him."

"What on earth are you talking about?" demanded their commanding officer. He refrained from calling them the idiots they plainly were. Kouric had commanded men for long enough to understand that there were times when telling them the average dung-heap had more intelligence, could in itself be a stupid statement. That was when money was involved. More than one officer had been murdered for that mistake.

"The Drac, sir," said one of the soldiers, using the local word for the Dragon.

"There is no such thing, trooper," said the captain dismissively. Once stories like that got hold, they were hard to dispel among the common soldiers. They were enormously superstitious.

"It's what the local people call Prince Vlad, sir," explained the soldier. "He is a monster, sir."

"They are having you on, spinning you a fine fairy tale," said Kouric.

"No, sir," said the soldier stubbornly.

Soldiers do not argue with their commanding officer. They know the penalty for that. So if any experienced officer has them do so, he knows something is very wrong. "Where did you hear this?"

"At the Green Bush, sir."

Kouric knew that he shouldn't even have had to ask. The inn was off-limits, but he knew full well that where there was ale, there would be troopers, and nothing short of a armed guard would stop them. "You're not supposed to shoot Prince Vlad," he said tersely. "You're supposed to arrest him. Those are your orders from King Emeric himself. Do you really wish to argue with him? The king is no story put about to frighten little babes. He is a real terror. If Prince Vlad was so powerful do you think he could have been kept prisoner? A hostage—and for years? Now get out there, get on your horses and get to your patrol."

They turned, and began to sheepishly stumble towards the door. One did half turn, and say: "What about our money, sir?"

"Go! You were stupid enough to waste it. You've lost it." If the blacksmith had any sense he'd return their silver. If he didn't, Captain Kouric was not going to look too hard for his murderers. The locals deserved some payback for their part in all this. No matter what the countess said, he was going to make an example of those who were trying to terrify his men with this story.

In a plain cloak, accompanied by one of his toughest sergeants, equally anonymously dressed, Kouric found his way into the taproom of the inn that night. The host was an old man with a severe limp. And he was giving free beer to the Croat troopers, which explained just why quite so many of the captain's men were prepared to risk his wrath by coming to a place that was off limits. There were a few locals. The captain noted their features carefully and sat down with his sergeant to listen. If they'd gone forward to the bar at least one of the men might have recognized them, but they stayed at the back, where the light from the tallow dips scarcely penetrated.

The speaker was so drunk that his words were slurred. He still had every trooper in the place clinging to them.

"—drank drank the mistress's blood. You could see it running from her throat." The man panted and sweated, just recollecting the event. "His skin is white, like something that's been dead. And he wears black clothes like a priest. And he walked right through the fire. Fire that was hot enough to kill the master's son, and burnt me like this, see." He pointed to his shriveled hair. "And I got out of there before him, long before him. It didn't burn him at all. You can't kill him."

The old man with the limp had come up to the table quietly, as they listened. He put down three mugs of beer. "On the house. You must stay here to protect us."

The captain had heard enough. He knew what he'd have to do. "Sergeant, we'll be shifting camp first thing in the morning." It was that or lose half his men to desertion. This Benedickt's story was obviously not invented for audience's benefit. It had spread to so many of the troopers already, that hanging the man would be a waste of time and effort. Counterproductive, in fact, since the hanging would simply give weight to the story.

Kouric's patrols still hunted for Prince Vlad. But there was a marked lack of real enthusiasm for actually finding him, and having to try to take him alive as they'd been instructed. Dead in a hail of silver bullets might be a better idea . . .

The captain was not a superstitious man. He would have to keep reminding his troopers just what the king did to those who disobeyed him. He also needed to send a message. Emeric would need more than the handful of soldiers he had in these hills, if they were facing a real armed insurrection.

He was not happy at the thought. The king of Hungary was known to ignore such messages and then, when troubles ensued, to demand the heads of those who had not warned him.

"Forty-two men," grinned Angelo. "A perfect number. Too many to feed easily, and too few to do anything with. They lack arms, or training, or even anyone to train them. King Emeric must be very afraid."

Just a few seconds before, Vlad had actually been feeling quite proud of his new army. Their loyalty touched him. Angelo's sarcasm touched him too, on the raw. But the gypsy was right, and Vlad could not forget that they had helped him to flee and draw off those who might have endangered his rescuer.

"Well, I have you and Grigori and Radu. Then there is me. So we have forty-six men. And I will recruit more"

Angelo shook his head. "No, Drac. We—Radu, Grigori and I—must go south now, and fast. There is business that we need to see to for our people. We will have to leave you. But we will be back. There are certain rituals between your house and mine that need to be renewed before we can have you crowned."

The idea of them leaving frightened him. In his shifting world, the gypsies had been Vlad's one anchor. True, it had been a very small anchor, which had allowed the vessel of his life to drift into new and dangerous waters. But everything else had gone.

"I am not sure where to go next. Or what to do."

The gypsy seemed amused. "Being a prince is a trade you'll have to learn without my help. I could only teach you how to look and behave like a gypsy, not the ruler of Valahia. As to where you will go ... I think that there is only one place for you to go and be safe for a little while, while you try to turn your men into a real army. The high Carpathians. It's wild, bleak and unruled. Bandit country. The Hungarians will not go there except in large numbers, and large numbers up there are hard to move around fast and unseen. You need time and a hiding place. Go up into the mountains and be very glad that it is still late summer."

Vlad decided that was sound advice. And those high bleak places called to him.

If he could not turn to the boyars for cavalry, leadership and training, he had to find some people he could trust to help with the instruction, or he would have to learn all of it himself.

But he was aware that twenty-seven horses and the contents of the boyar's strong box were not going to be enough.

Chapter 27

Erik and the Illyrian captain stood on the wall of the little fortified village, looking down on the braided river below. "That is the edge of our territory," said the Illyrian captain. He pointed. "Over that ridge are the lands of the Golden Horde. They will have seen us by now. They keep a watch higher up. Across that mountain, are the Bulgars. There is usually someone up there, too. I feel sorry for them in winter."

Erik nodded. "Our thanks, Captain. It occurs to me that I've yet to hear your name. I would like to tell my young friend, Benito Valdosta, how carefully you have watched over us. I do realize that you have dealt with two other groups of attackers, after the first incident on that pass. If we could formally introduce ourselves? I realize that it is late, but as they say, better late than never."

The mustachioed captain smiled. "In some cases, knowing could make you late, *Ritter* Hakkonsen. Benito already knows who I am. But as we part ways here, you may as well know my name. In these mountains I am called Iskander. And now, I see your men are readying themselves to ride. We will scout as far as the river bank. It is easy to ford at this time of year."

He turned and left the parapet. Erik went down to join the other knights. Manfred greeted him with a wave. Then frowned, seeing Erik's expression.

"What's wrong?"

"Nothing," said Erik. "We've just been hoodwinked a bit. Not that it did us any harm, I suppose. But Benito might've told us."

"I so love it when you speak in riddles," grumbled Manfred. "I suppose I should be grateful for the mental exercise."

"I mean that the Illyrian captain of our escort was none other than the Lord of the Mountains himself. Iskander Beg."

Manfred raised his eyebrows, and whistled. "No wonder his nose was out of joint when we were attacked. Eberhard is going to be sorely disappointed that he missed the opportunity to do some more politicking." Manfred smiled. "There is a rose in every patch of thorns. I'll save pretending that I knew until I need to irritate him about something. Still, we've got a day or two, surely."

"No. More like until Terce bell, if they have such a thing in these mountains. The river down there is the border, and our Captain Iskander has gone out scouting."

"Well, whatever happens we have learned a bit about him," said Manfred. "His logistics and staff work are far too good for some tribal chieftain lost somewhere in the middle of the mountains. My uncle would love to employ him."

Erik nodded. "True, although that's hardly a good

thing for us to tell the overlord of these tribes. The Illyrians might be as poor as Shetlanders, but they are just as proud of their independence."

"I suppose so. Francesca tried to teach me the fine art of tact and sensibility, but I mostly failed at it." Manfred mounted up, grinning. "Fortunately, from my experience, it is something that translators do for you. So how ready are you with the Mongol tongue?"

"Far from ready to act as an official interpreter," said Erik, tightening a cinch before mounting up. "My understanding is getting much better. But as for the speaking, I really think that I need a better teacher."

"But then our horseboy would have no practice in getting faster reflexes."

Erik jibbed his horse forward, "Knights!" He raised his voice to address all of them. "We are now on the borderline between Illyria and the lands of the Golden Horde. Our Illyrian escort will leave us at the river. From there, until we meet the Golden Horde, we will be taking full escort duty. Falkenberg, you will organize the prince's personal guard. Von Gherens, you will take the van. Proctor Kalb will take the rearguard. Knights Von Diderik, Kirsten, Von Taub and Wellmans, Hunsen, Dader, pair off. You will be scouting ahead. Kari, you are with me."

He and Kari would be even farther ahead, riding point.

Two of the Mongols, the rotund Tulkun and his sharp-eyed friend Matu, came up with their ponies. "We riding, scout. Meet Horde." He held a bunch of sky blue pennants in one arm and waved them about. "Put on, how you say, spear. Truce. Mother sun, father sky."

That would certainly ease any confusion arising from seeing a large party of foreign armored horsemen moving into their territory.

David had learned a fair amount since the incident on the pass. One of the things he'd learned was to look out for signs that the knights were expecting trouble. Even with the new sky blue pennants affixed to their lances, there was a sense of heightened awareness in the column. He, along with the baggage train, rode near the back, behind Manfred and his escort. By now he'd worked out that it was no use just wishing that he was riding even farther back, preferably on the way to Jerusalem. He looked and listened hard. There was entirely too much silence in these places. He was sure that any enemy could hear the passage of the knights from a good half a league away. In a nice crowded noisy city there were other noises to hide behind.

He'd never realized just how much he appreciated Jerusalem's Mongol overlords, until they were no longer around.

The country was more rugged here, along the borderland with the Bulgars. Bortai knew that was a blessing more than a curse. The terrain had provided the cover that had let them avoid an Arban that had plainly been out looking for someone. Now she prayed to the spirits of the land, to the tengeri, to the eternal blue sky, that they would not have to break cover to get over the next ridge. And they had to get over it and soon. She'd been scouting and spotted two Arban of search parties. Twenty men, all told. One to the west and the other farther east. The only way out was over the ridge.

Otherwise—had the pursuit not been getting closer—she would have been terribly happy. Kildai had awakened. He was confused, true. But two days ago she'd been less than sure that he would ever wake again.

Unfortunately, there was no way they could get the cart over that ridge. And she was not at all sure how he could ride. He seemed to think that she was his mother, dead five years now, rather than his older sister.

They had tethered the ox where it could graze reasonably well, and hidden the cart. With any luck those who were following them would lose a little time searching the area for them, not knowing that they'd moved on. Now it was a question of whether Kildai could stay in the saddle. She and Ion helped him into it. Surely, someone whose balance was that bad would fall? She thought they would probably have to tie him into the saddle.

But instincts honed by a lifetime spent riding came to Kildai's rescue. Even just sitting there, he'd put a foot into the far stirrup without any help from them. She had planned to ride on the same horse, in front of him. Now she wondered if he could stay in the saddle by himself.

But it was best not to take such a chance. At least Kildai was willing to let them tie his hands together, around her waist. Ion mounted clumsily—he had hardly ever been in the saddle. Leading the other horse, which was laden with such supplies as it could carry, they rode out, keeping under the trees, working their way ever upward.

As she had feared, the last section of the slope

offered no cover at all. It was just bare sheetrock with scattered tufts of grass. Looking back, she could see dust that had to be a large party of riders. There might be smaller groups trailing them also.

They simply couldn't afford to wait for nightfall. So she rode her mount out under the trees and onto a rough trail. As she had guessed would happen, she heard a distant yell and someone sounding a horn. She urged her horse into a canter. They'd save the galloping for later. Anyway, it was very likely that Ion would fall out of the saddle when they tried.

Coming over the ridge, she looked back again. The dust cloud had grown considerably. They were pushing those horses. And then, she heard a sound that she would have never have thought could be so sweet. It was a bell. She'd heard them before from one of the churches of the Vlachs who lived higher up in the Carpathians. No wonder they were hunting her hard. There must be a Bulgar village close by.

Crossing into Bulgar lands wouldn't stop the pursuit. But it did mean that someone—besides her—might just be shooting at them. If she could find some place to hide...

She wished that she knew more about the Bulgars and the border area. But her clan's holdings were far to the north. She'd never been down here and never had much interest before. The situation was complicated, if she recalled correctly. There were several conflicting peoples in the area. Bulgars, Illyrians, Hungarians. Bortai didn't really care. She just hoped that they would be furious with a raiding party and so busy fighting them that they wouldn't notice three riders fleeing.

❈   ❈   ❈

Erik had missed his guess slightly. They were ready in the woods on the far side of the river when the Terce bell rang out from the little white chapel in the village in the mountain-fold.

The Illyrians wasted no time, and engaged in no great formalities at their border. Iskander Beg simply rode up to Manfred, Eberhard and Erik. "Our mutual friend," he said, "has asked that you send word back, if you can, as to what is happening here. Of course he also wants to know what is happening farther north."

He grinned through his moustache. "He never asks for too much. There will be some men and good horses waiting in the village." He pointed to the little place they had just left. "In case you or a message want to return the same way."

"Our mutual friend, Benito Valdosta," said Manfred smiling. "If you knew him as well as we do, you would know that he always asks too much—and then usually gets it. Our thanks to you, Lord of the Mountains. Benito said that you took your honor very seriously here in the mountains. I take mine seriously, too, and I realize that you have paid us a rare honor. The Holy Roman Empire is in your debt."

Iskander bowed his head slightly. "I hope that I will have no occasion to wish to collect," he said, still smiling. "I hear a horn. It would seem that the Golden Horde are already aware of your presence. I think we will remove ourselves a little. Relations have not been of the best at times. I would prefer it if you met them somewhere close to the ridge. The land between it and the river is something of no man's land. We'd like to keep it like that."

In close formation, once the scouts were across, the knights clattered across the braided gravel of the border river, and into the woods. There was a faint trail, but it was obvious that it was rarely used. Erik, Kari and Tulkun the rotund Mongol rode ahead.

"Now, for heavens sake, Kari. Don't shoot the first thing you see that moves."

"It's best that way," said Kari. "Really, Erik. It avoids so many problems later." He was grinning as he said that, and Erik could only hope that he was joking. With Kari he never could tell. He always had at least four wheel-lock pistols secreted about his person. They were apparently not yet very common in Vinland and he had a fascination with the weapons.

Bortai felt her little brother slumping against her, but there was no way they could stop now. They needed to get somewhere closer to those bells, or else where they stopped would be where they died. She could hear a second horn being sounded. Their pursuers must be over the ridge by now.

The trail, faint though it was, did make travel faster. It zigzagged down the slope between some large boulders, each the size of a couple of gers. It was a good place for an ambush, and she might have considered the possibility, had there only been three or four enemies in pursuit of them. But she would guess by the dust that thirty or even forty was closer to the number. Only speed could help now. Fortunately, even two up, they probably weighed less than most warriors, especially this late in summer. Summer was drinking and feasting time.

That same speed nearly had them ride into the

people coming up the trail. For a moment, seeing just the scale mail and forelock of a Mongol warrior, she snatched at her bow. But then she noticed two other things. One was the man who was riding just ahead of the Mongol, in spiky, angular armor, on a truly magnificent piece of horseflesh. His visor was open. He had a chiseled face, and fine, almost white-blond hair. Obviously he was not a Mongol. In fact, he didn't look like he belonged to any people Bortai knew.

The other thing that really struck home was the sky blue truce flag on the lance of the Mongol. Then she saw more subtle differences. She'd never seen scale armor quite like that worn by this Mongol, and his tack was arranged slightly differently. The silver inset on his saddle was also something that she'd never seen before, as was the device on his shield.

But she knew what it represented. She'd heard of the Bear clan. They were part of the Red Horde. The Ilkhan. Not seen in Golden Horde lands for many years. Almost a thing out of legend.

Her frozen moment was interrupted by Ion falling off his horse.

Erik had heard them coming. Two or three horses, ridden hard. So, by the way he had drawn two pistols, had Kari. The Vinlander refused to wear much in the way of armor. He felt it slowed him down, which Erik had to admit was probably true. There was unfortunately nowhere to get off the trail. The path passed just between two of the huge boulders, leaving a space barely wide enough for four to ride abreast. Kari sidled up to a twisted tree that grew out of a crack and waited. Erik and Tulkun took firmer grips on their weapons, Erik dropping the point of the lance with its blue pennant to just above head height. Tulkun did the same with his spear.

They were ready for anything...

Except for a very beautiful young woman, riding tandem, with a young head lolling sideways behind her.

A woman who managed to control her horse, and to get a bow into her hand and an arrow on the string faster than Erik would have believed possible. Then it seemed as if she saw enough to dip that arrow-point, pull her pony to a halt—and still stay on it, bow in hand. It was a superb display of horsemanship as well as quick wittedness.

Just behind her, a second rider and a third horse came to halt. This rider, in rough homespun, showed no skill at all, unless it was in the speed with which he departed from the saddle.

In the stress of the moment Erik grasped for words. He'd never been too good at talking to girls, and in a foreign language...

Too late he realized what he'd said. That first carefully memorized sentence. He fumbled for the words to apologize, while turning puce with embarrassment.

As the man in homespun got to his feet, the woman started to laugh. It looked like she might just laugh herself out of the saddle too.

The boy up behind her needed help. Behind them, Erik heard the clink and clatter of the rest of the knights. His Mongol companion started to speak. Well, to do his best, between snorts of laughter. She replied to him.

He bowed deeply.

"The very people we are looking for," he said.

Just then another group of riders came around the bend. Also Mongols. They yelled when they saw the woman, spurred their horses, and dropped their lance-tips.

There was a sudden double boom. In the narrow defile, the sound echoed very loudly. The riders began frantically pulling their horses around. The shots in a place for an ambush might have been the cause. Or it could have been the solid mass of armor visible less than a hundred yards farther back down the trail.

Erik reflected that there was a certain inevitability about all of this. Firstly, he'd accidentally insulted this woman. Fortunately, she did not seem to take offense. Then she turned out to be from the clan that they were looking for. Then some other Mongols came around the corner intent on murder, which Kari and his too ready pistols had stopped. Now...

There were more Mongols coming around the corner. And the body of the knights was coming up, the weight of their great-horses and armor gathering momentum.

He finally got it all together. "Lady," he said, "can I offer you shelter?"

Since the events of the kurultai, Bortai had at least known what to expect of events. Yes, there had been a few surprises, such as Ion and the slave's courage and bowmanship. But here, when she thought that luck had finally run out for her and Kildai, it would seem that the spirits had taken a hand—although in a way no one could expect.

The foreign knight telling her that her mother was a

tortoise—plainly a fumbling attempt her language—had been so incongruous and funny that in spite of the desperate circumstances she could not help but laugh.

Now he had just proposed marriage. Offered her his ger.

There was no doubt that the tengeri had a sense of humor. An odd sense of humor.

But it would seem that her latest suitor had a lot of knights to prevent anyone killing her or her brother first. And in close, tight quarters like this, the greater maneuverability of the Mongol horsemen counted for little.

In a chaotic mass the Mongols turned and rode away. That was one of the actions that they were famous for. Some foolish enemies had mistaken such retreats for cowardice and panic.

Erik was not among them. He signaled a halt, and as the charge had not yet built full momentum, the knights slowed to a walk by the time they had reached him.

"Did you have to start a war?" demanded Manfred, who had somehow contrived to get among the van.

"As yet, hopefully not," said Erik. "Usually someone has to get killed for that. And I didn't see anyone go down when Kari loosed off those pistols of his."

Kari shook his head regretfully. "No. They're not as accurate as I'd like them to be. I think I may have winged the one."

"Then what in the name of all the saints happened?" asked Falkenberg.

"And just what should we do now?" added Von Gherens. "Retreat on the river?"

"I think that would be wise," said Erik. "There were some grounds for a misunderstanding."

"Like Kari shooting at them," said Manfred.

"To be fair, he only did that because they were heading for us full tilt with their lances out," said Erik. "It could have been nasty, otherwise. I think we'd better do a systematic retreat now while we can. They'll send an emissary down shortly, I should think."

Manfred nodded. "And who's the wench? There you are, on a barren mountainside, which I thought had a female sheep at best, and some beautiful girl comes out of the woods to find you. Why am I not this lucky?"

"I don't know. But Tulkun said that she is from the clan we're looking for."

"I admit that makes a pleasant change," said Manfred, turning his horse as Falkenberg gave orders. "Mostly girls just stare besottedly at you. This one at least has the common sense to laugh at you instead, even in the middle of a cavalry charge."

Erik blushed a dull red. "I may have greeted her incorrectly, in the stress of the moment. And her companion appears to be injured. We'd better see what help we can give."

Manfred raised his eyebrows. "Just what did you say to her?"

"I think you have enough to mock me about," said Erik severely. "Kari, you and the horseboy get on top of that rock. Everyone else is wearing armor, which doesn't help with climbing. Fire a shot if you see any sign of them coming back down the slope. And don't fire at them. Fire in the air, and then mount up and get down there. And come running anyway when you see us on the far side of the river."

He turned to the young woman with the boy on her back, whose eyes were open now but distinctly out of focus. In his rudimentary Mongol, Erik said: "If you will come with us. It looks as if the boy needs some help. We have those among us with some skill in healing."

She smiled at him. She had one of those smiles that ran all the way to her eyes, and dimpled her cheeks. "Thank you. You are offering your protection to him, too?"

At least that is what Erik thought she was saying. So he nodded.

"The clan of the Hawk is glad to accept." She was obviously stifling a gurgle of laughter.

He wondered quite what he'd said this time.

"Come on, *Ritter* Hakkonsen. Lead out!" yelled Falkenberg. As the man who had fallen off had remounted, they all rode back to the river.

On a field which was part of the floodplain of the little river, the knights formed up into a defensive square. The river was barely a stream now, but Bortai thought it would be a raging torrent in winter. The blond foreign knight had kept pace with her and Kildai. He had dismounted easily, something that Bortai was willing to bet was actually quite hard to do in such armor, without help. He produced a knife and she knew a moment of alarm, despite him having offered clan friendship. But it was just to cut the thong that she'd used to secure Kildai's arms around her. He lifted her little brother down.

Another one of the knights, a man with a scarred face and an eye patch, came up, along with the man from the Ilkhan Bear clan. She noticed there were several of the Bear clan in among the large party of knights. The tall blond man gently set Kildai down on a blanket that the dark-eyed man with his braided hair and the pistols had ridden up and handed to him.

She dismounted too. "What is wrong with him?" asked the man from the Ilkhan.

"His suns soul wanders the lands of Urleg Khan. Have you a shaman who can enter the spirit world below and call him back?"

The Mongol shook his head. "Maybe these Franks have someone. Their medicine is not as sophisticated as ours, but in spite of that, many of them get better. What happened to get him into such a state?"

"He was knocked off his horse during the great game at the summer kurultai. I think he landed on his head."

So these were Franks? She had, of course, heard of them. What were they doing here on the borderland of the Golden Horde? Was their word worth anything? Why did they accompany the people of the Ilkhan? And why did they carry truce-diplomat flags?

The Mongol nodded sympathetically. "It has happened to me. But I just broke this bone here." He pointed to his shoulder. "Mind you, I think that was from being kicked after I fell."

The one-eyed man knelt next to Kildai, opened his eyes and examined each pupil in turn. Very gently he felt at Kildai's neck, and then the skull.

He looked at her and asked a question.

"He wants to know how long he has been like this," translated the Bear clan Mongol. "And what happened to him."

She answered as best as she was able, feeling oddly helpless. Actually, she felt like just sitting down and starting to cry, as if she were a little girl again. It was just so good to no longer be carrying the entire weight of her little brother's health, and the clan's and their own survival on her shoulders.

Her relief must have shown in her face because the tall blond knight said something to the man with pistols. He took something out of a pannier, which turned into a simple saddle stool, with three legs and a leather top. The blond knight set it up and offered it to her with a small bow and a gesture.

He seemed to be avoiding using his few words of Mongol. She could understand that. A tremulous smile to her lips—not something she was very accustomed to bestowing on strange foreign knights. Or anyone else, really. The tremulous part worried her. She must not show such weakness.

The one-eyed knight stood up, dusting off his hands. He spoke again to the man from the Ilkhan, who translated. "He says the boy must rest quietly. He must stay still for some days. He should not ride, anyway."

Bortai shook her head, pointing back at the ridge. "If they catch us, they will kill us. We are far from our clan. We were," she decided to be economical with the truth, "separated from them during the big fight at the kurultai."

The plump Ilkhan warrior, Tulkun, was plainly shocked by that. "They *fought*? At the kurultai?"

She nodded. That had indeed been a shocking breach of tradition, but then tradition seemed to be weakening its hold on some of the clans.

"Clan fought clan." She pointed to Ion. If this man from the Ilkhan was going to be sympathetic, she may as well see if she could get some protection for Ion. "Our slave saw more of it than we did. He saw which clan waited in ambush for others, under the kurultai flag. They will kill him too if they find him."

"So, the clans have not yet selected a new khan?"

She shook her head. "As far as I know, no. The kurultai was broken before the vote. That means that Gatu Orkhan is regent."

"Ah," said the Mongol from the Ilkhan. "That is what the tarkhan Borshar has come to see to. We are not supposed to know," he said with a small smile. "And I heard and will bear witness that the *Ritter* Erik Hakkonsen offered marriage and kin-shelter. The Franks are under the envoy-flag of the tarkhan."

"Yes, but he did not actually understand what he said." Bortai smiled on the *Ritter*. That had been a generous gesture in a time when she had seen very few.

The warrior from the Ilkhan bowed respectfully. "The honor of the Hawk clan has not diminished. There are many who would have taken advantage."

The blond *Ritter* Hakkonsen spoke to Tulkun, who replied to him in the foreign tongue. He was speaking about them, that much Bortai was sure of. Behind him another knight rode over—the one who had shouted to him at what had almost been a cavalry clash. Now that things were not quite so fraught, she realized just how big the man was. And her first thought, incongruously, was a twinge of sympathy for the poor horse!

Fortunately it was a very sturdy animal, much like its rider.

❀   ❀   ❀

"She speaks too fast for me to understand all of it," said Erik. "What is the problem? They were hunting for her, weren't they?"

The Mongol nodded and replied in broken Frankish. "She was separated from her clan. Big fight at clan gathering—supposed to be peace for election of new khan. Fight start before khan elected. They very powerful clan, much honor. Old family. Clan the Ilkhan support for khanate. Family for ruler." He smiled. "You offer clan-protection. But honorable lady know it is just foreigner who does not understand what he say. Honor for foreigners not the same for Mongol."

Even though it wasn't intentional, the condescension in the statement irritated Erik. Manfred, now standing just behind them, leaned forward. "What did he say? I'm not sure I followed."

"The girl and—I gather the boy is her brother—come from the royal clan, if I understand it right. They got separated from their clan in a fight about the new ruler. In my misguided attempt to be polite, I offered them from what I can work out was an alliance and the protection of my clan. But our translator says that she understood that we foreigners don't have much of sense of honor and they don't expect us to abide by it."

Manfred raised his eyebrows. "And that is the core of the problem with our relationship with the Ilkhan, and probably the Golden Horde too. Erik, if I did not know you well enough to know you had already decided to do it, I'd order you to tell her that we foreigners have our own code of honor."

"No," said Erik. "This is not something that can be told. It must be shown."

Chapter 28

The great gray wolves ran on, covering the miles
with an easy, distance-eating lope. They conversed
as they did so, in the way of the wolf which is far
more complex than mere words, communication at
the level of scent, tiny movements and postures of
the head, ears or tail, with the smallest yelp meaning
many things through these filters. Human speech had
its advantages, and a greater range of vocabulary. But
now...this seemed very free. They had kept to human
form for a long time.

They paused on the ridge line, tongues lolling, with
the folds of the world trailing out raggedly to the lowlands. If anyone had been watching they would have
seen how the three blurred and faded and became
three men, lean gypsies in ragged bright clothes.

"We should be there by the hatching."

"At least now that we can run properly."

"And hunt properly."

"Still. There is much weighted against him. Perhaps
one of us should have stayed."

Angelo shook his dark ringlets. "No. He must find

the path himself, without us. We have done enough. Too much, without the compact."

"Times and circumstances drive," said Radu.

Angelo took out his pipe and played. The ancient threnody, sad, sweet and compelling, came back in echoing snatches, as if the land itself was answering. Perhaps it was. He stopped and let the silence of the mountains return.

Eventually, he spoke. "We are creatures of the compact, born to it and shaped by it. Without it, we will die."

Grigori shrugged. "So will he. So will his people."

"This is true. But that will be of no help to us."

"It's in the blood," Radu said. "I could smell it. He will come to us. Blood calls to blood."

"But it is still his choice and ours," said Angelo. "The compact is a thing of willingness. The blood must be freely given."

"And if it were not? If it were taken forcibly?" asked Radu, curious. "That would not be easy, but it could be done. There are magics..."

"It has happened before," admitted Angelo. "The hunger born of it is terrible, as are the creations thereof. When the time came on them... The creatures of the shadows stalked the night and fed on the blood of innocents. Or any other blood they could find."

Grigori shook himself, and spat. "Half-creatures. Loup-garou."

"Indeed. Neither man nor of the old blood, and not constrained by the compact. The legends still remain," said Angelo, grimly. "They are hard to kill."

"I still think we should have told him more," said Radu.

Angelo shook his head. "Part of the magic requires innocence. To take the step willingly, not knowing entirely what the risk or the price will be. Humans take innocence as virginity."

"It has parallels, I suppose." Grigori grinned toothily. "Although it does assume that a piece of skin equates with innocence."

"A large assumption, and sometimes false."

A little later they set off again. The moon would be full in three days' time and they had many miles to cover before then. The distance on a map was not so great, but there was a complex terrain both physically and spiritually between them and the heartland in the Fărăgas Mountains and the lacul Podragul.

And with steady inexorable precession, the syzygial dance of earth, moon and sun moved on to the point they had last occupied forty-four years and one month before. The exeligmos. The full turn of the wheel.

Duck eggs are frequently given to chickens to sit. Mother hen will dutifully turn them and them keep them the right temperature, until they hatch. To sit a wyvern egg, the wolf-people knew, you need a mountain. And not just any mountain. It had to be the one called Moldoveanu. It was a fitting place for such a thing.

Alchemists would pay a great deal for something as rare as a fragment of wyvern eggshell. The cave was littered with them, still golden in the candlelight.

Yet it would not be easy for anyone to ever find this place in the roots of the mountain. Were they to somehow evade those who guarded the place from within the dark trees on the lower slopes, climb the ravine, pass the waterfall and the guardians in the water, they would find the place itself was full of strange and unpleasant sulfurous reeks. The breath of mountains can kill, and here it was so bespelled that it would, if necessary, to defend this place. Set on a small fissure that steamed gently, the egg rocked. And rocked again. There was a sharp sound, like the touch of fine crystal glassware. A tiny hairline crack shivered across the iridescent gold surface of the egg.

From long experience the wolf people knew that the shivering would be matched in the otherwise still waters of the Lacul Podragul. This was not a mystery that they had thought upon, it was just the way that the mountain was. They knew better than to set up camp too close to the lake edge, because they knew what was coming next. On the steep rocky bluff they sat above their multicolored carts and tattered tents in the moonlit darkness, looking out over the water. They watched how the water suddenly shivered although there was no breath of wind. No one spoke. It was a time both enchanted and fraught with perils. The little ones within would be weak, and the shells were close to being as hard as adamantine. When they were full-grown, adamantine would be as soft as velvet compared to them. But now, they had to fight free.

In the cave, Angelo waited, as was his duty and right as the oldest. He had with him a flask of the only food that could nourish a young wyvern. A second crack splintered into the surface of the egg. There was nothing musical about this one. Instead it sounded like a wagonload of glassware crashing down a cliff.

Angelo knew that the Lacul would be a torment of waves now. He braced himself. There would be more. But at least there was a second crack. With creatures that had to be born as twins there was always the fear that only one would survive. He waited for the next assault on the egg and its membrane. A few moments later he was rewarded by a piece of shell ricocheting like shrapnel off the walls, and the appearance of a dragonish snout with a little sharp white egg tooth on the end. The baby snorted out egg-fluid, and sniffed, tasting the air. A second snout pushed its way next to it through the same gap, and repeated the performance.

Angelo realized that he had been holding his breath, and he exhaled in a long sigh of relief. The two noses twitched at him synchronously. The shell cracked and shattered with a noise like a chandelier cascading down several flights of stairs. Two pairs of little red slit eyes looked at him, and blinked simultaneously. Both gave a curious high-pitched creel and began struggling their way free of the egg membrane.

Mothers were reputed to gash their own breasts to feed their offspring. Perhaps they would, if they could survive laying the egg. Angelo had a flask of their mother's blood for them. No other substance would nourish the chicks. Fortunately, as long as it was kept from contact with the air, wyvern blood appeared to neither coagulate nor decay. Magic gave, magic took away.

It was a rare and wonderful blood and it was not only the chicks that needed it. Angelo did not know quite when the relationship between his kind and theirs had begun, or just how it had come into being. But their care of the hatchlings was an ancient and sacred trust. His people believed that without that blood the tribe would return slowly to its roots. Either a nomad or a wolf pack, depending on just who told the story. Neither was an option that anyone wanted to take a chance on.

This land was full of old things, creatures from before man's settlement. Most were subject to the compact. But only Angelo's kind were unsure just where they stood in it all, if it failed. All they knew was that it would cost them half of themselves.

Chapter 29

In Odessa a very frightened little man made painstaking notes about the number of wagons passing beneath his window. He was unsure if or how he would get the information to his paymaster. But if he had nothing to sell, he would never have the money to leave.

The work was dangerous, but Count Mindaug paid well.

The work was not actually that dangerous. True, Jagiellon was wise to the workings of agents and double agents. Spies and betrayal were meat and drink to him. Anyone attempting espionage on a military or political target of concern to the grand duke was indeed taking a great risk.

But economics was not. The Black Brain knew a great deal about several planes of existence. Mindaug's estimate was that he knew the least about this earthly one. Trade was something Chernobog had always understood poorly.

The demon was not subtle, no matter that he thought he was. To him, power meant that you took what you wanted. The only purpose of trade was to corrupt and to move spies into the territories of those who did not understand absolute power. Right now, Jagiellon judged that it was more important to keep his enemies in the dark concerning his preparations than it was to maintain the regular commerce of Odessa. So, he'd ordered the port closed. The cargo that would normally have been shipped out was piling up in the warehouses at the docks.

That also meant that Odessa was slowly starving. Mindaug's agents reported that people were even beginning to mutter against the voivode. At this stage, all that was involved were frightened and resentful mutterings. Things would have to get much worse for the utterly cowed population to even contemplate rebellion.

Mindaug knew that the voivode of Odessa poorly understood his overlord. He thought Jagiellon was merely a cruel and monomaniacal man who could possibly be reasoned with.

He would learn the truth, soon enough. And, unlike Mindaug, he would not have had the perspicacity to organize a means of escape before the demon's jaws closed on him.

Mindaug moved to the shelves to seek another book. All things considered, as vile a creature as she was, working for Countess Elizabeth was considerably safer than working for Chernobog. She was not actually a demon herself, after all. Simply someone who suffered from the delusion that she could trade with the greatest of demons and come out ahead on the deal.

❀　　❀　　❀

Jagiellon had had reports, but he preferred to see things for himself. So, in a supply tent in Odessa, a blank-eyed man roused himself from where he lay, rather uncomfortably. He was cold and stiff and walked, as a result, with difficulty and with a jerky and unsteady gait. No one spoke to him as Chernobog looked around the shipyard. They knew the nature of the blank-eyed man.

Neither Jagiellon nor Chernobog knew very much about shipbuilding. Jagiellon had never chosen to interest himself in such mundane tasks before he encountered Chernobog. Ships such as these that plied oceans of water did not occur in Chernobog's normal realm. However, both of them could recognize the signs of industry. There was plenty of that. Rigging and ratlines were being strung on some of the vessels already. Others were still being clad with their outer planking. That ran to plan, too: if they were going to be forced to wait for another season, they may as well build more vessels.

Chernobog left the human-vessel right there. Someone would take it back to the tent. Instead he occupied the body of a cavalry commander and looked out onto the vast parade ground. Jagiellon kept a far closer grasp on military matters than commercial ones.

Levies from across the lands that gave fealty to Grand Duke Jagiellon were engaged in drill. The levies came from several linguistic groups. Many of them were hereditary enemies. To a greater or lesser extent the Black Brain managed and controlled their officers. That required a vast capacity. But Chernobog had that, even if he sometimes poorly understood human soldiers' abilities and limitations.

The army being readied for the round ships—some forty thousand men, now—was but a small portion of the force that Jagiellon was mustering. He would have to strike in the north and the center, once he held the gate to the Mediterranean. For the last few years he had kept up a slow war of attrition, without major attacks, while building more reserves. He'd learned that it would take large numbers to bring down the Holy Roman Empire, given the capabilities of its current ruler.

This time they would feint north. The war-hardened Empire, led by the Knights of the Holy Trinity, would stop that attack, as they had many others. But the attack would be merely a diversion. Jagiellon thought the underbelly of Europe was soft and unprepared. With any luck, Emeric of Hungary would attempt to take advantage and attack either Italy or the Holy Roman Empire—not realizing that this would leave him vulnerable on his own eastern borders. Jagiellon would settle for a bridgehead into the heart of Europe through Hungary. The part of Jagiellon that was the Black Brain, Chernobog, cared little for these geographical conquests. But they were physical prizes which were not without value in the spiritual world. And besides, pouring across the northern Carpathians from the lands of the Kievan Rus would allow Chernobog to seize the physical earthly holdings of an old enemy, Elizabeth Bartholdy. There was a certain satisfaction in that.

Chapter 30

The sun kisses the high places, the cold roost of eagles and fugitives, before it shines upon the rest of the world. In the pale clarity of dawn, Vlad gazed out from the craggy edge above their small camp, loving the sheer limitless immensity of the folded shadowlands below. It had frightened him a little at first. Now he would die before he let anyone shut him away again. For a brief while his soul was at peace, in the vast tranquility of the place, away from the turmoil of conflicting desires and a world he understood poorly.

Could death somehow be like this? An endless, quiet, shadowy country?

The sun climbed slowly higher, becoming harsher and stronger, and people began to stir. They'd camped in a picturesque spot, in a small dell beneath a gray scree, with a craggy peak above it. To the right on the edge of the scree, a col led into another valley and deeper into the mountains.

Far, far below, Vlad's eye was caught by a flash of light. Vlad had discovered that he had very keen eyesight. He peered intently now, wishing that he had one of those telescope devices. Staring, his eyes picked up movements eventually. A column of horses, working their way up one of the valleys. Soon they would be hidden behind the ridge line as the valley turned away in its meandering.

Vlad knew all too well that that valley would eventually bring the horsemen to their camp. And it was very unlikely that it was a friendly column of several hundred horsemen.

He made his way quickly back to his camp. It was a very makeshift camp, tents constructed from a few ragged tarpaulins, and some lean-tos set around several cook fires, one of which was being blown into life.

"Best leave that," said Vlad. "The Hungarians are coming. I have seen a column of them heading up our valley. Wake everybody. No shouting," he added, seeing the startled fire-maker take a deep breath to do just that.

A few minutes later, two of the younger boys were leading the horses up to the col while those for whom there were no mounts began to slither and scramble over the broken cliff and down into the next valley. That left Vlad and twenty-one men waiting nervously amongst the top edge of the broken boulder scree near the col.

When he had planned the last ambush he had been filled with a kind of rash fury that expressed itself in cold-blooded, calculated killing. Now, he was just afraid. How had they found him here? The wait seemed interminable. He wished, desperately, that he had the experience, or that someone else here with him that knew what to do.

At last, a pair of troopers appeared at the foot of

the little mountain dell they had used for their camp. They were moving cautiously and halted their horses when they saw the rough tents. They turned, quietly, to ride away.

And then, while he was still holding his breath, Vlad saw it all come apart. Someone decided to shoot one of the scouts. He hadn't actually told them not to . . .

It was good shooting, all things considered. The one scout gave a gurgling scream as the arrow hit him on the breastplate and ricocheted upward, striking just under the jaw. His companion did not wait. He put his spurs to his steed and got away, as less well aimed arrows clattered impotently on the rocks, spearing the thin soil. Vlad heard a horn being sounded. And then, something worse—the sound of screaming from the valley behind them, where those without horses had fled.

Vlad simply did not know what to do. The Hungarians had obviously another column of horse coming up to take them from behind. Vlad's men were outnumbered, and would have been surrounded. Before Vlad could take a decision—something his little army were looking for him to do—the Hungarians came sweeping into the dell, lances out.

"Loose!" someone yelled. A ragged volley of arrows fell among the Hungarian knights, busy spearing canvas and flattening lean-tos. The knights were heavily armored, the horses less so. Some horses screamed. A few men fell, but the rest were now charging at the scree slope. Vlad's makeshift troops were no match for them. A handful loosed again, but most of them were scrambling for the col. Vlad stood up. He was damned, he decided, if he would flee merely to run into the second column. He would die here, and die free.

Seeing him stand his ground with a sword in his hand steadied three or four of his men who had not yet started to run. They began firing more arrows, yelling to their companions to come back and aid them.

Then, the invincible and terrifying Magyar charge slowed. It was not the pinprick of the few light arrows that affected them. Rather it was the utter folly of trying to gallop a heavy horse up a steep loose scree slope. The earlier flight of Vlad's men had started some rocks rolling down. A cascade of boulders knocked one knight from his horse.

Vlad stretched out his arms. "Push rocks, men!"

A heavy horse just does not change course or stop easily, even on a steep slope of loose rocks. Still, the charge—which had seemed so terrifying and unstoppable—scattered and broke up, as the Magyars tried to save themselves and their steeds. The scree, long undisturbed and appearing fairly stable as a result, had deceived the flatland knights. Perhaps they had intended to merely caracole and retreat, but now, in the sliding and rolling rocks and screaming men and horses, the order was lost. The booming of their pistols had not helped either.

In the dust and chaos Vlad knew only one thing: somehow luck had favored them. But what he should do next was a mystery to him.

The decision was taken out of his hands by someone tugging at his sleeve. "Sire, they are coming up from behind!"

Vlad took a deep breath. One of the reasons they had chosen this little dell as a campsite was that that it had had two valleys for them to flee down. The idea that they might need three had never occurred to him. Plainly someone had pinpointed their campsite exactly, and planned accordingly.

"To the horses, men!" They scrambled over to the col. The man who had warned him had a steaming horse. Vlad read into this that he had ridden someway down the valley before catching sight of the other group of Hungarians, advancing up that escape route. Vlad had heard the screams earlier, but he had to hope that there would still be a way clear. Well, there obviously wasn't.

"Mount up!" he said. "We are going back over. We will at least die like men."

They walked their horses above the scree and then down along the clear steep slope next to the cliff where Vlad had watched the sunrise—the route that the boys leading the horses had taken earlier. They were able to ride down, into the dust and shouting. It was very hard to tell quite what was happening down here. Vlad's men were no battle-hardened warriors. They were unarmored and poorly armed. True, most of the men had bows. But none of them could shoot from the saddle. So they had to resort to boar spears, a few pitchforks, rusty old swords—relics taken from above fireplaces—and even a few men who had nothing more than clubs, and axes intended for firewood.

The Magyars should have butchered them. Almost certainly the Magyar would have butchered them, had they come with a little advance notice, and not in the wake of the scree slide. By the time that it occurred to Vlad that in the books he had read, warriors gave a battle cry on charging, it was almost too late to do so. It was certainly too late to think of anything particularly inspiring. He settled for his own name.

It echoed hollowly, mockingly weak to his own ears. But that was obviously not how it sounded to his small band of followers. "Drac!" they yelled in chorus.

There were barely twenty of them left. Looking back to see if he was being followed, Vlad realized that the flanking party of Magyar had reached the col behind them. His pitiful little force was caught between two sets of enemies. But it was too late. The little ragtag group of rebels, all that remained of his army, had begun their doomed charge. All he could do was to wave his sword—he had no idea how to use it from the saddle—and race towards the chaos that had been their campsite.

At the top of the slope someone else yelled, "Charge!" And, "He must be taken alive!"

Vlad heard that quite clearly. It was the last thing he remembered hearing clearly for the next few minutes.

If there was one thing more stupid than trying to charge up a scree slope, it had to be charging down one. It was undoubtably the shortest way down, and in the dust and perhaps in the haste of the moment it might have seemed a good idea.

Vlad had no time to think of his enemy's logic. He was hacking at an armored man. This was not about swordsmanship. This was about survival. A pitchfork in the neck assisted his foe's fall. And somehow he was through to the other side of the Magyar troopers, with nothing but the trail they had followed up here in front of him, and the bulk of his force intact.

Emeric had some thirty-three battered men paraded in front of him. They were all that remained of a once-proud troop of a hundred and twenty that had set off on a well-planned dawn raid on the encampment of Vlad, Prince of Valahia.

"I think," he said, smiling nastily at his great aunt's beautiful features, "that you had better leave military matters me, Countess. I came expecting to find things in good order. Instead I find you have countermanded my instructions and made things a great deal worse. I did have my doubts. You are very skilled . . . in other areas."

He did not say that he had come because one of the captains whom he had seconded to her had sent a letter to his commanding officer, who had in turn carried it to the king. Emeric might need the man in the future. Besides, he thought it wise to let her think that he had guessed. Actually, the disaster had come as a rude shock to him. She was usually so devastatingly efficient.

She looked down her nose at him. "The operation was well planned. Your troops are inadequate. They were late. They should have arrived simultaneously at dawn."

He wondered if she realized that she had just reprieved them from drastic punishment. "Let us hear what they have to say," he said. He pointed to a trooper. "You. Explain."

The man was gray and shaking. But he was no coward, Emeric had to admit. "Sire. It was steeper than we realized. It took us much longer than we thought. Captain Genorgi had us out at midnight, riding up. We should have been in position hours before dawn. Everyone thought we would be, but we lost the moonlight in the valley. It was pitch dark and very rough going. We had to lead the horses."

"If you'd lamed my horses in that I would have had you flayed. But surely it had been scouted?"

The trooper nodded. "It's rough terrain, Sire, but not that bad in daylight. We just didn't realize that it was an ambush. A trap."

"And scouts?" asked the king.

"We had some Croats watching the camp from the other ridge, Sire. But they could only see fires. They didn't realize that the fires were a decoy. We'd have all been killed if our scouts hadn't sounded the warning. I was coming up the second valley. We killed some of their infantry. But when we heard the fighting, Captain Genorgi told us to leave hunting them and push on for the gap."

"And then?"

"We heard them massacring Lieutenant Mascaru's men when we got to the top. There were hundreds of them, Sire. Not just the forty peasants without weapons or training like we'd been told. All yelling 'Drac!' and cutting our men to pieces. Captain Genorgi gave the order to charge, and we rode to the rescue. But it was a trap. Prince Vlad... He's not human, Sire. He's a demon. He made the slope give way under us. I was lucky to get out alive."

"This may be temporary," said Emeric, and then remembered that he was not punishing them. "You did well. Now. Return to the ranks. I want to speak to someone who was with the other column."

The trooper was plainly unable to believe his fortune. He bowed and retreated.

"Well?" said Emeric. "Were there no survivors of Lieutenant Mascaru's column?"

Where had Vlad found a general with this level

of military expertise? Where had he found weaponry, knights, or at least cavalry? Emeric suspected treachery, and a far better woven plot that he had guessed at.

Nervously a man with a bandaged head came forward. "Me, Sire."

Emeric looked at him. A big man, but plainly shaken by the military disaster. So they should be. They were among his best. "And how many knights did they have?"

"More than us, Sire. A hundred at least. They took us in the flank out of the dust."

"And who commanded them? I need some ideas. Boyars have families." He smiled thinly.

The soldier looked nervous. "Sire, I think it was Prince Vlad himself. They were all yelling for him, or at least all yelling 'Drac!' That's what they call him. He's a huge man all in black clothes, black hair and a white face, and you can't kill him. I shot him at the top of the slope, but he didn't die. Then in the melee he knocked me out of the saddle just with his gaze. His eyes . . ."

The man shuddered. "I'll swear our swords barely touched." The soldier realized what he was saying, shut his eyes, and began to mumble a prayer.

It was all Emeric could do not to kill the idiot on the spot. This was exactly what he did not need. The Magyars prided themselves in the belief that they were the finest heavy cavalry in the world—as Emeric himself did. The accursed Knights of the Holy Trinity used magic, that was all. And now, here was an upstart little princeling who had shaken the confidence of his finest, shaken the very foundations of his kingdom. A man who was, it appeared, rapidly building a more terrible reputation than he himself enjoyed.

In a shallow cave that was barely more than an overhang, Vlad and his fourteen surviving men neither looked nor felt terrifying. They felt alive... but only just. Of the fourteen, only eight were not walking wounded. They were all still stunned by their first real combat, and the sheer ferocity of it all. Yes, they had escaped. Some said they had seen Magyar butcher Magyar in the chaos of rolling rocks and dust. It appeared that those in the dell had taken their rescuers—those that survived the scree slide—as yet more attackers. Whatever happened, Vlad's men had escaped with their lives—those who had not paid with theirs. But they had lost almost all of their food and the better part of their number.

Yet, somehow, Vlad's men regarded him as a hero. Vlad did not know what to make of this, but it filled him with shame. Still, he had learned one thing. Watchers were now posted. And there were several ways to flee carefully scouted. But he did not know quite what to do next.

The one thing he did not expect was for his watchers to be calling him excitedly, happily. He came to look. A sense of some relief washed over him. He recognized at least three of the men leading a party of perhaps fifty others. Not soldiers, or at least certainly not recognizable as such. There were a number of pack ponies, a few donkeys, and most of the men were carrying large bundles.

He tried to place where the three had been during that disastrous encounter. One of them, still with a horse, had been part of that terrible charge. The other two, one now leading a pack pony, had definitely been

with the group that had scrambled off on foot. Vlad
had thought them all killed. To his relief, he realized
that some of them must have got away.

That was a weight off his conscience. Perhaps generals with thousands at their beck and call felt little
for casualties. To Vlad, these men were still precious
companions. Yes, they were peasants and yeomen
farmers. But they were all he had. And they'd been
true to him.

He wished that he could make contact, somehow,
with Countess Elizabeth. She would have nobles
skilled in the art of war—something he knew far too
little of—willing to join and help him. She plainly was
a loyal subject, a vassal ruling Caedonia, one of his
cities, even if she was also a vassal of King Emeric.

He was delighted to see the other survivors. And
totally unprepared for the adulation of those who
accompanied them.

"Drac!" People bowed and cheered. "Bless you,
Prince!" They crowded round, incredulous and plainly
in awe.

Vlad smiled worriedly as he squeezed the shoulders
of one the men who had fled on foot. "Were there
any other survivors?"

"Some others, I think. We were scattered, Prince.
But thanks to you, some of us escaped when you taught
the Magyars a lesson. They fled like whipped dogs."

Vlad found himself so taken aback by this interpretation of events, that he was at a loss as to what
to say. The world inside the walls of his tower had ill
prepared him for the realities outside. That much he
understood. But did life have to be so illogical and
confusing? He had lost most of his men, had had

to flee their camp; had, in fact, barely survived. To Vlad's logical mind, that did not make him the sort of beacon to whom men would rally. Yet here they were, with more men than he'd lost, congratulating him on his victory!

It made no sense. Could they not see that he and a bare handful of men were huddling in a cave in the mountains?

"The story is spreading across the country, lord. Many thousands will answer your call now."

Bit by bit, as he spoke to his new recruits, Vlad began to understand. In the chaos some of the Magyars had fled, too. Vlad knew little about war, and of how King Emeric conducted it. But this much he did know: there was only one penalty for desertion—execution. On the other hand, even Vlad knew that Emeric was fond of painful deaths for those who had failed him. Desertion might have seemed a sensible option to some of those soldiers. It might be dishonorable and disloyal, but, for the second sons and minor nobility who made up the rank-and-file of King Emeric's elite, it might also have been better than returning and admitting defeat.

So. Desertion, and not just the scree slope, confusion and the few casualties that he and his men had been able to inflict, had made the difference—and painted a different picture of the battle. Very few of the survivors were in the two columns returning to face the penalties that their commanders, or worse, their king, might inflict upon them. But those who had chosen the course of honor, it would seem . . .

Had not chosen the course of veracity. They had vastly exaggerated the size of the force they had faced.

These new recruits earnestly believed that Vlad had inflicted a stunning military defeat onto the hated occupiers. Also, that he commanded a large force, and that he was a military genius. Their own eyes soon persuaded them that Vlad had no vast force. However, that just reinforced the belief that he was the greatest military commander that had ever breathed, to be able to inflict such a crushing defeat on superior numbers.

Besides, they wanted to believe. They would not let common sense stand in the way of that.

Vlad had little enough silver, very few horses, scant rations, and no arms. He did have, however, twice the army he'd had before. And there were more men on their way, apparently. Vlad wished desperately for wiser and more experienced counsel. He wished he knew how to make contact with the countess, or even the gypsies. He could talk to them. But he was wise enough to know that he could not truly take these people into his confidence. He needed them. And, even if their belief was false, he needed them to believe in him. So he walked off up the bare mountainside, to a place that he could sit alone and think. And pray. Father Tedesco had said that God would provide answers. Right now, those seemed to be avoiding him.

He would just have to do his best on his own, knowing almost nothing. Whatever that best was, it would have to include finding a larger camp and posting sentries. He had read of sentries. In a way experienced them, in the shape of the guards that had watched his tower. He just was not too sure of the exact details—such as how many of them, and what they should do, and for how long they should do it.

He walked back down to the encampment. It was, to his meticulous eye, a mess. Of course, it had been a mess previously, but then, as desperate fugitives organization had seemed a little futile. He cleared his throat. "Have we any men here," he said loudly, instantly stilling dozens of conversations, "who have any military experience?" He hoped he could find at least one common soldier from whom he could—without betraying too much of his own ignorance—get the details of how to set out sentries.

He got some seven men. And four of them, all comrades, were former sergeants from one of the levies that Emeric had raised in Valahia. "I need sentries posted, I need a better camp—this one is poorly ordered, and I need to train these men," Vlad began, wondering—as he knew little of how the military actually worked, if such men would know anything of what he needed. Perhaps they would have some ideas from watching their own officers.

They saluted. And turned away . . . But he had not yet finished speaking to them . . .

They seem to believe he had, however. And moreover they seemed to assume that he had ordered them to arrange these matters. To his amazement, Vlad discovered that they seemed to know precisely what to do. He watched them, covertly, determined to learn what to do next time. After a while he wryly concluded that the correct method was probably to tell several sergeants that you perceived a problem. Even if this was not quite the right way, and Vlad did not know if it was or not, it had certainly worked extremely well.

The cave with its handful of desperate survivors

transformed—at an almost magical speed—into a military encampment. The two sergeants drilling the newly formed squads might think that they resembled hopeless black beetles . . . and other fascinating and bizarre things, many of which Vlad had never heard of before, but suddenly they began to resemble fighting men. And strangely, despite the abuse heaped on their heads, they appeared proud, even if they were merely armed with staffs of green ash.

It left Vlad free to ponder other important questions, and to wonder if perhaps he should tell the sergeants about those, too—and how he could do so without shattering their confidence in him. He could hardly say, "Well, what do I do next?"

The one thing he was sure of was that they could not stay in one place for long. If the Hungarians had found and nearly destroyed them once, they would do so again. The others could delude themselves about his military genius, but Vlad had none, and he knew it. All he had was a logical, and very precise and tidy mind.

Chapter 31

Erik had noticed that the Ilkhan hunkered down on their haunches to talk. So he did the same next to the girl and her brother. Struggling to express himself in a language he barely had a handle on, he gestured quite a lot. "I have given the order. A thing to carry him on will be made for the boy. We have to travel. We look after you."

She stared at him, wide eyed. And responded with a high-speed chatter of which he understood only one word in three. It was not easy to string those words into anything coherent. How did he say "slow down?" The best he could manage was "do not gallop."

She looked at him, puzzled. And then started to laugh. That hadn't been quite the reaction he'd been looking for, but she did have one of those infectious laughs.

He saw that the pestilential horseboy had gotten back. "You. David. Come help to translate. And none of your silly tricks."

❀   ❀   ❀

Bortai had wondered just what she would do next. There was a little church and village up the slope. But it would offer at best temporary shelter. Given the numbers that now hunted for them, such a little village could not protect them, even were its people willing. And the foreign knight had said that Kildai should not ride any further.

She was rather puzzled when the tall blond foreign knight came and squatted next to them as if he were from the steppes himself. His accent was as strange as his words were limited. But there was no mistaking the kindness behind the words. It made her eyelids prick with tears, tears that she was determined not to show. He gave orders. He must command these mercenaries. It was odd that Ilkhan should resort to using a mercenary escort. But she could think of no other reason for these knights to be accompanying a tarkhan's party. Given the fact that they were coming from the west, either the Ilkhan had vastly increased their territories, or these knights had been hired to see them across lands not under Mongol control, lands where the locals were so ignorant that they would dare to attack a Mongol envoy. It was unlikely that either the Illyrians or Bulgars would have dreamed of it; they had had contact with the Golden Horde. But perhaps there were other tribes and kingdoms farther west with less respect. The heyday of Mongol power, Bortai knew, had passed.

Nevertheless, they were still a force to be reckoned with.

Then she got the actual meaning of what he was trying to say. He had ordered a litter to be made for them to carry Kildai in. And he made no mention of consulting the tarkhan. Well, perhaps that was just his lack of skill at her language.

She was a princess of the Hawk clan and she recognized his honorable conduct. He might be a foreigner, a sell-sword, but his behavior was far better than that manifested recently by many Mongols. Her reply, a little embarrassed, was perhaps voiced faster than it would otherwise have been.

By his puzzled look, she realized that she must be speaking too fast. And then he told her to stop galloping. It was so earnestly said that she had to laugh. She was behaving like a hysterical girl, and part of her was embarrassed by her own reaction.

He did smile when she laughed, though.

David looked at the Mongol woman. He was a Jerusalem-born thief. He had lived under the shadow of the Ilkhan all of his life. He was good at spotting details. Her clothing might be travel-stained, and torn, but it had been some of the finest weave. Her accent and tone reflected the same reality. This was one of their highborn, the kind that he avoided with as much care as possible. One step out of line and there would be no leniency. His first reaction was that he ought to back off and get lost. But he had learned by now that Erik's orders were to be obeyed, so he came forward and bowed very low, no matter how much his feet wanted to run in the other direction.

"She doesn't seem to understand what I'm trying to say," said Erik. "Explain to her that I'm having a stretcher made. I'll detail a few men to carry the boy. He'll get jolted around much less like that. We really need a well-sprung cart, but that doesn't seem possible. Tell her we'll get her back to her clan. I daresay somebody will be pleased to see her. The two of them seem to be good, ordinary people."

Unholy glee stirred in David's breast. Erik plainly did not realize that this was a high-ranking woman. Direct tricks, like the one that had nearly had him killed in the terrible criminal haven Corfu, were out. But he could certainly let the knight talk himself into a tricky position. And he would have grounds to claim complete innocence! Oh, bliss. It would serve them right for bringing him so far from Jerusalem. And it would be funny.

He would have to be careful, though. Stay close to the exact meaning. But Erik was going to be very embarrassed when it turned out that this was a very high muckety-muck, and he'd been treating her as if she were a commoner. Mind you, David had noticed that the *Ritter* treated Prince Manfred in much the same fashion. He knew that Erik was no noble. He'd asked Kari. But while he was at it he could tell her that Erik was of great rank. That meant a lot among the Ilkhan Mongol.

And then David realized that she was looking at him very strangely. Well, one of his ancestors somewhere had been one of the conquerors. He did have the eyes. In Jerusalem that was not uncommon. Looking like a Mongol had not stopped the local constabulary from watching him, unfortunately. He didn't have the forelock. That was strictly forbidden to lesser people, at least among the Ilkhan.

"Lady," he said in a tone of deep respect, "my master, the noble *Ritter* Erik Hakkonsen, says that he has ordered them to make a litter to carry your brother."

"I understood that." She looked at him strangely again. "How old are you?"

David wondered what on earth set her off on this tangent? What did it have to do with her? He was a little small perhaps. But he would swear that he had grown a good hand since leaving Jerusalem. His breeches bore testimony to that. "I am sixteen, lady."

"You look to be a little younger."

Well, he could be. Birthdays were not as religiously observed as they might be. He simply knew that he'd been born some time around the ascension of the new Ilkhan. But it was not a comment he appreciated.

"Sixteen," he repeated firmly.

"Tell your master that we appreciate his kindness. But we do not need to accept such charity."

"It is best for the boy," said Erik in his best Mongol, putting a neat end to David's plans for a flowery and mildly insulting translation. "We honor our promises."

Bortai had wrestled with the best. It was expected of a noble Mongol lady. Seldom, however had she been thrown as hard as this, and then as neatly pinned. First, a boy who could be Kildai's twin brother— dressed like a peasant. Could she possibly have got things wrong? It had been a few years since there had been much contact between the Golden Horde and the Ilkhan. But there was almost no imaginable way that the Ilkhan would be subservient to these Franks. If she recalled her histories correctly, the Franks had been among the allies of the Ilkhan against the Baitini. They had fallen out over one of the battles, where the Franks and their allies had failed, and the Ilkhan had been defeated. When the Ilkhan returned in force, the Franks too had been evicted from their holdings in Asia Minor. But that was all centuries ago. It still did not explain what this boy who was by all appearances as much of a son of the Hawk clan as Kildai, was doing as a serf. And, to make things even more difficult she was afraid that what this Erik said was true: she had to do what was best for Kildai.

Then the ridiculous side of it struck her. This foreign knight had proposed marriage to her. And in the jest of it all, she had accepted. And now he was saying that he honored his promises.

"Why does she keep laughing at me?" asked Erik plaintively.

Just at that point, a pair of men carrying a lance with the blue truce flag emerged from the woods on the far side of the braided stream. Erik looked up. "Hell's teeth," he said. "I'd better mount up and see what is going on. David, find Kari. I'm going to need someone else who is not in armor to help carry. In fact you will need at least four of them, to take it in shifts. Get Falkenberg to sort it out."

The boy ran off. He even ran like Kildai, Bortai noticed. The armored Erik got into the saddle with graceful ease and cantered off. Bortai was left sitting next to her brother. She had spent much of her life telling others what to do. Her mother had died in childbirth when she was just eleven. Much of Kildai's rearing had fallen on her shoulders. Yes, there had been many other older women to help with the practical day-to-day tasks, and her aunts had seen to her own very traditional upbringing... But she was still her mother's daughter. She had the final responsibility. She was accustomed to a role in the clan decisions. Now she watched as others dealt with their fate. She really did not like it. She could see no easy way of changing the situation, but it irked her.

Erik rode forward, escorting one of the Mongols, not Tulkun, whom he was developing something of a friendship with, but one of the others, to meet the Golden Horde envoy on a gravel bank in the middle of the braided stream. Erik could not really follow the entire discussion between the men. He did get some of the formalities, and some references to "Franks." At length the Golden Horde man saluted respectfully, and turned his pony and rode away back into the woods on the opposite side of the stream. Erik wished that he knew exactly what was going to happen—but it did not appear too threatening. This was something of a relief. By the way they rode, he really had a feeling they'd be tough opponents, especially on broken terrain.

A little later a party of four reappeared, still carrying the truce lance and Erik found himself riding out again. The new party from the Golden Horde was headed by a harder-faced individual, and as was protocol, two knights and two of the Ilkhan men rode out to meet them. This time Erik's party included Tulkun. Once again, Erik had great difficulty in following what was obviously a very polite. . . . but more insistent discussion. The one word that seemed to be being repeated quite often was "Bortai" with several gestures.

Tulkun held out his hands, pointed to Erik with

a thumb, and, grinning like a cheerful bear, sounded off at great length. The hard-faced individual peered at Erik then spouted at some more length. The only word Erik understood was "foreigner."

Tulkun replied. This time the only word Erik got was envoy. At least that's what he thought it meant.

The four turned and rode off again. "What was all that about?" demanded Von Gherens. "Are you selling them Erik?"

Tulkun grinned. "They want young lady from Hawk clan. I explain she under clan protection of him. Officer cross. Try to say that envoy-truce does not apply to foreigners. I have to explain to him that even our Tarkhan is not Mongol, but still under protection of Ilkhan. There is nothing they can do. But he does not like it." That idea plainly amused the rotund Mongol. They did seem to like laughing at these sort of things, Erik noted.

A further half hour later a plainly still more senior commander came down—amid worrying reports from the scouts that there were riders moving in the forest on the far side of the river, spreading out as if to flank them.

This time the tarkhan himself rode forward to treat with them. Erik would have loved to know just what he said, but he told the escort to back off. It must have been pretty impressive and effective however. He rode back smiling calmly. "They will escort us to the camp of the orkhan. Prepare to ride."

Bortai found herself being carried along by the tide of events. It was not entirely a bad direction to be carried in, but it would require care and careful steering to survive. She wondered just how deep the honor of her new protector ran. She got the feeling that it might be very deep indeed, despite his being a foreigner. On the other hand the honor of Gatu Orkhan could hardly be very much shallower than it already was. She could expect treachery and they would be heading back into the heartland of his support. It would also take them closer to her own people. Somewhere, somehow, she must seize the opportune moment to rejoin their clan. If Kildai recovered enough for them to ride it might be possible. Her thoughts also turned to the possibilities of using this serf David. The sight of him in the saddle would certainly upset rumors that Kildai was dead—if she could stop Kildai being seen by any others, while he was carried on litter.

And how was she to do that? She noticed the boy, David, hanging around as two of the foreign knights loaded Kildai gently onto a stretcher made from two strong poles and a piece of canvas. She called him over. He was visibly nervous. Good. "I do not know how to tell you this, boy, but do you own a hood? Something to hide or change your face perhaps?"

He looked even more alarmed. "I have a hooded cloak, great lady." He paused. Then curiosity and fear got the better of him. "Why?"

"You look like someone. Someone they would like to catch over there," she pointed across the ridge.

He looked very much as if he want to turn and run right then. "But I have never ever been there before."

"Yes, but you look very much like someone that the Raven clan want dead. I would wear the hooded cloak and keep out of sight as much as possible."

He bowed hastily and ran off. Bortai saw him rummaging in a pack a little later.

The *Ritter* Erik came back from the third parlay. He too bowed, but it was an easy, friendly bow. He was plainly unaware of her status, or else so highborn himself that he made little or nothing of it. "We explain you part of my clan. Protection of Tarkhan," he said in his awkward Mongol.

Bortai was uncertain quite whether he meant that they were under the protection of the envoy, or that he was there to protect the envoy. But whichever one it was, it plainly extended to providing for them. "I have asked *Ritter* Von Stael to see that you and your man are brought some food and drink. While we find out quite what is happening. Tulkun believes it will be no problem."

Bortai believed that at least on the surface General Okagu of the Raven clan would have to go along with the pretense that she and Kildai were protected. She was also sure that they would make a serious attempt to murder them. Of course, it would all be done under the cover of a polite fiction—if they were killed, some "renegade" would be caught and executed, and humble apologies conveyed. The killing would never happen in the public eye. But they would watch like a lynx in the forest, stalking a doe with a fawn, looking for the slightest opportunity to strike. She was sure right now that several of Okagu's officers were pointing out that at least they knew where she was now, and would be able to find a suitable opportunity somewhere. She would have to be as wary as that lynx-stalked doe. And when they got the chance, run for it.

She was also surprised by the thoughtfulness of

her accidental protector. She had seen that he was a very busy commander, and yet he had found the time to consider their needs. She'd noted that he had ordered scouts deployed both up and down stream, and on a high point behind them, as well as forming the knights up in the defensive square. For a barbarian, he was a good orkhan.

A little later, as she had expected, an honor guard rode down. Bortai found herself moving off at a walk, in the tail end of the column. Next to her two knights carried Kildai. His eyes were open again. He seemed, in her judgment, to be little less confused this time. He had at least called her by her own name. And while she was in sight he seemed content to lie still.

Erik rode close to Manfred. Yes, they were all in full armor. Yes, his charge was in the midst of a body of some of the finest knights in Christendom, but they were not *in* Christendom. This was a wilder, wider world. Nor had Erik been entirely comforted by the behavior of the Golden Horde Mongol. True, he had snatched a piece of their prey from their jaws. But surely that had been just a piece of petty inter-clan warfare? A set piece of triumphalism to hold one of the women of another clan for ransom? Or did things go deeper than that?

"Why are you so edgy?" asked Manfred.

"Something is not right about this crew," said Erik. "Yes, I know we didn't have the most auspicious start. But I talked to Tulkun—the short plump one. He seemed to think that it was just a bit of clan rivalry. The Hawk clan claim descent from Chinngis Khan. They're a bit holier than thou, or rather, more Mongol than thou, and it would be a big coup to capture part of the clan. But the girl seemed to think they'd kill her. She should know, surely. Tulkun thought it very funny, but he doesn't know these people and they're behaving more like bears with sore teeth."

Manfred grinned. "You spend your whole life looking for disasters, Erik. Our envoy fellows seems cheerful enough."

Erik grimaced. "It is always best to plan for disaster. Then when disaster happens, you can see how wrong your plans were."

Manfred shook his head. "In my experience you plan really well, Erik. It's just that usually the wrong disaster strikes."

"Yes . . . well. But the girl worries me. There is something not quite right about all of this."

"Nice looker," said Manfred. "And there is a charming novelty in seeing one of them laughing at you, instead of making calves-eyes at you. What did Falkenberg say about the boy?"

Erik shrugged. "From what we can work out, the kid had been unconscious for nearly three days before he started coming around. There is a possibility the spine is damaged but . . . well, by the way he's been jolted about—if it were damaged it'd be likely he'd be paralyzed. And his sister says he's moving his arms and legs. It's too early to tell. If a casualty stays in a coma for more than a week—things don't look good. Falkenberg thinks he's got a good chance of recovery. Of course keeping him still for a week or two would be best. But people with head injuries usually recover quite fast—especially youngsters—when they start to recover."

They had reached the ridge-top by this stage. "Well. The lands of the Golden Horde," said Manfred. "Funny they don't look particularly different from the other side."

"They do slope away to softer lands, by the looks of it," said Erik. "Anyway, it's the people, not the terrain, that shape a land."

Tulkun shouldered his horse up to them. "Lady say she have something to tell you. Stop knights sweating so much."

Erik looked around warily. "I better go and see what it is, Manfred."

"If you must," said Manfred. "Carrying stretchers on foot is good for them. Just as long as you don't want me to do it."

So Erik rode back—to where, as Tulkun had correctly put it, the knights were sweating along, carrying the boy. It was not that the lad was that heavy, but it was already bidding to be a warm day.

Erik greeted her, his tongue almost tricking him into the "tortoise" again. It was just close enough to make the accidental transposition easy. She obviously caught it, because she suppressed a laugh but not the dimpling of the cheeks. "I wanted to say I have a cart hidden down there. Maybe even an ox, still."

That would please the knights, even if it would probably jolt about more. Erik was sweating in his armor. Actually the only person who seemed to be feeling cold was the horse-boy. He was wearing an old hooded cloak Kari had given him. It was a good bit too large for him. Erik wondered if the boy was sickening for something.

Chapter 32

Across Europe there are places where old stones remain in cleared places. Moss grows on other rocks and even on the trees. Not on these stones.

Particularly not on the stones standing in their ancient ranks here. This was not a great or impressive circle; the stones were small and worn. Irregular. If it had not been for the lack of moss, they might just have been a random arrangement of rocks, not at all unusual for these mountains.

Humans often made the error of thinking there were merely two intelligences that shared this world: those who were human and those who were not. Of course, in reality, it was infinitely more complex than that. To begin with, there were facets of reality that mere flesh and blood rarely perceived, much less walked in.

But even on the earth shared with ordinary mortal men...other creatures, not precisely "mortal," walked. Some walked in darkness, others in light. Some were cloaked in flesh, others were less defined by the material world. Here of course, in her dark green heart, the wood sang ancient songs too. The forest was neither benevolent nor even truly understanding of animal life. It used and survived it, and sang slow songs of wood, water, wind and stone.

And blood.

Blood could bind.

Green cool eyes stared from the forest shadows at the glade and the ancient stones. Their blood was blue. There were others among the trees, further back, not wishing to be seen. It was twilight—a time when those of the day were prepared to meet the night creatures. And they had all come—or at least many of them. There were those who had chosen their own path and made their own arrangements with powers, such as the Vila. But the others... From hollow places in the hills, from the lakes and the streams, they came. Some would come forward when the syzygy called. Others would not.

The wolf-kind came to honor their side of the bargain, bringing the young ones to see and be seen, to receive the blessing and the binding of the forest, of the water and of the stone. Of all those who gave allegiance to the forest that once stretched from shore to shore before the ice-time... and again after, while men still huddled fearfully on the edges.

Men had grown more numerous and bolder since then.

The forest and its ancient denizens had given way. Everywhere, but here.

With a hiss the dragon-headed wyverns entered the glade. They were still of an age when every new thing was a delight—and possibly edible. Angelo and his kin stayed back, as was their right, on the north side of the circle. They were still. The time for howling was not yet.

There was no wind, but the dark forest moved and groaned.

Two sets of red eyes looked out at it. Eyes that burned like coals.

Utterly heedless of the magic and the dignity of the occasion, the two engaged in rough and tumble and then bounced around. The old ones looked on. There were few young ones anywhere anymore. These two had vast license, and both of them knew it.

They tasted the rocks, too.

The forest creaked, almost as if it was clicking its tongue in disapproval.

"The Dragon comes. They know it," said Angelo.

"But will he come here?" asked Radu.

"And then there is the question of blood," said Grigori, his long red tongue lolling.

Angelo sighed. "Go and chase down a buck or something. How do I know? How do any of us know? He will do what he will do. That, too, is in the compact."

"It's in his blood," said Radu.

"But will his blood be in it?" asked Angelo, looking at the shadows in the trees.

Chapter 33

In his throne room in Vilnius, that which sat behind the eyes of the grand duke was concerned by the continued absence of his new shaman. True, he could do without one. He had in the past. But having a shaman was less fatiguing. He would send fresh messengers to Karelia, with dire warnings. He did not like being kept waiting, or—although this was unlikely—being defied.

Jagiellon wondered briefly if there were some way to suck Count Mindaug—or better, Elizabeth Bartholdy—into the conflict he was stirring up in the lands of the Golden Horde. With the magical forces being unleashed, either one of them might with some luck be destroyed or at least damaged.

Neither of them existed in the spirit world to the degree he did. Mindaug dug for knowledge in print. He was clever, in that way, but in the end such knowledge was inherently weak. For her part, Elizabeth's power came from borrowing against her bargain. That made her formidable, for the moment, but eventually she would have to pay her side of that bargain.

But Jagiellon-Chernobog could not believe either could be that stupid. In the meanwhile he waited for his other plans to come to fruition. His targets walked cheerfully into his traps. What rich prizes to be so foolishly risked! Pawns, true, but pawns of some considerable value.

Magical communications were always fraught with risks. In common with several other religious sects, the Baitini believed themselves especially good at it, and protected. Chernobog knew otherwise, but if that was what they wished to believe, or that the drug enhanced their skills, he would not stop them. Like the belief that he would return them to power, they were welcome to their delusions as long as they were of use to him. As a fifth column within the Ilkhan they were very useful.

Jagiellon had received news of the progress of Prince Manfred of Brittany and his knights with some satisfaction. Although he had shattered the eastern dominions of the Golden Horde into a number of little khanates that served him, he knew that his hold on them was fragile. He needed to subjugate the Horde for once and for all. At a stroke now he would create a new ruler and a vassal, together with new enemies for them—the Ilkhan and the Holy Roman Empire. That would make the new western Horde's ruler very dependent on Lithuania's support.

The Baitini thought that, because of the visions of paradise he'd supplied them, that they were dealing with their god. That was amusing, insofar as the Black Brain Chernobog was capable of being amused. The Baitini earnestly believed that they were doing the righteous and honorable thing. Which, indeed, it was—for Chernobog. It was all about perceptions. Like their name, which had been a derogatory term until they embraced it.

It would be necessary to allow some of the lesser knights to escape. Perhaps a few, to give them a better chance of returning the news to the Holy Roman Empire. And at least one of the Ilkhan envoy's escort must return to the Ilkhan. Preferably they would have terrible tales of the other's vile duplicity and perfidy. He must brief his servant about that. He hoped the tarkhan's mind would not be so drug-mazed as to forget.

Chapter 34

"We need arms. And gold or at least silver. More horses. And probably food." Vlad spoke to himself. He did not dare say so to any other person. That would betray the weakness of his position and his own lack of knowledge. He knew he was the Prince of Valahia. He knew from Countess Elizabeth—he kept thinking of her—that his father was dead and that King Emeric was going to have him killed, as he had no further use as a hostage ... He was not entirely sure why he was of no further use. His mother still lived, didn't she? A tear pricked at his eye. For years he had avoided thinking of her. It hurt too much. He'd had a baby sister too. Where were they? Still in Poienari Castle, high above the ravine? Why could Emeric not just have forced her to act as regent?

He would go south, he decided. He had an army of sorts, growing daily. He bit his lip. He was aware of the problems in logistics. Just feeding them all up here in the mountains was a problem. Could he expect his good sergeants to solve that? They seemed very adept at solving other problems. It seemed a great deal to ask... and he had a feeling that he might not like their solutions. A raid on a village would not enhance his popularity. Nor was it honest. And that, he had discovered, was as important to his peasant army as it was to him.

Someone coughed, well off down slope. The sergeants had discovered... as had he quite by accident, and nearly fatally—that they should not try to sneak up on Prince Vlad. Where the speed and strength came from, he was not sure. But his men had learned not to toy with it.

It was one of the sergeants. "Begging your pardon, Sire. Sorry to disturb." What did they think he was doing? Plotting deep doings? He had too little to do. Too much time to think. Of the horror of men and their dying. Of the flames. Of gypsies that everyone seemed to despise. Of the creamy softness of the countess. Of the confusion of feeling she caused in him. "Yes, Sergeant Emil?"

"The outer perimeter guards found a man with a wagon on the trail. He said he was looking for you, Sire."

"Oh?"

"He says he is a loyal vassal. He has goods to sell." The sergeant sounded suspicious. "He sounds like a German. You can't trust them, Sire." The sergeant looked as if he wanted to say more... and then shut his mouth.

Vlad waited and then, when nothing more was forthcoming, pressed the issue. "What is it, Sergeant Emil?"

"Well, Sire," the sergeant said uncomfortably, "We could use food. And other goods... waxed flax, cloth.

It's cold here and not even autumn yet. I'd have confiscated all his goods and chased him off for a thieving German. But some of the men say you ... you'd not like that, Sire. That you paid good silver for everything. Only ... I have no silver, Sire."

"Then let us go down and see what he has to offer. I've been told my grandfather believed in honesty and that the country people still love him for that. I owe him for that legacy."

The sergeant twisted his hat in his hands. "Begging your pardon, Sire, that's true. But he was a mad bastard, too ... uh." He swallowed convulsively as he realized what he'd said.

Vlad nodded. "I know. I remember that even my father was afraid of him."

The sergeant nodded. "But he fixed those foreigner gougers properly. And he was harsh ... Sire, but fair. Not like King Emeric, who'll punish a man for telling him bad news, even if it is true. Or who'll kill the closest people to make an example."

They had begun to walk down the mountain toward the rutted track that crisscrossed the stream, using whatever flatland was available to continue up into the mountains. "I gather you have had experience of King Emeric, Sergeant Emil?"

The grizzled sergeant nodded. "He's like a rabid weasel, Sire. He kills for pleasure or for no reason at all."

There was already a crowd around the wagon, and business was brisk, by the looks of it. The jowled merchant and his assistant were busy.

The sergeant shouted something so close to a bear growl that Vlad did not quite catch the word. But the chaffering and noise stopped. Men stood rigid as if suddenly frozen to attention.

"And what is happening here?" asked Vlad, feeling his hackles rise as he looked at the trader.

The man bowed very low. "Your Majesty's loyal servant. Kopernico Goldenfuss, is my name, Sire. I trade in various fine goods..."

"At a price," muttered someone.

Vlad looked him over, not liking what he saw but unable to put a good reason to it. Yet...those feelings had been right in the past. "You know my grandfather's reputation, Goldendfuss? Honest weights, measure and fair dealing, or he made some appropriate adjustments to the weight and measurement of the merchant, I believe. He took the short weight off the scoundrel's belly."

"S...sire. I but took a reasonable profit for the risks and the transport..." the merchant stuttered.

"There are no risks. I accept that transport must cost something. What goods have you?"

"S...some fine cloth, Prince. And schnapps. And dried beef. I would be pleased to make a gift of a fine bright outfit for you, Sire. Not somber blacks. Scarlet and purple. Fit for a noble to wear..."

The rough wool had irked Vlad, as had the austere black of the priest's spare clothing. But this...scum thought he could bribe him. "My clothing is adequate," he said shortly. "I wear it with pride."

He was surprised to hear the troops cheer. He realized that for this conflict anyway, he would be wearing simple black clothes. "I could use a cloak, as could a number of my men. But I will have no more of your exploitation. I will buy your entire cargo at a fair price. It will be given to those who have most need. Give them their silver back. And consider yourself lucky. You will not be so fortunate twice." He turned to the sergeant. "I will have those goods back in the wagon, sergeant, and each man to get his money back."

The sergeant nodded. "And a close guard on that schnapps, Sire."

Vlad had not thought of what strong drink could do. He nodded. Looked at his small army and the expressions on their faces. "Every man will get some. But we cannot have any drunkenness. The Hungarians will cut your throats while you all sleep it off. The first man I find drunk...I will drown in it."

There was an almost imperceptible nod of approval from the sergeant. "Right. Form up. A straight line. With the goods and we'll see you get your money."

The merchant coughed, and bobbed his head awkwardly. "About my money, Sire..."

"You will be paid," said Vlad curtly, thinking of his scanty supply of silver.

"Of course, Sire. Your script is good."

Vlad suddenly put something he'd read into place. He'd read of promissory notes and usury without understanding them fully or bothering to find out much. So this was what it meant. He had the vaguest grasp of finance: he'd never really had the occasion to use money in the tower, and he was unsure just how princes got it. Taxation...but how did it work? What did he have to do? A series of accidents had led to a reputation as leader. As Prince. He'd been lucky. He'd made the right decisions...he thought. He desperately needed someone to advise him. He just didn't know things any fifteen-year-old peasant boy would know, let alone a twenty-year-old prince. But Vlad knew two things. Firstly, his hold on these people was strong but tenuous. Secondly, he needed them. Without them he was a child, lost and floundering. That much he'd learned among the gypsies, even before life became so much more complicated. He would be taken by his enemies. They might kill him. That he could endure. But they might imprison him again. He needed these people, if only to keep him from that. Besides, it would seem that he had inherited noblesse oblige. His father had drummed that into him from very young, and he had never quite forgotten it—and oddly, the old priest that had been allowed to visit him in prison had reenforced it.

But oh, for someone he could ask.

"A word, Sire." It was Sergeant Emil again. "I have taken the liberty of making Mirko the quartermaster for now. He served in Corfu, Sire. If that's all right, Sire?"

How did he expect Vlad to know? He barely knew what a quartermaster was. "I suppose so." That didn't sound firm enough, but it was said.

"I trust him, Sire. He's a good man."

"I did not trust that merchant."

The sergeant nodded slowly. "It was a bit odd. Traders don't travel up into the mountains with a wagon load of schnapps without a good few guards. Do you want us to tail him, Sire? There are a couple of men..." he coughed, "That, if you take my meaning, shot deer on land where they shouldn't have. They can move without being seen, at least as fast as man and a wagon."

Vlad had to think about what the sergeant was

saying. Ah. Poachers. He felt some doubt ... but ... he was suspicious. And it did feel right to be that, and to take some action, even though trimming the lard off the fat thief had seemed a better idea. "Tell the trader we want to buy more. He must come back."

The sergeant nodded. "We could use more supplies, Sire."

"We will not be here when this merchant comes back. Just in case. Just one man, watching the trail."

The sergeant rubbed his stubbly jaw, nodding again. "Yes, Drac." He'd noticed they called him that in times of stress or for greater respect. "I'll tell him, too, that most of the men are away. We only have some new recruits here."

Later, when the merchant had left with his empty wagon, they broke camp. Vlad was surprised at how quickly, and with how little fuss it could all happen. He was also surprised in another way just before they set off. His new quartermaster brought him a cloak. "Black, Sire. As you like it. Made up already ... But I had to get the girl to use some of the purple satin for a lining. There wasn't enough to go round, Sire. And best that it go to you, without the men fighting over pieces to give to their lemans."

Vlad took the cloak. It was stitched neatly, with a high collar, and lining of rich purple satin, and crimson inset to the collar. "What girl did this?"

The quartermaster looked as if he'd bitten into something unpleasant. "Rosa, Sire. I, um gave her some of the crimson for her trouble."

"I did not know we had a seamstress. I didn't know we had any women here at all. This is well done. But it is not safe for her to be here."

The quartermaster shrugged. "There's a certain kind of girl that'll always show up in the tail of an army, Sire. Your grandfather...he, um, was odd about it."

"Continue, quartermaster." He'd heard some fairly vicious stories about the old man.

The quartermaster plainly assumed he knew just how his grandfather had been odd. "Well, we didn't know how you'd stand on it, Sire, so we've kept them hidden."

"Do not hide things from me, Quartermaster. I don't like surprises. What are they doing here?" It was a statement of fact. Vlad was surprised to see the man cringe slightly, as if he'd said something sinister.

"Well...the usual, Sire. You know," Mirko said, rubbing his hands together.

Actually, Vlad was largely unsure. He'd been confined to six rooms in a tower, with menservants who barely spoke to him, since he was ten. His elderly tutor and priest had not taught him much about the world, let alone women. His occasional contacts with the court had been closely guarded and supervised. He knew men and women got together. He had some rather indefinite ideas about what happened then. He'd had some very confused and vivid dreams about it. Mostly involving death. "Why?" he asked.

Mirko shrugged. "Some of them have lost everything and had nothing else to sell. Some who want money. Some, like Rosa, who are too wild to keep to one man, Sire," he said uncomfortably.

"Oh. Well. Tell her I would like to thank her for sewing this for me."

Mirko blinked and swallowed.

Down the hill one of the sergeants bellowed. "Move out."

The quartermaster saluted. "Have to go, Sire," and scuttled away, plainly welcoming the interruption.

Vlad went to mount his horse, wondering just what he'd learned.

They rode or marched to the new camp that the scouts had located some days before. There was even a half tumbled down old shepherd's hut for him to sleep in. For some reason, his sergeants decided that it was appropriate accommodation for their prince. It was a gesture of consideration and respect. Vlad understood this. He hoped they would also understand why he had refused it. It had walls. Walls and a roof. And no windows. The thatch was old and rotten, and there was no door—or flooring. Yet it was still too confining for him now. For that reason, although it was a hovel, it reminded him far too much of his tower in Buda Castle. Walls might provide shelter, but they also provided confinement.

Instead, Vlad chose to bed down a little way away from the main encampment between some gray rocks that would provide some shelter from the wind, and privacy. He had always had privacy, and had grown accustomed to the solitude. The together-living of his soldiery he found hard. The men were used to sharing small accommodations with a large family. He had had six commodious rooms to himself, most of the time. He would have the stars and openness, and a quiet place by himself. His sergeants were welcome to the shelter and its fleas.

He was becoming quite a seasoned campaigner by now. He cut some heather for a bed. It did not look as if there was any chance of rain that night. So he did not bother with any form of lean-to. He simply laid his old cloak on the heather. He would wrap himself in the generous, thick folds of his new cloak after they had eaten.

That night as they were sitting around the fires— the schnapps had added a little volume and a little extra cheer to the troops, but they were anything but raucous—one of his sergeants came to him. "Sire, the poachers that Sergeant Emil assigned to follow that trader are back. You were right, Drac," he said with deep respect. "The traitor met a Hungarian patrol. They escorted him. And the men say the patrol was waiting for him. We will kill him if he ever sets foot in these mountains again."

Vlad digested this information. "I must forbid you from killing him, even if he deserves death."

The sergeant looked puzzled. "But why, Sire?"

"It seems probable that they will try to attack our camp again. When they do not find us there, they will probably punish him. However, I owe him an amount of silver. That debt must be paid. And then I will deal with the traitor in an appropriate fashion."

The sergeant saluted smartly. "I shall make sure that everyone knows that, Drac." There was something approaching reverence in his voice as he said that. Vlad wondered why. It seemed only fair.

As usual, he found himself sitting slightly aside from the rest of the men. He did understand that they felt this to be a measure of respect. It would also seem that they found themselves a little uncomfortable too close to him. However he had keen hearing. He did not think they realized just how much he eavesdropped, and how much he was learning from them. It was better than admitting he knew little of how to deal with people, let alone organize armies. The breeze brought to him wafts of conversation, some of which he could make very little sense of, and others like "... Knew it was a trap." Or "... he'll pay. Look at what he said he'd do for that German merchant."

Satisfied, Vlad took himself off to his rest. This time at least, he had made the right decisions.

He had found that he was quite a light sleeper— once he had recovered from the sheer exhaustion of his first few days as a free man. He had little fear that anyone would be able to sneak up on him while he was asleep. He also noticed that among the sentries the sergeants appeared to have one whose duty it was to watch over him. They were careful to leave him his space, however. He lay there looking up at the stars, somewhere in the region between wakefulness and sleep, when he heard a slight noise. A rustle of cloth. He was sharply and suddenly very awake, ears pricked, not moving but with every sense alert. His hand rested right next to his dagger haft ... and he waited. Vlad was unsure just how late it was. There were no sounds coming from the camp fires. And yes, that was definitely someone trying to move closer quietly.

There was also, now that his senses were so utterly keyed up, a faint scent. He caught sight of a black figure silhouetted by the moonlight. Whoever it was, was not particularly large. Ever so slowly, trying not to rustle cloth, Vlad drew his dagger. He closed his eyes, and then peered through a tiny slit, and tried to breathe easily and evenly. He expected the attacker to rush him at any moment.

What he did not expect was for the person to kneel

down, and say in a quiet but recognizably female voice, "Drac?"

Vlad rolled and stood up in one easy movement. In his hand the knife gleamed silver, as his cloak flared around him. The woman gave a small gasp of horror and held out her hands defensively.

"What are you doing here?" he asked, not relaxing. She had been looking for him, not a quiet place to relieve herself.

She giggled nervously. "Mirko said that you want to thank me. So . . . um . . . I came to be thanked, Drac." It was clear moonlight. Vlad could see that she was smiling warily at him. "I am Rosa. I sewed the lining into your new cloak."

Vlad slipped his dagger back into the sheath. "Ah. Yes. But why now, young lady? I very nearly killed you by accident."

"I did not want everyone to see, Drac. I had to wait until people were asleep," she said, her voice husky. He looked at her and saw how she looked back at him, brow lowered. She licked her upper lip. "Can we lie down among the rocks again? I do not want the guard to see me."

Vlad nodded. He sat down on his bed of heather again. She came too and pushed him back down gently on it, lying half on him, half next to him, her body soft against his, her lips brushing against his jaw line, hands running across his shoulders. She rolled slightly, and undid the buttons on her blouse. Moonlight shone on the full curves of her white breasts, and she began undoing the buttons on his shirt.

This was more alarming and confusing than merely being stalked by some killer. "What . . ." She put a finger to his lips and began to slowly, languorously kiss her way down his chest, unbuttoning as she went. She paused just short of the last button, and then slid her way up again, her breasts brushing against his chest. She put a leg over him and ground her hips against his. Then she sat up on top of him, rubbing her pelvis against him. She took his hands and led them up to touch the great soft globes and the firm nipple standing out from them. He felt the curve of them, touching and caressing, barely knowing what he was doing, but not wanting to stop either. He could feel his own pelvis thrusting up and against her. His body seemed to know what it was doing, even if his mind was less sure.

She rolled off him again and began to undo his breeches. He'd had strange and confused dreams involving this. She lifted her skirts and put her bare leg over him, and guided him into somewhere warm and wet and soft, and slid it down onto him.

Perhaps this was just one of those confusing and oddly relieving dreams again, he thought, as he thrust... she gave a slight groan, and pushed down onto him, moving rhythmically, and then panting, faster.

The stars looked down. They were quite small and reachable, really.

"I understand now. I did not understand what she was talking about," Vlad said later, thinking of Elizabeth. She was very different from this full ripe woman. To be admired, not—

"What?" asked Rosa, tracing a pattern on his chest.

"I did not know this was what men and women did," said Vlad, humbly.

She gaped at him in the moonlight. "You mean...
I was the first?" She asked.

He nodded.

"Well!" she giggled. "I was going to go, but I see
I have a lot to teach you, Drac."

Vlad did not do a great deal of sleeping that musky
scented night. On the other hand he did learn a great
deal about women, and indeed, about men. And the
world seemed a better, richer, fuller place. Rosa slipped
away just before dawn.

But she did promise she would come back. And
that he was a stallion. He assumed that that was a
compliment.

"We found these two riding around, Drac," said
Sergeant Mihai. "They claim that they are looking for
you. They say they need to speak to you and that it
is important." His tone said that he did not believe
them. "Poles. You can trust them nearly as much as
you can trust gypsies."

After their experiences of the previous day, Vlad
was not inclined trust anyone. But on the other hand
the gypsies had brought him here. They had treated
him well enough when he had fled in their company.
And besides the world, now that he had discovered
Rosa, was not the most evil of places. "I can hear
them speak, I suppose," said Vlad. It would help to
pass the time until nightfall.

"Thank you, Prince Vlad," said the short stocky
man. "Your man has the right of it. We are Poles.
But we have lived in these lands for twenty years, my
cousin and I. King Emeric gave us license to build
our workshop and ply our trade here."

"The bargains that my enemy makes scarcely bind me," said Vlad tersely.

"They don't bind him either," said the stocky man's companion, who was barely less broad. "He promised our families one thing, and we have found that he demands another."

"On the other hand," said the stocky man, "according to my wife, your grandfather kept his bargains, and paid fair price, and your father was a fair man too, as much as King Emeric allowed him to be. I took the liberty, Prince, of inquiring of some of your men while they walked us here, just what manner of man you are. They told me about a trader that was here yesterday. They told me that he had betrayed Your Highness. But that you owe him money and you will not see him dead until he is paid." He smiled grimly. "It was supposed to frighten us, I think. But instead it told us that we can maybe trust you. We wish to make a bargain with you, Your Highness."

That in itself was unusual. Vlad might be ignorant of the ways of the world but he knew this much: tradesmen and nobility did not mix. Tradesmen chaffered with the lower orders. They did not "bargain" with Princes. Any overt "bargaining" rapidly would end up being done at the sword's point. Most of Vlad's adherents adopted at least a mildly submissive posture and tone when speaking to him. This man looked him in the eye, and by the cut of his jaw was not good at being submissive to anyone. Vlad knew he should be offended. But he found himself liking the short, craggy fellow. "We are honest tradesmen," the fellow continued, holding out hands that were work-calloused, and that ended in thick stubby fingers. "All we want is to ply our trade and be paid fairly, and stay where we have built our workshops, and not be evicted just because we are not from here. That is what your grandfather did to foreigners."

"And with good reason, too," said one of the guards. "They were all thieves and rogues. And traitors, too."

The man ignored him, and continued to address Vlad, as if they were the only two men there. "We were offered land and a charter. Now we find our charter ignored and destroyed, and our holdings, our families and our lives threatened—just for plying our trade. Where does Your Highness stand on that?"

"I don't know," said Vlad, smiling despite the man's effrontery. "Just what is your trade, good man?"

The two men looked at each other, smiling slightly. The stocky solid fellow slapped his own forehead. "Forgive me. I forget, Your Highness. Everyone where we come from knows us. We're gunsmiths, Prince Vlad. Gunsmiths from Lwów. We fled from Galicia when Prince Jagiellon killed our prince. King Emeric's father gave us leave to settle, gave us a charter, in Harghita and Corona and the cousins in Várad. Józef Smerek is my name. This is my cousin Stanislaw. We are makers of fowling pieces, arquebuses, wheel-lock pistols. We settled here and we would continue our trade here, but now we are proscribed from doing so." There was no mistaking the fury in the man's voice at saying this.

"Smerek. They make good guns," said the guard, considerably more respectfully now.

"And there is the problem," said Stanislaw. "We make good guns. We sell them. The king's armies do not buy from us, but there are other customers. Not too many, but others. We make good guns, and we make them not too expensive. Then someone shoots one of King Emeric's Magyar officers with one of our guns. Shoots him dead, through the armor. And they catch him, find the gun, and now we are proscribed from following the family's trade. So the family sent a delegation to King Emeric four months ago to appeal the decision."

The two looked at each other again. Vlad saw how their shoulders were set in anger, the big hands balling into fists. Eventually Stanislaw spoke. He spoke in a cold, unemotional tone, very carefully and very deliberately, as if he was controlling a volcano of rage, but barely. "He tore up our charter. Ripped it apart and threw it in the dirt. And he had Papa Stanislaw impaled for daring to question him. For our part in killing his officer we were flogged. A hundred lashes for Edward and Thaddeus. I had to watch. I was the youngest. I got only fifty lashes—he told them to leave me alive to carry the message." He lifted his shirt, and turned, revealing the keloid mass of a terrible beating. "My brother Edward died there. Cousin Thaddeus died a week later."

Vlad looked. And nodded, slowly. It might seem a ridiculous punishment for such a thing, but he too knew Emeric's reputation. On the wrong day, the wrong word could earn you that sort of treatment. And that would have been just after the king returned from his disastrous expedition to Corfu. His temper had been very, very savage just then. "Fetch us some schnapps from Mirko," he said to the guard. Then to the two gunsmiths. "Come. Let us go and sit down and discuss the guns I wish to buy from you. And a new charter. One from me. I expect you to sell your guns to me, but I will not blame the maker of the tool for the use it is put to."

Vlad noticed his men were nodding, too.

The two looked at each other. "Yes, Your Highness," they said warily.

"My people call me Drac. Or Sire."

Józef looked at him strangely. "Drac...that means demon. Or Dragon. My wife is from the mountains."

Vlad nodded. "King Emeric may find I am a demon. The Dragon guards his own treasure. This is my treasure." He waved his hand at the camp. "My land and my people. Give me your fealty and you and yours will be my treasure, too. To be guarded. I will be both the demon and the Dragon for you."

He was surprised to see the stocky, solid men who had looked him in the eye so firmly suddenly kneeling in front of him. Tears were trickling down the faces of men who would not easily cry. "Drac." They said, almost in unison. Vlad found his hand being kissed.

"Józef can go back," said Stanislaw his voice cracking. "I have found my prince. I want to be your gunsmith, Drac."

Józef patted Stanislaw gently on the shoulder. "He is the best, Drac. He has even made cannon, though we were not supposed to. That is all we want. Revenge and to be your people. To belong."

Stanislaw nodded. "Yes," he said, his voice still thick. "To belong. To have a place we can call our own again. To have a prince who will be as loyal to us as we are to him."

Vlad reflected that he would have to go very far to find a better recruiting sergeant than King Emeric.

"You will both go back," he said, raising them up. "There are patrols, and you may fall foul of them. You may need each other for support. My men will see you on your way as far as possible. I want those guns. And then, Stanislaw Smerek, you can return to be my gunsmith. I am going to need you. And you and yours are mine. I will guard you to the best of my ability. I will have your loyalty and you will have mine."

They nodded. "Drac." It was a commitment. Heart and soul.

"They will not take us alive, or cheaply," said Józef with a slight smile. "Stanislaw carries more pistols about his person than most regiments."

Chapter 35

The knights found Bortai's cart easily enough. The bullock had pulled its stake and it took Kari a while to find it. He was a better-than-average tracker, Erik noted. He was as useful out here as he had been difficult in more civilized parts. The knights were glad that he had found it. So was Bortai, Erik noticed. It was probably all she had in the world besides a couple of ponies. Good horseflesh, but not on a par with that owned by the Ilkhan's escort. That was to be expected, naturally. Erik did not have Svanhild's eye for horseflesh, or utter passion for it. But he did like horses, and felt that he could tell a great deal about a man and his culture, from his horse. The Illyrians were not great riding people and generally the quality of the mounts of the scouts that accompanied them had not been of the best. Not that they didn't look after their horses, or were not proud of their steeds... but they came across as a people who fought on foot and fled on horses. The Ilkhan's men used and loved their horses... but the Golden Horde came across to Erik as men who lived in the saddle, fought in the saddle, and would probably mount a horse in order to cross the street in a town.

With three rather unexceptional ponies to her name, no wonder a cart and a bullock had seemed so important to the girl. Well, his own family were not rich—the lands at Bakkaflói had always been more beautiful and wild than really productive, although they grew good sheep and tough Icelandic ponies, and the sea saw that no one ever starved, but there were only little patches that were arable for rye and oats—so he knew what it was to be careful. And she smiled about it. She had an infectious smile, as well as a happy laugh—frequently, it seemed, when he was there. Erik was glad for her, although it gave him a pang of guilt. He'd never really thought he would enjoy listening to any woman's laughter again, after Svanhild. Svan had been quite a serious girl, most of the time. Except—he blushed, remembering—when he tickled her.

Finding the cart intact—and the bullock too, was a relief to Bortai. It meant that she could implement the second phase of her plan. With Kildai safely hidden in the cart, there was a chance that she could fool the Raven clan into thinking that the boy who looked like Kildai, was in fact him, and up and about.

There was of course one problem. He looked like Kildai. He ran like Kildai. But he did not ride like him.

She had to come up with an answer for that. But finding the cart, bullock and the things they had had to abandon was something to smile about to the tall blond knight. Her betrothed. She had to laugh a little. If that story got among the clan! And it was rather appealing and amusing the way he looked puzzled when she laughed at him. She felt slightly guilty. He had blushed so today. She chuckled to herself, a gurgle of welcome laughter. It had been rather pleasant to play such games after the life and death survival on the run for the last while.

She looked up from the cart to discover that he had just ridden up. And she was laughing again. He probably thought she was laughing at him. Well, at least he did not appear to be offended. She smiled and greeted him in his own manner. Perhaps his mother really was a tortoise.

He frowned, looking most comically puzzled. "I thought that was the wrong greeting."

Some demon from the lands of Erleg Khan made her reply, looking down demurely. "It is. But a man might greet his betrothed so."

He put his hands to his face. Shook his head. "I am sorry. That horseboy! He told me it was the right way to greet people politely. I wanted to learn your tongue. He taught me much rubbish." He blushed yet again. "I am glad Benito didn't know it was that sort of greeting. He would have killed me, let alone David."

"What?"

So in broken Mongol, assisted by Tulkun who had just ridden up, he told the story of how he had got the Darughachi to thus greet the tarkhan. By the time he had got to the part where his friend the Darughachi had the boy in jail she had to wave her hand at him—the one that wasn't clutching her pommel—to stop. She couldn't breathe and was in danger of falling out of the saddle. The plump Ilkhan warrior was in no better case.

❀   ❀   ❀

Erik hadn't seen quite how funny it could be before. But he had to admit, telling the story himself, in his broken Mongolian, that it was more than just a little ridiculous. He found himself hard put not to laugh, too, at their delight in the story. It would appear that the Mongols shared the same sense of humor as the plains tribes in Vinland. The plains tribes could be serious and earnest people. But they were also hugely fond of practical jokes, preferably very embarrassing and fairly direct ones. It was not a terribly subtle humor perhaps, but it was enjoyed enormously. Erik had liked the plains tribes. He found he liked the Mongols, too, so far. Well. He had not bound to the tarkhan Borshar. But perhaps he was more likely to get on with the rustic ordinary Mongol, than someone who was plainly more at home in the great cities of the Ilkhan empire, places like Jerusalem, Dishmaq and even the fortress-city of Alamut. Borshar seemed to spend a great deal of time in a trance-like state, paying little attention to the rest of them.

Erik rode back up the column to Manfred. "You seem to be getting along very well with your Mongol girlfriend," said Manfred.

Erik knew better than to rise to Manfred's obvious bait. "I was explaining how I came to use the wrong greeting. Fortunately, they seemed to find it quite funny. And there's no need for you to mock me about it."

"I wouldn't have dreamed of it," said Manfred with a totally unsuitable saintlike expression on his face. "I was just wondering if I should be learning the language. Or if she has any sisters."

"Learning the language is always good idea. Philandering in a strange culture probably isn't," said Erik.

"You never know," said Manfred. "There must be

a culture out there somewhere that thinks it's a good idea. I mean, I've never met any other girls who think that your face is something to laugh over. They normally go all starry eyed and moon over you." Erik cuffed him. "Ouch. You are supposed to be protecting me. Not inflicting me with injuries."

"I am protecting you. Your comments will get you killed elsewhere. I'm trying to teach you not to make them. Just you wait for rapier practice. Too much of you is covered by armor."

"Not another word, I swear," said Manfred, his grin belying the solemn words. "It is age, I am sure. Your face didn't used to be funny, now it is. We're all just used to it. Or afraid of you. That's why we don't laugh."

Erik threw up his hands in disgust. "Just you wait. You and that horseboy, David. I will choose my time and place."

Manfred laughed. "That hell-born brat. He's even more trouble than Benito was. Falkenberg and Von Gherens have both told me that he was born to be hung. At least Benito had the common sense to shut up and learn. This one keeps his mouth shut only when he's eating. And he's not even too good at that. Kari has had a rough time just teaching him to chew with his mouth closed."

Erik nodded. "Mind you, I've had less trouble from Kari since he's had to run after the boy."

"So now, instead of one source of trouble, you have two. I am not sure if you have gained ground, Erik. But no doubt this is some obscure Icelandic battle strategy."

"I think I'll ride up and check on the van," said Erik, shaking his head.

❀   ❀   ❀

Manfred watched him ride forward. He smiled quietly to himself. There had been a time, after Svanhild's death, that he had seriously feared for Erik's sanity and survival. He would never tell Erik, but he hoped that this Mongol girl seduced him, stole his heart, or at the very least made him laugh a lot. It had done Manfred's own heart good to see Erik smiling again. He would have to find excuses to send the Icelander to keep the lass company. Preferably on a cold, lonely night. Erik was no philanderer, but perhaps the girl could make up for it. In Manfred's experience, all but a few of them were willing to do just that, given the right opportunities. Erik was several years his senior, but in this, Manfred felt very much like an older brother. It would do the boy the world of good. And besides, she really was quite a looker. Maybe she did have a sister.

David was beginning to wonder whether dying of heat was any better than being murdered. The knights in their armor were complaining. And he, in this hooded cloak, felt as if he was going to melt entirely. Worst of all, it appeared that both Kari and Erik had noticed. "What are you wearing that thing for?" asked Kari. "It's hot enough to make a bear shed its pelt. Are you hiding something under there?"

"I'm just not smart enough to be seen among these noble Mongols," said David.

"These are nobles?"

David nodded. "Yes. Of course. They are Mongols. Like the knights, they are nobles. Well, not just commoners like me."

"In Vinland a man's as good as he can prove himself to be," said Kari. "I've never understood how just being born makes you something special. Maybe all nobles have tough births . . . but you never showed any worry with the knights. If these Mongols are what you call nobles, the knights should have troubled you just as much, eh?"

"They're foreigners. It's different," said David.

"Well, I'm not buying you some smarter clothes because you won't be seen dead in what you have. They'll just have to put up with you as you are. Or you can cook in that thing."

That was all too close to the truth. The part about being seen dead, and the part about cooking.

A little later, Erik had come past, doing his usual checks on the column and scouts. He had his visor raised within the column. He raised his eyebrows looking at David.

David had to admit that he'd at least tried to avoid being noticed quite so much by Erik, since the practical joke. He'd also tried to avoid any more temptation in this direction, especially after he'd been caught out. But the Frank's face did make it hard to resist. And he did feel that there was still some payback justified, even if Erik and Kari had saved his life from those barbarians on that island.

"Are you sickening for something, brat?" asked Erik. "It's as hot as a warm day in hell, or even a cool day in summer in Jerusalem."

David decided to play it for sympathy. "I am not feeling too well."

"I'd better get Falkenberg to look at you, then," said Erik. "He's as near to a Knight Hospitaler as we have with us. Mind you, I could ask one of the Mongols. Maybe they have a healer."

"Er . . . no. I'm really not feeling that sick. Perhaps I could just ride back to that village in Illyrian territory and wait until you all came back."

Erik snorted. "I don't think you'd survive, boy. The world out there is more complicated than Jerusalem. Maybe I can get you a ride in the Mongol lady's ox cart. You could hardly ride it worse than you do that horse. I'll go and ask her."

He rode off, and came back a short while later. He was smiling. That was enough to worry David. He had seldom seen Erik smile, and never for no apparent reason. "Come along, brat. The lady says she'll do you up as a pretty little Mongol boy. No one will ever accept that something as lowly as a mere horseboy will be smart enough to ride in a Mongol lady's cart. I've been talking to Kari. So if you're sick, or not smart enough? Either way we'll fix you."

David groaned. But he had learned by now that there was not much use in trying to resist Erik. Besides, he could lie down in the cart, couldn't he? No one would see him there.

Of course, when he got to the cart he discovered that the noble Mongol lady had her own ideas about what to do with him. It appeared that these included cutting his hair and dressing him up in her brothers deel. "I'm sure that they would hardly recognize you like that," she said, with a twinkle in her eye that he entirely distrusted. From the lofty height of his fifteen or possibly sixteen years he knew that women were usually not to be trusted, especially when they looked at you like that. And after they had asked you if your mother was a tortoise, definitely not.

On the other hand, it did appear that she was

going to let him drive the cart. That was more pleasant than riding as far as he was concerned. And he did rather enjoy wearing the fine clothes. He noticed several of the Golden Horde riders were plainly very impressed. He sat tall, forgot about the various ills of his life and played off the attitude and manners of nobly born Ilkhan Mongol. He doubted that they were that different to the ways of the Golden Horde.

Bortai had to laugh again. The tengeri were surely playing some complicated game with her life, and for that matter, with Kildai's. The foreign knight, Erik, must by now think that she spent her entire life laughing, principally at him. But he had told a good story, even in his broken Mongolian. Storytellers and singers were much liked and respected, the great ones as much as shamans and orkhans. He seemed genuinely concerned about the serf who looked so like her brother. Well, he did say the boy was much trouble. So was Kildai, except when the seriousness of being a leader of the Hawk clan was impressed upon him, which, sadly, usually lasted only a few heartbeats.

She was of course pleased to "help." She hoped she didn't look too utterly delighted by his request.

A little later Tulkun rode by again. He grinned at her. She beckoned him closer. Using every ounce of protocol at her disposal she addressed him very flatteringly. He grinned wider. "And what is it that the noble lady requires? When my wife is that polite to me, I know that she wants something."

"The wisdom of the noble warrior from the Bear clan stands as high as the eternal blue sky," she said, with her best smile. The one she saved, normally, for asking just how much a warrior would dare to wager on a wrestling match.

He chuckled roundly. "Oh, this is a large one. What is it that you desire, noble lady?"

"Just that if any of the people of the Raven clan of the Golden Horde should ask, my brother Kildai, as well as having been concussed, has broken his leg. It is not too serious," she said demurely. "You saw how they strapped it up and splinted it, did you not? It will make riding very painful until it heals."

He laughed again. "I suspect that this is a very clever trick. But I do not see that it will do me, or my master the tarkhan, any harm."

"No. And it will earn you the gratitude of the Hawk clan."

He nodded. "If any of them should ask me, I'll tell them that. You do not want them to think he can ride?"

"Something like that," she said, favoring him with a smile again.

She was pleased to see, a little later, after some quick barber work, and changing the boy into Kildai's beautifully embroidered deel, and even letting him wear Kildai's sword, that her judgment had been dead right. So long as they did not really get a close look at him or see him riding... The sword, too, he was plainly unfamiliar with. Ion was able to leave off driving the cart, and she let the boy take over with it.

This David seemed to be enjoying, which was something Kildai would never have allowed anyone to see, even if he did. And by the looks on the faces of the Raven clan escort, Tulkun had done his part too. It would make nearly as good a story as the tortoise greeting, if they got away with it. And there was some delight in playing such a trick on this serf from Ilkhan lands. No matter what his birth, he had shown himself to be a practical joker. A trickster. It was a dangerous way to establish your status, but it was both popular and effective. Of course any such trick always called for a reply. She smiled to herself; she was, in a way, repaying Erik for his generosity, and this David for his practical joke. Besides the look on the faces of the Raven clan made it all very worthwhile.

A little later the blond knight came riding up again. He was, she noted, ever vigilant. An orkhan who did not believe in merely delegating his responsibilities. She could understand why the tarkhan Borshar had hired such a mercenary, if he was going to hire such things at all. She'd seen quite a number of battle commanders, and this was one of the most methodical she had ever come across.

He looked at David. Blinked. Looked again. Then he motioned for her to ride next to him. They rode ahead a little. "He looks very like your brother. Clever. I should have seen."

And she should have realized that someone as vigilant as this would not miss the similarity. Or be taken in by the deception. She could only hope that the Raven clan was led by less observant warriors. "They look quite like each other," she admitted. "If they see him sitting up, they will not realize that he cannot ride away."

He looked at her keenly. "There is more, yes?"

He was entirely too astute. She nodded. "There is conflict between this clan and ours. Believing that my brother is recovered will worry them. That is good."

"I have a lot to learn about your people," he said. "Good luck with this."

His eyes, never still, scanned the countryside. "It is a fine, rich land," he said.

"Ours to the north is better," she said proudly. "What is your land like?"

"Mostly rocks," he said with a smile. "And very much colder. But when I have finished my . . ." he searched for words and ended up with, "serving." Which was plainly not quite what he wanted to say. "I am going back to Vinland. There is much good rich land there. I went there before," he searched for the word again, and had to settle for "serving" again.

Bortai had to smile at his description of his family's lands. Not many of the Mongol would admit to their lands being "mostly rocks," although in some cases it was true. It also explained what he was doing here. He was probably a second son. At least it would seem he had no plans to carve out a holding on Golden Horde lands, or, not yet. "So where is this Vinland?"

"A long, long way to the west," he said. "Across a huge . . . water, that takes us weeks and weeks to cross. My home is . . . part of the way. On a land in the water."

"An island. In the sea," she explained, resisting an urge to ask him if his people tended fish on seahorses.

He repeated her words, carefully. "And you would call them?" He supplied the words. And asked for a few others. It was amusing. But he never stopped looking out for trouble.

And when it came he reacted with speed and ferocity.

They had fallen back slightly and were now level

with David and the cart. He suddenly dived sideways, snatching the boy off the bench of the covered cart.

An arrow ripped through the covering of the cart. Had he still been sitting there, David would have taken it in the chest. Erik had somehow spotted it and in the process of removing David from its path he had also knocked her sideways, almost off her horse. She could not be certain that that was his purpose, but they were the only unarmored people there.

The responses from the Frankish knights were equally rapid, and plainly very practiced. Well, the movement of the knights was practiced and coordinated. What nearly frightened half of the Raven clan off their horses was the dark-skinned man and his hand cannons. He had fired four of them in to the copse, which the arrow had almost certainly come from, even before the steel-clad knights had got to a full gallop. Some hurtled towards the trees, the others closed in around them, as they pushed the whole column, including the poor ox and cart, into a run.

Bortai had pulled herself back into the saddle, and, plainly on orders from Erik, found herself between three steel-clad knights. The man with the hand cannons had leapt from his horse and onto the cart, a feat fitting of a Mongol warrior. The Raven clan obviously did not know quite what to make of all of this. It was apparent that although they were supposedly escorting the knights, the knights themselves were looking after the situation. A few hundred yards later someone—possibly Erik—called a halt. Looking back, Bortai could see why. The small column of knights that had detached itself, now accompanied by a couple of Arban of Raven clan warriors were returning. With a dead body.

Erik, still with the serf boy David across his saddle bow, rode up. He dropped the boy, who sat down abruptly panting and wild eyed at their feet. Erik was not laughing now. "I did not bring him to you to be killed."

"They are without honor," hissed Bortai, white with anger. She had expected treachery, but later, in the dark, when they could do it with poison or a thin-bladed dagger. She had never expected anything quite this blatant. True, had the boy been killed, and the knights and the man with the hand cannon been less rapid to react, the bowman would have got away. No doubt the Raven clan would have sent several Arban "in pursuit." They might even have brought someone back. Almost certainly, a dead someone. Possibly even the bowman. There would have been handsome and fulsome apologies. Blood money paid—they were under the escort of the Raven clan. It would have been a matter of considerable embarrassment. She would not even have been surprised if they did escort her home after that. She was not that important in their scheme of things. Killing Kildai plainly was.

"I nearly got killed," said her brother's look-alike, still stunned.

The man with the hand cannons had pulled the cart up next to them. He said something. The boy staggered to his feet. Bortai noticed that the man who had taken control of the cart was patting him on the shoulder with a sort of rough kindness. She felt terribly guilty. They did not look alike, but what if it was his younger brother?

"I'm sorry," she said humbly. "I did not expect this."

"You warned me, lady," the serf David said, gratefully.

That actually made her feel worse. It was conduct without honor. And without honor the Hawk clan was nothing.

The knights who had sortieed, together with two of the Golden Horde Mongols, Tulkun and a second man, and two Arban of the Raven clan came riding up. Bortai noticed that Erik's huge companion had made his way there, too.

Bortai let her fury explode within her. A little later, when she calmed down, she was not entirely sure quite what she had said to the commander of the Arban. It had included quite a lot of terminology that a well-born Mongol lady should not admit that she knew. The leader of the Arban was bright red, and the serf boy David was laughing so much that it looked like he would fall over. Tulkun and his companion were looking at her with a mixture of shock and amusement.

The commander of the Arban stuttered out the start to a reply.

Bortai, now that she had vented some of her spleen, demolished him in a few well-chosen words about the honor of his clan. And told him to go. Now. To remove himself from her sight, and to do the sort of job of patrolling that honor really demanded. She knew just as well as he did that the archer was from his own clan. She also knew that the humiliation would prevent them from trying in that manner again. It did not stop her from being badly embarrassed too, later.

"By Christ's blood!" said Manfred admiringly. "I don't understand a word of it, but I have heard drill proctors with thirty years' experience give a gentler chewing out. She's quite some spitfire, that girl. Take my advice: stick to the meek and mild ones. They're not as much fun in bed but at least you get to keep your head on your shoulders."

"She certainly was as shocked and angry as any one can be. She...has quite a rough tongue. I thought at first that she'd set David up as a decoy—a false target. I was fairly angry with her. He's just a fool of a boy."

Manfred shook his head and looked at the leader of the Golden Horde's little patrol slinking away like a whipped cur. "Are you sure she's just some ordinary woman, Erik? She was behaving like an empress back there."

Erik blushed dully. "No empress would tell a man to do that. No empress would even know the words. I didn't even know half of them, but what I did understand...well, I think perhaps she is woman who cleans fish. They are...um, inclined to speak like that."

"Still think you'd better take some steps. Fishwife or no, someone just tried to kill that boy. My suspicion has to fall on our escort."

Erik nodded. "Kari got lucky with a shot there. Normally those pistols of his are not particularly accurate, especially at that sort of range. Mind you, if they'd shot from close up they'd have killed him. I only had a few heartbeats of warning. I think he'll have to go inside the cart, and we'll have to put a full escort on it. I think, because I am trying to conserve our force, I will bring them inside your cordon."

"Makes sense to me," said Manfred. "If the targets are hidden inside that cart they can't tell just where they're dropping their arrows."

Chapter 36

Dana left the cart quietly, early, by the back. If she'd got up normally, before she'd covered thirty paces someone from the urchin pack would have joined her. And her mother would have moaned, just like yesterday, and the day before.

Mother moaned about quite a bit, starting with the clothing she was wearing.

"It's a nice skirt, Mother."

"It's a gypsy skirt! It's dirty and ... and vulgar. And how can you go barefoot, darling?"

"Tante Silvia says I have to look like the others, Mama, in case they come looking for us."

Mama had sighed. "Yes. But Dana. They're gypsies. Remember your position. And well, the men have a reputation. You must always stay with me ..."

"Mama. It's hot. The cart stinks of solder and Tante Silvia's herbs. And you don't need to worry about the men, I can't go anywhere on my own. Ever. There are always at least three of those girls with me. Always, Mother. And anyway, no one will ever know what I wore or did here. We're not going to tell them we

356

hid with the gypsies are we, Mother?" She didn't even try to explain that she'd found that the "gypsies" thought it really funny that her mother thought they were gypsies, just like the other bands that traveled the country. Those people were newcomers, and had come from the south somewhere recently...within the last few hundred years. These people said they'd always been here.

Mama had sighed. And cried. "I still think we ought to try and go to Cousin Dorrotea. Maybe they will have stopped searching by now. Maybe we'll be safe with my family. They could hide us in a situation more fitting to our station. It's so demeaning, this." The dowager princess had waved at the cart that was their meager kingdom these days, as if it were a garderobe. "And they're gypsies, Dana. You know what people say about gypsies."

Dana did. She had said some of it herself. They were rude, crude and vulgar, below contempt, the poorest of the poor, and of less regard than a serf. Only...something was wrong with that. They laughed at being sneered at and called gypsies. Not openly, but had laughed. Dana and her mother had only been among these "gypsies" for a few hours when she'd worked out that even the poorest ragged urchin looked down on her...well, not as far down on her as they did on ordinary people. She was of the house of Valahia. Almost as good as them, she gathered.

That would have done to her what it had done to Mama—driven her to sneer back...except for one of Dana's two besetting sins. The first—her temper tantrums and black fury, her mother tolerated. That was Valahia—as Valahia as her long straight black hair and pale skin. It was the second sin that drove her mother to despair, her insatiable curiosity.

It was a curiosity that had saved them. That was how she had found out that orders had come through for her to be taken to Buda, because Vlad—about to be transported there and crowned, had somehow escaped from his prison. Mama had not been able to bear the thought of losing another child...though what dire fate she thought was in store for Dana, she had not said. Instead, in a panic, she had sent them both fleeing.

And so here they were. Among the "gypsies"...who looked down on them and treated them like charity cases instead of their rightful lords. "We were here long before you, Valahia. It's our land. You merely live on it." And worse...she, Dana, was among people with some sort of secret...which they had no intention of telling her.

Well, she was going to find it out. So she'd pretended to be charmed by their rude songs, and joined in with their rustic behavior as if it was a great treat. Actually—having held up her nose at such things all her life—after a few days she'd got very used to them. She quite liked some of the pastimes they had showed her, involved her in. Some of the games—when she forgot to be superior and got carried away with the game—were clever and fun, too. She discovered that she liked winning.

She realized that they weren't quite games either after a while. They were teaching the young ones how to steal, and how to trick the settled people, which seemed to be their equivalent of schooling. She had to admit it was more challenging than deportment lessons. She decided that—as long as no one knew—being a traveler was possibly more fun than merely being a princess. Well, not the fishing in the lake. The fishing part was all right. It was catching the slimy things that wasn't. Blackberrying too. When you were hungry—and she had discovered hunger, too, along with the "gypsy" dances, and crude jokes and wild music—blackberries were good eating, despite the thorns.

"Look at your fingers, Dana!" Mama had cried in horror the first day. Then she had taken in some of the other details "What have done to your face? And your hair?" she had demanded icily.

"Green walnut juice. And Tante Silvia did my hair with hot sticks. I like it, I think."

"You look like a filthy gypsy girl. Not a princess."

She'd avoided rolling her eyes because it made her mother despair of her. But she wanted to; how could her mother be so—obtuse? "That's the idea, Mama. I need to look like one."

But this morning she had a very different agenda. She had noticed that at least two of the three main men, Radu, Angelo, and that eternally grinning Grigori sneaked off somewhere every morning. At least one of them was missing all day.

She'd even tried asking about it. Angelo had laughed at her. "Run and play, little girl," he'd said, cheerfully tousling her hair. She'd nearly exploded with shock and rage at his presumption. Then he'd said, "It's not for you to know."

She'd bottled her rage and tried to flutter her eyelashes at him, as she had seen some of the older girls doing. He'd laughed again. "The tricks you have learned among the pack, eh? Your brother is a dangerous man. You will be a dangerous woman one day. You'll need it. You'll be tall, just like him. I hope you ride better. He could hardly sit in the saddle when we brought him east."

"My brother?"

"I have said too much. What you don't know you can't tell."

As far as Dana was concerned, what she didn't know could very easily drive her mad. But other than the fact that he had plainly met her brother, he was not saying any more. She really hated that.

And they were up to something else. Something that kept the "gypsies" camped on this mountain in the late summer, when they would be normally be working the countryside. The other children let that much on, and they were so plainly pregnant with knowing something she did not, that it had even got her up early, before the sun had even peeked above the horizon. The grass was heavy with dew...and it was relatively easy to see where someone had walked out of the camp, heading away from the dark waters of the lake into the pine forests, up on the steep slopes of the mountain.

Looking carefully she just caught a glimpse of them disappearing into the forest margin. The dew was cold and wet on her bare feet as she hitched her skirts up and ran after them. She even had her blackberry basket as an excuse.

They moved faster than she possibly could, she knew. They'd never know she was behind them...

And then she caught a brief sight of gray brindled fur, white teeth and a very red mouth in between the shadows. She gave a small strangled gasp of a scream . . . but before she could open her mouth for a full-blooded bellow, Grigori stepped out from behind the low branches of a tree on the other side. "What are you doing here, little girl?" he asked roughly.

Dana was totally startled out of any pretense of hauteur. "I . . . looking for berries."

"Go down to the lakeside. They grow there. Go."

"There's . . . there's something in the woods. I saw it. Fur and teeth. A bear . . . or a wolf. I can't go on my own."

"Ah," Grigori said. "It is dangerous up here. It'll kill and eat the soft, tender meat. Now run. I will distract it. Run. Run quickly and do not stop until you are back in the camp. Quickly. Go."

From the forest came a menacing growl and Grigori drew his knife.

She needed no more urging. In a panicky headlong flight she ran downhill, jinking through the trees and tearing through the underbrush.

But she did not get very far. Less than three hundred paces. She hooked her toes on a tree root and went flying, landing so hard that all the breath was knocked out of her. She lay there gasping weakly, too stunned and breathless to get up, let alone run on, despite her fear. Even so, she tried, because of that, and as she struggled to a sitting position, she realized that the forest was still. There was no sign of a monster chasing her. It would have caught her and eaten her by now. There were no sounds of a desperate struggle while Grigori fought it off. There was nothing but early morning silence broken by a dove's mournful call.

She'd managed to sit up now, and inspect her ripped skirt and—by hitching the skirt up—her knees. They were both grazed and one dripped a little blood. Sore and with the increasing realization that she'd been made a fool of, Dana stood up. She did not turn down slope. Instead she walked determinedly—if a little cautiously—back up to where she had met Grigori.

There was no body. No mutilated dark-skinned gray-eyed man with his throat ripped out, and his entrails wrapped around the trees.

Dana took a deep breath as her temper rose. Not yet there wasn't. There might be when she caught up with them. They were laughing at her, no doubt. It had been Angelo growling, of course. And whatever she'd seen...well, they let the children wander around, freely; she'd discovered that the "gypsies" took good care of their own, contrary to their reputation. She'd seen how the older ones appeared as if by magic when two of the littlest children went too close to a landslip by the lake. Therefore there was no dangerous beast on the loose in the forest. They had just wanted to frighten her off from whatever they were doing in these woods.

She was of the house of Valahia. She didn't frighten. Not much, or for long anyway, damn their black hearts. She began to walk uphill again, far more determinedly now. It was steep going, and the pine trees grew thicker. It was quite a bit later when it occurred to her that they might not have been going this way at all. There were no tracks. There was not even a well-defined pathway—just the faintest of trails, which only existed in that several of the branches had been broken, possibly by some wild animal. She peered at the thick coating of old pine needles. Looking back she could see how she'd exposed little wet patches of their damp underlayer, just by struggling up the steep slope. Looking around there was no sign that the two larger, heavier men had made their way up here. No sign of any other disturbance... except on a tree about ten paces away, there were four deep gouges, cut at least a fingertip deep through the rough bark into the flesh of the tree. It bled gummy sap, in thin sticky pine resin trails.

She laughed. So that was what this was all about. Rosin. The right to collect rosin was a lord's right, which, of course they would get their peasantry to do. She'd heard tell that it was sticky, unpleasant work, saved for peasants not fit for much better. Still: It was a lord's right, just as the venison and wild boar were his. They would not take kindly to some gypsies stealing their property, even if they were not harvesting it themselves. She laughed again, louder this time.

And in the tree above the long scratches something stirred. Something of shifting colors, sinuous, and reptilian and spiky. With bat wings. The shape stared at her with slitted eyes that seemed to slide between a liquid copper and a fiery glow.

She wanted to scream, but she was actually too terrified to do so. Her eyes wide, and her heart racing, she began to turn ever so slowly, making no sudden moves. And then she nearly jumped clear to the top of the pine trees. Because, with a clatter and a thump, a second creature flapped down to the forest floor. The opalescent creature stood there on a pair of feathered legs, great curved talons digging into the moss, a long spiked tail snaked back among the trees.

It cocked his head and looked at her. And then, very obviously, sniffed at her. The other of the creatures flapped down, landing barely five paces away. She was trapped between the two of them. The second one stuck its scaly snout forward at her, and sniffed at her knee. The worse grazed knee.

Strange, liquid fiery-coppery eyes with crescent pupils looked at her. It was not, despite the bat wings, talons and long barbed tail, a very large creature. Barely the size of a graze-hound in fact. And skinny. She could see the ribs under the shifting greenish silver color of its scales. She could also see long sharp white teeth set into a red maw.

Then it said..."food."

While she'd been looking at it the other one had also come forward. "Hungry" that one said, and a long, forked, snaky tongue quivered out of its mouth, flickering over her foot and onto her leg with a ghost-like brushing touch.

Dana managed her scream.

"I wouldn't do that if I were you," said Angelo, standing and looking at her from where she would swear he had not been a few heartbeats before. "They're young and hungry. They can smell the blood."

"Help me..."

He smiled wickedly. "They are supposed to like tender young maidens. And the more royal the blood the better. Here." He reached into the sack by his side. Drew out a haunch of venison. Took a long thin bronze blade from his belt. Handed them both to her. "Feed them. Feed them before they feed on you." His tone did not suggest that he was joking.

Dana looked at the greenish-silver bat-winged

creatures in terror. Then the one that had not tasted her with its tongue butted her in the stomach so that she sat down. She was on face level now, and she could see the drool, and feel their breath on her face. And then the Valah fury came to her rescue. If she was going to die it would not be with a poor traveler mocking her. She got to her feet, and cut a long thin sliver off the venison. Ha. Stolen, poached venison! Royal game. The knife was razor sharp. It cut almost effortlessly. One of the creatures tugged at the bloody strip while she was busy. "Wait," she said sternly, and pulled the meat away from it and gave it to other one. She cut another strip while it stared at her, startled, and hurt looking. She fed it. The other was already demanding more.

The two creatures ate with noisy and messy abandon, and with as much haste as they could get the meat into their faces. The pace did slow down, as the haunch became a bone.

"Give them the bone, and come away," said the gypsy. "They'll argue about it, and then play with it and then eat it. They need it for their teeth."

"What are they?" she asked as she tossed the bone between them.

"Wyverns. Young ones. The last of their kind," said Angelo, taking his knife from her hand and cleaning it on the pine-needle mat, then on a scrap of cloth, before finally slipping it back into his pouch. "Now. You must promise me you will not come up here without us. Your word of honor as part of the house of Valahia, girl. We watch them . . . but they are hungry. And you are food to them, remember that. They do not yet care if food talks."

Dana had regained her temper, and her common sense. Besides, his asking for the word of a Valah appealed to her. "I swear. The word of the house of Valahia," she said proudly. "But you will let me come again," she said imperiously. "Our family are called the sons of the Dragon."

"We know. It is why we helped. We have dealt with your family from when your ancestor was just a hill clan chieftain. We stay out of settled people's affairs, normally. We need to keep you from becoming a hostage. There are things that need to be done. Sacrifices your father was not prepared to make because his son was a hostage." He jerked a thumb at the wyverns. "They are a secret. You must also swear to keep it."

Dana had no problems at all with being on that side of a secret. Besides, she suspected that there was more.

"Now you must go. I will see you to the edge of the forest, and you must go quietly back to your sleeping place. You will tell Tante Silvia I asked that she mend that skirt before your mother sees it. It is not good that you are out alone. There are more dangerous things on the mountain, and not all are satisfied with venison."

"You knew I was coming, didn't you?" she asked suddenly suspicious. He'd been in exactly the right place at exactly the right time.

He grinned again. Nodded. "We knew. This time."

Angelo waited until he had seen that she was all the way back to the carts and tents. Then he turned to Grigori who had ghosted down the mountainside behind them. "Old blood, that one."

"At least she never asked how we knew," said Grigori. "You took a chance there, Angelo. They could have killed her, and she them, with that knife."

"That is what this is all about, Grigori. Giving and taking chances. She could see them. I think we may need to rethink."

"It has always been the males of the line, Brother."

"The blood runs in both the male and the female, it would seem. They called to her, and she came, in spite of the fear. We may have to rethink. Blood is blood. And we cannot always choose. There is little enough of it left. And they accepted her, too."

Grigori raised an eyebrow. "I look forward to your telling Radu that. He is more conservative than I am about such things, although I will agree that the she-wolf can be more deadly than the male. I will go now and arrange that the little one of the House Valah is not alone again. There will always be some children with her. But I will think about what you say."

Dana, too, was deep in her own thoughts. Wyverns were a heraldic symbol . . . supporters in her family coat of arms. They were believed to spread disease, pestilence and poison . . . and yet, too, were symbols of strength. Which were these? Why did the gypsies seem to look after such things? Was there a reason, a real reason for them being on the coat of arms?

Chapter 37

David was glad enough just to lie down in the cart, and close his eyes and control his shaking. He had to admit—at least to himself if to no one else—he was badly rattled by all of this. He actually wanted to cry and might just have permitted himself a snuffle or two. Was the entire world determined to kill him? He hadn't even done anything to most of it, yet.

And if the entire world did have to be set on killing him, was it right that there should be quite so much world?

Pondering the unrightness and unfairness of it all, he might possibly have fallen asleep for a while. He was not certain. He had his eyes closed anyway. But the feeling that he was being watched finally penetrated his rest. He had grown up as a thief in a family of thieves in Jerusalem. The days of strict enforcement of the Yasa code were long gone, but even so, there were very few thieves in Jerusalem, and those that there were, were like David—very aware of being watched. They'd been selected for that. The Yasa code of laws had had those who failed, killed. Of course

368

that hadn't stopped him going against his instincts at that market stall on Corfu, where he could see that the stall-holder had her back to him. She had two small mirrors hidden among her merchandise...

Someone was definitely watching him. He opened his eyes a slit, wondering just how fast he could get to the knife in his boot. If they had tried to kill him with arrows...and failed, knives and certainty would be next.

It was the boy. He was half sitting up in the bed they had made up for him, staring at David. David opened his eyes properly and sat up.

"What are you doing here? And why are you wearing my deel?" asked the boy.

Perhaps because he had just managed to frighten himself silly again, David was less than respectful to this scion of a noble Mongol clan. "I'm here because your sister tried to get me killed instead of you," said David bitterly. "Which is why she made me wear your deel and sit out there, and get shot at. But she didn't tell me that. Oh no. She told me she was *helping* me."

The boy nodded slowly. "Bortai does that kind of thing. You get used to it," he said, quite as if he accepted this as a norm.

"I'll get even. Just you wait. All right, maybe she didn't actually know they'd try to kill me. But she tricked me," he said darkly.

The boy sniggered. "She *always* does that. You get used to it," he said again. "Oh my aching head. What happened to me?"

David had no intention of getting used to that sort of treatment from anyone, even a highborn Mongol lady. The very idea made him angry and frustrated, and although he knew he should be treating this boy with deference, he could not bring himself to do so. "You fell off your horse. Then you landed on your head. Knocked yourself unconscious."

"I did not! I do not fall off," said the boy indignantly. He paused. "Something knocked me off. I remember that. That and the Vlach. I don't remember anything else."

"I suppose you never fall off," said David, sarcasm dripping from every word.

Either the boy was totally unaccustomed to sarcasm, or the effects of being hit on the head were greater than David had realized, because he obviously failed to detect it. "Well. Not that often. And you?"

"At least I don't land on my head," said David, unwilling to admit that he had discovered that compared to the knights, and Kari, he was not a very good rider.

"Oh, I suppose you land on your feet," said the boy, showing that no matter how insensitive he was to being the target of sarcasm, he was expert at using it himself—and that he plainly took David for someone of his own rank, just a little older. "Where are you from? Your accent is very strange."

"Jerusalem. The greatest city in the world," said David proudly.

There was a longish silence. David eventually worked out that the kid—and he was a kid—at least a year younger than he was, was trying to work out where Jerusalem was. Everyone ought to know that. But maybe, on thinking about it, the kid had last been riding around at a kurultai, deep in this godforsaken part of the world. Someone from Jerusalem was not something he'd be expecting. "You're from the Ilkhan. Has Bortai got us away across the sea?"

"No, you're still in the lands of the Golden Horde. I came here..." the kid probably had no idea who the Knights of the Holy Trinity were, "with the tarkhan Borshar."

"Oh. I am very thirsty."

David sat up properly. "Hang on. I'll get Kari to call your sister to bring you something to drink. I don't know where to find anything."

"Kari?"

"Yes. He's driving the cart. He is mad. But don't worry, he's mostly harmless. He doesn't speak Mongol."

"You have a servant that is mad?"

Temptation, never too far from David, took a firm hold of him and steered his mind down to the reply he gave. It was bound to get him into trouble. But sometimes being in trouble was worth the payback. And he felt that he had a fair amount to pay Kari back for. "Doesn't everybody?" he said airily. "We humor him. He gets strange ideas. As I said, he's mostly harmless provided he doesn't get too excited. And he does a good job with the horses. We can't leave him to starve."

"Ah!" Light and respect dawned on the boy. "Lesser clans do. But we of the Hawk clan also take our responsibilities seriously. I suppose old Mette is pretty crazy. She still thinks I am in swaddling clothes," he said, grimacing.

David nodded, and pulled aside the door curtain. "Kari. The boy is awake. He says he's thirsty. Will you call his sister for him?"

Shortly Bortai came along with a skin of what was,

by the smells of it, kumiss. "Help me sit him up," she said.

"I can manage," said the boy rebelliously.

David felt he had the measure of the boy by now. He was still very afraid of the lady Bortai, so scared that his mind failed to make the connection that this was in fact her brother. In his mind the boy had somehow become a sort of younger brother of his own. "Do what you are told, you hell-born brat, or I will beat you," he said, sitting the boy up.

"Ha. You and how many others?" said the boy, not actually resisting. He took the skin of kumiss and drank.

"I think you must lie down again, Kildai," said Bortai.

He opened his mouth to protest, but David again, without thinking, waved a finger at him. He scowled and cooperated. "What's going on, Bortai?" the boy asked, once they had made him comfortable again. "How long have I been like this? I'm tired and weak. I don't like it."

"Longer than I liked either. Now lie still and get better because we may have to ride as if all the demons from the furthest corners of the realms of Erleg Khan are on our tails," she said.

"Now?"

"Not until we are across the great river," she said. "Rest."

He was already slipping into sleep. Or at least his eyes were closing. He opened them briefly and looked at David. "Bortai. Honorable clan. Look after old retainers. Mad ones."

She sat there watching him for a little bit. Kildai at least appeared to be sleeping. Eventually she asked. "What was that about, serf-boy?"

"I have no idea, noble lady," said David with his best attempt at insouciantly pretending not even having been in the same country as whatever had happened to cause whatever she was asking about. "He's been hit on the head. People get very confused by that."

"Yes. He keeps asking me how long he's been like this. And then he forgets he's asked. But this time he recognized me. He seemed to be a lot more with us. He seemed to listen to you. If I had told him to do that, even politely, he would have told me not to treat him like a baby. I am glad he had the kumiss. It's the first time he's asked for anything. You can live off kumiss."

David nearly said "Yes, but who would want to," but managed to bite his tongue in time. The fermented, mildly alcoholic mare's milk had come his way—well, he'd gone out of his way to steal it, because the noble Mongol still drank it sometimes. You had to grow up drinking kumiss to like it. Jerusalem had every other drink known to man, and of a long list David could make to try again, kumiss was near the bottom. You'd have to drink a bucket of it to get mildly tipsy, and he would throw up long before that. But she wanted reassurance, so he gave it. "Yes. I have heard some people eat nothing else all summer."

She scowled. "Yes. True. But the great Ulaghchi Khan forbade that." She looked at her brother again. "You are good with him. And I think it is probably safest for you in here. If he wakes again, call me. I need to watch for enemies."

"Erik is watching. Nothing gets past him, noble lady." He was beginning to believe it.

She nodded. "He is a great orkhan. But he does not know the Raven clan. They have no honor."

So David found himself on sick-bed duty. It beat currying horses. He looked forward to telling Kari that he would have to do that on his own again.

Some time later Kildai awoke again. David's hopes that he might have forgotten the last time or be lost in the confusion of concussion were dashed. Kildai plainly recognized him. "Can you call your crazy manservant? I need to pass some water. And I wasn't going to tell Bortai, but I don't think I can stand up. I feel so weak. But I really need to relieve myself. And I can't have a woman help me do that."

Later, when David had gone off to get himself fed, Bortai sat with her brother. He thought she was looking at him rather too keenly and too often, so he asked about the other boy. "He's not from any clan," said Bortai. "Although his mother was a tortoise," she said smiling.

Kildai looked at her. "Oh. He said he came from Jerusalem."

"Yes, he's with the Franks and the tarkhan."

Kildai had had a Byzantine tutor. His father had insisted. Bortai had learned more from the man than he ever had. The Byzantine knew nothing about the important things of life like horses, or the great game, or even about archery, war or hunting. Most of his attempts at teaching his charge about the history and geography of the wider world had passed into one of Kildai's ears and out of the other. A few errant bits had stuck. He knew that the Franks existed. And he knew that Jerusalem was in the lands of the Ilkhan Mongol. The Tortoise must be one of their clans. Strange, but maybe the Ilkhan had run out of good names.

Chapter 38

King Emeric was no rural hill shepherd who could track errant members of his flock by the smallest hoof indent. But the tracks here did not require that. The wagon had cut deep grooves in the turf next to the trail. He could see exactly where it had stopped. The fat merchant Kopernico Goldenfuss had definitely not lied about that. Of course, being a merchant he had probably lied about nearly everything else. Kneeling and shaking visibly before his king now, he probably wished that he had stayed there, or fled over the mountains, or done anything but return to report on the enemy's camp and how successful he'd been, and cheerfully demand the reward he'd been promised.

"I swear, Your Majesty. I swear they were right here. And they wanted that drink. They were paying me three times its price..." he plainly realized suddenly that this was perhaps not what he should be telling his overlord. "Dear God! It's their prince. He's the devil. He even looks like the black spy. He stopped them buying and drinking it. I swear it must have been him who made your plan fail. I did exactly as you bade me."

"Except to sell them liquor from my stores at an extortionate price. Which you somehow omitted to tell me," said Emeric coldly. He detested merchants. Chaffering scum. They always cheated him of his due. Well, sometimes it was important to remind them that a nobleman took at the sword's point.

"Honestly, Your Majesty, I had to do that," he babbled. "They would have known I was a spy otherwise. Any merchant would have done what I did. I swear it. Ask anyone. Ask my apprentice, he was there. They suspected nothing. They would have been insensible with the drink...please Your Majesty. I did my best."

"Except to steal from me. And fail me," said Emeric, putting his hands on the man's shoulders and letting pain arc through the merchant. The man screamed. "No, Your Majesty, aaagh! I never brought back any silver. Truly, I would have given it to you. All I got was the script of the prince."

"Which you failed to tell me about. And Prince Vlad saw through you, knowing you to be a thieving merchant." Emeric let the magical gift of his aunt's flow through his hands again. The man writhed in agony and then slumped, and toppled over sideways. Emeric had had this happen before, particularly with older men. He'd even had a few cut open to find out why. It would seem that their hearts were not equal to the burden the magic placed on them. He walked away, looking up the green valley, where, if this now dead merchant was to be believed, Prince Vlad of Valahia had quartered his little army. Well, short of necromancy he'd get no more from the merchant. But the man had mentioned his apprentice. Emeric had known that two of them had gone up. But he had not thought about questioning Goldenfuss's apprentice. He clicked his fingers. An officer-aide appeared as if by magic. Knowing that not to do so was a capital offense had worked so well with his aides. "Find me that merchant's apprentice," said Emeric, waving a negligent hand at the dead body. "And have that strung up as a warning. They'll not know he was dead first."

The officer left at to run, glad to find a task within easy reach, no doubt. He came back a few minutes later, sweating more than could be justified by the heat. "Your Majesty . . . it appears that the apprentice has run away. With his master's strongbox."

Emeric stared at the officer. "And how was this allowed to happen?"

"Your Majesty, it appears that the fellow took off when the merchant went to you to ask for his reward. Er. The man was not guarded at that time. He didn't even wait for his master to get in to see you."

"I see. You will find out who should have been guarding the wagon and the apprentice. Have them reduced to the ranks, and given twenty lashes."

Emeric looked in frustration at the empty valley again. It had been such a good, elegant plot. It must have been that accursed apprentice who betrayed it. It would appear that he had killed the wrong man. Emeric shrugged. There were plenty more where that one came from. Vlad had escaped him this time, but he could not hope to continue to do so. He was underarmed and sooner or later would be drawn out into open conflict. Then the superiority of Emeric's cavalry over some peasant irregulars would make the young fool rue the day he'd fled his quarters in Buda castle.

❁   ❁   ❁

The Smerek cousins had ridden through the night, luckily—and, in large part due to the intervention and wariness of their poacher escorts—had had no need to use Stanislaw's collection of pistols. Stanislaw had one in each boot—boots that had been specially modified to take them—three in his waistband, and in a double bandolier that had been made to fit under his loose cotte, a further four. He knew it was a way of compensating for being unable to do anything when he had had to watch the others die. But it would never happen again. He would start shooting first.

Now, at last, it seemed as if he would have help doing it. And if he had his way it would not just be nine of the bastards that died. His cousin—and indeed the whole family—wanted revenge. But they also dreamed of a place they could have and hold, of a lord to whom they could be as loyal as he was to them. Stanislaw only dreamed of shooting as many as possible. It had been the family—and principally Józef—that had persuaded him out of taking his arsenal of pistols and heading straight back to Buda. That would have killed all of the family. But now... well it would seem he'd found both revenge and a man to whom he could feel loyalty, and who would protect his family.

Riding through the dark on a tired horse, Stanislaw cried properly for the first time since the trip to Buda. It was as if a great weight had been lifted, and he had found that there was a God after all. He wanted to find a chapel, pray and make his peace, something he had been unable to do since Edward's death from blood loss and festering wounds after the beating.

Back in Harghita the family had met behind closed

doors to discuss the news that Józef and Stanislaw
had brought back from the mountains. It was not
hard for them to meet behind closed doors, after
all. There was no business anymore, and the very
neighbors shunned them, as if in fear that Emeric's
enmity would somehow contaminate everything they
touched. Across Valahia, no Smerek gunsmith was
selling anything. Cousin Anton, who had shocked the
family by going into the casting of bronze, instead of
sticking to firearms, was the only member still selling
his goods. For the rest of them, sitting with storerooms full of stock, they had been committing slow
economic suicide. The potential buyers still brave or
foolhardy enough to be interested had known that.
Known that the Smereks would eventually become
desperate enough to sell their businesses and stock
at any price.

The question that now faced the emigrés was whether
even that situation was not better than the risk they
now faced. But when Emeric had chosen to kill one of
the Smerek patriarchs on one of his cruel whims, he
had pushed the family beyond the limits of the caution
they had always exercised as refugee settlers. The entire
punishment had had the opposite effect from that which
Emeric could have desired.

A week ago they had been discussing the possibilities
of abandoning their holdings, going south and seeing
if they could somehow escape to Venice. When the
family had fled Galicia, they had come with little more
than ten sons, their tools and their lives. It had been
a long, hard struggle. It had seemed almost impossible that they would have to abandon all they had
built. Now that they had been offered an alternative,

380 Mercedes Lackey, Eric Flint & Dave Freer

loyalty for loyalty, which two of the boys assured them
that they at least accepted unconditionally, the entire
extended family moved towards open rebellion. They
had plenty of fuel for it.

The murders had been the match put to the fuse,
but there had been problems long before this. Before
the king's disastrous expedition to Corfu the family
had been offered the opportunity to make arquebuses
for the levy of infantry raised here in Valahia. It had
been their first ever military order. The Smerek family
had gone to it with a will. They wished to prove that
their weapons were superior, that they were reliable
as gunsmiths to produce goods on time. Then, in the
fashion of military procurement under King Emeric,
the order had been abruptly withdrawn. The family
had been left with storerooms full of arquebuses better suited to military use than their normal hunting
market. And then . . . when they had been attempting
to stave off bankruptcy, King Emeric had added the
final blow. He had probably thought it would be a
fatal one, though why he would want to destroy them
was a mystery.

He had not reckoned with the spirit that lay beneath
their stolid faces.

A thousand arquebuses waited for a better purpose.
The Smerek family were delighted to give them one,
even if they were only paid in a promissory note. But
they were not unaware of the possible consequences.
Sooner or later King Emeric would find out just where
those guns came from, and then there would be hell
and blood to pay.

They were willing to pay that, so long as they got
a good return in the same coin from King Emeric.

But very few of them were willing to let their women and children pay it for them. Some of the men would be returning to the mountains, with their tools, and a great deal of black powder. Others, the old, the young, the women and the infirm would be going south. Cousin Anton was not obviously connected with the family. Corona was far from the unrest. And it was far closer to flee from there to either Venice, or even possibly into Mongol lands.

Long before morning, firm plans had been made. Travelers set out, going south. Men remained, packing wagons, loading every weapon from their storerooms and display cases. They set out at dusk, having paid suitable bribes to get out of the town gates. There were too many bandits for most travelers to wish to be abroad at night. The Smerek men hoped that it would be bandits that they met, and not King Emeric's patrols. They did have men on good horses riding ahead, ready to pass through any checkpoint, and then ride back across country to give them warning. But they had also had help from Vlad's poachers.

Back in the town of Harghita few had noticed their absence. A neighbor. A man who had hoped to buy a gun, illegally, for a quiet and nasty act of revenge. Neither was telling anyone. Instead the town was buzzing with another, related story. The story of an apprentice who had fled his master's wagon ... and gone to give warning to the Prince of Valahia that his master had been on a mission from the King of Hungary. He had arrived on foot—at a deserted camp, not long before the Magyar. He'd hidden just in time, and seen his master die at the king's hand, and be hung for the crows and ravens. He'd sought refuge in the mountains with the prince...been recognized by the men. And been told that Prince Vlad had known of the treachery...and yet still had planned to honor his debt.

The story spread across Valahia, growing, like the tales of Vlad's vengeance, and his conquest of the Magyar.

Vlad lay with her in his arms. She was soft, warm and curved, and pressed against him. But when he asked, she pulled away. "I don't think I want talk, Drac. If you want to talk I will go elsewhere. There are plenty of men who do not want to talk. Do you not want me?"

"Very much. I had not known how much before... You have given me something very precious. I had never known a woman before you, Rosa. But...I have lived in a tower since I was a little boy. With menservants and an old priest and an older tutor. I don't understand so much. And you are the only person I can ask."

She was silent for a while. "Drac. You really are a babe in woods pretending to be a bear. I think that frightens me because I also want you to be a bear. Very well. I will tell you how I came to be a whore in your army's tail. And if you condemn me..."

"I will not do that. Not now. Not ever," he said gently.

She looked at him, considering. "You could be a bear in the woods, you know."

"But I need to be a Dragon. And to do that I need to understand."

"I was sixteen when my father married me off to an

old knight on a neighboring estate. We were freeholders, but not rich ... Mother told me that I would have
to accept that it was a woman's duty to lie there and
accept what men wanted and did. It was a woman's
burden, she said. She said it hurt and I would hate it,
but I would at least have the consolation of children."

Rosa was silent a while. Vlad waited. "She was
wrong. She was wrong about all of it. But no one
will own me. Not ever again."

Chapter 39

"I am worried," said Erik to Manfred, as they stopped for the evening.

"A normal situation," said Manfred. "What about this time? Besides a beautiful woman who keeps laughing at you."

"Believe it or not, that's part of it. Although not for the reasons you imply. I met and lost the only girl I will ever love."

Manfred said nothing. He'd learned that much from Francesca. Saying things like, "You'll get over it" or "there are other fish in the sea" were counter-productive, even if they might be true. Manfred had never been that seriously emotionally engaged with a lover. Physically engaged, yes. But he knew Erik was different, and did not know how to love lightly, and would never learn to. Manfred doubted anyone would be allowed to pierce that armor again. It was a pity, because Erik would never really get over it without someone else to take her place in his heart. But he knew his bodyguard, mentor, and latterly friend too well to do more than tease him, beyond a certain point.

"It was that incident when someone shot at the horseboy. It just doesn't fit, Manfred. The Mongols responded far too slowly...and the commander knew it was going to happen, if you ask me. That and the general...I don't know, feel. And the fact that they say we're going to have to cross the great river—I presume that must be the Danube. I feel like we are walking into a trap."

"You've been uncomfortable from the very start of this venture into the Golden Horde's lands, Erik. You've told me so at least five times now," said Manfred.

"It's the river, Manfred. Look, here, if things turned nasty...well, we are not that far ride from Illyrian lands. And if that Iskander Beg has less than a regiment's worth of men very close at hand I will be very surprised. They were there, watching, when we had our first little meeting. I spotted at least three scouts, and I'd bet Mongols did, too...but that won't be all. Iskander is like a good knife man. You won't even see the blade until he tries to kill you."

He gestured at one of the Golden Horde Mongol trotting past. "There are not that many of them. With our armor and our cohesion as a force...we could possibly get you back to that border-line. But not once we are across that river."

Manfred thought about it. Erik was by nature and by training one of the finest bodyguards in world. His instincts were preternaturally sharp. But this time...it just didn't add up. "There is of course their reputation for honoring the safety of envoys and diplomats," said Manfred. "And we are that, even if I must agree with you that this lot seem as trustworthy as the average adder. They don't like us, but there is not

much—serious—that they can do about it. Envoys
and their escorts are sacrosanct."

"It's an old reputation," said Erik. "Centuries old.
Things change. And the part that worries me most,
is that they are not likely to send your head in a bag
to the Holy Roman Emperor to tell them that it happened. The Ilkhan, by all accounts, are still known for
that honor to envoys, but if you die here—the blame
is likely to be pinned on Iskander Beg. Or bandits."

"The only part of your logic that doesn't make any
sense to me," said Manfred, "is why they would do
it? They have nothing to gain by it, that I can see.
Well, other than your little bit of Mongol cuddle. And
she's pretty, but hardly worth ruining the reputation
of centuries, and creating two major enemies if word
of it leaks out. And you know these things leak out of
even the most closed societies. Sooner or later, someone would tell a trader or a seaman. But I actually
have an entirely different worry for you. Something
that has been bothering me."

"What is that?" asked Erik.

"It seems to me," said Manfred, "that our entire
reason for coming on this expedition has fallen
apart. We hoped to meet and establish some form
of diplomatic contact with the leaders of the Golden
Horde. Now it appears, from what I can gather that
they are in a state which is very close to civil war.
They don't have a new khan. Their electoral kurultai
broke up in fighting. Nobody is in charge at the
moment. From the point of view of our agreement
with the Ilkhan: we have honored that already. We
have brought their tarkhan safely to Golden Horde
lands. Should we not be heading back? I know that

we haven't affected things as far as Jagiellon's fleet is concerned, but to be brutally honest, their civil war does us no harm."

Erik nodded slowly. "A point. I think you need to talk to Eberhard."

"For once I actually think I really could benefit by talking to old doubletalk," agreed Manfred. "Come with me. With any luck you will get your wish, and not cross the river."

They found Eberhard, "We have a problem—besides the fact that their women laugh at Erik," said Manfred.

"Would you give it a rest?" Erik scowled. "Manfred has a serious question about the entire mission. It would seem that our purpose—to treat with the new khan—cannot be achieved. I think we need to head back to Illyria." He did not say "While we still can," but Manfred could tell that he was thinking it.

Eberhard tugged at his short white beard. "Perhaps we need to talk to the tarkhan Borshar." Eberhard gave a wry grimace. "That is if the tarkhan is prepared to talk to anyone. My experience among the Ilkhan is that their diplomats are even better than the Ard Ri's speakers at the fine art of saying very little in very many words, for a very long time. Borshar seems to be an exception to that. Perhaps it's because he has to serve among us foreigners. I had hoped we'd learn something about the Ilkhan as we journeyed together. But he really is the most taciturn of men."

Manfred decided that if Eberhard thought the Ilkhan wordy, he was infinitely glad that he had not ended up having to deal with them, too. But he refrained from saying anything, something he wished that Eberhard would do.

Erik shrugged. "He looks almost as if he's in a trance half the time."

"Well, let's go and find out if he is talking at the moment," said Manfred. So the three of them went across to the encampment that had been set up for the tarkhan. Much to their surprise, he was not only welcoming but quite affable. He clapped his hands and sent his manservant to bring a bitter brew in little cups that he called kaveh, served with sickly-sweet little sweetmeats. Manfred would have preferred a glass of wine, but that was not on offer, it seemed. On the other hand Borshar was, this time, willing to talk.

"At the moment, until a new khan is elected, the orkhan, that is the war-leader, will oversee matters. It will be of great value for you to meet him. I will arrange for an audience for you, it will be an opportunity for you to present your credentials. He is a leader of great influence. I have spoken with these clansmen. He is trying to bring the kurultai back together again."

Erik had no time for diplomatic doublespeak. "Tarkhan, I am responsible for the security and safety of the prince." As an afterthought he added, "and Prince Manfred is responsible for your welfare. It is my task to assess risks. I do not like this situation. Quite honestly, I believe that we will come to the Danube tomorrow. I am concerned about crossing it."

The tarkhan raised his eyebrows. "You are here as part of my escort. You were honored with that status by the Bashar Ahmbien, the voice of the Ilkhan Hotai in Jerusalem. It is a matter of honor among the Mongol that an envoy and his entourage, and their escort will be as safe as if they are in their own homes. Do you question this?"

Manfred watched in some amusement as Erik, the blunt-spoken Erik, tried to avoid a major diplomatic incident.

"No," said Erik after a short struggle with his tongue and his conscience.

Before they rode out the next morning, Erik discussed the situation with Falkenberg and Von Gherens. He was not surprised to find the two old warhorses had similar feelings of discomfort. "They're supposed to be escorting us, protecting us, providing something of an honor guard," said Falkenberg. "They're not. They're guarding us, as if they expect us to break and run. When we rode that archer down—Kari had wounded him, half of them were all set to attack us instead."

"And if he wasn't one of their boys, then I'm a castrati eunuch from Alexandria," said Von Gherens. "We're riding into trouble, Erik."

"But from what you say, we can't easily get out of it," said Falkenberg. "I had a long talk with Eberhard last night. He said that to break off now would just about be a declaration of war. A deadly insult. I think it might be worth it."

"Unfortunately, Manfred doesn't. And in the end it is his decision," said Erik dourly.

"So what do we do?" asked Von Gherens. "Besides make our peace with God and go like lambs to the slaughter?"

Falkenberg touched his sword hilt. "We will make them pay a very high price for it. To the last man."

Erik bit his lip. Shook his head. "In a way, the

worst outcome for them is if some of the knights get away. A great deal of their power and prestige rest on their reputation. So does that of the Ilkhan Mongol, who do a great deal more business with us. Any kind of treachery here would force them into an alliance with us. We need to look carefully at the trap we are walking into. And then when they think they have us, give them a surprise or two."

The notion that the Mongols were not a great maritime people was upheld by the ferry boats. Erik's standards were set out in the north Atlantic. These things would have had a life span of moments in those great swells. Even on a river this size, Erik viewed them with trepidation. However, they did stay afloat for long enough to get them across the Danube. It was a vast river, and an intimidating barrier.

Looking upstream Erik could see distant cliffs. "What is that?" he asked one of their escort, pointing at it.

The man spat in the water. "Magyar," he said sourly. "Irongate."

Erik had been unaware of just how close they were to the edge of Valahia and Hungarian territory. Not that they would find any security or help there.

Once they had crossed the river it was still another four days' ride to the orkhan's camp. With every league, Erik's worries increased.

The camp was not far from the river. And Erik became aware of just how large the force assembled there was. There must be at least five thousand men there.

Erik looked at his pitiful force of knights, and put the heel of his hand to his head.

PART III
September, 1540 A.D.

Chapter 40

Vlad looked despairingly at his recruits' attempts to hit targets with their new arquebuses. He himself carried two of the Smerek pistols. And he could hit a target with them, while on horseback. This lot, it would appear, could not have hit a barn door from the inside. Wreathed in smoke, they fired at targets fifty paces off... and missed.

"Don't worry, Drac," said Sergeant Emil, when he commented on it. "They're as good as King Emeric's arquebusiers. Maybe better. The guns are better. And it's not about accuracy, really. It's about massed fire. They're not shooting at targets. They're just shooting at the charging mass."

"But will they even get that right?" asked Vlad.

The sergeant nodded. "We don't tell them so, but they're better than most levies. They'll get there, Sire. It's whether they can do so when they've got a regiment of Magyar charging down on them that you have to worry about. And if they don't, well, at least we won't have to worry about it."

"Why not?"

"Because we'll all be dead," said the sergeant with macabre humor. "If they break and run, we'll be run down and spitted. It'll be like a pack of wolves among newborn lambs."

"It's a small garrison, Sire. And we need to blood the troops somehow. And we need food and a victory," said Emil.

Vlad considered the rough map. So far every action had been a rearguard and defensive one . . . no matter how successful they'd been, he knew that sooner or later they would have to go on the offensive. "How well can we scout the area? We don't want to put our heads into a trap. We need to be able to get in, and get out. We still can't dream of holding a town."

The sergeant beamed. "That's why it is such a good target, Sire. We've sent scouts right to the walls. And there is one road in from Gara. It's a good two leagues off. There is only a garrison there at all because of the silver mine."

"Ah. Silver mine," said Vlad, keeping his voice even.

The sergeant looked uncomfortable. "Well, yes Sire. It's a wealthy little place, because of that. And it is your silver, Sire."

Vlad had had no idea how much war or an army cost, and of the influence of money, back when he had been a prince locked in a tower in Buda. He was better informed today. Plainly, so was his sergeant. "I will need to accompany the scouts," he said, thoughtfully.

Vlad was surprised how the knowledge that an attack was imminent galvanized his troops. They weren't supposed to know. Somehow they did. "You always do," said the quartermaster, when he commented on it. "Of course you get the place and time wrong, sometimes, Sire. But even the lowliest trooper has his ear to the rumor mill."

It made spies and the extracting of information from captives a lot more of a threat. He'd have to do something about that. Soon. After taking Gara.

Vlad was quite pleased with his plan. They made a night-march and then waited in the pease-fields just outside the town. There were scouts on the Lesu road, in case help somehow came to the relief of Gara's garrison. All the plans were made, the men instructed, primed and ready. At first light, a cart, heavily laden with hay, arrived at the gates. Demanded entry. On being admitted . . .

As the guard came down to demand to know just who they were, the two men took action. They were supposed to light the fuse that would set off the charge that would break the axle, and leave the cart stuck in the gate-arch. The Smerek brothers assured him it would be no more than a sharp crack, as if the axle had merely collapsed under the weight. Then with the gate open, Vlad's men would charge into the town.

The cart rolled forward and Vlad watched . . . as it all went awry.

Firstly, the guard was not prepared to let the men stop in the gateway. He belted the ox with his spear-shaft. The charge of explosive went off . . . A lot louder than a mere cracking axle. The guard started fighting the two men on the cart, and the gate . . . swung ponderously closed as they raced towards it. Someone on the wall above the gate fired on them. Vlad saw it go all wrong as an explosion roared and a column of flames leapt above the gate.

"Haycart caught fire," said Sergeant Emil. There had been a powder charge in the bottom in case the guard had stopped the cart outside the gate. More shots rang out over their heads. Vlad realized with gloomy certainty that they could not take the gate. And he'd lost two men. "Sound the retreat."

"Yes, Sire." The man winded his horn. "Well, back to the mountains. We'll need to move camp," said Vlad, determined not show any sign of the fury and embarrassment he felt.

The sergeant cleared his throat. "The boys will be over the back wall by now, Sire. No point in our going too far."

"What?"

The sergeant looked distinctly nervous. "Well, Sire. We're veterans of King Emeric's campaigns, Mirko and me. And the king makes these complicated plans. They go wrong nine times out of ten, and...well, we get punished for failing. So we got used to making a second plan or two. Just in case. The king usually isn't near at hand to know that the officers...um, modified things a bit. And that if they get a chance, the sergeants and men do it, too. But you're here, Sire, so you have to know. We had some of the men make ladders and wait for the commotion on this side."

Vlad was silent. Then he sighed. "I have learned three things from this, Emil. The first is that in war, things will go wrong. The second is that I need to have thought of a second plan."

"And the third, Sire?"

"To choose my officers carefully, and to listen when they wish to tell me about their experiences."

Vlad could hear the shooting now, from the far side of the small walled town. "Do we ride to join them or wait here?

"They'll open the gate for us, Sire."

Very rapidly, riding into the small town, Vlad realized that it was not only how to assault towns and conduct wars that he still had to learn about, but that the attack itself was only a small part of what he should have planned. He had won, yes. The small garrison had been outnumbered...and the survivors surrendered. And had been murdered out of hand, to Vlad's anger and embarrassment. And now his men seemed to have scattered into the houses and shops in an orgy of looting and mayhem. Vlad tried to round his men up, with limited success. He wanted silver, and he wanted food for his men. There was going to be precious little of either, at this rate.

The woman in the torn dress was screaming in terror as she ran, head down, not looking where she was going. She almost ran headlong into Vlad's horse. And behind her came...not the horrors of hell, but three of Vlad's own. "What do you think you are doing?" he asked them icily.

The men were already drunk enough for one to try to answer the question. "Victor's rights..." he said, his voice surly, doubt and shame making him angry both with himself and his prince.

She clung to his stirrup. "Lord, they killed my man. Save me."

"He's not dead. Jus' knocked him down..." A sense of shame now seemed to be returning to the men, the third one was sidling backwards, desperate to be away from what might have seemed acceptable, and a good idea, moments earlier.

"Hell's teeth, are you a pack of ravening animals?" Vlad felt the fury that had been building in him start to rise. "This is my land. My town, too. Yours too, damn you." He turned to the sergeant. "Sound that horn. Sound the retreat. We ride through the streets in one circuit. Any man who does not answer the call, I'll leave to get hung by the locals or Emeric, whoever gets them first."

"Sire . . . the silver."

"Devil take it, man. I'll have my due, brought to me. Not taken at knife-point over the raped bodies of my people's daughters. She could have been your sister, you animals. Sound that horn, Emil. And you three," he pointed at the would-be rapists. "Be happy that she got to me in time, or I'd make an example of you with the butcher's knife. Fall in."

The woman's eyes were wide. She knelt. But Vlad did not wait to hear what she had to say. He'd plucked the horn from the sergeant. He did not know how to blow it correctly. But he did. It made a noise . . . a horrible one. It was just as well. It stirred him from his fury, and spared the life of the three, who had not yet managed to get in place behind him. He handed it back to Emil. "Blow it. Properly."

They rode on, with the sergeant sounding the horn, and Vlad's men straggling onto the road behind them. They rode past the burned hay-cart, lying crashed where the panicked oxen had dragged it. The fire had spread to the next buildings. Vlad did not stop. He knew that not all of his men were behind him. He

supposed he ought to halt, do a roll-call and send a
few squads back to dig out the missing, be they dead
or engaged in sacking. But his disgust was such that
he just had to get away from there.

Part of that disgust was with himself. He'd known,
briefly, a surge of triumph, and a surge of lust. A
desire to raven, too. He'd turned it into anger with his
peasant recruits. He remembered them now, waiting
in the darkness. The half-frightened bravado. The odd
silences. The whispered prayers—he had very keen
hearing. How had it turned into this?

They were met barely half a mile from the town,
on a bend just short of the crest of the rise by one
of the scouts, pushing his horse as fast as he could.
"They're coming, Sire," panted the man. "Thank God
you are here. They're between us and the pass, already."

There was nowhere to run to. They could retreat
on the town... Vlad was damned if he would. "Let
us see if these men of ours can stand up to that
cavalry charge, Sergeant. It's that or, as you said, be
slaughtered like lambs."

Vlad's sergeants had been a silent group on their
retreat from the town. Now they took charge, positioning the arquebussiers on the ridge either side of the
road, and in a block, kneeling, standing and waiting
in the middle of the trail. Vlad and his handful of
"cavalry" waited too, off on the left flank. If anyone
broke through, they would have to deal with them.

They did not have long to wait. The fleeing scout
had plainly been seen in his panicked flight... but it
was also obvious that the cavalry had not expected to
find Vlad's soldiers so far outside the town, arrayed
for battle. Moving at a distance-eating canter, the

Magyar cavalry were a little strung out, but still in fairly close formation when the leaders, coming up to the ridge, saw Vlad's arquebusiers. To give the Magyar credit, they did not hesitate. Lances dipped. And to give Vlad's arquebusiers equal credit...the sight did not make them break and run. The first volley was a little ragged. But the second rank fired in an almost simultaneous discharge. Wreathed in powder smoke, the third rank fired—and the flanking arquebussiers cut loose, too. The charging cavalry fell, but did not stop.

Neither did the massed fire. The green irregulars worked as if this was a drill, and they were an experienced drill team. As if the Magyar lances were not out, dipped and racing towards them.

Gun smoke and thunder, and his men standing like a wall before the wave...would it overtop them? But the wave faltered and broke before the massed fire of the Smerek arquebuses. If the cavalry had realized that they were flanked earlier...or if they had realized just how shallow those flanks were...but they had not. The terrain had favored Vlad's men. The Magyar retreated—in bad order. They'd pushed the charge too hard and too far, believing that the enemy would break. When they had not, it had been they that had been broken.

"Stand!" yelled one of sergeants, when Vlad's stunned men saw the charge turn to a rout. "Stand, damn you. Recharge your weapons."

It looked then as if the discipline, so strong in adversity, might just break...the line was breaking up into men chasing after cavalry, cheering and yelling. Vlad had seen his troops come to pieces once that day, in victory. It wasn't going to happen again.

He rode up. "Back. NOW. Form up, and ready your weapons." His voice halted and held them.

Sure enough, the second rush came, this time with the riders caracoling and firing horse-pistols. Vlad exhaled sharply. Had they encountered a scattered rabble chasing after them, even this scanty remnant would have had no trouble riding them down. But the massed fire and the extra range of the Smerek arquebuses...turned the second advance into a bloody retreat, too.

Now Vlad's troops made no move without an order. The heavy arquebuses were recharged. Vlad sent his scouts out, and a few minutes later they began to march forward, through the killing zone. Vlad realized that they had in the course of one fractured morning passed from recruits into being soldiers. "They fought well," he said to Emil who seemed to have elected himself as his prince's aide-de-camp...well that, or watchdog.

"Yes, Sire. Shall I have a squad detailed to collect weapons from the dead? We're a bit short, Sire, though we have good guns, I'll grant. And we've got a few wounded there. Ours and theirs."

"Ours we take with us. Theirs we will disarm. We cannot care for them. I just hope we reach the trail back into mountains before we have to fight again." He turned to Emil, letting his guard slip, briefly, "How is it that they were such lions here, and such jackals back there?" he asked plaintively.

"Reckon there is a bit of animal, all kinds of animal in all of us, sire," said the Sergeant uncomfortably. "Most officers don't set the standards you do. It's... it's kind of normal. Armies do that."

Vlad looked at him coldly. Yes. There was a beast within him, too. But he kept it leashed . . . because . . . because if he ever simply let go he knew that it would destroy all in its path. And it would destroy him, too. "Emeric's army behaves like that. But these are my towns, and my people. I have come to liberate them, not use terror to make them my slaves."

Sergeant Emil was either a very brave or very foolish man. He shook his head. "You can't stop an army looting a bit, Sire. I'm sorry. I've spent too long as a soldier to believe otherwise. Maybe you, Sire, can stop them short of rapine, and murder. But ordinary soldiers . . . will take small things, Sire. They're poor men. And only human."

Vlad was silent. Then he said, "I will put up with them being only human. It's them being ravening animals that I will not. I will put up with them being humans because they have shown me that they can also be men." He sighed. "The animal and the man do war within each and every one of us, Sergeant. Me, too. We may not be strong enough to win every battle there, but if we lose more than the smallest skirmishes . . . if we give ground, the animal wins."

A quiet voice within him said "but sometimes the man may not be strong enough to defeat the enemy outside. Sometimes we may need that animal." He banished the thought. It frightened him. Like the animal darkness that rose in him sometimes, he could neither understand nor control it.

It was much later on the ride, when they were heading deeper into the safety of the mountains and his head was replaying the events of the day, that it occurred to him: why had the relief column come at all? And if he had not become so angry, they would have caught him with his men scattered through the small town, drunken and dispersed. He pointed it out to Emil. The sergeant nodded. "Yes, Drac. The men are already asking how you knew it was going to be a trap."

Vlad did not know how to answer. He felt a suspicion that legend was writing itself around him, in spite of himself.

He suspected it would betray him, one day.

Chapter 41

Elizabeth finished the last of the rites that would allow the dark messenger out of his entrapment in the pentacle, in safety. Safety for her, anyway. Crocell waited for her, at least with the appearance of patience. "You seek my master's assistance in the capture of Vlad, the Prince of Valahia," he said with a lift of the dark eyebrows, once he was free.

She nodded. "I have tried earthly means—Emeric's troops—first. When it became obvious that they were being misled by magical means I turned to my allies and the demons at my beck and call. We held the rite in my residence outside Caedonia. I tried a summonsing. It failed. He is peculiarly resistant to my magics."

"He would be largely immune to magics intended for humans. His blood is not entirely human..."

"I have for some years entrapped lesser creatures of air, fire and water to my bidding. Those summons did not work either."

"Because he is not that, fully, either."

"I have created mixtures before. I have forced the lusts of fire on wind. I commanded and constrained the results of that. I still have captive some of the results of those and other experiments."

"This is not the same. His is a willing sharing, an abandonment of some of the rights and powers of both to join in a union. It is a powerful magical bond, the greatest perhaps, the innocent giving themselves to the other in a willing self-sacrifice. The power generated by that willing union will transcend the givers. It may kill them or make them something more powerful. Powerful enough to resist the lesser demons you sent after him."

"Then I will need more power. I need power over him."

Crocell smiled. There was no humor or joy in that smile. "You already have. He is human enough to be seduced. And get him into a place of power, and by using the rite of Cthasares, you can strip some of his power from him. He is mortal. He can be killed as easily as the next mortal. Well. Fire and poisons are less than effective. But a bullet or sword thrust could kill him. Do not, however, try direct magics against him. Or even in close proximity to him. They may recoil and act instead on you."

Not to use her magical skills? That would be hard. She said as much.

"Passive constraints, spells on those who surround him may work. He is a danger. Why do you pursue him?"

"I want to capture a wyvern. I wanted him as bait. I have been informed by Count Mindaug . . ."

"He dabbles in dangerous and demonic traps, Elizabeth. He may be engulfed by one."

"So do I. And like him, I intend to outwit it," said Elizabeth, her voice chill. "Is the wyvern directly dangerous to me? You are constrained to speak the truth."

"Not directly, no. It is a vessel."

"I can break vessels if need be."

"True," said Crocell. "And these ones are quite young and fragile."

Elizabeth stared coolly at King Emeric. "You called me to ask me what to do next because Vlad of Valahia burned a town and shot one of your regiments of cavalry to flinders."

Emeric held his temper in check. He still was uncertain of his ability to deal with her. If he had to...it would be at long range. "I thought you might need to know, Aunt," he said, trying to match her coolness and failing. He'd been so certain that this trap would work, would deal with the problem rapidly and effectively. The deserter from Vlad's forces had sung beautifully. Vlad's scouts had been watching the town so...Emeric had come up with what he'd thought was such an elegant solution. What was one small town? One little garrison? Vlad's scouts had watched the town. Emeric's scouts had watched the trail down from the high mountains instead. When they were sure that Vlad's rag-tag army had gone...they'd borne word to the waiting troops at Lesu. Emeric wanted the little town to fall. While the sack was on...the rebels would be in one place. His Magyar could fire the entire nest, and kill any that tried to flee. Instead...it had failed. That Valahian swine had fired the town—ineffectually admittedly, and waited in ambush for the Magyar. Vlad of Valahia had never learned such tactics in his elegant prison. He must have an advisor who was as cunning as a snake. And thus Emeric turned to his own snake.

"I already knew. I have sources not available to you," she said dismissively.

He hated her. How he hated her. But he feared and needed her, too. "At least that will be the end of his support among the damned commoners. He burned their precious little town. They will hate him now."

Elizabeth shook her head. "I promise you that by now they are already finding ways to say that it was all your fault, Nephew. They will believe what they wish to believe. Do not concern yourself with the opinions of lesser people."

"That is what he has: an army of peasants," said Emeric angrily. "They are like lice. There are always more."

Elizabeth looked at her profile in the long mirror in his command tent, ignoring him. Adjusting the collar on her dress. Eventually he coughed. "So what are you doing about Vlad, Aunt?"

"Nephew. I know he is dangerous. I have always known that. You underestimate him, and the magic and powers concerned with him. I am moving to trap him... And I have to do it myself. I will have him, but like all good ploys it takes a little time to get him to betray himself."

"You do not fail, Aunt. You are the wisest, the cleverest person I know," he said ingratiatingly, doing his best at flattery. He knew that he wasn't very good at it, that she saw through his efforts. But she still did respond to it. If family rumor was to be believed it was her vanity that had entrapped her in the first place. They said that she had not been particularly beautiful—but that she had had a very good skin. She had gone to extreme lengths to keep it that way, he knew.

"And I will not fail this time. I play a long game, Nephew. For very high stakes."

He knew that. He also had a good idea just what the stakes were. He had considered it himself. But he had her, so why risk it himself? "So what do you need me to do?"

She shrugged. "Much as you are doing, I think. It has relatively little bearing."

"It has quite a lot of bearing on the Kingdom, Aunt. I . . . we, cannot afford a rebellion here. Not a successful one. Hungary would splinter," said Emeric, hoping to finally get her onto the plane of his real, physical concerns.

"Any rebellion will be short lived without Vlad of Valahia. He is their hope, their darling, and their leader. Without him as a rallying point you will have a few minor fires, but no conflagration, Emeric. I will remove him . . . and that which I seek."

"How . . . I mean he seems very good at evading us. When he finally comes out to fight he has to lose. So he hides and runs."

"I know where he is," she said calmly.

"Well, tell me."

"It would not help. I attempted that when I sent your soldiers in, to ambush him."

"What will you do to catch him then?"

She smiled sweetly at him. "I am going to join him. With my assistants. Training and preparing them is what I have done while you chased around futilely."

One day he was going to kill her. "Join him . . . ?"

"Yes. For a little while. And I will give him money and support so that he comes to rely on me. I told you he was dangerous. Here, in Valahia, not even I can just walk in and walk out with him. I could have done that in Buda. But not here. Not any more."

"He has a rag-tag army of peasant irregulars. How would they stop any decent force?" demanded Emeric.

She raised her perfect eyebrows. "How do you think he has stopped them so far? Military genius? This land works its own magic for him. If I could just ride in and take him I would. But it is far more complex than you would understand."

"I am going to crush him militarily," snarled Emeric.

"Good. Do. If you can," she said dismissively.

If the countess Elizabeth Bartholdy ever felt sorry for anyone, she could have felt sorry for this hapless idiot of a nephew of hers. He was so easy to manipulate, she barely needed the magical controls she'd set in place on him. She needed Emeric to press Vlad, to make him even more reliant on her. If Mindaug was right it was all a question of timing. The wyverns would not be ready yet, and neither would he. When they were, she must be in place. Tonight she would call the Vila, and hear how things went on the magical side.

Emeric looked resentfully at his departing aunt. One day he would really have to kill the bitch. He was fairly sure it would not be easy, but would be possible. In the meanwhile he had to consider his kingdom. He needed a pretender to the principality of Valahia. The Danesti...Well, they might prove more of the same; far more trouble than they were worth. His mind turned to Ban Alescu of Irongate. Ambitious. Wealthy from extorting every ounce off the Danube trade with the Mongols. And entirely dependent on their overlord. His mother had been of boyar stock.

And there it was; how obvious: The man was clearly a bastard older son of Vlad's father. Really legitimate of course. Emeric would see that the papers and records were prepared. It was Vlad's mother whose marriage was a sham, and Vlad who was a bastard pretender.

Emeric smiled in delight at his own cleverness.

In the green light from their eyes the Vila's wet, naked skin looked green, too. The rest of the pool was black as ink, the way they liked it. Elizabeth preferred slaves, but in the case of these ones, she was happy to at least pretend their relationship was one of equals. The leggy Vila-woman threw back her white-blond hair and looked out at Elizabeth from her pupil-less green eyes. Mindaug said they did not see as humans saw, but rather looked on essences. Elizabeth did not care. She had reached an alliance with them many years ago, and gave them their annual due of suicidal pregnant girls. Now, thanks again to Mindaug, she had found them useful allies. Yes, the others in compact—and there were some dark and wild ancient things—considered the Vila beyond the pale. But it did not stop them from knowing what was happening. It was from them that she had first heard of the compact, first heard of the wyverns... and the blood.

"They have hatched. They grow apace. The wolf people still guard them. They have been taken to be seen. To be imbued," said the Vila woman, her voice hypnotically low, purring and velvety. Elizabeth knew of the enchantments. She had taken steps against them. She used similar ones herself.

"So are the wolves with the Drac?"

The Vila trailed her fingers across her own flesh seductively. The creature could no more help doing that than humans could avoid drawing breath, regardless of the sex or interest of the audience. "No. They guard the wyverns."

"Excellent," said Elizabeth, smirking in satisfaction. The time would come for the changers. But she knew that they knew her for what she was. Vlad, her little spells had ensured, did not.

Chapter 42

The guard coughed warily, keeping a good safe distance from Vlad. Vlad scowled to himself. They had seen him angry. And now they were even more wary about him. Yes. He was a solitary man. But he did need some contact. He needed to know what they were doing. He needed to know what was happening. And right now they were probably too afraid of him to tell him. "What is it?"

"Sire, there is a party on horseback. They do not look like Hungarians. And there is a woman with them. What do you want us to do about them? They have a white flag."

"Have Emil detail two squads of arquebusiers to watch them from the ridge. Send one man to go and find out exactly who they are. Then come back and tell me."

Vlad returned to his thoughts. What had he done wrong? His men had not behaved like heroes. They'd been more like kill-crazed weasels. And then they had been heroes...

The guard returned. "She says to tell you that her name is Countess Elizabeth Bartholdy of Caedonia.

And she has come with a group of loyal boyars and their retainers to join Your Majesty's cause." The guard paused. Then he said, reverendly. "She is the most beautiful woman I have ever seen."

Vlad nodded his agreement. "Take me to her," he said, smiling for the first time since the sack and burning of Gara.

Elizabeth was surprised how much he had grown— not in physical stature, but in presence. He was as pale as ever. Well, his grandfather had been like that, apparently. She sensed other changes in him. She smelled things that ordinary mortals did not. And she smelled sex. Fury welled up in her. Had she had held herself back so that some sweet little thing could claim his innocence? It was hers. He was hers. To use, corrupt and discard. To bleed.

He bowed smiling. "Welcome, Countess."

"I am so glad that you still wish to see us, Prince," she said, laughing musically, exerting the full force of her charms. "Having run away from me like that."

He reached up a hand to help her down from her mare. She felt the spell there on his hand still traced on his innocent flesh with her spittle and her juices— when he had not even realized what she was doing to him. She activated the charm. And was a little taken aback to find that, if anything, his resistance had grown. With that spell he should have been her sexual slave, unable to resist her, to have ripped aside her clothes and raped her right there, driven by uncontrollable lust. Uncontrollable by him, at least. She could have controlled him, of course. Or driven him to believe he'd done it. But she might have allowed him to do it, beating vainly at his chest and screaming, just for the way it would destroy him.

But he merely smiled at her again. Crocell had been right.

She was going to find this woman, this little love that he had acquired, doubtless with tenderness and vows . . . and kill her. Horribly.

PART IV
October, 1540 A.D.

Chapter 43

Erik thought the large felt-lined tents which they had been assigned in the Golden Horde encampment were as defensible as a . . . piece of felt with a latticework of sticks. The setup was also such that the horses were kept in corrals some distance from their tents. "We will need to reorganize. We need to be able to keep our horses here," he said firmly. "And Tarkhan. We need to organize the tents in a defensive ring around your quarters."

For the first time since they had met him Borshar looked completely taken aback. "I will be staying in the quarters assigned to me by the orkhan. Not with you." His tone said "and thank heavens for that."

Manfred shook his head. "No, m'lord. The terms of our letter of safe conduct require us to accompany the emissary of the Ilkhan. Your welfare and safety is our responsibility."

"That responsibility ends here, among our own people," said Borshar stiffly.

Manfred smiled with ineffable urbanity. "No, m'Lord Tarkhan. These are Mongols of the Golden Horde. I know as well as you do, that they do not recognize the suzerainty of the Ilkhan. We cannot therefore abandon our duty of guardianship. To do so will violate the agreement and our honor. We will not permit that."

For a moment Borshar looked as he might dispute the existence of Frankish honor. But the Knights of the Holy Trinity, in full armor and watching, seemed to unnerve him. "Very well," he said. "Let me speak to our hosts."

"Erik will accompany you," said Manfred.

"Why?"

"I can pay you no higher compliment than to send my personal bodyguard with you. He is one of the deadliest men alive," said Manfred. "Besides he needs every opportunity he can get to hear the Mongol language spoken. He will be my aide, to make sure that translation is reasonably accurate, in the audiences you promised to facilitate."

Borshar nodded. "I am sure it can all be arranged."

And indeed, it was.

But Erik was unable to escape the feeling that the man was . . . almost pleased. Their new encampment was on the outer edge of the vast Mongol camp. And their horses were with them. But they had their backs to the river, and it was not a river that the armored men and horses could dream of swimming. There was some open land to the west, along the margin of the camp. Erik considered it as scarcely a better option than swimming. He was not surprised to discover that Falkenberg and Von Gherens regarded it in much the same light. It was a fairly somber Erik Hakkonsen who went back to Manfred and his new felt tent a little later, having extracted a modicum of information from the Mongol.

"I was wrong about how many men there are in this encampment," said Erik.

Manfred raised his eyebrows. "More I suppose?"

Erik nodded. "A Tumen. A regiment. Ten thousand men."

"And thirty thousand horses," said Falkenberg. "That's their strength. They can change horses and just keep going. They're lightly armored. I've yet to see a single firearm, but they're good with those bows. They put a lifetime of training into them. Our armor is more effective against arrows than a ball. But our horses are less well protected, and they are accurate."

"Their horses are small, though."

Von Gherens nodded. "As much as two hands smaller than ours. But I think they will be tough little animals. Not needing a feed of oats every day," he said, looking at Manfred.

"My horse needs it. It has a lot of me to carry," said Manfred. "So when are we going to get to present our credentials? If I am going to have to talk the sooner we get talking and get back out of here, the better."

"Ah, so you are feeling uneasy after all? I thought that was a good performance about our agreement with the Ilkhan."

Manfred shrugged. "Who wouldn't be nervous, surrounded by ten thousand men? Now if they were ten thousand women like that Bortai..."

Erik snorted. "You'd be in even more trouble."

"Probably true," Manfred acknowledged. "You should talk to her about this situation. I must admit I got uneasy when Borshar was so keen to abandon us. I know. I know. The Mongol have a long tradition of honor to emissaries. We have a written appointment to that effect. But... Go talk to the Mongol woman."

Erik went.

Bortai had watched and listened. How could she tell the Ilkhan's tarkhan that something was very, very wrong? Perhaps things were done very differently these days in the Ilkhanate. She had been told that they had become quite fond of dwelling in cities and palaces, not in the traditional fashion. But surely he knew where envoys and their escort should be housed? She looked for an opportunity to speak with him or one of his bodyguard, but the only person was who came to hand was her unfortunate Tortoise clan betrothed. She still couldn't think about that without a smile... well, outright laughter sometimes. And right now laugh was something she might as well do. She had put her head, and her little brother's head, right inside the lion's mouth. The tall white-blond Frankish orkhan had of course put his own head inside the lion's mouth, too, but that was the work he had chosen as a mercenary. But... She still did not want him killed. He made her laugh, even if he was one of the lesser peoples.

He bowed and smiled. "Obviously the things that worry me, should not."

"Oh. No," she said, feeling foolish. So he was not unaware. "You should be afraid. Very afraid. This is not the way a tarkhan should be treated. You should be in the encampment of the orkhan. Not here. The drinking and feasting should have already begun."

He looked troubled. "That may be my fault. I told them the first camp was not suitable."

"But it was not. It was an insult. Like this. You were placed with the new Arbans. The ... what is the word,"—she too had learned some Frankish from him, "the recruits."

"I knew something was wrong," said Erik heavily. "I had understood that there was honor in the way the Mongol treat a tarkhan. Now I have to get Manfred out of here. Somehow. We need a barge."

Since the last word was Frankish, she took a little time to work out what he wanted. And then to shake her head. Point to the wooden towers downstream and upstream of their camp. "Those have the ballista and arbalest...weapons for attacking cities. They practice on the... barges. Sink them. Throw large burning oil-vats at them. Even at night. It is full moon now."

The foreign orkhan looked as if he had swallowed something unpleasant. "They would have to defend against river attacks, I suppose."

"Yes. The Hungarians from Irongate have tried that. In my father's time."

Erik looked very thoughtfully at the towers. There was one not forty yards away. "Do you know anything about them? I mean, how they are defended?"

Her father had ordered their construction! Of course she did. But how would he know that? "Yes. I have been into one of them."

"So...how many guards?...and the door appears open. Is there a portcullis I can't see?"

It took a while to explain the portcullis. He plainly thought that it was some kind of fortification, not a siege tower. "Oh. There is no door. They are not for fighting from. They are for attack. We fight on horse. Not from behind a wall. Only the lesser people fight from behind walls."

"No door!" he said, incredulously.

"Sometimes a heavy blanket is hung to stop the wind," she conceded. "But the men would be trapped in there when there was fighting. A door would stop them reaching their horses." The horses were tethered at the base of the tower. When the grazing was finished, they'd move the tower a little.

He shook his head incredulously. "I saw the horses. I thought they were just being..." He searched for the word. "Bad," he settled on. It was plainly not quite what he wanted to say. "The weapons at the top. Could they be turned?"

It was her turn to look puzzled. "They do. To aim them at the river."

"I mean right around. To aim at the camp," explained Erik.

The idea had never occurred to her. It was shocking...and not without a savage pleasure. To drop a burning oil vessel on the Gatu Orkhan's own ger. A dream!...looking at his face, she saw it was not so. Not as far as he was concerned.

"I don't wish to ask you to betray your own kin," he said, mistaking the expression on her face. "But I have to at least create a distraction if we're to get out of here."

"They are no kin of mine. My clan are to the north," she said proudly. "Not one Mingghan...no, not even one Arban here is from the White Horde. We would have treated the tarkhan with suitable honor."

"He...doesn't seem unhappy. What is a Mingghan and an Arban?"

"An Arban..." she held up her fingers. "That many men. A Jahgun is that many Arban. A Mingghan that many Jaghun." She sniffed. "And it is not right. So: so you plan to leave the encampment? You should. You and the tarkhan are not safe."

Erik nodded. "That's been my reading of the matter. But it doesn't fit with the reputation of the Mongol."

Bortai had to admit to herself that it did not. Yes, Gatu and some of his henchmen had fallen far from the path of Ulaghchi and the Yasa code. But honor was still strong among the rank and file. Most of them would not dream of attacking the envoy, any more than they would pass a blade through a hearth-fire or pollute water. "You would find a welcome among my clan. Especially if Kildai were restored to them. He is doing better. He and the boy from Jerusalem talk a lot."

"Heaven help us. That David is pure trouble," said Erik with wary smile.

She nodded. "But he gets Kildai to do things that I could not."

"Probably things that will lead him into the trouble he likes so much."

Bortai shrugged. "It is tradition that boys of a certain age will do such things. Some of them die. Some learn. But Kildai cannot die. I have told him so."

Erik absorbed this with an inward chuckle despite the situation they were in. He did not have a vast close experience of women, but he had observed enough from Manfred's early conquests, Francesca, and of course his own iron-willed mama. He had a feeling that this young Mongol woman might be every bit as iron-willed as his mama. She might lack Francesca's finesse and skill in getting men to do what she wanted, but she probably would get there anyway. Without help. Erik felt faintly guilty. He had not compared her to Svanhild. It still hurt. And it always would. Svan had been different, she had been brave, yes, but not likely to get her own way, except that one would wish to make her happy.

Bortai interrupted his reverie. "Ion has gone out into the camp. He says they would not be looking for him here. I . . . I realize that I never knew a slave could have such courage. I knew they could be loyal, but Ion . . . he has risked his life for us. Do you have many slaves in your barbarian lands?"

Erik bit his lip. "In a manner of speaking I suppose. We have thralls. But there are few in Iceland now. They are more like family retainers, and Bishop Wulfstan got the Aetheling to pass a law that says the child of a thrall is a free-Carl. When we went to Norse Telemark the old system is still in place. But they do not . . ." he felt himself blush, "cut them."

"Cut them? Oh. You mean geld them. It is not common here. Common among the Ilkhan lands, I have been told. It was a custom there before the coming of the Ilkhan. We have found it best not to meddle in these matters among the subject people. They are easier ruled if you just remove that which irks them and leave them to their own traditions."

Just when Erik thought he was getting used to her, this part slipped out. She seemed an ordinary, if strong minded young woman . . . and then the Mongol attitude would come through, making her sound like a princess. An arrogant princess, at that. Iceland was too small and thinly populated and wild for such attitudes . . . and Vinland too big. "I must go and discuss this with Von Gherens and Falkenberg," he said stiffly. "Thank you for your help."

❈   ❈   ❈

Bortai watched him leave, feeling slightly forlorn. What had she said to offend him? He was certainly a fine orkhan, for a foreign mercenary. She understood, a little, why the tarkhan would use such men. They were nearly as disciplined as Mongols and very... regimented. If Erik had been one of the people he would have been a mighty general. She still needed to ask him to arrange some kind of distraction. The encampment was guarded, of course. But if she and Kildai and Ion could get out to the north, and go *through* the camp, with a horse apiece... well, there would be a Hawk-clan scout or three hiding in the hills, watching this encampment, unless they had been so defeated and scattered as to have no organizational skills left. Back on the north bank of the great river, they could at least ride.

She sighed. They'd gained some ground, it was true. Kildai's wits appeared to be as much back in his head as they ever were with a fourteen-year-old boy. They had some ponies—not the quality that she would have wished for, but better than nothing. They were on the north bank of the great river. But did they have to be right in the middle of Gatu's Tumen? Gatu had spaced them two Mingghan abreast along the river—more convenient for water than a normal diamond or a circle formation with the patrol Mingghan on the inside with the orkhan's personal Khesig. Plainly Gatu did not expect an attack. Her nails bit into her palms. Oh she would love it if the White Horde surprised him. But it was obviously unlikely.

The encampment of the foreign knights was obviously guarded, as Ion expected. But slaves went to-and-fro, doing the menial tasks slaves did. Ion joined them. He was terrified of being recognized. On the other hand... no one looked at slaves, and he knew just how to be one, and what to do. He kept his head down.

And was recognized.

But not by someone who knew of his fall from grace as one of Nogay's trusted slaves. "You. Here. Take this message to the ger of your master," said the commander of the guard on the foreign encampment. "It is from the Ilkhan tarkhan, or so his man said. I am not an errand boy. If he wishes me to carry messages he must speak with me himself."

Almost fainting with fear, Ion bowed and took the roll of parchment and hurried off. He had no intention at all of arriving at the ger of Nogay. But he was not about to tell the noble lord that. So he took the message and went.

"The other way, you fool," snapped the guard commander after him. So Ion went the other way until he was out of line of sight. He wished he could read. But at least he was away from the guard-commander. Ion was looking for two things... the best way across this camp, and some other slaves. Slaves liked to talk. And they always knew exactly what their masters were doing. Like Princess Bortai, he knew that something was amiss. And they would know what it was.

Of course the talk was all about the things that slaves found vital. Food. Punishment. Gossip about the sexual liaisons of their masters. There was nothing quite as pleasing as knowing something about his wife that he would not wish you to know... or that he did not know himself. Inevitably too, it was about the foreigners, and of course he had been seen leaving their camp.

"So how do they treat their slaves? Do they beat you often?" asked a grizzled oldster. "And what are the women like?"

"I've heard the men have no balls and the slaves have to service the women for them," said a younger one, hopefully.

Ion rolled his eyes. "And they all have six breasts."

"Really?"

"Don't be stupid. They only have four," said another slave, grinning. "Anyway, we'll find out tomorrow. What's the loot like?"

"Loot?"

"You know. Well, when the masters are finished with them tomorrow are there going to be any pickings for us?"

"They are quite wealthy," said Ion, fishing. "They keep their food in the plain saddlebags. The cloth ones."

"That's no use. Saddlebags are always taken by the masters. Can't you empty some out tonight? They won't take food when they divide up the loot."

"What about the other slaves?"

Ion did not tell them they had no slaves, or at least none with them. He would never have been believed. So he lied a little. That too was perfectly normal. You learned to cut through the chaff of lies to gain the kernel of truth.

And the truth was that the slaves were expecting a massacre. Advising him to keep out of the way in the morning. Hoping to secure a little loot that their masters considered too irrelevant in the aftermath.

And they too could not understand how this was to be. There were several who had seen Ilkhan tarkhan come from Kerch in years past. The emissary and the truce were sacred. Their masters knew that, too, and were troubled by it all, by the sounds of it.

But they were all looking forward to tomorrow... when whatever it was would happen.

Ion made his way back to the encampment, avoiding the way he had come in, and the captain of the guard, back to Princess Bortai, still with the little roll of parchment in his ragged cotte. He was a troubled man. Somehow they would have to get out of this camp, past the guards on the far side and then flee north tonight... for two or three days at the least, and possibly a week—his grasp of distances and places was rudimentary. He had always been told where and when to go, and when to stop.

Erik pointed at the rough map that they had prepared. "That is a kill-zone. They want us to try to flee along the river's edge. They expect us to go there."

Falkenberg nodded. "We exercised the horses along there. As if we were having a good scout around. There is a low berm between the Mongol camp and the river. The ground is marshy. Not good for a charge."

"Good place to get strung out, which is exactly what the Mongols liked, historically," said Von Gherens.

"This is all based on the assumption that we're going to have to break out of here by force," said Eberhard.

Erik looked grim. "Based on what I heard from Bortai, that is an assumption we're going to have to consider likely. We must prepare for it."

Eberhard looked like a balky mule. Erik was normally fairly tactful—by Erik's standards—with the old diplomat. "It's not a scenario that history holds likely," he said.

Manfred rubbed his jaw. "Prepare for the worst. Preparation hurts no one. And I don't like this either."

"For goodness sake don't kill anyone during your preparations," said the old man grumpily. "That would cause more problems than I think I could ever sort out."

"We have very carefully left Kari out of our deliberations," said Erik, "for precisely that reason. Now, has bombardier Von Thiel got some spare powder? We're going to need a large scale distraction. And do we consult with Borshar? Or at least his bodyguard? We may have to take him with us. . . ."

There was the sound of argument outside the felt-lined tent, including a very determined female voice, and a couple of words of Frankish interspersed with high speed Mongol.

"She can't keep away from you, Erik," said Manfred.

The knight on guard outside the tent was plainly no match for Bortai in this mood. He escorted the young woman inside. Manfred noticed that her hands were twitching into claws. If he'd been the poetic sort he'd have said that her eyes were spitting fire. The Prince of Brittany had met a few girls of that type and in that state over the years. You were wise to start running. He wondered just what Erik had managed to do. She appeared to be too angry to be coherent. She'd picked up a handful of words of Frankish from Erik, but right now there was just a torrent of Mongol pouring out of her. She pulled a roll of parchment out of her waistband and flung it on the floor in front of Erik.

"What's all this about?" asked Manfred, wondering just what trouble his innocent—in many of the ways of the world—friend, bodyguard and mentor had got himself into with the woman. He'd not seriously thought Erik would get himself involved with any woman again, let alone write letters to her.

"Something to do with Borshar," said Erik, holding up a soothing hand. He picked up the roll of parchment, and said something to her, which Manfred could only assume meant "slowly." Erik unrolled the parchment as Bortai began speaking again. Slowly. Too loudly, as if to a half-wit. After a few moments she got that under control too. She plainly had the sort of iron control that made wise men afraid. Manfred peered at the parchment in Erik's hands. It was in some foreign script, and most probably in some foreign tongue. He was fairly certain Erik hadn't written it, unless the boy from Jerusalem was a much better teacher than he'd seemed to be.

"She says," said Erik incredulously, "that this is a letter from the tarkhan to Nogay. One of the orkhan's generals. Her slave was given it to deliver to him. I am not following exactly why or how, but she did tell me earlier that he was going scouting in the camp for her." He paused. Listened to some more of Bortai's explanation. "Ah. The slave used to be in the service of this general. The man who gave him the message did not know that this was no longer true. So her man brought her the message. He almost forgot it. He did not know that it was important, as he does not read."

"We can't read it either," said Manfred. "But I gather the Ilkhan are not as out of contact with the Golden Horde as they would have had us believe, if they are sending notes to prominent generals. Or is he their spy?"

Erik spoke to her. She shook her head. Spoke some more. "She says the Golden Horde and the Ilkhan have exchanged emissaries in the past, yes, but not for five years now. But she says this," he tapped the parchment, "is treachery. They plan to kill us all."

"What? Explain. I thought they respected envoys and their escorts," said Manfred.

"Except that we are described by another word," said Erik.

"And that is?"

"Hostage takers," said Erik. "She says this note says it must be made clear to the men of the Blue Horde, that we are holding the tarkhan hostage."

"What!" came from several of the audience.

And now it was not just Bortai who looked furious.

Eberhard shook his head. "We have a writ of safe conduct, appointing us escorts to emissary of the Ilkhan."

"It seems it will not be worth very much. If we ever get a chance to show it to anyone..."

"The lady would have had to be one of the greatest actresses under heaven to have played that as well as she has," said Erik.

Manfred nodded. "True. But she could have been duped. I mean to get such a piece of evidence..."

"Which we can't read," said Eberhard.

"That I could very easily solve, in part," said Erik. "The little book of Mongol-Frankish translations that Benito gave me, gives the words in Mongol script— based on the Chinese I believe. Even a few words would do to verify the document. But someone else will have to do it. I need to scout. And I think I am are going to need Kari."

Erik's expression was as grim as any Manfred could remember seeing on his face. "I am afraid I can no longer promise, Eberhard, not to kill anyone in our preparations."

"What do we do about the tarkhan?" asked Von Gherens. "He'd do as a hostage, damn his eyes. Let him be what he claims to be."

Erik looked at Manfred. Who nodded, slowly. "Bring him here. Now. Do it with respect but with fairly massive force. I could use some explanations, if nothing else. It is our duty to escort him. We're going to take it very seriously."

Erik pointed to one of the knights. "Von Meul, take thirty of the knights, in full armor, and bring him and his entourage here."

But when they got to the large ger, the customary Mongol guards were not there. And neither was the supposed occupant. A slit in the rear, and darkness, had allowed them to slip away. It did look as if they planned to return—all their possessions were there. A guard of twenty knights was left, waiting.

"No," General Nogay said rigidly. "I did not get your message. I simply was warned by..."

He shuddered slightly. That happened quite often, when he thought of Grand Duke Jagiellon and his steel eyes. "The voice from Vilnius, of your coming some weeks ago. I was told, and passed the message onto Gatu that your escort were to die, barring a select handful. I was told that you would arrange a suitable pretext. The men will be unhappy about this."

"There is a guard commander that I will see flogged to death," said Borshar furiously. "I sent one of my men out to give him the message to be delivered to you. I did not want to be seen speaking to him myself. This may delay our plans a little. I had discussed the matter with General Okagu—who escorted us this far. It is necessary that the rank and file be told that they have taken me hostage."

"But I have been told that they have a writ of safe conduct."

"A forgery," said Borshar. "A tool to gain close access to the orkhan and kill him. They do not wish him to become Khan of the Golden Horde."

Nogay shook his head. "But they would surely die if they did that? No one would believe it plausible."

Borshar shook his head. "They are religious fanatics. They believe themselves secure in the promise of paradise if they die in the service of their God."

Nogay snorted. "I have heard of such madmen. Some of those out of Alamut were supposed to hold that mad belief."

He wondered why Borshar stared at him like that. But as the man's dilated pupils barely seemed able to focus, Nogay ordered food and kvass, and sent a messenger to the ger of the orkhan. He cursed mildly the loss of the slave he had used for such errands. Ion had been reliable and quick thinking, unlike this clod. He had a moment's regret that he had ordered the man killed. At the time it had seemed justified.

Neither of them noticed that one of Borshar's bodyguards, fat Tulkun, had slipped away.

When Bortai had heard Ion's declaration that there was a massacre of the foreign mercenary guard planned, she had taken it for the usual slaves' talk. Exaggerated and wildly fanciful, manufactured out of half-heard rumors. She had wanted more certainty about the disposition of horses and guards. He had told her what he could, and she'd regretted that he was no trained warrior. He missed things they would have noted without a second thought. Still, she knew more now... And then he'd remembered the roll of parchment he'd been given. Naturally he gave it to her. He could not read it himself.

She'd had to read it twice to believe it. At which point all her planning for their escape had gone for a long run out of the ger door—not as fast as she had, heading for the ger in which the foreign orkhan and his knights met. She'd been too furious to think about what she would do when she got there. It never occurred to her that anyone might not believe her. She was Bortai, Princess of the Hawk Clan.

She'd been a little taken aback that they had not instantly sprung to arms. It had taken a while to work out that the old white-haired foreigner doubted the truth of the entire matter. But Erik Orkhan, and his second in command Manfred—who was perhaps a war-shaman—did. Bortai wondered why it had never occurred to her before that the big man might be a foreign shaman. It would explain why he was always so carefully guarded. Enemies would stop at nothing to kill such a one. But the foreigners were different from the Golden Horde. Such a breach of honor, such a deception, would have had the Mongol onto their horses first and thinking and planning later. These lesser people were also less inclined to precipitous action. She bit her lip. It might not actually be a bad idea to behave thus, sometimes. Being cooler-headed was perhaps not a bad thing, when they were plainly facing a terrible war.

Such betrayal and insult would have to be repaid with a bloody finale. She'd been told as much by Tulkun, and seen it in their conduct. They had been an honorable escort, for mercenaries, drawn from lesser peoples. There was honor, and then there was Mongol Honor, and this tarkhan certainly had not lived up to it. At the same time, it occurred—belatedly—to her that a bloody death-battle was not going to help her in her stern duty: to get Kildai back to the Hawk clan, back to the White Horde.

Erik came over to her and bowed. "Lady, we thank you for the warning. It was an honorable thing to do."

She found herself coloring slightly. "I am Bortai." What more explanation was needed?

He nodded. "We need to get Manfred out of here, and keep him alive. We'll be riding right through the camp in about three hours' time. We will have to abandon our pack-train, and much of our gear."

"You flee?"

"We have a task ordered us. Manfred must be guarded. This does not appear worth much." He held out a piece of parchment with the royal seal of Ilkhan on it.

"May I see it?" she asked, meaning the seal. She was disappointed in their flight...and yet this shaman must be of great value, that they would put him before bloody revenge. They did not seem cowards.

"Certainly. Eberhard wanted to check it for loopholes. There are none in the Frankish," said Erik.

It was written in two scripts, neatly and with artistry, as such a document should be. She could not read any Frankish but the Chinese-Mongol script was clear and familiar. It was in every detail a writ of safe conduct for the escort of the tarkhan Borshar, and carried the seal of the Ilkhan. Bortai had written similar documents for her father. How dared anyone violate such a document? It would mean war.

And then it struck her. It would mean war.

War between the Hordes, as had nearly happened before Orkhan Berke's death three hundred years ago. War between clans as had happened after Ulaghchi Khan's death. It put a different slant on the need for flight. There would be time for revenge—once this piece of treachery—because it could be nothing but treachery—was dealt with.

As to why: she could see why it would be of great advantage to a power to the north to have the Golden Horde at war with the Ilkhan. Many unlikely alliances had been made by common enemies.

"We can offer little in the way of security for you and you brother now, I am afraid," said Erik. "We will happily take you along, but you will have to leave your cart and everything that cannot be carried on horseback. And is your brother fit to ride?"

"I think so," said Bortai, seriously. "If we stay we will be killed. And now that I understand this," she tapped the paper. "It is vital that you should not be killed. That you should present this—and the letter from Borshar to Berte at the great kurultai."

"I thought that was over and broken up."

"Yes. But we will hold a new one. Gatu Orkhan and his men will find themselves under the carpet."

"Under the carpet?"

"Yes. Nobles are put to death thus. Rolled in a

carpet and the horses stampeded over them," she said, relishing the thought. "I go to prepare Kildai to ride."

"Better put both David and him together on one of our spare mounts," said Erik. "They're a little bigger and better conditioned than yours, even if they probably don't have the stamina, and those two don't weigh much. David can keep him in the saddle. And Kildai can handle the horse better than the boy can."

He paused. "I would tell your brother that he does it for the Jerusalem lad's sake. David is not the rider that Kildai is. He'll be more willing to do it then."

Bortai smiled. He was a good commander of boys, not just men. She knew this break had a very poor chance of success and that the orkhan's Tumen would follow them like relentless wolves. But survive and defeat them they must. Or the Blue and White Hordes—that now made up the Golden Horde—would split, diminish and be eaten by the power to the north.

The ger flap swung open. A pair of knights stood there, escorting plump Tulkun, the Ilkhan tarkhan's bodyguard. "He keeps saying your name, *Ritter* Hakkonsen. He came back like a thief in the night. We don't understand another word he's saying."

Chapter 44

To say that Vlad found Elizabeth Bartholdy's joining of
his little army an unmixed blessing was not strictly true.
She and those that she brought with her—a selection of
minor nobles, and a handful of retainers who seemed
to do little more than minister to their masters. They
professed to be loyal to his cause, and expected more
than he and his army could offer, it seemed. He could
quite understand that Elizabeth was too frail and delicate
a beauty to sleep rough under crude canvas shelters
and eat the rations that his quartermaster had managed
to gather for the men. But every other man could do
so. The idea of sharing a rough bivouac with common
peasants turned soldiers, and having to train with
them, let alone share their food, was enough to rouse
protests from the boyars. Vlad found himself being very
short with that. He'd eaten with the men, bivouacked
with his men . . . huddled in the pouring rain without
any more shelter than their cloaks with them for that
matter. "When you bring me a regiment of cavalry or
even a whole troop of knights, I'll see you are quartered
and fed with the men you bring. In the meantime . . ."

"But this is an affront to our honor! To eat and sleep with the commoners!"

Vlad might possibly have felt that way himself, eight weeks ago, during his captivity. But now...well, he'd run with the gypsies, slept and fought side by side with his peasant army. They had given him loyalty and support when that was a rare thing. "It may be an affront to your pride," he said coldly. "I have noticed people confuse their pride with what honor is. It is an honor to serve in this army. My soldiers will conduct themselves with honor, or feel my wrath. Honor here is earned with combat and loyalty. It is not conferred or earned by others on your behalf. What you have is pride, and a false pride at that. Not honor. Not yet. Do you understand me?"

The florid-faced boyar, so lofty in his ornately frogged outfit a few moments back, almost cowered. "M...my Lord Prince. I did not mean...I mean the honor of my ancient house..."

"Is greater than mine?" said Vlad, realizing that his voice had risen, carrying to the nearby soldiers, who had stopped to stare. He moderated his tone. "We have few spare resources. I cannot pamper you."

It was easy enough to say that to the shocked boyar. The countess Elizabeth Bartholdy was another matter entirely. Fortunately, it seemed that she had come prepared. She had her two tire-women, and her tent—a small mansion of decorated canvas—was carried up on mules. Along with a bed and some other furniture. Vlad gazed longingly at the bed. It had been a long time since he'd slept on a mattress. Elizabeth watched him. "It is remarkably comfortable," she said, looking very directly at him with a slight quirk to her lips.

Vlad nodded. And swallowed. He was no longer the innocent he had been. But he was unaccustomed to dealing with lust. And she seemed to do that to him. It was . . . different somehow from the way he felt about Rosa. Hotter and more tempting perhaps . . . but with an uncomfortableness to it. As if . . . there was something wrong. There was, he supposed. He'd ill understood Father Tedesco's long ramblings about the sins of the flesh. He understood it better now. But somehow . . . it hadn't seemed wrong in the starlight, in his new cloak, with Rosa.

Either his lover had taken the testicles right off this cursed prince . . . or he was more proof against magics and plain seduction than most men. No. There was more to it than just the frequency or the quality of their coupling. She'd seduced men away from the most skilled courtesans before. He was, in some way, exceptional.

Elizabeth took little pleasure from sex. In the course of her quest for the dark powers that would keep her young, in the rites she had performed to agree to their compact, she had debased herself. Coupled with everything from a dog to a sequence of men and a woman of somewhat depraved tastes. She understood why these acts were essential to the entrapment. But other than the entrapment aspect, the tasting of forbidden fruit, she derived little pleasure from it. She did find a combination of sex and the inflicting of pain exciting. And immediately after killing, while there was still blood in her mouth, it was pleasurable too. But Vlad was not ready for such delights . . . yet. For him it would have to be tenderness, and the nauseating pap about love. That gave her a taste of bile in her mouth, as always. She needed to track his woman down and kill her. Soon.

Then she could enmesh this tender fool.

Chapter 45

Dana found herself going up to feed the wyverns every day. She wasn't quite sure how it had happened, just as she was not too sure how she had slipped into the life of the gypsies, or as they called themselves, the pack. She thought that name quite funny. True, Tante Silvia's cart could pass for the home of a packrat. The old woman and her tinker husband collected nearly every form of junk. Some of it they turned into things that they might sell. Some of it just accumulated.

It was among this clutter that Dana found treasures that she entertained herself with, and, quite accidentally objects that delighted the wyverns. They were mostly at an age when they were delighted by something that they could eat. Everything was tried for taste. Trees, rocks, pine needles. Dana had asked Angelo about that. "Surely it can't be good for them?"

He had just laughed. He did that a lot when she asked him questions. Dana just asked them again. Sometimes she got answers. "They don't like iron much. It won't kill them the way that it does to some fey. But they say it stinks. I have seen them eat very nearly anything else. It doesn't seem to do them any kind of harm. They are creatures of magic, not nature."

But they had held back from eating Dana's treasure. It was a glass prism. She could make rainbow-lights with it, and the two creatures loved chasing them, especially when she used a small mirror together with it. They liked to stand in the rainbow light and shift colors to match it, too. They were rather like fast-growing kittens without the furry cuddliness. They seemed to have a fascination with the light pattern. She could keep them busy for an hour, chasing it, hiding in it.

At the same time Dana was having trouble with her mother...who was convinced that her new interest in early rising and the deep woods was something to do with male gypsies. Mother had even tried to follow her. Dana had had to lead her back to camp after she'd got herself lost. Dana had become a bit more wood-wise now...and yes, she did always go with a male gypsy...who was not quite with her. But near at hand. But she had no interest in men. Not like that, anyway. The ideas mother got.

"Your father's mother said that the Valah always developed late. But did it have to be now?" said Mama, wringing her hands. "Dana...I have explained to you..."

"Mama, the dogs have more interest in me. They only marry their own kind, these people. And I have no more interest in them than they have in me. I just... like it up there." She actually had been noticing boys lately. There were some here that were exceptionally handsome, if you looked beyond the ragged clothes and the dirt. But the wyvern's watchers...they were old. Old men. Over thirty.

"You know Dana...men, men are, well some of them like young girls."

"Like the Hungarian commander at Poienari. He tried to touch me. I screamed, remember."

"Oh Dana. We should go to the Danesti cousins. I will organize for our horses..."

Dana knew she had to stop that. "They won't do it."

"Then I must make a plan."

Dana was still wondering just how she could distract her mother from a new flight, when Bertha took the matter out of her hands. She was actually trying to saddle their horses on her own late that night. Of course, as she had never saddled a horse in her life, and the camp only appeared to be asleep, things soon went awry. Dana, still half asleep, listened to her mother's hysterical voice. "You can't stop me. It's not safe here for my daughter."

Angelo's voice: "It is safer here than anywhere else in Valahia, lady. They still look for you."

"I don't believe you."

Dana could almost hear the gypsies shrug. "It's true, lady. We can send messages...if there is anyone you trust enough to ask."

"I could ask Cousin Alets." There was doubt now in her voice. "But could you really get a letter to him?"

"In Klosovar? That one is easy."

"But would you let me go, if he said it was safe?"

"Yes. But we have kept you safe so far, lady. Why are you worried now? The Drac is coming. He comes south with his army."

Dana wanted to ask about her brother. But she thought it might be a good idea to continue to pretend to be fast asleep. For now, anyway.

"It's not me," said her mother. "It's my daughter. She's..."

"She is as safe here as in her own home, lady. We watch her. She is the Drac's sister. That is important to our people."

"Yes...but she is not being properly...chaperoned."

There was some laughter at that. "Lady. You do not understand. She is the Drac's sister. No man here would touch her any more than if she was my own sister."

"And there are not many that would have dared do that," said Grigori, with a chuckle.

"He is married to my sister," explained Angelo. "But that was her choice, and with my permission. Who here would dare to ask the Drac for such permission? Your son is a great and terrible man."

"Vlad?" Her mother's voice was troubled. "I am so afraid for him."

"No need, lady."

"But he was such a sensitive little boy. And he got sick very easily...I can't think of him as a man."

Dana could hear the amusement in Angelo's voice "He has grown up a little. He is much taller than I am. And I have not seen him show any signs of ever being sick."

"Not even when the rest of us were sick from that bad meat," said Grigori.

"Oh. Taller than you? My baby. I begged them not to take him. I think of him every day...pray for him. It...used to make me cry. It used to make my husband very angry. You say that you could send a message? Could you send a message to him? From me?"

"We could do that. We will bring you a reply."

"But how would I know it came from him?"

"Ask him something only he would know. We can hope that he will also remember."

"It has been ten years," she said, doubtfully. "Does he remember me at all?"

"He does not forget very much. He was a prisoner and a hostage, and denied anyone to speak his own language to. He remembered enough to understand us. He used to sing songs to himself, he said." There was a pause. "He needs to be very strong now, lady."

"He is the House of Valahia!" said Dana, quite forgetting that she was supposedly fast asleep.

"Well said, little one," said Angelo. There was no surprise in his voice. He had known that she was there. They were almost like wild animals in their sensitivity to noises and things they could not possibly see. Dana wondered just how they did it. She suspected magic. More magic, they kept hidden from her. She'd searched the cart for talismans and magical paraphernalia. The trouble was: how could she tell it from the junk?

Chapter 46

Tulkun—the normally plump and cheerful Ilkhan Mongol bodyguard to the tarkhan—addressed himself directly to Erik. He was still plump. But he was anything but cheerful. He was plainly a disturbed and angry man, a man who was almost not capable of rational speech he was so furious. "They plan treachery!" He said slamming his meaty fist into his palm. He then broke into a torrent of rapid Mongol. Erik was only able to understand one word in five.

"Excitable fellows, these Mongols," said Manfred dryly. "I assume that he is telling you much the same as your young woman did?"

Erik nodded. "From what I can understand yes. It's a society in which treachery happens, but there are certain lines that you just don't cross. Ever. Honor is very important to them. It's all tied up with their status, or their idea of honor and the ancestors."

"I'm not too interested in why right now," said Manfred. "I'm more interested in just what we can do to counter the problem."

"In the long term it's that honor that could keep

us alive, but in the short term getting out of here seems to be the right answer."

Bortai interrupted them. "Tulkun him say talk for you." Then her Frankish deserted her and she began, slowly in Mongol, plainly choosing her words for simplicity. "The warrior Tulkun, he says he will speak for you. Tell of the plan to say you took hostage the tarkhan, using him and his status to try to get close to the orkhan to murder him. He and his bodyguard escaped without you knowing, so now you can be treated as you deserve. As treacherous lesser people. They now need to spread the story."

Erik groaned. "No wonder he looked a little pleased. We played right into his hands when we insisted he stay with us. But what is he doing this for?"

Tulkun shrugged. He had his composure now. "I am a master of the sword and bow. Not politics. I do not understand these things. But it is dishonorable. We are not hostages. And you have shown yourselves to be good men in your dealing with the noble lady from the Hawk clan, and in your behavior."

"They do this because they want war," said Bortai, tensely. "War between the Ilkhan and the Golden Horde. War as the orkhan Berke threatened before Ulaghchi the Great Khan killed him."

She was certainly right about the war. Possibly war between the Ilkhan and the Holy Roman Emperor too. Noble lady? Well, Tulkun was polite. And all Mongols were "noble," Erik recalled.

He turned to Bortai. "Would this work?"

She shook her head. "They will not give him the chance to speak. They dare not. They will come—tonight or in the early morning, to annihilate your camp."

Tulkun nodded slowly.

"We could go now and address them?" suggested Erik.

Bortai looked at Tulkun and Tulkun back at her. They shook their heads. "You need a gathering of the nobles. The orkhan, or at least the orkhan's henchmen and generals know. You would have to go from ger to ger. That is what they do tonight. Spreading lies."

Tulkun nodded in agreement. "They plan to say a message has been received from the tarkhan saying he is a prisoner. Then that he has escaped."

Bortai hissed between her teeth. "We could try, if we can evade the guards. Only, they know who to speak to. We do not."

Erik nodded. "Basically, your going out there would be suicide. For you and for us, because it could cascade this into premature action. And we want this on our own terms, not theirs. I see nothing much for it but to break out of here, tonight. How much time do you think we have?"

The two Mongol considered. "They'll let the drinking and the rumor-mongering go on for a while," said Bortai. "When the men are drunk they do things they would not do sober."

"And believe things they would not believe sober," said Tulkun.

"They'll drink?"

Both the Mongol laughed. "Ulaghchi the Great Khan tried to reduce it in accordance with Chinngis Khan's rules. But it is not easy, and the camp is the traditional place for it. You can stop the men when they go out to war, or on the hunt—the nerge," Bortai said.

"Well," said Erik. "We have a few hours. Tulkun, we plan to try and ride out of here. Tonight. We'll need to try and find some vessels—downstream I think, to get us across the Danube, and then we ride for Iskander Beg's Illyrian villages. We'll lose some knights . . ."

"Go north. Go to the White Horde lands," said Tulkun.

"White Horde?"

"The Golden Horde is made up of the western Horde—the Blue, and the northern Horde. The White. Lady Bortai comes from the White. They have lost much land to Prince Jagiellon and his allies. Lost clans and tribes too. But what remains is strong."

Bortai nodded. "You would be welcome and honored among my people."

Erik paused to translate.

Manfred looked skeptical. Eberhard, interested. "Their clan structure is quite loose. And there is a fair amount of intermarriage. It's how they cement alliances. Look, if we go north we may yet be able to sort this mess out. Word will spread . . ."

"If we go north we will have a lot more hostile territory to cross," said Manfred. "Next time, Erik, I listen to your instincts and the devil with diplomatic niceties."

"I think we may have to go north anyway," said Von Gherens. "Look, Prince Manfred, Erik, we are hugely outnumbered. And unless they're stupider than rocks, the first thing they will do is cut off our retreat across the river. They know where and what they're looking for. We're not going to find vessels nearby—that makes no military sense. And we won't find them in the dark, easily. It's what they'll expect us to do. By daylight tomorrow we can expect everything for a day's ride along the river to be guarded with a substantial force."

"So...we ride hard north. Somehow don't get spitted by watchful Mongols from this White Horde—am I right in saying that this is part of the kurultai breaking up? The two Hordes?"

Erik asked Bortai. She nodded. "Mostly this is true. We are also clan-blood with some Blue Horde clans, especially in the east. There are more that bind to the orkhan in the west and south."

Erik translated. Manfred bit his lip. "And this helps us how in the medium term?" He asked. "We can find short-term security to the north. But short of crossing the Carpathians into Emeric's territory, or maybe taking a ship on the Black Sea we will be stuck there."

"Well...I have a feeling that Benito and his fleet will be here in the Black Sea long before next summer."

"So we wait for that young jackanapes to bail us out again?" said Manfred with a grin. "Squire Crazykid. We're supposed to be getting information to him, not being rescued by him."

"I have a feeling he won't mind," said Erik wryly. "But it may not come to that. The Danube curves northeast, as I recall. We may be able to cross it, quietly, in secure territory."

Bortai had been concentrating intensely on the conversation—she had accumulated a few words of Frankish, but not that much—and asked Erik what they were saying. Erik explained.

"The war-shaman," she pointed at Manfred. "He that important to your people?"

"War-Shaman? I don't quite understand that word. He is . . . the third most important man in the Holy Roman Empire. We would not have let him come if we had thought the Mongols would not honor their reputation for the treatment of emissaries. The tarkhan promised to arrange for him to speak with the new khan."

Bortai looked at Manfred in some surprise. "Oh. I . . . did not understand. You are not mercenaries?"

"What does the last word mean?"

"Warriors who are paid to fight."

"Mercenaries." Despite the situation Erik had to laugh. And despite his anger, Tulkun nearly fell apart laughing. Of course Manfred wanted to know what about.

"She thought that we were mercenaries."

"I had wondered why a mercenary company was given a writ of safe conduct," she said, beginning to smile. "You must accompany us to the Hawk clan in lands of White Horde."

That was practically an order, Erik realized, coming from the sturdy but beautiful young woman. Despite her worn and plain clothes, she was anything but bashful and self-effacing. "And now I understand why you did not just want bloody vengeance for this betrayal. I thought maybe you were a coward. We must break out of here."

Which was what Erik had intended all along. He was surprised that it stung a little to know that she'd thought him a coward; after all, what should it matter what she thought? He nodded to her, keeping his feelings to himself. "Best to get David and your brother ready," was all that he said. "We need to organize.

We'll have to abandon our pack-train, and clear their guards and organize a distraction. Tulkun—do you ride with us?"

The Ilkhan bodyguard nodded.

"The party appears to have started out there," said Erik quietly to Kari. "Now you're not to kill anyone. Not unless it is them or you."

"They may see it that way," said Kari, cheerfully embracing the excuse.

"And I may not," said Erik grimly. "Always remember that I am more dangerous than they are. At the moment . . . we're still technically an envoy's escort, not at war with anyone, protected by these blue flags. Once they attack us, or we are out of here, out of this camp, with no more blue pennants on our lances, things are different."

They crept quietly forward. The greatest danger that Erik could see was that a Mongol in the siege tower might be alerted by their horses, tethered near the open doorway of the tower. They were dependent on Ion having done his work. The man had taken some kvass—a gift, apparently—to the five men in the tower. He had found one asleep . . . and the others glad to have the kvass on a rapidly chilling night. They were dicing, a common enough pastime among bored soldiery. Also quite an absorbing pastime. Their attention, such as it was, was focused on the still, broad, moonlit ribbon of river. Not on someone leaving, pulling up a picket-pin. The horses probably would not go far. But they would enjoy a little unaccustomed freedom to wander and find a bit of newer grass.

Erik had a squad of knights in reserve, but knights

had no skill in moving like thieves through the night. Kari was even better at that than he was. They'd dealt with the perimeter guard without any trouble.

They edged closer. Sure enough, the horses had wandered away. And the men in the tower sounded very cheerful over their game. Erik and Kari waited. As luck would have it two of them came down from the upper level to let the grass share some second-hand kvass. Erik and Kari were waiting as the first man stared in irritation at where the missing horses should have been. You could rely on a Mongol to notice that first. Next thing Erik and Kari had them from behind. The warrior had barely time to grunt before a knight came out of the darkness and helped Erik to gag and tie him. Von Taub, Erik noted, had helped Kari with his victim with a mailed fist. It was very effective. Bortai would not be talking to him for a while. "They wrestle better than I thought," muttered Kari.

"It's a Mongol sport," said Erik quietly.

"Among my mother's people too," said Kari. "I thought I was good at it."

"Even their women do here, apparently," said Erik. "Anyway. Let's get on with it," Erik pointed at the dark doorway. "You two—Von Taub, Wellmann. Come and add a bit more weight. The rest watch the door. No one gets away."

They went in. Erik realized that it would be less simple than he had thought. Access to the decking where the siege weapons were mounted—and the dice-players played—was a single, long ladder. Easy to defend, easy for those at the top to cry warning to half the camp. Well, there was nothing for it but to climb. It was not a ladder you could sneak up, either. It creaked.

But of course those above were expecting their companions to return. Erik took the last rungs at a rush.

Basically, it was going to be one against three... And he didn't want to kill them. That Bortai and Tulkun had agreed on implicitly: they were technically still under the truce flag. The Mongols—Golden Horde and Ilkhan—the old Red Horde, Erik gathered—held strongly to the concept of the moral high ground. If came to negotiations and recriminations—a knock on the head could be forgiven. The one who killed first, not so easily.

Erik dived up through the trapdoor and took the legs out from under a warrior who was just walking toward it. Maybe it was the sound of the armored men below. Something had stirred the fellow. Kari was up before the second yell or the two others had time to come their companion's aid. The one, poor fellow, had just woken up. Wellmann was just in time up to stop a knife-thrust to Kari's kidneys with the intervention of steel armor. The sleeper had been rendered comatose again. The other two... well, one had learned not to bite steel-clad fingers. The other still had his teeth, and a gag. There had been some noise... but the camp was fairly noisy anyway. It was sounding increasingly like a stirred up beehive, Erik thought. They passed the prisoners down, and waited in case anyone came to investigate the noise from the seige tower.

No one did. So Erik sent Kari to fetch the bombardier and his barrels of powder. The knights set to moving and resetting the siege weapons. They weren't trying for precision, just effect. In fact, the less precise, the better—it was paramount that no one end up dead tonight. Shortly they were hauling several small barrels upwards.

The bombardier was delighted with the trebuchet. Soon they were winding a long, long, careful fuse around the perimeter of the tower. The arbalests were ready with some bolts set with naphtha-soaked rags from a container the guards had kept for attacking the sails of barges. The bombardier had added a grenade to each, tied in place with thongs. The arbalests were aimed into the inoffensive night sky to the west. More cords and fuses were set hastily in place. Finally the main fuse was lit and they scrambled down the ladder—taking it outside with them, before heading back at a brisk trot for the camp.

Inside the circle of felt gers the horses were ready. Harnesses jangled. Armor clanked. Fortunately there were no Mongol guards watching the perimeter. They were watching the inside of the tarkhan's ger instead, tied and gagged.

Now all they had to do was wait. Watch the silhouette of the tower in the darkness. And hope the fuse burned down faster than the fuse of the Mongols in the camp. You could almost hear rumor and affront doing the rounds out there.

Someone out in the camp flung a burning torch from the darkness and noise of the camp. It bounced off the felt and landed still burning in among the horses. Kari dismounted and kicked it out. "I reckon it's started without our tower," he said.

"Just some troublemaker," said Von Gherens, looking pointedly at Kari. "You always get one."

"I hope you're right. When trouble comes, it'll come mounted. I'd prefer it if they still had to get to that point," said Kari. "They ride well."

It appeared that Von Gherens was right. There was no follow up on the torch. Instead...maybe five hundred heartbeats later, Erik spotted a fire on the top of the siege tower. That was as should be. Quite a good fire, by the looks of it.

Erik looked at grizzled bombardier. Even in the moonlight he could see the powder-burn marks on the fellow's face. "Count of five, *Ritter* Hakkonsen," he said serenely.

Erik checked the situation hastily. Everyone was mounted. Everyone was waiting. Ropes tied and ready, to pull down the ger blocking their way to the nearest through-path, through the encampment of felt tents. Horses nervous. They caught the excitement and fear from their riders. The boy David and young Kildai—making it look as if he were seeing double on one steed. Bortai and Tulkun close beside them. Erik could only hope her clan would be pleased to see them back, and that she saw things the same way its leaders would.

He signaled to the two with the ropes on the ger. "Now." It fell. "Lead out," he yelled, trusting the bombardier. They wanted to be moving when it all happened.

Somewhere in the distance a horn sounded, as, eight abreast, the knights rode up the low berm and into the main camp.

And off to the south a tower burned, and, suddenly, fire streaked into the sky. High up the grenades exploded in little flares of abrupt brightness. There was a sudden, startled silence from the noisy encampment. The knights rode warhorses and no horse likes fire or explosions, but these had been exposed and hardened to such things. They cantered on, calmly, moving forward as if this was what they should be doing. The knights had direction and purpose . . . which was more than the camp had. Now there was pandemonium breaking loose, the sounds of horns and yelling. And in the midst of it the trebuchet launched its little vat of black powder, to explode, thunderously and with a magnificent flare off to the west. At a steady trot the knights moved toward the outer northern perimeter, passing through a mill of men and horses—who were mostly heading west.

Erik was beginning to wonder if they might just, possibly, get away without even a challenge, when a squad of horsemen came riding toward them.

They could even see the outer felt tents of the encampment. Thinking about it, it was quite logical. Besides sentries, such a war-camp would have substantial patrols on horse *outside* the camp. The Mongols did not fight the way that settled people did. This was not a society that relied on the security of walls; instead they relied on the mobility of their horses. Every man in the camp was trying to get mounted. Some, outside the camp, had been patrolling and were sober and fully ready. And unless Erik was very much mistaken those horn-calls told the entire camp that beside the possible Hungarian bombardment and attack from the river, the foreigners were out of their encampment and on the loose. Erik only hoped the order to "stop them at all costs" had not been given.

By the reaction of the patrol, it had. An arrow

sang off armor, and the patrol—at least two Arban strong—had their lances out and were charging. They were very brave, very disciplined and very fast—and also very, very stupid. The horse-path between the gers was wide enough—in close formation—for ten horses. If they'd let the knights get out into the open, they'd have had all the space they needed for their famous charge, divide and retreat firing backwards technique. Here they had no space, and they had also misjudged the pace and potential acceleration of the big horses in the moonlight. The knights' column of eight nearly filled the horse-path. And then one of the knights peeled out of his saddle, an unlucky arrow finding a chink in his armor, on the edge of the gorget. "Charge!" yelled Manfred, beating the others, barely, to the order. The big horses, already moving at a fair pace did not have to accelerate from a standstill. They were a solid avalanche of armored horse-flesh and armed with longer lances than the Mongol carried.

From the middle-back of the column David felt as if he was somehow stuck on a runaway cart on a very steep incline. And what was worse his co-rider was urging their horse to go faster. There was a brief clash, but the column did not even slow down. Looking down, he thought he saw a man under the hooves as they burst out of the edge of the encampment and away onto to the steppe. The land around the camp had been denuded of trees. It was far too open for a boy from Jerusalem who just wanted to hide. Preferably in a nice alley. Ideally in Jerusalem. But anywhere would do.

They kept up the headlong momentum for, in David's opinion, far too long. Then the knights slowed their horses. Orders were yelled. Some of them peeled away from the column, riding back, and the rest continued at a trot. If there was one gait David hated, it was the trot. He was glad when they slowed to a walk, and then, after an explosion behind them, as the knights who had peeled away came back, they were back at a canter.

They rode on into the dark. "Orkhan Erik knows his work," said Kildai. "Good discipline."

Riding next to Kildai and David, Bortai was similarly impressed. She knew that they had merely escaped the first of the pursuit. But behind them the camp was burning in places. Possibly from the naphtha arrows, possibly from campfires kicked over in the chaos. The large group would of course be easy to follow, and those who followed would have plenty of spare horses, which these foreign knights lacked. They had a few, of course, but they were more remounts for knights whose horses were injured or killed. They could never hope over a longer distance, to match the speed of the Mongol. They were at least two days' ride from lands of the White Horde. Even there . . . the soldiers from the orkhan's Mingghan would possibly follow. It would all depend on how well those who had fled the kurultai had reorganized. The very fact that Gatu Orkhan had dared put their gers in an encampment on the northern bank of the Great River said he did not believe them well organized. It was likely the White Horde clans had gone east towards the marshy delta of the great river. They'd have lost gers, horses, carts . . . loot that would have kept the Blue Horde busy a while. Still, in the numbers that had been at the kurultai, it would have been risky to attack them. Gatu Orkhan also knew the tactics of the Mongol well. Many a retreat had been turned into a victory. That could be especially true if his westerners tried to attack the White Horde in the marshlands near the mouth where the Otter clan held sway. No, it was likely the fleeing clans had fled in disorder... and had been allowed to do so. Gatu Orkhan would assume that he could take them at his leisure, that they would either change allegiance, now that Hawk clan was headless, or could be eaten up piecemeal. She sighed. At least, she hoped he had thought so. Blue Horde was larger and more numerous than White these days. It had been for this reason that her father had wanted to press the conflict northwards, to reestablish the lost lands and liberate the clans.

She saw how several scouts peeled off from the column. Very professional. If they'd had larger numbers and more horses they'd have been a force to reckon with. As it was... she wondered if they'd be better off on their own. They could move much faster, now that Kildai seemed to be riding reasonably well.

Erik, circling the column with Von Gherens, tallied men. "One dead, three injured. It could have been much worse," said the older knight.

Erik knew it could have been. But he also knew they had days of flight ahead. And that he had a very scanty force. He could barely afford to lose one man. If they were trapped by larger numbers, they'd lose many more. His foes knew the terrain. They rode faster and lighter. And they were far more numerous.

Erik was afraid for his charge.

Chapter 47

Elizabeth, for the first time in her long career, wished she knew a little more about the military. She'd never really paid the least attention to it. It had always seemed such a clumsy way of solving things when she had magic, murder, seduction, and treachery as possible options.

She was almost sure generals and princes did not normally lead their men on night-sorties and raids. Emeric didn't. Perhaps that was why he lost so many battles. Perhaps it really was necessary or just wise. But right now it was interfering with her plans. She really did not like that. She'd come, with a small but well-trained staff of suitable "loyalists"—if they'd known that they'd been chosen as expendables to make sure that her departure with Vlad was not interfered with, they might have been less loyal. She'd expected to be able to seduce him, work out where his defenses were. Overwhelm them, seduce him and get him back to her nearest facility. She had a suitable nunnery a little farther south down near Caedonia. She really really needed to get off this vile primitive mountain. She hated it. Yes, she'd put up with far worse to gain the power she had. But she'd done it so that she would not have to do this sort of thing.

Well, she'd mostly done it for power and a perfect skin, and the appearance of a seventeen-year-old. She had all that provided she used the treatment—the blood.

She ground her perfect teeth in frustration. She could seduce—by magical means granted to her—anything that was still breathing. She just couldn't do it long distance. Vlad had acquired certain protection, had some power. He'd also taken the edge off his appetite with some other woman. He still should not have been willing to go off in the night. All she had been able to do was to get him to take one of her boyars with him.

She looked at herself in one of the mirrors she had had transported up to this place. She always had at least three mirrors. She liked to see what she had paid such a price for. It was very satisfying. Looking at her eyes she detected just the tiniest hint of a line developing. It was the sun up here! Thank heavens winter was coming. The leaves were starting to turn, and it would start to snow one of these days. She looked at her eyes again, and then at the other telltale areas. She'd need more blood, and soon. Royal blood if possible. She wondered what had happened to the girl. Vlad's little sister. Thirteen. Such a desirable age, thought Elizabeth, her lips quirking into a smile. Perhaps she would catch the girl, seduce her and then kill her slowly, with the whip and much screaming, before draining her of all that delicious blood. She would have to do it over a bath, so as not to waste any. She licked her lips slowly. Well, she would ask the Vila. Perhaps they would know where she was hidden.

In the meantime she needed to take some steps to investigate the military. She walked outside into the darkness to find suitable material. Vlad had put one of his best men to guard her tent. She supposed it was a compliment besides being convenient. "Sergeant," she said. "What is your name?"

"Emil, Countess," he said, looking like a suitably hypnotized rabbit. He smelled. He was under-washed and his raiment was shabby. There was definitely stubble on his chin. Well, she thought, needs must when the devil drove. And the devil drove her, drove her harder with each passing year. "I need you to come and help me with something inside my tent, Emil," she said, exerting her will, stirring her magic. And her hips. He stood stock still. For a moment, an awful moment, she thought that she had lost her power somehow. That it was not just Vlad, that the magic of this vile land was robbing her of what she had given a mortgage on her soul for. Then he stepped forward and took her breasts in his big coarse hands. She ignored the roughness of them and, reaching her hand between his legs, led him into the candle-lit interior of the tent. She reflected that men were all the same. Once you had them by the testicles, their bodies, their hearts and the minds they contained would follow, for you to do whatever you wished with. And of course if the bodies didn't follow, then you could always have pleasure of ripping the testicles right off. Her victim gasped in pain. It gave her sufficient frisson to say: "I'm sorry. Did I squeeze? Let me kiss it better." She did, expertly and at length.

She let him undress her. He would suffer later for the careless handling of the velvet.

She had arranged the mirrors suitably. At least watching herself was pleasurable. More pleasurable than his desperate rutting. "You are so enormous," she said throatily. It pleased him and he pushed her thighs higher. Ha. She'd experimented with a few nonhumans that had seriously threatened to split her. Them she'd had to restrain. That had been back when she'd been curious about whether size or shape would provide her with pleasure. She'd since found that it was all in her mind. Inflict a little pain—or better, a lot—and the dwarf Ficzko could give her more satisfaction.

She could have bespelled him to believe he'd had the wildest orgy of his life. But she needed to lay some deeper enchantments on him. His spittle—on her breasts—his blood—she'd have that on her fingernails from his buttocks in a minute, when she faked a climax—and his semen. She'd bind with chains that would make him her absolute slave. Chains that would evade magical detection, after a day or two. These spells altered the nature of the victim. They drew on what was there, but usually controlled. They drew on the beast in the man. That thought and sticking her nails into him was some consolation.

Afterwards, when the stupid rabbit was done, she lay there between her candles—the fool had not even noticed the number or the pattern—and traced the sigyls of binding on his forehead, chest and thighs, with the inks she had just collected.

And then she started to question him on the military and other matters she wanted insight into. He was in no state to realize that, however. He thought, now, that he was enjoying another round of exquisite pleasures, an illusion built within his own mind. She didn't need to put up with it twice.

"Who is this woman Prince Vlad is sleeping with?" she asked.

"Rosa," he answered. There are no real secrets from sergeants in an army camp.

"Some pretty little village maiden, who loves him dearly?"

"She's a whore."

Elizabeth was almost angry enough to kill Vlad right then.

Chapter 48

Vlad did not think much of the seat of the boyar volunteer Elizabeth had sent with him. Actually, if it wasn't for her, he'd have said his father was dead right, and he'd be better off without them and told the man to be off.

They'd been in the saddle barely five hours and the man was behaving as if Vlad was going to cripple him. Vlad thought he should send the fellow to the gypsies to train. He wondered what had become of them. He must set enquiries in motion, talk to one of his sergeants. It was an amazingly effective way of finding anything out, he'd learned.

He noticed how the leaves were turning, and indeed, starting to fall. That was another worry, more pressing than a saddle-sore boyar, or even what had happened to his gypsy rescuers. He just hoped that they were all right. Mind you, they were competent enough, and tough and fast enough. They were thieves too, and he'd become a little more accepting of this, with distance. He was never going to like it, but on the other hand, he might have to become one himself at this rate. Winter was coming and he had more recruits every day. Peasants and craftsmen, though, to a man. Other than the few nobles that had come with Elizabeth—and thank God for her loyalty and help— his support seemed to be best among the poor, or at best, tradesmen. He needed money to provide for his men, and he needed a places for them to over-winter. It would be cruel in these mountains. They would die under canvas and lurking in caves. He had a few more weeks in which to take a few villages at least.

He also needed to secure some horses. A lot of horses. His men fought best on foot—they were no knights. Smerek guns made them a decent fighting force, and, if he had enough men, and enough guns, he'd deal with any knights that King Emeric could send into these mountains. But they needed to be mobile, and the guns and horses and food had be paid for or captured. Vlad permitted himself a smile. King Emeric was going to be in for a nasty surprise with the new light four-pounders Stanislaw was making for his prince. Cannon—even mere four pounders, that were mobile and could be transported about in wagons or carts, or even, if need be, on mules—were going to change the battle equation. Still, like the carts and wagons that Vlad had found that he and his forces were accumulating, they had to be stored, and moved. And they could not move as fast as the infantry, let alone his mounted men.

Mounted men. They really weren't cavalry, his men, just men with horses. Mounted infantry was the best way Vlad could describe them. Still, they were more mobile than his camp followers' carts and wagons. It had obviously got around that he was their longed-for prince... with a shortage of accommodation for his soldiery. More men were turning up with a covered cart than without one, these days.

"Can't I stop and rest for a while, Prince Vlad?" whined the boyar.

"We'll rest when we're there," said Vlad, wishing for the tenth time, at least, that he hadn't agreed to take the man along. The rest of this troop were his best men. It mattered not at all that some were poachers, ex-bandits and rogues. They were his forward scouts. The rest were good shots and the steadiest men he had. He'd had Emil and Mirko pick them out, and then let his feelings govern the selected ones. He was getting better at trusting those feelings.

"Where are we going?"

It was not a question Vlad wanted to answer. Not after his experiences in Gara. "A little ambush," was all he said.

"We're a long way out of the high mountains," said the boyar, who seemed to assume he was at liberty to interrupt Vlad's thoughts at will, and speak to him without the respect Vlad had come to take for granted. He tried to make his volunteer armies more comfortable, confident enough to address their prince... until of course he found someone like this who took it all too far.

Vlad did not say anything. They were a long way from the security of those mountains. He was aware of that. Some of the recruits had been bandits in those mountains. They still had networks of contacts. Nothing moved in the high mountains for forty miles without Vlad or the sergeants being told. In the lower lands Vlad felt far more nervous.

But then King Emeric wasn't going to send his pay chests through the high passes.

"Where are we going?" The boyar asked again.

"Where the Drac needs us to go. Now hold your tongue," said Mirko . . . and suddenly realized that the man outranked him by birth. "I'll go and check on the rearguard, Sire."

The boyar looked after the man. "You tolerate such insolence, Prince Vlad?"

"He forgot to whom he was speaking, my lord." said Vlad. Elizabeth had brought him these allies. He ought to appreciate them. Besides they were of noble blood like himself.

"I hope you'll demote him and let me discipline him for you, prince. That's what your army needs. More discipline."

Vlad disagreed, but said nothing. And he was going to have to find some way to avoiding this happening. Mirko was a good and valuable man. He wasn't quite as good as Emil, but Vlad had felt that he owed Elizabeth some duty of care. There were some rough men in his command, and she was a lady of high degree. Besides, she'd freed him from the tower; he would never forget that, and he would always be in her debt. It made him uncomfortable just thinking about her. She did odd things to his feelings. He should not lust for her, but he did.

A rider came up out of the dark—one of the scouts. "All clear ahead, Drac," he said respectfully. "And good hiding places next to the ford. Lots of cover."

It had been hard to guess that from the map. Vlad was relieved. Now all he needed was the scouts to report on the retreat-routes. Vlad was fairly sure this was not a trap. But he took no unnecessary chances any more. Information trickled in from all over now—it was amazing how it had picked up, in the weeks since Gara. He had this convoy, wagons under heavy escort, confirmed from two separate sources, let alone the tip-off that had come from the Smerek cousins down south. He had to move south too, and soon.

They positioned themselves carefully on both banks of the river in the gray light of a misty dawn. The ford was little more than a broad shallow area, with an entry and exit cut into the steep bank. The place really could use a decent bridge, Vlad thought. Like the roads it was not something that Emeric believed in spending money on. Vlad had had to swim and ford far too many cold mountain streams to not appreciate bridges.

And then there was just the inevitable waiting. Waiting with this annoying boyar, who kept asking him questions. Vlad tried asking a few of his own. The man had seen some military service as an officer with the levies that Emeric had raised from Valahia. But his experience and knowledge of military strategy seemed to amount to obeying the orders he had been given, and disciplining his soldiers. That didn't seem to stop him wanting to know all about Vlad's strategy and plans. "So what do you plan, Sire? When do you hope to meet him in battle? What cities are we going to lay siege to?"

Vlad had not discussed his plans with anyone. Part of the reason for this was that he had not had a clear strategy when he had started, besides trying to survive. Now it had evolved into at least a medium-term strategy in his head. It still amounted to "survive" but extended to "and look after your troops." Eventually, tired of being polite, Vlad sent the man across the river to the soldiers he had positioned to cut off the retreat.

First came three squads of Emeric's cavalry, sixty men in all, clattering and splashing through the ford, cursing the water. Then came the two heavily laden wagons, both with a driver and an armed guard next to him. Behind them, another squad of twenty cavalrymen. Bored cavalry. No one ever tried to steal from King Emeric. He had the unpleasant but effective habit of killing, slowly, and visibly, a suitable number of the closest locals. If that didn't work as an adequate deterrent, he would massacre a little farther afield. Vlad had to admit that he had chosen this ambush site to pay the king back in his own coin. The nearest settlement was one of German and Hungarian miners. If Emeric reacted with his normal tactics he was going to lose the support of those foreigners too.

Vlad by now was reconciled to the fact that no military operation followed any sort of plan, after the first shot had been fired. All he could do was to train his men well and plan for as many contingencies as possible. When, inevitably, something you hadn't thought of came up, at least the training would stand you in good stead.

This ambush was no exception. Gunfire, a single shot, began just too soon. The second wagon was not quite down the slope into the ford. The driver however tried to urge the horses on rather than trying to turn. Even if the massed volley of fire did not catch the cavalry bunched and unaware, it was still very effective. The water reduced the ability of cavalry to maneuver, reduced their speed to that of a walk on dry land, and gave them no place to run or regroup.

Out of the morning river mist Vlad heard the sergeant Mirko's "fire at will."

With his handful of horsemen Vlad waited to deal with escapees. Sure enough a few made it, having driven their horses up the bank rather than up the cut roadway. They were brave men, and now, behind the ambushing arquebus infantry, tried to ride them down.

Vlad rode into them instead. "Drac!" yelled his men—and that, and that alone, before the clash of arms, seemed to take the heart out of the surviving cavalry. They panicked and tried to run. It was a short, bloody fight. Vlad learned another lesson. A retreat in good order might be survivable. Panicked flight was not.

A little later he met up with Mirko. The sergeant-cum-quartermaster was plainly uneasy. "Sire . . . I have to tell you something. That boyar. He tried to sneak off just before the attack. I told him I'd shoot him dead if he didn't stay just there, Drac. He threatened me, and . . . well. You heard the shot before it all happened. He started yelling at me. Said I was peasant scum, and had no right to tell him what to do."

"So you shot him."

Mirko looked startled. "No Drac. He tried to shoot me. One of the boys hit his pistol arm with an arquebus. That's why I'm still talking to you. Then the shooting started."

"Where is he?" asked Vlad.

Mirko chewed his lip. Looked awkward. "He ran off, Sire. Someone shot him again. But he got away."

Vlad nodded slowly. "I want two men, Mirko. I want the man who struck him with the arquebus. And I want the man who shot him."

"Sire . . . they only did it for the best," said Mirko,

standing up for his men. He had survived Emeric's army, where he would never have done that. But he had—gradually—learned that his new commander was different.

Vlad illustrated how different he was. "I know. That's why I am promoting them. We need more sergeants. They need to learn to shoot better, though. And to deal with such idiots faster."

"He . . . the boyar is one of our overlords, Sire."

Vlad shook his head. "At best he was a fool. At worst a spy and a traitor. And he seemed to forget that *I* am *his* overlord. Well. He is a boyar no more. He's a peasant and a deserter. Five gold forint for the man who brings me his head."

Mirko grinned. "It's a public service that most of the men will do for free, Drac."

"In the meantime, we need to get a move on, to get those wagons unloaded and onto the horses and to heading back into the mountains. I think we'll take the road along Drumhos valley. That boyar may know too much about the other possible routes. We'll also be moving camp again. Send a man on a good horse with my instruction. I told Emil we'd probably do it."

"Sire!" said Mirko, saluting respectfully and grinning.

A few moments later Vlad heard Mirko telling the troops to jump to it. And two wary looking young peasant recruits came out of the mist and saluted. "Sire. Sergeant Mirko sent us to see you. He said to say it was about that boyar."

"Ah. He is not a boyar any more."

"No Sire. He is. He was alive, S . . . sire," stammered the one with the thatch of black hair and a single solid eyebrow.

"He is, yes. Unfortunately. He just is not a noble-man in my realm anymore. I will have both his lands and his head for cowardice and treachery. Now, what are your names?"

The surprised looking soldiers took a moment to absorb this. "Viorel, Sire," said the solid-browed one.

"Brudhos, Sire," said the stolid second man.

"Very well, Sergeants Viorel and Brudhos," said Vlad with a smile. "See that you work on the accuracy of your shooting. And now get back to helping load the pay chests out of those wagons. I'll not have them looted. That's your pay and the pay of the rest of our men up in the mountains, in there."

It was the sort of work, Vlad noted, that men could go to with a will. He reluctantly admitted that there was an element of bandit in even the best of men, even himself. Like the animal, the hard part was keeping it subservient to the good man in there, too.

King Emeric, in the temporary quarters he had appropriated from one of the local overlords, got the news of his missing pay chests later that same afternoon, along with an injured boyar. The man had lost some blood and ridden more than thirty miles. He was pale and clinging to the saddle when Emeric saw him from the windows of the room which he had set up as his operations center. The Croat officer with him was not much more cheerful looking when they arrived and dismounted. "Now what is it?" demanded Emeric irritably, as the two men were shown into the drawing room. He'd been going through reports from the various districts and towns in Valahia. He had invested little money or effort on spies here, in this subject kingdom. Now he wished that he had done more.

"Your Majesty. The army pay wagons have been attacked and robbed," said the Croat captain, not wasting any time in getting to the point, getting the worst over with.

Emeric flung a fragile inkstand—a beautiful piece of Venetian glass and silver—hard enough to smash onto the thick turkey carpet. "Damn your eyes. Did I not order them escorted with at least three squads of cavalry! This country is rotten with thieving bandits. Find the nearest settlement. Crucify five men, five women and five children until they talk. The local peasantry and burghers always know, and always sing. And then burn their homes. You know that. You've served with me long enough. I remember your face from Corfu."

"Your Majesty, I took steps against the nearest village. Then...this man came to us."

Emeric looked at the obviously wounded man. He looked and dressed like one of the minor nobility of this benighted principality. The wounded man was not in chains. If he'd been one of the brigands, he would have expected a brutal and efficient officer like this Croat to make sure of that. In fact the officer would probably have made him sing, and then followed the pay chests already, if that was the case. "Who are you?" said King Emeric, his eyes narrowed.

"The boyar Pishtac. From Cluj," said the man uneasily. His right arm hung useless at his side.

"And what do you have to do with my army's pay chests?" asked Emeric.

"They were taken by Prince Vlad. I tried to stop it...to warn..."

Emeric walked up to him. "Taken by Prince Vlad indeed. He is in the high Carpathians. His ragtag peasant army don't dare come down."

The Croat officer coughed. "Your Majesty, there were four squads with the pay wagons. Eighty men on horseback. They were all killed bar two—and they bear out what this man says. They were attacked by well-armed well-disciplined men, who fired in massed volley. The villagers heard it, too. And the two survivors confirm the attackers calling 'Drac.'"

Emeric scratched his chin. He hated losing his gold, far more than he hated losing men. Men bred. Gold had to be dragged out of a reluctant population. His tax men were good at it, and he had given them almost unlimited powers, but there was never as much as he wanted. "Tell me what you were doing there," he said to the boyar. "And how come you failed to save my gold."

"I tried, Your Majesty."

"Tried is not good enough," Emeric said, preparing to vent some of his rage on the man. The fellow's next words changed his plans.

"Countess Bartholdy said I was to go with him," said the boyar, cowering back. "I couldn't help it. Honestly, Your Majesty. I did my best."

Emeric let his hands fall, and turned to his factotum. "Get this man a chair, before he falls down. And then all of you get out of here. I need to question this man alone." He looked at the quaking boyar. "And give him some brandy."

Soon, the boyar was seated in a comfortable armchair. A large glass of very good brandy, held clumsily in his left hand, clattered against the boyar's teeth, and spilled down his shirt. Emeric smiled. "Now I need to know where Vlad of Valahia is. And I need to know exactly what he is planning. And, of course, I want my gold back." Emeric paused. "And I also want to know just what my dear aunt is up to."

The glass nearly ended up on the floor. It was good Venetian glass, Emeric noted. He would have his people look into just what the local lordling was paying in taxes. "She's a witch."

"No, strictly speaking I believe that she is an enchantress. She dislikes and despises witches. She has done a great deal to eliminate pagans from my lands, and has destroyed the *stregheria*. But that is beside the point, right now. First Vlad of Valahia. What does he plan?"

"I tried to get him to tell me, Your Majesty. But the man...if he is a man, and not a demon..."

"He's a man. He's going to be a dead man when I catch up with him. So what does he plan? Did you glean anything of value? Your own life depends on this, Boyar. Give me what I need and you'll have lands and life. Otherwise, I may become angry. You wouldn't want that."

"Your Majesty...mercy."

Emeric sniffed. The man had fouled himself. Bah. Where there no real men out there? "Of course. Just tell me all that you can. And I will decide if it is enough for rewards...or punishments." He wondered if torturing one of her creatures was worth the risk. Probably. She really did not care.

"I can show you where their camp is. On the map. I made sure that I could find it again."

Emeric let him show him, and two of his generals, who carefully ignored the stink of the man. If Vlad knew this fool had run off, he'd already have moved. But he was moving a large encampment. There would be traces.

The rest of the questioning did not go so well. The one real and substantive piece of information the boyar had to offer was that Vlad had been very interested in the cost of horses, and where to buy them. Well, that little avenue could be closed. Emeric would forbid the sale of horseflesh. But the man could tell Emeric little that he didn't already know. The boyar was not deep in Elizabeth's confidence. Emeric suspected that Elizabeth had set some form of compulsion on the man. He would do whatever she ordered him to do. That unfortunately didn't tell Emeric what Elizabeth wanted this man to do.

Eventually Emeric let the boyar leave. Or rather, be taken away to a chirurgeon. Not because he'd been as cooperative as possible but because he stank and kept fainting.

PART V
November, 1540 A.D.

Chapter 49

"The seasons move, the stars dance in their ancient courses and fiery portents are seen in the sky," said Radu, who was prone to a poetic turn of phrase.

"And besides that, it is getting damned cold," said Grigori. "The first snows will be here soon. We need to move."

"And the foraging is getting thin around here," said Radu.

Angelo shook his head. "Another week at least. They are still too small. They need the vents at night. Soon they'll be big enough to walk the woods on their own. We need to teach them to hunt."

"It will be easier than feeding them. They're getting more voracious by the day."

"They're just growing. They'll slow down soon enough." Angelo had been through two hatchings before. The pack lived far longer than most ordinary humans as a result of the magical blood, but he was beginning to feel his age a little.

"Just as well, or there would not be enough game

for them in all Valahia, let alone on this mountain," said Grigori, stretching.

"It's just forcing you to run a little more," said Radu. "You said you liked to run. You said that we spent too much time riding when we were with the Drac."

"So who is going to take the dowager duchess's letter to the Drac? It's time he came south anyway," said Grigori.

"You. It'll give you a break from hunting for food for the young ones," said Angelo.

"So I get a longer cross-country run instead. Alone, no doubt." He didn't sound too unhappy about it. Well, Angelo knew that the new Drac, his survival and future preyed on their minds. Once the Drac had merely been the man of a river priestess, and then, his sons, hill-chieftains. And back then the protection he afforded the pack was small. But for centuries now, that protection had been growing. And with the coming of the travelers from the south...well, they were convenient cover for the pack. But they did carry the potential for persecution with them. And the pack knew they were outnumbered, and if they failed, if the wyverns failed, and if the Drac failed, the other nonhumans would not help them.

"Take one of the youngsters with you. You can teach him a bit about hunting on the way," said Angelo. Radu would complain later, no doubt. But Grigori was the best at fitting in with humans. He was more flexible than Radu. And it was time to start to groom some new blood to lead the pack. They could be in for some very tough times, if the Drac failed...but for the first time, they had a second throw of the dice with the younger sister.

Later that afternoon Grigori and young Miu set off, loping quietly through the trees. The little Besarab noticed they were missing. She didn't miss much, that girl. Tante Silvia said she'd been fiddling with the all the rubbish in the cart, obviously looking for something. Well, the blood grail would just have to be hidden from her.

When Vlad arrived back at their camp with the pack-train, the camp had already been largely dismantled. For the last month it had been practical to divide the camps up. This was far from the only base that Vlad had ready. He had hidden food stores, and spare weapons. He even had the Smereks safely secreted in a cave that had been refitted as a makeshift smithy. The men were used to moving. Used to not knowing where they would go, until they actually left. Vlad thought it worked very well. It would make them hard to find.

It appeared that the gypsy and his young companion hadn't found it so difficult. They were lounging next to a large rock when Vlad rode up.

Vlad leapt down from his horse in delight and hugged Grigori, rather to the gypsy's surprise and disapproval of their other watchers. Vlad did not care. He'd missed the ragged men, and the music... And he owed them. He owed them a debt even greater than that he owed to Countess Elizabeth Bartholdy. "Angelo? Radu? Are they here, too?" he asked eagerly.

"Too lazy to make the run, Drac," said Grigori with his usual wicked wolfish grin. "This is my young cousin, eh. Young Miu. I brought him along for company."

The young man bowed. He was a younger version

of Grigori, even with the same gray eyes. "Drac," he said, bowing. "They did say that you were very tall. But you are even taller than I thought. You look very like your sister."

"My sister?" said Vlad, puzzled. The last time he'd seen her she'd been a big-eyed toddler. He could barely remember her.

Grigori fished in his ragged patchwork cotte and pulled out a sealed letter. "We have them—your mother and your sister—hidden and safe on Moldoveanu mountain, Drac. This is a message from your mother."

Vlad's guilt nearly overwhelmed him as he took it. He had been so busy first surviving and then building up an army and fighting King Emeric's troops that he had not even given a thought to his own family! True, he had not seen, or been allowed to hear from them for ten years. But that was no excuse. He tried desperately to reconstruct the image of his mother in his mind. He had done his best not to think of her, for so many years. But he could still remember the songs she had sung to him. She'd been big...then. But so had everyone. He had been a small boy.

He opened the letter, breaking the seal of the house of Valah...two wyverns supporting the rooted crown. Eagerly he unfolded the page. Just one page of a neat, slightly crabbed handwriting.

"Dearest son," he read. His eyes blurred. She had always called him that.

He tried to get a grip on himself. Surely all mothers addressed letters to their sons thus?

"What have you got there, Prince Vlad?" asked the countess Elizabeth, musically.

He bowed. "A letter from my mother."

"So nice. And what does she have to say? Where is she?"

"I . . . haven't managed to read it yet," he said, feeling foolish.

"Poor boy. Can I read it for you? Where did it suddenly come from?"

"Oh, the gypsies brought it for me," he said, gesturing—and suddenly realizing he was gesturing at nothing in particular. He blinked. Where had they got to while he'd opened the letter? "They've gone," he said lamely.

"To be expected, Prince Vlad," she said, waving a languid hand in front of her nose. "Gypsies. Dirty and untrustworthy, everyone knows that."

"Well . . . they have looked after me. They, er, they have helped me a great deal."

"I doubt if they did it for you, Prince. They have their own agendas. And they will desert you when they are done with those purposes." She looked him from under lowered lashes. "They're said to be ritual murderers, you know. They use blood magic. Every adult gypsy man must rape and kill a non-gypsy child. The shared conspiracy and secrecy binds them. They have plans, evil plans, for you."

He gaped. Thieves yes. They were . . . although they seemed to have a code of honor, a line which they did not cross. But murderers? Why? Why had they brought him home?

"They practice dark rituals every day. Defile churches . . ."

"I lived with them for weeks. I never saw anything like that."

"You can't trust them, Prince Vlad. They will seduce

you into their own evil ways with their blood magic. And then abandon you."

They had left him...but they'd brought him home, too. Protected him. Perhaps for their own ends... He didn't want to argue with her about it. "If you will excuse me, I must read this letter," he said.

"Let me read it for you," she said with a devastating smile.

Reluctantly, but unable to resist, he handed the letter to her. "How is it that you look so young, Countess?" he said admiring her smooth skin. Vlad was not versed in feminine looks or ages. He assumed that she must be a little older than himself. In references to the passage of time at court she'd mentioned things that had happened some years ago. "You could be twenty-five."

She nearly dropped the letter. He was surprised at the poisonous look that came over her face... It was the first time he'd seen her look anything other than serene or smiling. It made her look a lot older. "I do not thrive outdoors. Now, let me read this for you. "Dearest son, it begins."

She somehow made it sound very commonplace.

Grigori could scarcely believe that they'd got away. What was SHE doing here? Yes, he knew that the old woman kept out of the public eye too much in the Magyar lands. What was she doing so openly here? The pack had never hunted the Pannoian plains, so they knew her less well than they might. What he did know, frightened him. Grigori wished desperately that Angelo was here, rather than young Miu...even if it had been Miu that had smelled her and warned him.

By the Old Ones . . . she *stank*. Age and decay and fear. The terror of others, rubbed into her decrepit flesh. How the people around her could stand it . . . human noses were really inadequate. He shuddered to think of it. They'd barely got away in time, and right now, the farther away the better as far as he was concerned. What was the Drac doing consorting with such a one? Had she entrapped him? Were they all doomed, the pack, the Old Ones, the compact?

"And now," said Miu, rubbing his nose as if that would rid him of the scent that still clung there. "What do we do, Uncle?"

Grigori wished he knew. His instinct was to run. But they'd been charged by the Drac's mother—rather repetitively, it seemed to him—with bringing back a message from her son. She, and possibly the little one, were their second chance, maybe their only chance if the old woman had her hooks into the Drac. They would run off if no message came back. The two women, Grigori knew, stood very little chance if they left the gypsy encampment.

"Back off and watch," he said, finally. "We need to see him. When she is not around. She'll be watching for us, too. And she'll kill both of us pretty quick if she gets her hands on us."

Elizabeth Bartholdy could barely contain her rage. She had to get away from here. She needed blood *now*. Preferably young and noble. Twenty-five! Damn this upstart boy. But he was too ignorant to lie. He really thought so. She'd given the devil a lien on her soul to remain forever seventeen. Of course he'd set conditions. But these days it seemed that she could

barely go a week without her bath. And even moving
between her various establishments, and with her rank,
and deliberately keeping a low profile—she was beautiful and people did ask suspicious questions when she
remained that way—it was difficult to find sufficient
victims. She needed their pain and terror as much
as their blood. It all took time. And if word got out,
real confirmed word, there might be repercussions.
Nothing that she couldn't deal with, but enough to
make hunting for victims harder. She'd had to fake
her own death, once before, before returning as a
cousin—just as beautiful, but with golden hair.

And then there were the damned gypsies, as they
called themselves. Ha! Did they really think that
she did not know what they were? As soon as she
got back to her tools and paraphernalia . . . she had
enough . . . there had been tiny amounts of wolf-saliva
on that message. She'd deal with them. Nets and iron
would work.

The nauseating pap in this mother's letter was
almost the final insult.

Vlad looked ready to burst into tears. Useless soft
fool.

She had to get out of here. Had to. Even to entrap
him she could not stay another day—especially as it
seemed that they would be doing nothing but moving,
and, it seemed as if he would be off campaigning for
days after that. She had her agents in place now. They
would bring him to her establishment near Caedonia.
She needed her blood. She was obviously showing
her age. "I am sorry, Vlad," she said, caressing his
cheek. "I have also had messages that I must go and
attend to some business." The dismay written on his

face was comical. She had worried, just a little, that he would be able to resist her. He did resist more than a mortal should.

She touched his cheek. "I am trying to recruit you some more men and of course, money. Politics, dear. Not your forte, but something every ruler needs to master."

He made an effort and smiled. "I will ask you to do it for me."

For a very brief moment she was almost tempted. He would make such a good front for her. Better than Emeric. Emeric needed power, and Elizabeth, to stay on the throne. Vlad they might just follow because they loved him. And oh, how she could corrupt that. She smiled at him again. "It's a hard task. But if you are to assume your rightful place you'll need more than just the support of the commons, Prince Vlad."

"Better men than Boyar Pishtac, I hope," said Vlad rather curtly.

He was plainly a little stung by her reference to his troops as commoners. They were, of course. But they were loyal to him. She would erode that, given time. Not that it was important, really. He would be in her clutches and drained long before that became relevant. "Oh?" said Elizabeth, raising her eyebrows. "What did he do? I haven't seen him. I will chastise him."

Vlad shrugged. "He fled when we clashed with Emeric's troops."

She was startled. He shouldn't have been able to do that. He was supposed to find out what Vlad's plans were. She thought she'd soothe Emeric with such information. The prince had said to her twice that he really needed someone to help him with strategy. That he could talk to. And then Pishtac had run off.

It was this place. It had a negative impact on her workings. It was affecting her! She was quite right that it was a good time to leave. "I will send word. His family will be dealt with."

"But . . . just because he was a traitor . . . does not mean that they are," protested the young prince, showing his naivete. He obviously had not understood any politics yet. "I think, Countess, that he was in the pay of King Emeric. He could betray you."

She sighed. "Perhaps I was too trusting. But he will not dare speak ill of me to the king. I promise that." She toyed with the idea of letting Emeric "capture" her and luring this fool into a rescue. But first she needed his blood to stay in his veins until it suited her, and second, he might just succeed. He should not have been able to do what he had done, without either support or money. It had to be magic. She wondered, just for an instant, if she *could* harness it. Or if he, too, had made his compact with her master. It would be typical of the dark lord to set them against each other. A game for his demons to play. A betrayal of hopes. But no. The boy was still an innocent, if not virginal.

Her hands twitched. She'd done something about that woman, anyway.

"I am still sorry that you must go. But so must we. I expect Emeric will be hunting us. I will arrange a suitable escort to see that you are not intercepted," He said.

"Emeric is unaware of my sympathies. Even if Boyar Pishtac has betrayed you and I, he can hardly have reached the king. And it would take a direct instruction from the king before any lesser soldier would dare to act against me. And I have legitimate reason to be here in Carpathia. I have my estates at Caedonia and the nunnery there—which is where I will need you to meet me, Prince. I will have some special things arranged by then."

He bowed. "I will be there, Countess. Nothing would stop me."

She smiled graciously at him. She had him. She need spend no longer in these unappealing and rude circumstances. "There is one other thing you could do for me—I don't need an escort, but your mother and sister will need them. I can provide them with safety and shelter at my estate. Emeric will not look for them there. But you'd better send some of your best men to protect them. And be aware that the gypsies may not want them to go. They keep them as hostages, I think."

She'd struck home with that one. "I'll sent Emil. And fifty of my best. I'm just not sure where to."

"Emil? Is he the man you set to guard me? It is no use sending fifty men, Prince Vlad. The gypsies will hide from them. Just send Emil to be their bodyguard—and to help them steal away. He is so trustable." She smiled. "I will need his help in packing up my things."

"I will order him to assist you," he said, smiling gallantly. "Or could I help you myself?"

She lowered her eyelashes. "Such work is beneath a prince."

"I would gladly do it to help you."

"Ah. But I would not demean you thus," she said. "Emil will do very well. A prince must show the commons that he knows his worth."

❋   ❋   ❋

Vlad thought about the need to show his men that he was indeed a prince. It puzzled and worried him. He'd lived with them, eaten from the same pots, slept rough next to them...they still treated him with deference. In the end he concluded it was probably good advice if the men did not know you. His men did. They'd built a legend around him, to believe in. It almost didn't seem to matter what he did.

The business of getting the camp moved, and seeing Elizabeth safely off occupied Vlad for most of the rest of the day. His scouts—and the mountains seemed alive with those who would bring word to him—reported some Croat scouts, that they had shot at. The days had long gone where King Emeric's scouts or indeed anything less than a few hundred men could move freely in the north end of the Carpathians. Someone, somewhere would shoot at them.

But at close of day, he had something of a surprise for his men. They were volunteers, serving him out of loyalty and the hope of eventual reward. And of course the chance of some loot. Vlad knew that, and had seen the effects of the desire to loot. He hoped to ease that desire a little.

"Parade the men, Mirko."

It was something he had not done very often, and it plainly surprised his partisans. They drilled in formation to shoot and to march, but not to stand. He'd sat with the quartermaster sergeant earlier, and found that his little army had grown more than he'd realized. He had—including the scouts and the men in the two smaller camps—just over a thousand men. Barely a bite for Emeric's armies—the king could field eighty thousand, if he called up levies, and possibly more.

But still, for a prince who had arrived as a vagabond in his own duchy, a vast step up. He still did not have enough arquebuses for them, but the Smerek brothers had quite a manufactory going. They were—Vlad did not ask how—getting components up from their old workshops and contacts. Cast-brass barrels for the little cannon, too, had come up from the south, somehow bypassing Emeric's checkpoints. But they really needed a far better and more stable base, one where they could actually machine the weapons from scratch. That too was on Vlad's mind. The Smereks were getting a substantial chunk of the money that King Emeric's paymasters should have been handing to his troops. So was the quartermaster. But Emeric had been paying seven times the number of men, and of course, officers, who were paid much more generously. And this had been the money for the next quarter. Vlad knew regular pay would be beyond his means . . . but for some of his peasant irregulars this would be the first money that wasn't copper that they'd ever touched.

The men were a little wary. Their clothing was for the most part the worse for wear, and the colors tended toward mud. For some reason they'd all taken to wearing three goshawk feathers in their hats. It was as close to a uniform as they had. It was becoming known as the Drac's symbol—that was why he'd had Emil and the two men he'd sent south take them out of their hats.

"Men, I have called you together because I wish to reward you for your loyalty to me. It has not gone unnoticed, I promise. Thanks to the courage of the men who accompanied me on last night's ride, Sergeant Mirko will be holding a pay parade."

They began cheering. He raised his hand to still them. "I will reward those who serve me well and loyally. That is my word."

"Drac! Drac!" they cheered.

It was later, just before he headed off to find some food and rest that he saw the gypsies again. Looking wary. He was both angry and a little uneasy. Why had they vanished like that? Still, he owed them a debt. He walked up to Grigori and said so.

The gypsy laughed, a return to his old self of their journey together. He had always laughed, while Radu took things seriously. "We don't need your gold, Drac."

"We can take it anyway," said young Miu cheerfully.

"Shut up, boy," said Grigori, cuffing at his head. The young gypsy dodged. "He wants finery. He thinks it may impress a certain young woman."

"She likes me anyway," said Miu.

"I was looking for you. I have despatched Emil, my trusted sergeant, and two of my best men to be guards for my mother and sister. Tell them I am coming south..."

"Your mother said we were to wait for a reply. And that you were to quote the song she always sang to you. If you remember it."

"Of course I do! Let me find parchment, a quill and some ink. Do you think you could find my sergeant? Or I can send more men with you."

Grigori raised an eyebrow. "We watch, Drac."

Vlad was glad enough to find his bed that night. But although he was tired he waited for Rosa.

She did not come to him.

Chapter 50

In Vilnius the man-monster with the steel eyes decided that, when his rule extended from the icy shores of the north to the hot heart of Arabia, he would see to stamping out the production and use of certain drugs. Yes, they had been useful. Chernobog had found it far easier to deal with mazed minds that wanted to believe they had seen paradise and dealt with their god. But right now, when he needed to either organize a pursuit or punish his servant, the tarkhan Borshar was too full of the narcotic to be completely coherent.

They'd been right inside his mouth...and somehow the valuable prizes and the conflict their death would stir up had slipped away from the sharp teeth that had waited to rend them. That would still happen, but not in the time and place of his choosing, which angered him.

To add to his fury, one of his sailcloth manufactories had caught fire. And the news Chernobog could glean from Venice—where the monster dared not venture, not even in spirit—and other points of the

Mediterranean, was that the west was readying itself for a spring attack on Constantinople. The city should hold, even if the Venetians had somehow managed to work out a way to fire massive forty-eight-pound bombards from the decks of their vessels without sinking them.

Alexis must be warned of that. The Byzantine emperor should concentrate his guns on the seaward walls, to keep the enemy ships out of range. That was if Alexis could be kept from alternating between his depravities and total panic. He was a weak reed, but at least it meant that he was corruptible and malleable.

Chernobog turned his questing mind across the distances to his newfound disciples and their demands for visions of paradise and translucent virgins, and investigated the state of the Ilkhan and his agents' penetration and readiness. He found them a worried group. The overlords had at last deigned to notice their activities. Nothing had been done, yet. The Ilkhan Hotai the Ineffable was a large, lethargic man, but that was not true of all of his generals. Some of them were definitely looking at Alamut. The Baitini cult were nervous and looking for reassurance. Tiresome as it was, Chernobog would give them that reassurance. After all, so long as the Ilkhan were in a state of chaos and civil war they would be too busy to interfere with the other plans that the Black Brain had.

He wondered just when his new shaman would be here. The delay was becoming insupportable. It was far better that the shaman risked his life in the dangers of the spirit world than for Chernobog to assume that risk himself. He wondered what his enemy beyond the Carpathians was up to. As usual, her demonic assistants defended that area from his view, as the church shielded Rome, and the Servants of the Holy Trinity shielded the Holy Roman Empire.

In realms far removed from this physical world, but yet with ties to it, Chernobog was aware of the powerful and ancient wild magic stirring in the Carpathians themselves. Mountains have deep roots, some into planes beyond most human ken.

He hoped that Elizabeth was stupid enough to meddle with mountain-power. It might be a match for the host of lesser demons that protected her. Her master, like Chernobog, would never risk that close an encounter. If Elizabeth dared to meddle, she might find herself abandoned.

In his chambers in Elizabeth's castle, Count Mindaug was entertaining similar thoughts. There were certain places in the world that the wiser sort of magic-users avoided. Corfu was one of them—as King Emeric had learned, not so long ago.

The Carpathians were another. These mountains had their own ancient forces, which it was best not to meddle with.

All the more so, because it was inherent in such old and pagan powers that their geographic scope was limited. On their own terrain, they could be fearsome. But only on that terrain. In their very nature, those forces could not extend their sway beyond their limited realm.

Mindaug was not at all happy to be in Elizabeth's castle in the northern stretches of the Carpathians. But at least, unlike the countess, he was not attempting to meddle personally in those mountains. He thought she was quite mad to be doing so. Of course, she was quite mad to begin with.

He pulled another book down from the shelves. Far better to explore such dangers in print, from a suitable distance.

Chapter 51

Irongate. Irongate was the prize. Of all the castles in Valahia, no other had the capacity to earn income on that scale. With control over the Danube, it was a valuable and strategic place, which King Emeric would not, could not leave in the hands of someone who was less than completely loyal to him. Ban Alescu had known that, had schemed very carefully to become its master. Marriage was the key, and power. It was simply unfortunate that the law only permitted one wife.

The answer was of course to bury them, and he had done that. He had accumulated power, but he had further ambitions. That was his nature. But up to now he had been content to eat, slowly, into the lands and possession of his neighbors.

Now, looking at the letter from Emeric he saw a way clear to become overall ruler of the Duchy of Valahia. And then Emeric would have to look to keep the throne of Hungary under his backside, thought Ban Alescu grimly.

He wondered just what his mother would say when she found out about her secret marriage. He grinned.

A good thing his father was dead. And of course the Dowager Duchess Bertha of Valahia might be less than pleased. He had met her and her daughter, several times. Her husband had been a weak vacillator, unable to take control of his nobles, and not able to stop Hungary's steady encroachment on his productive heartlands in Trans-Carpathia. The Mongols had taken and held all the lower lands to the east, and Emeric was nibbling away at his principality from the west. The prince had been left with control of a few strategic castles in the passes, and even those had garrisons of Hungarian troops.

Well, he would, of course take up the king's offer, but there was no way he would allow himself to be a puppet prince half-controlling a rump principality. He wanted the degree of control that the man's grandfather had had.

He turned to one of his footmen. "Have my scribe sent up. And tell him to bring with him some of the best parchment."

The man hurried off. It was only once he had gone that it occurred to Ban Alescu that there might be more to this proposal than first met the eye. What had happened to the Prince of Valahia's son Vlad, named after his terrifying grandfather? He'd been a hostage in Buda. Had Emeric killed him? Alescu had been too wrapped up in the affairs of his own fief to pay much attention to local politics in Valahia.

The scribe hurried in with quills, ink and several rolls of parchment. He bowed respectfully, trying not to spill the ink. He was from Valahia, a native, if the Ban recalled right. "Bergen. Tell me about the son of the Dowager Duchess Bertha..."

"Prince Vlad, your lordship," said the scribe, eagerly. "His army grows by the day. They say that he is coming south. Are you going to make your submission, my lord? That's most wise. They say that he is his grandfather reborn."

The Ban steepled his fingers, and sighed. A complication. Emeric had said that he merely wanted Alescu to step in to avoid rival claimants to the Principality causing a civil war. It appeared Emeric was in fact trying to foment one. Well, that did not mean he would not take the king up on his offer. Just that the price would be higher. And he needed to find out more about this Prince Vlad. Which of the nobility cleaved to him? What sort of force did he have? It had to be substantive or Emeric would not be holding out such offers.

"What can I write for you, my lord?" asked the scribe.

"I think I shall do it myself," Ban Alescu said. "But I will still need the parchment and quills. Leave them there on that table."

"Yes, my lord."

The fellow was obviously disappointed. So Vlad was taking the fancy of the middle rank of society. And the scribe plainly knew more—rumor if nothing else—than his master. Rumor had to be sifted, but there was usually a shred—just a shred—of truth in it somewhere. "So, do many of the nobles of Valahia make their submission to the prince," he asked idly.

The scribe scowled and shook his head. "A handful of boyars only, my lord. They'll pay a high price for that, I think. Although . . . it's said that the countess Bartholdy has joined our prince." He sounded doubtful about that.

Countess Elizabeth did own several estates in Valahia—one not more than thirty miles from here.

She also owned extensive lands in Slovenia and Hungary. She was the aunt of the king. And a stunningly beautiful woman, apparently. There were many rumors about her. But why would she back a young Prince Vlad against her own nephew?

Ban Alescu had met King Emeric, and after due consideration, he rather thought he could imagine several reasons why. The question was, which side should he himself back? It did not seem that Vlad had much support. All the same, natural caution suggested that he stay out of it all, until he could clearly see who was winning. One didn't want to be the first to make one's submission . . . or the last. It wasn't an easy, clear decision, like hanging gypsies.

The scribe cleared his throat. Ban Alescu roused himself from his thoughts and waved him away. It would take a little more investigation, and a lot more consideration. Whatever happened, he, Ban Alescu of Irongate, was going to emerge richer and more powerful from this.

Oddly enough, at that very moment,. Vlad was receiving his very first submission from the nobility of Valahia. It was a fairly rough and ready submission. The Székely people of Carpathia might have been expected to stand with the King of Hungary—their language was much the same. And, in their seven seats along that part of the montaine region, they far outnumbered the Vlachs. Unfortunately, King Emeric had decided their status of being untaxed and able to administer themselves, and provide their own judges and juries, was not one that suited him. He'd forced Radu, Vlad's father, to introduce the feudalism he preferred, and the taxes he preferred too. Radu hadn't managed to prevent it, or stop the Buda-bred district overlords being sent in, but he had managed to let the Székely know that this wasn't his idea.

All three Székely classes had ended up subservient to the new barons... Not just to the Count of Valahia. Suddenly they remembered, remarkably, that they were the proud Kabar people with their own traditions and beliefs, and not Magyar. All this Vlad discovered when he spoke to the messenger who met his column on a pass.

Primor Gabor Peter wanted—said the messenger—to know whether Prince Vlad respected the rights and privileges of the Székely, as his grandfather had agreed to. Vlad had had a long day's ride, and was still deeply disturbed by Elizabeth's departure and Rosa's disappearance. He was more than usually blunt. "What are those? And do these Székely recognize me?"

The messenger—with interspersions from Mirko— not always polite ones, as the Székelers were not much loved by the Vlachs—explained.

Vlad sighed. He could remember his father's bitterness with the boyars. But he could not recall these... primors? "What is a primor?" he asked.

"A captain of the Horseheads," explained the messenger, making things clear as mud.

"He's like a sort of lord," said Mirko. "But they're not born to it. There were some serving with me in the Corfu campaign. I'll say this for them, they're nearly as good fighters as the Croats."

"Better!" said the Székely messenger. "I am a Horsehead. I am a freeman and own my own horse!" he said proudly.

"And how many Vlachs serfs do you have?" asked Vlad.

"They don't mix. Székely live together with other Székely," said Mirko.

"We live together on the seats that were granted us, to keep our traditions," said the Horsehead messenger. His head looked fairly normal to Vlad.

Vlad thought about it. His support, so far, barring the few boyars that had come with Elizabeth, was entirely from the Vlachs peasantry, Vlachs townsmen and occasional freemen. He turned to Mirko. "Tell me what you think?"

The sergeant grimaced. "We need them, Drac. And they're not the worst. Not Germans or Magyar."

Vlad nodded. "Tell Primor Gabor Peter I will meet him. If he will recognize my rule, and provide me with support, I will restore the privileges of the Székely, at least of those who recognise me."

The Horsehead bowed respectfully. "I will tell the primor," and mounted and rode off with the sort of skill that did lend some credence to what he had said about the Croats.

A little later—not very much later—they must have been near at hand and waiting—a group of well-armed horsemen came up and dismounted. "The infantry are back at our fortress," said their leader, dismounting. Up to this point Vlad and his ragtag army had operated from the high Carpathians to the west. The east—a narrow strip of foothills and debated lands—had been somewhere they'd not ventured. The Golden Horde lived over there.

The primor and his Székely lived where the Golden Horde stopped . . . Or perhaps, where the Székely had stopped them. The Primor Peter looked like a fighter, there were tales in the scars and the broken nose, in his armor, that was somewhat dented in spots, although well polished. "I have hung a few Magyar troopers on the gates as a welcome flag, Drac," he said, cheerfully, going down on one knee. "My bandits brought me the news you were coming at last. Welcome, Drac, to Ghîmes."

It was a small welcome, from a small place. But it came with a fortress—really a castle—and thirty Horseheads and a company of a hundred and twenty-five footmen—archers and pikemen.

"Bandits, Primor?"

The scarred man grinned, showing a missing tooth. "It's easier to use them than to chase them. I collect tolls from caravans passing through to trade with the Golden Horde. A few merchants try to avoid that, and me. And there has always been a problem with bandits in the high Carpathians. So I rounded up a few and told them that I'd pay a bounty on any parties they spotted for me, but nothing if they robbed them first. If they robbed them I would hunt for bandits. I hate competition," he said, laughing heartily. "I'll house them in winter. You don't want to ask too closely whose serf some of my men used to be, before they ran off and tried their luck on the highroad."

Vlad found himself torn between an instinctive liking of the hard-bitten primor, and disapproving of the fact that he was plainly little more than a robber himself. But he had come to offer his fealty, his men and his home, to his overlord. That had to count for something, surely?

They ate, and drank at the primor's table that night.

Vlad was not afraid of treachery this time. His own men patrolled the walls, and they outnumbered the primor's by ten to one. Vlad noticed details. Weapons were well cared for and clean. The food was on the rustic side—better than they'd had for the last while, but simple and wholesome. This was not a rich castle. It was also one that was no stranger to attack. So Vlad asked who did the attacking—besides merchants who did not wish to pay toll, and bandits who did not wish to accept a small share of the spoils.

His host laughed. "Besides those two groups. The Golden Horde. We trade with them. And the young bucks in their number will raid up here. We don't try to return the favor too often. Got the pants beat off us last time we did. Never even think about stealing their horses. They don't take kindly to it. But the clans don't try Ghîmes itself. I spent good money on cannon. We command a good field of fire from up here. Outlying farms are more the target."

"Can you buy them?"

"Cannon? Not as easily as I'd like."

"I meant horses."

The primor nodded. "Yes. Mind you they sell us their breakdowns. Never the best. And they want a steep price for them. You're better off buying in Valahia or even farther afield. The Horde sell sheep and even cattle cheaply enough, but they have more horses than cattle, and don't part with them as easily. Their horses are tough but not overlarge. You'd struggle to find a horse big enough to carry you, my Prince.

"Well...I want them for my infantry."

The primor blinked. "Why? They are infantry. You can't turn them into cavalry, Drac. A man needs a lot of experience in the saddle to be good enough to stay in it in battle."

Vlad smiled. "We play 'hide and seek' and 'catch as can' with King Emeric's forces all over the mountains, Primor Peter. We need to move far and fast, and still be reasonably ready to fight and then run again. And we may be able to help you with a few cannon. I have my own gunsmith. Come winter I will need a better work place for him."

The primor tugged his beard. "I can see that. Mind you, you will need men to hold the horses. It's a bit like what our bandits do here in the mountains. Shoot at us, and by the time we get there, they've moved to where we've just come from because they know the mountains better than we do. Makes it hard work to chase them. Well, if that is what you need them for, the Mongol ponies will be the right animals for you. But you'll need a lot of horses. You'll have to go and treat with one of the clan-heads for that. It'll cost you some gold, Drac. But I'd love to have your gunsmith. He can have whatever he needs here. King Emeric is not going to take this place by force, and if he tries by siege, well, winter is coming fast. We are provisioned for it, and they can freeze their butts off out there. The snow will be thick out there. You will just have to come and relieve us, Drac, if we need it in the spring."

Vlad was fairly sure that a mere twenty well-provisioned and armed men could hold this little fortress on its little promontory on the gorge edge for a long, long time. Getting siege cannon up here—if you could get them up the mountain road (and the carts had had a hard enough time of it), meant bringing them along the road below the castle. The Ghîmes defenders could roll rocks on them, never mind the fact that they would be right under cannons and bowshot from the castle.

"So . . . how do we trade with the Golden Horde? I have some gold, and I need some horses. We could probably use some mutton for winter provender, too."

The primor sucked at the gap in teeth. "Normally I'd say wait around for a clan rider to come up with some sheep or a few ponies. It happens most weeks. But they're not coming up at the moment. Something is going on out there. Still, for the numbers of horses you'll want, Drac, that wouldn't work anyway. You'll need to take a fairly strong party out there, with truce and trade flags—we can help you with those, and deal with a clan head. They have plenty of stock. It's all a question of their being prepared to sell much. Mind you, going out into their lands is always a chancy business."

Vlad sighed. "I need to get my men provisioned and quartered before winter. I certainly can't wait. We will have to go out there, whatever the risks."

"You need to go looking like merchants, Drac. Take a good few carts. But you also need a good strong force of well-armed men. Normally a trader negotiates for an escort . . . they get much better prices out in the lowlands. It's a balance with the Golden Horde. You need to be worth trading with, but too strong to make raiding and looting worth while. That's the advantage of doing it here, under the guns. It's a pity you can't take a fortress and cannon with you. They're a bit heavy to move," said the Primor Peter with a chuckle.

Vlad bit his lip. "Cannon. Well I can't take the fortress, but we have some good four pounders. Stanislaw has made us some special ball shot. Many little balls. It will devastate cavalry at close quarters. It will devastate anything. But we tried firing from the carts. It shakes them apart worse than mountain trails do. We have to take the cannon off and fire them from a mount on the ground."

It was the Székely primor's turn to look thoughtful. "Draw the carts and wagons around and put the horses inside and cannons in the gaps. There are very few firearms among the Golden Horde. They're too good with their wicked little horse-bows. It takes heavy armor to stop those arrows. But a cart and some faggots should do it nicely. We can spare you the faggots."

"Thank you. But won't they burn very well?"

The primor smiled. "There is a hole in every great idea. Bags of sand would be heavy."

"What about bags of wheat?"

"Well, it would be lighter. And you could eat it. Put the faggots in with it and if they used fire against you, you could always make bread."

It was said in jest. But Vlad could see how it could work for his arquebusiers. A wagon would be better than a cart. But you could take a cart where the wagon would struggle. In more open terrain, and possibly with some oxen—far slower but stronger... He would think more about it. And ways to defend against arrows.

Vlad bedded down that night in a private spot, but bivouacking like most of his men. They assumed that it was to show solidarity with them. It was actually because he hoped, desperately, that Rosa would come to him. He'd been trying to spot her for the last two days. She could be in one of the carts... He was afraid to ask. He had ventured a vague question to Mirko. "Are all the camp-follower women still with us?"

The sergeant had shrugged. "They come and go, Sire."

He did not own her. He knew that. She'd said as much to him.

Chapter 52

Manfred had never seriously weighed his own mortality. He would live or die. It was a philosophy that was common among the Celts with their rather inverse view of the world and afterlife. What he found himself doing, on this expedition, was to suddenly start thinking of the mortality of others, and he didn't like his own conclusions. These were men who had come thinking they were merely providing an escort, and now they were running for their lives. The reality was that the knights were going to be easy to follow, and outnumber. This was the Golden Horde's country; they would have all the advantages. "Erik," he said, riding up next to his bodyguard and mentor. "Should we try scattering? As a group we have very little chance to avoid being followed. A solitary knight or three might get across that river."

Erik was silent. And then shook his head. "I have considered it, Manfred. Look, it is possible that I may still have to try to get you away, and leave the rest to make as long and messy stand as possible. I don't like the idea, but Falkenberg has already suggested it. But the reality is that the knights would be easy prey on their own. Only Kari and myself have much in the way of skills needed to move undetected across enemy terrain. Talking to Bortai, they'll use their ten-man squads—Arbans—to hunt us. They've cleared a lot of the forest for grazing lands. The country is fairly open as a result, and they're mobile and fast. This is, sadly, what they do best. They train their soldiers in these massive hunting exercises in which they enclose a huge area and then literally close in and kill everything. The entire point of the exercise is not to let any game at all escape. We're going to be that game, unless we can keep breaking their line and heading north."

"Looking at the stars, we're heading west."

"Northwest. There's rougher country up there, towards the border of Hungary. Still a few areas of dense forest—apparently more so farther south, unfortunately. Better for us to fort up if we can find a defensible site—because that's the other possibility. We get the Mongols away—Bortai and her brother, with Tulkun. The woman has already showed she's pretty expert at evading pursuit of any kind. They may, or may not, be able to raise her clan to come to our assistance. Tulkun seems to think that they would. I suppose it depends on what actual cred-ibility the clan puts on the word of a woman and a boy, and a Mongol from another Horde. Tulkun is a good fighter but he's no ambassador. And the truth is that the Mongols don't seem to put much value on non-Mongols."

"It does seem a little extreme, and a fairly thin hope," said Manfred.

"Our hope here is very thin," agreed Erik.

"Judging by the temperature tonight—having roasted

us a few days ago, we might just get snow to rescue us, too," said Manfred.

Erik nodded. "It'll be dropping off a lot faster in those mountains we can see. I've wondered just whether it might not be worth taking our chances up there with Emeric's Hungarian forces. They might allow you to be ransomed."

"Emeric . . . not after Corfu," said Manfred. "Not for all the money in the west." Anyway, he thought to himself, perhaps he had some value, but the others would be killed. They might as well take their chances here in lands of Golden Horde. And with a bit of luck . . . get away to Illyria. While there was life, there was hope. It was a platitude, but he was not Celt enough to give in to fatalism just yet.

Erik was not relying on hope. Rather he was relying on rivers, forest and booby traps, and the knights' experience in signaling to each other by means of horn-calls. Kari was off scouting so Erik split his small force in two . . . which, on the face of it, seemed like insanity. But there was logic in his insanity. The two parties had the same point as an objective. They'd be relatively close to each other. And if one of the two columns encountered scouts who were foolish enough to engage or be seen, horn-talk would see to it that they could act as relief for each other. Even if one group ran into a large group that surrounded them, the Golden Horde Mongols would scatter from a direct charge. That seemed a given and sensible tactic. The heavier horses and armor of the knights meant that they could punch through Golden Horde ranks—it just wasn't expected to do the heavier knights any good. The Golden Horde would reform and pick them off, one by one. Numbers, and a lack of any near-at-hand refuge were on the side of their pursuers. But perhaps, just perhaps, flexibility was on theirs.

Bortai struggled with her decision-making. She and Kildai could move faster than this. They had remounts. Not of the quality of the knight's horses but still better than no remounts. And the Golden Horde ponies had more stamina, and carried less weight. Should they leave the knights? Allow them to ride rearguard? Go to call the Hawk clan—or rather the remnants of it, to their rescue? The flaw, besides the lack of honor in this course, was that the orkhan was not that stupid. She'd bet that flanking Mingghans had been sent riding north. There would be, of course, an element of doubt in the minds of the orkhan's generals. Would these foreigners flee north or try to recross the great river? But her presence—and Kildai's presence—would make northward seem likely. She saw how the party was split, and the direction they were taking. The heavy country against the mountains would favor the smaller party in some ways. Erik was a shrewd orkhan. He just needed more scouts. It seemed logical to offer her services, as well as Tulkun's.

Erik seemed a little taken aback. "But... you are a..." he struggled, either with the concept or the language, "lady," he said, eventually.

"Do ladies not do such things among your people? I am a Mongol of the Hawk clan. In war a woman must do what there are no men to do. That means we must fight and ride now."

"Um." Erik took a deep breath. "It's not quite like that with us. But... well when we fought on Corfu... I learned that necessity can make deadly fighters of

women. Thalia . . . A friend's wife, showed us that. If
you will scout a path ahead for us, lady, we would be
grateful. You will ride with her, Tulkun? I would be
happier with a warrior—" he seemed to realize he was
saying the wrong thing, and stopped.

Tulkun beamed. "She could kill me, Erik."

The Ilkhan Mongol at least knew that. But it appeared
that he knew her lineage. They had talked about wrestling. Princess Khutulun was a legend. Khutulun had
defeated scores of suitors before Ulughachi had arrived
at her father's gers, without the horses to make the
wager . . . and still she had taken his challenge. Bortai
had always wondered just why her great grandmother
had lost. Bortai had a strong inclination to take on this
orkhan and show him a thing or two. Perhaps she would
if they won free of this mess, even if he was one of the
lesser peoples. An odd thought tickled her mind: what
would she do, if, by some fluke, he won? Intermarriage
happened . . . but never that way around.

Erik explained what he wanted, what natural defenses
he was looking for. He was good, Bortai acknowledged.
The Mongol strategy here would be to get onto the
flattest most open country and run. But Erik clearly
understood that they could not do that, and that the
people tracking them followed stray livestock when
they were not at war. She wondered what the Hawk
clan and its allies—if it still had any—were doing now.
Normally the clans would disperse for winter. Family
groups would move the herds to lower lands. But now . . .
now she would bet the gers were being moved into the
foothills and the clan was gathering for the war that
seemed inevitable. Inevitable and wrong.

Chapter 53

It seemed odd to ride away from the high mountains—
and not by night, but in the open. But skulking, the
Primor Peter had assured him, would mean an attack.
It made a kind of sense, Vlad supposed. Anyone
skulking was up to no good. They had a reasonable
force—some two hundred men—twenty Horsehead
Székelers and another fifteen who had joined Vlad's
infantry—enough to fight and yet not be an invading
army, and a fair amount of gold. Basically, all the gold
he had left . . . he had spent the rest on organizing
winter billeting for the remainder of his men. He had
requisitioned four wagons and twelve large carts. Vlad
wondered why with "requisitioning" at their disposal
so many thieves resorted to theft. He had faggots . . .
and sacks. If they had time they could always fill them
with soil. And canvas. And a fair number of barrels,
which the thirsty had discovered disappointingly, did
not contain beer. An arrow would pass through stout
canvas . . . but as Mirko pointed out, not going at the
same speed it went in, and not with a burning oil-
soaked rag. The rag would stay behind. Putting out

a fire on stretched canvas was a lot easier than in
faggots. Vlad had been surprised at just how much
his quartermaster-sergeant had liked the whole idea.

"It's easier for the troops to keep their heads, Sire,
when a they've got a barrier between them and men
on horseback. We should try it against King Emeric's
troops," said the sergeant.

"But it's only a farm-cart, Mirko."

The man shrugged. "Better than nothing when you're
on foot and you've got a knight riding straight for you,
Sire. Knights usually eat footmen for breakfast, unless
the footmen have numbers and guns ... or walls. This
will take the walls with us. It could work. Especially if
we stick some pikes out of the gaps and on the top of
the carts. Landing on a pike could put a horseman off
trying to jump into any gaps."

So, with lots of fifteen-foot pikes, an array of
arquebus and horse-pistols ... and some twenty small
cannons, they set off. Vlad had felt that he might be
overdoing things. Primor Peter had assured him that
he wasn't. And Peter wasn't the sort of man who could
be thought timid and overcautious.

So far they'd seen no one. Not for nearly four days, as
they wound down to lower lands. That didn't prove anything, the Székelers gleefully informed him. The Golden
Horde clans were very traditionalist. They moved with
their herds. And there was, likely as not, to be a horseman watching them from a copse on a hillside. They
could ride up out of nowhere and they were good with
their bows. Pick a man out of the saddle and be gone
before anyone could do anything about it. The trade
flags would of course tell them that the party wanted
to trade and not engage in warfare. It apparently was

no guarantee that the Golden Horde clans would not decide that they would engage in the warfare, and it did say the caravan was probably worth looting. "We're on the edge of Hawk clan territory. They're traditionalists, hold by the Yasa code. On the other side are the Mink. And they're more into opportunistic looting."

"We'll just have to hope we run into the Hawk clan then."

The Székeler primor nodded. "They've got their own code of honor. But the Hawk are far, far tougher in a fight. The Mink are all right. Just less disciplined."

The man had hardly said that, when a warning horn-blast shattered the apparent tranquility. It was followed by a scout riding hell for leather back to the carts. The raid came quickly, but, thanks to the Székeler outrider's warning they had time to circle the carts and wagons. Men were still trying to un-hitch when the first arrows came.

The Mink warriors learned a thing or two about disciplined, massed fire in the next few moments. Vlad's men even managed to get one of the small cannon unlimbered and primed and ready.

The result of this, and the arquebusiers firing from shelter, was that a rather ragged attack turned into a rout, after barely two volleys and a single cannon-shot.

The Székeler Primor Peter tugged his chin. "We'd best be moving on. Fairly fast. Those were young bucks out for some looting. What's left of them will be heading for the clan's orkhan."

"Orkhan?"

"War leader. You just gave some of the Golden Horde warriors a bloody nose." He pointed. "I would say that there must be ten dead and twice that wounded out there. We have only a few arrow-wounds, nothing life threatening. They're going to be angry, and upset, and just a little bit afraid. That'll make them keen to deal with this new threat." He grinned. "Mind you, it could cost them dear, by the looks of it. This idea works better than I thought it would. We need to organize some sally-ports."

"There were far fewer of them than of us," said Vlad warily.

"Yes, maybe seventy. But that would be enough, normally. One horseman is worth a good few infantry, and more so of mere merchants. The worst the Mink expected was to be fought off, but with us having to abandon some of the carts and goods and flee. They expected the balance of the losses to be with us."

"Well, let us head towards another clan's lands before they make it true," said Vlad. "We can still be attacked by night, or on the move. And a larger force will overwhelm us then, I think."

The Székeler primor looked at him, thoughtfully. "You know, Drac, the stories that reached us about your military victories... I'm a fighting man on the borderland. I thought that they were just stories. That you were lucky and a better military tactician than King Emeric's commanders... but that's not hard. They typically use an anvil to crack a walnut. In places where there is no space for an anvil, the walnut can survive. But I was wrong."

"No. You were right," said Vlad, glad to admit it. "I need help. So far I have learned all I know of war from my sergeants."

The battle-scarred captain laughed. "It's a good place to learn from."

"I have found that," said Vlad seriously. "But it is difficult because they do not realize that I am ignorant."

"They know, Drac. You can't fool sergeants. Not for long. But they must believe in you."

"They do. And I cannot fail them. I need to learn more generalship."

The primor nodded. "I see why they follow you, Drac. I think the Székeler people will, when we hold our council of seat-captains at Udvarhely."

This was something Vlad had hoped for, but not expected to happen easily. "I still need to learn more generalship, Primor," he said, as the scouting Székelers rode out and the first cart began to roll. "Can you teach me?"

The man laughed again. "I am just the captain of a handful of horsemen, and a border fort, Drac. I will teach you what I can. But you need more."

"I know that. But it has been hard to find anyone to ask."

That, several days later, was something that Vlad could have said about the Golden Horde, too. They'd seen rich lands, and huge numbers of sheep and enormous herds of horses. They'd seen a few—very few—riders with them. Showing discretion could also apply if you were a Mongol shepherd, they'd kept away from the well-armed party. There were plenty of rutted cart tracks from the Golden Horde's own migrations. There were signs of where encampments had been, recently. They just weren't there, now.

Vlad had talked a great deal about combat with the primor, getting a grasp on the tactics of light cavalry. The Székely drew their origins from some earlier wave of horse-warriors sweeping out of the east, and had kept many of the traditions and organization and warfare-style, although they were more settled now. He also learned how the Székely stayed a people who were so apart. Feudalism as such did not exist in their lands. Lands were held in common, and a man could work what he could till. It made for relatively less powerful leaders, and a strong commons. "There are fewer Horseheads than we need, Drac. We have had no taxes until Emeric, but also no roads or bridges. It's a hard country."

Vlad could see how much richer this lower land was. Much of the forest had plainly been cleared away and burned to make more grazing, and there was a lot of it. And a lot of grazing animals on it.

So where were the all the people?

It was plainly worrying the primor, too. "It smells like trouble, Drac. I'm beginning to feel that we should head back up into the hills, horses or no horses. And please, Sire. Don't even suggest helping ourselves."

Vlad shook his head. "I would not do that," he said seriously.

The primor nodded. "I'd heard that. You know, Drac, it's a good thing you ran away. King Emeric would have put his appointees between you and the people. We need you."

"I was helped to escape. Emeric was going to kill me."

"Oh. We were told that you were going to be made our prince. Why did they wish to kill you, Sire?"

"Because my father was dead," explained Vlad. "I hear that the king planned to put the Danesti in my place."

"Oh. It was one of them who told the Székely council you were coming back," said the primor, surprised. "He seemed very certain. And quite . . . relieved, Sire. So I was just surprised."

So was Vlad. He'd accepted unconditionally the certainty that he was to be executed. Surely Elizabeth Bartholdy could not have been wrong?

Like the way that Rosa had disappeared ... there were too many mysteries. Too many things he did not know or understand. He felt he was being moved about a game board he couldn't see by forces beyond his control, and he really did not like that.

PART VI
December, 1540 A.D.

Chapter 54

The great wheel of heaven turns and there are forces chained and liberated in regular sequences by the rotation. Even in ancient Babylon the workers of magic had established that. Earth, sun and moon are yoked together, in a long and endless dance. And the pattern repeats. Every nineteen thousand seven hundred and fifty six days it completes one full cycle. One great turn. The blood moon returns when the shadow devours the moon and the old magics are made strong again.

The wolf-people lived by the moon. They had known these things for always and always, before the Dacian tribes, before the Romans. Back when these forest-cloaked mountains were not the last refuge of the first ones. Before blades cut at the forest. Before iron. Before bronze. When the only things that cut were sharp-edged stone, and tooth and claw.

Now the ancient cycles called, called the children of the wolf back, back to their cradle-lands. Back with worrying word. Grigori ran through the daylight, and the young one ran beside him, in the easy lope that was the way of their kind, even when they were tired and harried. As Grigori had expected she had tracked them, sent her servants, possessed and driven men, to hunt them. She was afraid of the Dragon. Not of them. Against the Dragon she moved circumspectly now, wearing her cloak of lies and a mask of magical deceit. Against the wolves she deployed her minions. She had plainly gone back to her place of evil and immediately set her forces out to wait.

They only had teeth. The foes had steel, and she directed them in their hunt. Not all the cunning of the old wolf had shaken the pursuit.

But a man, even in daylight with her guidance... was still just a man. There were five of them, with steel blade and firearms, in a narrow defile. More close behind. Dozens.

Grigori did not wait for them to fire. The first one died with his neck snapped as the great wolf pulled him down. They had nets. Heavy, weighted nets. One flung his, enmeshing Grigori and the next man. Another tried to catch Miu. In the folds of the net Grigori's white teeth ripped again, finding a throat. To tear and shake as something stabbed him in own vitals.

Despite the agony he changed. Only hands would do to free himself of the net.

Miu was younger and faster. He slipped the net and tore the hamstrings of the one who had speared at his uncle. He was younger and less skilled, too, so he failed at the clean snap of the neck as he bore the other victim down. A bullet burned across his side from the last man still standing. The man drew his sword. Staggering, bleeding, free from the net, Grigori turned on him, with nothing more than a rock.

Miu worked tag now, ignoring the pain as the man, predator moments before, tried to keep the blade pointed at the white-fanged wolf and the man holding his own intestines in with one hand and a rock in the other. The wolf darted in, ripping flesh and tendons on one leg. And as the man turned slashing at it, Grigori closed swinging the rock at his head, oblivious of the blade that cut at him.

The man Miu had merely felled to the ground had found his feet. He fired at the tangle of man and wolf. Hit man. And man-wolf. But not...the wolf. Miu was merely bullet-burned from the previous encounter. His leap was neither elegant nor anything but a fury of savage biting and scrabbling paws but he knocked the man down and they rolled, the desperate man wrestling, trying to fend him off. Miu bit at his face and arms, and eventually found the jugular. Once he'd torn it, he kept biting in fury. Then he got a grip on himself and pulled free.

The man he'd so cleanly hamstrung first was quick to finish off. He turned back to his uncle.

Grigori was half changed. The vast bloody muzzled wolf-head, the gray eyes unseeing, maw contorted in a last defiant snarl, teeth in the throat of the foe... .set on a man's torso.

Miu knew that he could do nothing more for him. The other hunters would have heard the shots. He nosed the letter from his uncle's pocket, and took it in his teeth He bowed his great head respectfully, briefly and turned to run on, again.

The hunters would find something they all believed in, but had never seen. That was unavoidable. If the Drac, or his sister, did not renew the compact, they

might all be hunted like this. And the little ones of
the pack were easy prey.

Full of fear and hatred for the old woman and her
magics, Miu ran on alone. His kind were not solitary,
and he was very afraid. Instinct said to hide, but the
passing time pulled at him to run. To return to the
heartlands.

Emil looked at his hands, looked at how his nails had
been pulled away from the quick, and how the dirt was
still stuck there. He shook his head trying to clear it. It
was full of such terrible visons, like a cobwebbed maze
of nightmares, with the same horror at every turn, no
matter how he tried to flee from her, from the memory
of her head at such an unnatural angle, and a dribble of
blood leaking from the corner of her mouth. And now
he was trapped, condemned and doomed. There seemed
no way out of what he'd done. He'd buried her. There
was still dirt under his nails from his efforts to make
that shallow grave. Why had he killed her? Rosa had
been a friend of his, in the way that she was a friend
of half of the camp, including the Drac. It was all so
confused, so misty in his head.

He was so very afraid. And still so very compelled
to do what he had to do.

"Where do we go now?" asked one of the men he
had taken with him.

He couldn't answer at first, still knotted up inside
with guilt and fear and uncertainty. He couldn't possibly escape the consequences of what he'd done.
Surely, surely the Drac, or even Mirko, would realize
that something was wrong, that he had chosen the
worst, not the best.

Emil waited for an answer that he knew would come unbidden to his mind. An instruction. A direction from the power that had usurped his mind, the power that controlled him and drove him. Until now, it had had him pursuing a wolf hunt for days, but that was over now, it seemed.

His orders came. "We need to go northwest for a little to avoid the Hungarian patrols. After that we go south again."

"It's amazing, Sergeant," said the pockmarked soldier, the one who was always trying to butter him up, "you always seemed to know exactly where they're going to be."

He did. Because she did.

In her southern bastion, the nunnery she had had constructed on her estate near Caedonia, Elizabeth once again allowed herself to revel in the amenities of life that she felt were a necessity. Fresh linen, well-cooked hot food, and suitably inflicted pain were what made life worth living. That and the use of her power. She had had a little vengeance on the wolf-changers, but they were easy enough to track, magically. It was very satisfying to use her power again. It would appear though, that one had avoided the fate she had in mind for them. He was dead.

Her sendlings were supposed to have brought them back to her, alive. She had ideas and uses for humans that could become wolves, interesting and terror-filled uses. Well, the other would be an interesting addition to her menagerie, when she finally caught him, but there were other matters more pressing to deal with. Along with the other preparations that had to be made, she was going to be busy. Some things she had to do herself. The staff here in the nunnery were all entrapped in her darkness and could not betray her, but still, some things had to be done by the worker of the magic. There was much labor, which she despised, in the ritual.

She turned her attention to those other matters, and was rudely interrupted in her exercise of inflaming the lust of the victim for tonight's bloodletting. She could not make them love her, but lust, yes. And that was a good enough substitute for Elizabeth Bartholdy. The moment of betrayal when they realized that she had not brought them to the desecrated chapel for a passionate, shameful, but desperately desired tryst, but to be defiled, tortured and killed for their blood, was always sweet. And only Emeric would dare to interrupt her. He was almost too gauche to live.

"We will see each other later, Narine," she said smiling at the daughter of some small provincial noble, knowing that the poor girl was desperately in love with some ineligible merchant's son, and was now terribly conflicted by the enchantment that her hostess, so sympathetic, had set in her flesh.

When she was found dead, it would be suicide. Or perhaps she would arrange things to make it appear that the little merchant's boy killed her ... The sacrifice-to-be was not a peasant girl with no relations and no one to notice if she disappeared. The body would have to be found, and still be recognizable. Noble blood was riskier, but it would do more for her complexion.

"Grooming your newest victim?" said Emeric, not caring how offensive he sounded.

Really, he contrasted badly with young Vlad. Emeric

was stupid and willfully sadistic. Vlad was not stupid, and the streak of bloody murder and fascination with pain that was in him was well controlled... it would be entertaining to free it. And he could lead... She put the thought away from her. Crocell had warned her of his danger, and although she liked to toy with danger, she would never willfully endure a long-term threat that she could not utterly subjugate. Vlad was unnaturally strong, and seemed to be better armored to resist or throw her coercions off. Better to endure this crass puppet, even if he was getting far too many ideas of his own. She sniffed. He stank. He'd always been a little erratic about bathing. "What is it now, Emeric?" she said tartly.

"I've been south to see Ban Alescu of Ironguard. I don't trust him. He's ambitious."

"We've dealt with ambition before, Emeric. Put a little fear into him."

Emeric nodded. "I did that. And I think I'm going to find a town to make a similar example of. There's too much support for that little upstart. Ban Alescu told me he was popular with a number of burghs. Besides I want some replacement coin for my pay chests from them."

"Besides taxes." She knew he'd increased those.

"Sometimes taking all of the substance at once is a more worthwhile exercise than bleeding them slowly."

Bleeding them slowly. She'd never thought of that. She could keep them alive for a while. Let them replenish their blood. Occasionally even the stupidest fool could say something wise. She smiled on him. "So long as it is not too close to here. I have things happening that I do not wish disturbed."

"I have a list. Ban Alescu is not to be trusted, but he's a useful source. More effective than my own spies have been. I'm bringing another thirty thousand men in, over winter. The first ten thousand will be arriving in a few days. I'm going to make these mountains untenable, and remove his support by ensuring that the towns remain mine. Then we can strike before Vlad is ready in spring. Now, I came to ask what you could tell me of his troop numbers, disposition, weaponry and so on."

She shrugged. "They are on the move. He seems to have mostly peasant levies with arquebuses."

"I'm going to have to take steps against the freemen and peasantry in this part of my kingdom. Punish some relations."

He really was not very bright, thought Elizabeth. He'd bite off too much and have a civil war on his hands. He did have enough troops to put one down. It was not something that Vlad and his partisans could win in the long term, even if Elizabeth was going let him survive. Then it occurred to her that it had been a while since she'd been around civil strife. It was a good time to find plenty of displaced people looking for sanctuary. And people went missing. "What a good idea," she said. Once Vlad was gone, it could always be fixed.

Ban Alescu sniffed. He could only smell cloves. He had always considered himself the biggest, wiliest and nastiest dog in the pit. Now, although he'd burned the soiled breeches, and washed himself repeatedly, he knew that he was not. That shame and abject terror would live with him for the rest of his life. His mood was as black as the weather outside. And that was very black indeed. Rain was sheeting down. Not all of it could wash away the shame and embarrassment. But, he thought, allowing himself a moment of satisfaction, he might not be the biggest and nastiest dog in the pit, but he was still wily. He'd successfully convinced Emeric that several of his rivals and the towns and cities that fell in their ambit were sympathizing with and supporting Prince Vlad.

He had the sworn declarations now of a nursemaid, and a bishop, who attested that his mother had married Radu—Vlad's father, in secret, and that he, Ban Alescu, was the offspring of that union.

Ban Alescu doubted that many people would believe it. Or that Emeric cared whether they did or not.

He sniffed again. He absolutely could not smell anything beside the cloves in the pomander he toyed with. He really must make plans. Ones which would oblige his overlord. He was afraid to do otherwise.

The wyverns had begun to roam, and to hunt on their own. But it was raining. She could have brought them food. They licked their lips and looked at her, considering.

Dana had grown accustomed to them by now. She knew that they were dangerous and capricious. But she liked them anyway, and they, it would seem, liked her, too. "A bit of rain won't melt you. And Angelo says that you need to learn to hunt or you will be reliant on others always."

"Hunting is good. But the rain makes it harder to smell prey."

"And winter is coming, Radu says. We need to be fat before winter. So do you."

Winter was coming, and despite the wyverns and the fascination of the strangeness of their hosts, Dana was beginning to long for the comforts of a real bed and a home. She also wondered when Grigori and Miu would be back, and what news they would bring from her brother. She wondered just what he would be like.

Chapter 55

Armor protected a knight. They tended to love it, despite the weight, the layers of padding, the inflexibility, the smell and the temperatures inside it. A knight in armor was worth twenty peasant levy footmen, and four light cavalry. Of course, they did not really approve of firearms. Besides the flux, the other thing a knight in armor dreaded was rain.

Right now, Erik welcomed it. It was mixed with flurries of sleet. Delightful! Absolutely wonderful! Even if only David, in Kari's old hooded cloak really had a chance of staying half-dry. To think, the boy had been roasting in it only a few weeks ago.

It was just what a large party of horsemen attempting to hide from a far larger search party needed. They consolidated the two parties of knights, when the rain started. Visibility was terrible and there was no point in losing each other. They'd had to stop to rest and where possible change horses. You couldn't expect even an enormous warhorse to carry something the size and weight of Manfred and his armor for too long.

Rain found its way into the cracks and chinks of

the spike-shouldered armour, into the quilted liner. A cloak helped only so much. Erik flexed and moved as much as possible. Sighed. They'd have to stop and oil joints soon. As soon as they could find a good spot. But hopefully this would discourage the pursuit. He said as much to Bortai.

Bortai crushed that hope. She shook her head. "It will make you harder to follow, yes. But they will know which direction you are going now. They will follow hard. We still have many leagues to go."

"About how many?"

She shrugged. "I think it should be possible to reach Hawk lands in about three days if we continue to travel as fast we are now. But they may follow us even there. Our clan will be weakened and in disarray from what happened at the kurultai."

They'd done a day, perhaps a day and half of traveling so far. Even in the rain, that was a lot to ask of their luck.

"Once we cross the Iret river..."

That was another drawback to traveling across this country meant for grazing. Not only had the Mongols indulged in widespread tree-clearing, there were very few bridges over the rivers. They'd had to engage in two very dangerous exercises in fording, and Erik was afraid of getting trapped against a natural barrier like that again. "This river...is it very..." He struggled for the word. "Fat?"

She chuckled. It was a very infectious chuckle. Warm and...comfortable. And right now that was very welcome. "Wide," she said. "It has some fords and an old Roman bridge. I will find them for you. I know that country well."

Erik wished he knew this country well, too. But the best he could do was to deploy scouts. He had them in layers. Knights innermost, Tulkun and Bortai, next, and Kari ranging, ahead. He had done some of the latter ranging, too. But in this rain it was hard to even guess the lay of the land.

He was about to ride out a bit farther when Kari rode up. "How am I supposed to keep my powder dry in this? There is a river ahead, with a decent ford a little east of us. I might have seen some riders lurking there. It's hard to tell the difference between a horse and a man and a tree in this."

The hairs on the nape of Erik's neck lifted. A ford—a good one—was a perfect place for an ambush. It forced the knights to use one spot, and it would slow the horses down, if they were forced to charge, or tried to flee. "Scout upstream. I'll send Kirsten and Wellmann downstream. We'll halt here for a bit of a rest. We're overdue for one."

Kari came back a little later. "You can force it about a half a mile upstream. Not easily or safely. By the trail the ford is where most people cross. But that tree I saw... It has moved."

"Hmm. Do you think that tree saw you?"

Kari nodded. "I'd guess. I went to the water's edge. Trotted part of the way in."

The two knights returned. "We saw a Golden Horde scout. There is a small settlement a little way downstream. Just a few huts."

That was rare enough in this country. The Golden Horde had taken a very different attitude from the Ilkhan. The Ilkhan kept the cities of the land they'd conquered. They made relatively tolerant overlords,

apparently. They were certainly pleasant enough in
Outremer. Here, at least, the Golden Horde seemed
to have allowed very few of the cities or even villages to survive—at least that they'd seen so far. Erik
resolved to ask Bortai about it. Later. "Any boats at
this little settlement?"

"Looked like there might be. That was probably
why there was a scout."

Erik went back to confer with Manfred. "I don't
suppose you've found an inn with good mulled wine
and eager serving wenches?"

"No, but an ambush on the river. And we'll have
to cross it. No easy way around, and we can't afford
too much time looking for one. Besides, any of them
would probably be guarded, too. And the scouts almost
certainly know we're here."

"It's what I'd have done, in this weather," admitted Manfred. "Well, there is a world of difference
between being surprised in ambush and riding into
one ready and primed."

"There is Kari's ford, upstream."

Manfred shook his head. "I know that mad Vinlander. His idea of a dangerous ford is most people's
idea of swimming. And men in armor don't swim."

"We could put a rope across. We have some rope."

"It'd take too long, Erik. By the time we had half
the men across, the Mongols would have heard the
commotion, and come riding up both banks. We'd be
divided and worse off than riding into their ambush."

"I was worried about that. Well, what I'll do is to
put a few men across—and then we'll ride into the
ford—"

"I'll ride into the ford. You take Kari and the

horseboy and the girl and her brother across. Tulkun. Maybe a dozen others. And then we'll ride across the ford. Nothing takes the wind out of an ambush as badly as being attacked from behind, when you're the one supposed to be taking someone by surprise."

Erik liked the idea of leaving Manfred not at all. But, he was forced to acknowledge, the small group attacking the ambushers would need a very decisive and effective commander. Charging into the ford simply meant giving the order. So that was what they did.

The other "ford" Kari had found was merely a slightly shallower place in the river. But the water, though high, was not that fast moving. Kari and he took up positions upstream and downstream, watching for patrols. Erik brought some twenty knights across, having chosen men with stronger horses and of smaller stature. It was still a tricky, slow exercise. It took them the better part of an hour, and they were all very wet. Kari was fussing about his firearms and his powder. Von Thiel would be too, Erik knew. The bombardier had his little cannon—barely worth calling that, but the bombardier loved it—strapped onto a spare horse. Erik had wondered about leaving it behind. But it could yet be a little surprise for their foes, and besides, it had not been worth arguing with Von Thiel about.

They rode quietly downstream towards the main ford. As with most complex plans something went wrong...A pair of Mongols on horseback. They, however, were just as surprised...and had little time to do anything about it. Kari didn't even get his beloved wheel-lock pistols out. Bortai and her brother had both had arrows on the string, and let fly as soon as the vague shapes in the rain resolved into figures. They were very accurate; two riderless ponies shot off into the storm.

Bortai did not turn so much as a hair. The boy looked quite pale, but not as pale as his companion. David's eyes were wide and frightened as they rode past the corpses. "The horses will tell them there is a problem," said Bortai, fitting another arrow as if she did this every day of her life. Erik thought about how he had worried about her scouting for them. And felt a little foolish. "No matter. They'll have enough problems soon. The main ford didn't look very deep, and Manfred will take the knights into it at speed, if I know the man. He'll not wait for us. We should hear the shouts any moment now."

And a few moments later, they did.

They rode hard themselves, pushing their horses. Erik did not like to do that, with the cold of the water in their muscles, but there was no help for it. And then, they were practically on top of the ambushers firing arrows at the charge. Kari cursed as one of his pistols misfired. The second did not. And the ambushers, who had dismounted and hidden in a brake of hazel on the upstream side of the ford, found themselves the ambushees, caught between two sets of foes. The rain made it even more uncertain, hard to guess at numbers. The Golden Horde, taken at a disadvantage or no, were consummate warriors, even trapped between two sets of attackers. A knight on Erik's left went down, and then a second. The air was full of the sounds of battle. It was bitter hand-to-hand conflict. But the attack from their undefended flank had cost the Mongol warriors dearly. For one they were cut off from their horses, tethered further back, and for a second thing the two-pronged attack had allowed the charge across the ford to gain full momentum and get the van of the knights across and among the dismounted Mongols... and they were not able to retreat and mount because of the second attack. On horseback or at range they were deadly opponents. On foot with the heavily armored horses and knights, they were at a huge disadvantage. Still. It was grim work, and not as one-sided as it could have been. Nor was it as complete as it could have been. Some—not many—of the Mongol managed to get to their horses. Despite the flanking encirclement by Von Gherens and his van platoon, in the misty rain, at least one managed to escape.

Erik saw that Bortai had dismounted and was methodically cutting throats. He swallowed. This was no tame and delicately reared girl from the soft lands of Europe. "Gather our wounded and dead and let's move out!" yelled Manfred. "We'll see to wounded when we're in a defensible position."

"Get their horses," added Erik.

They stopped on a hillock some half a mile off. "They're onto us now," said Manfred, listening. There was a distant sound of horns.

"Yes. But we're outside their cordon, I think. They will have to chase us, and we have another forty-four horses."

"And we are down four knights. And Hunsen is not likely to survive. And I have another nine wounded," said Falkenberg grimly.

"Fit to ride?

Falkenberg shrugged. "We will tie them in the

saddle if need be. I think they would get little mercy from our foes, judging by the conduct of the woman."

Kari, in the act of repriming his pistols paused and grinned. "She'd fit right in on the Vinland plains. I could get to like these people."

Erik had to admit to himself that he could get to respect them, anyway.

Bortai had done her duty, as a good Mongol should. But she too was reassessing how she regarded these foreigners. She'd built up some respect before, when they had responded to the attack on Kildai, and when they'd broken out of the orkhan's camp. Now her attitude was beginning to border on awe. True, this was this Prince Manfred's Khesig. They had opened up that ambush like an overripe melon. She had been through ambushes before. The northeast frontier with the half-bloods and clans that had fallen under the sway of the grand duke had seen to that.

She rode over to her little brother. He had seen some actual conflict before, riding with Father. He was drooping in the saddle. "He needs to rest, great lady," said David, without a hint of his normal cheekiness.

She bit her lip. "If he rests now, it will be in the grave."

Still, she was desperately afraid: if he didn't rest now, it might be in a grave anyway. And they were so close ... It was hard to be sure, but she would guess that they were somewhere between four and seven leagues from the Hawk-clan lands. Surely the clan had scouts out? But would they aid a party of foreign knights?

❀ ❀ ❀

Examining the state of his forces, Erik weighed the possibilities. It was getting on into the late afternoon, he judged, although it was hard to tell in the black weather. Time, in a monastery somewhere, for Vespers. He could use some quiet prayer and reflection...and a meal and some rest. He took a deep breath. "They expect us to run, Manfred."

"I would expect that, too," said the prince. "So shall we go back to that little settlement and see if they have an inn. With beer, food and beds?"

Erik shook his head. "It's an idea with merit, despite the fact you said it as a jest...I hope."

"Well, my best real hope is that the rain slacks off soon. Anyway, a hamlet here would probably only offer us fleas."

"There were some cliffs upstream of where we crossed. We might find some shelter there. A cave or something," offered Kari.

"It'd be a big cave to take all of us. But yes, that is what we'll do. Double back a little, rest up, rest the horses and maybe even organize a little food. It will be dark soon. And five or six hours will make a lot of difference to the battle condition of the men, and give us a chance to treat the wounded, and bury our slain with honor."

Soon they were making their way into the wooded gorge. The dream of a cave to hold more than a hundred men and horses was a wild one, but the soft rock did provide a long—several hundred yards—of shallow overhang. There was even some reasonably dry deadwood that had ended up there. "Small fires. Hidden behind a screen of rocks," ordered Erik. "And we'll have hot mulled wine and some bread for everyone. The horses need to picketed in the shelter if possible. We don't have much in the way of oats for them, but we may as well use it all. Nose-bags, *Ritters*. And see them rubbed down first, before you see to that armor," said Erik singling people out for orders. "Proctor Kalb. See to a guard roster. We will not spend more than half the night here. We'll need someone outside the gorge, hidden."

"Well, not as good as an inn," said Manfred. "And no beer, and I'll bet scanty rations of wine. But at least the rain is letting up."

"I hope it is with us tomorrow."

Manfred nodded, his face serious. "I hope so. And now I'll see to the burials, Erik. It's a small honor and a sad duty. But these men died, and died bravely, for me."

It was a side you did not often see of Manfred. But it was a side that had grown, and grown a lot, since Venice. Manfred would make a good Duke of Brittany. He might even make a good emperor. People followed that kind of honor. Erik nodded. "We will come together for the final laying to rest, Manfred."

"And I owe you an apology, old friend. You were right. We should not have crossed the river."

"No man really knows that, until he crosses the river," said Erik somberly.

"I have a feeling that that is not just the wide one we crossed you refer to. Well, I'll leave you to philosophy. I have graves to help dig."

He would, too. And the knights, being the kind of men they were, would appreciate the signal honor he gave to their fallen comrades. Erik, for the millionth time, found himself thinking of Svan. Trying to recapture their moments together, in their too short idyll. He felt guilty, a little later, when he found that he had transposed her face with someone else's.

Bortai realized that the tengeri must want her little brother to survive, to encourage this madness. The weather that given them shelter was clearing. She knew the signs. If they rode hard, now, they could probably reach the Iret by dawn . . . this stop would slow them, even if it rested those large horses of theirs. They were magnificent beasts, but not as tough as the Golden Horde ponies. Look how they were pampering them. . . . It was a good thing, really. They'd not manage to graze much in this situation. And, unlike the Golden Horde horsemen, the knights had few remounts. There were going to be some very unhappy ponies used for carrying all that steel when they rode on. But once she and Ion and the boy from Jerusalem had seen to Kildai—given him some kumiss and seen him slip into what was hopefully just exhausted sleep—she had work to do. There was no time for her to rest. First she must find some white fabric somewhere. And then some charcoal sticks.

She had never felt less artistic in her life.

David, for the first time in his not so long life realized that there were, maybe, more important things than just getting back to the streets of Jerusalem. Perhaps, just perhaps, there was something in this knightly honor business. His eyelids prickled with unfamiliar tears as the five knights were laid to rest, a simple cross of tied sticks at their heads, the last salute of their comrades as a final farewell. The flight, the river crossing, the fight, Kildai sagging against him . . . It was a sea of experiences that he found was overwhelming his small world. Exhaustion took him to sleep, still questioning the values he'd always thought true.

All too soon—an instant after falling asleep, he was sure—Kari roused him. Maybe more gently than usual. By shaking, not with his usual toe in the ribs. "We need to saddle up, boy."

"What happens today?"

Kari shrugged. "We run. Probably get killed."

David looked at the crosses above the earth mounds. The moon was out and the rain had stopped, and he could see them clearly. He bowed his head slightly to them, feeling a little odd, but as if it was owed to the dead.

Would the knights salute him? Would there be any of them left to do so? All his life had been spent knowing that the one thing you did not do was to openly defy Mongol power. Now it would seem that he was going to die doing so. "Have you got a sword for me?" he asked quietly.

Kari paused. "You'd probably cut your own ears off." He looked thoughtful, then bent down and pulled a small wheel-lock from the top of his left boot, and straightened up and held it out to David. "Here. And I've got a decent spare knife somewhere." He felt around in a saddlebag, while David still looked at the small heavy wheel-lock pistol in the moonlight. "Ah." He pulled out a scabbarded hand-and-a-half blade. Passed it hilt first to David, who stood with a pistol in one hand and a knife in the other, wondering what to do.

"The scabbard has belt slits," said Kari, taking the pistol from him. "Put it on, and don't try and get clever with the knife. Never threaten anyone with it. If you need to use it, take it out and push it into them. Knife fighting takes more skill than a sword, and we don't have time to teach you, but 'just thrust' sometimes works." He then showed David how to use the pistol. "It's intended for the boot-top. Put it there. Use it if you have to, not for fun. Remember, just point and squeeze the trigger. She kicks like a mule. And now we need to get a move on."

In the darkness when the moon was obscured by scudding cloud, the emptiness of the big world outside Jerusalem seemed even bigger. But David felt the new weight in his boot top and the blade on his belt. It seemed a little less intimidating.

Chapter 56

The knights' night ride towards the Iret ended all too soon, as Bortai had feared, with the dawn, bloody fingered, and they were still the better part of a league from the river. There had been less clearing of the forest here—they could see the Hawk lands across the river where trees had been cut and burned for more grazing-lands. Here there were several old oxbows thick with willows and more copses than open land, before the braided bed of the Iret. And, as was inevitable in relatively flat landscapes, they soon saw that they'd been spotted. Bortai could see two groups of riders—at least a Jaghun—a hundred men—each, coming up from the east, and another, coming down from the west.

The column of knights formed a defensive phalanx, with their triple crossed shields giving some shelter... But if the forces of Gatu Orkhan were moving so openly in relatively small numbers here, they must have little fear of the Hawk clan. The constant attrition of the mounted archers would slow the knights, and more and more of the orkhan's men would arrive. The horses would tire, they would be forced to make a stand, probably be cornered, and eventually be killed. It was the nerge hunt way. Bortai had cut a rough lance and attached her handiwork of last night to it. She unfurled it and put it up into the rising light of mother sun. The charcoal hawk stood out against the dun—the nearest to white she been able to find—of what had been a spare shirt taken from one of those they had overcome.

Tulkun looked at it. And beamed. The knights around them merely looked puzzled. The knight Erik was somewhere else in the tight, disciplined column, but Bortai jockeyed her way closer to the huge man she had at first concluded was their battle-shaman. She wished that he had some magic up his sleeve. Perhaps it had been magic that had allowed the knights to survive this long, to know where the ambush lay. She searched for her few Frankish words. "Sky flag?" she said. "On lance?"

He frowned and then obviously got it. Shrugged— quite something to do in the angular plate armor. Gave an instruction to the knight next to him. "When we stop. Cannot do it in gauntlets." He tapped a steel clad glove.

"Give for me?" she asked.

"Von Gherens. Can you tell the lady where to find one?" said the Prince.

He nodded.

A little later a furled envoy-truce pennant was handed along the tight formation to her. It was less than easy while they were on the move, but she managed to attach it to Tulkun's lance, just below the head. Soon that fluttered in the breeze, next to the charcoal Hawk.

An arrow clanged against armor.

❀   ❀   ❀

From the rearguard, Erik watched the Golden Horde Mongols closing on his pitiful little column. He'd spotted the first scouts just after first light, before the dawn. Since then he'd watched the arrival of a first company to the east, joined by a second company, and then a third coming up from the west. The Mongols had been ahead of them. Well, he'd expected that when he'd rested the knights. The Mongols knew the country. They would have ridden through the night, changing horses, and there would be more men behind them. The knights could not outrun them. They needed a refuge, or place to stand. Erik had gambled on them finding one. It had been a forced gamble. Yet... They'd needed to rest the horses last night.

It seemed as if luck had not favored him, this time.

His keen eyes had picked out the best spot to make a stand. It wasn't very good. A low bluff near the river, still holding some trees, near a big swampy looking oxbow of the old river channel. If he read it right, the oxbow would limit the fronts on which they could be attacked, and, given his second plan, might allow them to retreat on the river at nightfall. Like nightfall, that was still a long way off.

The company now closing from the west dispatched a party of ten riders, galloping in to fire at the knights and retreat.

At this stage all they could do was to rely on their shield-wall and armor. To react would slow them down. Soon the Mongols would begin darting in to attack the tail of the column. Then the rearguard would have to deal with it.

Erik heard the pops of Kari's guns, saw a skirmisher,

made confident by the lack of response and thus come in too close, almost fall from the saddle, and race away, clinging to it. Erik smiled grimly. That would keep them a little farther off. Emeric had his Magyar knights carry horse-pistols. It was high time the Knights of the Holy Trinity did the same. If they lived through this, Erik was determined to see that Manfred's guard at least carried them.

Kari had put them off more thoroughly than Erik could have hoped. They plainly were less used to firearms than most western troops. The Mongols kept a great deal farther off. But eventually, as Erik had known they would, a charge was made by one of the groups of pursuit. Von Gherens and thirty knights peeled off and turned. The clash was a brief one. The light, mobile Mongols knew they had no need for head-on conflict, yet. They turned and retreated and Von Gherens and his three squads galloped back.

The enemy knew that they could do this all day... and that the knights could not. It was a contest of stamina against strength, and Erik was sure the enemy numbers would increase too, as the day wore on.

They'd lost another knight by the time they gained the low bluff. It was farther to the river than Erik had hoped, a little less than a mile. The bluff itself was not more than thirty-five feet higher than the surrounding land. It just appeared bigger because it still carried a good stand of oaks.

At the end of the bluff was a small knoll, with a few left-over boulders that had helped this little spit of land resist the erosion to the valley below. Erik had formed an outer defense line, still mounted, on the edge of the trees. The other knights he had dismount, at least while the enemy themselves regrouped. They'd be foolish to try a frontal assault, and the spreading branches of the trees would help deflect arrows lofted at the knights. The oxbow, still half-full of stagnant water, and densely fringed with willow made a natural moat of sorts around two thirds of the bluff. The enemy would send men across it, of course. The Mongols were lightly armored and used to rough terrain. But they'd probably wait until they had a lot more men. They only had, by his estimate, four hundred now, to the hundred and seventy-odd Knights of the Holy Trinity. No, first they'd surround them and then send men along the ridge line using the trees for cover. Erik found bombardier Von Thiel. "They need a few little surprises, on that ridge, Von Thiel," he said.

"I've enough powder to plant a few charges, *Ritter* Hakkonsen. In some of this loose rock—it'll be like shrapnel," said the man cheerfully.

Erik was glad not to be on the wrong side of his cheeriness. "And we'll be needing some intervention when it comes time to get out of here, Bombardier. Maybe, when you've finished that, you can rig us a mangonel of some sort. And there's your little cannon. We need to keep them from easy bowshot, and clear a path when it comes to charging out of there."

"They don't seem too familiar with black powder," said the bombardier. The expression on his blue-pitted face said he intended to teach them all about it, the hard way.

"Well, save the lesson for when they need it most." It was all they had. Erik had the feeling that it would take magic, prayer, and the intervention of decent sized force to survive here for long. If they had another five hundred men, this would not be an easy place to take by anything but overwhelming force or siege tactics . . . but he didn't have five hundred men, and it was quite possible that overwhelming force was coming. He went to study the terrain, and to consult with his proctors and Manfred.

So this was how it would all end, thought Bortai. In sight of the ancestral lands of the clan. Not that a final run would have taken them to safety . . . but it would have been good to be there. The ancestral tengeri would have been pleased that they had come to die among them. The Hawk clan could, drawing on the sub-clans sept to them, had at its height have raised three Tumens—thirty thousand men. And now . . . here on the borderland, in plain sight, Gatu Orkhan dared to bring his ragtag Jahguns to pursue the Hawk banner. There would have been more dishonor if it had been on the other side of the Iret, she supposed.

The man with the blue-pocked face came to her. She understood only one word in ten. But then Ion came along, and by gesture, she understood that he wanted Ion for some digging. Well, Ion, poor slave, at least had not done as much carrying of armor. She went along. The pockmarked-faced foreigner was burying some bags. Treasure? Why? And why did he want Ion? Unless he planned to kill him. That was not going to happen, or at least not at the hands of these foreigners! But if they were meant to be hidden. . . . Why was he was laying trails of powder?

The ways of foreigners were strange. Perhaps it was

some religious ritual. She'd been impressed, despite herself, at the rites they enacted for their dead, the night before. She kept a wary eye on the forest. The orkhan's men would be in it, farther back along the ridge, in as solid a line as possible, making sure that no one fled through the trees. They would advance, slowly, closing the noose, as more and more Jahguns turned up. Now was when the Orkhan Erik ought to have split his forces, and hidden a small part, to escape, if that was his intention.

Perhaps she should have told him that.

He came riding up. "Ah. Lady Bortai. I need to ask a few things about the river. You said you know this country?"

She nodded. "That is my clan-lands on the other side of the river. But they will follow us even there, I think. They come through the woods now. We are encircled."

"Not for very long," said Erik. "*Ritter* Von Thiel is setting up the trip lines, with wheel-locks to trigger the charges. When those charges go off, it is going to wreak havoc in their surrounding force. I think you, Tulkun and your brother and man and . . . I can spare you two men, should leave along the ridge. I'd send Manfred too, but he won't go. Let your people know we're crossing into their lands tonight. Now . . . how deep is that river? It's braided and looks crossable."

Bortai was filled with a number of conflicting emotions. Firstly, disgust that he thought that they would abandon their escort. Yes, it made sense. Well, it would, if the cordon of men on the ridge could be broken. But even a charge of the knights could not do that in the rocks and dense trees. The orkhan's men would be on foot, several deep. It would be good war tactic if they could break through, and the Gatu Orkhan's men were somehow not aware of it. Her father had talked enough about strategies and tactics for her to know that. But she did not wish to do it! Not even if it were possible. Secondly, she was puzzled. He mingled Frankish words with his rudimentary Mongol. Charges? And the war-shaman would not go? Why? "What do you mean?"

"I don't really have time to explain, but get your man, your brother, young David and I'll send Dader and Von Stael with you. You'll probably have to lead your horses. After the explosions." He smiled at her. "Good luck, Lady Bortai. I'm sorry we could not escort you all the way home." He bowed and rode off, leaving her even more puzzled. She went in search of David and her brother.

The boy from Jerusalem was able to explain. "The bombardier has set charges along the ridge. And trip-lines. I was setting those. When our enemies come, he will make it explode."

Bortai had to weigh this. She'd seen the explosions used to aid their escape from the orkhan's camp. She'd seen some cannons before, used up in the Székely on the borderland in the mountains. They inspired respect. The Horde would have bought them, but for Ulaghchi Khan's objections . . . and the reluctance of the Hungarians to selling. But . . . could this, would this, make a hole in the cordon? And was it not her duty to her people and her clan and her brother to take him out along the gap created?

"I am staying here," said David, abruptly, before she could even mention his going. "And, no noble lady. I don't know why. I think my wits have gone missing."

"It is orders from Erik Orkhan." Out on the marshy floodplain she could see two more Jahgun riding closer. These must be some of Gatu Orkhan's better men. They were in much closer formation than the ragged-chase of the earlier three Jahguns.

Two knights rode up, bowed to her. Spoke in Frankish. "They say Erik has ordered them to accompany you," translated David.

"But..."

And then, in the fashion of military plans, things went wrong. The Gatu Orkhan's men who were in place had plainly seen the ordered Jaghuns riding up from the east, and wanted the glory themselves. Someone must have given the order to push the pace through the forest.

Bortai spent the next few moments fighting to stay on her horse, and being terribly glad Kildai and David were not mounted yet. The foreign knights were plainly far more used to explosions, and so were their mounts.

She could easily believe, now, that the cordon had broken. The other thing she could see—glancing out onto the floodplain—was that beside the disarray of the Gatu Orkhan's besieging troops—whose horses had also not liked the explosions on the ridge, was that the oncoming Jahguns had begun to charge... As had the foreign knights, taking some advantage of the confusion.

But what made her heart leap was the banner that was unfurled and the clan shields exposed. "Hawk!" she yelled in delight.

Kildai whooped.

❀   ❀   ❀

Erik had expected a good hour's grace until the skirmish line, that was doubtless moving down the ridge, got to them. It made no sense for the Mongols to push the issue until the companies of horsemen he could see approaching on the floodplain were available and integrated. They'd be facing nearly five hundred foes then... And still have several hours before dark. If he was an enemy commander he'd expect them to try to flee in the dark.

The explosions on the ridge took him by surprise. Had they gone off by accident? It could happen so easily. But the bombardier had told him their men were all pulled back...and he could hear screaming. By the looks of it one of the Holy Trinity proctors had seen the opportunity presented by the chaos and taken the sortie squad out to punish the Mongol.

Then he saw Bortai, followed by her little brother racing down from the hillside at a full gallop. She was waving her home-made flag and yelling. But he'd told them to escape along the ridge! Had she misunderstood him? The two knights he had assigned to her were riding behind Bortai and her brother, but were being out-paced. They looked more like pursuers than an escort.

Then he saw the banner of the oncoming companies and understood. "Mount up! Mount up and form up."

Falkenberg, already in the saddle rode across. "What is it, Erik?"

"Help," Erik pointed. "Possibly. Those two companies that are fanning out there. They're from Bortai's clan. See their banners and their shields."

"They're a little outnumbered," said Falkenberg.

"Not if we join them."

The older knight grimaced. "Be a little awkward if they're also after our heads."

"Might be more awkward if those two get killed," said Erik. "Because at the moment it looks like we're chasing them, not sheltering them."

Bortai had barely got to the water-meadow, when she realized just how premature her action had been.

The charge by the two Jahgun of Hawks was not going to reach her before she reached the chaos that was the Gatu Orkhan's troops. They were some distance from the small sortie of knights. She could yet have handed Gatu a victory in his troops' defeat. She and Kildai turned, heading back for the bluff and the trees. An arrow narrowly missed her.

And then the heavy steel of the foreign knights, lances out, came galloping down from the wooded fringe of the bluff. The Gatu Orkhan's men, realizing that the oncoming Jahguns were foes, now found that they were between their enemies, and worse, their men were disorganized and divided. Many chose the option of flight, then and there.

Bortai allowed herself and her horse to be carried along with the foreign knights, holding her makeshift lance and flag up, as they galloped toward the Jaghuns of Hawks, scattering Gatu Orkhan's men like chaff, riding down the few who did not choose to flee. And then, the charge began to lose momentum as at the end of the willow-fringed oxbow, they came face to face with the Hawk clan.

Bortai tried to shoulder her slighter pony forward, yelling to the clan. This could all still go wrong . . .

Kildai, with years of experience at the great game,

was better at it than she was. He'd forced his way into the front, and was waving.

The two sides were still coming towards each other, at a slow canter now, and then breaking into a walk, as the Hawk warriors began yelling, lifting their lance-points high. She could hear Kildai's name being called. As the foreign knights ported their lances, Erik and his prince came through the press and made a space for her to ride out to greet her brother's men.

"I think they're glad to have them back," said Manfred. "They seem to know the boy. Enough of them were calling his name."

Indeed, grinning, laughing, backslapping—until told off by Bortai—warriors surrounded the two. Tulkun was respectfully greeted. They seemed a little taken aback by the knights, and unsure how to deal with them. Slightly warily, seemed the general consensus. But Bortai was not having that situation. She was a forceful young woman, thought Manfred to himself. She rode back to Manfred and Erik, accompanied by an older, scar-faced man. "This Banchu, son of Makai. He lead this Jahgun. He with father," she patted her chest, "in Khesig."

Manfred bowed. It seemed safe. "What's a Khesig?" he asked Erik.

"Imperial guard, I think."

"So they're the children of a fellow warrior. A well-known one. No wonder they're getting such a welcome."

Bortai proceeded with introductions, in Mongol, to the two of them. Maybe Erik followed some of it. All Manfred understood was Erik's name.

"It appears that you are going up in the world," said Erik, grinning. "I am a war khan. If I follow right, you're getting the credit for the bombardier's explosions from this Banchu. He's impressed. But he says there are more of this Gatu Orkhan's men coming."

"I think we should take this opportunity to get out of here, don't you?" said Manfred.

Erik nodded.

Chapter 57

In the mazed world of smoke-inspired paradise dreams, the tarkhan Borshar moved suddenly from tranquility to agony. He jerked convulsively, spasming, his face contorted into a rictus, his throat torn by a horrible scream of rage. The tarkhan had not, when he slipped into the trance, expected his communication with the greatness to be agonizing.

Partly, that was just because the Black Brain poorly understood the frailty of humans. Its closest contact with them was with Jagiellon, who was not frail. But mostly it was because both parts of the Black Brain, the man who had once been Grand Duke Jagiellon and the ancient and powerful denizen of planes far beyond and below the ordinary, were angry. Indeed, furious.

Could these stupid tools not manage a simple straightforward murder? The Baitini were a society of assassins. They spent their lives in practice and prayer, blast them. Killing a few pawns should have been a joke. They were masters of the poison, and the cunning blade.

Now the pawns were on the loose again.

And they were dangerous pawns. Pawns that had turned victory into defeat for him on prior occasions. He did not like the fact that they were now much closer to his heartlands. It seemed ridiculous, but...

"They must be hunted down and killed."

Over the last few years the Black Brain had so subverted the Baitini that they obeyed him unconditionally. He had orders. Borshar would do his best, or die trying.

But his influence, Borshar informed him, was limited. The breach of tradition had frightened and upset even Gatu's loyalists. The Mongols believed the spirits of the land favored the foreign Knights of the Holy Trinity. Or that they practiced magic, to have survived.

"I will give you magical powers to call on the afrits and lesser creatures to do your bidding. Let them believe you too are a powerful worker of magic."

The Baitini tarkhan thanked him devoutly for so favoring him.

Chernobog knew what price the user would pay, eventually, for what were actually rather limited powers. But that was not his problem.

The Black Brain now turned its attention southeast to see how the Baitini dream of capturing the empire and ruling it by the code assassin was succeeding. They prayed and tried to reach him. Because, right now, they had need. That in itself was not a bad thing, the part which once had been human informed him. Chernobog and Jagiellon were one and the same now, but still the part which had once been Prince Jagiellon did have a better grasp on human affairs. No matter what the Baitini and their fifth column insurrection achieved, chaos among the Ilkhan was a good thing. It would make physical conquest easier, later.

He turned his attention now to the shipyards and the burgeoning encampment outside Odessa, using his puppets to inspect the work.

Here he found much that pleased him.

Then he was recalled to his throne room by a messenger who had returned from Karelia in the far north.

Bringing strange, worrying news, and no shaman.

"They will not come. They flee before me, Prince Jagiellon. We caught one, eventually, but he was just a minor healer. Of no use to you, Your Highness. We tortured him until we got some answers. Something is moving up there among the hunting tribes and reindeer herders. Something is acquiring their names. It seems they would rather die than come to your service as a result."

The messenger did not understand, but Chernobog did. The shamans of the north believed everything had true names. And if one had their true, secret names, they had to obey. There were ways of protecting those names. There were ways of ferreting them out. Obviously some shaman had become expert in the latter, and was choosing to defy Chernobog. That had to be investigated and dealt with.

Chapter 58

Vlad was glad to see Golden Horde riders at last. Well, riders not intent on raid and pillage, or at least not of the carts right now. That was just as well because there were at least a thousand of them, riding in formation, the scales of their armor bright in the early morning sun, their Hawk banners flying. They came up just after Vlad's small expedition had broken camp and begun to move, on what Vlad had decided was the last day of this vain pursuit. The horsemen must have been traveling from before the dawn, and were moving quite rapidly. A commander rode over. His grasp of the Valhaian tongue was probably why he had been sent. "We do not wish to trade, merchants. We are at war. Go away."

That explained the lack of people if not the herds of sheep and horses they had seen. "We only wish to buy horses..."

"We do not sell those. Now, go back to the mountains. And leave any of our people you see there in peace, or we will follow and wreak a vengeance that will be talked about among your tribe for a thousand years."

So the women and children—and possibly some of the men had been sent to take shelter in the mountain foothills and the dense forest, the great Codrii Vlasiei that still had not been cleared up there.

"We do not fight women and children," said Vlad stiffly.

"Why not?" asked the Hawk commander. "They are fitting foes for you."

And on this casual insult he turned and rode off.

Vlad felt the black fury rising in him. He would dismember the upstart...

Except that the man was already several hundred yards away, moving back to the column of horse at a rapid canter.

Vlad took a deep breath, and tried to calm himself, with limited success. Primor Peter waited until he done so. "Which way will you have us go, Drac? I think closer to the mountains might be a good idea, for all that roads are not so common."

"We just give up? We go home?" asked Vlad incredulously.

"We don't have a lot of choice, Sire. We really do not want to get caught up in their inter-clan warfare. That has been what has stopped them pushing west for the last hundred years. It settled down under the last khan, but he was set on reuniting his people south and east. The fights between clans are vicious. They'll kill us just for being there, most likely. We might as well turn around. There is no sense in making them angry."

Vlad found himself furious, let alone them being angry, but not knowing what else to do. They began to turn in a wide curve, and headed northwest. The column of men and horses were soon a mere dust trail.

Worryingly, several hours later, they could see another dust column. "Maybe the attackers will sell us some horses." said Vlad, still irritated. "We'd better make a circle and get the cannon and pikes ready. They are not likely to give us a chance to trade."

So they did. They had found a slight rise with a boggy stream behind them.

"So what has happened to the Hawk clan?" asked Bortai as they rode, surrounded by a the bulk of the two Jahguns, who all, it seemed, did not want to let them out of their sight, "since that night at the kurultai?"

"Much that needs to be put right, Princess Bortai," said Banchu. "We lost fewer men than we'd thought at first. It was chaos. I think Gatu's plans went wrong, too. But without Kildai and without you...the clan was coming apart. Most of the sub-clans...have gone their way. They have not formally renounced ties...but no men come to take their place in our regiments. We've called. We just hoped to hold our own. We expect Gatu Orkhan to ride across the Iret soon. He will conquer all that do not make submission to him. He is promising rich rewards to those who do. He seems to be awash with gold, Princess. That much we have heard. The clan itself is divided. Gatu is showering wealth around—no one knows quite where it has come from. Gold is tempting: But most wish to resist. The anger about the attacks at the kurultai...that has not happened in centuries. He was shamed by that. We expect him to extract a heavy-vengeance price for it. We will make them pay in blood for doing so."

"We will," she said with grim certainty.

He nodded. "Things will be different now that you and the young khan are back."

He paused, coughed. "Who are these foreigners? And why are we bid to treat them as if they were royal envoys?"

"Because that is what they are."

The officer blinked. "But they are foreigners. I mean, we owe them a great debt for sheltering our young khan ... and they fight well, it seems. We had scouts out, watching, from early this morning. We watched, we saw your flag ... They are formidable for a small group of foreigners ... But Princess, they are not Mongol."

"No," she paused. She knew that although she was speaking to Banchu, at least ten other horsemen in ear-shot were taking in every word. She took a deep breath. "They are not without honor. Their code seems ... nearly as deep as our own. And Tulkun and Kildai will testify— they make war differently from the Mongol, but they are, at their own place of choosing, as effective as our people. Their discipline is very good. And they force their enemies to fight on their terms. And the big man is a noble among them. So is their orkhan."

Banchu rubbed his jaw. He plainly did not wish to disagree with her. She could almost read his mind: she was a woman, yes, but a noble and respected one. Moreover she was one of the best wrestlers that you could wish to see. A few men had been foolish enough to wager they could beat her ... "Maybe against Gatu's men. Not the Hawk clan."

"We will see. But now ... I must tell you of treach-ery. Of a breach with the ancient tradition. Of honor— from these foreign knights, from this man of the Ilkhan—and of black dishonor." She gestured to the warriors who rode near her. "Come closer. I will tell this tale many times. But you will be first."

Bortai had been trained in the storyteller's art. It was a noble and respected, and, indeed, much loved art among the Golden Horde. And she had a story that she could see would become even more widely known and loved than that of Khan Ulaghchi and Khutulun. Even if they lost the day, and Kildai and the whole of the Hawk clan was hunted down and killed, this story would endure. The Hawk clan did not have gold to match that of Gatu. But they had honor and tradition. And she would weave that into a story that would be worth more than any tainted gold to the people of the Golden Horde. And so, to a spellbound audience she wove a tale of magic and treachery, of the hand of the ancestral tengeri, of heroism and blood. Interspersed with some laughter. The Hawk warriors loved the tortoise story as much as she had. It was to be hoped that they would not encounter any foes soon, or some of the men were going to be in no state to fight.

But by the end of the tale they were in no mood to laugh.

And Erik was being referred to as Tortoise Orkhan. It was appropriate, in some ways. The armor. The determination. And the vicious bite. But they would learn he was faster than most tortoises, she thought, laughing a little to herself.

David had watched the two Golden Horde nobles career off to join their people. Kildai's abrupt action in mounting and departing had taken him by surprise. He'd scrambled to find another horse, and then just stopped. He'd thought...well. He was wrong. He took out the wheel-lock pistol from his boot and marveled at the mechanism of it. In Jerusalem he would have been executed for even being in possession of such a thing. He must get more ball and powder, learn to reload. And to actually shoot at something. Sometime. The way things had gone on this expedition he would.

Then one of the two knights that had been assigned to guide and escort them to escape came riding back. "The boy says you are to come. But to wear your cloak with a hood. At least that's what I understood from Tulkun." The knight looked at the pistol in his hands. "What are you doing with that thing? It's dangerous."

"Kari gave it to me. He said I'd chop my ears off with a sword."

"As likely to blow your foot off with that gun." The knight rubbed his eyes. He was a big solid man. "I nearly cut my own head off with my first sword, let alone my ears," he said seriously.

"Will you teach me?" David nearly bit his own tongue off. But that burial and the honor shown... it had stirred something he had not known existed inside him.

The knight looked equally startled. "Why? I mean, boy, a sword is a knight's tool. Not the first choice..."

"Of a thief," said David, shocking himself with his own honesty. "But no thief would choose to be here...I saw my first real fighting yesterday, *Ritter*." He bit his lip. "I was there when *Ritter* Kalb died. It was horrible. I had never seen a man die before. Then...they put his sword on his chest. And the prince himself saluted him. And said that he was with God."

"I was Kalb's squire when I entered the order,"

said the knight, his voice rough with emotion. "And if any man . . ." He stopped. "Wait here."

It was an order. David had never been much good at obeying orders. This time he stood. The knight rode down onto the field of combat, dismounted and picked up a Mongol sword. David had seen just how hard it was for an armored knight to get into the saddle. He could only marvel at the athletic strength of this man, who got back up without help or a block.

The knight rode back. "Here," he said, handing the blade to David. "This will have to do until we can get you a decent straight Christian sword. Bear it with honor. Now mount up, and see that you take good care of my gear. Squire."

"But . . . I am not nobly born."

The knight shrugged. "There have been a few commoners accepted into the order over the years, boy, in cases of heroism, or exceptional peity. We swear an oath of poverty and equality before God. Mind you, Abbot Störer will probably have my guts out and chase me round a tree. I'll make you no promises, boy. But while we're here, away from the Chapter House, you can serve as my squire."

Erik rode beside Manfred as they splashed across the Iret. "Well, this is a more friendly reception," said Manfred. "What do you think, Eberhard?"

The old diplomat looked surprised at being addressed. "I think we are lucky to be alive, Prince Manfred. And I have been utterly wrong about the Mongol treatment of diplomats and envoys. So I am reluctant to say what I think until we see a little more. But they are smiling at us."

"They were laughing like madmen earlier," said Erik. "Bortai had them in stitches. I thought some of them were going to fall off their horses."

"Probably telling them how well you speak the language," said Manfred. "And how you make her laugh. Next thing you'll have her big brother and an axe, asking you what your intentions are."

"Don't be silly, Manfred. I can see you are overdue some fencing practice. Or a bit of wrestling."

Manfred grinned. "Why don't you go and wrestle with her? I'm not the one making them laugh."

"Don't be ridiculous, Manfred," said Erik, blushing.

The problem with the Iret was that it was no barrier. The Hawk clan had men and horses as a barrier, not a deep river.

The only detail was right now they did not have many men. Riders had been dispatched. The clan had managed to field nearly fifteen hundred men... a far cry from the thousands that made up the Tumens of yesteryear. Looking back to the south, Bortai could see dust.

That could only be a lot of horses. And the heavily armored knights and their steeds simply did not have the stamina that the Hawk riders did. Nor did they have several changes of those huge horses of theirs. Yes, they could ride smaller ones, borrowed from the Hawk clan, but they were big heavy men, in big heavy armor.

They were going to have to stand and fight, again. And this time there would be a lot more troops coming against them, and not much in the way of natural help from the terrain. It was flat and open.

If Gatu dared to cross the Iret, he must have some thousands of men at his disposal. He must also have an idea of just how weakened the Hawk clan and all their allies and sub-clans were. And, Bortai realized, an awareness of just how much he had to lose if Kildai's survival and the story of the treachery began to circulate.

Chapter 59

Vlad looked out from that fragile fortress of carts and wagons. It was clear now that there were at least three large groups of riders on the plains. One smaller group ahead. One very large group trailing them and, off on far flank to the east, another group. Probably the Hawk clan regiments that had told them to get off their lands.

"How long until they get here?" Vlad asked the Székeler primor.

The man shrugged. "They are riding hard. We have enough time to dig our own graves if we start now," he said, morosely. Yet his actions belied his tone. The Székely had a chance, if they fled. Most of Vlad's men did not. Yet they showed no signs of running. Vlad decided that he could come to like and depend on these men, despite their odd ideas about hereditary overlordship. It was worth putting up with it, for their support. "Let us dig graves then," he said. "We will dig them outside the wagon-square. We can decide on who is buried in them later."

The primor nodded. "They might fall in them. It'd slow the horse charge."

So they dug a trench along the edge closest to the oncoming men. And when they still had time, on the second side, too.

Erik had been scanning the horizon for a suitable piece of terrain to take advantage of and hold. He'd talked to Manfred about it. In theory Manfred was in command. And if it came to strategy of war he would command. But for the details of day-to-day tactics, Erik managed the men with Von Gherens and Falkenberg. This alluvial plain was flat and had been cleared of trees. They were riding again toward rising ground, but the mountains or even the woodland was far off. But what was that? He rode across to the fringe of the accompanying Mongol and asked, in his best attempt at the language.

The man bowed respectfully, and smiled. He, too, squinted at the white structures ahead but off a little to the southern side. "I don't know, Tortoise Orkhan." He put his heels to his horse and rode forward. Erik could see him pointing, while he pondered on what the man had called him. That horseboy! Still, he thought, his ears red, the man had seemed a lot more respectful and communicative than the ones who had escorted them from the edge of Iskander Beg's lands. He had noticed that Tulkun's friendship stemmed from the original incident. Perhaps being laughed at was worthwhile sometimes.

The Mongol came back, accompanied by Bortai, Kildai, Tulkun, Banchu and another officer. Erik noticed how much taller young Kildai sat. Today no one would have suggested that he needed someone to help to keep him in the saddle. Plainly being among his own people had done the boy a great deal of good.

"We think it is some traders," said Bortai. "They come down from the mountains sometimes. We will go that way. Gatu's troops may stop to loot. To the east are more men we think from the Hawk clan," she pointed. "The traders will perhaps buy us a little time."

Erik had noticed the dust plume—even in the wettest country hundreds of horses will raise dust. It was grim luck for the traders, but... "We'll need to rest our horses soon, lady."

"We will call a halt and mount your men on the spares we have," said Bortai, decisively. She was a forceful woman. She didn't even ask the officers. She had the makings of a great one herself, he had to admit. And the Mongols were very effective during the halt, and remounting the knights. Erik knew and understood the need. But he couldn't help feeling sorry for the Mongol ponies and also hoped that they would not find themselves having to fight from their backs. A knight and his warhorse were a unit. That was why the Knights of the Holy Trinity made the knights care for their own beasts.

They rode on towards, what Erik could see now, was a small enclosure of wagons. Perhaps the poor traders had made a sheepfold out of it. Gatu's troops were plainly driving their horses hard, and had gained slightly while the the knights were being re-horsed. Now they were perhaps two miles back.

Vlad shaded his eyes and peered again. "Tell me my eyes deceive me," he said. "Those are not Mongol. They're western knights."

"Some are Mongol. The same banner—the Hawk as the men we encountered this morning. They're being pursued." The Székely Primor looked professionally at the scene. "A few hundred men, being chased by several thousand. The men chasing are starting to deploy flanking companies."

"What is the device on the shields of the knights?" demanded Vlad. He could see it well enough. He just wanted some else to confirm it.

"Three crosses, Sire."

The Knights of the Holy Trinity. It fitted with their archaic-looking spiky armor. But what were they doing here, in the lands of the Golden Horde? Well, whatever they were doing, they were the enemy of Hungary. Vlad spoke fluent Frankish. And he was seized by one of those impulses he had at first tried to ignore, but had learned not to. "I need my horse," he said. "And a lance with, if we have one, the flag for truce."

"You're not going out there, Sire? They'll have to turn and fight soon."

"Yes. And we're going to be overrun. And so are they," said Vlad, swinging himself into the saddle. "So let us see if we can stand together."

He rode out of the small sally port gap they'd made, alone, towards the oncoming horsemen. Somehow it felt right, even if he was about to get killed. He had always been alone...

"One of the traders is coming riding out to us. Good horse," commented Falkenberg. "Now if the Mongols had nice fresh steeds that size, we'd have real mounts to give the chasers a run for their money."

That was, Erik knew, the basic problem they faced. The two companies that had come to their rescue had ridden long and hard to do so. Even their spares were tired horses. The knights were too big and heavy for them, really. And their pursuit plainly hadn't ridden as far or as hard.

"I can't see that the Mongols are going to want to talk to him."

The man pulled the magnificent black horse to a halt. He did not, Erik admitted to himself, look in the least like a trader. Tall and dark haired with very pale skin, he was dressed entirely in unadorned simple black, except for his cloak, which had a rich purple lining. "Hail, Knights of the Holy Trinity," he called out, in slightly accented but clear Frankish. There was no trace of fear in his voice, and he sat as straight backed as a lance on his fine horse.

"You are in the middle of a battle, sir," called Erik.

"I know. I am Vlad, Duke of Valahia. I have two hundred arquebusiers and twenty cannon there," he pointed at the square of wagons and carts. "And a handful of cavalry. I propose an alliance of convenience."

"You've got *twenty* cannon?" That was the bombardier.

The man on the black horse nodded. "Small cannon. Four pounders. But loaded with grape-shot."

The bombardier beamed. "Worth twenty men each, I would think."

The column of knights and Hawk Mongols had come to a halt. "What does he say?" demanded Bortai.

"He has cannon. He wants an alliance of convenience," Erik explained.

She translated and elaborated. "Cannon" plainly made some impact among the Hawk clans. "The Székely fortresses have them, on the border. They can do much damage."

"Those will be larger cannon, but yes," said Erik. "What do you want from us, Duke?" he called out. Was Valahia not part of Hungary?

"Draw them onto us, and counterattack once they have felt the the cannons." The pale man seemed very sure of that strategy.

"I think we are doing the first part anyway," said Manfred, looking back. "I say yes. We should do this. We have very little choice."

Bortai turned to Erik. "You are a great orkhan. Well versed in this kind of war. Banchu and Feyzin they are leaders of Jahgun. One hundred men. They are good fighters. But this is not what they know."

"Tortoise Orkhan says yes," said Erik. Bortai looked enormously embarrassed. He turned his attention to the two Mongol commanders and addressed them in his best attempt at the language. "They catch us. We can run, but they catch us. We have to fight. Why not here? It will win us some time." He pointed. "More Hawk clan come." He pointed at the black-haired pale skinned man: "He asks to do what we must do anyway."

The two Mongol officers looked at the duke and then at Erik. And nodded.

"We have a deal, Prince Vlad," shouted Erik. The man rode closer, smiling. There was a magnetism about him, for all his odd looks.

"Good," he said. "There are no women and children among those who pursue you, are there?"

"It . . . seems unlikely," answered Erik, taken aback by the question.

"Excellent," said the Duke of Valahia. "I would want it remembered by the Hawk clan. If you have any wounded . . . or women and children, we will give them shelter. Position your people behind the wagons, so they will have to ride around two sides of the guns. Be careful—It's very boggy down to the east of us." He waved and turned his horse and rode away.

"What he say about the clan?" demanded Bortai.

"Something about there not being women and children among the enemy. And giving shelter to the wounded, and women and children."

"Oh."

Kildai shook his head. "No!" he said, firmly.

Erik got the idea that the boy was just as strong-willed as his sister.

Gatu's forces were sacrificing formation for speed. They'd be in bow-shot soon. Erik drew a deep breath. Time to marshal the troops. He knew the right attitude would be to send some of them on, with Manfred, but Gatu's troops were already moving to flank them. Instead he trotted them around to the back of the encampment. The knights returned to their own slightly rested mounts. And Erik sent two of the knights, both too wounded to have been riding, had there been any choice, and Ion, and the bombardier *Ritter* Von Thiel to the wagon and cart stockade. David, however, refused. The boy was looking terrified, and stuck close to *Ritter* Von Stael, one of the two men he'd ordered to accompany Bortai and the escape party. The big taciturn man pointed a gauntleted hand at the boy. "He is learning to be my squire, *Ritter* Hakkonsen. His place is behind me."

Well, Kari and latterly Falkenberg and Von Gherens had informed him the boy had the devil in him and a grave reluctance to learn anything but devilry . . . Von Stael was welcome to try. Erik had more on his mind. Bortai was not going either. But the Mongols hated to be penned. And even resting their horses a little...well, they had some chance of escape during the chaos of a battle.

There was not a great deal of strategy to explain to anyone, which given his grasp of Mongol, let alone of battle terms, Erik was grateful for. It amounted to getting Mongol companies to form up behind the knights. Shoot at will. Charge when given the order. Erik did not add "and hope like hell the rest of the Hawk clan military show up soon."

"The sun is already past the noon-mark," said Manfred. "We have a handful of little cannons and unknown allies in that fragile little fort, the hope of relief, and nightfall. I am not sure which to pin my hopes on."

"That's a lot of cannons, if they can use them. And Gatu's men are not expecting it," said Erik.

The enemy, seeing that their prey had stopped, stopped themselves and marshaled their own men. Sending companies out to form a neat flanking on both sides. Erik had the satisfaction of seeing the riders sent east return to the main mass of men, which was beginning to move slowly forward. Good. The bog to the east must be such that the horsemen thought it was broken-leg-for-horses country to charge across. The plain back on the other side was black with riders, riders vying for position to get at them first.

A war drum and it began. First at a trot, and then accelerating.

They intended to roll right over—or at least close around the little wagon and cart square. They had the entire plain to circle around the obstacle—with the exception of the bog to the east, and they chose to charge straight towards it under, it was to be admitted, the cover of archery.

They did not expect the defenders of the wagon-and-cart square to not even fire an arrow back at them... until they were less than seventy yards off and beginning to sweep around the sides, with some riders even heading for the narrow eastern flank.

And then, in near unison, the cannons were fired.

Ritter Von Thiel, the bombardier, had wasted no time in asserting his skill. He'd immediately gone to the cannon. He carried the kind of authority—as well as having unlimbered a small cannon from his pack horse, that said "I know guns." Despite his having no words of Valahian, and only four of Hungarian, two of which were unfit for a soldier of Christ, Vlad saw that he was getting the men to adjust things slightly. Vlad left him to it, and went about bracing his men. Their survival would depend on cool heads. They were outnumbered... Vlad judged by something like five to one, even including the knights and the few hundred Hawk clan Mongol. But his men were still remarkably calm. He realized, with terrible responsibility, that they believed in him. That they had somehow deluded themselves that he was a great military leader. The only nervous ones were the Székelers, which his men seemed to find very funny.

The charge began, and Vlad found himself at one with the Székelers. But he could not let it show. Mirko and his arquebusiers, and the cannoneers all waited on his word. It would be cannon, arquebus, rank one, rank two and then rank three. Hopefully then it would be cannon again, possibly with some relief granted by the cavalry. They had concentrated their forces on the foes that faced them, even repositioning two of the cannon.

Arrows began to pepper down on the canvas screens, punching through them and into the faggots, as the men waited for his signal. He watched as their death began to gallop towards them. The squat, blue-pockmarked faced knight coughed. And said "cannon."

It stopped the almost-trance that he had been in. "Fire," he said.

The noise and smoke were enough to have Vlad fighting for control of his mount.

Mirko may have given the order to fire to the first rank of arquebusiers. Vlad did not know. This was the first field test of the Smerek cannons—they'd been fired before, and the crews manning them had each done so... but never en masse and in a relatively confined space.

The crews looked as stunned as he was.

The arquebusiers were, however, loosing off at Mirko's signal. And the Knight of the Holy Trinity was prodding the gun crews back into action. In control of his horse now, Vlad looked out at the field of battle.

Gone were the ordered companies. Instead it was all chaos and blood.

"That prince has nerves of steel," said Manfred, when the cannon finally roared. "I thought he must be in collusion with them."

"I was about to call the charge myself," admitted Erik.

"Now?"

Erik nodded. "It'll take a while to get the cannon ready again." He shook his head. Looked at the little wagon-fort. "I thought it looked like a stupid idea."

Manfred raised his lance. "It is. Unless you are stupid enough to run headlong at it. But there are always plenty of military fools. Sound the charge."

"A quick in and out, eh, Prince Manfred," said Falkenberg, raising the horn.

Manfred nodded. "Hit them while they're confused. And then let's hope they want to try again, rather than attack us."

Gatu's forces were indeed confused. And badly mauled. This had seemed an easy, quick victory, one they had been in a hurry to achieve before any relief arrived. They'd expected the defense of desperate merchants and of a vastly outnumbered small group. Cannon . . . belonged in castles and fortresses. Not here on the plains. They were relatively unfamiliar with them anyway.

So: The last thing they expected was cannon and then massed fire, and then, finally a disciplined charge. The knights smashed through and rode over the resistance, the tightly packed and totally panicked nature of Gatu's troops taking away their advantages of mobility. It was horrid carnage, and largely one-sided too. And Erik, too, learned something about the use of combined forces that he would keep in mind for the future. The Mongol horse-archers were ideal for covering the retreat.

Manfred had sounded that, just when it seemed they had routed the enemy. Erik had to smile. The prince had learned from Corfu, and listened to the description of the favored Mongol tactic. "Flee and let

your foes over-extend. Turn and cut at their flanks."
Not this time. Soon they were back behind the lee of
the little wagon fortress. And the cannon, in a more
ragged volley this time, fired again.

"Now what, Manfred, gentlemen?" asked Erik, as
the knights marshaled again.

"They won't try a frontal attack again," said Von
Gherens. "That has cost them dearly."

Falkenberg snorted. "Never underestimate the
stupidity of some commanders."

As it turned out Falkenberg was right. They did try
again, before attempting a wide flanking movement.

Inside the wagon fortification, Vlad also could not
believe that they would attempt to charge again. Looking out on the field of battle, still full of the dying...
the horses had had the worst of it, it would seem.
Or perhaps no one would drag an injured horse off.
And yet, here they came again. Now, there was no
thought of bypassing the fortress to attack the men
on the far side. No, they flung their arrows and then
themselves at the wagons—concentrating their attack
on one side, meaning that they had less cannon-fire to
face. They came on, and on. And died, in the grave
ditch and up against the pikes.

And still kept coming. Until, this time, the knights
and Hawk clan Mongol came around both sides of
the fortification. Vlad's hard-pressed men, under the
instruction of the bombardier carried a cannon from
one side of the square enclosure to the other, and,
using a dead horse as a rest, fired over the top of the
ramparts, up in an arcing shot, and into the press of
men beyond the actual fighting. That again caused a

rout. What had begun as a totally one-sided conflict, in terms of numbers, was not that any more.

Vlad watched as they regrouped, plainly at a range where they felt safe. The squat bombardier was of another opinion, and wanted them to share that opinion. He had, by hand-signs and yelling, got one of the Smerek guns positioned on an earth mound so its barrel was at a steep angle. And he had one of the few solid balls that the Smereks had provided Vlad with. And what looked like a touch too much powder to both Vlad and the gunners. Maybe it did to the knight too. He made them all back off and take shelter when he lit the touch hole.

Vlad watched. The shot actually grazed the far edge of the massed troops. In terms of damage it was probably the least effective shot they fired that day. But it scattered the forces that had been being marshaled.

"If they get any farther away they'll lose sight of us, Prince," said the bombardier. "You have very good guns and terrible gunners. Have they never fired a cannon before?"

"Once. In practice," admitted Vlad.

The man slapped his thighs, laughed and shook his head. "They'll need a lot more practice."

Vlad nodded. "I had not realized . . . I did not know how effective they would be. My gunsmith wanted us to have them. I thought they would be good against fortifications . . . I thought they might impress the Golden Horde."

"Oh they're impressed, all right," said bombardier. "I don't think they want to come back. Their commanders are having a hard time persuading them, right now. They'll probably try to attack Prince Manfred and the Mongols with him, avoiding you next. We need to elevate some of the guns and get a bit of range. The prince and knights can stay close and we can keep the Mongol out of bowshot. If they want to close with them, they'll have to come in range of the arquebusiers and grape-shot."

"Who is Prince Manfred?"

The bombardier looked at him as if he were missing his wits. But nonetheless he explained. "The son of the duke of Brittany. The Holy Roman Emperor is his uncle. We were his escort to Jerusalem."

Vlad had struggled with concepts of distance and geography, probably because he'd been confined so long. But one thing he was sure of: this was not the usual route between the Holy Roman Empire and Jerusalem.

The bombardier proved correct. The Mongols took a wide arc, before coming riding in from the northwest. And now they were spread in a wide skirmish-line to allow for less massed targets. "Now it comes down to fighting, man to man," said Vlad. "I have twenty good men. I think when the conflict gets closer, we will go to the aid of our allies."

The bombardier grinned. "Just don't let them use you as a shield from your own guns. I'd be wary. I think there are more problems coming."

"For us?"

"Now that's a hard question, Your Highness. But I saw signs of large numbers of horses out there earlier, and I don't now. Means someone is resting them for action, probably."

"We passed I would say a thousand men. Well, ten companies of Hawk clan Mongols back there."

"Could be. It would equal the odds very nicely if

it was. But I've been a Knight of the Holy Trinity for twenty-three years, mostly up on the Swedish borderland, and if I have learned anything it's that you never gamble in conflict, Your Highness, pardon my saying so. You know who is there when you see them. Until then, expect the worst and prepare for it. I like this idea, with the carts and the wagons. But what of some good oaken boards? Instead of the canvas."

"If we survive this, I intend to make some improvements. The wagons are better than the carts. And we need better ways of moving the cannon around— Look. They're rushing."

"And our men are proving the superiority of column over line."

That was indeed the case. In order to avoid the murderous fire from the wagon and cart fort, the Mongol attackers had spread out into a long skirmish line.... Which the knights with their superior weight and reach of their lances, had simply ridden straight through, cutting the line in several places, taking Hawk clan Mongols through with them. "They're going to herd them in to the guns. You'll want to range them carefully."

And then there was the sound of horns to the north and east. They could see the dust, now.

"They circled," said Primor Peter. "Typical Mongol trick."

The effect of the horn-calls and distant war-drums on the attack was as catastrophic as the cannon fire.

The attack, already in trouble, became an exercise in rapid departure.

"Let's help them along," said Vlad to the primor. So they sortieed, although, frankly it was an unnecessary exercise. And then ... it wasn't. The foemen turned again—trying to flee west. For a brief while it was hot and heavy fighting against men who wanted to be elsewhere, and were not prepared to let the twenty Székelers with Vlad stop them. Vlad was glad when they were joined by a number of Knights of the Holy Trinity. They and the knights were content to let the Mongols flee. The Hawk clan were not.

And riding across the field came the reason the flight had turned to a chaotic rout. More Hawk clan warriors, some joining their fellows in hunting down the invaders. Some coming closer. Vlad stood his ground. A ground littered with the corpses of those who had fallen during the initial two assaults on cannon, carts and wagons.

He was surprised to recognize the lead horseman as the man who had ridden over to tell them to leave. The warrior pulled his horse to halt. "Are these your women or children?" asked Vlad grimly, pointing at the dead and dying on the field of carnage.

The Hawk officer blinked. Plainly recognized him. That was hardly surprising. Vlad had realized that he did not look like many others. "No . . . these are the Gatu Orkhan's men."

"Oh. They were so easy to kill, we thought they might be women and children," said Vlad dismissively.

The Mongol looked at the body-strewn field. And shut his mouth, which had hung open like a cave-maw. He shook his head. And then said humbly, "The Hawk clan is in your debt, foreigner. I spoke without knowing."

"We had some help from your clansmen," said Vlad. "They are chasing what's left of Gatu Orkhan's men."

"We had heard . . . the young khan was here. And the princess Bortai."

Chapter 60

Bortai had been among the first to work out what the Mingghan of Hawk warriors that came to their aid was doing. They surely realized that Gatu had at least three or four thousand men to thus venture into Hawk territory. They—from what the the two Jahguns had said, knew that they were outnumbered, mustering barely a full Mingghan—a thousand men. Yet they could not desert her and Kildai. So they had sent a few men and horses to use General Subatai's trick. Harnessing horses to logs to make dust. Sounding horns and drums where they were not. That was what gave it away to her. No Mongol general would betray an attack until it was too late. Creating the impression that they were a far larger host and coming from exactly where they had not seemed to be. It was a masterful stroke. She'd told Tulkun. And one of the knights. He'd looked puzzled and steered her toward Erik.

It did separate her from her brother. She was less worried than she had been. A handful of the the Jahgun had been determined to become the part of the young Khan's Khesig, his imperial guard. And what better way than to surround him and fight bravely? He had a guard of at least twenty. He would just have to cope without her. And she'd told them that if they ran off after Gatu's men, they would wish they were dead.

She saw Erik. And then saw that some of the Gatu Orkhan's men were making a last effort to leave the field with some honor. Or at least with her.

It was a mess, thought Erik. And this was always when things went wrong, when people got killed. When they thought it was all over. He was keeping close to Manfred for that reason. And then he saw Bortai riding toward them, alone, and straight into trouble.

There were four of Gatu's men, and there was at least seventy yards between her and the knights. Erik put his spurs to his horse, and Manfred was right beside him. Von Gherens was just behind them. But Erik knew they could never get there in time. His heart knew the agony of remembering the same situation with Svanhild's death.

Only...this was Bortai, not Svan. She was not going to wait to be rescued. The first of the four got an arrow through his chest. The second barely missed being slashed out of the saddle with her knife stroke. She'd dropped the bow, and had a blade in her hand. She didn't kill him, but his right arm was gashed to the bone. And the third, taking no chances and using his lance, got the thrown knife through his throat.

That left one man, who suddenly realized this fact. He swung his sword in a vicious arc that would have— with the pace of his pony—probably decapitated her... If she'd been in the way. She wasn't. She'd dropped over the side of her horse, and the blade scythed above her. The fellow suddenly realized that three knights' lance points were heading straight for him, and attempted to turn, to flee... to find Bortai had beaten him to the turn and was just behind him. She used her momentum and his weight to cartwheel him out of the saddle, under the galloping hooves of the advancing horses. The knights lifted their lances. And she smiled sweetly at them and waved. Dismounted to recover her knife and bow.

"This is why I disapprove of women in combat," said Von Gherens.

Manfred guffawed. "Ten more like her and there wouldn't be any combat. No wonder she laughs at you, Erik."

A little while later—the knights massed again—they rode across to the cart and wagon encampment. The Duke of Valahia came out to meet them.

"So, Your Highness, what brings you out here on to the lands of the Golden Horde?" said Manfred, conversationally, after formal introductions had been made.

"Well, I am at war with King Emeric of Hungary," explained the tall, pale-skinned man. "I have raised a small army, mostly of Valahian peasantry. I came to buy horses for my army."

There was a rather stunned silence. "Er. Don't you have a quartermaster-general to do that?" asked Eberhard, probably the most skilled at filling in gaps.

The Duke of Valahia smiled diffidently. "I probably ought to have one. Making war is a new profession for me."

Manfred looked at the killing field. Men were out dealing with the wounded, and looting. Putting down horses that were too injured. "God help King Emeric if this is what you do while you're still new to it. Shall we find a place away from this carnage to have a stoup of wine, and talk? Emeric of Hungary is no friend of ours."

Vlad nodded. "I too would like to know what the Knights of the Holy Trinity are doing here in the lands of the Golden Horde?"

Manfred laughed. "It's a long story. And a dry one, like all long stories."

Vlad was torn between suspicion of people who wished to befuddle him with drink, and a desire to get to know these knights, and their prince. The signs of piety and yet skill in warfare appealed to him. Well, he had found that alcohol had little or no effect on him. If they hoped to dull his senses with it they were in for a shock. "Come into the enclosure," he said. "We have had very few losses in there. It was much more effective than I had hoped. The cannon too were very much more deadly than we expected. As I said, I am still learning..." his voice trailed off. "Although such death must grieve any Christian's soul."

Several of the knights nodded.

Vlad found that encouraging, despite his own strange, suppressed desire to walk among the dead and dying. He was morbidly fascinated by it.

They sat and talked. Vlad's quartermaster had only some beer to offer, but the knights provided a small cask of wine. Feeling he needed some support, Vlad asked the Székely primor to join him. "I speak very little Frankish, Drac. Just what I learned from the whores in the tail of Emeric's army when I served on the western border. Not suitable for high company."

"I need you. Even if you say nothing." He wondered again, for the thousandth time, just where Rosa had got to.

The Székeler shook his head and smiled. "No, Drac. We need you. I think you can count on the support not just of me and the people of Ghîmes, but the Székely. You have what we need. Honor, courage and fairness. Those are rare attributes in princes, and the Székely will follow one that has all of them. But if you want me, I will be there. Besides, I like a goblet or two of wine."

After a while, Vlad had lost his earlier caution and merely enjoyed talking to people whose world was wider than his, and who, it would seem, knew much of what he needed to learn. And they felt . . . wholesome.

The talk went on deep into the night, only interrupted by a respectful Hawk clan officer who came to ask if the envoys and traders needed anything. "I think we need to clarify your status a bit," said Manfred.

Vlad smiled. "We will need to trade with them, if we are to fight Hungary. It will make trading easier."

That brought laughter. "It'll put them off raiding other traders, that's for sure."

That night, after the talking had finally broken into yawning, and the men had retreated to bed, Vlad pondered what he had learned. The world was a bigger and more complex place than he'd known. And there were, he decided, forces of good and evil in it. He liked to think he was part of the good. But he still wondered.

Here, on the edge of Hungary, dependent in many ways on it, he was in a poor position to ally with the Holy Roman Empire. Yet... they seemed—to judge by this small sample—a people he would want to ally with.

"He's a lost cause," said Manfred, cheerfully. "No allies, no money, no officers, no powerful friends, except this countess... I think I should conclude an alliance with the fellow on my uncle's behalf. Besides the fact I like him, it'll infuriate Eberhard."

"When it comes to fighting your way up from nothing with nothing... he has proved he's far from a lost cause. But he really does have huge holes in his knowledge of the world. Being confined and isolated like that for all those years has shaped him in some odd and unpredictable ways," said Erik.

"And kept him from learning a lot of things which he'd just have to unlearn. Look, we're trapped, for now, in this part of the Golden Horde territory. Let's take him in hand, Erik. He can, at the very least, be a thorn in Emeric of Hungary's side, and keep the man busy rather than interfering with our affairs."

Erik nodded. "Those are good troops he has, especially when you consider they were peasant volunteers six months ago. Well disciplined, and willing to die for him, I reckon. And the light cavalry, the Székelers, are not bad either. Not as good as the Mongols, but on a par with the Croats."

"And like any elite, they resent the fact that Emeric has passed them over for his Croats. I gather the Croats will take pay in money, and the Székely want it in less tangible things. They're hardened with constant attrition by the Mongol clans."

"The Mongols are better, though. And they out-number them. How come they haven't pushed into Hungary?"

"From what I can gather, two reasons. One, the terrain. They don't like mountains, they don't like forests, they like open plains, and their way of life is shaped to that. There are also a lot of fortified buildings up there, things it would be hard for them to take. And second, since the time of their 'Great Khan' Ulaghchi... they've been through a number of periods of civil war, with no strong leadership. Ulaghchi pushed east and north, recapturing lost territory, pushing further. Much of that land was lost again to Lithuania and Jagiellon."

"And Eberhard ferreted out something else about this Khan Ulaghchi. Apparently he was a rabid traditionalist—you remember that hamlet next to the river being literally the only settlement we'd seen? He issued an edict against settled dwellings. Said they made people corrupt and soft. Didn't approve of gunpowder much either."

"He could be right," said Erik, with a chuckle. "No inns and no wine—think how tough you'd be."

"Yeah. And how miserable. But as the old windbag pointed out, it means that they have no real manufacturing base either. If you can't make it from a sheep or a horse, you have to take it from your foes."

"Or buy it. People in towns buy sheep. And I need some sleep before morning. I have a feeling that tomorrow is going to be even more complicated."

Nothing, thought Bortai, was ever completely simple. Yes, they had managed to get home to the clan. Yes, they had handed the forces of Gatu Orkhan a lesson, and a defeat that would have other clans steer clear of

Hawk lands, and conflict with the Hawk clan, for many years. It was a defeat that had been inflicted, largely, by a force a quarter of the size of Gatu Orkhan's. Moreover, they had taken very few casualties, and inflicted vast numbers of deaths and maiming among the enemy.

And now some of the Hawk clan were saying that they should seize the cannon from the trader who had aided them. They were pressing her, as they could not press Kildai. He had ridden off with his "Khesig" to "do things he had to do."

She was not sure quite where Kildai had got to.

But it had been somewhere in the direction of the wagon-cart fortress.

David could have told her. At least, once he had got over the disorientation of being woken up after very little sleep after one of the most exhausting days of his life, he could have. The guards on the rough encampment of the knights had recognized and admitted Kildai. They'd had been polite but firm about Kildai's escorts. Kildai had been relieved. He did not want them listening in. Nor was he too keen on them seeing David. He had a feeling that it might be useful if the two of them wanted to get away...

Before the kurultai...before his uncle's death, Kildai had been happy. He had had no real responsibilities. He'd been the nephew of the orkhan, and the great grandson of the Great Khan. He did not remember clearly, as Bortai did, when their father had been orkhan. In the months leading up to kurultai...he'd been aware that he was being pushed forward as the Hawk clan's claim to rule the Horde. But he had not really believed in any of it. It wasn't actually going to happen.

Then had come the accident... If it was an accident. He suspected sorcery still, even if no one but David seemed to believe him. That had suddenly made him aware of a whole lot of the realities he had not known about before. Now...it seemed that the clan itself thought that somehow...He was the khan. To them anyway.

And they were asking him to decide on things he'd never even thought about. He could ask Bortai... but...but...he had spent the last few years rebelling against that. And it would be, in terms of his authority, a mistake. He knew that much.

So instead he turned to someone he could trust. Someone who knew a little more of politics and the world than he did. Someone brave enough to not carry a sword into combat so that he could keep Kildai upright.

David blinked. "How would I know?"

Kildai hoped his face did not betray his disappointment. But of course it did. David laughed. "You wake me up and ask me what to do about the trader. What trader, you idiot?"

David knew, by now, just what high company he'd been mixing with. But the habits of the last few weeks of near constant contact and amicable bickering, when he hadn't known it, died hard. And his brain was still fuzzy with sleep. The idiot part had come naturally. What he didn't expect was Kildai to grab him...not to wrestle him or cut his throat for such disrespect, but to hug him. "They expect me to know everything," said Kildai, in a distinctly watery voice.

"Ach, so what do they know?" said David roughly. "So tell me. Who is this trader?"

"The man with the cannons. He is with some Székeler guards. The clan do not like the Székely. The commander of the Mingghan says we must take the cannons."

David covered his eyes. "Is one war not enough? That's not a trader, Kildai. No trader has a whole lot of cannons. That is the Khan of Valahia. He said so to the knights. I heard him. And they believe him. Wait. I'll ask *Ritter* Von Stael—"

"No," Kildai said, warily.

"He's a good sort, Kildai. He made me his squire." David was still incredulous about this.

"I need... No one must know. But I need to ask you. So: he is a khan, really? And the Székely? The officer of the Mingghan has something against them. But some of my Khesig say that he tried to raid one of their forts... I don't know. They say he said he came to buy horses."

So David spent the next half an hour solving the problems of the young khan. Mostly he solved them the best way he knew, by the logic of the back streets of Jerusalem, and with a bit of common sense. Often Kildai seemed to have that, too. He just needed a bit of reassurance.

"If you're worried, just tell them that you need to think about it. And that only a fool makes big decisions in a hurry. Von Stael said that to me today. Then you can ask me." David did not add, "and then I'll ask your sister," although he thought it, and wondered just how he could manage to do that.

Kildai nodded. "Yes. Now I will go back. The Khesig will be worried. And I need to step in and stop anything more happening tonight. You are right."

❀   ❀   ❀

Bortai was a worried woman. She'd already quietly asked three men to go and find Kildai and get him here. She felt, in her core, that the trader should be left alone. They'd fought together, as brothers of necessity, against Gatu's troops. She had some support from the commanders of the Jaghuns that had accompanied them over the Iret—although they too were tempted. The Mingghan that had arrived later... well, they felt that it would be a rich booty, and too valuable in the war that was coming. Yes, the traders had aided the young khan, and they deserved some mercy. Well, most of them felt that way. The commander of one of the Jaghuns felt they should leave them alone. That he was mad, and should be avoided in case it was a sickness that spread. But his and Bortai's voices were the only openly dissenting ones, and it was only the respect that she commanded, and that her father had commanded that had held matters in check for this long.

Then Kildai entered, accompanied by a close guard of those who had elected themselves his Khesig.

The question was respectfully put to him. Bortai's heart sank. Protocol demanded that she could not speak to him first. And he was a boy of fourteen. A good rider, but what did he know, really, of such things? He would let the officers lead him.

Kildai took his time in answering. Sat down. Looked thoughtful. She knew him. He was play-acting the part. She'd seen him do it...

"Only a fool," he said calmly, "starts a second war, before he has won the first."

That was accepted as wisdom, which, indeed, Bortai thought it was, from him. It made sense, and was an

argument she might have used. It just didn't sound
like something he'd have come up with on his own.

Kildai continued. "And only a fool does not scout
his enemy's position and know whom he is attacking,
before he presses the attack."

"What do you mean, young Khan," said the commander of the Mingghan, a little patronizingly.

That was a mistake with Kildai. He pointed at the
the commander. "I mean your counsel nearly led us into
another war. He is not a trader. Those of us who saw
him in war, know that. Those who arrived later, did not."

It was a cutting comment, a little unfair. But . . .

"But he had trade flags. He said he wished to buy
horses," said the officer who had been insistent that
he was mad.

"I say again," said Kildai. "He is no trader. Your
scouting is not good enough."

"Who is he then, young Khan? A spy. A conqueror
with two hundred men?" That was said a little sarcasti-
cally by the commander of the Mingghan.

Kildai shook his head. "He is the khan from over
the mountains. He told us so. And I have been making sure. My scouting is careful."

The trader, well, not a trader, according to Kildai,
had spoken in Frankish when he had ridden up to
them. But she'd only understood part of it. The part
about an alliance of convenience. But how had Kildai
understood more? And then it came to her, and she
understood just where he had been. The horseboy.
Well. So far the little devil's advice had been good.
She must talk to the orkhan Erik about this. She
would need to say a few things that boy, and also to
have an eye kept on him.

"But then . . . what does he want here? He said he wanted to buy horses."

"Probably exactly what he says. Horses."

"But we do not sell our horses . . . some old ones, bad animals maybe. But a khan would want the finest . . ."

"We don't know. Maybe he wants to give them to the Székelers," said Bortai, which provoked a fair amount of laughter.

"Anyway," said Kildai. "Who said anything about selling him *our* horses?"

The entire audience was stilled. "We'll sell him our enemies' horses. We may even give him some for free."

That provoked uproar. Horses were the measure of wealth. Kildai held up his hand for silence and it came, reluctantly. "Gatu Orkhan has gold. And wars cost that. We will need gold, which we can't take from Gatu, easily. But this day we have taken at least two thousand horses. Let us exchange them for gold, if this khan has it. We'll keep the best ones, of course."

Bortai was sure now that David had fed him this. She'd listened to him talking to Kildai. He seemed to know a great deal about the value of horses. But she found herself in agreement with him on one thing. There was no point in starting a second war. Instead they must use this so-called Khan to win this one.

Vlad was greeted the next morning by a respectful messenger from "the young khan." Could they meet?

He took the Primor Peter with him. They were escorted to a small encampment away from the field of battle. He was surprised to see that they really meant "the young khan." The boy looked as if he was in his teens. They were introduced, also to several of the other Mongols, some of whom were definitely the military commanders. The introduction seemed to provide the young boy with a fair amount of satisfaction. "My people told me that you were a trader. Wishing to buy horses. Not a prince," translated one of the men.

"I am a prince fighting a war. I need horses." This too was translated.

"So you were scouting to raid," said one of the older men, sardonically. At least, if the translation was faithful it was darkly said.

Vlad stared him down. "It is beneath my honor to steal. I told your men. I wish to buy horses."

Vlad did not allow his gaze to waver, as this too was translated. The officer did not seem pleased. But it made an impact. Vlad was not too sure it was a positive one. But the boy nodded. Said something to one of the men. The Székely Primor gaped. "He is giving you horses."

The translator explained. "The young khan has ordered that you be given your share of the battle-spoils. Fifty horses. The young Khan wants to know: for what do you want the horses?"

Vlad explained. The translator guffawed. Slapped his knees. And translated with difficulty. The other Mongols found it equally funny.

Eventually the question was asked "So, you do not want our fastest and best then, for the earth diggers, the eaters of vegetables?"

"No. Good sound placid animals. Not warhorses. And I wouldn't mind buying some sheep too." Vlad was a little prickly. True, his men were mostly peasants or poor freemen. But their cannon and arquebuses had brought down enough horse-riding Mongol light cavalry yesterday. More than the Hawk clan Mongols had. But if they wanted to deceive themselves, well, maybe it was best that they did. As long as they sold him horses. And some sheep. It appeared they were willing to do that. Selling "good" horses ... spirited warhorses, or parting with them in any other way but by brute force, was sheer foolishness. They could be used against them. But to sell the slow, solid slugs to men who could not ride ... well if the khan from mountains was stupid enough ... And sheep. Sheep were plentiful and cheap. The Mongols were chortling with glee, when he started talking gold. And then they were eager to discuss future business.

They parted with mutual goodwill, each, it appeared, having got what they wanted. It was rather pleasant.

Outside, Vlad was surprised to see the officer who had told him they did not sell horses. The man bowed, warily. It appeared that at least one of the Mongols had decided that he did not wish to fight Vlad. "Khan. My brother was with the Jahgun that escorted the Lady Bortai and the young Khan. He says you are terrible in battle. You saved some of their lives. I spoke foolishly before. But I spoke for you last night."

Vlad could honestly not remember much of the the sortie that had turned ugly. He hoped the man did not mean "terrible" as in "not good." "We all say things we don't mean. I promise this. I do not harm women and children. In fact, if they need it, we will provide shelter and protection during the war."

The fellow seemed even more taken aback.

Chapter 61

"You are our honored guests," said Bortai. "Most of the clan are back against the edge of the mountains and in the forest. You understand. Things looked bad for the clan. Now they are much better."

Erik wondered how they were so much better. Yes, with Vlad's cannon and arquebusiers, they had given a part of Gatu's army a bloody nose. But Erik had established that that was really quite a tiny army by Mongol standards. The country was fertile, it was covered in flocks and herds. Every man was a light-cavalry man. Apparently armies of forty or fifty thousand had fought over it in the past. And it looked like they were heading into more such internecine warfare. But he thanked her, politely. Manfred had said that he ought to be polite to a girl who could take on four warriors and win. That or start running. Manfred was forever making that sort of joke. Erik had just come from another meeting with Vlad. It appeared that he, too, was eager to have them in his demesnes. He had been devastatingly honest about that, and the size of his army. It was something that would have horrified most dukes, and Erik found refreshing. "Our real desire is to return to Illyria," Erik said, smiling.

"That may take a little while," said Bortai seriously. "Of course, we will do all we can to make it possible. But it may take well into next spring..."

Erik wondered if she was merely optimistic, uniformed or just being kind. Civil wars could drag out for years. Still, she was just a soldier's daughter, even if he'd plainly taught her more about combat than most warriors. What would she know about civil war?

"If we are your guests—at least until we can return to Illyria, do you think it would be acceptable to have some of the knights accompany Prince Vlad back to his men at Ghîmes? It is just a small mountain village, on your border I believe. We have been talking about training some of his men."

She blinked. "Why?"

Erik struggled to explain in the limited vocabulary he had. He was getting better at the language, but he still had extreme limits on what he could say. And he found he put in Frankish words when he lacked Mongol. He wondered quite what she understood. "Our clans are on the other side of the Khan Emeric."

She scowled. "He tried to invade the lands around Irongate in my father's time."

"We have the same problem with Emeric. Prince Vlad is at war with him. The enemy of my enemy is worth helping."

"Not always. Sometimes the enemy of your enemy is worse. Best if they both fight for a long time and weaken each other."

That was remarkably astute if rather cynical for a mere soldier's daughter. "In this case the prince is weak already. We would help him to become a little stronger. That way he could fight harder."

The dimple appeared. "Yes. He wants to put the eaters of vegetables on horseback. He asks for horses that have no fire, because they will fall off ones that do have spirit and speed." This reduced her to giggles and then outright chortles.

"Well. You can see that he does need our help," said Erik, grinning.

Bortai, her shoulders shaking, agreed. "It will take a little time before the clans will agree to a new kurultai. I hope before spring. But first there will be winter. Probably a time of raids and much politicking. Gatu may try again. With force, this time. But that is too close to Mink lands for us to keep our guests as safe as we'd like. There are Székeler fortified villages farther south. Arrange to meet him there."

"Then you do not think the Hawk clan will raise any objection to it?"

Bortai dimpled again. "I think the young khan will be happy to have you there. I will need to speak to your horseboy."

"Oh, he has gone up in the world, Bortai. He is a squire now. Von Stael seems to have tamed him. It's odd. That knight is a big serious fellow, not too clever, who spends more time on his knees than most. And yet he has the horseboy following him like a puppy."

He was, for a foreigner, very polite. Not asking directly for Bortai to influence Kildai—not that Kildai did not know, too, of the debt they owed to this man and to his prince. She liked him. It was the way he treated her like a respected equal—except that she

MUCH FALL OF BLOOD 609

had had to prove her skills at arms...he *did* accept that now. She still needed to teach him a few things about respect for her wrestling skills. If he was a Mongol, she would ask him if he had any horses to wager. She blushed slightly. She could almost be tempted to fight to lose.

It was almost as if he didn't know who she was. Then a shocking, hilarious thought occurred to her. Maybe he really *didn't* know who she was. After all, she'd been mistaken about who Prince Manfred was—and he had dressed as a noble. The idea was crazy enough to make her smile. And the puzzled look on his face, enough to send her off into helpless laughter. Really. The tricks of the tengeri!

"Did I say something wrong again?" he said warily.

"No," she said, trying to keep a straight face. "I will ask one of the officers to convey you word from the young khan." This was just too amusing a game to avoid. It was a practical joke that would delight the clans for years. Of course half of them would have to be in on it. And the story would soon spread to the other half. If only she could keep a straight face. But he thought that she laughed a lot anyway.

"We need to stay on good terms with the Mongols of Hawk clan. I've just had a message from their young khan saying that they would find it acceptable for us to base ourselves at an encampment of theirs near the Székely fortress at Berek. It would be possible to organize some training together." Manfred coughed. "It's a little awkward, as I gather from you that the Székely at Ghîmes are supporting you...."

Vlad nodded. "I wish to move south this winter

anyway. And Prince Manfred. I have a lot that I wish to learn. Let me ask the primor."

The scarred captain nodded. His Frankish was limited, but he understood more than he was willing to speak. "Berek is cousin," he said tapping his chest. "Székely declare for Drac, anyway."

Vlad looked earnest and addressed the man in Hungarian. After a while he said. "It will probably be possible, Prince Manfred. Primor Peter says the Székely will decide to support me. I don't know. But if it doesn't happen, I could send a messenger to the young khan. They have already arranged that we will be in contact. I suspect they found us very profitable to trade with. It's not really something I know very much about."

Manfred grinned and slapped him on the back. "You say that about everything. And then show us just how successful you can be at it."

Vlad looked startled. And then smiled shyly. As if he had never had a physical sign of camaraderie before, thought Manfred. "I really don't know very much about anything, Prince Manfred."

"Call me Manfred. We're equals, I suppose. We've fought together. And Erik never calls me anything else."

"Except 'idiot,'" said Erik. "Strictly speaking, the Althing of Iceland recognizes no titles outside of the League of Armagh. So if I call him 'Prince' I am committing a crime. Or I would be back home. I am oath-sworn to the *Godar* Hohenstauffen to defend and train him in his *vanderjare*. You must understand, it is not the relationship of a prince and his retainer, and I owe no loyalty to the Empire or deference to his title. Only loyalty to the *Godar* Hohenstauffen, in repayment of an old family oath. It has made me old before my time, but he is growing up quite well."

Ah. So Erik had noticed, too, and was making an effort to make the Valahian prince feel more accepted. "It is not easy," said Manfred, "to find someone who will call you by your first name, who wants nothing from you, and will occasionally beat you."

"I was beaten," said Vlad, his voice flat. "Emeric had his torturer beat me. Several times. When I first was taken to Buda when I was ten. They chained me and beat me. On the king's instruction, so I would learn who my master was. Then I was taken to watch the impalement. The king had them bring a stake and place it here." He touched the seat of his pants. "He said that that was what waited for me, if I forgot. Another time he had his men hold me above the pike. I was scared and started to struggle. Emeric said it would be good if I made them lose their grip on me, as I would impale myself. I . . . I had to hold very still. I was young and very afraid."

Manfred and Erik were both silenced. Eventually Manfred said, "I think it is time that someone pulled Emeric off the throne and onto one of his own pikes. Erik did not do that to me, Prince Vlad. He wrestled with me, and drilled with me, and fenced with me. That was the kind of punishment he inflicted on me. He taught me how to be my own master."

The pale face was motionless as if Vlad was wrestling with some inner demon. And then he smiled. "Call me Vlad . . . Manfred. And *Ritter* Erik, I would be grateful if you would fence with me sometime. I have never learned to wrestle."

Erik nodded. And reached out to squeeze the

man's shoulder. Manfred knew Erik well enough to
know how atypical that gesture was. "I'll fence with
you and even teach you the basics of wrestling, with
pleasure, Prince Vlad. It's a skill that is sometimes
useful in combat. It is a major winter pastime among
the people of Iceland, where I come from. I am
Erikur Hakkonsen. Mostly the Franks call me Erik.
I will stand your friend if you need to pull Emeric
down. I owe him for the death of Svanhild anyway.
His war caused that."

"Me, too," said Manfred.

Manfred saw Vlad swallow. Then he nodded, and
put out a hand. "I have a need of friends, Erikur.
Manfred. I... I was very alone."

"Well, you are part of an odd brotherhood now.
We will have time to wrestle a bit, eh?" said Erik,
obviously acutely uncomfortable, shaking the hand
that was extended to him.

Vlad and his men and their wagons and carts left
the same day, accompanied by an escort of Mongols
and a herd of horses. Sheep and more horses would
follow, in a few days.

Manfred and Erik had gone to say farewell. The
knights had paraded and saluted him, something
which—by the enormous smile, had delighted Vlad.
Manfred reflected that he had probably seen a hundred guards of honor. Vlad probably had not seen
one before.

Vlad and his men had followed the most direct
route—now that they had guides, and stopped at
encampments that they must have passed—all hidden

in folds of the landscape and bits of the old forest. Plainly the Hawk clan had been keeping a low profile, but if alcohol—at least the alcohol you got from kumiss—had any effect on Vlad he could have got as drunk as many of his men did. The news they brought was welcomed by the Hawk clan camps. Usually with an eagerness to drink kumiss together. Fortunately Vlad could keep it down and be polite. And the relief and outright happiness at the news of their "Young Khan" having returned to the clan, and the defeat handed to the followers of the Gatu Orkhan, was infectious. It could have taken them a month to traverse what had taken them a week, quite easily, except that the Mongol escort plainly had orders, too.

The fortifications at Ghîmes were in sight when their escort of Mongols rode up and announced that they had to return to their regiments. And the sheep would be here within the week.

Vlad and the horses rode to the village to a rapturous welcome.

"Well, Primor. I see that you brought them back," said a smiling, elderly Székeler.

Primor Peter waved and gestured at Vlad. "No, Father. The Drac brought us back."

"Greetings Drac," called the oldster. "Your men believed you would be back. They think that you are immortal. We thought you were all dead, thought it would save on food for the winter," he continued cheerfully, showing that Primor Peter was not the only Székeler with a morbid sense of humor. "There are several fat burghers from the lower lands waiting to see you. We thought we might send them on after you."

Primor Peter paid his respects and left immediately

with four of the Horseheads from Vlad's expedition to
the eastern plains, for a meeting with the seat-captains
of the Székelers. "I will deliver them to you, Drac.
I have some stories to tell." he said. "It was a great
honor to have been there. I have stories to tell my
grandchildren of the day we defeated the Mongols
on their home ground."

Vlad went to see what the several fat burghers
wanted.

Some of them were quite substantial. And all the
representatives from the cities of Kölholm and Feketahegy were worried, afraid and desperately hoping
that Vlad would prove to be half the man that his
men and rumor had made him out to be.

His arrival with more than eight hundred horses and
a sea of tales of war and success against the feared
Mongols buoyed that hope.

The reason for their coming was rapidly told to
him. Emeric's Magyar and a regiment of Slovenes
had gone to Vajdahunyad, one of the towns that, all
of the men there assured him, was the most pro-
Hungary in the entire duchy, with a large expatriate
population of Poles and Germans. For no good reason
they had sacked the place. The king himself accused
it of being a nest of traitors, and of supporting the
pretender Vlad, instead of the true heir to Valahia,
Ban Alescu of Irongate. King Emeric's troops had had
a three-day raven which had destroyed half the city,
killed many of the citizens, and left their daughters
and wives raped.

The towns of Kölholm and Feketahegy had themselves had clashes with Ban Alescu. And—although
this was unspoken—Vlad might be a pretender, but

he wasn't a rabid weasel. And they were desperate
for protection against the same thing happening to
them. Their gates were closed, their walls manned.
But they knew they could not stand against the forces
that King Emeric could turn lose against them. So
they'd come to offer their cities' submission, fealty
and support... in the hope that the duke would in
turn deal with Emeric's troops. The fact that the cities and towns were reeling under new, heavier than
ever taxation, and open confiscation of assets, had
not helped Emeric's popularity with the third group
of burghers. Their town was full of billeted Croats,
and they wanted them out...

Vlad listened. He needed them. He also knew that
there were resources in the towns he was going to
need if he was to succeed against King Emeric. He
was grateful for the long lecture he'd had on the subject by the white-haired old man in Manfred's party.

"Yes. I will accept your submission and fealty. But
there are two things I will require of you."

They listened warily. "First, no more taxes paid to
Emeric. No succor nor sustenance for his troops."

They cheered that.

"And of course, instead, half that tax comes to
me. I will need it to defend the duchy. And do not
dream of cheating me. My men will tell you that I
am my grandfather reborn. Remember how he felt
about dishonesty? And how he punished that. I would
suggest you remember that, and explain it very carefully to your guildsmen. Oh. And I will also require
three large wagons and dray horses of each city of
over a thousand souls and a hundred men for my
armies for every thousand. Smaller towns will send

me levies proportional to their size. Now go and tell
your councils. Tell them what you have seen, and that
those are my terms."

Three days later two of the three returned, along
with representatives from another two towns, and three
boyars with whom the Ban of Irongate had conflicts.

The next day brought the last of the first three
back and yet another two smaller towns. And nearly
five hundred sheep. And the Primor Peter.

"How are things since I left, Drac?" asked the
captain of the Horseheads.

"I should go down to the plains to buy horses more
often. I leave and seven cities send their representatives
to make their submission to me," said Vlad, shaking
his head in amazement.

Primor Peter beamed. "And the Székely seats have
declared for you. They recognize you as the true Count
of Székely. Valahia rallies to you, Drac." He looked at
his little village. "And it all comes to Ghîmes!"

"It may not for too much longer, Primor," said
Vlad, with inherent truthfulness.

"Oh I know that, Drac," said the primor placidly.
"It's a small place. There are better passes. But it
was here that it began. People will remember that."

"They will also remember you, Primor Peter. I
think I will call you the father of the battle wagon."

Winter was settling fast on the mountains. Temperatures were barely ever over freezing during the day, and
snow lay on the ground in many places. This did not
stop Vlad. He moved his headquarters to Berek, and
the training and the preparation went on. The towns
that had declared for Vlad knew a rapid return on
their fortunes, as Vlad turned the money into casting

cannons—with the Smerek brothers supervising, and setting up a new factory for arquebuses—and supplies of equipment, and fodder and provender.

The knights, having little else to do, were drawn into training.

"I thought it a stupid idea. But this business of mounted infantry could just work in this terrain," admitted Falkenberg. "The infantry of his are still useless in a melee, but they can stand together and fire together. They're disciplined and better than most of the sweepings Emeric has for footmen. And they cover a lot of ground and get there relatively fresh. They carry a lot of ammunition and provender. Prince Vlad lacks heavy cavalry—he's got about thirty boyars and their loyalists—maybe a hundred heavy cavalry in all, and Emeric's Magyar will ride right over them. But the Székely make very good light cavalry, and there are a lot of them."

"And then there are those battle wagons of his," said Erik with a smile, knowing this would provoke a reaction from the rather conservative Falkenberg.

It did, but not the one Erik had been expecting. "I told him to put some spades in those wagons. A trench will stop a charge and an earth wall will stop bullets and arrows. Like the wagons. They won't stand siege, but they'll bring cannon to field warfare. He's going to put more cannon in those Székely fortifications too. They were built to stop the Mongols, but they'll work just as well against Emeric." He paused. "Or the Golden Horde if they decide to try the pickings across the border. Bombardier von Thiel is drilling the cannoneers."

"If I was Ban Alescu of Irongate, I'd consider the

value of my head, above my desire to claim a duke-dom," said Manfred, coming in. "And it's a good thing we've got drilling to do. We don't seem to making much of this diplomatic headway. Old Eberhard is busy enough talking to elderly generals, and we're being treated like royalty, but if it wasn't for Vlad, I'd be bored."

"The Hawk clan khan is still consulting some sha-man called Kaltegg," said Erik, who had had this from Bortai, yesterday afternoon. "No insult is intended. Anyway, the diplomatic stuff will only really start after they manage to have another kurultai and elect a new Khan."

Manfred put his helm down. "Bortai: the gospel according to." He turned to Erik. "Has your girlfriend infected all the other Mongol in the place? They only have to see you and they start grinning. How is she, by the way?"

"I wish you'd stop that, Manfred," said Erik, his ears glowing with the guilty knowledge that he'd gone to look for her only that morning. "She's away. They seem to be using her and Tulkun to spread the tale of Gatu Orkhan's perfidy. I suppose she has the common touch."

"And the drill sergeant's command of invective, and can take on four armed men and win. I'd run if I were you," said Manfred cheerfully. "Mind you, I don't know if it would help. She rides better than you do. I saw her on a blood mare that most princes would give their eye-teeth to own. I wonder where she got that?"

"She said she got it from a wager," said Erik. And then realized what he was being led into, and scowled.

Chapter 62

Kaltegg Shaman was a wizened old man with piercing blue eyes. Those eyes—very un-Mongol eyes, and his outspoken attitude, had been the principal reasons for his falling out of favor with the clan-heads, and particularly with their father and uncle. Bortai was more than a little nervous about going to see him.

They went through the appropriate rituals of greeting and gifting before business could be discussed.

"It is good that you have overcome your father's prejudices and come to see me, Khan Kildai, Princess. You will need a battle shaman soon. Much evil has been raised against you."

Bortai did not, or not directly anyway, want to point out that she was here more out of worry about her brother's health, than a desire to reinstate the shaman. But perhaps . . . they'd lost a powerful shaman back at the kurultai. "Kaltegg Shaman, the Parki Shaman said we should bring Kildai to you when his suns soul wandered in the lands of Erleg Khan. He is better now. But I thought it might be wise to consult you."

"You have your mother's wisdom. She was very angry

with your father over the decision to make Parki the clan shaman. He was a good man, my apprentice. But times like these we need more than good. Come. I need to examine your brother, and visit the worlds above and below to check on his souls."

Now that she thought about it, Bortai had been aware that her mother and father had not seen eye to eye on the subject of the shaman Kaltegg. Well, that did raise him in her estimation a little. Her father had been an excellent orkhan. But her mother, with her descent from Princess Khutulun, had had great status. And, as Bortai remembered, a lot more common sense than her father about social issues. Father had been rigid about tradition.

The shaman began his rituals and his dancing and drumming. And then went off into the spirit-worlds.

A little field mouse, striped and inquisitive, peered from the slumped man's shirt. Bortai found herself wanting to laugh during what was a very solemn rite.

At length the shaman surfaced again. "I have made you whole, Kildai Khan," he said. "You suffered a very powerful magical attack. Someone wanted you dead, young Khan. You will need some protections. I shall see to it."

"I told you I never fell!" exclaimed Kildai. "I was pushed off by a big hand."

The shaman nodded. "A hand from the north, young Khan."

He raised an eyebrow at Bortai. "It is acceptable to laugh at Kreediqui, my mouse. He does not mind. And he is very curious."

"I think," said Kildai, decisively, "That we need you to come back to the great camp of the clan, Shaman. I ask this as the Khan of my people."

The old shaman gave her brother a wintery smile. "And how do you feel about marriage, young Khan?"

Kildai's forehead wrinkled. "I think I would like to avoid it for a while. I have people trying to arrange one for me already." He looked warily at the shaman, expecting the next arrangement.

The old man gave a little snort of laughter. "That was what I fell out with your father and his brother about, finally. Arranging marriages. It might be useful for the clans, but it's not always good for the people. I get to see the results. Besides the children, I saw the sickness caused by the conflicts of souls. Some souls do not bind well together, and a marriage must be a melding of souls if it is to be a healthy place to raise young warriors."

Kildai frowned. "That makes sense."

"That was what your mother thought. Your father thought it caused problems if women chose their own bridegrooms," said the shaman, gathering his possessions. Some were prosaic like little bottles and a tools. Others were decidedly odd. Stones. Some wing pinions. Small bones. A tooth.

"Oh," Bortai could see that her little brother was out of his depth here. So was she, a little. "But there is always the challenge for the bridegroom. Princess Khutulun did that. It must always be acceptable. And father always let me choose..." She'd turned down a number of suitors. And fought with seven. She had of course beaten all of them.

"The rules for his own daughter were different. It is often like that." His tone said Kaltegg did not approve.

"That is true, I suppose," admitted Bortai.

Kaltegg smiled. "There is a spiritual selectivity to

these things. Just as there is in the creation of a shaman. You can train and try...but the tengeri choose who they will work with. It is not arranged. Not at the final point."

PART VII
January, 1541 A.D.

Chapter 63

"Are they too stupid to learn!?" Emeric snapped angrily. "Instead of taking a valuable lesson from Vajdahunyad, I have reports here of towns and villages daring to refuse my men entry. Turning billeted troops out in the dead of winter. And not paying their taxes!"

Elizabeth looked bored. "They can always be brought to heel, Emeric. Do not concern yourself with small people. The boyars have been loyal."

"Most of them, yes," said Emeric sourly. "But the Székelers are going to be landless peasants by summer. They're really going to understand the meaning of losing their so-called 'privileges.'"

"Without Vlad they will fall apart. They'll be glad enough to come cowed and licking your boots then."

"With or without Vlad they will fall apart. Or I will rend them in pieces, come spring. I have ordered a mobilization. I'll have forty thousand men here, before the spring."

"He will be gone before spring and you can just send them all home again."

"Not before I've taught those towns a very painful

and direct lesson for daring to oppose me. I'll have more men on pikes than Vlad's grandfather did. Every village, every hamlet will get a very pointed reminder. At the moment we can't do too much because of the snow. Anyway, we have the devil finding even the male peasantry now. They're deserting their boyars in droves."

Elizabeth shrugged. "A few women and children should do it. They seem to get that message."

Jagiellon looked at the sweating Nogay.

It was, in magical terms, a great effort to achieve such a materialization.

Normally it could only be done if both the participants were magically skilled. But this Golden Horde general was totally unskilled. Jagiellon had yet to decide whether it was going to be worth sending him back. Of course, Nogay's body was actually still in a ger in the territory of the Golden Horde. But what the spirit does not know, it can do little about. Nogay thought that he was here. Whether the Black Brain let him return would depend on what the man had to offer.

"Gatu Orkhan prepares to raid north. It is late in the season for a major campaign. They will not expect him."

"And this benefits me how, Nogay? I have provided you with much gold for an army and a complaisant khan, who would turn them loose as I wished on the Bulgars and Constantinople."

The Horde had enjoyed several years of relative peace, and abundance, after a long period of civil wars during which Lithuania had devoured much of the northern territories of the Horde. Once their lands had stretched as far east as the Kirgiz Steppe and south to the Caucasus on the other side of the Black Sea. Capture and subversion had brought Lithuania lands and vassal states right down to Odessa. Some of the old parts of the Golden Horde lands had been cut off, and reverted to small khanates. That suited Jagiellon, since those could be devoured at will.

In part, Jagiellon had intervened in the politics of Golden Horde simply because that would stop them raiding his shipyards and pressing north. The murder of Gatu's rival for the khanship had failed. But even the failed assassination of the more obvious heir apparent Kildai had given the Grand Duke of Lithuania months of peace to continue building. The fleet was nearing readiness.

If a civil war was the best that Jagiellon could hope for, instead of another army of horsemen to turn on his foes, it was still better than the alternatives.

"Khan, we will win. We outnumber them and they have nowhere to run. They are trapped between us and Hungary."

"I will allow you some time to try this. Finally, the matter of the tarkhan Borshar."

"Yes, Khan?"

"He is skilled at killing. Use him, but circumspectly. Remember, as I have told you, he believes my sending comes from his god. His mind is less than clear, much of the time. But I have gifted him with certain magics. I believe that may impress the primitives. Now go."

The demon now turned its attention to other matters. There were strange stirrings in a far-distant spirit realm. Those seemed to have ties to the northern regions from whence he once drew the shamans to service in the court of Jagiellon.

It had attempted to investigate. But so far there were just currents, and dark mist.

Chapter 64

Bortai found herself worried about the legend-horse she was riding. Yes, that had been her intention, when she'd told the story. It had indeed spread like wildfire, even crossing clan lines. Unfortunately quite a lot of people had embroidered on to it. Fat Tulkun for a start. He enjoyed storytelling and could be led into it, very easily, with just a small amount of kumiss. He was being given enough to float a boat. And the more he drank, the more grandiose the story got, with more embellishments. The Mongols loved it. Tulkun could probably live out his days in the lands of the Golden Horde as a successful storyteller, growing fatter with every ger he visited.

He was the one who had furnished the details about Tortoise Orkhan. Must be a lost clan, he'd said with a twinkle, from far off Iceland. She was sure that he'd said it as a joke. The only trouble was most of the Golden Horde Mongols—even the clan-heads—were, as often as not, illiterate. Many of them had never seen the sea . . . So, naturally, their language had changed after all this time. That was why he struggled to speak it in a way that Mongol could understand . . . It was living in the ice that had made their hair so pale . . .

Of course he *had* to start that story *after* she had let a few people into the joke that Erik—Tortoise Orkhan, thought that she was just a soldier's daughter. She'd subtly pumped him as to what he thought her status was. The daughter of a warrior from the imperial guard? That was true, in a way. Her father had commanded that Khesig, before he became orkhan. By now, it seemed, she would struggle to find a person in the entire Mongol nation who would not earnestly tell the foreign orkhan that she was a humble Mongol maid. Some might even manage to keep a straight face. And they all thought it was *romantic*. It added a dimension to the story that brought all the women, even the ones whose clan had nothing to do with the Hawk, into an eager audience. She hadn't realized that she had had a reputation of being as unapproachable as the Princess Khutulun, before Khutulun had met and fought the Great Khan Ulaghchi—who was at that time a homeless, impoverished exile, traveling incognito as a wandering hire-warrior—and he had won her diamond-hard heart. She could see the parallels they drew. It wasn't true, of course. Erik was an outlander. *Not* a Mongol. How could they think he was a Mongol with his features and his fine white-blond hair?

It was gradually brought home to her that most of the women didn't care. And many of the respectable maidens would be very willing to drag him off to the nearest patch of woods, or just behind the family ger if there were no woods handy. A patch of snow would do. And he might need it, judging by some of the very leading questions being asked.

And Kildai, *dear* little brother, thought it absolutely, screamingly, funny. He had heard, from David, a fair amount of lore about Erik. It would seem her brother's horseboy friend, and closet advisor, knew a great deal about the man, and probably thought it just as funny, thought Bortai, savagely. "Well, brother," she snapped finally, "you are so full of big talk. You would be well served if it was true. If I ran off with some foreigner. What would you say then, eh?" Her suitors had all been arranged. But the clan—via its heritage from Princess Khutulun—believed in the right of refusal. So far she'd found little reason not to use it. Of course, being Bortai, she'd used the traditional way to get rid of the suitors. And unlike Khutulun, she'd found few men prepared to wager a hundred horses against her hand.

"I'd say it served both of you right." Then, as he occasionally did, her little brother surprised her with his own seriousness. "I think maybe Khan Ulaghchi had it wrong, Bortai. The Ilkhan still rules, and they allow intermarriage there. And let us be honest, it happened here too. Everyone claims that they're descended from Chinngis Khan himself. But half of them don't look any more Mongol than the Székely do. And look at David. He looks more like a Mongol than most Mongol do. But he isn't."

Bortai knew that was true. Some Golden Horde Mongols even had blond hair. . . . Hair dye worked well. "But that is them. Not us. We *do* know our ancestry. And I am not interested."

"That cuts both ways," said Kildai. "David says women everywhere try to get his attention. He doesn't even know that they're alive. David says he was in love with some Vinlander girl, and she got killed."

"Oh. Tell me about it? What else did he say?"

"I thought you weren't interested?"

"He is a good man. Very kind. A clever orkhan. I can want to know about him without being interested... like that." Bortai felt unusually foolish. As if it was she who was fourteen and he who was twenty-three.

"Then ask him about it."

"I will."

"Her name was Svanhild."

"What a strange name."

She had resolved to let Erik know that this foolishness had gone far enough. Or possibly just to avoid him. Unfortunately, when they met the next day she managed to do neither. He smiled. Looked faintly concerned. "You are pale. Let me get you a seat. Something to drink?"

And that brought back memories of his kindness when they had fled and he had rescued them on the edge of Illyria. She rubbed her eyes hastily. "I am fine."

"I haven't upset you... or offended you again have I? I am not very good at your language."

And that brought back his initial greeting and the offer of his ger to her. She really must make sure that he did not say that to any of the over-eager maidens. It could get him into all sorts of trouble. The thought of some of their probable reactions to this invitation brought a snort of laughter.

"That's better. I am more used to you laughing at me."

She rushed the ditch. "Orkhan Erik," she blurted. "Tell me about Svanhild?"

His face went bleak. More bleak than she'd ever seen it. "Manfred. He can't leave well enough alone..."

"N . . . no. It was David."

"Oh. He had it from Kari, I suppose. Kari was a Thordarsen retainer."

"I am sorry. I did not mean to offend . . ."

He smiled. It was a sad smile, but a smile nonetheless. "It's all right. I suppose . . . I suppose that it is just that everyone avoids mentioning her to me. You're the first person to do so, I think."

"Would you tell me? Tell me about her?"

He was silent for a while. And then he nodded. "Yes," he said. "Yes I think I would like to do that. I'm . . . scared to remember. But I am also afraid that I might forget. I loved her with all my heart," he said, quietly. "I would have died for her. I very nearly did. Benito saved me. Manfred kept me alive. And sometimes I wonder if they should have."

Bortai shook her head vehemently. "The tengeri decide when it is your time. Besides *she* did not want you to die. I know this." And it was true. She did.

She squatted down. Motioned to him to do the same. "Now. You will tell me. She would want the story told. I would want mine told. And she would not want you to be unhappy."

So Erik Hakkonsen talked. The language limited him, but he was a man who had always struggled to express emotion anyway. At first it was hard. A trickle of words, gently encouraged. And then it was like a torrent, as if a dam inside him that had wanted to burst for a year had finally given way.

Then, when the last part had been told, Bortai said something which healed a wound inside him that he thought would be open there forever. "Her spirit must run with the great horses across heaven. What more could any woman have desired: to have loved and been loved like that?"

"I wanted to give her so much more."

She looked at him sternly. She could be very imperious in her looks. "It is not what you wanted to give that is important. It is what she wanted to receive. You gave her that. Never doubt it."

Chapter 65

"I had the slut killed, of course. But it does downgrade Vlad's value. And increase his sister's."

Mindaug nodded politely, to disguise his true thoughts. Elizabeth Bartholdy was far too reliant on demonic power. Did she not realize that in magic symbolism was vital—but that it was superseded by actuality in spells of these sorts? It was true enough that virginity was symbolic of innocence and purity. But in a rite such as this, what mattered was the spiritual, not the physical, reality. A woman who had been drugged before being violated was still pure, whereas a woman with an intact hymen did not necessarily qualify.

There were those who went to their weddings with that hymen intact, and had no more innocence than a brothel keeper. Elizabeth knew nothing of Vlad's sister except her age. And that too was no guarantee that she had been allowed to stay virginal in the magical sense. Look at Elizabeth herself. She had probably not been spiritually virginal since the age of five.

They walked across the chapel. It would be impossible to tell, without the most minute examination, that the cross had been broken and rejoined with a mixture of excreta and menstrual blood. But the pentacle on the floor was easily enough seen once the carpet was rolled back. A carpet was very unusual in a chapel, but no one asked why she had had it placed there.

There was a little inscription in Latin beneath the cross. Hard to read unless you came very close. *Pater noster, qui erat in caelis.* "Our father who was in heaven." Foolish to have such visible evidence. But that was an intrinsic part of the worship and the magic of the path she had chosen to follow. To flaunt and taunt. To claim that one's survival was a demonstration of their master's power.

It was none of his business. If she wanted to take chances, that was her problem. Mindaug was merely here to help her set her trap. The altar would be well used, for the orgy of blood she needed. The dungeon was already filling with the material she had collected for it. It just lacked its prime victims.

The trap would remove much of the Dragon's magical power. Make him—or the girl—an easy prey for her spells. Make the reversal and defilement she planned possible.

The count wondered if Elizabeth realized that it would affect her, too, inside the circles. She would be as mortal as Vlad, when she went inside the area of containment, to the altar. Mindaug himself would certainly not take such a risk. The Dragon was . . . dangerous.

Not since she had discovered the wyverns, had Dana had so much excitement. It wasn't entirely pleasant.

Miu had returned from the north. Alone. With bad news for the tribe. They were in shock and mourning. And yet there was some good news—in the shape of a letter from her brother. Dana was beginning to wonder if words could wear out with reading. Her mother was certainly trying.

And then came a further surprise, in the shape of three scruffy looking men. The gypsies were suspicious. But Miu recognized the leader of the party as just what he claimed to be: one of Vlad's trusted sergeants. Emil respectfully informed Dana's mother that they had been sent to help guard them, and to provide escorts for them. Prince Vlad was deeply concerned about their safety.

Chapter 66

They'd had a flurry of snows and cold, bitter weather, and then the skies had cleared a little. Vlad took advantage of the lull in winter's fury to organize some exercises with his mounted infantry. He also took this as an opportunity to visit and put his stamp on the Székely fortified villages. He went farther south along the mountains than he'd been before. The Székeler were, if anything, too hospitable. They had been the barrier to Mongol raiders for centuries. The valley of the river that the Mongols called the Iret had been one of the routes Vlad had followed. It was steep, snowy and forested. The tale of his exploits on the plains had spread, and besides, some of the new cannons had arrived in their fortress. Cannon from their overlord! Overlords took, they did not give, especially not weapons that might be used against them! He was plainly mad, but great. The Székelers there took him to a ridge line where he could see far into the lowlands. And pointed out something no prince fighting a war wants to see.

A large army. At least twenty thousand strong. On the move. In winter.

The Mongols had done that historically, Vlad knew, using frozen rivers as roads, using speed and the unexpectedness of an attack in winter to destroy their enemies. "It's all right, Drac. They're not coming up here. They're hunting the women and children from the local Mongol clans. We saw them root a bunch out. They have them in a stockade a bit farther down the Iret. There is a war going on down there."

Vlad took a deep breath of the dry, cold air. "Do you know where the stockade is?" he asked, weighing matters in his mind.

The Székeler nodded. "You can see it from Coltii."

"Take me there. And I will need two of your best riders to bear a message for me back to Primor Gabor Peter who is in Berek with my troops. I need it done as fast as possible. They must get a change of horses at Csomakrös. The Primor Peter will carry the message further."

Within the hour the messengers were off, eager to prove to their count just how fast they could be. And Vlad was off to go and look at the stockade.

It was pale predawn. Erik and Manfred were at their usual morning's fencing. They always attracted a few watchers. Manfred noticed, with amusement, that Bortai was always there, despite the cold and the hour. She and Erik seemed, heh, to be frequently seen together. "Prince!" called someone from the sidelines.

"Up swords." They stopped.

Manfred recognized the fellow as the taciturn scarred man who had commanded Vlad's handful of Székeler cavalry on the plains. He did not speak much Frankish. But knew enough to say "Message for you, Prince," and hand Manfred the roll of vellum.

The fellow was staying in Berek with Vlad's growing corps. He seemed, for his sins, to have been saddled with preparing Vlad's gun-wagons and their crews. Vlad's encampment was a good mile and a half farther into the mountains. The Székeler captain must have left well before first light to be here already.

Manfred unrolled the message, and rapidly saw why. He handed it to Erik. "Here. Your Mongol language skills are going to be needed for this. Bortai," he beckoned to her, and the young woman came over from where she had squatted with two others.

Erik read the letter. Turned to listening Bortai. "It is a message from Prince Vlad. The khan over the mountain. You need to get a message to your generals. He says that there is an army of some twenty thousand across the headwaters of the Iret. They have captured some of your people. He says that he will make the attempt to free them."

Bortai did not pause. She turned to her two companions and let loose a high speed stream of orders. Erik could follow only about half of it. She was even sending them to her brother. At a run, by the looks of the way they took off.

"What else does he say?" Bortai demanded. "Translate every word for me. It is a long message, I see."

Erik looked at Manfred, who nodded. Erik did his best.

"To my fellow Prince, Manfred. Greeting. Friend I ask you to convey news with all possible speed to the Young Khan of the Hawk Clan. There are an army of, by my . . . I do not know this word in your tongue, it means 'he thinks but does not know precisely' some 20,000 men on horse who have crossed the upper Iret. They have

ravaged one small encampment, taking some prisoners.
My men say they are mostly the women and children.
They are being held . . . I think 'a wall made of logs.'

"We have a watch on this from a nearby moun-
tain ridge. If they try to move them—if possible I
will attempt to liberate them. I only have some three
hundred of my mounted infantry here. I send to
my officer, the Primor Gabor Peter, a letter of safe
conduct for up to five hundred of the Hawk clan, to
be escorted by the same officer to come to their aid.
They still owe me some three hundred sheep, which
I do not think I will get from the invaders.

"My regards to you and my friend Erik.

"Yours etc.

"Vlad"

Several more Mongol men, officers by the looks of
them, came running up.

Bortai bowed to the primor. "Will you wait? I will
see to it that food and drink are brought."

She strode off, talking nineteen to the dozen with
the officers.

Manfred clapped the Székeler Primor on the shoulder. "Our ger is just there. Come and get out of the
wind and have some wine and bread. They will send
you Kumiss—we offer wine. Erik, tell one of these
hangers-on to find Bortai and tell her that they can
find the primor at our ger, at our fire."

The primor's Frankish was limited, but he knew
both "wine" and "fire."

The most terrifying thing about the Mongols was
just how fast they could mobilize their forces. Bortai
returned with two generals a little later. They were
both embarrassed, and yet eager to take the opportunity

offered. The worst aspect of it seemed to be that it was across Székely land. Both for Székely and the Mongols, it would seem. "How about if we form part of the escort," said Manfred. "That way the Mongols can be escorted by us, and we will be escorted by the Székeler Horseheads."

Bortai clapped her hands and nodded. Translated. It appeared that would be a great deal easier for both sides . . . But could extra steeds be found for the knights? The Mongols wished to push through at speed.

"Anything they can do, we can do better," said Manfred. He was to regret that statement later. "And maybe the primor can send messengers ahead so that we won't be met with a hail of defensive arrows." Amusingly this had to be explained to the man in Mongol, which he understood better than Frankish.

They were in the saddle and riding by Terce, with five hundred Mongols, two hundred and thirty Székeler Horseheads—all that could be ready in time—and a hundred knights, leaving the injured and a guard for Eberhard. The trail was icy but mercifully relatively snow free. The Székely primor said that would not be true for very long. The Mongols had brought no less than five changes of horse. They intended to press very hard.

Manfred was soon regretting his statement about anything they could do he could do better. But he was pleased, too. He'd seen Erik smiling at the Mongol girl. And her smiling back. He knew a lot more about women than Erik did. Somehow those two had broken through each other's defenses. Now all he had to do was contrive to leave the two of them alone together. But she was seldom alone. There always seemed at least three female chaperones hovering. And five or six men-at-arms who seemed to have nothing better to do than be there. Not too close, but there. He was none too sure who she was in their society, but he also knew more about society than Erik did. If she was a simple Golden Horde maiden, the daughter of a warrior in the imperial guard, as Erik believed, then Manfred was a Breton fisherman. Hell, then he was a Breton fisherman's daughter. But if that was the game she wanted to play...

She'd accompanied them on this ride, too. For once without her female chaperones, but if anything, more guarded. How she'd got away with this would be another tall story, thought Manfred, with a grin. She'd probably tell Erik it was to act as liaison between the knights and the Mongols or something. Erik spoke their tongue adequately for that purpose. He spent enough time practicing it, and he had a natural gift for languages that Manfred could only envy. Besides they had the Székelers. Manfred had to smile about that, too. He'd thought the source of the conflict was the raiding... but it turned out the sticky point was about wives. Marriages, particularly among the wealthy and powerful Mongols, were often arranged. They were ways of cementing clan ties. Sometimes there was mutual love and attraction... sometimes there wasn't. Mongol women were not reared to be complacent doormats. Not surprisingly, a small number of Mongol girls did what any sensible lass would do if she didn't like her marriage: leave. Which, if you didn't want to be fetched home again, meant one of two things. Another clan—or up over the border, where a girl with a few horses could find a replacement husband very easily—and he could be of her choosing. Sometimes the deprived spouse tried quite hard to get her (and the horses) back ... Of course to Mongols it was always theft. But the Székely were very Christian, and also, more significantly, *not* confident enough as warriors to go raiding into Mongol turf. "Marry a girl with a few good horses" was a promotion for them—a man could become a Horsehead. But only if she came with horses.

It meant most of the Székelers spoke at least some Mongol, and neither side trusted or liked each other much.

Some secrets are impossible to keep. Kildai's Khesig had got far too used to David, and their young master's visiting and consulting and talking and, yes, the two of them behaving like a pair of young hooligans, to think anything of it. He looked a lot like the young khan, but not if they actually stood next to each other. David was treated with tolerant respect that he found much more disturbing than the way Kildai talked to him. Kildai was just ... a kid. A kid brother he'd dressed, helped to the toilet. Rather as if he, David, had not been the youngest brother of the family.

David had had little enough time to spend with Kildai, though, since Von Stael had "adopted" him. The knight was just too good—good to the edge of saintly—David had to admit. Erik or Kari would have seen a scam, and given him a clout. Von Stael earnestly believed the best of his squire. There was no skill or difficulty at all in putting one over him ... so David found that there was really not much fun in doing it. Besides ... it would hurt his knight. Von Stael would never be sharpest blade on the rack. But he would be the most reliable and consistently work the hardest. And he was intensely proud when David did things right. It was unfair. He didn't want to disappoint the man.

The result was that he had worked harder than he had in his life. He was already putting on muscle. And sleeping like the dead.

But now he had some liberty at last. Von Stael had gone with Prince Manfred and Erik. David, however, was not taken along.

So he went to see Kildai...who had ridden off too, to join the regiments in the field, to attack the orkhan's invasion in the flank.

So David thought he'd go for a ride on his own—an idea that six months ago would never have crossed his mind. There was nothing else to do. And no need to wear a breastplate, or helmet, for the first time in ages. He waved to the guards—they all knew him and the odd privileged position he enjoyed. He rode off to see what the back of the nearest mountain looked like.

It looked like it was occupied by five incredulous men he'd never seen before in his life. Men who had just seen a main chance presented to them on an unguarded horse. Without as much as a bow with him.

Vlad greeted them. With relief—on seeing the Mongols—and delight at seeing the knights. "The palisade is guarded by two companies. We had considered taking them on, but we were afraid the women might not trust us."

"More likely to trust you too much," said Manfred. "But anyway. We're here. Let's decide on a strategy."

However, to the Mongols the plan was very simple. Those were people of their clan. Theirs to rescue.

They deeply appreciated the news, and the safe passage. Bortai, in rather broken Frankish relayed that. She seemed to feel it was right to speak to him in Frankish. "But the war-khan... He wishes to know why? Besides the sheep. Why the safe passage?"

"Tell him it was because of the children. I was taken as a child to be the prisoner of my worst enemy. I will have no other child suffer the same." Vlad had a quality that most politicians and generals would give half their wealth for: When he spoke there was a deep earnestness about him. He was very believable, even if the listener didn't understand a word of it.

Bortai nodded. Translated. It plainly struck home with the audience. Manfred made a mental note to tell Bortai just exactly what Emeric had done to the scared little boy that Vlad had been. "But orkhan he say: this is our fight."

"If that's the way they want it, sure," said Manfred. "What are you going to do once you break them out of there?"

"They will be tired and scared. Some are wounded," said Vlad. "You have our permission to bring them back here to the fortress. Then we will give you safe passage back again."

Bortai translated. The surprise on their faces was quite funny really. The officers talked among themselves. And then the senior officer bowed low. Manfred assumed that what he said was "thank you," in Vlachs.

The knights, the Székelers cavalry, Vlad and his mounted infantry and Bortai and five Mongol escorts remained behind, to watch the action from the ridge line that Vlad had observed the palisade from.

The Hawk clan's five hundred men didn't waste

time and energy on strategy. They just rode down to the palisade as if they had every right to be there and started shooting. They drove off the guards, broke open the wooden stockade, and began mounting the captives on to spare horses... when the enemy strategy became clear. The captives weren't just prisoners. They were bait.

Only... any attempt at rescue had been expected... to come from the plain, not the mountains.

There were a lot of men and horses hidden in the forest. All that saved the Hawk clan rescuers was the fact that—as they were supposed to sortie from the plains and not the mountains—the ambush had been positioned below, down slope, from the palisade. The ambushers, instead of cutting off the retreat, now had to gallop in the chase.

Vlad took in the scene. Turned to his troops. "Mount up," he shouted.

"What are you going to do?" asked Manfred.

Vlad pointed. "I should be able to get my arquebusiers to there—in the woods where the valley narrows, on the south of the track. The Székeler cavalry must stop them in the woods, while we retreat."

Manfred nodded. "Give me fifty of your light cavalry and I'll take a charge right across the column, there. We'll go up that valley diagonally opposite."

"There are several thousand of them, Manfred."

"They will be strung out in a long thin column by then. No one can move that fast in the forest, so they'll be on the trail. I want your Székeler as guides, and to cover our backs, because we'll have to leave through the forest. Ask if we can get back over to your fortress up that valley."

The inquiry was made, and the troops divided and

set off. The Hawk clan were fighting a systematic retreat, pushing the former captives ahead, and slowing the pursuit with arrows. But once again they were in a situation where their horses had been ridden, or made to run far, and their foes were fresh.

The women and children and a handful of the Hawk clan came galloping along the trail. Behind came the Hawk clan, turning and firing from the saddle, in full flight, with the last of the riders not more than thirty yards from the van of Gatu Orkhan's men.

Vlad had his men in a treble row in the edge of the wood. They waited. "On your command, Sire," said Sergeant Mirko.

Vlad waited until the van was almost past his men. "Fire!"

They were firing into the side of the column. Not as massed a fire as Vlad would have liked—the target was strung out. More a task for marksmen than his men. Still, at forty yards, it was hard to miss all the horses. And that was what his infantry aimed for. And the impact was devastating. The Mongols had met infantry before. They destroyed foot-soldiers. They hadn't really had to deal with disciplined massed fire before, though. It was not a feature of the Bulgar warfare, or their opponents to the north—who were mostly light cavalry like themselves—or even Székely who used a combination of light cavalry and fortifications defended by infantry. Emeric had companies of arquebusiers, but they had not been deployed here. The Székely had been left to hold this border.

Vlad did not wait. His men mounted up and raced back up the narrow road. What they lacked in horsemanship they made up for in the freshness of their mounts. The Székelers covered the retreat. In the distance Vlad heard the clash of arms. The knights. He could only hope they would be all right, and rode on . . . to be met by Hawk clan warriors . . . turning to help cover the retreat. Cheering. A mile farther up, with the last of the sun touching the mountain tops, he halted his men again. Formed them up and stood ready.

For a charge that never came. One of Székeler primors rode up. "They're retreating, Drac. They obviously think that this is one big ambush!"

With a screen of scouts behind them, Vlad and his men and the Hawk Mongols also retreated on the Székeler fort, in the dark. The knights and the rest of the Székely Horseheads were there, already tending to the wounded and the rescued women and children.

"How did it go, Manfred?" asked Vlad, seeing the prince. "I did not mean to drag you into my wars."

Manfred waved a hand dismissively. "This is more like the Mongol wars. We hit them a little late, after your volley. But they were still badly disordered by it. We sliced through them like an axe through a cabbage. No serious damage at all. Well. Barring Erik."

"Erik is injured?" asked Vlad worriedly.

Manfred beamed. "Yes. Bleeding and being tended to by a lovely Mongol lass."

"It is not serious?"

Manfred guffawed. "Oh, it is serious, all right. But the wound isn't. And now I need a drink and we need to discuss what steps to take next. You just tweaked the beard of quite a large army down there."

"I will deal with it."

"Of that I have no doubt. But friends are around to help with these little things. And I gather the Hawk clan think they owe you, now."

"Three hundred sheep."

"They might throw in a few horses, with fighting men mounted on them, now."

Bortai examined the cut carefully. "You were very lucky, Orkhan Erik," she said severely.

He winced. And then schooled his expression. "That is not actually the way it feels right now."

"There are bits of fabric in the wound. They must come out."

The arrow had slipped, somehow, between the lames of the shoulder spaulder, and cut across his shoulder and chest, the point stopping against his collar bone, close to his throat. It must have been fired from very close and by someone who had dismounted—or been unhorsed, more probably. Another inch more force and it would have cut into Erik's neck. As it was, if he survived Bortai's ministrations, he'd live.

"I am going to have to sew this up," she said firmly.

"What? It's not that serious."

"It will heal much faster. And with less scarring." She looked at his muscled, scarred torso. "You have enough scars already. Don't worry. I have sewed up a number of horses." She turned to her assistant—one of the rescued women. "I will need some snow. It slows the bleeding and numbs the skin."

The little woman bobbed. "Yes, Princess." Then she looked at Erik. "We call everyone princess in our sub-clan. It's not as if she were royalty or anything." She giggled and ran off.

"What was that about?" asked Erik.

"I have no idea," said Bortai firmly, blushing. "You should worry instead about what tomorrow will bring instead. The orkhan will come here in force tomorrow."

Erik moved, winced slightly and was told to sit still. "He may. But I think he'll regret it. I smell snow on that wind."

She nodded. "It is that time of the year. But what provoked the khan over the mountain to intervene? To ride to the rescue?"

Erik shrugged, and regretted that too. "I think it is the sort of thing he does, Bortai. He's a complex man."

"One better to have as a friend than an enemy. I have heard from several men who saw him in battle. He is very brave. Very strong."

"I saw him, too. He fights like a madman."

"Yes. But I think a very honorable madman. There is someone in great trouble about those sheep that were not delivered," said Bortai. "Ah. Here is Mira with the snow. You will have to hold still."

Erik did. But it struck him that being shot was a lot quicker.

The next morning showed that Erik had been right about one thing. The weather was atrocious. However a force of Mongols did get up the pass. Cannon and even more snow forced them back.

The Mongols, the rescued women and children, the knights and the Székelers and the infantry spent another two days of heavy weather at the fort, before things lifted much. And then it was a Székeler relief force of some thousand men and horse, and sleds, who forced their way through the drifts.

It was an interesting time, Erik reflected later, for

people being forced to get on with each other, and
to be forced to swallow prejudices and soup together.

Deep in the snowy forest, General Nogay saw the
battle-magic of Borshar fail in its purpose. That had
been the centerpiece of his ambush, too.

Borshar had the ability, acquired suddenly from his
god—or so he informed them—to cause fits in the
riders he touched and to fling small thunderbolts. The
Mongols had been impressed, for they were deeply
superstitious about thunder and lightning.

Unfortunately, Borshar's range was limited and he
was a poor rider. So they had missed the ambush, by
being in the wrong place. And then they'd been too
slow to catch up with the fleeing Hawk clan rescuers, which had kept Borshar from using his magics.
That might also have kept him alive, of course, when
the pursuit had run into withering fire from enemy
arquebusiers.

Nogay's limit was finally reached. The Ilkhan
emissary had demonstrated his power, showed it on
a rebellious Arban . . . and now, in the mountains, he
said that the power had deserted him.

"I should do the same to you. Leave you here to
die in the snow."

Nogay had learned a lesson, then. However ineffectual the Ilkhan man had been in the ambush, he
was a deadly hand-to-hand fighter. He'd had Nogay
off his horse and on the ground before he realized
what was happening. With his blade against Nogay's
throat, the tarkhan had spoken softly. "This is my skill.
Not open warfare."

Chapter 67

"To think that we came to bind our sub-clan to the Hawk banner," the nearest man said, smiling cruelly, "and here is the richest prize in all the lands of the Golden Horde. Gatu Orkhan will cover us in gold."

David knew that he was in dire trouble. His first thought was to flee. His second was to tell them they had the wrong person.

And neither was going to work.

Instead he tried pure arrogance. He must show no fear.

"Do you really think," he said, "that I am here, unwatched? I came to consult with the tengeri, with the eternal blue sky about this war. For this I must be alone. But the Khesig is never far away. Listen."

It stopped them. Stopped them right there.

And there was silence.

"You wish, Khan," said the leader of the group.

Just then a branch did crack higher up the slope. It could have been the weight of snow. It could have been anything.

The group froze, again.

But the leader was made of sterner stuff. "Let us take his head and ride!" he said, spurring his horse forward. He was only seconds in front of the next man.

. . . And sprouting an arrow through his throat. David not wait to think where it had come from. He had his sword out—following the drill Von Stael made him exercise so painstakingly. He and the next man clashed—and he was lucky, or Frankish sword drill was different or better. He cannoned into the next man and both of them lost their seats . . . and David the sword. They rolled together. David, desperate, bit. And somehow broke free. And as the man on foot and the remaining two closed . . . he had the pistol out of his boot. Cocked the lock and fired.

At that range he could hardly miss, but he did his best. The recoil pushed him back, and spun the attacker around—blood and tissue flying. It startled the hell out of the other two riders' horses.

David stood there, spent wheel-lock in one hand, Kari's knife in the other.

"Who will die next?" said another voice. There was the sound of a galloping horse, too. David risked a quick glance. There was a Hawk man, an arrow to his bowstring, up slope. Presumably a scout or a guard. And riding up the trail, hell for leather, was Kari.

The two men stood. But David was a thief. Used to reading his victims. He knew they were going to try something. And it didn't look like run. "Dismount," he said, imperiously.

They wanted to do no such thing. "You came to see me. What kind of respect do you show, when I am on foot? Dismount or die, now."

He raised the empty pistol, hoping they could not

see how badly his hand was shaking. One of them
slid off his horse, keeping it between himself and
the pistol.

"You, too. And do not try to hide behind your
horse. Unless you wish to die. Do what I say, and
you will live."

There were other riders coming, coming to see
what the shot had been about. The second man got
off his horse. Went down on his knees.

David thought he was going to keel over in the
snow, right there. But it wasn't over quite yet. "We
will need men who are good at seizing the initiative,"
he said quoting Erik, in an entirely different context,
a few days earlier. He pointed the knife at a dead
man. "But not fools."

The Hawk guard had now ridden his horse over.
Kari was just up slope, a pistol in each hand . . . some-
thing David wished he had. The Hawk dismounted.
"Take my steed, Young Khan," he said.

And somehow David managed to get himself into the
saddle. It was no small feat, as his head was whirling.
A patrol of several men had closed with the group.

"These men came to offer their clan's alliance,"
said David. "See to them."

And somehow he managed to turn and ride off.
With Kari right next to him. Handing him something.
Another one of his pistols. David reached down to take
the one out of his boot and realized it was extremely
sore. And that he was bleeding.

"Just keep me in the saddle until we're out of
sight," he said, clinging onto it for dear life.

He did not remember getting back to their camp.
But they must have, because someone had bandaged

him and put him to lie down in the ger he shared with Von Stael and three other knights. That was where he was when Kildai came to visit him.

"I hear I have a reputation for mercy that I do not want," said the boy. "I want to take their heads off, and not accept their homage! They were probably spies anyway. They have never allied with us before." He scowled. "And now I have had to let them go."

David—for whom the last bit of time had been very vague—said, "You're back!"

Kildai nodded. "I nearly found your souls in the land of Erleg Khan. You idiot!"

"Ha! I did a pretty good you. Better than when your sister tried to make me out to be you. Ow. Gently."

"Serves you right," said Kildai. "I get a long cold, boring ride and an enemy that runs away. You get to kill and disarm fifteen attackers. And spare the lives of those who make their obeisance."

"It was only two," said David. "And it was mostly luck...and I didn't like it much."

"One actually. The one you shot. He bled to death. I think you came off worse than the one you stuck with a sword. He just landed on his head. But the story is now officially fifteen. And growing."

Kildai looked at him. "I did not realize that there were other people of importance in my world. Except the clan, and the Horde. I do now."

David had begun to grasp enough of politics to realize just how important that could be.

PART VIII
February, 1541 A.D.

Chapter 68

Vlad found that attempting to cobble together his rule over the duchy was complicated by the atrocious weather and snow. That and the bad roads. The attempt of Emeric's troops to oppose him was equally hampered by the same. Only Emeric's men also had to contend with a hostile local population and Vlad's highly mobile infantry and light cavalry—who knew the country and knew where and when traveling was possible. Still, Vlad was now the de facto ruler of a j-shaped section of Valahia. The holdout was in the southwest, where Ban Alescu of Irongate held sway, and the lands away from the Carpathians where Emeric and his troops effectively enforced the myth of the new true duke. Rumor—slow and garbled—had it that the boyars were having a hard time of it there, enforcing the will of Emeric. Vlad had already had two grisly packages delivered from new supporters in the lands he now controlled—at least for the winter: the heads of two boyars.

He'd also had more money and news from Elizabeth. Both had been very very welcome. She was incredibly well informed about the movement of King Emeric's troops.

Vlad knew that spring and summer would be bitter warfare. He would, by the information trickling east, face the full might of an angry Emeric. Many thousands of troops, a lot of heavy cavalry—something he had very little of himself.

Since the incident with the rescue of the women and children from the stockade, relations between the Hawk clan Mongols and the Duke of Valahia had been remarkably amicable. It had given him something he'd previously lacked: a source of food for his troops.

"It's a problem," said Bortai to Erik, at one of their frequent meetings, with the dimple that betrayed the fact that she was trying to keep a straight face. "For the last century at least, the sub-clans have kept their restive youngsters from causing too much trouble by sending them off to go and raid the Székely. Loot is important. And so is keeping them from starting fights with other clans or going off wife-stealing."

"I thought that was forbidden," said Erik.

Bortai shrugged. "Yes. But the Yasa code was poorly enforced after the Great Khan's death. Clans spent more time fighting each other than anything else. It has crept in a little again. It was the way the Mongols did things. And we are retentive about our traditions and beliefs."

"I suspect that they're popular with men who have little other chance of finding a wife."

She dimpled. "Probably. Older men marry too many wives. Still, if the kurultai goes to plan . . . we will give them plenty of opportunity for warfare to the north and east."

"Your people could do worse than to strike a deal with Vlad. They can provide you with what Eberhard calls a manufacturing base. And they are a good market for your sheep."

"And our breakdown horses." Bortai giggled. "The generals were saying—after the fight in the pass—that we should really sell the Khan-over-the-mountain better horses. And then they were saying 'no, eventually he'd use them against us.'"

"Still. The Holy Roman Empire proves that very different people can live at peace. They turn the aggression outwards."

"Chinngis Khan proved that," said Bortai, cheerfully.

Erik nodded. "But I don't think that light cavalry can ride over all opposition any more. Cannon and fortifications have gotten better."

She nodded. "And men softer. More...living in cities."

"Is that all bad? I wouldn't choose to do it, but for others..."

She pondered that one. It was plainly an idea she'd never contemplated. But the one thing about Bortai was that she would think about new ideas. Intelligently. She was, Erik suspected, just as traditionalist as his mama. But she had some flexibility and adaptability. "I suppose so. For other people. Someone must smelt iron and grow grain. But not me, please. I like space. Even the lands of the Golden Horde grow too crowded for me," she said with a chuckle.

"You should see the plains of Vinland," said Erik, dreamily. "You could ride for a month and not see the end of them. And there are few people there. There were no horses, and without horses people cannot survive there. The distances are too great."

They ended up talking about Erik's daydream until Manfred came looking for him. Erik was embarrassed. Where had the hours gone?

They rode, as planned, to see Vlad. And, as the weather turned too miserable for the drill they'd planned, ended up talking about strategy for Vlad to use the next summer.

"In truth, we're relying on massed fire," he said to Manfred, when asked about what he hoped to do about heavy cavalry.

"If you hold most of the castles and fortifications, that may work. At the moment," said Erik with brutal honesty, "You're relying on the ability of your infantry to run away on horseback and your light cavalry to shield them in their retreat. Come spring Emeric will have more light cavalry than you can muster, and you'll need places to run to, because between the Croats and his knights you're going to get herded and crushed. But if you tie up his men trying to take castles—and being attacked if they don't, it will improve things for you. Infantry firing cannons and rolling rocks and pouring boiling oil can stop heavy cavalry."

Vlad nodded. "I am sending messengers southwest. To the man Emeric wishes to replace me with. I have received messages from him."

"Expect treachery," said Manfred.

Vlad blinked. "Oh. I suppose so."

"I think I had better lend you Eberhard of Brunswick. He's used to double-talk and what it means. And he can fill you with his theories about what a state needs."

Vlad nodded eagerly, completely missing the sarcasm. "I've thought a lot about it. Roads and bridges, I think . . ."

"Excellent. Just the sort of thing he'd say. Now if we can introduce you to Doge Dorma, you could start on trade, too," said Manfred.

"The Danube has such potential," said Vlad, not noticing Manfred's expression.

"Ban Alescu has sent a message to Prince Vlad."

Elizabeth shrugged. "You said that he had proved a weak reed, Emeric. That he'd not managed to rally anything but the area he effectively controlled to him, anyway. Kill him and start afresh."

"It's a bit more complicated than that, Aunt. Vlad has somehow reached an accommodation with the accursed Golden Horde. The Mongol numbers and strength have built up over the last few years. They've been turning their attention north, up till now. Nothing but petty nuisance raids into our territory."

"I sense this is all going somewhere, Emeric," said Elizabeth, allowing just a hint of asperity to creep into her voice. "So why don't you actually tell me what you are getting at. What does this have to do with Ban Alescu of Irongate?"

He scowled at her. "Just that. Irongate. At the moment he controls the little river traffic that there is. The Danube is a gateway to Hungary. One I need to control. That traitor Vlad could offer the Mongols: Irongate and access to my inner kingdom. If they did come up on barges, they could land anywhere. Attack anywhere. Especially if he sells them cannon. He has somehow, curse him, found someone to make him guns and cannon."

"Oh. Well, set your mind at ease about that. I have certain allies in the waters of the Danube. I can take your unfaithful vassal's castle away from him. Just like that." She snapped her fingers. "Shall we have a look and see just what he is doing.?

Emeric nodded delightedly. "And I wonder why I had never thought of using the barges myself. I'll have some prepared. With cannon."

Elisabeth did not say, "good, that will keep you busy and out of my way for a while," or "your father wasted time and money on that idiocy," but she thought it. Instead she said: "I will foment some distrust of the Mongols with Vlad. Send him some tale of planned treachery. That will help."

Emeric rubbed his hands in glee. "Come spring they're in for a surprise," he said, as he followed her into the room where she had suitable preparations made for the summonsing of a minor demon. She had had other plans for the summonsing, but those could wait. A pot bubbled slowly on a charcoal brazier in the far corner. She went and stirred it, on her way to collect the candles.

"You've taken to cooking, Aunt?" commented Emeric, sniffing.

"Merely rendering fat for certain special candles. Certain tasks cannot be done by underlings, as you know," she said coolly. "Sometimes you will have to see to doing something about this unseemly haste that priests show to baptize babies."

"It makes you look like a hedge witch."

She looked down her nose at him. "I do not like the comparison or implication, Emeric. My power is not drawn from old ambivalent goddesses or herbs. I've done my best to stamp that out."

She took out the candles and made the nine circles

complete. Wrote certain names in an ink that was very prone to clotting despite the spells she used to counter that. A small blot could change meanings, and free something that might, at best, devour her. Elizabeth often wondered if that, or symbolism, was why it was required for these summonsings. She called up something that made Emeric blench. Not her. She'd seen worse. Although, this one was a tricky one. "I abjure you once. By the dark power that is given to me by great Lucifer, by Ashteroth and Baal'zebub and all the lesser names: show only the truth." She repeated it thrice.

The thing in the pentacle smiled toothily. It had many teeth. "Of course, mistress. As if I would do otherwise."

"Not now, you won't. Show us Ban Alescu of Irongate."

An image appeared, as if floating in the air. The man was seated and eating soup. He was a rather noisy soup eater, and they could hear him clearly.

"It is fish soup. Sterlet," said the demon.

Emeric sighed irritatedly. "How valuable—"

And someone said, "M'lord, there is a messenger here from Prince Vlad."

"Show me this messenger," Emeric snapped.

The demon ignored him. Showed instead the Ban putting down his spoon, and taking the message, and reading it.

"Let us see what it says!" shouted Emeric. Elizabeth had to push him back. The fool would have broken the enclosure.

The Ban, of course unaware he was being watched, smiled. It was not a nice smile. "'He will be just in addressing my claims.' Ha! Now the horse-trading begins."

He set the message aside, and continued to eat his soup.

At length someone coughed. "Will there be a reply, m'lord?"

The Ban nodded. "Oh yes. But not until I have thought it over. See the messenger fed and given a bed."

"He would not stay, m'lord."

"How trying. But the last messenger got there. Now what do we have after this soup?"

Emeric's General Muiso was was doing his best to avoid conflict without telling his master. "It would be difficult to take his fortress. The island is well defended. It is about a mile long and walled. Then there is the citadel itself... Your Majesty, it would be possible to take it by siege—but there are fields on the island itself. To bombard it from the water is not to be thought of, to bombard it from land... firstly the range, and secondly it is in the mouth of the gorge. The terrain is vile. Steep. Forested. It will take time to get the guns up there, and they're going to be farther away from the island than will allow us any accuracy. The city of Orsoua and the castle there—his secondary fortress, would be easier," said the general. He coughed. "And, Your Majesty, the Irongate gorge is not easy to navigate. There are some cataracts, the Prigada rock... It is possible, Your Majesty, but far from easy. Do you wish me to make preparations to seize the castles? We will need to commit quite a lot of troops to it."

Emeric slammed his fist into his hand. Sighed. "No. I will see if...alternative means cannot be made use of."

"Yes," Elizabeth Bartholdy said. "In the middle of the water, isn't it? Yes, there is something I have wanted to try for a while. They do not like being dry, of course. But the river spreads its net a long way. With the power I will release from that blood...I think soon men will run screaming from it. But the island will do for a start. The Irongate will be in the hands of those who will devour ships' crews that come too close."

"You talk of power, Aunt. But all I seem to have done with your machinations this time is lose it. And send my money to my enemy," said Emeric sourly.

"Ah. But that is because you look too closely. You do not see the syzygy. The pattern between great events. The old ones on the land have held power for a long, long time. But once power lived in rivers—some seven thousand years ago. There are carvings on the stones beside it that show you the evidence. And the river-things did not share that power; they were worshiped and took what they needed from their acolytes. That time will come again, but this time, I will rule. I will control all of them. I have had an arrangement with the Vila now for many years. I give them what they desire; now I will give them more—for a price. And I will take the other ones into bondage, for my purposes." She laughed.

"Seven thousand years. Surely there is nothing left."

She snorted. "It draws its strength from the forces of nature and the stone of the mountains, the movement of the sun and moon, and those will soon be in alignment."

"Who and what are these things you seek to bind?"

"Various ancient magical rulers. And wolves."

"Wolves?"

She shrugged. "The wolves made a compact with a tribe of stone-workers. And between them they made a compact with a power of air and fire. The forest, the Leshy, which gives allegiance to the earth, joined with them. But the compact must be renewed. If one, just one, the one that draws from all of them, can be constrained to make the same bloody bargain with the last of the old water order, my Vila friends..."

Emeric shook his head. This was out of his depth. He took part in some rituals. He used a few simple spells. But Elizabeth had destroyed the other magic-users and workers far more thoroughly than the Servants of the Holy Trinity had. "How did you find all this out?"

"I have my sources," she said loftily.

She did. Demonic ones. Emeric could only hope that she had checked them against more tangible and less deceptive sources.

Chapter 69

Vlad had ridden—despite the weather—down to the Hawk encampment. He was a familiar face there now. The Mongols had, Erik gathered, decided he was mad. Mad in such a way that he should be humored. Stories of his campaigns had been leaking across to the Golden Horde via the Mongol speakers among the Székely. That merely reenforced their belief that he was mad, and dangerous...in a good sense as long as you were on his side. The Székelers of course took vast pride in him, did everything possible to claim him as one of their own. He was the Count of Székely, as well as the Duke of Valahia. They preferred to call him the former, on every possible occasion.

But Vlad did inspire respect, even this side of the mountains. He seemed to have no real notion of personal safety, often riding alone, even across into Mongol territory, always sleeping apart, yet living with his men. He'd confided to Erik and Manfred that he hated being enclosed by walls. Manfred had taken the opportunity to pass on to the generals of Hawk clan that a suitable gift would be a small felt ger. No gift could have pleased Vlad more: it was just too cold to sleep outdoors in this weather. Those driving sheep and horses west reported that he lived in it. This totally unintended flattery raised his profile still further among the Mongols, who despised those who lived in fixed dwellings.

He was greeted as if he was an honored emissary by the patrols. No one made any attempt to escort him to the guards around the actual camp. Even those merely saluted. Bortai commented on it as he came riding toward them. "He's a trustable man."

"Yes," said Erik. "But I really do think the Mongols have the right of it. He is a little mad. He's a good man ... but on the cusp of being dangerous at times. He's terrifyingly strong, too. He's not a great swordsman ... just powerful." Erik had long since got used to saying exactly what he thought to Bortai.

Bortai nodded. "I would not wish to be his enemy. A sane man will ride away from a fight he cannot win. A madman will attack you even when you know that he cannot. Sometimes such a man takes down many."

Vlad rode up to them, and greeted them politely. "Friend Erik. Lady Bortai. I need to consult with you Erik, and Manfred. And then with *Ritter* Eberhard, about a separate matter."

"Manfred thinks that he should just move up there with you. Like Bombardier Von Thiel. Manfred has just finished with drill." Erik had had to forgo that for the last few weeks whilst waiting for his wound to heal. It was healed, really, by now. He'd started stretching and working it from when the stitches came out. But it was pleasant to rest and talk. And it did Manfred the world of good to put the knights through their drill instead of having Erik do it. A prince ought to know how to do that, Erik thought, faintly guiltily.

They went to find Manfred. He was experimenting with a curved Mongol blade, which he put aside when he saw his visitors. "Ah. An excuse for wine. Have you managed to get us any more, Vlad?"

The duke nodded happily. "I have more merchants traveling every day. They use sleds, now. Which, as the roads are bad...winter has its advantages."

"Some spies, no doubt."

Vlad nodded again. "But as Eberhard pointed out, the news they take back to Emeric is hardly good." He took a deep breath. "It is about that that I wish to speak to you. I have had two letters from the southwest. One is from Ban Alescu. He says that he wishes to meet. That he wishes his castellans to hand over the keys to his fortifications. He will become my vassal. In exchange...he wants certain guarantees. And of course certain territorial increases."

"Talk to Eberhard," said Manfred. "But in a nutshell, do you trust him?"

Vlad shook his head. "It may be that Emeric forced him into the position that he is in. But I would not meet with him without some force at my disposal."

"Hmm," said Manfred. "If you are going to a rendezvous with someone you don't trust, be there early, scout carefully, and make sure you have numbers and space to run."

"And the other letter?" asked Bortai. No one would have dreamed, by now, of asking her to leave. And her Frankish was improving. Perhaps not as fast as Erik's Mongol—but they both tended to mix languages. That made the learning natural. Erik had noticed that she had an absolute fascination with the written word. Of course she could not read Frankish script. But she could—and did read—their own, which was apparently derived from the Chinese. He wondered where she'd learned. It was an unusual accomplishment for anyone who was not a noble, he gathered. But then Bortai broke the rules. She was still the only person that he could talk to about Svan. It had brought him great relief—to the extent that it didn't hurt all the time any more.

"Ah. The other letter. That is far more frightening to me." Vlad rubbed his pale cheek. "My good friend and advisor—the Countess Elizabeth—has been consulting with some practitioner of the magical arts. Now, I know little of these things. I am, I hope, a Christian soul, although I fear for that, sometimes."

"Eneko Lopez—who is one of the finest theologians of Christianity, and also one of its better mages, once said to me that while men feared for their souls, God did not have to," said Manfred. "But anyway, go on?"

"She has had word about a piece of pagan black magic, a blood ritual of sacrifice and torture. She says that her mage has told her that the gypsies probably wanted me for this end. She says they are in league with practitioners of the dark arts. Their errand boys, were the words she used."

"One of the other things Eneko always said was that evil really existed," said Erik. "But . . . he has also said that some of the pagan forces were not overtly evil."

"We had experience of that, in Venice, especially," said Manfred.

"Yes, but she says that they have performed certain scryings and auguries. It is all set to happen on the night of the thirteenth. She says that she is organizing magical and religious safeguards—she is the patron of several nunneries, at her estate, near Caedonia. She asks that I go there, with all haste." He looked at Bortai. "And she includes a warning that the Mongols plan to betray me and attack my forces while I am away."

Bortai stared incredulously at him. Turned to Erik. "Say in my own language!"

Erik found he had no choice but to comply. Bortai said several bad words, showing her soldier-family antecedents.

She stood up. "Khan-over-mountain. I swear to you on my great grandmother's grave. We plan no treachery. This woman lies." Then Bortai moderated her tone. "Or she has been lied to. I go now, to the orkhan of the clan." She stopped mid-turn. "If we wished to kill you," she said, "we could have done so many times. Here or on the trail. Instead the patrols watch over you!" She stormed off.

"That's true enough, Vlad," said Erik.

"I know. But, well, other than the fact that she does not like the gypsies, who have been very good to me—kept me alive and hidden—all the other information Elizabeth has sent me has proved true," said Vlad, unhappily. "That is why I told Bortai about it . . . I feel, well, welcomed here."

"You are," said Erik. "Trust me on this, I've been in a Mongol camp where we were not. They like you and trust you, Vlad. Bortai was saying so earlier. I hope this does not spoil that relationship. You could use peace and trade with them. And a mutual defense against enemies. With allies like them you could stand off Emeric."

Vlad nodded. "I know. And that is why I came. Alone."

Erik saw a group of the Khesig guard coming riding up. "I think Bortai has stirred up a hornet's nest for you. I think you must tell them just what you said right now," said Erik.

The Khesig-men rode off with Vlad. Respectful but . . . uneasy was the right word. The camp was a large one, by now, as large as a market-town. It was incredible how Bortai seemed to know everyone, that she could do this so quickly, thought Erik. But everyone did seem to know her. Erik had even had several strangers tell him what a lovely simple country girl she was.

"Vlad does raise Cain with great ease, said Manfred. "Why was she swearing on her great grandmother's grave of all things?"

Erik shrugged. "Whenever Bortai gets excitable, her great grandmama pops up. I hope they put a good heavy gravestone on her," he said with a smile. "Khutulun. Ancestors are important here. The Mongols reckon that they're still around looking after the living. And I suppose she was someone important."

Vlad looked at their grim faces. Every one from the young khan to the general was looking either offended or just furious.

The young khan spoke. Vlad noticed another boy, one who looked very like Kildai except that his hair was not shaved Mongol style (but looked like it might have been) and with his arm in a splint, stood at his side.

The translator was there. "I hear you believe us treacherous."

Vlad shook his head. "No. That," he said, remembering Erik's advice, "is why I ride to your camp alone."

The translator translated. And Vlad could almost feel the tension in the great ger drain away as the implication of this sank home.

"If I did not trust you, then I would not have told you. And I would certainly not have ridden here alone to do so."

That too took a few moments to sink in. But a few of the assembled officers nodded their heads, thoughtfully.

"The person who sent me this information...has not been wrong before. She sends me much information about the movement of my enemy's troops. She has many contacts. She has found many supporters for me," explained Vlad.

"We do not plan any such thing," said Bortai.

The boy with his arm in a splint said something to the young khan, diffidently.

Bortai was listening in and clapped her hands. "Ah. The letter. It say 'Mongol.' Not Hawk clan? Not White Horde? Is maybe Gatu Orkhan!"

That made sense. Vlad felt himself smiling.

One of the other officers—the one who had led the Mongol relief of the prisoners from what proved to be a trap—spoke.

"General Pakai, he ask, your spy says the attack will happen when you go to see spy-woman about magic?"

That was about the gist of it, although Vlad had never thought of Elizabeth Bartholdy that way. He nodded.

The general spoke again.

"General he say, you are an honorable man when

we rescue women and children. He will come with you as a hostage. Hawk clan attack your people..." the translator drew a finger a cross his throat.

Bortai and several others chimed in immediately. Obviously volunteering themselves.

The boy spoke. Which translated to, "We will also send Shaman Kaltegg. To protect you from evil magic."

David found himself called into the presence of Kari, Erik, old Eberhard and Prince Manfred later that day. "*Ritter* Von Stael says that you tell him you were present at the meeting of Vlad and the young khan," said Erik.

"And I would like to know why they have a young Jackanapes like you in their royal tent, but for all that they treat us very well, we have yet to be invited," said Eberhard.

"We see everyone from their generals to even young Kildai and Bortai every day," said Erik, defensively. "I've been meaning to ask you, David. Has Kildai been adopted by the...what do you call them, Khesig. The elite troop."

The devil that seemed to leave him when he dealt with Von Stael was back, with delight, in David. Sometimes people really couldn't see what was waved in front of their own noses. The Golden Horde—especially the White Horde, and naturally, extra especially the Hawk clan, still put a lot of store in the show of austerity that the Great Khan had instituted. That didn't mean that one could not see who was rich and powerful. It was just more subtle than these Franks were used to. Oh what a prize jest! It was rather like desert tribesmen persuading foreigners that sheep's eyes were a delicacy, especially reserved for guests. Half the Golden Horde were laughing at Bortai's trick, and playing along much better by now. "Oh yes. He's a sort of mascot," said David. "Because he got away from the orkhan. And his father was quite well known to the old Khesig, you know. I get called on because I know him, and I speak Frankish. They want to know about the knights. I tell them a lot of good things."

"A pack of lies if you ask me," said Kari.

"Sometimes," admitted David, and ducked.

"So tell us what happened with Vlad."

"But that would be betraying confidences," said David as righteously as Von Stael himself.

"Don't make me angry," said Kari.

David shrugged. "Bortai got them frothing like new beer. Magic and the spirits are really important to them. And they're very touchy about honor. The prince calmed them down pretty quickly. They like him nearly as much Bortai likes Erik. Ouch!"

"Keep to the point," said Kari. "Or I'll box the other ear. And you be grateful I got there first."

David caught Erik's, and, more intimidatingly, Manfred's glare and hastily continued. "Well, I pointed out that the warning might be about the Gatu Orkhan . . . which it might, and then old General Pakai, he chirped that he'd go as a hostage. Just about all of them offered themselves. So a bunch will be going with him. And just in case it's Gatu, the Hawk clan and their allies are going on an exercise to the possible passes. Oh, and some hairy old shaman is being sent along with Vlad."

"And us," said Manfred. "We're going to protect his soul and stand his friends. And Eberhard is going along to do his negotiating with this tricky piece of work from Irongate."

A day later, again in one of the better breaks in the icy weather that they'd had, Vlad, and a substantial part of his army, rode south. They were accompanied by the Knights of the Holy Trinity and some twenty Mongols, including Bortai and three other young women, and a short, hairy old man with a marked bouquet and very bright eyes. He didn't smell unwashed or anything, thought Erik. The shaman just made Erik want to sneeze.

Vlad rode with the knights, and not, for once, with his own men. "Friends," he said, his voice reflecting an inner turmoil. "I am so glad you are here with me, with the holy crosses around me. I . . . I truly fear for my soul. Something is dragging at me. I must go south . . . southwest. I must. I cannot even sleep properly waking repeatedly, wanting to go. I think someone has set a compulsion on me. It's as if a great tide is dragging at me."

Later that afternoon when they stopped for the night, Erik repeated this conversation to Bortai. Who in turn took him to see the old shaman.

The old man looked thoughtful. "There is a spell on him. I saw that when I first met him." He shrugged. "But the spell does not work properly. Not on one like that, no. I can clean it away. It is just on one arm."

Erik sneezed.

And again.

"Sorry. It's the pepper."

"What?" asked Bortai.

"Pepper. Can't you sbell idb?"

They both looked at him strangely. "No," said Bortai. Erik knew it was a spice they used a lot of. He backed away from the old shaman a little. That was better.

The shaman peered at him. "Witch-smeller?"

"What?" asked Erik.

"You smell the users of magics, yes?"

"Not that I know of."

But it came to him, later, that he had smelled odd things when they'd encountered magic before. A dusty smell of snow with the magics out of Lithuania. Less pleasant bouquets on Corfu. It had never occurred to him that others might not smell the same things. How did he know if other noses were smelling what he did?

It did seem to impress Bortai enormously though. They found Vlad. Praying.

"The Mongol shaman says he saw a spell on you, Vlad. He says he can take it off."

"He can?" asked Vlad, eagerly. And then, "But... isn't he a pagan?"

"Almost certainly," said Erik, keeping a straight face.

"And he say Erik is ... What is the word, Erik?" said Bortai, grabbing his arm with excitement, her eyes sparkling.

"I didn't really understand it. He said that I was a witch-smeller. But I can't say I understand it."

"Do you think... he could help me?" asked Vlad. "I mean, would it be a sin? I feel as if I must run south." Vlad rubbed his forearms and then said, rather desperately: "Is it not true that the power of prayer, the name of Christ and the cross trump all pagan magics? Let us go, friends."

Erik had seen various enactment of Christian magic.

This was different. Noisier for starters, involving a lot of rhythmic beating on a small drum. And oddly, the old fellow passed out. Bortai assured him it was quite normal. That he merely went into the spirit world to do what had to be done. Then Erik simply had to go out to sneeze. By the time he came back, the old fellow was washing the back of one of Vlad's hands. The water turned a rusty reddish brown. And it smelled rotten. The shaman put the entire wooden bowl into the fire, along with a considerable muttering and various fluttering passes. The fire devoured it.

"Feel any better?" asked Erik.

Vlad took a deep breath. "No. All I can think is that I miss Rosa more than ever. I have to find out where she has gone. But I still must go south. Pardon me, my friends, but I must go pray again."

"What was it?" asked Bortai, when he had left.

"Sexual spell. For lust," said the old shaman grinning. "To trap and hold. Nasty spell. You don't need that, eh."

Erik blushed. Bortai gave the shaman a look that, if looks could kill, would have the old man in the realms of Erleg Khan right now.

There was no need to bring that up. None at all. It had been a perfectly unrelated airy enquiry earlier, about whether love charms really worked.

Chapter 70

In the moonlight, twisting tendrils of the freezing river mist crawled over the outer wall of the island. The guard trudging between the towers had his mind on staying warm, rather than on any possibility of an attack.

She was sitting on the battlement.

Naked.

Wet.

Her eyes were empty and glowed green.

He screamed and tried to flee.

She caught him easily.

So many of the others had drowned themselves in the freezing river, rather than be caught.

Barely a handful made it to the boats, and only two of those boats reached the shore.

The fishes would feed well.

The Ban Alescu was not in his fortress that night. He was discussing troop dispositions with his boyars in his city of Orsoua.

Chapter 71

The "gypsy" encampment was finally breaking up. Dana thought it odd to be moving. This place had been their home for months. But they were travelers, and the sense of something long awaited about to happen was almost palpable.

The wyverns had gone. She'd been up this morning, avoiding annoying Emil and his guards, back to their usual place. But the wyverns weren't there. Miu was.

"Where are they?" she demanded.

He pointed up slope, towards the snow-clad peaks. "They go back to the lacul Podragul. It is covered in ice now, but they will break the ice. It is important that they go there to ask the old questions."

"Old questions?"

"Of the water. And the things that live in it. The time is coming."

"I don't understand."

"Neither do they, and that is important," said Miu annoyingly. "And like you, they will get no answers. Now, your watchdogs are looking for you. You want me to create a distraction while you get back to the camp?"

It would be a wolf.

She wasn't supposed to know, but she wasn't that stupid.

The gypsies had converted their carts into sleds. They went east, for the track across to the Olt valley. It was hard traveling, and, from what Dana could gather, they were expecting the Jiu valley—where she found out they were headed—to be worse.

Dana found it all incredibly irritating. She wanted to go straight over those snowy mountains, straight as an arrow southwest. She eventually said so.

Angelo nodded. "That is where we go, little one. But we have to go around the mountains." He seemed satisfied. Dana was not. She wanted to get *on*. It was pulling her. And they were going the wrong way. She rode some of the time. It was a better option than sitting in the cart, listening to her mother.

Elizabeth consulted her scrying tools. Excellent. They came. They came from the Olt Valley with the girl, and also from the northeast. Vlad.

Excellent! She must send Dorko and Ilana-Jo into Caedonia to buy some extra provisions. She sniggered. Why, they'd be entertaining soon. By the looks of it the girl would be here first. There was no time for seduction. It would be straight into the dungeon with her. She could scream with the others. Elizabeth had taken serious measures, both physical and magical, to ensure that they could not be heard. She still had fifty of Emeric's troops at her disposal. They would be useful for snatching the girl from the wolves. She had been very busy putting up magical defenses against them,

because they would be desperate to get the girl back...
especially once they realized their foe had Vlad too.

It was a good thing that Emeric had gone to Irongate.
She didn't want him getting any of his silly ideas about
Vlad or his little sister. Irongate should keep him happy.
Of course, he couldn't actually go into Irongate. Or
past it. No, not any more. The place was infested with
a river's worth of beautiful naked women with green
empty eyes.

She laughed nastily. The local people would be
taking some priests along to try to exorcize them
soon. A pity that they could only get there by boat.
Drowned priests appealed to her. She suspected that
the Ban would be all eagerness to reach some kind
of accommodation with his overlord. It was a pity he
had not been in the island-castle. Her spies said that
he was marshaling rather a lot of his followers. He
was strong among the southern boyars.

Dana was wholly unprepared when it happened.
She was riding a little way behind the caravan of sleds
and horses. As usual, her brother's three men were
riding close by. They looked...edgy, she thought. And
then, suddenly, at a gallop they came towards her.
"Hungarian Patrol!" they shouted. "We must flee."
And they swept her along with them, up a trail into
a side valley. She clung to her horse.

And then there was a rude surprise. At least half
a company of King Emeric's soldiers. Waiting.

One of the three tried to draw a firearm...and
was promptly killed.

Dana had never seen death before. Not...close.
"You...murderer!" she screamed.

Emil—the sergeant in charge of the other two—grabbed her. "We need to move," He said, as the troopers calmly shot the other man. His voice sounded very odd. Almost a sob.

Dana bit him, but it didn't help. He didn't even seem to notice. They tied her up. And tied her to the saddle.

The troopers pushed their horses along the trail someone had painstakingly cleared of snow, obviously deliberately for this purpose. They covered several miles before coming to a bleak stone castle.

There she was cut free of the horse. The troopers plainly had no intention of staying. She, and that vile traitor Emil, walked up the stairs to the heavy doors, with the sound of their departing hooves in her ears.

Emil knocked. The door was opened . . . by a dwarf. A man with a thoroughly venomous expression. "Come. You are expected."

They were marched down several corridors, and to a large, luxuriously appointed salon, heavily furnished with mirrors.

It appeared the person expecting her was fond of seeing her own reflection.

That was not surprising. She was truly celestially beautiful. Her skin was exquisite and her hair so gold it almost glowed. She had a little rosebud mouth. Dana had expected King Emeric, or some general. But not . . . her.

Emil groveled at her feet, but she did not even seem to notice. Instead she walked over to Dana and raised her chin with a perfect forefinger. "What a lovely child," said the woman. "My favorite age. But I think we need to restore you to your true appearance first."

Dana felt her hair twitch and straighten. "The complexion too, I think," said the witch. Looking at

686 *Mercedes Lackey, Eric Flint & Dave Freer*

herself in one of the mirrors Dana saw the brown stain drain away, leaving her skin its usual white, with just a touch of color at the cheeks.

Dana had been alternately frightened and angry, and plotting revenge ever since the kidnaping. Now... she was just terrified.

"Beautiful! And so virginal and afraid," said the woman. She licked her lips. "Almost I am tempted to play, now. But your brother comes. He should be here before Vespers."

There was a big beefy woman, with a face like cold pork-fat standing waiting. "Take her below, Dorko."

Dana was propelled away. And when she tried to lie down rather than cooperate, she was picked up like a screaming, kicking sack of meal and carried. Her last view of was of Emil, still on the floor. His expression was both adoring and, somehow, anguished.

Hearing the sound of gunfire, they halted. The small army was moving with a strong perimeter of scouts, with two companies ahead, mounted infantry and Székeler cavalry, and another riding the flanks, with a fringe of scouts beyond that, wading their way through snowdrift and forests—this was not territory which had declared itself for the new duke.

A Székeler primor galloped up and reported, "The scouts found signs of a large group of horse. Fifty or so. We followed them. They were Hungarian soldiers, Drac."

"I thought your informant said that there were none within seventy miles and Caedonia was ready to declare for you, Vlad," said Manfred.

"I suppose they could have moved. Where have they gone, Primor?"

"We're burying most of them, Drac. We asked the survivors some questions. They say the king himself was here three days ago, with a thousand men. He's gone south, to Irongate. They were supposed to join him. They say there are no other troops near at hand."

"I do hope the Countess Elizabeth is all right," said Vlad. "She has played a difficult double game for me."

"Well, provided there are no other nasty surprises, I think we'd like to make the castle before dark. It's going to be a bitter night."

"It is nearby," said the primor. "Maybe half a mile away."

They rode on, and soon could see the turrets on the skyline. It was a monolithic place, with looming high walls of featureless dark stone, broken only by tiny window-slits. "She's a wealthy woman," said Manfred, impressed.

The snowy silences were suddenly torn by a terrible howling.

"This is a bad place, Drac," said the primor. "Listen to those wolves."

"We have two thousand men, Primor. We should be able to cope with a few wolves."

The man looked doubtful. "They say," he said darkly. "That wolves can turn to men in these foreign parts"—as if they were ten thousand leagues away, instead of twenty leagues from his village.

Mirko grinned. "Ah, but they also say that the king of the wolves of the mountains, also answers to the Prince of Valahia."

Soon they were at the castle gates. The gatehouse was empty, and the gates open. They rode on to the great hall itself. Vlad dismounted and walked up the steps to the great doors. These were flung open.

"Why, Vlad!" said the stunningly beautiful blond woman in the doorway, flanked by the footmen who had flung it open. "I was expecting just you. Not an army."

She didn't sound wholly pleased to be receiving one.

"It is hard for me travel without one, Countess. Especially when we found some of Emeric's troops waiting for us," said Vlad. It was odd. They said that absence made the heart grow fonder. But seeing her, Vlad realized it was not so. He had felt conflicted before. Now...she was very beautiful. A lovely woman in the flower of her youth. But he missed Rosa.

"They can't come in here, Prince Vlad," she said, glancing at the troops.

"Then we must leave and find lodging elsewhere, Countess. It is cold and I will not have them sleep outdoors tonight. You told us Caedonia was ready to declare for me, and it is not. They fired on my banners," he said, grimly. He gestured at the castle. "It is a large establishment. Can you not make space for them? They'll bed down in the halls if need be."

Elizabeth was furious. There was going to be some servere punishment for a lesser demon. He had deliberately deceived her. Deliberately! He had *not* shown her this force. "It is Emeric's doing," she said angrily. "Caedonia *was* ready to declare for you. But he led a force up here. I managed to send him chasing off to Irongate."

She paused. "Well. What can't be cured must be endured. Caedonia is my city. I will have messengers sent..." she saw Vlad's expression. Was he becoming even more resistant to her magics? "Not tonight. Tonight, somehow we will cope. I just ask that you order the men to stay out of the cloisters!"

She looked onto the field. At the bright silver shields and their three red crosses. She wanted to be sick. How did they get here? If there was one thing she feared... "Who... who are they?" she croaked. She would lash that little demon with white fire.

"Ah. Let me introduce you," said Vlad beckoning them closer. Several knights dismounted. "These are my good friends. Prince Manfred of Brittany. *Ritter* Erik Hakkonsen of Iceland, and the good *Ritter* Eberhard of Brunswick. Remember how you said that I was weak politically. Well, I have found a wonderful advisor!"

Elizabeth bowed, recovering herself. Manfred of Brittany. Here? Well, what a prize for little Emeric. Manfred's Icelandic ladies'-delight companion looked a little unwell. "Forgive me for being so abrupt. I was... rather surprised. Come in. If you will pardon me I will go and speak immediately to my castellan and chatelaine about arrangements for your men." She turned to her dwarf retainer. "Refreshments. Mulled wine, Ficzko."

The dwarf bowed. But the look he gave Vlad was one of unmixed hatred and fear. She would have to discipline him.

Erik struggled to control his stomach. How could they live with the stink in here? Something had died and was rotten. Castles stank as a rule. You got used to it. But perhaps he had been outdoors for too long. It didn't seem to be bothering anyone else.

She would have to delay. Her castle, her castle stables... they bulged indecently. The passages were full of common men-at-arms. Lascivious commoners, devouring her with their eyes. Did they not know who she was?

Well, no. That was the point. Anyway, she still had three days. The moon and the sun were still moving toward their appointed places. Tomorrow she would send the troops off. She would bring intolerable pressure to bear on that stupid mayor, by magical means, tonight. Well. She could not chase them all out. She would have to allow Vlad the appearance of having a guard. Perhaps thirty or forty men. She could manage to deal with twice that number easily enough.

The Knights of the Holy Trinity worried her most. They were protected, curse them. On the other hand... they could be trapped. Confined to a wing, while she did her work on Vlad and the girl. Then the two could be magically prepared for the rape, murder and bloodletting that she planned to turn their ancient ritual into. Oh yes, the Prince and Princess of Valahia would share blood. Her share would be all of it. Every drop drained from those bodies. And a dark rite and a binding of the water-dwellers. First of course they would need to be driven into her net. Betrayal and self-disgust would break their wills. She could start on the girl tonight...

Then she realized she couldn't. Not even with her abilities. There were just too many of them. She couldn't even walk down her own corridors. And she would need all her power tomorrow. She would even forgo the seduction—stopping just short of actual penetration, that she had planned for Vlad. But he was no longer a virgin. Would it matter? The book had clearly stated "innocent and willing" were requirements for the blood-letting. Count Mindaug had assured her that bending Vlad's and Dana's wills to her purpose would work. They would be "willing."

❀   ❀   ❀

On the snowy hills beyond the barrier she had set up, very nearly the entire pack—only old Silva, left to tend Dana's mother—men, women, and children roamed. The barrier held them back. But...she would have to lift it. Have to move them to the place at the head of the Jiu valley where it all began.

And somehow they had to stop her. The wyverns might have the power to cross the barrier. But they were busy, busy with the call. Calling the ancient dwellers of the forest to come to the open place, the place of stones...to be betrayed, enslaved and killed.

In the filthy cell, Dana cried. No one came. But there were others, weeping. Screaming too. Eventually, Dana found something. Her courage. Her pride. And she began to sing. A hymn. A prayer. It seemed the only thing appropriate for this place. *"Áve María, grátia pléna, Dóminus técum. Benedícta tu in muliéribus, et benedíctus frúctus véntris túi, Iésus Sáncta María, Máter Déi, óra pro nóbis peccatóribus, nunc et in hóra mórtis nóstrae. Ámen."*

"Hush," said someone in a nearby cell. A frightened tearful child's voice. "They will hurt you if you sing...that. Maybe even kill you."

"They dare not let me live," said Dana, trying to keep the tremor out of her voice. "So I may as well sing. God may hear me. And when they kill me, God having heard me will be of more use to me." She began again. This time, by the third repetition, the other child in the nearby cell began singing, too. More voices joined. Some called for them to shut up. Some still screamed or cried.

Vlad had found a place to be alone, and outside the walls. On the top of a turreted tower, he had them erect his little ger. And he stood, breathing great breaths of icy air that no one shared, that was not confined by walls. He felt faintly guilty at taking over Elizabeth's castle like this. But the welfare of his men came first.

A wolf howled out the night. Vlad gave in to his inner self. He howled back. And was answered by a chorus...

"Talking to the wolves?" said Erik.

Vlad smiled. "They can go south. I must stay here."

Erik looked at the ger.

Looked at Vlad. Looked at the ger again. "Do you mind if I share your quarters tonight?" he asked abruptly. "I can't take it down there. I have a bedding roll."

Vlad felt a little nonplussed. He liked his privacy. But... He nodded. "Of course."

Erik smiled. He looked a bit pale. But perhaps it was the moonlight. "Thank you."

Somewhere, far away, Vlad could hear someone singing the Ave Maria. A sad, young, woman's voice. Sad yet strong. It must be one of the nuns.

"Where is Erik?" demanded Bortai. "The tall blond man..."

"I know who you mean," said the shaman grinning at her. "Where are your chaperones, Princess?"

"Down the hall, eating. They do not worry about you," said Bortai calmly. "Now, have you seen Erik?"

"The witch-smeller was looking unwell. Maybe he went to look for some air," said the shaman.

"You really think he is a witch-smeller?" It was something of very high status among the Horde.

"I think so, yes. He is untrained though. No one has taught him. But I see magic and the workings. He smells it. There is much here. This place is full of spells."

"I don't like her," said Bortai abruptly, feeling foolish. She sounded like a jealous young fourteen-year-old. "Her smile isn't real. It doesn't go to her eyes."

The old shaman nodded. "She is full of spells. All over."

"I'd better find him. We should leave this place."

The shaman nodded. "The tengeri here...are afraid."

"I'm not going without him," said Bortai, knowing that she was being stupid and utterly transparent.

He nodded. "I think that would be a mistake." He pointed to Manfred, making his way past. "Perhaps he will know."

Manfred did. He laughed. "On top of one of the turrets, with Vlad. Both fast asleep in that felt tent. How they got it up there I do not know. They're a sight. Both sleeping with their swords laid like crosses on their chests."

"They are all right?" That was how they had laid the knights for burial... "They are not dead?"

Manfred shook his head. "Trust me. No one snores quite like Erik. He and Vlad were doing a beautiful duet. He woke up when I looked in. He sleeps like a cat. I was worried about him, so I went to check," said his overlord. He grinned at Bortai. "You'll get used to the snoring, really, after a week or two. Francesca had a very ladylike little trumpet. She used to get very angry when I told her about it."

"I do not know what you mean," said Bortai a little stiffly. Maybe she didn't understand as much Frankish as she thought.

He grinned. "We'll see. Good night. I don't think I'll find entertainment or even strong drink tonight."

Chapter 72

Elizabeth's morning was no more pleasurable. The city of Caedonia was one of the largest and richest in all Valahia. It was also her backyard. Emeric had made sure it would stay loyal. He had troops garrisoned there, and a loyal council, and town elders.

She had to turn all that around. Of course she didn't really want to surrender it. Just get rid of the bulk of Vlad's troops. And given the short time she had available, it would be hard to set up as a trap... still, with magical communications, she thought she could do it effectively.

Vlad had ridden to Caedonia that morning. All the fools in the city had to do was hide and wait until the billeted troops were asleep that night.

The gates were open, as she'd ordered. Vlad's troops entered the city, with him at their head.

And then it had all gone wrong.

The city had greeted him like a long lost savior. Vlad got the sort of rapturous liberator's welcome that Elizabeth was sure Emeric had never got from these ingrates. They'd also greeted Vlad with a gibbet.

With her people hanging from it. And far from hiding the troops that had been there to deal with matters that night, the towns-people were desperately eager to help flush them out. Even though it meant burning a few of the town's buildings. Most of the Slovene troops had been far too willing to surrender, offering their own officers' heads as tokens of this.

And Vlad had been far from pleased with them. He seemed to take no pleasure in the hangings, and ordered the bodies taken down for a decent burial immediately.

"There will be no more hangings without the process of law," he told the town representatives bluntly.

They were stunned. As she had been. But...once it sunk in, they were not displeased...except, as the head of the goldsmith's guild pointed out, one of the men they'd hung was the chief justice imposed on them by King Emeric. "And he'd have hung us, not those that deserved it," said the goldsmith.

Vlad had rubbed his chin. Nodded. "A reasonable point. I like the Székeler way of doing it. You will elect your own chief justice in the future. He will answer first to God, then to you when he faces reelection. Every ten years, shall we say. And of course finally to me."

There was a another silence. The goldsmith—Elizabeth resolved to remember him—coughed. "Wouldn't that diminish your authority, Drac?"

Vlad shook his head. "No. Not if you think about it. It will, I hope, increase the respect and affection my people hold for me."

The goldsmith took a deep breath. "It does mine, Drac."

Vlad had them eating out of his hand, damn him. And he didn't seem to care what power he was giving up, and how long it would take her to set the city to rights again. She might just have to burn it down and start afresh.

And worse, the process took time. It was after None, the ninth hour of the day, and already heading into dusk, before she got back to her estate. To add to her irritation, they had not shed enough of his retinue to make her happy. The knights were still with him. And so was the little contingent of Mongols she hadn't noticed before. There were several women with them, who might be usable.

She excused herself fairly soon after they got back, leaving them to dine without her. First, she needed to make sure that the knights would be trapped in the wing they were to be quartered in. Then she would go down to her dungeon and begin work on the girl. At midnight, she would summon Vlad to the chapel.

Bortai had refused to stay in the comfortable lodgings that a wary—but eager to impress—town had offered the Mongols. No, they must remain with the Khan-over-the-Mountains, she had said in what she hoped was a polite fashion to the translator. It was odd that her Frankish was now far more fluent than the few words of Vlachs that she had. Of course a number of Vlachs words had crept in to the Mongol vocabulary via the slaves. That brought a moment of guilt to her. If Ion had been with them he could have spoken to these people. But of course you could hardly take a Vlachs slave into

Valahia. He would run away... He deserved more than the rewards he had been given.

She felt like a prisoner herself in this place.

The guests had finally retired... and Elizabeth's work was done. The knights would not leave that wing. They were walled in.

On the handful of Mongols and Vlad's Székely guards, she'd merely settled for locking them in, and binding the doors with minor magics.

Elizabeth had taken Dana and the girl from the next cell for the start to her work. They would almost certainly have spoken. And her watchers reported that they'd been trying for heavenly aid. Both of them.

"One of you broke my rules," she said. "One of you was praying. One of you two will be cleaning human excrement from the cells with your hands. After your face has been rubbed in it."

To the peasant child that would be disgusting. To the daughter of a noble house far worse...

"It—"

"Be quiet until you are told to speak, peasant brat. Lady Dana. Was it you?" That first denial. That first lie. The first choice to let someone else take your punishment... oh it would be sweet.

"Yes," said Dana. "It was." And she began to sing again.

"Gag her," hissed Elizabeth. "Gag the little bitch. Strip her naked. I want her intact. But a beating and then you can sodomise her, Janos. Bring me my whip."

She would break her. If need be she would do it by magic. But first she'd bleed a little.

The little thing fought like a wildcat when they tried to take her clothes. They ended up tearing them off.

"It is pulling me apart," said Vlad.

He was, Erik noted, sweating. It was cold enough to frost the battlements. In the background the wolves howled.

"Let us go down to the chapel. It's at the entry to the nunnery," said Erik. "Prayer will help."

So they walked down. The place was oddly quiet, as if something was swallowing even the sound of their footfalls.

They went. Someone was plainly preparing to clean the enormous chapel. Perhaps because of the attached nunnery it could take several hundred people. The pews had been removed, and it was very big and empty. The huge carpet that had given such unexpected comfort to their knees had been rolled back. They walked up the steps to the dais and knelt at the altar below the ornate sliver cross. Fat candles burned there.

Vlad bowed his head . . . and then stopped. "Erik. Do you read Latin?" he said.

Erik nodded. "Yes."

Vlad pointed to the small inscription below the cross. "What does that say? Was I taught wrongly?"

Erik had seen the familiar words. Not really read them. Now he did, translating. "Our father who was in heaven—"

He turned around to look at his companion and his eyes were caught by a pattern. He looked instead at the floor behind them. "Vlad," he said quietly.

"We need the knights. I think we have stumbled on something that we need their help with."

"What?"

"Look at the floor."

Exposed now, they could see they stood in a pentacle, inset into the floor. The altar was inside it, the point going up into the nave of the chapel.

Neither said anything. But Erik could swear that he heard a dark chuckle.

And somehow the passages seemed to have twisted on them. Ten minutes later they found themselves back at the doors to the chapel.

"Draw your sword," said Erik.

Vlad did, warily.

"Reverse the blade and touch it to the ground."

Erik felt a vague jolt as he did so. "I wish we were in full armor," he said. "Now... It's that way."

It wasn't easy because the candles kept going out ahead of them...but this time they found their way to the door to the wing where the knights were housed.

Only there was no door.

Just massive stone blocks and mortar, visible in the moonlight from the arrow slit.

Erik pounded on it.

It was no illusion.

"And now?" said Vlad.

Erik took a deep breath. "Dark magics, friend. Very black." He pondered for a moment. "It is the antithesis of Christianity. It opposes us well. Let's try the Mongols. That shaman of theirs...was something different. The door should be down those stairs and to the right. Let us see if that is stone too."

It wasn't.

But it wasn't opening either.

There was not even a crack that they could get their swords into—although they could see the crack in the moonlight. To the touch it was smooth. It felt like glass.

Bortai had endured a tough evening. Not only was she less than comfortable in this place, but their hostess had talked to her. That had meant in Frankish—a second language for both of them. The countess spoke it fluently, however. She was ... polite. She had pried into Bortai's private life. Whether she had any suitors. It was something many women might wish to know. But not on first meeting! Bortai had been coy about her relationships and her rank. She'd stuck to the theme of "simple Mongol warrior's daughter who speaks some Frankish: that was why she was here." She'd been uneasy speaking to the woman. The countess was, quite literally, flawless. Her skin showed none of the tiny signs of wind, sun and weather that Bortai was aware that her own skin showed. And everything, from her teeth to her eyebrows, was perfectly symmetrical. That wasn't natural, surely?

Then the woman had excused herself, saying she had work to do. What work? Those hands had never as much as pushed a needle. She had just wanted to get away from them. Bortai had not found it possible to talk to Erik. He'd kept away at the only time they could have mingled, when their hostess was talking to her.

And now ... her unease was terrible. She took Magdun, one of her accompanying chaperones, and went to find the shaman Kaltegg. She found the old man laying small stones on the floor in a complex pattern by the door. He kept tapping his little quodba drum.

"Some bad things out there," he said. "But this is a strong country if you reach deep enough. The bad is new."

"Let us try our swords as crosses against it."

Erik nodded. "And maybe...I think a psalm?"

Vlad had a deep, clear tuneful baritone. Erik was not very musical, but he had a strong voice to follow...

And there was a sound from inside.

They both heard the singing. The shaman smiled. "Ah. He reaches for the deep bones of the land. And it gives him strength."

"That is Erik's voice, too," said Bortai and tried to open the door. It would not open. She called to him.

The shaman came and tried it as well.

Then his eyes narrowed and he reached into his pouch. He pulled out a small doeskin bag, opened the drawstring and took out a pinch of something. He blew it at the door. And the door slammed open to reveal two startled looking men, Vlad and Erik.

Without thinking about it Bortai ran out and hugged Erik. And then backed off, hastily.

"My magic is stronger than her magic," said the shaman, grinning like a rather mischievous boy. "Really, I think it is just different. She draws on demons. I draw on the land and the tengeri of it."

The noise had roused the entire Mongol contingent, and, armed and half dressed, they had come out into the passage.

"We have a problem," said Erik, simply, with no

further ado. "We have found some terrible magic, vile and black, and somehow there is a wall shutting the knights in. Can you help us?" The Mongols only waited long enough to arm up completely and get boots on—which was wise, because a man that stepped on something sharp in a fight was a cripple and useless. They followed Erik and Vlad through the hallways. It was dark, all the candles in the sconces having gone out, and the moonlight being limited by the paucity of windows. The shaman muttered. He reached into his pouch. Felt about...and came out with something that looked like a little fluffy ball of light. He teased some strands off it. Handed each of them some of the threads. "Moonlight," he said. "I catch it in the fine lambs-wool and keep it. Tie it to your helmets." It helped.

Thus lit, they came to where the door to the wing that the knights were in should be...and now a very solid wall stood, keyed in to the arch.

The shaman nodded thoughtfully. "Very clever. Real stones," he said, tapping them. Erik was not tapping. He was pounding. It did make a noise, but not much. If there was any sound from inside, they could not hear it.

Vlad and Erik tried singing at the door.

"Real stones," said the shaman. "Magic on inside. Maybe they'll hear you, but I don't know."

Vlad stopped. "I think we need to find Elizabeth," he said. "She has to be involved in this."

So they went along to the countess's rooms. The confusion spell of earlier seemed to have dissipated, and they found it with no trouble. Erik had given up on finesse and politeness. He tried the handle, it opened, and he barged in to the room.

It was a very opulent chamber. It led into an even

more opulent bed chamber. No one was in either. They found three other rooms—a walk-in wardrobe full of clothes—more than a princess would own. Then a dressing room, all with more mirrors—even one over the bed—than any person would want . . . and another room. A place of magical paraphernalia, some rather unpleasant in nature. There were bones . . . black ones. There were things in bottles. Some of them were alive or at least moving . . . The place stank. And she was not in it.

But the shaman had teased a single blond hair from the inlaid ivory brush in front of the mirror in the bedchamber. He held it up. Tapped his drum. The golden blond hair fluttered as if in a strong breeze. "Follow," he said.

They did.

It led them downstairs, and downstairs again . . . to a blank wall.

"Walled off again?"

The shaman walked closer. Touched it. "Is not real."

He had to try several things before a pattern of gray stones laid before the wall made it suddenly flicker and become a heavy, studded door, reinforced with iron, with a solid bar, and large lock. Only the bar was slid open, and the key was in the lock. Erik turned the key and pushed. It opened into a dark passage, leading down. And the sound of screaming came out of it.

Vlad led the way into the maw. Erik was just on his heels.

Dana bit her lip savagely. She would not scream again. It gave the countess too much pleasure. The countess had shed her clothes, too. Somehow that was less obscene than the other women who had held her, in their parody of nuns' robes, even with wimples on their heads . . . with cut-aways on their breasts, between which upside-down broken crosses swayed.

The countess leaned over. Dana could feel her nails on the whip-cuts. She stepped around those who held Dana. Licked her fingers. A little blood trickled down from the corner of her mouth. "I can feel my skin refresh," she said, her voice thick and throaty.

Dana said nothing. It was all she could do not to whimper. But while she could, she would not. She'd screamed the first time . . . not the second or the third.

"Let us see how she does with the pain of others," said the woman.

More of her vile pack held the peasant girl. They simply pulled up her thin dress and the countess brought her whip down. She screamed. So did Dana.

"My brother will come. And he will hang you or burn you, you witch."

The countess laughed mockingly. "He is here already, you poor little fool. How do you think I caught you? Who brought you to me? His man."

Dana closed her eyes. And began to sing. Her voice felt small and weak. "*Áve María, grátia pléna . . .*"

Those holding her nearly let go. Dana struggled with every ounce of her strength. And somehow it was enough. She was free. They snatched at her. And she ran, pushing aside the little dwarf.

And somewhere down the passage, the singing of strong men's voices answered her—clean and wholesome and strong. She ran frantically towards it, as Elizabeth and her obscene nuns followed behind her, like a pack of slavering beasts.

❀　　❀　　❀

Erik wondered if they had entered hell. Or at least the earthly version of it. The first room they came to was plainly a torture chamber. It had a rack, a "bed of no rest," a grate with shackles suspended over a fire-pit, and a wheel. Various instruments for cutting, burning, and tearing flesh were hanging from the walls. And there was a large bath with meat-hooks above it.

The entire small group stayed very close together, swords and knives at the ready.

They moved deeper into this place of horrors and came to the cells, and some had children in them. Vlad pulled angrily at the locked door, and those within cowered away and screamed.

Just then another quavering scream came down the passage. And then moments later, a girl's voice, singing. The same voice, and the same song, that he and Vlad had heard on the battlements. Vlad answered... and they ran towards it.

A naked, pale, dark-haired girl came sprinting desperately toward them, pursued by the harpies of hell. Leading the harpies was a equally naked woman.

The Countess Elizabeth. And with her came the terrible stench of decay.

Erik raised his sword. "That which cannot abide the name of Christ, begone!" he shouted.

The pack halted... and the girl flung herself towards them. "Dear God. Help me!" She panted.

Vlad and Erik stepped forward, and pulled her between them, to shelter behind them. They stood, swords out and ready.

"Elizabeth?" said Vlad, incredulously.

The countess smiled. She might have perfect features, but it was smile of pure evil. "Vlad," she purred.

"Come to me. I crave your body. I need to couple with you now."

Vlad stared at her, his pale aristocratic face expressionless. And then he said: "You foul, unhallowed bitch. I should treat you as my grandfather treated all his enemies. Get away from me!"

If he had kicked her in the stomach he could hardly have had more of an effect on her. Her face was anything but beautiful just then. It took on an expression that could not be described as anything other than fiendish. She raised a hand covered in streaks of dried blood and pointed a talonlike finger at Vlad. "By Ashteroth, Baal'zebub and all the lesser names. I command you to come to me. I command your lusts! Come and rape me!" she screamed.

By the cold fury on Vlad's face, it looked as if he would very much like to impale her—but not in the way she wanted.

"Let's get the hell out of here," said Erik quietly. "There are more of them behind her. And they have weapons."

Vlad nodded.

They began to back away, slowly, swords at the ready.

"You cannot resist!" screeched Elizabeth, her voice cutting across the shadows like a poisoned knife "No man can resist me! My magics command you!"

"Not anymore," whispered the shaman behind them. "I washed the spell away."

All Erik could do was to thank heaven for that.

Elizabeth did not seem to understand that her power over Vlad had been broken. She continued to call on demons, and scream at Vlad to come and violate her. . . . Perhaps it had been a long time since anyone had escaped her. But it eventually did sink in. "Seize them!" she screamed.

The passage between the cells was full of her minions. They surged forward in a suicidal rush, literally running themselves onto the blades.

It wasn't killing them that was the problem. It was their sheer numbers. In the end Erik and Vlad and their companions won back to the torture chamber. Two of the Mongol men had maneuvered the bath, the grate, and the "bed of no rest" onto the stair. As soon as the last of the rearguard were past they managed to upend both pushing them against the ceiling, until they jammed—partly on the body of one of the "nuns."

They gained the top of the stairs.

The waiting Mongol general slammed the door when they were up. Slid the bar. Turned the key.

"There may be another way up. There seem to be hundreds of them," said Vlad, still pointing his sword at the doorway, breathing heavily.

"The woman will use her demons to open the door," said the shaman, tracing a pattern on the floor with a small bundle of feathers.

"Stables," panted Erik. "And some clothes for the girl."

Vlad had already unbuckled his cloak. Turned to offer it to her. She shied away from his face, horror on hers. "What is wrong? he asked.

"You're Vlad! You betrayed me to her!"

"No. I . . . I don't even know who you are."

"Looking at her, I would say she's a relative of yours, Vlad," said Erik, trying not to look at anything but the face.

"Dana?" said Vlad, incredulously.

"Yes," she spat. "Traitor."

Bortai handed the girl her cloak instead. Dana wrapped it around herself eagerly. "He is a good man," Bortai said. "Not a traitor. Would he be here if he was? Now we must go."

Vlad nodded. "We'll be back with an army and a battering ram."

"And a rope. That woman is rope-ripe," said Erik grimly.

They hurried down the corridor. Vlad was plainly hurt, confused and shocked. Erik fell back so that he was next to the young girl. Bortai had an arm around her. "Lady Dana? Why do you think Vlad betrayed you?"

She was sobbing a little, and holding onto Bortai.

"She told me. I said Vlad would come. She told me he was here. And he was. And his man took me away from the g…gypsies." She started to cry in earnest now.

Erik understood now. "I swear this by all that is holy." He touched the cross on his surcoat. "Your brother has been with us, and us with him, for the better part of the last week. We have only just arrived in this place of devil-worshipers ourselves, yesterday. I believe Vlad was as entrapped as you were. And I swear on the cross that we will protect you and see that no harm comes to you."

"Who are you?" she asked.

"*Ritter* Erik Hakkonsen of the Knights of the Holy Trinity, at your service, milady," he said, making a small bow, as they walked.

That got a tremulous smile, despite the tears. "You have to free the others down there, she's…she's *evil*."

Erik nodded. "Incarnate, I think. Look, this is

plainly a Satanist cabal. And I'm no theologist, young lady. But my friend Eneko is. And he once described Satanism as not pagan, although it sometimes steals pieces from it. It's a parody, a deliberate perversion of Christianity, not a religion itself. And one of its core tenets is deceit. Betrayal and deceit. That is why Satan is called the father of lies. So, anything she said to you was probably not true. That's how she works."

The girl was plainly made of the same tough steel as her brother. "But Emil. He did come from Vlad. Miu said so. And Miu does not tell lies," she said fiercely.

Vlad had plainly been listening. "Emil? As God is in heaven, I sent him to guard you. He was my trusted sergeant, and I certainly never ordered him to bring you here! You and mother—" he paused mid-step. "Mother? Is she down there? I must go back."

Dana shook her head quickly, before he could run back down the way they had come. "She's safe with the gypsies."

Vlad wiped his brow. "I don't really remember you, you know. You were just a tiny thing, in your first dress... But Mother. Dear God... I miss her."

That plainly broke through her distrust. Dana took a step forward and hugged him, fiercely. He, after a brief moment, responded. She winced. "Ow."

"What is wrong?" he asked pulling away.

"She beat me."

"Her back is bleeding," Bortai observed dispassionately.

"Elizabeth will suffer for that," said Vlad grimly.

"No," said Erik, equally grim. "Die, yes. But we are exactly what she is not..." He realised that he was dictating about something that had nothing to do with him. "I spoke out of turn, Vlad," he said. "It's your principality and your sister."

Vlad nodded. "But you spoke well for me. I could be...worse than her, fixing it."

"Can we get to the horses?" said Bortai. "You can talk later!"

But by the noise, they'd left it too late already.

Someone shook Manfred awake. It was Falkenberg, and with him *Ritter* Von Stael.

"Prince Manfred...I am sorry to disturb you... But we seem to have been locked in."

"Probably don't want us molesting the nuns," said Manfred, yawning and stretching.

"Possibly, Prince."

"How did you find out?"

"We heard a few odd noises. The guard," Falkenberg gestured at Von Stael, "thought they'd have a look. The door appears locked."

"Could be an innocent measure of security," said Manfred. "But we'll explain in the morning. I'll need a battle-axe."

Falkenberg allowed himself a little smile. "I know you well enough by now, Prince Manfred. I've had one fetched. Should be waiting for us at the door."

It was. So were twenty knights in the final stages of hastily donning full armor.

Manfred raised his eyebrows. "You're taking this seriously, Falkenberg."

"No, Prince Manfred. I'd have them all up and in armor if I was."

Manfred took the axe from the knight who held it out to him.

He swung hard at the wood above the latch.

The door cracked, but held. Manfred swung again, putting his full strength into it.

The heavy oak shivered and split.

And swung open a little way.

But then, it stopped.

Manfred reached forward and pulled it aside.

The candles shone on a wall. A wall of stone blocks each weighing at least a hundredweight. And mortared. Manfred reached through and touched the stone. It was real, and quite solid.

The knights gaped at it.

Manfred turned to Falkenberg. "Full armor. Everyone. And make it fast."

Falkenberg, himself already armored, gave the orders. The knights left at a run. He then accompanied Manfred back to his chamber, to help him get the steel on, and also to talk.

"Those blocks. Are they real, Prince?"

Manfred nodded. "And the mortar is dry. This is magic, Falkenberg. But whatever it is, it is not good."

"So what do we do, Prince?"

Manfred pointed at the floor. "The castle is a stone shell. Those are oaken floorboards. And our ever so beautiful and charming countess is going to do some explaining."

Vlad and his tiny party found their way blocked. So they hurried down another passage. And then another.

"We're being herded," said Erik.

"Where to?"

The answer appeared in front of them.

A man—dressed like a well-off peasant, wearing a

hat with three feathers in it. He had haunted, desperate eyes, thought Erik.

"I have a way out for you," he said.

In a vast stride, Vlad reached the man, grasped him by the front of his tunic, hauled him up off the ground and slammed him against the wall, holding him there with one hand. "Emil! You traitor."

"I have a way out for you," the man gasped. "Follow me."

"Why did you do this to me?" Vlad hissed, his face contorted with fury—and then he looked at Erik, and Erik looked soberly into those eyes that were dark with a terrible rage, and the fury was replaced by something colder and more rational. He shook himself, like a wet dog, and put his prisoner down. "You have a few seconds to make your peace with God," he said, his tone icy. "I will not execute you un-shriven."

Vlad had felt the dark tide rising. And then Erik, friend and, dare he say it, conscience, intervened. Vlad was grateful. . . . and still determined. But that wild rage was channeled now. A desire for the truth, the truth at all costs, flowed out of him. The man fell at his feet.

The shaman said something.

"He says there is spell written all over the man," said Erik.

The Mongol shaman came forward, did what looked like a little dance in place, threw some powder over the man, spat on his finger, and rubbed it on Emil's forehead. Emil gave a choked cry. "Drac. Kill me, Drac. Please forgive me, but kill me, for I do not deserve to live. She made me do it. She wanted me to betray you now, again. To take you to her chapel.

She draws all that is evil in a man, drives him. I killed her, Drac. I strangled her while the countess watched. Then she lay with me again next to her body. God, I had to have her. I did what she told me."

"Who did you kill?" asked Vlad, although, somehow, he already knew.

"Rosa. The countess was angry about her—"

Vlad felt his blood go cold. His sword-point dropped.

"Forgive me, Drac," the man pleaded.

But Vlad knew that he never would. "God may," he said bleakly.

The question of what he would do with this man was taken from him, seconds later. He only just had time to raise his sword. Emil, screaming, arms flailing, flung himself at them. He literally impaled himself on three swords.

Vlad's was not one of them.

His sister pressed against him. Put an arm around him.

"We've got to go on, Brother," she said.

Vlad did not want to. He was an inner maelstrom of ice and fire, raging. He did not care if he died. But his little sister needed him. He might not know her, but he *felt* her, bone of his bone, blood of his blood. They were of the same flesh. She needed him, and it was his duty to protect her.

They pressed on. Erik saw how Vlad fought now with an almost insane rage and strength. It should have made him easy to kill. But their opponents who had plainly escaped the dungeon were not of any particular caliber. Elizabeth chose her men-at-arms for her "religion," not martial prowess.

They could win free to the stables, still. And then Erik realised they would not. Not down this passage anyway. The countess had finally stopped fighting them by force of arms and was using her magic.

Something all shadow and ire roared out of the darkness; they all looked to the shaman, who looked to his talismans and powders and then just shrugged. "I do not know this thing," he said. "We must run."

Shadows wrapped it so that it was impossible to see, but there was no doubt that if it got them, it would kill them.

And then the shadows cleared. Whatever this monstrous thing was, it was pushing a wall ahead of it. All they could see was a block of stone, Stone, so tightly fitting the passage that it ripped the sconces from the walls, as it advanced on them at a slow walk. They could only retreat.

Back, back, towards the chapel.

Chapter 73

They had little choice: go into the chapel or be crushed, because whatever was behind that wall was strong, obviously strong enough to push them ahead of it or crush them beneath it.

So they backed towards the chapel like a herd of wild cattle, with Dana in the center and swords facing their retreat and the wall.

Earlier only the candles on the altar had burned.

Now candles burned in all the sconces. Black candles.

And Vlad felt a sudden exhaustion. A strange empty numbness, as if somehow, he had been cut off from that black tide of strength that had, until now, sustained him.

There was no one there. The place felt oppressive to Erik ... as if they had somehow walked into the middle of a summer thunderstorm. The moving wall stopped just short of the chapel door. The shaman looked around as they stood hard against the doorway, not wishing to go any further. He shrugged. Took out a little bottle of liquid from his pouch-stash and drank some. A magic potion of some kind?

"Strong brandy," he said and offered the bottle to Erik. "I buy it from the Vlachs. You want some?"

Erik felt that he could use it. But he shook his head. "Give the little girl some. She needs it."

Dana certainly did. She was at least part of the way into the shock that follows after mortal combat, by Erik's judgement. Still, she was a tough young lady. Her teeth clattered slightly on the bottle. She coughed and spluttered a little, but the brandy did put tiny spots of color in her white cheeks.

The shaman got out his little feathered drum and tapped it.

The sound seemed to be absorbed.

"Strong magic," he said.

That was all he said because he—and the rest of them—fell over.

It was as if every bit of strength had drained out of them at the same time that something invisible enclosed them in a skin of stone. Erik found he was unable to move a muscle. He couldn't even breathe, and felt his vision darkening. Then the grip loosened slightly. He could breathe. Just not move.

The doors behind them opened. Another door at the back of the chapel did, too. The countess's people came in, women in those obscene habits, men in filthy uniform tunics, picked all of them up, like so many staves of wood and carried them to the center of the chapel.

"Prop them up. I want them to be able to see," said the countess's voice from the shadows.

Something was set behind them. The terrible rigidity of their muscles eased just a tiny fraction.

Elizabeth Bartholdy walked up to them from somewhere out of Erik's line of sight. She looked down at Vlad and his sister. "In here I have taken some long and complex steps to make it safe for me to use magic against you. I was strongly advised not to try it out there." She smiled down on them. It was not a pleasant smile. If Erik could have shuddered, he would have. "Now we can begin."

Why did they always have to *talk* at times like this? Was it just that they needed an audience to appreciate their cleverness?

She stared down at Vlad, pondering a moment. "For the bloodletting rite to be performed, I learned that you had to be willing innocents. Mindaug says that actual virginity may not be necessary, but that you should be willing is." She nodded, her attention no longer on Vlad, as if now she was talking to herself. "I shall take no chances. I have both of you. One virginal, and one not. And by the time I am finished with you, you will be willing to perform my will. As for innocence, Mindaug assures me—and I do not think him wrong this time—that that is what allows you independence. You will take part in our little Sabbat tonight. And I will call on my master to bind your wills. I gather nothing less will do it."

She smiled another of those terrible smiles, her attention on Vlad again. "My little grandson Emeric will be so pleased."

She waited, her head cocked to the side, in an listening attitude, then laughed mockingly. "Ah. Of course. You can't reply. This is such an effective spell. I had to be careful, with you consorting with those vile knights. This magic is particularly good against men and Christians."

Her glance slipped to Erik. "Well, let us prepare.

Then I will come and fetch the first sacrifice from your company. This young woman here has all the right qualities." She kicked Bortai. "It's her or your sister, Vlad of Valahia. And I need your sister's virginity." She said it in Frankish. She obviously wanted them to understand.

She walked away, and stood sharpening a knife next to the altar. Cages were carried in. A cat. A black rooster. A goat was led in. And then a row of five young terrified children, boys and girls ranging in age from about eight through to the edge of puberty, who were dragged to the points of the star.

Erik looked on in sick horror, and prayed. Begged for strength for his arms and legs, just for an instant.

The Satanists began chanting—a depraved, vile perversion of a Gregorian chant. The huge crowd began a bizarre, obscene dance, writhing and stroking their own and each others' bodies, except for those who held the victims. Some began coupling on the floor.

And Erik saw a little striped field-mouse crawl out of the shaman Kaltegg's tunic. It very purposefully darted down to his pouch, burrowed into it, and emerged with a large feather. A hawk's pinion feather. The mouse dragged it over to Bortai.

In the meanwhile Elizabeth had proceeded with her butchery. She was cruelly and brutally methodical. To Erik it looked as if the walls behind her seemed to glow red. But perhaps it was just his rage and desperation.

And then they came for Bortai. Dragged her, limp and unstruggling to the blood-wet altar. Pulled her, spread-eagled onto it. The dwarf, like some evil misshapen gargoyle, his swollen manhood exposed through a cutaway in the priest's cassock he wore, clambered onto the altar. The chanting had stopped now. The other victims were being spread-eagled too. Erik prayed. Prayed as he had never done before.

The field mouse dragged the wing-pinion across his hand. It felt like the worst pins-and-needles he'd ever had. The dwarf walked up his victim's body and then knelt to tear her deel.

Bortai head-butted him so hard that you could hear his nasal bones crack across the room. He fell back. And Erik, still feeling as weak as a newborn kitten, staggered to his feet. It was at least twenty yards to the altar. His new "Algonquin" hatchet flew. Elizabeth Bartholdy was obscured. But the man holding Bortai's wrist was not. And if she could head-butt . . .

As the man holding Bortai fell over, Erik staggered desperately towards them, trying to get his sword up.

Elizabeth watched, stunned, as Ficzko fell back off the altar, onto his overlarge head. The girl kicked Dorko in the stomach. Mascon fell, an axe in his back, and the Mongol girl's right hand was free. Anna had lost her grip on the other leg, and Ilona got flung right over the altar. And the Mongol girl had a knife. And staggering up toward the dais was the blond man, with Vlad and another Mongol leaning on their swords, but getting there.

Elizabeth was trapped between them, but they were plainly still weak. So would the girl be. And there was only one of her.

"I am not a man, and my windhorse is strong. Stronger than your magic," said the girl who had been going to be her victim.

A pagan. The spell that she'd used to paralyse would be weaker on her. No matter! The room was full of her followers. And Elizabeth had her magic. She called on the lesser demons that she had bound to do her will. She would turn this victim into a burnt offering.

Nothing happened.

With a gasp of disbelief, Elizabeth called forth her nails. Her deadly toxic nails.

Nothing happened.

And then she knew real fear. And came to the horrible realization that activating a spell to cut Vlad off from his source of power ... had left her in the same position.

No matter! Elizabeth still had a knife. And she had used it for many sacrifices.

Too late, as her sacrificial knife went spinning, and her intended victim's knife entered her chest, did she realize that the sacrifices didn't usually have the chance to fight back.

Erik had hewed one of the countess's sacrificial assistants down and managed to get behind Elizabeth ... trying to raise his sword again, when Bortai pushed her own blade right into Elizabeth's heart.

Erik wasn't taking any chances. He managed a thrust anyway.

In his years of fighting, he'd had a sword go into flesh often enough before.

This time it slid in far more easily than it ought to. Bortai was slashing at Elizabeth's perfect throat as the countess fell.

Only it wasn't a perfect throat.

It was the wattled neck of an old crone. An incredibly fragile old crone. She hit the floor, as Erik pulled his sword free, and her round stomach spilled maggots and putrefaction.

There was silence.

And then terrible screams of horror from her acolytes.

On the hills the wolves felt her barrier fall. They surged in a great pack towards the castle.

In his own chambers, Count Mindaug shrugged philosophically. Elizabeth's recklessness had ended the way such folly usually did. He had warned her, after all, as was his duty. Well. Admittedly, the warnings had been very subtle.

Time, now, to escape. To Buda, he decided. As distasteful as he found the prospect of working for Emeric, the king of Hungary seemed his best option.

A moment later, Mindaug was gone. The chamber was filled with a cloud of smoke and, oddly, a single mirror hanging suspended in the middle. The count enjoyed his little jokes.

Chapter 74

There was silence. And a nothingness, except for a hall of mirrors before her. Elizabeth's agony didn't come from the wounds. Her whole body hurt. And, in the mirrors from which there was no escape, she could see that the body was old. Not even that of a crone. So decrepit it almost looked like a corpse.

Crocell came stumping forward.

"This was not my bargain," she croaked.

"Oh, I think you will find that it was," said Crocell.

"I was going to be young and beautiful forever! You betrayed me. You lied."

"Of course. That is what we do. This is the way all such bargains end."

"But I was his loyal servant! You were, too!"

Crocell shrugged. "In our master's house there are many slave kennels. There is nothing else. You should know that Mindaug had betrayed you anyway."

"Curse him!"

"He is accursed, but your curses no longer have any effect."

"What did he do?"

"You set about a great binding spell. One of deep demonic compulsion, with the perquisite sacrifices and atrocities that you humans require. Vlad and his sister are not ordinary mortals to be easily bound to your will. But he had successfully arranged for you to perform the rite of Cthasares, which nullifies all workings of magic and the drawing on powers within the sphere of protection. Of course all workings performed outside, even on objects within the sphere, still work. But not spells cast within it. You should have been outside, but in your folly, you were inside with them. Therefore your binding of their will would not have worked, despite you following all the forms and rituals precisely. The moment that Vlad and his sister were out of there, they would have both drawn on their bond with the land. I think they might possibly have been driven mad by what you planned them to witness. They would have woken the wildfire. Called the winds down. Shaken the earth. Probably killed themselves, and you. But under no circumstances would they have gone near the place of stones. And for them to stay away was precisely what Count Mindaug wanted."

"But he wanted a corrupted compact. He showed me how to do it!"

"No. He wanted to destroy the compact that already exists. End the truce between the forest, earth and fire and man. The old ones would lose eventually, of course. In the process, he found rituals and spells to take control of members of each faerie group. But they are protected thus far by the compact, because they share."

Crocell waved his hand. "However, that is all behind you now. It is time to begin your eternity of beauty."

Elizabeth looked at herself in the endless hall of mirrors, knowing that what was to come would be torment without relief. "The prisoners cannot leave the sphere of Cthasares without me. They are trapped there until they join me here. The place is bespelled to resist the Knights of the Holy Trinity, too."

The thought did not offer her any comfort. And soon she was hardly thinking at all.

Chapter 75

The floor of the wing in which they had been imprisoned was made of sound eight-inch oak boards, laid on even thicker joists. Good oak was common just over the mountains.

They were no match for a determined Manfred and several other axe wielders.

Hauling timbers clear, they tried shining a light down, but couldn't see what was below them. Eventually they settled on sending down David tied on a rope, with a candle. "At least if it is a cistern we can pull you back up, boy. Wouldn't like to try it with Manfred," said Von Gherens.

It proved to be a refectory, some fifteen feet below. David tried to haul a table under the hole. But even without his injured arm, it was too heavy. So they lowered the next knight. And the next. Then David, with the candle, found the the pantry and the pantry ladder, which, on top of the table made the descent plausible for the armored men.

David had, by this time, peered out into the passage,

as it suddenly occurred to him that someone should be curious about the noise they were making.

It was very dark. Not a brand nor a candle to be seen.

"Tell someone we will need candles," he sent the message to the last knights up in their quarters. In the meantime he raided the pantry. Looking for candles, of course. He found some tallow dips, and a pasty.

The knights stepped out into the passage, with candles . . .

Which promptly went out.

They returned to the refectory, and lit them again. The candle went out as soon as it was in the passage. "Brothers," said Falkenberg. "There is some form of dark magic afoot in this place. Let us try a good psalm."

"And surround them with steel and the sign of the Cross," said Von Stael.

As long as they kept the candles or tallow dips inside the phalanx of steel, as long as the singing continued, they had light. It did mean that they weren't going to be able sneak up on anyone.

Before long they started finding dead bodies.

"No one we know, is it?"

Manfred turned the woman's body over with his boot. Looked at what she was wearing. "I really don't think so," he said. David, from the center of the phalanx, was glad that he couldn't see it, by the sounds of Manfred's voice.

And then they heard the chanting.

"Sounds like a Gregorian chant. But there is something very wrong with it," said Von Stael, as the rest of the knights kept up their singing.

"Well, let's go and see just what it is."

But it was very clear that they were being opposed somehow. Misled down passages that took them away. They arrived at the refectory again. "Cruciform swords... and we will walk widdershins. Not try to follow the sound."

They were definitely getting closer.

"Something huge scraped along this passage," said someone. "Look at the scratches. And the sconces have all been ripped off the walls."

David could see that. And yet the knights kept advancing.

Then there was a silence... followed by screaming. Horrified, angry screaming, and the candles suddenly burned brighter.

A knight held one outside of the steel wall.

It stayed alight.

"Onwards!"

They moved forward at a rapid pace.

Ahead were the open doors to the chapel, across a wide hall, spilling running people. People who took one look at the knights and their shields with the triple cross and ran off down the hall, as if their tails were on fire. Some of them weren't covering those tails too well, thought David, peering through a gap in the steel elbows. And then suddenly the crowd who had fled down the hallway were trying to come back. Screaming.

The knights, shoulder to shoulder, big men all, pushed forward through the crowd—who wanted to flee, not attack. The steel wedge made its way into the chapel.

And stopped. Lightnings arced across the lead knight's armor. He fell back onto his companions.

❊   ❊   ❊

In the desecrated chapel, the prisoners found themselves able to move more easily. It appeared that most of Elizabeth's "congregation" could move, too. All they seemed to want to do was flee. That was just as well, as by sheer numbers they could have overwhelmed the handful of Mongols with Vlad, Erik and Dana.

Erik still stood looking at the last putrefying remains of Elizabeth, his sword at the ready. She stank less in death, and the rapid decay, than she had for him in life. Bortai too stood for a frozen moment. And then they both fell together, Erik holding her and her holding him as if there would be no tomorrow. Well, a few moments ago there had not been.

Most of Elizabeth's retainers were pressing to get away from them. But not one of her followers, who had just sat up from where he had landed next to the altar. "You killed her! You killed the mistress!" screamed the dwarf, running to the oozing, rotting pile, from which bones already protruded. Time had caught up with her with a vengeance. Erik lifted his sword.

"He is so small," said Bortai.

Erik looked at the vicious little eyes, the hate-contorted face and the too large head. "Sometimes we need to remember evil can also reside in those less fortunate. We should judge a man on his deeds, and not on his appearance. And no matter what misfortune he has suffered, nothing can excuse this."

Her slave sprang, snarling, at Bortai. It was the last thing he ever did.

Dana began to sing again. The same song, but there was a triumphant thankfulness in her voice. After a moment Vlad joined her. And then another voice. One of the other victims that had been brought by the Satanists, was sitting hunched and terrified, but still managing to sing.

They found four of the would-be victims. Alive, frightened and desperately grateful.

"Let's get out this place," said Vlad.

But they could not.

The crowd that had escaped the chapel had pushed away from the knights. All but one. He was a boy of about ten and he had flung himself against them and clung to *Ritter* De Berenden's knees.

The others were adults. And all of the others only wanted to get away. The knight called to his companion—who happened to be Manfred. Manfred too realized the difference. "What's he saying?"

"Hungarian gabble, Prince Manfred," said the knight. "That and the name of Christ. Here. Maernberg. You have some Hungarian. See if you can understand."

The knight pushed his way over. Knelt in front of the boy who was still clinging like a limpet. Spoke to him. The child, sobbing, spoke. The big knight picked him up. Held him. "He says that the devil was in there. And then the woman and blond man killed her."

Manfred looked at Falkenberg.

"Erik," they said together.

"We have to get inside there," said Manfred.

"Knights will lock arms, reverse your blades, ground the tips and we will advance. Singing a glad song to the Lord," ordered Falkenberg. "Take that boy, David. You. Maernberg. Guard them."

"You may need a Mongol speaker, sir," said David. He did not want to go into that chapel. But Von Stael was going, and he knew a squire's place.

"Then we'll fetch you. Move."

So David found himself holding a Hungarian peasant brat, with huge, tear-streaked eyes. The kid looked half starved. So David gave him the pasty he'd stolen. The boy looked as if he expected it to turn into a scorpion. But he held it. "*Ritter* Maernberg. What's eat it in Hungarian?"

"*Eszik*." The knight said. "They are shouting something about hell-hounds out there in the halls."

The knights, still singing, moved forward slowly into the chapel, energies crackling and cascading off their armor. It was designed for this. Magic had been the main advantage of the grand duke's armory against the Knights of the Holy Trinity, once. Still, this was very strong magic.

But so was cold steel.

Erik spotted the coruscating mass pushing through the door.

All he could see was lightnings.

"More devilry," said Bortai. She still held his hand.

Her two chaperons were comforting the former victims—as much by smiles and kindness as by speech, as they did not share any common language. The shaman was busy attempting yet another trance. He'd been deeply upset about how the chapel seemed to affect his abilities. He'd barely been able to use his familiar and a very powerful talisman. Vlad and Dana were talking earnestly. The four other Mongols were testing the barrier, systematically.

And now a fiery thing of sparks and lightnings was coming in to attack them. Erik wondered just how he could protect them from this, when he suddenly started to laugh. He recognized the shape of the spiked shoulder bosses and the helmets, even when they were dancing with little lightnings.

"Did I say something funny?" asked Bortai, a dimple appearing.

"No. That's not another problem. It's the knights trying to rescue us. Look, you can see their feet."

"So how do we get to them?"

They eventually solved the problem by crawling between their legs.

It was undignified but a lot better than staying in the chapel with the corpses.

The minute he crossed the pentacle threshold of the chapel, Vlad felt it come back. As if he'd been a tree that had had its roots severed. Power and strength flowed back into his limbs.

"I'm alive again," said Dana, incredulously.

The circle of steel opened, visors lifted, and they found themselves in a circle of smiling knights. "What the hell have you been up to without me?" demanded Manfred grinning, squeezing Erik's shoulder.

"Hell is the right word," said Erik. "We've been in the portal of it. We owe our lives and probably our souls to Bortai."

"To Shaman Kaltegg. He break spell. I just kill devil-woman."

"We have trouble, *Ritters*," said someone.

Manfred groaned. "What is it this time?"

"Hell-hounds, Prince Manfred."

Vlad stepped forward. Here, back in his strength and power, he'd deal with any hell-hounds.

And then his sister began to giggle and rushed toward the eyes and teeth and fur at the rim of the candlelight, pushing past the knights.

Vlad followed, willy-nilly.

They weren't hell-hounds.

They were big, bristling gray wolves. And Dana flung herself at the leader of the pack. Wrapped her arms around his neck. "What took you so long, Angelo?" she said thickly.

Vlad felt—strange. As if this was something he had known, or *should* know, or had expected without knowing he had expected. And he was not afraid of these wolves. Not at all. They felt—like friends.

"You are not supposed to know this, girl," said a familiar gypsy voice.

It sent another jolt of not-memory through him.

Dana stood up. Stamped her foot. "I'm not stupid, you know. I worked it out long ago."

"I am," said Vlad, shaking his head, trying to work out how the wolves could be gypsies or the gypsies wolves. . . .

"The king of the wolves has a pact with the prince of the land," growled Angelo. "I see that you broke her enchantments."

That sounded right. More, it felt right. Things he still didn't understand with his head settled into place around his heart and soul, and Vlad nodded. This was exactly how he had known in his bones that Dana was his sister. Understanding could come later. "We did. Now we need to round up these servants of hers before they escape. And there are prisoners in her dungeons to be freed."

"We guard the stable yard already."

"A rescue, a rescue!" shouted someone in Székely Hungarian. "The prince is surrounded by wolves!"

Vlad had to do some hasty explaining before anyone could spit a "gypsy." It was a good thing that the Székelers were so loyal to him.

It was a busy night—what was left of it. But by morning they had the last of her servants ferreted out—good noses had been a great help—and penned in the refectory. The building had been searched from cloister to dungeon, and nearly forty young victims found and liberated.

Vlad did not want to think about the ones they had been too late for.

But the knights held a requiem mass for them, in the courtyard, at dawn.

Somehow the strange wolfish dogs had disappeared.

A caravan of gypsy sleds arrived just after Terce, as a group of horrified town elders from Caedonia were being escorted through the secret dungeon.

Chapter 76

Vlad was a man torn by conflicting emotions: a terrible sadness and rage, and yet a deep joy.

He'd lost Rosa. He still had to come to terms with that. She'd said "no man can own me." And she was right, now.

He'd lost faith in someone that he'd thought he could trust. In a world of shifting sands, Elizabeth had been someone he'd trusted and relied on. Some of that, he realized, had been because he'd been enchanted. Then there was his sergeant, Emil. He had to lay that, at least in part, at Elizabeth's door.

And yet he'd found others to trust. A sister he'd never known. Erik. Manfred. The Primor Peter. The Mongols—Vlad realized now that if Elizabeth said they were his foes, the opposite was almost certainly true. And of course his mother.

She had held him. Held him as if he might be torn from her arms again. It was very lovely...but by afternoon he was beginning to understand why Dana had said that she was a bit "clingy."

Above all of that he had an enormous desire to

go to the southwest. Dana said she too was almost unable to resist walking away from the castle, and heading for a place she knew how to find, without ever having seen it or been there.

And somehow the wolf-"gypsies" were at the heart of much of it. Vlad decided that he'd better finally get to the bottom of the entire matter. So he went to call on them.

They greeted him with wary politeness.

Very wary politeness.

He stood before them, no longer the bewildered, confused, boy-man who had never used a sword in anger, never ridden or even walked in the free air from the time he had been taken hostage, never been with a woman...

Now he was a leader. A prince. And princes had rights. "I want answers."

Angelo turned to Radu and the younger Miu. They looked at each other. Even in human form there was something wolfish about them. "Don't know if we can give you any of those, Drac. The whole point is that you should not know anything."

He shook his head and looked them in the eyes, sternly. "The point is that I already do. And in talking with Dana, I have found out a lot more."

The three looked at each other again. Vlad realized that they were talking. Not in the fashion of men, but in the fashion of wolves. There were certain small, subtle signs.

"She is of an age when it is somewhat harder to deceive about these things," conceded Radu. "Older people will see, too, but they will not allow themselves to believe what they see. We do not deceive them. They deceive themselves. And that suits us well. There are rules, Drac. Magic is like that. Even seemingly wild magic."

"We have to be innocent and willing," she said.

Vlad had not even noticed that Dana had come to join them.

The gypsies looked startled.

"She told us," said Dana. "The old woman, as you called her. She was not too sure what innocent was. I think she'd forgotten."

The three men grinned. And they were very wolfish.

Vlad sighed. "Suppose you just tell us what you are. I already know that you are sometimes wolves and sometimes men."

"And they are not gypsies," said Dana.

The three grinned again. "We think we can do this. It will be enough for now. We will tell you that. And then, if you are willing, you will come with us to the place of stones."

"Is that," Vlad pointed, "over there?"

The wolves nodded. "It draws him," said Angelo.

"And her," said Miu. "Look."

Vlad did. He could see her staring intently down the line of his pointing finger, nodding.

"So what are you?"

"Wolves."

"Not gypsies."

"They are newcomers to our range. From the south. Very convenient," said Radu. "We prefer people to think that that is what we are, too. We have been as we are now for seven thousand years."

Vlad shook his head. "Why? People despise the gypsies."

"Better despised than feared and hunted to extinction. People don't like gypsies, but they don't fear them. They fear men who become wolves, and wolves who become men, although we are even less danger to them than the gypsies. There is an ancient fear. Like us, the gypsies are travelers. We migrate across our lands with the seasons," said Angelo.

Radu contined. "Wolves cannot coexist with men. A wolf is stronger than one man, most of the time. Wolves work together to add to that. But there are far more men, and they are more cunning than wolves, and also work together."

Angelo nodded. "If we fought . . . men would suffer. We are strong and cunning, and work as a pack. But in the end humans would win."

"But each can live together . . . if each would just give a little. The world can be better, richer place . . . for men and for wolves. Men are settlers. We move. We do much of the trade and much of the movement of information in your land. We deal with less desirable creatures which both men and wolves regard as pests. We take our prey from the land—but we take less, and we do not take men. In turn we have become more like men."

"We would not give up being wolves, but we would not give up being men, either," said Miu.

"We need to hunt and to run," said Radu, repeating as if from a litany.

"But fires and plum dumplings are good things," replied Miu.

"Each takes something from the other, each gives," said Radu.

"And tomorrow night . . . it may end. We may become

men or we may become wolves. We cannot stay both without it," said Angelo.

"There must be blood," they said, together.

Vlad took a deep breath. Looked at his sister...the two of them talked wordlessly rather like the wolves did, in tiny movements of the face and eyes. It was a language, Vlad realized, that just the two of them shared, that neither had to learn. The wolves had saved him from Elizabeth's clutches, earlier. Brought him home, to his land, where he had been able to grow strong, to come into his birthright. They had never lied to him. They'd let him deceive himself. He could trust them with his life. He was wary about trusting them with hers.

She told him that they'd saved her and her mother from Emeric, watched over them...there was more. Some of which he almost understood. It involved wings and fire. And a dark lake. They were dangerous. But dangerous did not mean that they could not trust them.

Brother and sister nodded simultaneously. Still... a blood ritual, Elizabeth had said.

"They're wolves," said Dana, answering his unspoken fear. "They like blood. They see everything in those terms."

"I only have one question further," said Vlad, knowing that he could not ask the questions he would like to—was his soul in peril? Was this black magic? It was certainly not Christian, not over seven thousand years. Yet...they had been saved by Bortai and the pagan shaman, who had found Elizabeth as evil as he had. Would they...his mind shied away. His sister was a young virgin. That evil woman had attached some significance to that.

"We will answer, if we can," said Radu.

"Why tomorrow, and why there?"

"Two questions, but we can answer both."

"It is the place where the first bargain was made with the man of the river-people. It must be renewed, and a period was set on that, a time when the magics needed would be strong. Tomorrow night at midnight is the eclipse of the full moon. It happens in a regular pattern. A pattern known from ancient days."

Chapter 77

There is a circle of stones, not a particularly remarkable circle...the rocks are not large or exceptional in any way, except that moss will not grow on them, nor snow lie on them. They are just on the edge of the forest land, with the wild and rocky heath to the north and east, and the river to the west.

Forest cloaked this land for always, so long ago that it lies in coal measures beneath it. Yet the Les were not the first.

Water ran here before them, and life stirred in it. But Voda too was not the first.

Stone, rock from before the very plants, stuck their ancient bones into the sky here. And the stone which is the land has life within it. Creatures of silicon with veins of metallic ores, and jeweled eyes...are here too. They are not the first either.

And then there are the creatures of wind and fire, fused by ancient magics. They are not the first, either. But they are children of the first.

They all waited for the alignment. The time when the forces of the sun, the earth and the moon finished their long stately measure and bowed to each other, before starting the next long dance. The choreography of that dance was echoed in the piping of the wolf-king.

Vlad and Dana waited with the wolves. "We are neither one thing nor the other. That is why we get to bring you to the blood-rite."

There was an inevitability about this, this time and place to which he had been drawn, been driven. This rite that his mind knew nothing about, but his heart somehow recognized. No matter what—this had to be. It had to be done. Or too much would unravel for the mending, and there was something out there, black and horrible, that would make use of that unraveling.

But... a blood rite. If someone was to be sacrificed—

"If there is any killing... or dying. I will do it. Not Dana," said Vlad abruptly.

"You don't own me, Vlad," said Dana equally abruptly, completely unaware of the effect that her choice of words had on him.

"No. I don't. But to love someone is to wish to protect them."

"That's a good start," said Radu. "Come. It begins."

The moon shone down clear and cold... except that something had taken a bloody bite out of it. And strange snaky bat-winged shapes flew across it... And circled to land.

"The wyverns!" said Dana.

"Hush," said Angelo. They walked forward. The forest creaked and swayed. And from the depths strode a tall slim man with long greenish white hair and a beard.... He was more beard than person. He seemed to shrink as he came forward, until he was a small, stooped man with long thin bare arms and legs, and protuberant eyes.

From the heath came a giant. A being of oddly shaped stone. In daylight he would have looked like a rock tor or a stony ridge. Now in the moonlight they could see him for what he was.

And from the water came a woman. Brushing the water from her hair, and the moonlight shining on scales.

"We have come as we were constrained to."

The shadow ate the moon, turning it bloody.

The wolves howled. The forest moved, creaking. The earth groaned. Only the water was silent. There was a pattern to the sound. It was the very tune that Angelo had used to call Vlad.

"Will you renew the compact?" hissed the wyverns.

"What is the compact?" asked Vlad and Dana as one.

"Ah, good. The first condition is met. They are innocent of purpose."

"Pure of heart."

"But what is it?" asked Dana.

"We swear that it is good for the land."

"But not without pain and price."

It was hard to tell just from whom the words came. They seemed to come out of the very air itself, and echo around the circle of strange creatures. Vlad's mind knew he should be afraid, or if not afraid, certainly aghast at these beings that were not even out of the stories he had read or been told. Vlad's heart knew better.

"Then the second question: are you willing, children of man?" Now it was only the two wyverns speaking. Dana looked at Vlad, and he at her. The unspoken communication was made, and Vlad was desperately glad to have her there.

The shadow covered the moon and they were bathed in a bloody light.

"Yes," said Vlad.

Dana hesitated a moment longer. "Yes."

"And you, Fărăgas, king of the wolves?" asked the wyverns together.

"Always. It's blood," said Angelo, grinning toothily.

"And you, Leshy, lord of the forest?"

His voice was like the cracking of branches. "With him, yes."

"And you, Zem, lord of stone."

"Both. The man for stone, the woman for earth," rumbled the stone-giant.

"That's different," said the wolf.

"And you Voda? Queen of the ancient river?"

"She never agrees. The first compact was made because of her. The men of the river came to us, after we had made our bargain," whispered Angelo.

"Yes," said Voda, her voice the sound of many rivers, "this time we will agree. To her anyway."

The wyvern flicked their claws out. "And we, for fire and air, we will bind ourselves. Let the blood flow. And let us share blood together."

"But what do we have to do?" asked Vlad, still expecting—and dreading—some form of sacrifice.

"Willing but innocent," said the one wyvern.

"And very stupid," said the other.

Dana stamped her foot, and they both looked at her, mouths agape with silent laughter. Vlad's mind still dreaded, but his heart eased.

The wyverns dipped their heads, sharp amusement

still in their eyes. "We share blood. Blood from each other's veins, and bind ourselves into the protection of the others."

"Each of the lords of the nonhumans gives up some of their power to the human lord, and the human in turn binds himself to us, and to our protection. The blood that runs in your veins is a product of that, anyway," explained the wolf king. "That is where you get your strength, your resistance to poisons, your ability to tolerate fire, and your fine hearing and smell from. The last part is from us," he added, with a hint of pride.

"Except there is a woman this time, at last. And the waters will bind to her," said Voda. "That will give you power over flow, and those within our rule. There are those who walk outside it."

"Come. It is time," said the wyverns impatiently. "Where is the grail?"

"At your feet," said the wolf, pointing to a stone chalice.

"I thought it was just a bowl," said Dana.

"It is. What else is the grail?" said the wolf.

"Come closer, so that we can make you bleed," said the wyvern showing talons and teeth that could take a man's head off.

"Er. I have a sharp knife."

"No metals. Only talon and tooth allowed." The wyverns smiled toothily. "Trust us."

Vlad understood now, finally, that that was actually what this was all about. About trust. So he held out his wrist. As did the others.

The claws were sharp.

"Press it together with mine," said Angelo.

Wolf-blood flowed in his veins. And then he did the

same with Leshy. With Zem. And with each wyvern in turn. With each new mingling the blood in his veins tingled with more and different power, and he began to feel things that he had no words for. It was intoxicating. He wondered if this was how other men felt when they were drunk.

The river-queen withheld. But she'd shared with Dana. Then they held their wrists over the grail, and the blood mingled, shimmered and then began to glow.

Or it could just have been that the eclipse was over.

And then—the bowl was empty.

"They thought it must have a hole in it the first time," said Angelo. "It has been shared. For some reason, you men..."

"You humans," put in the queen of the rivers. "Not men."

"Humans," said the wolf, "Share it with the land, not your kind. The land in turn shares its strength with you. You—and those of your blood, and it gets spread around—will always be strongest here, in ancient Valahia. And you can staunch the bleeding now. We can go back to the sled, and out of the wind."

The Leshy was the first to leave, bowing and walking away, becoming taller as he went.

"They hate being awake in winter. Only the pines are really available then."

The stone giant groaned to his feet. Soon he was just another rocky outcrop.

The river-woman looked at Dana. "You could bring us back toward the old order, you know."

"You never give up, do you?" said the wolf.

"No. Water wears down all things in time," and then she too was gone.

"She's weaker now. The flow was much more powerful once. But the Rhine is stealing her water," said the wolf. He looked at the two wyverns. "I believe we have a buck or two back at the camp. Shall we go?"

They went.

"You wanted us afraid," said Dana, a bit resentfully.

"Afraid and yet prepared to trust us. And to sacrifice yourselves if necessary for the greater good. The rest of us are constrained to be there. We cannot refuse to be there. But mortals must come of their own free will. So they must be afraid, yes."

"But I was constrained," said Vlad. "I have felt this place drawing me for, oh, months."

The king of the wolves shrugged. "It comes of mixing the blood. You are born a little like us, and we, a little like you."

"But why?"

"The story goes thus. Who knows if it is true? 'A man and the king of wolves were once trapped by a blizzard in a cave near the stones. The wolf had a broken leg from falling in with his prey. The man—his wife was a priestess of the river, and he was as near to a chief as she would let him be—had come out to die. He too had fallen in, and was cut and concussed.

"The man wanted to die. To walk away from the river then, was to die. The forest was Leshy's, and he suffered no humans lightly. Leshy and his tree-folk misled and starved those that tried. The mountains were Zem's domain. The old ones were very powerful then, and their fey followers more numerous than men. Only wolves roamed both forest and heath. But humans... They had a compact with the queen of the river. They worshiped her. Carved statues in the sandstone and kept them behind the hearth. And she gave them fish and some safety. Some safety... yet the women of the water—you would call them the Rusalka, or the Vila—had taken his son. And then his young daughter, too. The boy had been a handsome man, and the Vila like those. She had been pregnant against the wishes of her family; the Rusalka preyed upon such unhappy girls.

"His wife kept the river goddess's stones behind the hearth. But the river queen did nothing. She let the children be taken, because the Vila are not hers, the Rusalka are not hers. They are magical creatures that breathe air not water, creatures of forest and water, and thereby answering to neither.

"The man was desperate, unhappy and afraid. Unhappy enough to talk with a wolf. The wolf listened. The man talked more. And after a while he came over to the wolf and splinted the wolf's leg. They shared blood in the process. They could hardly do otherwise. The wolf could have, should have, ripped his throat out. They both would have died. Instead the man made fire, butchered the buck with his stone knife. They ate and waited out the storm. And then the man built a ramp so they could walk out. And the king of wolves saw the man was walking into Leshy's domain again, to die. So he brought him back. Back here. And, as he had hunted with the wyverns, so he brought them here, too. They hauled stones—a ring of stones—so that they could sit on them and talk."

"Wolves don't talk," said Dana.

"They don't share caves or allow men to tend their

wounds, either. This was the king of wolves. Now do
you want the story or not?"

Dana put her finger to her lips and nodded.

"That was a magical place and a magical time. They
had shared blood. Become more like each other. The
man did not want to live by the river and eat fish
and lose his children to it. He wanted to run in the
forest and hunt deer. And the wolf had learned, too:
he wanted fire—warmth in winter. And already men
were cutting their way into those forests.

"The wyverns called the kings of the forest, the
mountains, and the queen of the water to that place.
And told them what these two had done. He was wise
in the workings of magic, and could read the signs
in the dance of heaven. He told the others what was
coming, and that they should make a bargain—which
would let the man roam free ... but would also pre-
serve the rest of them.

"The forest and mountains made the bargain. The
river would not. But it was laid upon them, then, that
they should return to this place periodically—and in
those days the only measure of time was the moon,
the eclipses—to see if they would share blood again."

There was a silence. "The queen of the river never
has before."

The king of the wolves, Angelo Fărăgas, looked at
them in the unblinking way of wolves. "We thought
we had two possible chances. You, or him. We did
not understand then. The lord of the forest will make
no pact with women, and the queen of the river no
pact with men."

Chapter 78

Vlad and his sister looked...different. Erik could not quite put his finger on how, but they both seemed more confident after the two days that they'd been away with the gypsies.

Both he and Manfred tried asking what had happened, but got polite variants of, "I really can't say. Please don't ask me. But it was good and it was important."

They returned to Elizabeth's castle, by Vlad's request.

"I think," he said to Dana, "that it should be destroyed."

She nodded. "Utterly."

They walked up to the building. Put their hands on it. And turned and walked away...quite fast.

"I think...we should gallop."

Glancing back, Erik saw that the castle was on fire. And then an earth tremor nearly shook them off their horses.

"God has fix bad place," said the Székely Primor in poor Mongol, looking back.

"You might say that," agreed Erik. But privately he

suspected the cause was nearer at hand. Whatever Vlad and his sister had done—and in his precise bodyguard's way, he noted bandages on their wrists—he suspected that foes really didn't want to invade their territory.

It was interesting how Vlad had made his younger sister a de facto co-ruler. They did almost nothing without discussion. Or at least an exchange of glances.

They rode southwest for the meeting that was scheduled with the master of Irongate.

Erik noticed that they had wolves scouting for them now, as well as a small gypsy contingent, riding along. The little deception amused him. Being in Venice, and then around Benito and Maria . . . had changed him, too. Really there was only good and evil, and the forms it took mattered not at all so long as you knew which was which.

Chapter 79

Emeric had expected to find Ban Alescu frightened and homeless...if alive. What he had not expected was to find Ban Alescu, frightened, homeless...and sitting with a field army of his boyars and all their retainers, with intent to kill someone. Emeric had more troops—by far—than the Ban. What he didn't have was them right there.

"My castle. My jewel...has been taken over by... If I am to believe the idiots, blood drinking naked women from the river," snarled the Ban. "What sorcery is this?"

Emeric met question with question. "What are you doing here with an army?"

"I expect Prince Vlad. I had set a trap for him. I was going to make an end to him," said the Ban, grimly.

"Oh." That put a different complexion on the Vila having seized Irongate.

"He has stolen a march on me by sending his demons to take Irongate. And if these fools get to hear of it, he may defeat me yet. I had the survivors executed before the story spread." The Ban looked gloomy. "If he really has this sort of power, I had better make my submission. And you, too, I think," he said to his overlord.

Emeric was shocked almost rigid by this forthright speech. It wasn't derogatory...it was just matter of fact. It infuriated him. And then he remembered where he was, and the small number of troops he had at his immediate disposal. He could kill this man... if he could reach him. The Ban was standing a good safe distance off. With difficulty, he controlled himself. "I have sorcerous powers at my disposal, too. I will deal with these Vila. After you have dealt with Vlad."

The Ban gave a nod. But it was a very curt nod. "I will await you in Orsova castle. Bring me his head," said Emeric, choosing to ignore what he did not wish to see.

"If you are going to a rendezvous with someone you don't trust, be there early," Manfred had said. Well, they had two days in hand. So Vlad sent scouts, scouts whose ability to move in the dark and undetected was far better than that of most humans. They'd had warning. It appeared that the towns did not like Ban Alescu.

"There are thousands of men camped in the forest," reported Radu.

"He has mobilized his boyars, Drac. Just as they warned us in Bucova."

"You can't believe everything you hear," said Vlad. "They also said he'd filled his fortress in the Dunrea with man-devouring drowned women, and that he killed everyone who tried to speak of it. They say worse things about me, up north."

"Oh, down here, too," said the primor, cheerfully. "They want you to be terrible, Drac. To terrify children, or their enemies, depending on how close the enemies are, or how bad the children are being."

"What sort of forest is it, Radu?" asked Dana.

"Mostly pine." The gypsy's eyes gleamed wickedly as he said it.

"Well," said Manfred. "If he's sitting in the forest with his loyalists... He isn't guarding his towns and cities."

"Irongate might be a bridge too far though," said Erik, looking at the map.

"He can surrender that one," said Vlad.

Standing at the appointed time on a knoll-clearing above the meeting place, Ban Alescu could hardly believe it. He'd expected an emissary, more conditions... Yet the man—that all the towns of Valahia were hailing as military genius, who had beaten Emeric at every turn, had ridden blindly into his trap. He was out on the open fields with a small contingent of knights, waiting for Ban Alescu to come and make his submission. To escort Vlad to his castles, and present him with the keys.

Ban Alescu shook his head. He turned to tell his trumpeter to sound the advance. He had no intention of being part of it. Vlad was apparently a demon of a fighter. It was probably as much of a rumor as his military skill.

Only... there was no trumpeter next to him on the knoll. Just a rather saturnine man in bright but patched gypsy clothes. "Lady wants to see you," said the gypsy laconically. "You have implied that she and her brother are bastards and that her mother is an adulteress. She's a little upset with you."

The Ban reached for his sword. His horse reared. He fell off in a most undignified fashion, and found that something was standing on his chest. Hot breath that smelled of meat was blown into his face from between very white teeth. Big teeth.

"Call off your dog. I have eight thousand men in these woods."

The gypsy laughed softly. "In the woods, eh? In the pine woods. A very bad place to keep them. Leshy and his people are wild and bad tempered at being woken at this time. And making them bad tempered is nearly as bad as calling Miu a dog. I hear you've been hanging gypsies, Ban. It seems that you're a bit like a bad-tempered bull. Maybe you need a nose ring." Sharp white teeth touched on his nose.

"I wouldn't pull away. You have a fairly long crawl ahead of you. Or you can get up and walk, if you behave yourself. The Princess Dana of Valahia wants a good explanation. A nice walk will give you time to think of one. And I think you may find you're better off than your men. It could take them a week to get out of the forest. A week in winter out there could kill some of them."

Ban Alescu walked. He was unused to walking. And the woods seemed very dark, and very empty.

They got to the open field. His troops surely had to see him—he had very recognizable gold and white enamel-inlaid half-armor—and charge. The woods had been jam-packed with them.

The forest looked a little different now. Unfamiliar, somehow. Was that a dragon-like shape above it?

A young woman and a group of men rode over to him. He remembered her face. He'd been very flattering to her last time they had met. Her father had been Duke of Valahia then. And then with shock he recognized the men with her, too. They were the city elders from Mehadia and Herkulesfürdö. His towns. With a sinking heart he realized that that was probably not true anymore. "It is very odd that you should not have chosen to mention that your mother was married to my father when we met last, at the reception last year at Poienari castle," Dana of Valahia said. "Perhaps you would like to explain how you suddenly claim to be my father's legitimate heir, both to me and these good people?"

Her brother did not even bother to watch what she was doing. Vlad continued to stand and look at the forest. It appeared to be moving.

The Ban knew that he lived or died on a young girl's whim. And she did not look very sympathetic. He grovelled. "It's not true, Princess. It was not my idea, I swear. King Emeric did it, Princess. I . . . had to go along with him. He would have had me killed otherwise."

She did not appear impressed. She was quite young, but had the speech and diction . . . and sarcasm of a much older woman. "Really? Even in your impregnable fortress at Irongate, that you bragged about?" she said dryly.

"You filled it with your monsters, and killed my men," he said.

She seemed mildly taken aback by this. "What sort of monsters?"

"Naked women with long green-blond hair."

"I assure you," said Princess Dana primly, "if I had anything to do with them they would have been decently clothed."

She began to turn away. "What are you going to do?"

"Deal with them, I should think. I don't think I approve of nudity."

Ban Alescu had realized that whatever else was

happening, his army was not coming to his rescue. "I meant...what about me. I came to make my submission. If you have the power to take my best castle by magic...and to destroy my troops..."

"We had nothing to do with your castle. And your troops are merely lost. That can happen in the woods, especially with a little mist. As for your submission: Vlad and I do not deal with traitors. When we found the ambush you planned, we decided we'd had enough. You are stripped of all your titles and possessions," she said. "I would find a stick and start staggering for Hungary if I were you. I've been told," she gestured at the town elders, "that you are not much liked here. All we wanted from you was a public renunciation of your claims. We have that, now."

A nervous general interrupted his master's inspection of a river barge. Emeric was still in love with his idea of taking them down to flank the Mongols, and opening a route to the Black Sea and conquest of the east. Perhaps even Constantinople. It was a great city, but Alexis was a soft nut to crack. The general coughed. "Your Majesty. Some of Ban Alescu's boyars have just reached the town."

"Excellent. I hope they have that upstart Vlad's head."

The general coughed again. "No, Your Majesty. In fact all they seemed eager to do was to buy more horses and keep running. I think we should retreat on your garrison at Resicabánya. We will have twenty thousand men at your disposal there."

Emeric stared at him in horror. Was this to be another Corfu?

Chapter 80

Once safe in Resicabánya, surrounded by his garrison, Emeric allowed his panic to subside a little and fury to take hold. The coward must have surrendered. He'd even talked of doing so! Well, he, Emeric, still had control over Irongate. And while winter would make major troop movements difficult to impossible in the mountains, what did Vlad really hold? A strip of worthless mountains, and adjacent towns. They could be given similar treatment to Irongate. Or did that require them to be surrounded by water?

Emeric settled down to pen a message to Elizabeth. She had never refused to help him, when matters had really got out of hand. The letter was carefully worded—he certainly did not want her to take offense, and, on the other hand he did not want his message to fall into the wrong hands—Vlad had either taken cities and towns while travelling down to the southwest or had bypassed them. Of course Elizabeth would be able to hold off invading armies, single-handed if need be. The messenger was a tried and trusted one, and Emeric knew all he had to do was to wait.

And he did.

It was nine days before the messenger returned. With the message, undelivered.

The messenger—who had taken messages to Elizabeth's castle before—was a troubled man. "Your Majesty, the castle is gone."

Emerich stared at him. The man was surely mad. "Gone? It can't be gone,"

The messenger sweated and was pale as death. "It's a ruin, Your Majesty. A burned out ruin. I went to Caedonia to try to find out what happened. The town has fallen to Vlad . . . and I didn't have to ask. I was told by everyone who had a tongue. They have some of the children that were held prisoner in her castle. They say the countess was in league with Satan himself. Some of the local dignitaries were taken there by Vlad's troops. They saw for themselves evidence of the devil worship in her castle. They were very full of it. And the Countess Elizabeth Bartholdy is dead."

Emeric had to sit down. The room was full of roaring sound. He knew it was just in his head. "Definitely?" he said weakly.

"Definitely," the messenger said. He paused. "Your Majesty. It is well known in Caedonia that you were a guest at her castle. There is much suspicion about you."

Emeric stood up. "I am going back to Buda. There are people I need to consult."

He did not know what to do. He had hated her, but relied on her also. And now he was alone. Suddenly he was aware of just how desperately he needed her. Vlad must have found a far, far more potent magic worker. Emeric was afraid. Someone who could defeat her? That was almost unthinkable. And it meant that he was exposed, too, to other enemies. He knew full well that she'd murdered many threats to his throne. He was less than confident about dealing with them alone. And then there was the enemy to the north. Elizabeth had told him what Jagiellon really was: the Black Brain, Chernobog.

The answer came to him, on the journey back to his castle: He would obtain the services of her servant Mindaug himself. For all that Elizabeth had made some disparaging remarks about the count's timidity and bookishness, there had been no mistaking her genuine respect for Mindaug's knowledge.

That was all Emeric really needed, after all. Simply the knowledge. He could provide the boldness the count himself lacked.

In Orsova the survivors of the Irongate were very glad to tell their new prince about their ordeal.

Vlad and Dana had absolutely no idea what they were talking about. Fortunately the king of the wolves was better informed.

"Vila. They have always stood outside the compact. The queen of the river does not rule them. They are creatures of both bank and water, spending time among the willows and in the slow backwaters of rivers and in lakes and ponds, and they breathe air. Strictly speaking her sprites stay within the confines of the water, and can breathe water. The Vila are an ancient evil. They seduce young men. They're said to be unfortunate girls who drowned themselves after getting pregnant . . . but they like to kill. I think they like desperation, and will take the young girls as they take the young men."

"If the river queen can't deal with them, what can?" asked Dana.

"I think it is more a case of 'won't' than can't," answered the wolf king. "But they could." He looked at the two wyverns, peering doubtfully at the island fortress.

The two wyverns looked at the water.

"It's wet,"

"And cold.

"And runs too fast."

"On the bank it would be a different matter."

"You are a pair of babes," said Dana. "You fly."

"Not over running water. Not if we can help it."

"All forms of magic have their natural limitations, and it is likewise with magical creatures," explained the wolf king.

"Then we'll just have to deal with it ourselves," said Vlad. "What are the Vila's limitations then?"

"Iron. Fire. And they need to breathe air."

"We could drown the island. Block the river with an earthquake."

"That's not something used lightly," said Angelo. "Earth ties to earth. Move one piece and another must move, too."

"We could take the knights in boats—"

"They'd sink the boat."

Dana spoke up. "I am able to affect the flow of the water. Let us stop it."

"And then?" asked Vlad.

Dana smiled at the Wyverns. "You two don't mind still water do you?"

They exchanged one of those speaking glances, first with her, then with each other. "Not fond of it. But we can fly over that, yes."

Vlad stood up. "I will go and see the priests."

"Priests?"

"As the wolves have explained by their desire to appear gypsies: people fear the unknown. They do not trust real dragons here. With reason, they are wary of the old powers. They were strong here once. So let us give them something else to believe responsible. I will have the priests on the shore exorcize it. During the night you two can fly over and deal with our green-haired naked women. Then in the morning we can go over and find that prayer worked. And who knows: It may even do so."

Dana liked the idea. "I think we should get the townspeople to sing hymns across the water from the island, too."

Vlad nodded. "The more involved they are, the more they will believe."

In the dark of the night two batwinged shapes flew across the still water. The Vila, sitting combing her long, greenish tinged blond hair on the battlements did not see them come. She was too taken up with her narcissistic admiration of herself.

"Fshhh," the wyvern said, taking the end of the blond hair in a taloned forepaw and slashing another claw across the rest, with a movement more like scalping than cutting. The Vila, shorn, screamed. First in outrage, then in horror, realising what she was facing, as the wyvern shifted colors. She tensed to run.

"Where are you going to run to?" asked the wyvern. "The water won't hide you. And the forest will not give you shelter. You've traded one off against the other for too long."

"And anyway, you will run straight into me," said the other wyvern.

By the next day, when Dana and a small delegation of priests and knights went across, the island was a peaceful place, and very empty.

The only sign of the terrifying women was a large hank of wet, greenish blond hair, next to the battlements.

Dana was close to being considered a local saint. It seemed some measure of fear was a prerequisite for the Drac, but his little sister...she could be a lot better than she actually was.

"The land on the other side of the river—it seems sparsely populated," said Erik.

"Yes. It's Slav land. Nominally ruled by King Emeric, too," said Vlad.

"I wonder..." said Erik, tentatively. "Is there any chance of getting a messenger across it, down into northeastern Illyria? It can't be more than five or six leagues...to the village of Gorlac."

"Dangerous for a man," said Angelo. "Easy enough for a wolf. We can do it one night."

"Would you please?" Erik asked politely.

The king of the wolves nodded. "From what I hear we owe you for saving the girl."

So, at long last, Manfred was able to send a detailed report of his whereabouts and the situation in the lands of the Golden Horde. It included a statement from Tulkun, and Bortai, in Mongol script, destined for the Ilkhan.

Erik was willing to bet few sword strokes could wreak as much havoc as those sheets of paper would. Of course it might take until next spring to get them to where they might do some good.

Chapter 81

The winter, having being fairly mild, turned into a harsh season, with more snow. Vlad was able to do little more than consolidate, drill a little, and wait for spring.

To the east, the Golden Horde put aside inter-clan warfare in favor of keeping warm, and, of course, passing the time. A lot of babies would be born nine months later. And, naturally, a lot of stories were told. This was the time of year to strengthen and maintain the core of Mongol tradition, mostly by word of mouth. The story of Tortoise Orkhan was a popular one, across the White Horde, and the unaffiliated and disaffected part of the Blue Horde. It was repeated, more clandestinely, even among the women folk of the clans closest to Gatu.

The orkhan called a meeting of his closest advisors. "It is like being pecked to death by sparrows. Every day we get more demands about having a kurultai to choose a new khan. Do they not think that I know what they're doing?"

"In spring—"

"We cannot wait until spring. If we wait until then, we seven in this ger will be the last left," Nogay said glumly. "We've spread gold like water. And all she has spread is this story. And they prefer tradition and stories. The women coo about the romance of it."

"Besides," said another adviser, "they have made an alliance, or at least a truce, with the khan over the mountain. He has let them pass through his territory. They can flank us or raid our gers while we try to fight the White Horde."

"Let us call for a new kurultai," said Gatu thoughtfully.

"You might have lost an election then, Orkhan," said General Nogay, "which is why we took the actions we did. You would definitely lose an election now."

"Yes," said the orkhan. "But you have told me that we have a skilled assassin. Borshar has brought us nothing but trouble so far, not the help we were promised. So let us see if he can be of other use."

Nogay looked thoughtful. "Kildai was supposed to die with the spell that knocked him off his horse. The ancestral tengeri look after that one. He would have to be killed in such a way that no suspicion fell on you, Orkhan."

After Emeric dismissed Count Mindaug, he felt some anxiety over his offer of employment. Mindaug had taken the offer—and gratefully, to all appearances. But the King of Hungary could not help but be somewhat worried.

Emeric's grasp of magic was rudimentary, compared to that of Elizabeth's. In the past, the countess had seen to it that competent practitioners whom Emeric could co-opt were few and far between. She had killed anyone who might rival her, and taken into her own employ those like Mindaug who posed no threat but were highly skilled.

The result was that Emeric had no good way to oversee the work of someone like Mindaug. He didn't know enough, himself. He would have no choice but to trust the count's word for such things—and trust was not something that came easily to the King of Hungary. It didn't come at all, actually.

Still...

He decided he was fretting too much. Elizabeth had never given any indication that she feared treachery from Mindaug, after all. The count's faults were those of fear and timidity—hardly the traits one would expect from an ambitious schemer. Emeric would simply have to see to it that, in a crisis, he overrode Mindaug's inevitable hesitations.

Chapter 82

"The orkhan and the khans of the clans of the Blue Horde have sent tarkhans to negotiate a kurultai!" announced Bortai excitedly. "The generals and the khans from the clans are discussing safeguards with them."

Erik found himself in turmoil on hearing this. He ought to be glad. Bortai was plainly pleased, the election of a new great Khan for the Golden Horde would hopefully end the civil war situation, and this after all would clear their way to their completing their mission. But... for the harsh months of winter, he had spent part of nearly every day with Bortai. She and two or three female Mongols—often different ones, escorted discretely by a few warriors, always came to make sure that they were well provisioned, and that they had no needs. Once Erik had found out the protocol that Mongols would follow among themselves on these visits, he'd had a word with Manfred and they'd turned them into showpieces of good hospitality. This had certainly done them no harm in the eyes of their hosts. They were an intrinsically traditional society, placing value on such things. The result had been that the knights were now almost regarded as a slightly odd Mongol tribe . . . and that Erik was even more fluent in Bortai's tongue—and she in his. And of course that his feelings for her had grown. She was . . . different from Svan. Always would be. But she was as true as steel, and laughed a lot.

And now they would be parting. And he still was none too sure what to do about it.

"Will you be going to the kurultai?" he asked.

"Oh yes, definitely! I will be giving my testimony there, before the assembled clan heads."

"I will miss you," The words were out before he thought about them.

She looked at him a little oddly. "But you will be coming with us."

"Um . . ." How best not to give offense?

She understood. "It will not be like last time. First . . . The clan khans have agreed. And second, our army awaits less than a league away. Third, it will take place on our borderland. This time it is not us who are far from home and isolated. And finally, this time we are prepared. Let them dare. Few, if any clans will stand for it twice. They have tried to pin the blame on us for last time. It has not worked. The honor and reputation of the Hawk clan towers above them. The best they can hope for is for people to accept is that it was a mistake."

"I have to consider Manfred's safety." And yours, he wanted to say, but held back. How had he got himself into this situation? He'd said that he would never love another woman. That his life was duty . . . And also, well, just how could he do it? He had no real idea of the protocols involved in proposing marriage to a Mongol woman. And...was the idea at all acceptable to her? Was he?

She nodded. "*We* understand the sanctity of a tarkhan and his escorts."

Which was important, but not quite what he needed to know, right now.

Bortai had become very, very good at reading Erik. She knew him now for the reserved, intensely honorable that man he was. She'd long since moved on in her thinking from considering him a foreigner and some kind but lesser person. He was just...Erik. A man who loved neither lightly nor with anything less than his whole being. She too saw complications. A Mongol woman moved, with her bride-goods, to the ger and lands of her new husband. She had long since realized that the horseboy had lied about Erik's noble antecedents. And she found that she really didn't care. She'd met enough young nobles whose nobility amounted to a title and wealth. In Erik...well he had that inner quality that set him apart. But just how did she persuade him to take that next step? And...was she ready to cast clan, tradition, and all she had lived for aside for a handsome foreigner?

Her heart said "yes."

Duty and common sense said "no." Or at least, not yet. But part of her said she should ignore the smiling chaperones—who were very good at turning a blind eye—and just kiss him.

Duty won.

Narrowly.

The wolves knew roughly where to start searching. And the noses of the wolves were keen. It did not take them that long to find the shallow grave, and to open it up.

Vlad stood silent looking down at fabric that he recognized. At her remains.

Finally, he turned away and said quietly. "No man could own you. But you...owned me. And in part you always will." He took off his black cloak with its rich purple satin lining. "Let us wrap her in this. She will have a real burial, with honor, in the churchyard. My debt to the Lady Bortai is deeper. But I will purge this earth of Elizabeth's descendant, too. Emeric of Hungary was Elizabeth Bartoldy's legacy. Destroying him will be Rosa's."

Kaltegg Shaman looked at the two boys and chuckled. "You are willing to do this, boy?" he asked David.

David nodded. Once he would have shied as far as possible from it. But he been a different boy then. A person to whom the walls of Jerusalem had been the walls of the world, and to whom self had been all important. Now...he knew that had been a very small world, and that self was part of larger whole.

"You know that they will try to kill you," said the shaman.

"That's why I came. That's why I made Kildai come."

"It is my task and my risk!" said Kildai.

"Shut up, you," said David cheerfully.

"How can you tell me to shut up? Have you no respect?" demanded Kildai. But the shaman could tell by the way he said it, that it was a rhetorical question.

He smiled to himself. The young khan needed this. And the boy from Jerusalem needed him, too.

"Nope," said David. "You know that by know. So tell us, Kaltegg Shaman, can we do this? They will try to kill him. I know it. He knows it. Last time they tried by magic. I think that is what they will do again. I've talked to Von Stael. He says that I am doing the right thing."

The shaman nodded. "Yes. I believe it will be a magical attack, and a strong one. I believe it will be directed at Kildai Khan. I believe that the force that will provide the spell does not know Kildai Khan. They must have got hold, somehow, of some of his essences. Blood. Skin. Hair. Maybe even clothes. Thus it was that the force was able to be released at him, while he rode in the great game." He looked at Kildai, sternly. "You were lucky to survive, Kildai Khan. But this could work. The spell will be directed at the wrong person—if they require that it should be by direct indication of the victim. I think this is true. They *must* point you out—focus the ill-wishing on you. Otherwise Kildai Khan would die, even though he be hidden from them."

David nodded. "So, until we have dealt with Gatu Orkhan, I will be you. And you be me—wearing steel and riding with the Knights. And the two of us will have to keep apart."

The shaman nodded. "I will do what I can to protect you both."

The kurultai must have had ten thousand tents.

"A small gathering," said General Pakai. "People are wary. But every clan has sent some representatives."

"And a lot more wait, and watch, just a few hours away," said Bortai.

They rode on.

The huge camp was very edgy. Clan representatives and soldiers had gone ahead, setting up gers, preparing the sections of the kurultai. The camp was a large ring, allowing access to the open steppe beyond, without crossing the camp of any other clan. White Horde was on the northern and eastern side, Blue on the southern and western. In the middle was a large open area, with a dais for the clan heads. The sub-clans would be obliged to settle for the grass. But the camp had been chosen well: it was set about a low dell, which had been cleared of snow, making a natural amphitheater.

The Mongols, who normally dressed in rather plain clothing, making it hard to tell a khan from a commoner, had broken out their finery. Erik hardly even recognized Bortai, in the rose colored and patterned deel of embroidered fine cloth and doeskin boots. The clan must be making sure that their prize witness looked the part.

The knights rode in the rear of the column. There was a disturbance up ahead and Bortai rode on to see what it was.

David lay on the ground and fitted epileptically. The Khesig had formed a defensive circle around him. The shaman Kaltegg had already made a circle in the snow and was beating his drum, chanting.

As Bortai pushed her way through, David sat up. By the time she got there he was being helped onto his horse.

"Are you all right?" she demanded.

"No," he said, crossly. "I feel like I have just run fifty miles, and been pounded with rocks."

"Magical attack," said the shaman. "I have the flavor of the attacker now."

"Oh, good," said David, clinging to the saddle. "That makes me feel better. Why didn't you stop them?"

"I did not know who it was, or what form it would take," said Kaltegg. "I do now, boy from Jerusalem. And if you had been Kildai, the attack would have killed him. Now, it will rebound."

Bortai rode back and evaded Erik, to make sure that *Ritter* Von Stael's "squire" in peaked helmet and high-collared cloak was all right. And to reassure Kildai that David, too, was fine. They managed a swap around later in the Hawk camp, and a little later Kildai, looking as fit as a young colt, rode off to the first session of the kurultai.

"You will be called," Bortai explained to Erik. "A little after me, I think."

"What happened earlier?"

"The horseboy transferred his debt to you, to us," said Bortai with a twinkle. "He will be all right. And he is a brave boy."

"Better than he was, anyway," said Erik.

A messenger came looking for Bortai, and she went to face the clan-heads.

"There was some consternation at seeing Kildai there," said her escort, grinning.

"You have noted carefully who did not expect him to be?"

"Of course. But we already knew."

Bortai stood and spoke to the crowd. She had a

good, strong carrying voice. She told her story well. She had been taught to do so, since story-telling was a skill of great value. The audience responded appreciatively, with suitable laughter, and appropriate gasps of horror in the right places. Pointed looks were cast at the orkhan.

Afterward one of Gatu's pets got up. "It's a good story," he said, "if hard to believe."

The audience hissed. They wanted to believe. "But tell me," he went on. "The effects of a fall onto one's head, as we all know, can weaken the souls of the body causing fits. Is it not true that the young khan of the Hawk has had such fits since then? Making this tissue of silly lies a necessity? The clans cannot have a leader who will fall from his horse."

Bortai drew herself up for her reply—and Nogay, he who had been tarkhan to the north—suddenly began gibbering and shrieking, and then, with foam on his lips, began to spasm and jerk uncontrollably. He rolled down the slope, his back arched with a peculiar choking, gurgling and screaming as he thrashed about, fighting unseen demons. Eventually he lay still, his head at an odd angle.

"No," said Bortai, smiling sweetly. "You must have confused Kildai with General Nogay," she pointed. "That was no fit, though. That was a curse. A spell cast by Nogay—which has come echoing back on him." She sniffed disdainfully. "His souls do not have the strength of my brother Khan Kildai. His ancestors do not watch over him. They have turned away from him in shame. Some people will do anything for gold. But it does not go well with the spirits if they do so."

The lifeless corpse of Nogay bore mute witness to

what she'd said. That and the fact that Nogay had indeed come from relative obscurity to become very rich. The advisor who had raised what he had hoped would be a clinching point, supported by a fit from Kildai which never came . . . shrank down again, close to his master.

"It has been said, though, that the clan Hawk gave shelter to truce breakers and, worse, those who took hostage an honorable tarkhan of the Ilkhan of the Red Horde."

"Many things have been said. Not all of them are true," said Bortai calmly, although she raged at the implications. "We say that the clans were deceived into truce breaking, into attacking those who came honorably acting within the writ of safe conduct they had been given. If there is dishonor, it is to those who told such lies." She walked over and kicked the corpse of Nogay. "Here is one. The other traitor to both the Red Horde of Ilkhan and those whom he was supposed to be the emissary to . . . is the tarkhan Borshar." There was a gasp of horror at this. A tarkhan was immune to any form of punishment. It made things complicated. "I have here," she held up the documents, "bearing the great seal of the Ilkhan Hotai, a writ of safe conduct to the Khan Manfred of Brittany and his retinue of Knights of the order that is called 'the Holy Trinity' as escorts of the tarkhan Borshar. I call the warrior Tulkun of the Bear clan of the Red Horde to be our next witness to this."

Tulkun had been fetched. As he strode in, the escorts left to fetch Erik. They had decided to let it be Erik, because he spoke—badly, it was true—the tongue of the people.

Tulkun was a good fighter. He was not a particularly good speaker.

The tarkhan himself rose, lazily. "What you have here is a case of double-tongued speaking. A traitor himself, accusing me of treachery. Yes, they had a safe conduct, but planned treachery and used me as a hostage. This Tulkun is a traitor and without honor, who has sold his clan and his people to the foreigners. I say the honor of the Golden Horde demands his head."

There was a growl of assent from a lot of throats.

Bortai held up another piece of paper. "There is one more thing. A document that has come to our hands. It was given to Captain Feldu for the late General Nogay. Written by the tarkhan."

Bortai read it out.

And was aware of a group of armed men who had entered the central area of the natural arena.

"A forgery," said the tarkhan, waving a dismissive hand.

Bortai was aware of the fact that the nine men who had accompanied Tulkun and the tarkhan Borshar were closing on them.

"You know that this is the kurultai. That the spilling of blood is forbidden," said Bortai, turning toward them.

They bowed. "We know that. We have not come to spill blood," said the leader of the small group, Matu. "We escorted the tarkhan from Jerusalem. We have come to bear witness that the warrior Tulkun speaks the truth. He is an honorable man."

"I carried the message to the captain from the tarkhan Borshar," said another.

There was an audible hiss of indrawn breath from the watching crowd. You could see the red rage-lights in their eyes.

The tarkhan shrugged. "Politics. There is nothing

you can do about it. I am a tarkhan of the Ilkhan, with all the rights granted between the fellow people of the Hordes. Send me home, if you can."

"There is something I can do about it."

Bortai turned to see that Erik had entered the amphitheater.

"Who are you, foreigner, that you dare to raise your voice at the kurultai," said Gatu Orkhan. "There is no limit on the spilling of blood of non-Mongol."

"He is protected by the same writ of safe conduct. He is a Knight of the Holy Trinity," said Bortai.

"Nonetheless. Borshar Tarkhan may be unwelcome in the lands of the Golden Horde, but no one can raise a hand against him," said the orkhan.

There was an outcry at this. "He has shamed us. He has brought us to the brink of war with the Ilkhan." The crowd seethed like angry bees.

Erik held up his hand. Someone in the watching crowd said "He is the Tortoise Orkhan!"

There was ripple of interest and amusement through the crowd.

"Let him speak!" called several voices.

Erik bowed. "My thanks and my respect to the clan heads of the Golden Horde." He pointed to Borshar. "There is a man who has tried to engineer war between the Golden Horde and his supposed master the Ilkhan. He has tried to engineer war between the Holy Roman Empire and Golden Horde—for, and he knew this well, had his plot succeeded, and had my Khan, Manfred of Brittany, been treacherously murdered, it would have meant war. Probably war with the Ilkhan, too. He does not serve the Ilkhan. He serves the Khan Jagiellon. The source of much gold."

"I serve only God," said Borshar, above the hubbub.

"And anyway," said Bortai. "He *is* protected by his status. No matter what he has done, no matter what he has been accused of, no Mongol may raise a hand to him, let alone cut him down."

"I am not a Mongol. And if you read the words of our writ of safe conduct carefully, you will see that it says we are to defend the tarkhan from outside threats. Those words are specifically used."

"So?" said the Gatu Orkhan.

"So it does not say that I am obliged to defend him from myself," said Erik, throwing down a gauntlet. He didn't know if this gesture meant anything to the Golden Horde. But it was the traditional way of issuing a challenge. By the cheers they understood.

"If no one was holding me back," said Tulkun, looking around, "his bodyguard would have to defend him. Although we despise the son of Dishmaq."

The Ilkhan's men suddenly found themselves being held by grinning Golden Horde men.

"You cannot spill blood at the kurultai," said Bortai. "And a foreigner spilling the blood of one of our blood..."

"We'll wrestle," said Erik.

The crowd cheered deafeningly. Erik had gathered it was an even more popular entertainment here than in Iceland.

The tarkhan came forward. "You son of Iblis. Your death will be a suitable lesson. And our Lord has desired it in my dreams. Besides, you insulted me."

Tulkun said, "Erik. He trained at Alamut."

An assassin.

Bortai felt her blood run cold.

Erik was a great fighter. She'd seen that. But no foreigner had skills at the noble art compared to the Mongol. And this Borshar would have been taught to kill in many ways.

Erik loosened his sword belt. "Can some of you help me out of my armor?"

Erik knew enough about Alamut, the assassins' castle, to be wary. But Borshar was not equally wary about the Knights of the Holy Trinity, or Icelandic wrestlers.

Erik changed that quite quickly. He threw Borshar hard over his shoulder. The man from Alamut rolled with practiced ease. But he did not come forward with such unwariness the second time. And Erik noticed he was flexing his fingers and that each nail had been sharpened. Borshar plainly wanted him to notice. "There is a death on each nail, dog. The peacock angel waits for you."

As Erik expected, he tried to kick Erik in the crotch. Erik helped his foot in a neat arc upwards. And then the fight was on.

Erik smelled the sudden stench of magic and slapped the assassin, with cupped hands, simultaneously on both ears. Erik didn't quite know why he'd chosen to do that, but the miasma of magic-use cleared.

Erik was limited in that Borshar's nails really might have a poison on them. And he did not want to make the man bleed.

Within two minutes, though, he knew how it would end—and by the growing look on his face, first of surprise and then of desperation, so did Borshar.

The Alamut assassin was very skilled at unarmed

fighting, true. Probably even more skilled than Erik, in terms of sheer technique.

But skill and technique are not all there was to fighting—fighting of any kind, much less wrestling. There was also strength, stamina, and most of all the near-instant reactions of a body that trained constantly.

Borshar was good. But he had done little exercise since leaving Jerusalem. Erik trained every day, for several hours, and had for many years now. There was probably no man alive who was in better fighting condition than he was—and if there was such a man, it certainly wasn't Borshar.

There could only be one end. Again, Borshar was just that little bit too slow in his reactions, and again Erik slammed him to the ground. When he came up, the Alamut assassin drew a hidden knife from his boot.

The audience hissed. Bortai cried out a warning. But Erik had been expecting something like this. He evaded the knife thrust, seized Borshar under the arm and threw him over his shoulder. Then he followed the half-stunned Borshar to the ground and slid both arms under the assassin's armpits. In an instant, Erik had his hands clasped behind Borshar's neck and heaved him to his feet.

The huge audience was silent. That was a deadly hold and they all knew it—provided the man using it was strong enough.

Erik was immensely strong. Much stronger that he looked, with his lean frame. Not quite as strong as Manfred, true. But quite strong enough.

His muscles heaved. Borshar's eyes seemed as wide as saucers. The assassin's arms flailed about uselessly, the knife slipped out of his grasp.

There came an audible crack. Erik heaved again, just to make sure the spine was severed, and then let Borshar's lifeless body fall to the ground.

There was no blood. Not a drop.

The other thing there was none of was Gatu and his inner circle. They too had realized soon enough how the match must end, and had used the distraction of the fight to make an escape.

As soon as someone realized this the meeting broke up in chaos. Men ran for their horses.

Erik, standing panting a little, asked Tulkun just what was happening. "They fear that he will try to mobilize his personal guard into an attack. They are all that is available to him, because most clan heads are here. Even from the Blue Horde. And he will have almost no support now."

Erik sighed. "It never ends. Give me a hand with my armor, would you?"

Erik was about two-thirds rearmored, when Manfred and the knights came riding up. "We're invited to join the hunt, Erik. According to Bortai, that's a signal honor. We brought your horse."

So, tired or not, Erik found himself riding out that afternoon as part of the Mongol hunt.

Only the prey, it seemed, had kept a river-barge on standby.

With only one candidate the election of the new khan was rapidly accomplished. Also, even if the knights had been included in the hunt, it was not an affair for non-Mongols.

By midmorning the next day, a summons came for Manfred and Eberhard. Erik stood up to accompany

Manfred, but the guard-captain of the escort Arban respectfully shook his head. "No, Tortoise Orkhan," he said. "It is only an invitation to Manfred Khan and his advisor. They say that he can take only one knight—a *Ritter* Von Stael—with him as a bodyguard."

"They think you're dangerous, Erik," said Manfred, grinning. "Serves you right for killing notorious assassins."

"Who is going to translate for you?"

"Lady Bortai will be there," said the Mongol guard-captain.

Erik had to be happy with that. He rather wished she was here with him instead.

He had to wait several hours before Manfred and Eberhard came back. In a roaring good humor. A little drunk, both of them. "You didn't miss much, Erik," said Manfred in a voice that said exactly the opposite. "The new Great Khan's a crusty old devil, but very generous with his wine. Real wine, especially for us."

Eberhard sat down on the three-legged stool. "The Emperor will be very pleased with the outcome of this adventure, anyway. We have powerful new allies, flanking Lithuania."

But Manfred seemed oddly lugubrious, all of a sudden. He shook his head. "I'm not so sure how well this is turning out. Erik is in real trouble."

"Me?" said Erik.

"Yes, you," said Manfred. "The Great Khan of the Golden Horde thinks you're a fine fellow. At least three clans want to adopt you for doing the Golden Horde a favor with the tarkhan Borshar. But the Great Khan has heard that you're trifling with the affections of an innocent, poor young Mongol maiden. He thinks you should approach her kin to ask for her hand or back off."

Erik blushed to the roots of his hair. "Does everyone know my business? I suppose going to see Kildai would be a start. Although, Manfred, I don't know how these things are done among the Golden Horde. I've done something wrong. They all seem to have heard the story of my first greeting to her. And every single one I meet, from grandmothers to generals, seems to be smirking and sniggering."

Manfred's attempt at keeping a straight face failed. "Well, I thought the innocent poor young Mongol maiden was going to tear the new Great Khan of the Golden Horde's head off."

"I'm not surprised. She...can express herself." Erik blushed again. "But...I will keep my distance if that is what I am supposed to do."

"Well, maybe she's just waiting for you, Erik. You know, they marry them off young here. She's quite old to be single. She might be desperate enough to take you, in spite of your looks," said Manfred, laughing again.

"You've had far too much wine."

Eberhard nodded. "Especially as we have to ride to see Vlad of Valahia this afternoon. The new khan wants to discuss a mutual nonaggression pact. He asked us to act as his intermediary."

"Which is one step from miraculous, considering their history," said Erik.

"But common sense," said Eberhard, "if they're going to try to expand north and northeast. It would leave them with an underprotected long flank."

"Anyway, so you'll have a nice long cold ride to think about it," said Manfred.

But it was less of a ride than they had anticipated.

They had barely gone two leagues when they were met by Vlad, a company of his Székelers, and an escort of Mongols.

"I have come to propose an alliance. Emeric of Hungary is pushing through the Suceava river valley. It appears that he is coming to the lands of the Golden Horde, not to attack Valahia. He has some forty thousand men."

"You want an alliance?"

Vlad nodded. "Whatever he is up to, we will be next. Dana and I are quite weak in the north. The heart of our power is in the Fărăgas Mountains, but we may not be able to resist there either. So: it comes down to strength of arms. It will take me a few days to gather my troops, and bring them north onto the lower lands of the Golden Horde. I do not have great numbers, but I do have the wagon-forts and the cannons. We can be the anvil, and the warriors of the Hawk clan can be the hammer. Between us, I think we can defeat the Magyars."

"I think you'd better ride on," said Eberhard. "It won't just be the Hawk clan, any longer. There is a new Great Khan and he will be pleased to see you."

When it had become apparent that his operations in the lands of the Golden Horde had failed of their direct purpose, Jagiellon sat on his throne and scratched at lice absently. The intellect that had largely devoured him was deep in thought. Factors to consider were many, complex and varied. Somewhere on the Black

Sea was a hostile fleet, although his own fleet was larger. But the shipyards on the Dniepr still held the bulk of his round ships. The camps outside Odessa held thirty thousand troops, waiting. If he could not take his troops to Constantinople by sea, perhaps they could go through the lands of the Golden Horde.

That would not be easy, of course, but... The grand duke's agents had told him that Emeric was attacking the Mongols. Jagiellon didn't think the Hungarian king would defeat them, but for Lithuania's purposes he didn't need to. All he had to do was bleed the Mongols and remove them as an obstacle.

That would be enough. True, the power in the Carpathians would remain, and it was nearly unassailable. But that power weakened quickly as it left its mountainous heartland. Chernobog could magically shield a force moving at speed past those lands toward Constantinople.

Yes. It would be enough.

PART IX
March, 1541 A.D.

Chapter 83

The lumbering wagons had trundled through the night to be here, to set up the mobile forts, each with a goodly trench and earth rampart, and their cannons ready. There were six of them, each considerably larger than the original makeshift one that Vlad's men had contrived.

The mounted infantry were out on the gently rolling hills, along with the Székeler light cavalry, harassing and drawing out the Hungarian heavy cavalry. The Székelers inflicted steady pinpricks of damage and fury, never stopping to allow the greater numbers and mass of their opponents to catch up with them.

In separate little battles, the Croat light cavalry were taking a battering. There were fewer of them than Emeric needed, for one thing. For another, the Székelers had local guides and used the mounted infantry as bait.

By the time the scouts sighted the wagon-forts, Emeric and his commanders were almost desperate for an enemy that would stand and fight. The Hungarian troops had had little respite since the campaign began, suffering small attacks day and night and facing a hostile local people.

For once, Emeric left the tactics to his commanders. They sent some of the Croats forward to probe the forts. Those could be avoided if they appeared too well defended. The Croats came within fifty yards of one of the forts, at which point they came under desultory arquebus fire.

"They're well enough dug in, Your Majesty. I would say they have been using them as reprovisioning points, camps to defend themselves against Mongols. Still, they're just earth embankments, wagons and a few pikes. Something of an abatis, but they're short of trees.

"One of the encampments," the scout added, "the one in the center, flies the flag of the Duke of Valahia."

Emeric grunted his satisfaction. That was what he had planned for. A battle with Vlad of Valahia here would make more sense than an endless campaign in the mountains, with its castles and fortifications, and a mobile enemy using the terrain to nullify the advantages of numbers and heavy cavalry.

Emeric directed two thousand of his troops at each fortification, in a simultaneous attack. "They plainly expect to come to each other's aid. This way, they can't."

In the wagon-forts, the covers were being taken from the guns. Fixed pikes were being positioned and anchored. And the waiting had started.

Instead of scouts and infantry, Emeric's commanders had apparently decided on speed and weight. The charge, the heavy cavalry's standard method, raced forward, to the brave sound of battle cries.

Under normal circumstances, that charge would have crushed the enemy. Magyar heavy cavalry were feared, and for good reason. But here they encountered fire they'd never expected in an open battlefield. At barely one hundred yards, the bastard culverins of the wagon-forts cut loose, firing cloth bags full of shrapnel.

The slaughter was horrific, especially of the horses. The charge collapsed almost instantly. And as the Hungarian cavalry began retreating, Mongol cavalrymen came in pursuit. The retreat became a rout.

Emeric's fleeing cavalry disorganized the rest of his army, as often happened in such instances. If the Hungarian troops weren't rallied, this battle could turn into a disaster.

More than anything, the situation called for a commander with steady nerves and the ability to instill confidence in his officers. Or, to put it another way...

Anyone except Emeric.

The King of Hungary began screeching furious orders mingled with threats that were as pointless as they were blood-curdling. The result was simply to confuse his staff officers.

The Hungarian army began coming apart, here and there. Infantry units began breaking and heading to the rear, following the cavalry. Naturally, the Mongol cavalrymen targeted them immediately. Steady infantry, well-organized and armed with either pikes or guns, could withstand cavalry. But routed infantrymen were easy prey for cavalry—any cavalry, much less Mongols who'd been trained since boyhood in the great Mongol hunts.

Emeric turned to Mindaug. The count was perched on a mule perhaps ten yards away.

"Do something!" he shrieked.

Mindaug managed not to shake his head. Barely. As he had feared, his new employer was prone to hysteria. From a purely military standpoint, the situation was not yet desperate. True, the initial headlong and reckless Magyar cavalry charge had been bloodied and battered, and the Hungarian army's morale was fraying badly. But there was still time for Emeric to rally his forces, and those forces still outnumbered those of his enemy. Under such circumstances, to turn toward magic would just be further recklessness.

"Your Majesty, I would recommend—"

"Do something!" Emeric looked to his immediate bodyguards and pointed a finger at Mindaug. "If he doesn't *do* something—quickly!—then kill him!"

Mindaug was sorely tempted to produce a harmless but dazzling display of magicry. That would, after all, constitute "doing something"—and it was obvious from the confused expressions on the faces of Emeric's guards that they had no real idea exactly what the king wanted. Which was hardly surprising, of course, since the king himself had no clear idea.

Just *something*.

The problem, of course, was simple. Someone as familiar with the black arts as Emeric should have known perfectly well that battlefields were terrible places to wield magic. There was far too much iron present, more than you would encounter almost anywhere else.

Iron and magic did not mix well. Only the strongest magics would work at all, and the end result was always uncertain.

"*Do something!*" the king screeched again.

Mindaug shrugged. So be it. He began chanting the necessary phrases.

If this magic went badly, it was likely to go very badly indeed—and there was a simple countermeasure against it. Hopefully, the enemy would overlook that countermeasure, because of its very simplicity.

And if they didn't... Well, Mindaug had long since prepared his escape. Too bad for the King of Hungary, then. But he was a loathsome fellow anyway.

Kaltegg Shaman was not happy about the dispersal of the magical protections at his disposal. He had wanted, and very badly, to station the knights with their curiously spiked armor at each of the mobile forts to help disperse magic, but it seemed that was out of the question. The knights stayed together, in a group. And the shaman had not had enough time to direct the cobbling together of iron and steel junk into dispersal-rods for all the forts, either.

The tengeri were uneasy. The air-horses were unhappy. The shaman could only wait for whatever the foe might throw at them, and hope that he could think of something to deflect it.

When the attack finally came, it was not the raging storm of magic on the spirit plane he had expected. Instead it came subtly, so subtly that at first he did not recognize it as an attack. It came as a lowering of the spirits, of energy. A dimming of the senses. It crept over him slowly, so slowly that he did not even realize what was happening until a wounded man he was tending began to weep and say a word that Shaman recognized as meaning "mother." Yet that man was not about to die, was an old and experienced campaigner, and should not be acting like a boy in his first combat.

And that was when the shaman knew, with a start, that the enemy had a truly skilled magic-user. A subtle one! He was doing his work in such a way that the knights had not been alerted. This was no Elizabeth Bartholdy, to bombard with demonic energies. This was a thing of long patience, indirection; the mind of an ambusher at work.

Just as the shaman realized that, there came a sound that he did not recognize from the farthest fort on the line. An explosion that seemed far too loud and somehow wrong. And then, another.

From the Sky-Runners came the word, whispered magically into his ear.

The cannons are exploding.

Frantically, the shaman began his drumming. And the Sky-Runners began to cloud-dance in time with his rhythms. They could not disperse the cannon-killing magic with iron and steel—but perhaps they could with air and fire and music.

He sensed, rather than saw, the farthest fort fall, its cannons turned deadly to the occupants, their bodies riddled with bronze shrapnel.

He redoubled his efforts, sweating.

It is not enough, came the strained word from above. *We need more help.*

The shaman rarely prayed as such. The spirits with which he dealt could be bargained with, or coaxed, or rarely, coerced. The gods, on the whole, preferred mortals to help themselves, which was right and good, if harsh. But the steppes were harsh, and had grown strong warriors—and a child never becomes a man if he is protected every step of his journey through life. The shaman agreed with that in principle.

But at this moment, he prayed. *A little help, Powers. Just a little, or the enemy will engulf us.*

And that was when it started, beside him.

The singing.

Not the knights; that, he might have expected. And not a battle-hymn such as the one they had sung to confound the evil woman. This was the horseboy, David, his voice still on the high side of tenor, high enough to pierce the battle-noise and carry over it, even though you could hear the faint tremolo of fear in it. And it was a simple song, a simple melody by the knights' standards, and what sounded like simple words.

The men around him took it up. Quickly, the shaman altered his drum-pattern to follow the beat of the words. There was power in this song, as there had been in the knights' battle-hymn. There was magic, too. And, it seemed, a greater magic than he guessed because soon *all* the men in their fort were singing it, and in three different tongues! The song carried out to the next fort, which took it up, and the next, and the next, and then the knights themselves sang it in their deep, thundering voices. Even his own people, the Mongols, seemed to sense the meaning of words none of them understood much of, and chanted nonsense syllables to the same tune. The Sky-Runners altered their dance to match it, and pulled the power of the song up to the sky, *and power descended from the sky to match it.*

The song somehow formed a protective shelter over the forts and the men in them. No more cannon exploded.

The shaman gave himself up to his drumming.

Luckily, the Hungarian king was too enthusiastic about the initial success of Mindaug's spells to notice that the count was now murmuring very different words.

As Mindaug had feared, the enemy either knew or had discovered by accident the countermeasure. And this countermeasure was building rapidly. Whoever that tenor was in the enemy ranks, he had enormous power. Mindaug wanted to be nowhere in sight when the enemy's counter-magic swept the field. The soldiers would panic; the horses, panic even worse.

Emeric must have realized, finally, that something was amiss. He turned toward Mindaug, his mouth open. To question, perhaps; more likely, to shriek more threats.

But Mindaug was gone. Where he and his mule had stood, there was now nothing but a cloud of smoke. And, bizarrely, a small mirror suspended in mid-air. Emeric could see his own reflection in that mirror, gaping. He clamped his mouth shut.

And then, suddenly, it was over. The Hungarian army simply disintegrated. The Mongols harried the edges of the fleeing mob. Vlad rode forward with his Székelers to accept the surrender of those who were sensible enough not to try to escape—or simply too stunned. The backlash of the spell unleashed by the Hungarians seemed to have struck the Magyar soldiers like a club.

Vlad's peasant soldiers found King Emeric, as they engaged in the looting of the corpses of their former attackers. Emeric was pretending to be dead himself.

That was a foolish ploy, given the finery of his

apparel. One of the soldiers recognized him and moments later he was surrounded. The soldiers kept their distance—the Hungarian king had a reputation of his own for black magic—but they called out to their commander.

Prince Vlad rode over to see what all the shouting was about.

"I give you my surrender," said Emeric sulkily. "As one lord to another. Keep these peasant carrion away from me."

One of the soldiers laid hands on Emeric. He reacted, foolishly, by using his pain touch. The soldier screamed and backed away. Now in a rage, Vlad got off his horse and strode over to the King of Hungary.

Emeric seized him as well; and, indeed, his touch was quite agonizing. But Vlad simply ignored the pain. He seized Emeric's hands in his own and, with one mighty shoulder-heaving wrench, broke both of the king's wrists.

Emeric screamed. Vlad flung the king to the ground, half-stunning him in the process. Then, seized Emeric by the scruff of the neck and shook him like a terrier shakes a rat.

"D'you want us to impale him?" asked one of the Székelers, grinning savagely. "Won't take but a moment to sharpen a stake."

Emeric nearly fainted with terror, suddenly realizing that he could be on the sharp end of his own favorite method of torture. "Please. I beg you!" he squealed.

"You threatened me with that, once," said Vlad harshly. "I spent long hours thinking of doing the same to you. But I have seen what cruelty unleashed can bring. Still, I will not suffer you to live."

He turned to his men. "Build a gibbet and find a rope. He hangs, right here and now."

It didn't take long. Many of Vlad's men were skilled carpenters.

Emeric screeched throughout. Once, frantically, he tried the pain touch again. But with both wrists broken, he couldn't get a decent grip on the Prince of Valahia. Vlad cuffed him half-senseless, then.

That was something of a mercy, perhaps, since the Hungarian king was too stunned to be very aware of his surroundings. Which were, of course, quite unsettling. The gibbet went up almost as if by magic.

Emeric regained his senses when he felt the noose fitted to his neck.

"You can't do this!" he screamed.

"Yes. I can." Vlad heaved on the rope. Given his great strength, Emeric went up like a bag of linen. He kicked for a time, and then died.

Vlad tied off the rope to a strut on the gibbet and then gazed upon the dangling body for a few moments.

"Rosa," he said, and turned away.

When the fires were burning for the night, and men were feasting and drinking, Kaltegg Shaman sought out David, in the midst of the knights.

He found the boy by the side of the one that had designated himself as David's mentor. "Boy," he said, without preamble. "You did a good thing. You helped with the battle magic, and maybe more than you know." He nodded at the older knight, who was looking at him curiously, but without any hostility. "Translate. Tell your master."

With a look of astonishment on his face, David did so. The knight nodded thoughtfully. So did the others that were near enough to hear. So. They recognized what had happened, too.

"So, tell me. That song. What was it? Some magic spell this man taught you?"

David's brow creased with puzzlement, as he translated again. The knight laughed.

"No," the knight replied in terrible Mongol. "Is child's sing. I make him teachings of Church."

David blushed a deep crimson, but raised his chin. "My knight is giving me religious instruction, and he taught me the first hymn all children are taught, and it was the first thing that came into my mind. I couldn't remember the battle hymns, but I could remember this."

Tortoise Orkhan came into the firelight, and caught the last of David's words.

"The song? The boy is right, it's one of the first hymns any of our children are taught. They say Saint Hypatia—she was a sort of holy person, like a shaman of shamans—wrote it herself. I think it must have been translated into every language we've ever come across, which is why every Christian knows it." His brows knitted for a moment. "It's about how everyone of good will, no matter what face of God they worship, is united in the eyes of God. I'm no poet, but I'll try a translation for one of the stanzas."

His eyes closed for a moment, then sang softly.

"From lands of endless ice and snow, to sand-filled desert winds that blow, all men of good beneath the sun, hold this pure truth that we are one."

"It goes on like that for three or four verses, each

one ending in 'we are one,'" said David. "I like it. I don't care if it is for children."

"Things for children are inclined to be very pure," the shaman said gravely. "Simple is not bad. The simplest things are likely to be quite profound."

He could well imagine that a saint had put her hand to those words. Even in translation, they had power.

Not enough power, however. So. Kaltegg studied the boy David. This one would bear watching, he thought.

Chapter 84

The waiting game, decided Dana, was not one that she was well suited to. Everyone, including the wyverns, was away at the war. Dana hadn't liked her first brush with killing. She'd actually been very glad to agree that it would be wise for her to stay here, in Berek. But now she was bored and worried. She learned from the villagers that Vlad rode down to the Mongol encampment quite often. So, accompanied by three wary guards, she did the same. It too was full of women, waiting...

Including Bortai. Dana had really bound to the Mongol princess in the time from their traumatic meeting in Elizabeth's castle to the taking of Irongate, and their return to Berek.

Bortai was also finding the waiting hard. "Khutulun rode with her father's generals. I think I should, too," she'd said. And then had to explain why she couldn't, who Khutulun was and from there, it was a short step to Erik, and what he was doing, and more importantly, wasn't doing. And what her brother had said. And...

Dana found herself trying to comfort someone

who was probably ten years older than herself. And who was a lot more worried about Erik than she'd admitted to anyone else.

"He's..." Bortai fumbled for words. "I'm stuck in a stupid practical joke that everyone in the entire Golden Horde thinks is hilariously funny. And the worst part is I think that I will have to stay in it. Erik...I think if he knew that I was a princess...that I have a bride's portion of many horses and flocks, he'd run away. He has told me so often that he was worried about what Svanhild's family back in Vinland would think of her bringing home a near penniless Icelander." She sniffed, defiantly. "I'd have him in the clothes he stood in. And half of the Golden Horde women would have him out of them before he could open his mouth to protest. And now I don't even know if he's alive. I should have told him that I loved him."

"He's alive," said a voice behind them.

Bortai turned, and had a knife out, pushing Dana back so fast that Dana hardly had time to squawk her own surprise.

"Come out," said Bortai to the dark back of the ger.

"Phiss. What are you going to do with that little knife? Steel's no good on us. It needs to be stone and magic at that."

Dana stamped her foot. "Come out. It's a wyvern, Bortai. You know. The creatures we have a pact with. They can make themselves very hard to see. But they won't hurt us."

"Might eat you," said the wyvern, gradually appearing out of the darker area of the ger. Dana knew it had been there all along, but looked like it was coalescing out of the shadows.

"No you won't," said Dana. "Have you been at the battle?"

The wyvern shrugged its wings. "A lot of magic. The shaman is good at it."

"My brother..."

"Is alive. His usual happy self. And so is Erik, and so is her brother," said the wyvern. "They sent me to tell you. But it does bring me to ask some questions about mating among you humans."

Dana hugged it. So did Bortai.

"I don't think we can cross the species line," said the wyvern. "Besides. I think I am female. I wanted to ask you about mating."

"I know a lot about breeding horses," said Bortai, grinning with relief. "And that is quite revealing."

Dana was more tenacious. "Have they won? And when will they be back?"

"They hanged someone called Emeric. And the clans are chasing down the northerners. They've crossed the Dniestr, I was told to tell you. Now about this breeding. Is it necessary to mate with one's brother? We've been looking at you humans and wondering."

Bortai looked startled. "It's not a good idea. Well, we do it sometimes with horses, and dogs. But new bloodlines strengthen the animals...And humans just shouldn't."

"We become a little more human with sharing of the blood. Still, we only have one chance to breed. There were many of us, once. But we are few now. We are the only two left here."

"Explain?"

So the wyvern did.

Both women were left silenced and discomforted. Finally Dana asked: "Isn't there another way?"

"Not that I know of. But I don't know everything... yet," said the wyvern.

Three days later the knights came limping back, accompanied by the surviving Székelers, and the mounted infantry. The wagons and the rest of the infantry were heading back into Valahia by a less steep route to the north.

The Mongols followed five days later, full of victory and loot, after a sweep that had taken the Golden Horde as far as the Bug river. They reported seeing ships flying the winged lion at anchor off Odessa.

Erik had come through the entire encounter with no worse than dented armor. And yet he was a troubled man. He finally went to talk to Manfred about it. "Am I fickle?" he asked.

Manfred smothered a snort. He didn't even try to pretend that he didn't know what Erik was talking about. "About as fickle as a whale-fish is small, Erik. Go and propose to her."

"I'm not exactly sure how to do this among the Mongols."

Manfred slapped him on the back. "I'll find out for you. Leave it to me. I have contacts."

Erik closed his eyes. "I shudder to think."

"Trust me," said Manfred. "The Great Khan himself speaks to me."

"You can't get Bortai to translate!"

"No. I'll take young David."

"That is worse! I mean...look what he got me into last time."

"He got her to notice and like you," said Manfred cheerfully. "What you may not know, and I do, is that she's a very popular woman. Had scores of suitors."

"I would think every man in the lands of the Golden Horde has tried. She's exceptional," said Erik, earnestly.

"Well, personally I'd advise you to run, and to run now," said Manfred, grinning. "She's got a tongue on her that could skin an ox."

"Good. I prefer them without skin," said a sibilant voice.

They both had their swords out. "Wyvern," said Erik, with relief. "Back there. What are you doing here, beast? Go back to Prince Vlad. Or his sister."

"Learning about human courtship. Dana sent me to find out just what you were doing."

Manfred snorted. "Everyone knows your business, Erik. Let me go and find David. Relax. Von Stael has quite reformed him."

Erik groaned. "Only with Von Stael, Manfred." He looked at the wyvern. It was not a very large creature, but he'd seen just how deadly it could be. "Are you going to go away, too?"

"No," said the creature. "I thought I'd stay here and tell you a Mongol tale."

Erik was about to protest. "It is Bortai's favorite. Actually, it is the Golden Horde's favorite story. It's their founding myth you might say." The wyvern preened. "I am a creature of myth. It's important to understand them *I* think."

"There is sometimes a grain of truth in them... somewhere," admitted Erik, curious.

"Oh, yes. Somewhere. Most of the story is usually wrong," said the wyvern.

"But they tell you how people think. Tell you about the culture."

"And pass the time between meals," said the wyvern.

"Are you going to tell me this story or aren't you?" asked Erik, sitting down. It beat pacing and waiting for Manfred.

"The story of Princess Khutulun and Ulaghchi."

"So they were real characters? Ulaghchi was the Great Khan. In what the Golden Horde feel was their golden age."

"Indeed. It is a song-poem. It goes like this..."

Erik listened. It was indeed a compelling story.

And when it was done, the wyvern faded away, blending its opalescent scales with the background and disappearing like a morning mist.

Erik shook himself. It had been a magical experience...well, it had been. He was aware that he'd heard snatches of the song before. It was obviously popular. And certainly held some clues as to how some people got married... Back then.

"Daydreaming?" said Manfred, grinning and smelling of wine. "You have to go and see her brother, Erik. David will take you."

Erik had never attempted to find out where Bortai lived. It was, however, exactly as he imagined: a simple, neat ger, with simple poor possessions. Every single person in the entire encampment, however, seemed to be between him and his destination. Grinning at him. There were even some of the Great Khan's Khesig hanging about, throwing bones near the ger. They were not the most soundproof structures on earth, Erik reflected as Kildai, playing host, gave him kumiss.

Erik did not last very long at the politeness. "Kildai,"

he swallowed. The boy was fourteen, and the impudent David, who hadn't gone away, perhaps a year older. "I want to marry your dau...sister."

David sniggered. But Kildai nodded seriously. "You realize that she does not have a very big bride portion," he said.

"I would take her if she had nothing at all," said Erik. "It's not important to me, if she'll have me."

Kildai looked thoughtful. "That doesn't seem a very provident thing to do. I do expect you to look after her. She would not be content to dine on vegetables like a Vlachs slave. Will you be able to feed her? And you do know that she snores? Especially when she drinks too much."

Bortai had been sitting talking to Dana, when the wyvern arrived as silently as only it could. "He is talking to your brother."

Both of them stood up headed towards the great ger. "Not in there," said the wyvern. "In some little store tent at the far side of the camp. My brother is listening to them."

Bortai arrived there, scattering people, curious, sniggering people trying to listen in. Just in time to hear her brother, prompted by his little friend no doubt, tell Erik that she snored.

"This has gone on long enough," she said angrily, bursting in. "Stop it. He's a good man..."

Kildai laughed. So by the sounds of it did half the audience outside.

"They are playing a practical joke on you, Erik. It is my fault."

He smiled at her. "I snore, too."

Kildai stood up. He was still smiling. "All right, Sister."

He faced Erik. "As her brother, you have my permission to pay court to her. But . . ." he held up a hand, looking much older than his years, "You will also need the permission of the Great Khan of the Golden Horde. And he is a different person from me."

"But . . . !" protested Bortai.

"No buts," said Kildai, firmly. "Erik is not of the clan, not of the people. You are a very important person to me, to the clan. He must go and ask." He looked every inch a khan, and she was proud of him, even if he was playing games with her. There was an element of payback there, she had to admit. Some of it was . . . fair. "I will see you in the ger of the Great Khan. You may want to ask your Khan Manfred to come and stand as your friend," he said to Erik.

Erik nodded. "Bortai . . ."

"Go," said Kildai, sternly, above her protest.

Erik went back to Manfred's ger.

"We can't have you going like that," said Manfred looking at him. "I've a spare cotte. And Falkenberg. Come and trim his hair."

It took quite a while before Erik was considered ready. Manfred seemed to be in no hurry about it.

They walked together up the hill toward the great felt tent. People cheered. Manfred waved a lordly hand. Erik just walked.

The ger was a huge structure, needing whole trees for support. It was full. But people moved aside to let them pass.

Erik and Manfred came at last to the Great Khan's

dais, and his chair. There, standing next to it, was Bortai. Looking as if she would either burst into tears, rip someone's ears off, or turn and run. Her face was very pale.

The Great Khan, dressed as befitted his station, looked at Erik.

"You're supposed to bow," said Manfred, prodding him.

Erik wondered whether he should turn and run. But he looked at Bortai instead. She looked as if she was going to faint. She was holding onto Vlad's little sister. So he smiled at her. And bowed respectfully to Kildai.

"You may advance," said the General of Khesig, Pakai. They walked forward.

Kildai smiled. "Erik Hakkonsen. I have spoken to your khan. I conferred with the khans of the various clans, with my generals, and with my war-shaman. I have not forgotten that when every man's hand was raised against us, you stood as our friend. You did not know who we were, and you expected no reward. Your honor is a bright beacon." He stood up and walked over to Erik. "You are supposed to kneel," he said quietly.

Erik did. Kildai kissed him on both cheeks. "Let all of the clans of the Golden Horde know that this man is now one of us. To strike a blow against him, is to strike a blow against the Hawk clan, the people of Golden Horde."

The people in the ger—and, by the sounds of it, right across the camp joined in the pounding of shields and cheering.

Eventually Kildai held up his hand for silence.

Erik had had time to think. Time to look at Bortai. Time to understand what the wyvern had said to him, and what it meant to the Golden Horde. And more importantly, what it meant to Bortai.

"Now," said Kildai. "You had something to ask me about the Princess Bortai."

Erik shook his head slowly.

The vast ger was still.

"No," he said. "I have spoken to her brother, Great Khan. Now I must challenge her."

Kildai beamed. "You are one of us! But so far seven men have tried. They wagered a hundred horses, as is tradition. I think a few more might also have been that courageous, but that is a lot of horses."

"Khutulun's suitor wagered a thousand horses," said Erik. He noticed that David was also there, grinning, and whispering a translation to Manfred.

There were murmurs. Smiles. The people seemed pleased that he knew the story.

"But I do not have a thousand horses," she heard Erik say.

Bortai was as tense as drawn bowstring. Her gut was twisted up in a knot around her heart...

"Hell's teeth, Erik. I'm good for a thousand horses," said Manfred expansively. "Make it a thousand and one. I can't have you outdone by some other fellow. I will stake you a thousand and one horses, my friend. Any day and any time."

Someone translated. The crowd were silenced. A thousand and one horses! That put the wealth of the foreigner at a level that most Mongol could not dream of. That the foreign khan put such a value on the Tortoise Orkhan was quite a revelation.

Erik stood still for a few moments, aware that he

was being watched by most of the flower of Golden
Horde clans. Slowly he shook his head.

Bortai felt the bottom drop out of her world.

"No!" he said. "I will only wager what I have. And
that I will do."

"And what is that?" asked Kildai.

"I said, Great Khan: I will wager what I have.
Everything."

There was a stunned silence.

"It's not much. My horse. My gear. My land. Myself.
My life if need be."

He turned to Bortai as if there were not several
thousand people watching. As if they were the only
people there. "Will you accept my wager?"

Bortai, for the first time in a lifetime of telling
people exactly what to do, found that she had no
voice. She sniffed determinedly. Maybe he knew the
story. But it didn't matter. She knew Erik. He spoke
from the heart, with absolute and utter conviction.
He knew and understood the honor he was giving
her, here, before the assembled clans. It would be
remembered. It should be remembered. She still
found her voice was weak. But she could nod, and
say "yes," so quietly that only he could hear.

The clans, however, could see the nod. "Fight!"
the chant began.

"Fight! Fight! Fight! Fight! Fight! Fight! Fight!
Fight!"

The center of the ger was cleared. Erik faced
Bortai. And he really did not know what to expect.

He learned quickly enough. Wrestling is a matter
of strength among some people. Among the Mongol

nobility, it was a martial art—as well as a marital one. It was about using your opponent's weight and strength. And, however Bortai felt about him, she was not going to give him an easy time of it. Fortunately, he knew how to land and how to get up again. And she wasn't actually trying to kill him. After a few minutes, Erik was glad of that, and stopped remembering that his opponent was both smaller than him, and a woman. Instead he fought to survive, and hopefully, to win. Fortunately, the school of skills she had did not entirely match his own...of course that also meant that she knew throws that he didn't.

Bortai's heart sang. At last she'd found a man who...understood. Understood the balance between honor, duty and love. And, what was more, could wrestle. The honor he'd given her had to be repaid. She certainly could not lose easily.

And then, as he twisted neatly behind her, taking her arm in a pinion hold that she did not know, she realized that she would not have to.

And then, he let her go. Stepped back. "I would never defeat my wife," he said, smiling.

She bowed, acknowledging a worthy foe. "But perhaps you would kiss her," she said, smiling back at him.

They did.

Maybe the crowd cheered.

She didn't notice.

Maybe they would tell their children and grandchildren that they'd been there.

She didn't care.

Chapter 85

"Caesar. It has been done and the babe and mother lived to tell the tale," said Falkenberg. "But it takes a skilled surgeon. Someone like Marco Valdosta. It is neither safe nor successful that often. But it has been done."

"Explain," said Dana, knowing that there was a listening wyvern in the ger.

So the knight did. Dana swallowed and was brave. But she wondered if she should tell him that a wyvern would be accompanying them on the Via Engatia.

"So, you are married," Vlad beamed. "Congratulations! I am hurt that I was not invited, but at least Dana was there."

"Well... I didn't even know that I had proposed," said Erik, "And been accepted, months ago, before we even met you, Vlad. But we'll be having another ceremony in Iceland. You'd be welcome at that," he said ginning like a man who had just discovered that the world can be a very good place sometimes. It was after Terce, and Bortai and Erik had just emerged from the same ger.

Vlad looked a little puzzled. "You had proposed?"

"I didn't have a very good grasp of the language," said Erik. "It was the second thing I said to Bortai."

She held on to him very proprietorially. "And I will make sure that he says it to no other young maidens! I need all of him." She licked her lips. Dimpled. "Again. I am teaching him the art of wrestling."

Erik blushed. "So what is the news out of Hungary?" he said hastily.

"Chaos. If I had the men and the inclination I could go a-conquering. But I have neither," said Vlad. "I have consolidated my duchy. And that is good enough. It will take years to fix what needs to be fixed. I came because Dana sent word you would be going south to take the Via Egnatia home."

"Well, yes. But the news is that some vessels have been sighted nosing their way up the Danube. Venetian ships. So we wait now for them. We plan to ride down there in few hours.

"Then we will have the gifting ceremony," said Bortai. "You will come, Khan-from-over-the mountains?"

"But of course, if I am invited. What will I have to do?"

"The bride and groom sit together. The bride's father or protector brings her portion, and puts it around them. Then the guests each place a gift for the couple around them. There is a big feast, and everyone gets very drunk. Usually some people fight," explained Bortai.

So Vlad joined them in the ride down to the Danube.

Sitting in the chairs, holding Bortai's hand, Erik was almost too stunned to take in the steadily growing pile of golden jewelry and coinage growing around them, until it got to waist high. "I hope they stop before they cover us."

Bortai smiled at him, laughing a little. "But I must be at least as rich as you. And anyway... it is part of the legend. Gold... they can always find more gold. But dreams and honor are more precious. This is the story which will keep their honor burning bright forever. They want to have been here, to have been part of it, to have added to the pile around the poor Mongol maiden and her khan."

The following is an excerpt from:

INVASION

Book One of the
SECRET WORLD CHRONICLE

MERCEDES LACKEY

with Steve Libbey, Cody Martin
& Dennis Lee

Available from Baen Books
March 2011
hardcover

INTRODUCTION

The blue-skinned, blue-haired woman known by the callsign "Belladonna Blue" leaned into the oval hatch of the captain's cubby. She was already suited up in her white, full-body nano-armor, with only her head exposed. Her helmet was under her arm.

"You've got about two hours, Vic. Make the most of it."

Victoria Victrix nodded. She hoped someone was going to be around to read the file when all this was over.

She began to type, hesitantly at first, but picked up speed as she went to make the most of what little time there was left.

Whoever you are that's reading this, you might not know that the real genesis of where we are now was back in 1935.

That was when the first metahumans first started showing up in Nazi Germany, paraded before screaming crowds at Hitler's rallies. The very first to appear were "Vaterland," and his sidekick, "Hitlerjungend." Then came the one the rest were named for—"Ubermensch." And honestly, nobody thought they were anything but propaganda blow-ups using stage-magic and fakery until the Blitzkrieg started pounding across Europe. But there were more of these "Ubermenschen," and all by themselves they were the equivalent of entire battalions and tank-corps. For a while they had it all their own way, too.

817

That changed during the Battle of Britain; the waves of fighter-bombers were being led by a Nazi who had reflexes like nobody's business and hardly needed a plane at all.

The Black Baron.

Bullets literally bounced off him. His "plane" was a frame with eight machine guns and an armored engine. He could pull maneuvers that would easily have sent anyone else into full blackout. He was an unstoppable one-man fighter-squadron. And he was cutting the RAF down at the coastline.

One of those RAF pilots was Lt-Commander Nigel Patterson, whose plane burst into flames and disintegrated around him under the Baron's guns.

Except "Nige" didn't die, because something happened to him in that instant. Out of the explosion burst a fireball that was a man, who proceeded to punch holes with his body in every Nazi fighter-bomber in that formation. Then he landed on the frame of the Black Baron's craft, ripped the control-cables and fuel-lines out, and punched the Baron square in the nose for good measure, knocking him out. The Baron's "plane" folded up and plummeted. Maybe the Baron could survive bullets, but he couldn't survive a terminal-velocity fall with an armored V-16 engine crushing him. He turned into a red smear on the ground.

Spitfire, the first of the Allied supers, was born.

Time after time, again and again, it happened during the War. Nazi, Italian Fascist and Japanese metas would show up and kick butt for a while, and then something bizarre would happen on the battlefield. Suddenly they were facing someone that could take them. That changed the way the war was fought. The metas battled it out one-on-one, gladiator style, leaving conventional forces to win or lose the battles. And after the war was over, the metas that didn't much cotton to law and order just moved on to crime. Which was where Echo came in, funded by the eccentric but charismatic nephew of Nikola Tesla who had a boatload of his uncle's inventions and the savvy to make them pay off handsomely. Echo organized the old metas from former WWII vets and recruited new ones, bundling them all into a single organization. And for a while, well, things in the world looked a lot like the comic-book writers from before the war used to picture them. Every city had its Echo HQ, and you'd see the occasional meta-villain pulling off something extreme and your local Echo OpTwo or Three would take him out, either alone or with a team. People got used to it, and couldn't remember a time without metas, actually. They collected trading cards and action figures, and wore buttons with their favorites on them, like they did with ball players. Metas got legislated, with the Extreme Force laws and the Control Officer mandate. Echo built special containment prisons for meta-villains. It was a lot less scary than the threat of the A-bomb, and then the H-bomb. And a lot more marketable.

Echo's main HQ was in Atlanta, because Yankee Doodle and Dixie Belle got married right after the end of WWII and settled there, and they were the pride of the US Meta-human Corps. Atlanta was pretty central, fairly modern, and had access to about anything, but was not Washington DC or NYC. Andro Tesla wanted to keep Echo away from the US centers of politics.

Then came the day that everything changed. My friends and I were right in the middle of it.

Who am I? I'm Victoria Victrix Nagy, magician, meta-human, romance writer, and hacker, at your service. I'll *try to chronicle what happened. I'm not a reporter—I'm trying to pull together notes and stories, write this all down as best I can and I hope I don't screw it up. I'll give you the truth, as far as we know it. You'll know the mistakes we made, and hopefully someone will have a record of who was a hero, who gave all, and just how much we lost. And for us, for me, this is how it began*

   Welcome to our nightmare.

CHAPTER ONE

Before the Storm

MERCEDES LACKEY, STEVE LIBBEY,
CODY MARTIN AND DENNIS LEE

Atlanta, Georgia, USA: Callsign Eisenfaust
I Minus 24:00:00 and Counting

Eisenfaust hunkered in the shadows of an alleyway outside a bar. At the end of the block, a stark white wall terminated the nighttime darkness like a false horizon, surrounding a brightly lit tower with windows as slender as a man's arm: the Echo Security Facility, one of the most heavily guarded buildings in the United States of America.

He had survived the plane crash—as Germany's greatest pilot, he knew how to ditch a plane—but he hadn't counted on the flimsiness of twenty-first century aircraft; his broken arm throbbed, not quite healed yet.

Better than the fate his pursuers had encountered in the Andes. He almost wished he was back in the jungle stronghold, just long enough to mock the Commandant who had stolen his beautiful Valkyria from him.

Ah, Effi. Your betrayal cut deep.

He would not fall prey to the foolishness that won Valkyria. Eisenfaust had fought for the Fatherland, for his fellow Deutschlander, for the freedom his people deserved. But this...this was madness.

And in keeping with his *nom de guerre,* he'd crush it under his fist. But he needed allies, and he needed time to plan.

Slowly, he made his way down the dim street to the Echo compound. These American *ubermenschen* would surely be surprised by the identity of their uninvited guest.

The guard at the gate eyed him. "The campus is closed, sir."

"I wish to speak to your commanding officer," Eisenfaust said. "Fetch him at once."

"Ah...right. You'll have to come back tomorrow. We open at nine A.M."

"I have no intention of waiting." Eisenfaust scowled at the enlisted man. "Your commander—bring him."

A second guard stepped out of the booth, wary of the increasing tension in the air. "We can't do that, sir. Please step away from the gate."

Eisenfaust cursed under his breath. Even the Allied Aces had shown him more deference than these flunkies. He pointed at the Security Tower. "That is my destination. If you cannot assist me, step aside."

Both guards reached for their sidearms. Moving with the inhuman speed that made him Germany's greatest aerial ace, he swatted the guns out of their hands before they could level them in his direction. The two men gasped.

With his good arm, he flattened the first guard with a blow to the chin. "I will find him myself!" he exclaimed furiously. The second guard knelt to seize his gun; Eisenfaust booted the man in the side, hurling him back into the booth.

With a contemptuous sniff, he kicked the guns aside and walked to the door of the detention facility.

In wartime Eisenfaust would never have been so careless as to simply leave the guards unconscious, but his goal was not to kill these men. He was here to make his presence known. Eisenfaust opened the glass doors, approving of their weight; the bulletproof glass was two inches thick and obscured the lobby.

"Stop right there, mister." The speaker was a fine example of American manhood: tall, wide shouldered, a face with mongrel features, topped with a swath of light brown hair. His black Echo uniform sported epaulets decorated with the Stars and Stripes. A thick metal gauntlet on his right hand glowed with plasma energy—and was directed at Eisenfaust.

"*Guten nacht*, my friend. I am told you have rooms for rent."

A score of Echo guards with rifles lined up behind the meta. "We have plenty of room for punks who smack our people around. Don't make me use force."

"Good. I was hoping to speak to someone with authority." He drew himself up into a salute. "I wish to turn myself in."

"Now that was easy." The meta motioned the guards forward, who circled Eisenfaust. "Take him in, boys. Watch those hands."

Eisenfaust gestured to his broken arm. "You have nothing to fear from me, young man. I am a colleague of your father's." A guard handcuffed his wrists, eliciting a wince of pain.

"I doubt that. Pop died over twenty years ago, and I don't think he ever managed to buddy up to a German after the war."

A tinge of doubt crossed Eisenfaust's mind. "I . . . I

am sorry to hear this. He was a fine warrior, the best I ever faced."

"Huh?" The metahuman looked at him closely. "Now you're messing with me. You can't be a day over thirty."

"You are correct, in a sense." The shackles clanked as he offered his hand. "I am Oberst Heinrich Eisenhauer of the Uberluftwaffe of the Third Reich." He paused, enjoying the look on the young man's face. "Your father, Yankee Doodle, knew me as Eisenfaust."

The meta looked from the hand to Eisenfaust's face. "Bull," he said at last. "He died fighting the Allied Aces. In 1945."

"Then your father told you about me. Clearly you carry on his legacy."

A succession of expressions passed over the American's face so quickly that anyone lacking Eisenfaust's metahuman perceptions would not have registered anything but a frown: first surprise, then reflection, then the cold, strategic calculation of a man used to secrets. His bluff bravado returned in less than a heartbeat.

"As Yankee Pride, yeah. And we're a little too savvy to let some Nazi fetishist get his rocks off by pretending to be a dead Nazi war criminal. Did you leave Hitler's brain in your Panzer tank out front?" Yankee Pride backed off as Echo guards seized Eisenfaust's arms, wrenching his broken arm. "Put him in a holding cell under suicide watch until we can ID this wingnut."

The guards began to drag Eisenfaust down the hallway towards the cell block. He called out: "Ask your mother! Or Liberty Torch! Or Worker's Champion! They knew me. They *feared* me! They will recognize me!"

"Save it for the shrink, Fritz." Yankee Pride replied. He tapped at controls on his gauntlet, gesturing oddly at Eisenfaust for a moment.

Eisenfaust calmed himself. He assumed the Americans would be suspicious of a man claiming to be one of their country's greatest foes. He would overcome their doubts.

"You're taking me to a cell?" he asked a guard. "Is it secure?"

"No one's ever gotten out of Echo," the man sneered.

"That's admirable." Eisenfaust gave the man a prophetic smile. "But it's who will try to get *in* that concerns me."

Las Vegas, Nevada, USA: Callsign Belladonna Blue
I Minus 6:37:22 and Counting

The name on her badge said "Bella Dawn Parker," but Bella's Las Vegas Fire Department callsign was "Blues." Not because she sang them, but because she *was* blue—blue-haired, blue-skinned, a metahuman.

Metahumans didn't stand out in a city like Lost Wages, where you could stand waiting for the bus next to a Russian acrobat, a seven-foot-tall transvestite in Cleopatra drag, a guy with an albino anaconda wrapped around his shoulders, and five Elvii, and all anyone wanted to talk about was the Rebels' football scores

She was the Rookie in Station 7 of the Las Vegas Fire Department, Alternate Driver of Rescue 2, Paramedic Parker, EMT-4, the highest EMT rank there was, and not so coincidentally a registered OpOne with Echo Rescue.

There'd been a huge dump fire earlier that had taken hours to put out and had occasioned a three-station roll-out, so everyone was starving. They all rolled back about two A.M., Oh-Dark-Hundred, and it was her turn to cook, which mean they were getting spaghetti, easy to reheat. Rarely did anyone in a firehouse get to finish a sit-down meal.

She lounged back and watched the guys trundle in, mostly still wet from showers. They still stank a little of burnt rubber.

"Hey Blues?" One of the other rookies looked over at her as he was dishing himself out red sauce. "How'd you get to be EMT-4 so fast? You're only what, nineteen? Twenty?"

"I slept with the instructor," she smirked. "Naw, it's actually a lot less dirty than that. I started taking the EMT courses while I was still in school. They needed me at ball games and stuff, and they wanted me legal. I got the jumpstart 'cause Echo Rescue tapped me for the touch-healing when I was twelve."

"Damn, there goes my bet—"

New York, New York, US: Callsign John Murdock
I Minus 6:22:17 and Counting

John Murdock sat on a bench in an out-of-the-way corner of Central Park with his face buried in his hands, laden down with a feeling that could only be described as "soul-weary," assuming there were such things as souls. Since he'd found this spot, he'd never seen anyone else use it. Possibly because it was a frequent target for pigeons. With his eyes closed, he tried to shut out the happy ruckus of ordinary folks having a cheap good time.

In the middle distance, he could hear a street preacher sounding off. And then, from somewhere behind him, the sirens of three cop cars wailed as they gave chase. He'd stopped looking for somewhere to hide whenever he heard sirens about a year ago, but the sound still made his nerves twitch.

Whoever they were chasing wasn't giving up without a fight.

Probably there was no one in this park that could hear what he was picking up; the sounds of gunshots under the sirens. Single shots, all semi-auto. Handguns, then.

Then he picked up something else. Micro-jets, tearing through the concrete canyons, on a vector that would converge with that of the sirens.

Echo jet-pack. Whatever the perps had done, it had to be bad to earn them metahuman attention. *Tough luck, chumps. Cavalry is comin'.* He leaned back, sighing heavily. *Like you're one to talk, chump.* Every time he heard something like this, ten years of training to protect the innocent warred with five years of paranoia, but as ever, survival-instinct and the paranoia won. The sounds ended with no way of telling the outcome—other than that the meta with the jets had clearly triumphed, since they spun down a minute after the shots ended.

He shook his head. Things, little things, really hit home for him when it was bright and sunny out, like it was today. There were days when he wondered why he had ever been born. They were happening a lot more often lately, and this was one of them. And "never been born" all too easily morphed into "better off dead." He was close, close to that point of no return, but he'd kept on living so far and damned if he was going to give up now. Sheer stubbornness maybe, or just the bargain-basement revenge of outliving the bastards that had put him in this position in the first place.

He stood up, tired of feeling sorry for himself. He started walking away from the park, skirting on the periphery of the tree line, and kept going for several blocks, letting his mind go blank. Funny how people thought of New York as a terribly dangerous place to live. In fact, it was more like a series of vertical villages; people knew each other, went to the same little snack-shops, bought milk at the same bodegas. The fact that he didn't belong in any of those little enclaves, made the gloom wrap around his soul even tighter.

Eventually, he found a bar; a real Irish neighborhood joint that must have been there for a century, the sort of place that firefighters and steel workers went to after putting in their shifts. Alcohol wasn't really a cure, but it sure worked wonders for the short term. Six A.M. might be early to start drinking by most people's standards but nobody in this bar was keeping track.

But he wasn't going to get any trouble here as long as he didn't start any himself. At six feet even and two hundred pounds, he wasn't huge, not by the standards nowadays, where you saw Echo metas that were the size of park statues, but he wasn't a pip-squeak either.

Mostly, though, it was the way he moved and held himself that made trouble avoid him, recognizing him for a fellow predator.

Inside the door, he looked up. There was a patina of hard use and age on everything. He strode up to the bar, spying a whiteboard listing the drink prices. *Cheap.* It was the first bit of good news he'd had all day. Money was running out. It went fast in this town, even when you were sleeping rough and making do with the showers at the Salvation Army. Be time to find a job soon, under the counter pay, shady construction work, janitor...he hoped he wouldn't have to go on the gray side of the law. Still, he figured that he had enough to get drunk with, and maybe even some money left over for half of a decent meal. Or one full meal at a soup kitchen and a real bed at a flophouse.

John sat down hard on the wooden stool, resting his elbows on the worn counter in front of him. The bar-keep was busy having a conversation with a middle-aged couple at the right end of the bar. John knew what the barkeep saw; a customer maybe, but one that wasn't going to spend a lot of money, even by the standards of this place. Clothing nondescript. Jean jacket, white shirt, and cargo pants; clean, but they had seen too many hard wearings and washings. His brown hair, a little too long and uneven, hadn't seen a barber for a long time. Compact muscles and expressionless grey-green eyes, like two cold pebbles, also said he might be trouble, as did the callused knuckles. Fingerless gloves. Fist-fighters tended to wear those. John rapped his knuckles against the counter a few times until the bartender tore himself away; he was an older man, with shock-white hair and a day old stubble shading his chin. "What'll it be?" he asked, his tone shaded with impatience as well as wariness.

John looked up wearily, meeting the bartender's eyes, and shoved a ten-spot toward him. "Whatever's the house special."

"House rye, dollar a shot, coming up." The barkeep really *was* in a hurry to get back to the conversation. He shoved a half-full bottle—John's eagle eye measured the contents as just about ten shots-worth—and a shot glass across the counter at John, and turned back to the couple. He resumed his banter, stopping short to eye John up. "We'll be having you pay as you go, too."

Echo Headquarters Atlanta, Georgia, USA:
Callsign Eisenfaust
I Minus 02:32:15 and Counting

By day, the Echo detention facility hummed with energy. Metahuman prisoners could not be afforded the same liberties as conventional convicts: no exercise yard, no recreation room, no library. Even the classic prison pose, leaning against the bars with hands useless and dangling, was denied them. The reinforced steel doors contained grills that afforded a limited view of the corridor.

Some deemed it cruel. Most considered it necessary due to the unique nature of the metahumans. Ordinary criminals could be disarmed, metas couldn't. Metapowers were, by law, lethal weapons that had to be registered with local law enforcement and the government.

Eisenfaust paced his cell. After his death-defying escape from the clutches of the Thule Society, confinement was maddening. These imprisoned men and women were scum, and to be interred with them, even by choice, grated on his nerves.

The grill at the foot of his door slid open to admit a tray with his lunch. "Guard," he said. "I have waited for your commanders to speak to me for far too long. Where is Yankee Pride?"

"Out doing his job," the guard answered abruptly.

"Why has he not contacted me? I told him I have critical information, a matter of national security." Hand pressed against the door, he perversely longed for the typical iron bars of a jail.

"Sure you do."

The guard tapped a button with his foot. The serving grill slid shut with a final clatter. He stepped back behind the food cart.

"You're all in terrible danger," Eisenfaust said, his voice becoming strident with urgency. "Please, you cannot ignore this threat for long."

The guard sighed. He leaned against the door. "Listen pal," he said. "If it'll shut you up, I can tell you this: they're sending an Echo Support detective down here to interview you after lunch. Save it for her, okay?"

Without another word the man wheeled out of sight.

Eisenfaust stepped back, mind racing. A detective? Hardly an official, but at least someone who was trusted to report on matters of consequence.

He felt momentarily giddy. "*Danke*," he called down the hall.

"Dankay? What kinda nonsense you spouting?" The rough voice came from the cell directly across his. The face behind the grill was black; blacker than a human should be.

"*Deutsch, mein freund.* German. It means 'thanks.'"

"You ain't been here long if you're thanking the CO's," the black shape said. "You probably think you're in here by mistake."

"*Nein*. I asked to be here."

The voice laughed, a coarse bark. "Didn't know stupidity was illegal."

Eisenfaust scowled. "I suppose you're incarcerated for rudeness."

Again, the staccato laugh. "Not me. Robbery with Metahuman Powers. Aggravated Assault. Resisting Arrest."

"You're lucky Echo is so permissive. I'd have killed you on the spot."

"O ho ho, big man. You're scaring me. What're you in for?"

Eisenfaust thought for a moment. "I killed one hundred and twelve men that I know of."

Silence fell upon the corridor around them.

"Yeah?" The black shape moved away from the grill, his voice smaller.

"Yes. Shooting. Bombing. By plane, by pistol...two with a knife. One with my bare hands." All necessary deaths in wartime, he told himself, though in this den of thieves he took some relish in trumping their claims. No criminal can exceed the sins of a man at war.

"Damn."

"So in my eyes, you're all mere amateurs. Worse, your crimes were committed for selfish reasons. I fought for my country."

Every ear seemed to be turned to their conversation. Eisenfaust flushed. His story wasn't for these lowlives; only Echo and their metas were his peers, regardless of what cause they served.

A high pitched voice sang out from his right: "He shut you up good, Slycke!"

"Go to hell," Slycke rumbled. "My daddy served in 'Nam. Killed him a dozen gooks and brought back their fingers on a string. This guy ain't no different, except..." His voiced trailed off. "Who'd you serve under?"

"Haven't you guessed?" Eisenfaust paused for effect. "Adolph Hitler."

The corridor erupted with angry shouting. The guards came through in squads, banging on the cell doors with energized prods and calling for order. Eisenfaust took his meal to his seat and smiled as he picked at the cornbread and ham. Soon he'd meet with the detective and give her enough tidbits to earn him an audience with the master of the house.

Alex Tesla.

Atlanta, Georgia, USA: Callsign Victoria Victrix
I Minus 02:23:56 and Counting

Victoria Victrix Nagy stood in her cozy living room, surrounded by the sandalwood scent of her candles, by the armor of her shelves of books and music and movies, and stared at the closed door of her apartment, gathering her strength and her courage. She was about to do battle, as she did about every two weeks, and the fight was going to require every resource she could muster. She checked, once again, to make sure that her protections were in place, that she was covered from chin to toes with not so much as a millimeter of skin exposed. The battle she faced was inside herself, and she faced it every time she had to leave her apartment.

And it wasn't getting any easier for standing there.

She took a shuddering breath, felt her throat closing, her heart racing, heard the blood pounding in her ears. And the fear, the terrible, blinding, paralyzing fear spread through her, making her knees weak, her hands shake.

But there was no choice. She had to eat. It was time to do the grocery shopping, panic attacks or no panic attacks.

<Come on Vic,> she heard her cat, her familiar Greymalkin, say in her mind. <You can do this. Do it for me. I'm out of tuna, and the kibbles are almost gone.>

That did it. That broke the hold for a moment, as Grey had probably figured it would.

"Selfish beast," she said aloud, with a shaky laugh.

<What did you expect? I'm a cat, not Mahatma Gandhi.>

On the strength of that laugh, she got to the door, and opened it. There was no one in the hallway, with its worn brown carpet and forty-watt lighting. It was people that triggered her panic attacks, not places.

She chose her time and day carefully. It was early afternoon, the day of the All-Star game. Those people who were not at the game, or the pregame events, or thronging to glamorous parties, in hopes of getting a glimpse or even an autograph of some movie star, or on the streets hawking cheesy giant foam hands and sun visors, were either at work, or at home. No one sane went anywhere, unless you could do so without resorting to any major streets or, god forbid, the Interstates. The traffic reports said that within a mile of some of the Star Parties it was taking an hour to go three blocks. The grocery stores would be deserted. Earlier this morning there would have been a last-minute run on the staples of the day: beer, hot dogs and buns, beer, ice, beer, soda and beer. Now bored employees would be bowling in the empty aisles with frozen turkeys. Fortunately, the neighborhood of Peachtree Park would be spared most of the horror of the day. It was a blue-collar working-class neighborhood, but the workers had, for the most part, long since retired to their thirties-era bungalows. There wouldn't be many barbecues here today; the residents were inside to watch the game, sensibly isolated from the unseasonable heat (ninety degrees in February!) and the bugs, and especially from the "Georgia State Bird," the mosquito. So the streets should be as deserted as if it was four A.M. on a Sunday.

She made it down the hall to the elevator, an ancient model complete with brass grill inner doors. She pushed the button for the first floor, and the old cage shuddered and made its slow descent. There was no one in the lobby. Her sneaker-shod feet made barely a whisper against the worn-out gray linoleum as she crossed the lobby and let herself out through the front door.

The parking lot was full. This was, after all, a fifteen-story tall apartment building constructed in an era when people took buses and streetcars to work. The parking lot was always full, and those few residents who didn't own a car could command a nice little monthly fee for the use of their assigned space. Vickie's was as far from the building as physically possible, because the super knew that she only moved her little econobox when she absolutely had to.

It looked as if there wouldn't be much in the way of

cloud cover today, and cars would turn into ovens, even with the air conditioning on. It was only around nine A.M., but this was going to take her...a while. Her little light blue, nondescript basic-mobile was parked under a giant live oak, which could be a nuisance in acorn season, but its shade was nice now. She could actually hold the steering wheel without using oven-mitts.

Once in the car, she let out a sigh of relief, and waited for the trembling in her arms to stop. The first hurdle was cleared.

Actually driving was not a problem, even when there were other cars on the street. It wasn't rational, but her gut regarded the car as a safe little shell, and the panic eased back to jitters as she negotiated the narrow, thirties-era streets. Peachtree Park wasn't a trendy neighborhood, and it certainly had seen better days, but it wasn't a slum. Cracking and peeling paint, and aging roofs, stood in contrast to the immaculate yards.

At the border of Peachtree Park and the next neighborhood of Four Corners, things were changing. There was an interstate exit that fed Four Corners. There had been demolition and rebuilding in the fifties, then the seventies, and now again. Here was the chain grocery Vickie made her pilgrimage of fear to whenever the supplies got too low. As she rounded the corner, she prayed that she would find the parking lot empty.

It was, and again she breathed a sigh of relief. There was nothing there but five identical semi-truck trailers—odd, but—

Well, it was the day of the All-Star game, and it was entirely possible the drivers had realized they were never going to get anywhere today and had rendezvoused here to watch the TVs in the cabs and have an impromptu party of their own.

This was the least of her worries. In a moment, she would park the car. She would have to get out of the car, and walk to the entrance of the grocery. Only a few feet but—there would be people there. People who would stare at her, the way they had looked at her—after. With revulsion. With loathing. With hatred—

Get a grip. This is now, not then. They're just people. People here for groceries, nothing more.

But her palms were sweating now, and her short hair was damp with sweat, her mouth was dry, and as she turned off the ignition her hands and arms were shaking and she had to force herself to reach for the door handle, then to pop the door open. She was hot and cold by turns, her stomach so knotted that she was getting sick and regretting that cup of coffee and morning toast....

It would probably take her two hours to convince herself to leave the car.

—end excerpt—

from
INVASION: Book One of the Secret World Chronicle
available in hardcover,
March 2011, from Baen Books

The following is an excerpt from:

HARD MAGIC

BOOK I OF THE GRIMNOIR CHRONICLES

Larry Correia

Available from Baen Books
May 2011
trade paperback

One general law, leading to the advancement of all organic beings, namely, multiply, vary, let the strongest live and the weakest die. The appearance of esoteric and etheral abiliites, magical fires and feats of strength, in recent decades are the purest demonstration of natural selection. Surely, in time, that general law will require the extinction of traditional man.

—Charles Darwin, *On the Origin of Man and Selection of Human Magical Abilities*, 1879

— PROLOGUE —

EL NIDO, CALIFORNIA

"Okies." The Portuguese farmer spat on the ground, giving the evil eye to the passing automobiles weighed down with baskets, bushels, and crates. The cars just kept coming up the dusty San Joaquin Valley road like some kind of Okie wagon train. He left to make sure all his valuables were locked up and his Sears & Roebuck single-shot 12 gauge was loaded.

The tool shed was locked and the shotgun was in his hands when the short little farmer returned to watch.

One of the Ford Model Ts rattled to a stop in front of the farmhouse fence. The old farmer leaned on his shotgun and waited. His son would talk to the visitors. The boy spoke English. So did he, but not as well, just good enough to take the Dodge truck into Merced to buy supplies, and it wasn't like the mangled inbred garbage dialect the Okies spoke was English anyway.

The farmer watched the transients carefully as his son approached the automobile. They were asking for work. They were always asking for work. Ever since the dusts had blown up and cursed their stupid land, they'd all driven west in some Okie exodus until they ran out of farmland and stopped to harass the Portuguese, who had gotten here first.

Of course they'd been here first. Like he gave a shit if these people were homeless or hungry. He'd been born in a hut on the tiny island of Terceira and had milked cows every single day of his life until his hands were leather bags so strong he could bend pipe. The San Joaquin valley had been a hole until his people had shown up, covered the place in Holsteins, and put the Mexicans to work. Now these Okies show up, build tent cities, bitch about how the government should save them, and sneak out at night to rob the Catholics. It really pissed him off.

It always amazed him how much the Okies could fit onto an old Model T. He'd come from Terceira on a steamship, spending weeks in a steel hole between hot steam pipes. He'd owned a blanket, one pair of pants, a hat, and a pair of shoes with holes in them. He'd worked his ass off in a Portuguese town in Rhode Island, neck deep in fish guts, married a nice Portuguese girl, even if she was from the screwed up island of St. George, which everybody from Terceira knew was the ass crack of the Azores, and saved up enough money doing odd jobs to come out here to another Portuguese town and buy some scrawny Holsteins. Five cows, a bull, and twenty years of back breaking labor had turned into a hundred and twenty cows, fifty acres, a Ford tractor, a Dodge pickup, a good milk barn, and a house with six whole rooms. By Portuguese standards, he was living like a king.

So he wasn't going to give these Okies shit. They weren't even Catholic. They should have to work like he did. He watched the Okie father talking to his son as his son patiently explained for the hundredth time that there wasn't any work, and that they needed to head toward Los Banos or maybe Chowchilla, not that they were going to work anyway when they could just break into his milk barn and steal his tools to sell for rotgut moonshine again. His grandkids were poking their heads around the house, checking out the Model T, but he'd warned them enough times about the dangers of outsiders, and they stayed safely away. He wasn't about to have his family corrupted from their good Catholic work ethic by being exposed to bums.

Then he noticed the girl.

She was just another scrawny Okie kid. Barely even a woman yet, so it was surprising that she hadn't already had three kids from her brothers. But there was something strange about this one . . . Something he'd seen before.

The girl glanced his way, and he knew then what had set him off. She had grey eyes.

"Mary mother of God," the old farmer muttered, fingering the crucifix at his neck. "Not this shit again . . ." His first reaction was to walk away, leave it alone. It wasn't any of his business, and the girl would probably be dead soon enough, impaled through her guts by some random tree branch or a flying bug stuck in an artery. And he didn't even know if the grey eyes meant the same thing to an Okie as it did to the Portuguese. For all he knew she was a normal girl who just looked funny, and she'd go have a long and stupid life in an Okie tent city popping out fifteen kids who'd also break into his milk barn and steal his tools.

The girl was studying him, dirty hair whipping in the wind, and he could just tell . . .

"Fooking shit damn," he said in English, which was the first English any immigrant who worked with cows learned. He'd seen what happened to the grey eyes when they weren't taught correctly, and as much as he despised Okies, he didn't want to see one of their kids with their brains spread all over the road because they'd magically appeared in front of a speeding truck.

Leaning the shotgun against the tractor tire, he approached the Model T. The Okie parents looked at him with mild belligerence as he approached their daughter. The old farmer stopped next to the girl's window. There were half a dozen other kids crammed in there, but they were just regular desperate and starving Okies. This one was special.

He lifted his hat so she could see that his eyes were the same color as hers. He tried his best English. "You . . . girl. Grey eyes." She pointed at herself, curious, but didn't speak. He nodded. "You . . . Jump? Travel?" She didn't understand, and now her idiot parents were staring at him in slack jawed ignorance. The old farmer took one hand and held it out in a fist. He suddenly opened it. "Poof!" Then he raised his other hand as far away as possible, "Poof!" and made a fist.

She smiled and nodded her head vigorously. He grinned. She was a Traveler all right.

"You know about what she does?" the Okie father asked.

The old farmer nodded, finding his own magic inside and poking it to wake it up. Then he was gone, and instantly he was on the other side of the Model T. He tapped the Okie mother on the arm through the open window and she shrieked. All his grandkids cheered. They loved when he did that. His son just rolled his eyes.

The Okie father looked at the Portuguese farmer, back at his daughter, and then back to the farmer. The grey eyed girl was happy as could be that she'd found somebody just like her. The father scowled for a long time, glancing again at his strange child that had caused them so much grief, and then at all the other starving mouths he had to find a way to feed. Finally he spoke. "I'll sell you her for twenty dollars."

The old farmer thought about it. He didn't need any more people eating up his food, but his brother and sisters had all ended up dead before they had mastered Traveling, and this was the first other person like him he'd seen in twenty years, but he also hadn't gotten where he was by getting robbed by Okies. "Make it ten."

The girl giggled and clapped.

NEW YORK CITY, NEW YORK

The richest man in the world stepped into the elevator lift and looked in distaste at the gleaming silver buttons. The message had said to come alone, so he did not even have one of his usual functionaries to perform the service of requesting the correct floor. Rather than soiling his hands or a perfectly good handkerchief, he sighed, tapped into the lowest level of his Power, and pushed the button for the penthouse suite with his mind. Cornelius Gould Stuyvesant, billionaire industrialist, could not tolerate filth. A man of his stature simply did not get his hands dirty.

He had people for that.

The steel doors closed. They were carved with golden figures of muscular workers creating the American dream through their sweat and industry under a rising sun emitting rays as straight as a Tesla cannon. He sniffed the air. The elevator car *seemed* clean. The hotel was considered a five-star luxury establishment, but Cornelius just *knew* that there were germs everywhere, disgusting, diseased, tiny plague nodules just itching to get on his skin. Cornelius understood the true nature of the man that was staying in this hotel, and he must have ridden in this very car. Cornelius shuddered as he squeezed his arms and briefcase closer to his sides, careful not to touch the walls.

He could afford the finest Healers. In fact, he was

one of the only men in the world that had an actual Mender on his personal staff, but nothing could stop the blight of a Pale Horse, and it was that foul Power that brought him here today, reduced to a mere caller. Cornelius had tried to seek out others, once under a gypsy tent on Coney Island, again in a tiny shack in the Louisiana Bayou, but those had been frauds, charlatans, wastes of his valuable time. He tapped his foot impatiently. After what seemed like an eternity, the doors whisked open.

A tuxedoed servant was waiting for him, an older negro with stark white hair. The servant bowed his head. "Good evening, Mr. Stuyvesant. Mr. Harkeness is waiting on the balcony. May I take your coat, sir?"

"Not necessary. My business will not take long."

The servant studied him with cunning eyes. "Of course, sir. Would you care for a drink? Mr. Harkeness has a selection of the finest."

"As if I would drink anything *here*," Cornelius sputtered. The notion of ingesting something from the household of a Pale Horse was madness. "Take me to him immediately."

"Of course, sir." The servant led the way down the marble hall. Carved busts of long-dead Greeks watched him from pedestals, judging. Cornelius hated statues. Statues made him prickly. Even the giant idolized bronze of himself at the new super-dirigible dock bearing his name atop the new Empire State Building bothered him.

Lots of things made Cornelius Gould Stuyvesant uncomfortable, including this servant. He did not like the way he had examined him, like he was being sized up. The information he'd gathered on Harkeness indicated that the man surrounded himself with other like-minded Actives. There were many who would kill a Pale Horse on basic principle, so it made sense to have loyal staff with Power for security. He idly wondered what kind of Active the old servant was. Probably something barbaric, like a Brute, or even worse, a Torch. That would seem to suit a race that was so easily inflamed by their passions.

"Mr. Harkeness is through here, sir." The servant paused at the fine wood and thick glass door leading to the balcony. He turned the knob and opened it. "He prefers the fresh air. Will there be anything else?"

Cornelius did not bother to respond as he stepped onto the balcony. His time was valuable, more valuable than any man in the world, more valuable than emperors, kings, tsars, kaisers, and especially that imbecile, Herbert Hoover, and the very idea that he was reduced to having to take time from his busy schedule to meet someone on their terms rather than his was blatantly offensive.

To further the sleight, Harkeness was leaning on the balcony, overlooking the city, placing his back toward the richest man in the world, as if Manhattan were somehow more important than Cornelius Gould Stuyvesant, himself. The balcony lights had been extinguished, so as not to hamper the view. The city was illuminated forty stories below by electric lights and flashing marquees. Thousands of automobiles filled the streets, bustling even at this hour, and overhead a passing dirigible train floated in the amber spotlights like a herd of sea cows. Cornelius snorted in greeting.

"Mr. Stuyvesant." The Pale Horse didn't bother to turn around. His voice was neutral, flat. "I was just admiring your marvelous city. Have a seat."

Cornelius felt a single drop of sweat roll down his neck. It was shameful, but he found that he was actually frightened. He glanced at the pair of chairs, fine, stuffed leather things that in any other scenario would be inviting to rest his ponderous bulk, but at that moment, all he could imagine was the horrible diseases crawling on the cushions.

"I said have a seat," Harkeness repeated, still not turning around. His accent was indeterminate, his pronunciation awkward. "You are a guest of mine. I would not harm a guest. I am a civilized man, Mr. Stuyvesant."

Cornelius sat, vowing that he would throw this suit into the fireplace as soon as he got home, then he would have his personal Healer expend a month's worth of Power checking his health. He would probably burn the Cadillac car he had traveled in, maybe the driver too, just to be on the safe side.

Harkeness left the railing and took the other seat. He did not offer his hand. He was older than Cornelius had expected, tall and thin, face lined with creases, and blue eyes that sparked with an unnerving energy. His hair was receding, and what remained was artificially blackened. His tailored suit was as fine as could be had, and his tie was made of silk as red as fresh blood. He smiled, and his teeth were slightly yellow in the dim city light. "Smoke?"

Cornelius looked down at the wooden humidor on the table between them. The cigars were sorely tempting, but the very thought of touching his lips with an item tainted by Harkeness' evil made his stomach roil. "No, thank you."

Harkeness nodded in understanding as he puffed on his own Cuban. "Straight to the chase then. I was informed that you were looking for me."

"Nobody can ever know we spoke," Cornelius insisted. He was the founder and owner of United Blimp &

Freight, the primary shareholder in Federal Steel, and the man that bankrolled the development of the Peace Ray. He'd sired children who had gone on to be ambassadors to powerful nations, senators, congressmen, and even a governor. A Stuyvesant could not be seen consorting with such sordid types.

"I assure you, I am a man of discretion." Harkeness exhaled a pungent tobacco cloud, not seeming to notice his guest's discomfort.

Cornelius cringed, trying not to inhale smoke that had actually been inside the very lungs of such a pestilent creature. "You are a hard man to find, Mr. Harkeness," the billionaire said, aware that he had to tread carefully. Even with eight decades of mankind dealing with the presence of Powers, of actual magic, to the point that it was just an accepted part of life in most of the world, the Pale Horse was such a rarity that most still considered them to be a myth, crude anti-magic propaganda created to sow fear and distrust in the hearts of the masses. "Men of your . . . skills . . . are especially rare."

"Yes . . . What is it you were told I am?" Harkeness asked rhetorically, examining the ash on the end of his cigar.

Cornelius hesitated, not sure if he should answer, but growing tired off the awkward silence, he finally spoke. "I was told you are a Pale Horse."

Harkeness laughed hard, slapping his knee. "I like that. So . . . biblical! So much nicer than plague bearer, or grim reaper, or angel of death. That title has gravitas. Pale Horse! You, sir, have made my day. Perhaps I shall add that to my business cards." His pronunciation was stilted, with pauses between random words. Cornelius found it almost hypnotic, and realized he was nervously smiling along with the other man's mirth.

Then Harkeness abruptly quit laughing and his voice turned deadly serious. "So, who must die?"

"You presume much," Cornelius said defensively.

"If you just wanted to merely curse someone and make their hair fall out, or to give them boils, fits, or incontinence, there are far easier Actives to reach than I." Harkeness' smile was unnerving. "People come to me when they desire something...epic."

The industrialist swallowed and placed his briefcase on the table. He unlocked it, then turned it so that Harkeness could see inside. It was filled with neatly stacked and meticulously counted bank notes and a single newspaper clipping. Cornelius quickly snatched his hand away before the Pale Horse could touch the contents, as if his Power might somehow be transmitted through the leather.

The Pale Horse did not seem to notice the money. He gently removed the yellowed clipping, took a pair of spectacles from his breast pocket, set them atop his hawk-like nose and began reading. After a moment he removed the glasses and returned them and the clipping to his pocket. "An important man. Very well...What will it be? Bone rot? Consumption? Cancers of the brain or bowel? Syphilis? Leprosy? I can do anything from a minor vapor to turn his joints to sand while his skin boils off in a cancerous sludge. I am an encyclopedia of affliction, sir."

Cornelius bobbed his head in time with the litany of diseases. "All of them."

"I see..." Harkeness seemed to approve. "Very well, but first, I must know..."

"Yes," Cornelius answered hesitantly. The hairs on the back of his neck were standing up.

"Why? A man such as you has no shortage of killers

to choose from. Why not a knife in the back? A bullet in the head? You yourself are a Mover, why not just invite him to a balcony such as this and shove him off? It would even look like a suicide, which would be particularly scandalous in the papers."

"How—" Cornelius sputtered. His Power was a secret. "Me? A magical? Who told you such slanderous lies?"

Harkeness shrugged. "I have a trained eye, Mr. Stuyvesant. Now answer my question. Why do you need me to curse this man?"

Cornelius felt his face flush with anger. No matter how dangerous Harkeness was, Cornelius Gould Stuyvesant was not about to have his motives questioned by a mere hireling. He pushed himself away from the table and rose, bellowing, "Why you? I do not want him dead. That is far too good a fate for one such as he! I want him to suffer first. I want him to know he's dying and I want him to pray to his ineffectual God to save him as his body rots and stinks and melts to the blackest filth. I want it to hurt and I want it to be embarrassing. I want his lungs to fill with pus. I want his balls to fall off and I want him to piss fire! I want his loved ones to look away in disgust, and I want it to take a very, very *long* time."

Harkeness nodded, his face now an emotionless mask. "I can do this thing for you, but first, I must ask, what terrible thing did this man do to deserve such a fate?"

The billionaire paused, pudgy hands curled into fists. He lowered his voice before continuing. He had planned this revenge for years. It was only the purity of the hate for his enemy that drove him to this place. "He took something...*someone*...from me. Leave it at that." Cornelius tried to calm himself. He was not a man given to such unseemly outbursts. "Will that do?"

"It is enough."

Cornelius realized he was standing, but it did make him feel more in control, more in his element. He gestured at the open briefcase. "I was given your name by an associate. I believe that this is the same amount that he paid for your services." Rockefeller had warned Cornelius about how expensive the Pale Horse would be, but it would be so very worth the money. "Take it."

The other man shook his head. "No. I don't think so."

"What!" Cornelius sputtered. Was he going to try and shake him down for more money than Rockefeller? *The nerve.* "How dare you!"

Harkeness leaned back in his chair, puffing on the cigar. He took it away from his mouth and smiled without any joy. "I don't want your money, Mr. Stuyvesant. I want something *else.*"

Cornelius trembled. Of course, he'd heard the odder stories about the Pale Horses, the rarest of the Actives, but he had paid them no heed. He was a man of science, not superstition. Sure, he had magic himself, nowadays one in a hundred Americans had some small measure, but it didn't mean he understood how it actually worked. One in a thousand had access to greater Power, being actual Actives, but men like Harkeness were something different, something rare and strange, themselves oddities in an odd bunch. Hesitantly he spoke. "Do...do you want...my *soul?*"

This time Harkeness really did laugh, almost choking on his cigar. "Now that's funny! Do I look like a spiritualist? I'm certainly not the devil, Mr. Stuyvesant. I do not even know if I believe in such preposterous things. What would I even do with your soul if I had it?"

That was a relief, even if Cornelius wasn't particularly sure if he had a soul, he didn't want to deed it over to a man like Harkeness. "I don't know," Cornelius shrugged. "I just thought..."

Harkeness was still chuckling. "No, nothing so mysterious. All I want is a *favor*."

That caused Cornelius to pause. "A favor?"

Harkeness was done laughing. "Yes, a favor. Not today. But someday in the future I will call and ask for a favor. You will remember this service performed, and you will grant me that favor without hesitation or question. Is that understood?"

"What manner of favor?"

The Pale Horse shrugged. "I do not yet know this thing. But I do know that if you fail to honor our bargain at that particular time, I will be greatly displeased."

He was not, by nature, a man who intimidated easily, but Cornelius Gould Stuyvesant was truly unnerved. The threat went unsaid, but who would want to cross such a man? The industrialist almost walked out on the absurd and frightening proposal, but he had been planning his revenge for far too long to turn back now. If the favor was too large, Cornelius knew he always had other options. Harkeness was deadly, but he wasn't immortal. It would not be the first time he had used murder to get out of an inequitable contract.

"Very well," Cornelius said. "You have a deal. When will he get sick?"

Harkeness closed his eyes for a few seconds, as if pondering a difficult question. "It is already done," the Pale Horse said, opening his eyes. "Isaiah will see you out."

Isaiah joined his employer on the balcony a few minutes later. Harkeness had gone back to admiring the view. "Could you Read him?"

"He's very intelligent. I had to be gentle or he would've known. He's got a bad tendency to shout his thoughts when he gets riled up." The servant leaned against the concrete wall and folded his arms. "He even thought I might be a Torch. Can you believe that?"

Harkeness chuckled, knowing that Isaiah was far more dangerous than some mere human flame hurler. "Was he truthful?"

"Mostly. He absolutely despises this man."

"For what he did to him? Wouldn't you?"

Isaiah sounded disgusted. "Stuyvesant is utterly ruthless."

So am I, Harkeness thought, knowing full well that Isaiah would pick that up as clearly as a high strength radio broadcast. "You don't get to such lofty positions without being dangerous. I'll have to curse him quickly. Arranging a meeting should be easy enough. Stuyvesant will be expecting immediate results now."

Isaiah left the wall and took one of the cigars from the table. "I liked your little show, with closing the eyes and just wishing for somebody to die and all that. That's good theater."

Of course, even he had his limits. He would actually have to touch the victim, and it took constant Power thereafter to keep up the onslaught against the ministrations of Menders, which he already knew this man would have. This would be an extremely draining assignment. "Whatever keeps Stuyvesant nervous," Harkeness shrugged. "I do like the new term though. It suits me."

Isaiah quoted from memory as he clipped the end from the Cuban. "And I heard a voice in the midst of the four beasts, and I looked and beheld a pale horse, and the name that sat upon him was death..."

"And hell followed with him," Harkeness finished, smiling. "Appropriate..."

"If the favor you ask of him is too difficult, he'll have you killed."

Harkeness had suspected as much. "He could try. Wouldn't be the first."

"The man's got a phobia about sickness. The Spanish Flu near did him when it came through, been worrying him ever since." Isaiah said as he lit the cigar. "He's scared of you."

"Good," the Pale Horse muttered, watching the people moving below, scuttling about like ants, ignorant little creatures, unaware of the truth of the world in which they lived. The Chairman was about to change the world, whether any of the ants liked it or not, and that meant war. Many ants would be stepped on, but that was just too bad. It was unfortunate to be born an ant. "He should be..."

BILLINGS, MONTANA

Every day was the same. Every prisoner in the Special Prisoner's Wing of the Rockville State Penitentiary had the exact same schedule. You slept. You worked. You got put back in your cage. You slept. You worked. You got put back in your cage. Repeat until time served.

Working meant breaking rocks. Normal prisoners were put on work crews to be used by mayors trying to keep budgets low. They got to go outside. The convicts in Special Wing got to break rocks in a giant stone pit. Some of them were even issued tools. The name of the facility was just a coincidence.

One particular convict excelled at breaking rocks. He did a good job at it because he did a good job at everything he set his mind to. First he'd been good at war and now he was good at breaking rocks. It was just his nature. The convict had single-minded determination, and once he got to pushing something, he just couldn't find it in himself to stop. He was as constant as gravity. After a year, he was the finest rock breaker and mover in the history of Rockville State Penitentiary.

Occasionally some other convict would try to start trouble because he thought the convict was making the rest of them look bad, but even in a place dedicated to holding felons who could tap into all manner of magical affinities, most were smart enough not to cross this particular convict. After the first few left in bags, the rest understood that he just wanted to be left alone to do his time. Occasionally some new man, eager to show off his Power, would step up and challenge the convict, and they too would leave in a bag.

The warden did not blame the convict for the violence. He understood the type of men he had under his care, and knew that the convict was just defending himself. Between helping meet the quota for the gravel quarry that padded the warden's salary under the table, and for ridding the Special Wing of its most dangerous and troublesome men, the warden took a liking to the convict. He read the convict's records, and came to respect the convict as a man for the deeds he'd done before committing his crime. He was the first Special Prisoner ever granted access to the extremely well-stocked, but very dusty prison library.

So the convict's schedule changed. Sleep. Work. Read. Sleep. Work. Read. So now the time passed faster. The convict read books by the greatest minds of the day. He read the classics. He began to question his Power. Why did his Power work the way it did? What separated him from normal men? Why could he do the things he could do? Because of its relation to his own specific gifts, he started with Newton, then Einstein, finally Bohrs and Heisenberg, and then every other mind that had pontificated on the science related to his magic. And when he had exhausted the books on science, he turned to the philosophers' musings on the nature of magic and the mystery of where it had suddenly come from and all of its short history. He read Darwin. He read Schuman, and Kelser, Reed, and Spengler. When that was done, he read *everything* that was left.

The convict began to experiment with his Power. He would sneak bits of rock back into his cell to toy with. Reaching deep inside himself, twisting, testing, always pushing with that same dogged determination that had made him the best rock breaker, and when he got tired experimenting with rocks, he started to experiment on his own body. Eventually all those hours of testing and introspection enabled him to discover things about magic that very few other people would ever understand.

But he kept that to himself.

Then one day the warden offered the convict a deal...

— end excerpt —

from *Hard Magic: Book 1 of the Grimnoir Chronicles*
available in trade paperback,
May 2011, from Baen Books